Blood of the Reich

a story of a Ring

Blood of the Reich

A Novel

Mike Whicker

a Walküre book

For

All those who have served,
serve now,
or will someday serve
honorably in the branches of the
United States military in wartime or peace.
Army, Navy, Air Force, Marines, Coast Guard
and
For the honorable members of law enforcement.

This book is dedicated to you.

Blood of the Reich

a Walküre imprint

This is a work of historical fiction.

ISBN: 978-0-9844160-0-4

Printed in the United States of America

Contents

Part I

Friendship needs no words – it is solitude
delivered from the anguish of loneliness.
— Dag Hammarskjold

Chapter 1

Soap Operas

Cincinnati, Ohio—September, 1943

"Do you think Deborah will sleep with Robert?"

"Of course, Penny," said Clare. "She's after his money. But I'm hoping he'll find out she slept with his brother for the same reason. If Robert finds that out he'll send her packing."

The commercial for Ivory soap ended and Clare and Penny returned their attention to the radio.

Clare's custom was to stay home on Saturday night, cook dinner, and listen to the soap operas. She did not mind this routine. It was a habit grown accustomed to in high school, and after all these years the routine was comforting.

Occasionally she tuned in *Fibber McGee and Molly* or *The Shadow*, but the soap operas were her favorite. To Clare, any kind of love story was wonderful, even a love story with the bickering, backstabbing, and constant infidelities of the soap operas. To have someone love you for a moment, Clare thought, would be enough. Even if he changed his mind at least you would have a memory. No one could take that memory away. Yes, that would be enough—a memory of love.

Clare resigned herself to the fact that she would never have that memory. Thanks to a bout with polio when she was four years old, Clare limped. She knew many polio victims much worse off than she; nevertheless, the limp limited her mobility so Clare picked up extra weight each school year until she weighed 220 pounds when she graduated from high school. If that were not enough, a bad case of acne scarred her cheeks and forehead.

High school.

Clare had an easier time then during her younger years. The bold elementary school recess taunts of "fat, crippled cow" quieted in high school to stares from boys and snickering by girls when she walked by. The stares and laughter stung Clare, but she determined to not show it, devising clever ways of turning her head away at just the precise moment, or looking down at a piece of paper she carried. Her schoolmates would have to understand that this paper was of ultimate importance, she had to read it at this exact moment, and therefore she could not be aware of their gawking and snickering.

In high school, she even worked up the courage to attend one of the dances her senior year. Of course she had no illusions that a boy would ask her to dance, and none did. But if nothing else was accomplished, she at least showed them that the hurtful treatment at school did not damage her too badly. By her early twenties, the acne had left although many scars remained, and Clare resigned herself to the fact she would always be heavy. The myriad diets always ended the same: lose a few pounds then gain them back along with a few extra.

Now, at thirty, Clare was on her own. Three years ago she left her small hometown in southern Ohio to begin a new life in the big city after finding a job with one of Cincinnati's newspapers. Clare typed obituaries as well as birth and wedding announcements for *The Cincinnati Observer,* and had been trained to operate the newspaper's teletype machines.

Clare enjoyed independence. The Lamar Apartment building where she rented a room was a tad dingy, but her apartment was economical and a quick bus ride to work. She could afford to live here without asking for help from her parents, who had lost almost everything during the Depression. Someday, after a raise or two, Clare planned to find a better place.

Moving to Cincinnati had been the right decision for Clare. Life for the aesthetically unacceptable was easier in a big city. Life ran faster and people had less time to pay attention to Clare's flaws. And she made a close friend.

Penny lived on the same floor as Clare and they met soon after Clare moved in. The two had much in common. Like Clare, Penny was a typist; she worked at an electrical supply warehouse downtown. Also like Clare, Penny had physical flaws. Penny was a diabetic and the disease had not been kind. A chronic lack of appetite and daily insulin injections, which Penny gave herself, had over the years emaciated her body. Penny seemed a walking skeleton, so painfully gaunt that her frailness drew gasps when she was out and about. Twice since they became friends, Clare had to administer a sweet concoction of orange juice and sugar to bring Penny back from a diabetic seizure.

Probably the biggest difference between Clare and Penny was in their dreams for love. Clare long ago gave up on a romance, but Penny still clung to the hope.

The two women drew close and shared company whenever time was theirs. Clare had succeeded in getting Penny hooked on the radio soaps, and several times each week the two met in Clare's apartment to tune in. Both women enjoyed predicting the storyline: who would fall in love with whom, who would soon be cheating on whom, and with whom. Clare and Penny spent hours discussing which character was next in line for a broken heart.

Another subject of conversation was their third-floor neighbors. It was a quiet floor. Except for Clare and Penny, little interplay took place among the third-floor residents. Mrs. Rausch, an elderly widow, was pleasant enough but her hardness of hearing made conversation exhausting. A Chinese couple with two teenage children lived on the floor yet seldom were seen; the entire family worked long hours at a Chinese restaurant a few blocks away. Mr. Hinkle, the building's maintenance man, had an apartment on the third floor, but like the Chinese family, Mr. Hinkle was seldom around, spending much of his day in the building's basement boiler room. Grouchy old Mr. Teller lived next to Penny. Mr. Teller had little to say unless to complain, so people left him alone.

One other resident of the third floor was a young woman who moved in a month ago. Clare guessed her to be mid-20s. Both Clare and Penny thought this woman looked terribly out of place in the Lamar Apartments. The newcomer was blonde and beautiful with a lithe figure and a movie-star face. But like some other residents of the third floor, this new neighbor was seldom seen. Clare and Penny occasionally spotted her coming or going, but any attempts they made to strike up a conversation with her were rejected pleasantly but quickly. Once, after Clare saw the mysterious newcomer return to her apartment, she and Penny knocked on the woman's door. Their knock was quickly answered and Clare invited the woman to listen to the soap operas with her and Penny that evening. The woman politely thanked them for the offer but quickly declined and then gently dismissed them by slowly closing the door.

This woman became more and more a point of conversation for Clare and Penny. Why was such a beautiful woman not married? Was she lonely? But a woman so beautiful would never be lonely unless she chose to be, and no one would choose to be lonely. Clare and Penny concluded that the woman, surely a crusher of hearts, instead suffered from a broken one, and they resolved to continue their efforts to offer friendship.

Clare and Penny's extensions of kindness and efforts to get to know their enigmatic neighbor proved unsuccessful until one afternoon when Clare returned home with a bag of groceries. Because of her limp and obesity, Clare struggled with stairs and stopped each flight to catch her breath. As Clare rested on the second-floor landing, she heard footsteps and turned to see the mysterious neighbor ascending the stairs. Clare smiled at her. The woman took the bag from Clare's arm and walked with her up the last flight. Clare made small talk and once again invited the woman to listen to the radio that night with her and Penny. That evening, Clare and Penny were surprised when they answered a knock and found the young beauty standing in the hall.

They stuck to the plan and listened to the soaps. Clare easily offered a running commentary on the characters, and filled in their new friend on the various romantic intrigues. The woman, who said her name was Anne, listened but said little and responded only in generalities when, during a commercial, Clare or Penny would ask a question.

"Where are you from, Anne?"

"My family moved a great deal when I was a child. I really have no hometown."

"Do you have a boyfriend?" It was prying but Penny could not resist.

"No."

All of Anne's answers were such. Clare and Penny learned little about her that night, and she had not visited again despite an open invitation. That was a week ago.

◊ ◊ ◊

It was Tuesday when Penny told Clare the big news.

"I have a date Friday night."

Clare squealed with delight. "Who is he?"

"His name is Roger. I met him last week at lunch."

"Tell me all about him." Clare was full of questions. "You say you met him last week? Why didn't you tell me?"

4

Penny blushed. "Wasn't anything to tell until now. I never thought he would ask me for a date. He just recently started eating at the diner where I usually eat lunch. He started talking to me one day. Then he came back the next day and we talked some more. He's an auto mechanic."

"What does he look like?"

"Slim, dark hair and eyes." Penny was a bit embarrassed and downplayed the news. Neither of the women had had a date since they became friends and Penny worried about Clare's feelings. The worry was misguided. Clare was genuinely excited for her friend.

"So what are your plans?" Clare asked. "Will I get to meet him?"

"We're going to a movie. Saturday he's going to pick me up here at seven. I gave him your apartment number. I'll introduce you then."

The days leading to Friday were delightful for Penny and Clare. The two went shopping not once, but several times, and they never tired of the endless decisions concerning shoes, hair, and makeup. Clare would suggest, Penny would consider, and then one or the other would change her mind—Clare as often as Penny.

Finally, both women decided Penny would wear a dark green skirt and a white blouse. Penny bought a pair of white cotton stockings to cover her painfully thin legs (Penny was very self-conscious about her legs and she thought the stockings made them look a little better). In one of the stores, Clare saw a small, pinned hat the same green as the skirt Penny picked out. Clare showed the hat to Penny, who liked it, and Clare insisted on buying it for her.

Now Saturday, Penny was ready for her date by six o'clock.

At 7:30 Roger still had not arrived. Clare dreaded the thought of Penny being stood up after their week of excitement. Finally, just before eight o'clock, they heard the knock. When Penny opened the door, Roger stood there alongside another man and a woman. Roger, apparently unaware that he was late, made no apologies. He explained that the others were friends he was giving a lift. Clare heard Roger tell Penny he would drop these friends off on the way to the movie theater. Penny let the group into the apartment and introduced Roger to Clare.

Penny told Roger she would grab her coat and they could be on their way, but as she turned, Roger grabbed her arm, swung her around, and slapped her viciously across the face. The frail Penny flew backwards and fell onto the couch. Clare stood there stunned, her brain refusing to register what her eyes just witnessed. When Clare

5

did react, she screamed and rushed toward Penny. The other man stepped in front of Clare, grabbed her hair, and punched her in the mouth. Blood spurted from around broken teeth as Clare dropped in a heap.

As Clare lay on the floor, time seemed in slow motion. She heard the men ask Penny about money and jewelry, but Penny was in shock and could only call out for Clare to help her. For that the men beat her more. When the second man noticed Clare crawling toward Penny he kicked Clare in the stomach. The woman they brought with them disappeared into the bedroom, apparently looking for money or anything of value. Finding neither, she returned with a broom and used it to beat Clare. One blow hit Clare across the left eye, swelling it shut. The woman continued to beat her with the broom until Clare stopped crawling. The men continued the beatings of both Clare and Penny; the woman who came with them watched, laughed, and encouraged the men.

Clare, still conscious, screamed again for help. *Why will no one come to help?* she thought, barely able to move.

The men also found little of value while ransacking the small apartment, which provoked them further. Clare saw Roger use a knife to cut off Penny's clothes as she lay unconscious on the couch, leaving only the green hat Clare bought her. Clare tried once more to crawl toward Penny, but knocked over a shelf of figurines when she tried to pull herself up from the floor. The second man complained that the noise might summon help and suggested they leave.

"Yeah, let's get out of here," Roger said. "These two whores are so disgusting I'll never get it up anyway."

"Here, use this," the woman said and handed Roger the broom.

As Roger prepared to rape the unconscious Penny with the broom handle, the other man pulled off Clare's pants and undergarments, leaving her naked from the waist down. He punched her again in the face. Clare fought to remain conscious.

"Don't take any more of her clothes off," said the other man. "I'll puke if I have to look at it."

Suddenly the apartment door swung open and the three attackers stopped. The room went silent. Clare had vision only out of her right eye, yet she saw what her attackers saw.

Anne stood in the opening.

Clare didn't want her to suffer the same fate as she and Penny. "Run, Anne!" Clare fought to shout through a mouthful of blood. "Run away!"

Instead of running, Anne stepped into the room and closed the door behind her. The men looked at each other with a look of disbelief.

"No!" Clare sputtered through the blood. "Run!"

Anne glanced around the room and looked at each man before speaking. "Boys, you've got it all wrong. I'm your date tonight."

"Who the fuck are you?" Roger demanded. The three intruders stood silent, the attack on Clare and Penny abandoned momentarily if for no other reason than astonishment in what they were seeing. Anne smiled, her hands behind her as she casually leaned against the door.

"You heard Clare. My name is Anne. I live down the hall. I heard the party and I thought I'd invite myself."

Roger and the other man exchanged glances.

"You want to join the party?" Roger asked then turned back to the others. "I think we can invite this bitch, don't you?"

The other man laughed, and the woman smiled. Roger stepped toward Anne. As he moved forward, Anne brought her right hand around from behind her. She held a gun, which she pointed at Roger. She pulled the trigger twice. Instead of a loud report, the muffled sound heard was not unlike that of brief, low static on a radio. The bullets ripped into Roger's chest. He fell forward into Anne's skirt and then slumped to the floor—a look of horror in his eyes.

The other two attackers stalled in disbelief, and then the man fumbled in a pocket and pulled a switchblade. As he flipped it open Anne shot him in the face: again the crackle of the gun's report surprisingly hushed. The bullet tore through the man's teeth and exited through the side of his mouth. He spun and fell to the floor.

Anne saw the woman eye the broom. "Bad idea," Anne said as she aimed the gun at the woman's head. The woman froze.

The second man, still conscious, managed to get to his knees. "Don't kill me, lady!" the man pleaded as he held his hands to his wounded face. Surprisingly, he could still speak after the bullet's journey through his mouth, but the words were garbled through broken teeth and blood. "It was his idea!" he said, pointing to Roger.

Anne ordered the man to shut up and told the woman to get on her knees. The woman obeyed and remained silent, but the man continued to beg loudly for mercy. Anne shot him in the groin. He screamed and folded over. Anne kicked him in the head, like someone who had done such an act before, knocking him unconscious.

Anne lowered the gun to her side and refocused on the woman. "And what am I to do with you?"

Chapter 2

An Ancient Punishment

Cincinnati—Friday, September 10, 1943 [same night]

District 1 Police Station

"Frank, go home. What are you trying to do, brown-nose the major so you'll make lieutenant?" The question came from Glen Shafer who had just checked in for the night shift.

Frank Ault ignored the ribbing. He hated paperwork, especially backed-up paperwork, and he didn't want this batch waiting for him when he came in tomorrow. He wanted to finish his report on an arrest he made earlier that day. Scores of Appalachians moving their families to Cincinnati for war jobs created tension between the newcomers from the poor hills of West Virginia and eastern Kentucky and some of the city's longtime citizens. Around lunchtime, a brawl broke out between a group of Appalachians and locals all in line to apply for jobs at Aeronca Aircraft in Middletown, a plant manufacturing *Defender* airplanes for the Army. Normally a homicide detective sergeant did not handle a simple brawl, but Ault was only a block away when he heard the call on his car's RCA.

When typing, Ault used the two-fingered *hunt-and-peck* method. Finally finished, he ripped the paper from the typewriter, signed it, tossed the carbon into a nearby wastebasket, and threw the top copy into the box on his desk for finished reports.

Now he turned to Shafer. Although Ault outranked Shafer—Ault was detective sergeant, Shafer detective—protocols of rank were ignored. The two men had been friends since they went through the police academy together fourteen years ago.

"Yeah, Shafer, I'm trying to make lieutenant so I can promote you to my job. That's the only way you'll get a promotion, if a friend takes pity on you."

Shafer laughed and lit a cigarette. "Screw you, Ault. How's the wife?"

"Fine."

"I read her article the other day about the graft going on in the city council. You have to hand it to her, she's never afraid to open a can of worms." Shafer chuckled.

Ault's wife, Elizabeth, worked as an investigative reporter for the *Cincinnati Observer*, and was well-known locally for her exposés on corrupt politicians, unethical business practices by local corporate leaders, reports on high profile criminal trials, and hot-topic crime investigations. The latter had caused Frank Ault numerous headaches in the past when his wife worked to scoop a story concerning a homicide he worked. The article Shafer referred to was published two days ago. After snooping through documents for the better part of three months, Elizabeth Ault revealed that an influential city councilman was awarding building contracts without proper bids to a friend who owned a large construction company.

"Yeah, I imagine that guy is scrambling to cover his tracks." Ault remarked.

The telephone on Shafer's desk rang. Ready to leave, Ault rose and reached for his hat on the window ledge next to his desk.

"See you tomorrow, Glen," Ault said.

Shafer ignored him and listened on the phone.

"He's just leaving for the day, Major," Shafer spoke into the receiver but looked up at Ault who had turned to leave, but now hesitated. Each Cincinnati police district was commanded by a police major. Now past 9:00 p.m., the major would be at home or at some social affair. Why the call? Ault watched Shafer's surprise at what he was hearing. "What's the address?" Shafer scribbled on a piece of paper and listened for another moment. He looked again at Ault as he spoke into the phone, "Right, he's still here. I'll tell him."

Shafer, who had a habit of slamming down the receiver, set it in the cradle gently.

"Let's go, Frank. Dispatch called the major at home. All hell has broken loose. Some kind of massacre at an apartment building off Elm Street near Washington Park. He wants us to meet him there."

Shafer drove. Under light and siren, they skidded to a stop in front of the Lamar Apartments in less than five minutes. A young, uniformed patrolman stood outside talking to a few civilians, probably neighbors.

"Do you recognize him?" Ault asked Shafer, referring to the young cop.

"No."

As the detectives approached, Ault flashed his badge to the young officer. "I'm Detective Sergeant Ault; this is Detective Shafer." Ault looked at the young man's badge. "I don't recognize you . . . *Christian*."

"I'm Officer Christian," the young man said needlessly. He was sweating and on edge. "I was transferred here from District Four two weeks ago."

"How long have you been on the scene, Christian?"

"About twenty minutes. I went up to the room with my partner as backup. When we knew we had cleared the room for a threat, he sent me down here for crowd control."

"Who's your partner?"

"Joe Lawrence. He's inside."

"I know Lawrence—good, veteran cop. Is Major Cantrell here yet?"

"No sir, at least I haven't seen him."

"What's happened here, Christian? Give it to me quick."

"Hell if I know. One guy's dead for sure, another shot. Blood all over the place. Three women beat up. One is . . ."

Ault interrupted. "I assume you radioed for an ambulance."

"Yeah." Christian nodded.

"What floor?"

"Third . . . no, second . . . no, third. It's the third floor."

"Okay, stay here and keep the crowd back. The whole neighborhood will be on the sidewalk when more cops, the ambulance, and the coroner get here. And calm down, Christian."

Ault and Shafer entered the building and climbed the stairs. On the third floor, residents stood in the hallways bewildered, unaware of what had happened.

"Where?" Ault asked an old man.

"The cops went in Clare's room." He pointed down the hall. "What's going on?"

Ault ignored the question. The apartment door stood ajar. When Ault and Shafer entered, they saw Officer Lawrence leaning over a man curled up on the floor. Lawrence pressed a towel to the man's groin, trying to stop the bleeding. Lawrence looked up.

"Jesus Christ, Frank," Lawrence said. "Look at this mess."

Even a seasoned homicide detective and tough cop like Frank Ault was forced to do a double-take. Blood colored many places on the linoleum floor and plaster walls. Besides the bleeding, groaning man Lawrence attended, another man lay in blood behind the door, eyes

11

open and glassed over. Ault recognized the stillness of death and the look in the eyes of the dead—Ault always thought it a look of disappointment.

Across the room, a heavy-set, badly beaten but conscious woman knelt crying beside another badly beaten woman, this one gaunt and frail, who lay on a couch. It looked to Ault like the thin woman was unconscious. The heavy woman tried to care for the thin one, covering her with blankets.

Then the unbelievable. A third woman, naked, sat on the floor, arms spread out with her wrists impaled to the wall—crucified—with what looked like kitchen meat knives. Blood ran down the wall from her wrists, and her head hung forward, like that of Christ on the Cross.

Chapter 3

Elizabeth to the Scene

[same night]

None of the victims was in any shape to answer questions. The only fully conscious victim was the heavy woman, and she was in shock, rocking back and forth and crying. Ault, Shafer, and Officer Lawrence attended to the victims as best they could until help arrived. The three policemen knew better than to pull a knife out of a stabbing victim so the crucified woman remained as she was until the ambulance medics got there. Ault threw a tablecloth over her for modesty, the handiest thing he could find.

"You're going to need backup," Ault told the medics when they entered the room. Two more ambulances were summoned along with the fire department. Ault asked Shafer to notify the crime lab team. Ten minutes after the firemen and crime lab investigators showed up, the crime scene photographer appeared in the doorway, just in front of the police major, Ed Cantrell. Before long, the street in front of the building swarmed with police and other people who needed to be there along with many who did not. Officer Christian dealt with the crowd of curious that Ault had predicted, establishing a police line he guarded with a second uniformed officer. On the third floor, Ault stationed another officer outside the apartment with orders to keep the other residents away from that end of the hall.

As soon as the medics took over for the police, Shafer began questioning the perplexed residents of the third floor. Ault found an old, stooped man who said he was the building manager; he had just begun questioning the man when he heard a voice behind him.

"Hello, Frank."

It was Elizabeth. He knew she would show up, but this was fast, even for her.

"I hope traffic patrol did their job and issued you a speeding ticket," he said to his wife.

"Such a kidder," she said. "No, I don't need to rush now that you have the new RCA at home.

"I thought we agreed you would not turn that on when I'm not home."

13

"I was dusting it off and it accidentally flipped on."

"Sure, I should have figured that would happen. I'd like to chat but I'm a little busy right now, and you shouldn't even be up here."

"What happened, Frank?" Elizabeth ignored his admonition. "The young cop on the street said a man was dead and a woman was nailed to the wall."

Christian! Talking to the press—a typical rookie mistake. But Ault was not surprised; Elizabeth often ferreted information from those who should know better. A good-looking woman, she knew how to put on the charm.

"I don't have time to talk now, Elizabeth. This is a bad one. I'm sure the major will hold a press conference in the morning, and I'll fill you in on what I can later."

Ault knew this would not stop Elizabeth from snooping, and he could not stop any reporter, including her, from doing their job as long as they did not interfere with the police investigation. Ault went back to the crime scene room to check with the lab men. As he passed the officer stationed outside the room, Ault gave him instructions.

"See that woman at the end of the hall?" Ault pointed to Elizabeth who was now talking to one of the residents.

"Yes, Detective," the officer answered.

"That's a reporter. Don't let her near the room, even if she tells you she's my wife."

"Right."

As Ault stepped through the door, he made way for two medics carrying the injured, unconscious man out on a stretcher.

"What's his chances?" Ault asked one of the medics.

"Don't know yet."

Other medics had removed the knives from the impaled woman's hands and she was now on a stretcher. Semi-conscious from loss of blood, the woman mumbled weakly and incoherently. Two other medics from the Fire Department tended to the heavy woman and the frail woman, both now sitting on the couch. Glen Shafer found some shell casings and handed one to Ault. Ault recognized them as .32 caliber. Doctor Steven Hagan, the Cincinnati coroner, hovered over the dead man behind the door.

"Anything yet, Doc?" Ault asked.

"Looks like at least four bullets were fired," said the doctor. "Two are probably still in this guy's chest; no exit wounds in the back of his shirt that I have found, but he's been lying in blood so we'll have to

14

wait to see for sure after we get him cleaned up at the morgue. Looks like the guy they just hauled out was hit a couple of times. I heard you ask about his chances. Shot in the face and abdomen. The face hit isn't life-threatening; he must have had his head turned slightly. The bullet went in one cheek and out the other—took out a few teeth. The other bullet entered the left lower quadrant abdomen—might have taken out the sigmoid colon, but it missed the femoral artery or the guy would be dead already from exsanguination."

"Drop the doc jargon, Steve."

"He'll probably make it. The gut shot didn't sever an artery or he would have already bled to death, and the bullet was probably stopped by the pelvic bone. If so, that's a good thing. We can remove it from his ass without complications."

"It will be a .32 slug you take out. How about the women on the couch?"

"Both have various contusions and abrasions from beatings, but they are in better shape than the other three, especially this guy," said the coroner, referring to the dead man. "But if you're wondering about questioning them, you'll have to wait, at least till tomorrow. Both have swollen jaws and can barely speak, and they are in various stages of shock. Nearest hospital that can handle this is Christ. That's where they'll be. The one nailed to the wall will need a transfusion and will be in La-La Land until she gets one. But she should make it. Her heartbeat is high but steady."

With questioning of the victims on hold, Ault helped Glen Shafer search the room. They found no gun, but only one conclusion came from that—the dead guy was not a suicide shooter. Two purses were found and searched. Driver licenses revealed two names: Clare Miller and Penelope Lindauer. Ault sent Shafer down to the street to enlist some uniforms to look for a gun that might have been thrown out of one of the apartment windows. When Shafer returned, he reported no gun. They would search again outside in daylight tomorrow morning, but if no gun was found then obviously none of the victims was the shooter.

He was out there somewhere, or maybe it was *they.*

Chapter 4

Cantrell Preps for the Press

Saturday, September 11, 1943

Ault awoke and looked at the clock: quarter to seven. He left the crime scene about 2:00 a.m. and hit the sack around 3:00. Since becoming a cop he was not much of a sleeper, so he was satisfied with getting the four hours.

Becoming a policeman seemed logical for Frank Ault, not because of any familial legacy like some of his colleagues who came from a long family line of cops. His father was not a cop, nor his grandfather or uncles. It had more to do with a preordination by disposition. Frank Ault grew up a tough kid in a tough neighborhood where, for a tough kid, becoming a cop or a crook were two of the most plausible career choices. Ault flirted with the latter during Prohibition. As a teenager in the Roaring Twenties, he earned money unloading trucks from Canada delivering heavy loads of illegal hooch to some of the local speakeasies.

When the time came to choose a life's path, there was no dramatic epiphany that saved him from a life among the low. Without giving it much thought, one day Ault walked into the neighborhood precinct station and told the desk sergeant he wanted to be a cop. Simple as that.

After the academy, Ault started out walking a beat. Hardy with his fists (in his twenties, he won the police boxing tournament four years in a row, still a record), his beats were always among the roughest. When a vice detective in District 1 retired, someone suggested Ault to the major. Vice calls for tough cops, and Ault got the job. He spent two years in Vice learning how to be a detective before moving to Homicide nine years ago.

Ault sat up on the side of the bed. Elizabeth still slept. He was glad his wife did not get a look inside the room last night. As a big city reporter, she was not immune to witnessing tragedy and the results of human cruelty, but last night was different. At 37, Ault had seen more than his share of horrific scenes, yet last night was a first. He had never seen a human impaled to a wall. He was glad Elizabeth did not see it. If she had, he knew she would not be sleeping.

16

Besides the gruesomeness of the crime, many details about the case baffled. The building manager could identify only two of the victims: the heavy woman, and the frail woman. Both lived in the building, and the crime took place in the heavy woman's apartment. Their names turned out to be the names on the driver licenses found in purses. The rest of the third floor residents were at home at the time of the crime except for a Chinese family and a young woman. All residents present last night were questioned and none heard gunshots. Others who live on the floors above and below also heard no gunshots. Most of the third floor residents, at least the ones closest to the apartment, were elderly and Ault found out quickly during questioning many were hard of hearing, so not hearing a scuffle or possible shouts for help was believable, but unless they were all totally deaf, gunshots that nearby would be heard—and none were. The impaled woman had no identification, neither did the man who was alive when carried out, and the manager could not identify them. The dead man's wallet offered up a driver license with a name.

Last night the major ordered Ault and Schafer to be in his office with a preliminary report at 9:00 a.m., but that was still two hours from now. Ault was impatient to question the victims. Doc Hagan said the heavy woman would probably be the first victim able to answer questions. Also, Ault wanted to talk to the doctor who treated the victims when they arrived at the emergency room, and he knew the emergency room night shift ended at 8:00 a.m.

In twenty minutes Frank Ault had shaved, dressed, and was on his way to The Christ Hospital.

Ault was no stranger to the medical staffs at the various Cincinnati hospitals, and they always knew why he was there. An emergency room nurse summoned the doctor on duty who would be familiar with the victims' conditions. Ault had no need to flash his badge.

"Good morning, Doctor Lamphier." Ault offered his hand; the doctor shook it.

"Hello, Frank. You gave me a mess this time. The dead man is at the morgue. The body was here about an hour while the paperwork was processed, then we shipped it over. Doctor Hagan accompanied the body in the ambulance and told me he would perform the autopsy this morning at ten o'clock. He knew you'd be on his butt to get it done."

"And the others?"

17

"I think they'll all make it. The man's the worst. He'll be here for awhile. To me, the bullet looks like a .25 or a .32, but that's your department. The slug is in the lab. The bullet went through the colon but missed critical organs and arteries. The pelvic bone stopped it. Fractured the bone."

Doc Hagan guessed right about the colon and the pelvic bone, Ault thought. The detective felt no need to verify that the slug was a .32. He let the doctor continue.

"All three women were badly beaten, but they should recover. One of them is a diabetic so we have considerations there."

"How about the woman with the wrist wounds?"

"Somebody beat the living daylights out of that woman. We had to pump a lot of blood into her. The wrist wounds were enough to slowly bleed her out, but nothing like severing an artery. The punctures were between the two bones of the forearm—the ulna and radius—in almost the exact same spot in each wrist."

"What do you make of that, Doctor?"

"I don't know; other than wrist slashes for a suicide, I've never seen such duplicate wrist wounds. And as I said, these aren't slashes to open an artery, just puncture wounds." The doctor thought for a moment. "Could they have been self-inflicted, say before the beating?"

"No, not self-inflicted." Ault didn't tell the doctor about the impaling.

"Then someone wanted to inflict pain, and he knew what he was doing."

At 9:00 a.m. sharp, Frank Ault sat down beside Glen Shafer in Major Ed Cantrell's office. Little had come from Ault's early-morning trip to the hospital; all the victims had been sedated during the night and none had yet come out of it. The doctor told Ault that the woman named Clare Miller should be able to answer questions by late morning.

"Give me an update," the major ordered. Cantrell, 51, had been a cop for 27 years, had paid his dues, risen through the ranks, and was well-respected within the Force.

Ault responded. "Dead man was killed by two gunshots to the chest—.32 caliber. He had a driver license on him and we fingerprinted the corpse. Name is Roger Beck. Glen ran a background and the guy has a rap sheet longer than a soup kitchen line—in and out of jail since he was a teenager—several small-time burglaries, petty theft charges. One assault, which he did two years for."

"Salt of the earth," Shafer interjected.

"The other victims are all expected to make it," Ault continued. "I dropped by the hospital this morning on my way in. Couldn't question anyone—they had all been sedated, but the doctor said at least one of the women should be coherent later this morning. When we're done here, I'll head back to the hospital."

"Who are the other victims?" Cantrell looked at Ault.

"Ran the prints on everybody, but besides the dead man, the only one we had a file on was the other shooting victim. His name is Duane Rudd. This joker is only nineteen, but he's another guy whose career goal is to be low-life. He's been stealing cars since he was fifteen and has spent time in the reformatory. A year ago he was charged with attempted rape, but beat the rap when the woman changed her mind about testifying. No outstanding warrants at this time. We still don't know who the woman is who was nailed to the wall. She had no I.D. and her prints aren't in our system. The other two women are residents of the apartment building according to the manager." Ault referred to notes in front of him. "The room where the crime took place is rented to a Clare Miller, one of the victims. And one of the other victims—a Penelope Lindauer—lives down the hall."

"Who called it in?"

"We don't know," Ault answered. "There are only two telephones in the building. The manager has a private line in his apartment, and there is a pay phone on the first floor. The dispatcher who took the call told me the caller was female. I figure the caller was one of the old ladies who lives there but doesn't want to get involved."

Cantrell nodded, "What is your initial impression of what we have here? I have to tell the press something at ten o'clock."

"Hard to form a notion yet about the shooter and motive, Ed," Ault said. "Four shots were fired that no one heard. The women who live in the building, Miller and Lindauer, had clothes missing and torn, and someone had ransacked the place. After Glen told me the backgrounds of the two males, we both thought of a break-in, assault and robbery of the three females. The manager said Miller and Lindauer are friends. I asked about husbands and he told me the two women are single. No one on the third floor knows much about those two. Looks as if everyone there stays pretty much to themselves. No one could give us any leads on family for notification; one old lady said she thought the

19

Miller woman was from some small town near here but she didn't know which one. Don't know about the third woman yet, the manager didn't recognize her. I figure she's a friend of Miller and Lindauer and was just visiting when the break-in occurred—a wrong place at the wrong time deal for her. As for the men, maybe they had a third partner who turned on the others when they came across something valuable—wanted it all to himself—but then it doesn't seem likely there would be something of much value in that apartment. The entire building isn't much farther than a half step away from slum status. But until we can question the victims, it's hard to say. Right now all we know is there is some lunatic out there who kills people, nails women to walls, and is running around with a silencer on his .32."

"Silencer?" Cantrell asked.

"No one heard any gunshots."

Cantrell took half a minute to think. "I'm not telling the press about the woman nailed to the wall. That'll bring the loonies out of the woodwork. Every rag reporter in the country will descend on us. And it will be to our advantage to have that confidential when we bring in a suspect. If the suspect starts talking about the specifics under interrogation, we know we have something."

Right, Ault thought. That was why he did not give the doctor at the hospital any particulars. But there was a problem: Elizabeth. Ault didn't tell Cantrell that the young patrolman—Ray Christian—told Elizabeth about the woman impaled to the wall. He didn't want to get a young cop just starting out in trouble. Ault would look up Christian himself and take him to task for shooting his mouth off. And Ault didn't need to worry about Elizabeth telling another reporter that information; his wife was the ultimate newshound and would never share a scoop with the competition. But he had to get to her before she submitted her story. He knew her deadline for the next morning's paper was 10 p.m. By the time Elizabeth had put together any facts about the crime last night, it was too late to get the story in this morning's newspaper—a stroke of luck for the investigation.

Cantrell continued, "I'll tell the officers who were on the scene, and the medics who were there last night to keep it zipped about the details. Frank, it's your case. You'll have to deal with Elizabeth. She'll be all over this one."

You got that right, Ault thought.

"Glen, you're the partner. I'll get you moved back to day shift."

Shafer nodded.

"Let's get this thing resolved," Cantrell added. "If the guy in the hospital was one of the perpetrators, we need to know so we can detain him. With two gunshot wounds, he'll be in the hospital for a while, but still, with no outstanding warrants, when he recovers he walks out of the hospital and disappears. Frank, give me an update this afternoon after you've talked to some of the victims."

"Okay." Ault rose.

"Gentlemen," Cantrell concluded, "we have a bad guy out there . . . a very bad guy. Let's find him before we go through this again."

Chapter 5

Miss Miller Covers Up

[same day]

As they left Cantrell's office, Ault asked Shafer to check with the lab for any updates then join him at the hospital.

Reporters were already inside the conference room where Cantrell would hold his press briefing. Frank Ault knew he would find his wife there, and he knew she would be in the front. Elizabeth was always at the front of any group of reporters. If she couldn't charm or flirt her way to the front, she used her elbows. He caught her eye and motioned for her to join him in the hall.

"Elizabeth," Frank always called her *Elizabeth*; she did not like *Liz* or *Beth*, "I need a favor. I have to ask you to keep some of the details of the case confidential, at least for a while."

"Like what?" she eyed him with suspicion.

"The part Officer Christian, that rookie cop on the street, told you about. He called it 'a woman nailed to the wall' I think you said."

"Are you kidding me?" she frowned. "No way! That's a big story."

"Look, Elizabeth, we need to find this guy quickly, and it won't help matters to turn the case into a public circus. I promise that you'll get to scoop it when the time comes."

"So Cantrell is not going to mention it?"

"No."

"I don't know, Frank. That's asking a lot. That detail might get me a special edition." She paused as if she had to consider it. Frank knew she was working an angle. "I want to be the first reporter to see the photographs, and I want to see them at least twenty-four hours before any other reporter."

"That will be up to the major, but if I tell him you played along with the department's request about the details on the woman, I bet it might sway him."

"And you'll tell me everything you learn during the investigation?"

Frank had to smile. She knew he would not do that. "I'll tell you what I can, Elizabeth. We've been through this before. I'm limited on what I can tell you about an ongoing investigation. You know that. I have to get going. Just tell me there won't be anything in tomorrow's newspaper about the woman with the knives through her wrists."

Elizabeth nodded reluctantly. "As long as Cantrell doesn't mention it, I'll sit on the 'crucified' part of the story for tonight's deadline. That's all I'm promising for now."

"Fair enough," Ault agreed.

"I hope you appreciate how hard sitting on a detail like that is for me, Frank. That's huge."

"I know. You're a good girl. Thanks. Are we meeting for dinner tonight?"

"I guess."

"Where?"

"Meet you at Sano's at seven," Elizabeth answered. "If you can't make it—as what happens most of the time when you're on a big case—call and leave a message for me in the newsroom. If I'm not there, I'll call in and check for a message at six-thirty. I don't want to be sitting on my rear end in a restaurant waiting for a husband who will never arrive."

"Okay."

"It's Saturday," Elizabeth reminded her husband. "You'll need to call for reservations."

"Right."

[10:30 a.m.—The Christ Hospital]
"Hi, Cookie," greeted Ault. Cookie was a nurse at The Christ Hospital. Not only did they now run into each other occasionally because of their respective jobs, Cookie and Frank Ault went way back. Cookie was from the old neighborhood, and she and Ault knew each other growing up. They even dated for a short time in high school.

"Oh, hi, Frank. How's everything?"

"Fine, and you?"

"Okay," Cookie answered. "But you don't have to keep sending us more business—five in one night, Frank?"

"Good job security for you, Cookie. You know I'm always looking out for you."

Cookie smiled, remembering a time when they were teenagers. A man snatched her purse while she stood outside a hat shop looking at a window display. Two months later, the man was arrested for another crime and his photograph and address (on the other side of town) appeared in the newspaper. The article said he was out on bail. Cookie saw the newspaper, recognized the man, and told Frank. Frank chased the man down and followed him to an infamous speakeasy known for its rough-and-tumble crowd. Though just a teenager, Frank walked into the speakeasy, beat up the guy, and took from him the amount of money he stole from Cookie plus enough extra to buy a new purse.

"That's right, Frank. You always did look out for me."

As they spoke, a different doctor from the one he had spoken to that morning, but still one Ault recognized, approached the nurses' station. The doctor also knew Ault.

"Two of the patients are conscious, Detective," the doctor said without Ault speaking a word.

"Which two?"

The doctor picked up a chart. "Clare Miller and Penelope Lindauer. They were lucid enough about an hour ago to confirm their names. The Lindauer woman has a broken jaw we had to wire. She cannot speak. We confirmed her name by writing it on paper and asking her to blink twice if it was correct. It was dicey with her for a while last night. She went into diabetic shock after they brought her in. We're keeping her in intensive care."

"Doctor Lamphier told me this morning the Miller woman should be able to answer some questions by now," Ault said.

"That's right, although she has been through a lot of trauma and is badly beaten. Her jaw wasn't broken like the Lindauer woman's, but Miller's jaw is swollen and she lost a couple of teeth so it's difficult for her to speak. Please keep it as brief as possible."

Ault nodded. "How are the other two?"

"The man is also in intensive care. The woman is recovering, but has three broken ribs and a broken nose—besides those wrist punctures. I thought I'd seen everything, but that's a new one—straight punctures through both wrists. What's the deal with that?"

Ault was evasive. "We're not sure yet. If you don't mind, Doctor, I'd like to see the Miller woman now."

Cookie led Ault to a ward where three beds lined each side wall, six beds in all. Curtains drawn around each bed formed small cubicles. Cookie opened one of the curtains enough so Ault could enter. Although the woman lying in the bed looked much different from the woman Ault saw last night—the blood was gone, replaced by bandages that hid much of her face—Ault knew she was the same person. To verify he looked at the woman's chart at the end of the bed: *Clare Miller.*

Because he did not want to question the woman within earshot of other patients, Ault asked Cookie if Clare Miller could be moved to a private area for a few minutes. Cookie checked with the doctor who agreed. A male orderly rolled Clare Miller's bed to a small, unoccupied room down the hall.

"Do you want a chair, Frank?" asked Cookie.

"No thanks, Cookie."

Cookie left. Ault stood beside the bed. Clare Miller's half-opened eyes stared at the ceiling.

"Miss Clare Miller?"

The woman's eyes opened wider.

"Miss Miller, I'm Detective Frank Ault with the Cincinnati police." Ault held up his badge so she could see it. She adjusted her eyes, but did not move her head. "Miss Miller, I'm here to find out what happened to you. We're going to find and bring to justice the person or persons who attacked you. Can you understand me?"

The woman muttered a weak *Yes.* She began shivering. Ault unfolded a blanket from the foot of the bed, added it to her covers, and asked: "Is that better?"

"Yes."

"I know it is difficult to speak, Miss Miller, so I'll ask questions you can answer with 'yes' or 'no' or very short answers." Ault paused. "First, I'd like to identify the people in your apartment last night."

Clare interrupted. "How is Penny?" The words came slowly and were nearly inaudible. Ault moved closer.

"Penny? Ah, Penelope Lindauer. The doctors tell me Miss Lindauer will be okay. She is a friend of yours who lives in your building, is that right?"

"Yes."

"And the other injured woman? We haven't been able to identify her. I assume she is another friend, is that right?"

Suddenly fear appeared in Clare Miller's eyes. "No!" She said it loudly and winced in pain. Ault tried to calm her.

"That's okay, Miss Miller, just relax. You're safe here. No one can hurt you. You say the other woman is not a friend. Is she one of Miss Lindauer's friends?"

"No, she . . . beat us, too."

"The other woman also beat you and Miss Lindauer?"

"Yes."

"And you said 'too.' Did any of the men we found in your apartment last night beat you and Miss Lindauer?"

"Yes."

"Both men beat you, or just one?"

"Both, Roger . . . and other man." Tears welled in Clare's eyes.

"So you're telling me that both men and the unidentified woman all took part in the beatings of you and Miss Lindauer. Is that what you're telling me?"

"Yes."

"You identified one man by name. So you know Roger?" Ault used *know* instead of *knew*. At this point, Ault saw no benefit in telling her the man was dead if she did not pick up on that last night when she was in shock and disorientated.

"Yes."

"How do you know Roger? I realize this will take a few words, Miss Miller, but please try to answer. Take your time."

"Penny met him . . ." her voice cracked. "He . . . asked her . . . a date."

"So Miss Lindauer—Penny—met Roger somewhere, and he asked her for a date."

"Yes."

Ault paused and thought for a moment. "So this Roger fellow asked Miss Lindauer for a date. Then when he showed up for the date he had these other people with him? The other man and the woman?"

"Yes."

"Then they attacked you?"

"Yes."

"And there was another person with them, a person with a gun. Is that correct?"

"No."

"No? There were gunshots fired, Miss Miller. Are you aware of that?" Ault thought perhaps she was unconscious from the beating when the shots were fired.

"Yes."

"So you saw who fired the shots?"

"Is Anne okay?" She suddenly seemed to change the subject.

Ault hesitated. "Anne? Who is Anne? Are you telling me there was another woman in the room?"

Clare Miller paused, as if she was thinking. "No," she said and diverted her eyes, ". . . nobody . . . I was confused."

"Again, Miss Miller, did you see who fired the gun?"

Another pause. "No."

"You didn't see the person, or you saw the person but don't know who it was—which one, Miss Miller?"

"Did not see," was all Clare Miller said before she closed her eyes.

"Miss Miller, just a couple of more questions for now. Are you still with me?"

Clare Miller's eyes remained shut, as if she had fallen asleep.

Chapter 6

Is Anne Okay?

[same day]

A frustrated Frank Ault found and informed Cookie that the questioning was over for now, and Clare Miller was taken back to her ward. Ault could usually tell when someone was withholding information, and that thought occurred to him, but maybe Miller was still loopy from medication. And the strange question she asked about Anne: *Is Anne okay?*

Ault knew Penny Lindauer could not answer questions, so he found the doctor and inquired about the other victims. The male gunshot victim was still sedated and unconscious in intensive care. The unidentified woman, the one Clare Miller included among the attackers, had awakened. When Ault learned her bed was one of the six in the same ward with Clare Miller he summoned hospital security.

"The anonymous woman in bed four must be removed from this ward immediately," Ault told the hospital guard. "It's likely she will be charged with a crime, and she is in the same room as one of her victims. A man in intensive care named Duane Rudd will also be charged. See to it that he is isolated when he leaves intensive care. I'll have two police officers here in a few minutes, and we'll station officers outside their rooms around the clock until those two can be released into police custody."

The guard nodded and summoned orderlies to move the woman. She was awake and groaning as they wheeled her bed down the hall. Her wrists were heavily bandaged, as was her chest to support cracked ribs; both eyes were blackened from a severely broken nose and the side of her face swollen. Ault guessed her age at early-30s, although that was hard to tell because of the condition of her face. He walked beside her bed as it was taken to an elevator, showing his badge to the woman as the elevator door closed.

"Ma'am, I'm Detective Sergeant Frank Ault with the Cincinnati police." Ault did not tell the woman she had been identified as one of the attackers.

"I need more morphine!" The woman spoke clearly despite her swollen face. "Tell one of those cow nurses I need more morphine."

28

"It's coming."

"Where are they taking me?"

Ault lied. "Someplace where you'll be more comfortable, a room all to yourself." That last part was true. "We're very sorry this has happened to you. Ma'am, I need your name so we can notify your family, or whomever you wish us to notify, that you are here. And we need your name for the police report, of course."

The woman avoided the question. "What happened to Roger and Duane?"

The woman did not realize it, but her question about the two men told Ault a great deal. For one thing, it confirmed Clare Miller's statement that this woman was with the two men, and her failure to ask about the condition of the other two women spoke volumes to the seasoned detective.

"I'm sorry to have to tell you Roger didn't make it." Ault watched her carefully and saw little reaction. "Duane is in intensive care, but the doctors think he'll pull through."

The elevator door opened and the orderlies pulled the bed out into the hall. A uniformed police officer was waiting.

"What is this?" the woman demanded. "Why's that other cop here?"

"Lady, you've been identified as one of the attackers, and I'm placing you under arrest for felony assault on Clare Miller and Penelope Lindauer. When you are released from this hospital, you'll be remanded into police custody. An officer will stay outside your room as long as you're here. Now, I need your name."

"Fuck you, asshole. Instead of harassing me, you should be out there finding the bitch that did this to me!"

Four minutes later, Frank Ault walked back into Clare Miller's ward. He would have preferred to have her bed moved again, but did not want to alarm her. A radio sat on a shelf in a corner of the ward. Ault turned it on to make it harder for other patients to eavesdrop. When Ault opened the curtain surrounding Clare's bed, a young nurse's aide was holding a spoonful of soup to the injured woman's lips. Clare seemed startled to see the detective again so soon.

"Miss Miller, you certainly awoke quickly." Despite her bruises and bandages, Ault could see the color drain from her face. Ault smiled, and then spoke to the aide. "Miss, I'm a police officer and I'll take over helping Miss Miller with her lunch. Will you excuse us, please?"

"Well . . ." the girl hesitated. "Okay, I guess it's all right."

"Thank you." Ault took the spoon from the girl and dipped more soup from a bowl on the tray table. He lifted the spoon to Clare's mouth. She looked wary as she sipped.

"Miss Miller, can I call you 'Clare'?"

"Yes."

"Clare, I think perhaps you were not quite honest with me when we talked earlier."

Clare's expression shifted from wary to worried.

"Let me tell you why I think that," Ault went on. "When I asked you who fired the shots, you immediately asked me about a woman named Anne. I thought this strange because, until that point, you had been very focused and helpful in answering my questions. Suddenly you changed the subject, or at least that is what I thought you did at the time. But now I believe maybe you weren't changing the subject. You weren't changing the subject, were you, Clare?"

Clare said nothing, but looked even more apprehensive. Ault dipped more soup.

"I guess it's human nature, Clare, even for police, to think a man is at fault. And almost always that is the case. Men commit, by far, most of the violent crimes. But not always, right, Clare?"

Ault didn't expect an answer. He felt sorry for this innocent victim, but it was time for her to fess up. He laid down the spoon and spoke sternly.

"Now I want you to listen to me very carefully. First of all, I want you to know that when Penny Lindauer is moved from intensive care, she will be placed in another wing of the hospital where you won't be able to talk to her and get her to corroborate your story. And lying to the police, especially about a serious felony, is a crime that holds considerable consequences."

Clare started crying. Ault returned to his friendly-uncle demeanor.

"You know, Clare," Ault said, "after I found out from the woman who attacked you that the person who attacked her was another woman, I started thinking. If someone could do that to a person—pin a human being to a wall with knives—I bet that person would not have qualms about firing a gun, regardless of their sex. What do you think, Clare?"

Clare continued to cry. Ault did not wait for an answer. He went on uninterrupted as he handed her a tissue from a box by the bed.

"Then the name you mentioned—Anne—suddenly rang a bell. I remembered that two residents of the third floor in your building were not home last night when we arrived on the scene. One was actually a family, a Chinese family, and the other resident of the third floor who was not accounted for was a woman named Anne Brown. I have a feeling that Anne Brown is your Anne, and your Anne fired the gun, didn't she, Clare?"

Ault waited.

"Anne saved us," Clare said through her tears. "She saved Penny and me."

Chapter 7

Anne's Room

[same day]

After Frank Ault finished questioning Clare Miller, he radioed police dispatch from his car and instructed the operator to get a message to Glen Schafer. Ault now wanted Shafer to meet him at the Lamar Apartments instead of the hospital. As he guided the unmarked 1941 Plymouth out on the street, Ault did not bother with the siren. The detective held no expectation of finding Anne Brown at home.

At the apartment building, Ault parked on the street behind a marked police car. Another uniformed officer had taken Officer Christian's place outside the building. At first, Ault was surprised he did not see any newspaper or radio reporters hanging around, but after checking his watch, he remembered Cantrell would be conducting his press briefing. The reporters covering the crime would be at the station.

Two men from the recently-formed forensics team were working in Clare Miller's apartment when Ault entered. Police investigations were much different now from when Ault first made detective in 1932. In 1938, two-way radios were installed in every police car in Cincinnati, and with the success of the FBI crime lab in Washington during the 1930s, some of the larger city police departments created their own crime labs. The Cincinnati Police Department was among the first, having started its crime lab in 1934.

"What's the latest?" Ault asked, not directing the question at either man.

"Lots of prints," one answered, "and we found one bullet lodged in the woodwork over there." He pointed. "We almost missed it. It went right into a small gap between two boards. The slug is pretty distorted, but I'd guess a .32. It looks as if it passed through something before it entered the wood—maybe one of the victims. We'll know for sure after we get it back to the lab."

"It is a .32," Ault confirmed. "My partner found the shell casings last night. They're downtown."

Ault found the manager waiting in the hall—a stooped, craggy-faced man with a bulbous nose made purple by his love of the bottle.

32

Last night the old man bordered on hysterical; now he looked disheveled and frazzled.

"Sir," Ault began, "last night you told me one of the third-floor residents who was not at home when I arrived is a woman named Anne Brown. What can you tell me about her?"

"Ah . . . Anne? I don't know much about her. She just moved in a month ago. Just paid her rent last week for a second month . . . paid early."

"Have you seen her this morning?" Ault knew the answer.

"Ah . . . no."

"Does she live alone?"

"Yeah."

"I'd like to see her apartment."

"Ah . . . see Anne's apartment?"

"That's right."

Too exhausted to wonder at the detective's request, the man led Ault down the hall. The old man knocked on the door and called her name twice, then found a key from a heavy collection hanging from his belt and unlocked the door.

"Stand back and stay here in the hall," Ault ordered as he stepped through the door. Ault felt no need to pull the Smith & Wesson .38 snub from under his suit jacket.

The room was small and spartan. One framed picture of a bowl of fruit hung over a small couch. An old Emerson radio with a broken dial sat on a small table that cried out for varnish. One armchair, the upholstery worn thin like the faded linoleum on the floor, sat at an angle to the couch. It had been a long while since paint on the walls was wet. One window only, the view a trash-strewn alley.

Ault looked into the kitchen and was surprised to find a bathroom off of it. Residents of most apartment buildings like this one usually shared a common bathroom on each floor. But it was the bedroom Ault wanted to see. He expected to see dresser drawers flung open and clothes hangers on the floor, evidence of frenzied packing. Instead, everything was in order. He prowled through a couple of drawers, careful not to disturb any fingerprints. Clothes were still there, folded neatly. Only two items in the room seemed out of place: a folding card table and a wooden chair sat at the foot of the bed, crowding the room. Ault had to turn sideways to walk between the table and bed. He always looked in trash cans when he searched a room. In the bedroom wastebasket he found a newspaper, an empty paper cup, and a few short pieces of wire. Ault pulled out a strand of the wire, examined it briefly, then put it back. Later he would examine the room more closely, and call in forensics to turn the place inside out. Now, though, he wanted to gather some information about Anne Brown. Ault stepped back into the hall where the fearful manager waited.

"Anything wrong?" the man asked Ault. "Is Anne dead too?"

"No, no. No one is in there. I'm just following routine procedure. There is nothing to worry about."

"Nothing to worry about!" the man shouted.

"Calm down. I know this is tough for you, but we're going to get to the bottom of this, and I'm sure there is no further danger. Police and our laboratory people will be around here for several days, and if we think there is any danger we'll post a police officer here for as long as needed. You and your tenants are safe. Okay?"

"Yeah."

"I do have a few more questions. Did the room come with the furniture?"

"Yeah."

"About Miss Brown. I'd like for you to give me a physical description."

"Nice looking gal."

Ault realized he would have to spoon-feed the questions. "How old would you say she is?"

"Ah . . . twenties I reckon."

"How tall is she?"

"Ah . . . not sure, maybe about the same as me."

"You're about five foot eight. Is that right?"

"Yeah."

"What color is her hair?"

"She's a blonde woman."

"Blonde hair, so she's Caucasian?"

The old man stared blankly.

"A white woman?" Ault had to clarify.

"Sure, I don't rent to no niggers. What kind of man do you think I am? I only rent to white folks and Chinamen. Chinamen smell bad but at least they work and pay their rent. I try not to rent to Appalachians even though they're white. They tear up and cause trouble, and somebody told me they marry their sisters. I want to keep my place respectable."

"Yes, I can see you have a first-class place here." Ault could not avoid the sarcasm, but the old man nodded, missing it. "Getting back to Anne Brown, do you know the color of her eyes?"

"Nah."

"You said she is 'nice looking.' What do you mean by that? Pretty face? Nice figure? Both?"

"Both, I reckon."

"Slim figure or full figure?"

"Regular, I guess. She's a sturdy gal."

"What do you mean by *sturdy*. You just said she has a *regular* figure. Are you now saying she is heavy set?"

"Nah, just healthy lookin', I reckon."

"Buxom?"

"Regular, I reckon."

"Anything else you can tell me about her appearance—any distinguishing marks like a birthmark or a mole, freckles, an unusual nose, anything like that?"

"Ah . . . not that I saw."

"Do you have some kind of application she filled out when she rented the apartment?"

"Nah."

"Where does she work?"

"I don't know."

"When someone rents from you, you're not curious about where they work? How do you know they'll be able to pay rent?"

"None of my business where they work. If they don't pay the rent, I kick 'em out."

"What is she like? Friendly, outgoing, or maybe quiet and shy? Anything about her manner you can tell me?"

"Her manners are fine, at least when she first showed up and I showed her the room. After that I didn't talk to her much. Said a few words last week when she paid for a second month. That's about it. She pretty much kept to herself."

"Okay, mister, thanks for your help. If you do happen to see Anne Brown again, whether it's here or out somewhere, I want you to call me right away. Do you still have my card I gave you last night?"

"Yeah."

"Good. And I want you to leave the door to Anne Brown's apartment unlocked. Police will be going in and out of her room over the course of the next few days. The room will be off-limits, and we'll put our own padlock on the door. It will be just temporary. And you said you already have the rent on her apartment for another month so that won't hurt you from that standpoint. Right?" Ault knew the old coot would worry about his money.

"Yeah . . . I guess that's right."

Ault thanked the old man again and told him that would be all for now. As Ault turned to walk back to Clare Miller's room, he saw Glen Shafer coming up the stairs.

"What's up, Frank?" Shafer asked. "I was on my way to the hospital when I got the call telling me to meet you here. Do we have a lead on the gunman?"

"Yeah, we have a lead. You better hold onto your shorts."

Chapter 8

News Leak

[same day]

Cincinnati police major Ed Cantrell sat behind his desk talking on the telephone. When Ault and Shafer entered his office, he motioned for them to sit down.

"That's all we have right now, Chief . . . yes . . . yes, and I will keep you updated. Frank Ault and Glen Shafer are handling the case and they just entered my office. If there are any new developments I'll call you right away . . . Okay." Cantrell hung up and directed his attention to the two detectives. "The news about the woman pinned to the wall with kitchen knives through her wrists didn't stay a secret very long. Last night a reporter from WLW radio followed an ambulance back to the hospital and cornered one of the medics. I didn't know until the peckerwood reporter asked questions about it at the press briefing. When the other reporters heard about it all hell broke loose. The news people are already calling the person responsible 'The Crucifier.' It's already been on the radio. The entire city knows about it and the mayor called Chief Weatherly about the case. That was Weatherly on the phone."

Cantrell leaned back in his chair. "Okay, what do you have, Frank?"

"The person we are looking for is a woman."

Cantrell stared at Ault for a long moment. "What did you just say?"

"The person who fired the gun and nailed the woman to the wall is a woman. Her name is Anne Brown, or at least that is the name she is using. She is . . . *was* a tenant at the Lamar Apartments. She hasn't been around since the incident happened last night."

Shafer added: "Like they say in the movies, 'she's on the lam.'"

"Thank you Jimmy Cagney," Ault replied.

"You're welcome." Shafer grinned.

Cantrell ignored the quips and thought about what he had just heard.

"A woman. Are you sure?" Cantrell wanted to verify.

"The woman nailed to the wall confirms that her attacker was a woman. And Clare Miller, the woman who lives in the apartment where the crime took place, backs that up. At first, the Miller woman tried to protect this Anne Brown, but she finally came out with it."

"Miller tried to protect the attacker?" Cantrell was incredulous.

"Clare Miller claims Anne Brown was not one of her attackers. Miller said the woman nailed to the wall was one of the attackers, along with both men. She told me this Anne Brown came in during the attack and saved her and the other woman, Penelope Lindauer."

Cantrell raised his hands to stop Ault. "Okay, let's back up. Give it to me from the beginning, everything you know for sure. First, tell me about Miller and Lindauer, and the people who attacked them."

"Miller and Lindauer both live on the third floor of the Lamar Apartments," Ault began. "They became friends. The Lindauer woman, apparently while out and about, was approached for a date by Roger Beck, the dead man. Lindauer gave him Clare Miller's apartment number because Lindauer got ready for the date there, and she wanted to introduce Beck to her friend. When Beck showed up at Miller's apartment to pick up Lindauer, he had the other man and the woman with him, and that's when they attacked Miller and Lindauer."

"Have you charged the other guy and the unidentified woman yet?"

"Yeah, and I have officers at the hospital."

"No information yet on the unidentified woman?"

"She refuses to give her name," Ault answered. "A run on her prints came up empty, at least here in town. She's a real honey—called me an asshole and told me to fuck off."

Shafer chuckled: "Sounds like she's a good judge of character."

Cantrell, tired of the wisecracks, glared at Shafer. "Cut the shit, Glen. This case is already building up to be a goddamn circus." He returned his focus to Ault. "So where does this Anne Brown come into the picture, Frank?"

"Brown apparently heard the Miller woman's calls for help. Brown entered the room—calm as a cucumber according to Miller— and put an end to the attack using a .32 with a silencer that just happened to be in her possession. Killed one attacker and almost killed another. Fired four shots and all hit their mark. The only bullet that was not still in a victim had gone through the surviving guy's face before it lodged in the woodwork. Then Brown made the female attacker take off her clothes and for an encore beat her up and nailed her to the wall with knives from Miller's kitchen."

"Christ," Cantrell muttered to himself, then asked Ault: "You said a minute ago that Anne Brown was the name she is using. Do you have reason to believe that's an alias?"

"We have a woman with a very common name—a good alias name, lots of Anne Browns in the world—who looks like Miss America living in a rundown apartment building where everyone keeps to themselves. She's a deadeye with a handgun *with a silencer* and is not afraid to prove it on people. . . ."

Cantrell interrupted. "Okay, I see your point. You're right, probably an alias. Any leads on her whereabouts?"

"No."

"What did you mean when you said she looks like Miss America?"

"She's approximately mid-twenties, about five seven or five eight, blonde hair, attractive. That's all we have right now, but I have the sketch artist on the job. He'll talk to the apartment building manager, tenants, and the victims. I told him we need a sketch as soon as possible."

"Well," Cantrell concluded, "we'll need that sketch published in the newspapers. I might as well release to the press that our suspect is a woman. Holy Jesus, when the press hounds get a load of this, they'll be happier than a gang of goddamn Japs that just fell into a vat of saki." Cantrell hesitated for a brief moment. "Anything else?"

"Just one more thing," Ault added. "Last night I checked with dispatch for the name of the person who called it in. The dispatcher who took the call told me the caller was a woman who hung up before she could ask for a name. I didn't think much of it at the time. We all know that happens. People, even good people who will call to summon help for someone in need, many times are hesitant to get involved personally. At the time, I figured the caller was one of the old ladies who lives in the apartment building. But after finding out that our shooter is not a man, I went back to the dispatcher and asked more questions. She told me the woman's voice did not sound like that of an old woman, and get this, the caller reported that two women had been attacked at the Lamar Apartments and needed help, gave the address, and hung up. *Two women. . .*" Ault stressed. "Anyone looking into the apartment would have immediately seen the other three people—the dead guy was right by the door—but the caller mentioned nothing about anyone else. It's obvious the call was made to get aid for Clare

Miller and Penelope Lindauer and the caller was not concerned about the others."

Ault ended with his conclusion.

"Anne Brown called us."

Chapter 9

The Dangers of Eggplant

[same day]

Like most Cincinnati residents, Frank Ault's ancestors had come to the United States from Germany. Along with St. Louis and Milwaukee, Cincinnati makes up America's German Triangle. The town's German heritage dates to the 18th century, and 60 percent of the people who live in this southern Ohio city proudly acknowledge their German roots—despite America's war with their ancestral homeland. After all, most of Cincinnati's German-Americans argued, it was the Nazis' war, and the Nazis were a political party not representative of average ethnic Germans, whether they lived in the United States or back home in the Fatherland. True, before America joined the war in late 1941, many Cincinnatians supported the America First Committee and the German-American Bund. Both were legal, isolationist organizations opposed to the United States getting involved in the European conflict. Some Bund members went even further and embraced Nazi ideology and praised Germany's revival under Adolf Hitler. Pro-Nazi German-Americans in Cincinnati were never huge in number, but they were boisterous and dedicated. After all, the Nazi sympathizers preached, Hitler had brought Germany out of ruin. *Your relatives and friends back in Germany now have jobs, and all those rumors about mistreatment of the Jews are simply propaganda by New York Jews and their minions in Washington trying to seduce America into war.*

But when Germany and Italy declared war on the United States a few days after Pearl Harbor, everything changed. Cincinnati's German-Americans proved their allegiance to America. They went to work in the many local war industries and not merely for the good pay but also to support the war effort. Their sons and brothers joined the armed forces to fight for their adopted homeland (although many asked to be sent to the Pacific theater). Membership numbers in the Bund nose-dived, and the few pro-Nazi German-Americans who remained steadfast were forced to keep their views secret and any meetings clandestine or risk a visit from the FBI.

Yet not everyone in Cincinnati was an ethnic German. Smaller bands of other immigrant groups, including Irish, English, and Italian,

41

arrived and sprinkled out into their own neighborhoods around the city.

In the heart of one of these ethnic neighborhoods sat Frank and Elizabeth Ault's favorite restaurant. *Sano's* was located in an Italian neighborhood a stone's throw from the Ohio River. The restaurant was small—only seven, maybe eight tables—and not much to look at from the outside, but the place was clean and authentic, with delicious home-cooked Italian fare. The Aults ate there regularly. The owner, Giacomo Sano, emigrated from Naples in the early '30s and Americanized his first name to *Jim*. Sano brought his family with him, and now his three sons served as the only waiters; his wife and two daughters worked in the kitchen.

Sano's had no parking lot. Customers parked on the street or in an alley beside the restaurant. Frank Ault arrived at 6:30 (a half-hour early). All the spaces on the street and in the alley were taken so he parked in the next block. When he entered the restaurant, every table was occupied. He then remembered Elizabeth's warning to call in reservations. Jim Sano spotted Ault and approached.

"Ciao, Frank," Sano said with a heavy Italian accent.

"Hi, Jim." Ault did not say *ciao* though his wife would encourage him to. He always felt ridiculous trying to speak a language he did not know, even a simple greeting. Ault did not like people who put on airs, and anyone who acted as if they could speak a foreign language when they in reality could not, put on airs in his opinion. "I'm meeting Elizabeth here, but I forgot to call ahead."

"No-a problem." Sano waved over one of his sons and told him to set up a table for two in a small, vacant area near the back of the room. "I hope-a you do not-a mind being back by the kitchen."

"No, not at all. I appreciate you going to the trouble. Thanks."

A small table and two chairs appeared quickly. A red and white checkered tablecloth, place settings, and an unlit candle covered the table within seconds. Frank Ault sat down, ordered a beer, and waited for his wife.

Frank Ault met Elizabeth Cullen five years ago. She was 25 at the time, and not long out of college. Twenty-five was a couple of years older than Elizabeth had originally planned to be when she earned her degree, but her father, who was quite wealthy in the '20s, lost nearly everything on Black Friday. With her family unable to help financially, Elizabeth worked her way through college. Determined to never return to what she called "the bad old days," Elizabeth grew ambitious and driven to succeed, sometimes to the point of ruthlessness. When they met, Elizabeth had just landed a job as a reporter. The powers-that-be at the *Observer* decided to start her off covering inane events like society gatherings and movie premiers, but Elizabeth would have none of that. A tall, green-eyed, sylph beauty with a Chaucer gap between her two front teeth, she quickly beguiled her bosses into giving her a shot on the crime beat. It did not take Elizabeth Cullen long to make a name for herself; now Elizabeth Ault was Cincinnati's highest profile reporter. Since her photograph accompanied her byline, it was not uncommon for her to be recognized while out and about. She was a local celebrity, and Frank Ault had had more than one restaurant dinner interrupted by her admirers.

Frank loved his wife. Unfortunately, their jobs sometimes conflicted and caused a professional friction that most married couples never have to deal with. Still, Ault considered himself a lucky husband. Elizabeth had smoothed some (not nearly all) of his rougher edges, even if he had resisted mightily, and he knew that was a good thing. He enjoyed his life more now than he had before she walked into it. As far as the job clash, dealing with that was difficult, but, after all, their jobs are what brought them together.

They met when she was a rookie reporter and assigned to cover a case he worked. Elizabeth boldly asked him to dinner one night—doubtless to coax information about the case out of him, he reasoned. Despite her ulterior motives for asking him out, the cop and the reporter hit it off. They dated for a year. Seven years her senior, Frank had flirted with marriage twice before he met Elizabeth but never made the commitment. This was the first marriage for both.

Anthony, one of Jim Sano's sons, had just delivered the beer when Elizabeth walked in. In addition to the food, Frank liked Sano's because the clientele was mostly neighborhood Italians who dined there often. Here Elizabeth was a familiar face, not a celebrity they were seeing in person for the first time, and the regulars left them alone. Jim Sano greeted Elizabeth, escorted her to the table, pulled out the chair and held it for her. Frank stood while she hung her purse over the chair back and sat down.

"It's my lucky day," she kidded. "You actually showed up. I called the newsroom to see if you had canceled and was surprised there were no messages, but I figured you'd stand me up anyway."

"Stand up the queen of Cincinnati journalism?" Frank returned the kidding. "Who would dare?"

She looked around. "Why are we back here by the kitchen? You forgot to call in reservations, didn't you, darling?"

"No, I didn't forget. I requested a place near the back for privacy."

"Yeah, right."

Jim Sano delivered menus, and Anthony arrived to light the candle and take Elizabeth's drink order.

"Anthony, prendo un bicchiere di Barolo." She smiled at the young man.

"Molto buona, Signora." He nodded and left.

Frank looked at her. "They all speak English, you know."

"So," she shrugged, "it's classy to speak in a foreign language. And, since I know you're wondering, I ordered a glass of Barolo, Frank. That's wine."

"The most expensive wine they have, I'm sure?"

"Sure it is, but you're buying so why should I care?"

Frank grinned.

"Besides," she added, "you're saving a lot of money with that cheap beer you drink. What do you have there, some local brew a guy made in his basement?"

"I asked for that but Jim doesn't have any," he joked and took a long swig.

Anthony returned and set the wine on the table in front of Elizabeth. She ordered dinner without opening the menu.

"Anthony, prendo la melanzana parmigiana. E'stato delizioso ultima volta." Then she looked at her husband, "Eggplant—it was great last time. You should try it."

"I hope I can get something with meat." He turned to the waiter. "Anthony, do you have meatballs today?" This was not an absurd question; some meats, including beef and pork, were rationed and restaurants received limited supplies. Frank Ault's having meatballs on his plate depended on how many meatballs Sano's had served that month.

"Yes, Mr. Ault, we still have meat." The young man had spent the better part of his life in the States, and even though he spoke fluent Italian, when speaking English he sounded like any other Midwestern kid.

"Great. I'll have meatballs and spaghetti, with some of those fried peppers your mother makes."

"Marinara?" Anthony used the word to remind Ault that at Sano's, as in Italy, spaghetti did not automatically come with tomato sauce.

44

"Yeah, thanks for remembering."

"Okay. Should I bring you another beer?"

"Sure."

As the young man walked away, Elizabeth said, "I wish I could get some gasoline as easily as you get your meatballs. The scuttlebutt going around the newsroom is that the government might reduce the gas ration from five to three gallons a week. I can't do my job on three gallons of gas a week. I'm cutting every corner now, no pun intended, with five."

"If I know you, you'll find a way." He winked.

"And I'm down to my last good pair of stockings."

"They need nylon and silk for parachutes."

"I might go to the black market," she threatened.

"Then I'd have to arrest you. Hey, that would be a scoop for you. I can see the headline: 'Famous reporter sends stories from inside the hoosegow.'"

"That would be okay if I could have a good-looking cop frisk me."

"I did that the other night."

"I said 'good-looking.'"

Frank laughed. Elizabeth sipped her wine.

"I guess you know that the details about the woman stabbed though the wrists were brought out at the press briefing," she said.

Frank knew it was coming. He knew Elizabeth would be perturbed about losing the scoop. "Yes, Cantrell told me some reporter from WLW chased an ambulance back to the hospital last night and cornered one of the medics."

"You realize you cost me an important news story. It's not every day someone in Cincinnati gets crucified."

"No one knew that the WLW guy had that information. He blind-sided Cantrell with it at the briefing. Besides," he added, "your newspaper can't beat the radio to the punch even if you were going to come out with it."

"A special edition might have. I could have called in the facts about the woman to the newsroom before Cantrell's briefing."

"Elizabeth, I was honest with you. We wanted to keep that information under our hats, at least for a while. We have an ongoing investigation and we're looking for a suspect. Having every detail of the crime out there for public knowledge doesn't help us right now." He took a drink of beer and tried to change the subject. "How's your brother doing?"

"He's okay. Mother got a V-mail from him a couple of days ago. He's still in the Aleutian Islands and wrote that it's turning cold."

"I guess when most people think of the Marines in the Pacific, they think all the fighting is happening on hot jungle islands. I know that's what I thought until you told me a few months ago about your brother fighting the Japs in Alaska."

"At least the fighting is over where he's stationed," Elizabeth added.

"That's good. Maybe he'll be there for a while and get a break from combat. They're probably keeping some Marines stationed there to discourage the Japs from coming back. That's good for him—better to be a little cold than to have bullets looking for you."

Elizabeth nodded. Talk of bullets reminded her of an unpleasant incident involving her husband. "That guy who took a shot at you a couple of years ago is still in prison I assume?"

"Yeah, he'll be there a long time."

"That has to be scary—to be shot at, I mean."

"It is scary," Ault agreed. "And it only happened to me once. Just think of what it's like for the troops. Some of those guys get in battles that last for days or even weeks, being shot at every day, bombs dropping around them, worrying that their next footstep might be on a land mine. . . ."

"That's enough, Frank. I don't want to think about it."

"Sorry, honey." Elizabeth had a brother in harm's way. Even though she knew of the dangers, he should not have said it.

The food arrived. Ault thought it a good opportunity to lighten the mood so he made up a lie.

"You better be careful eating eggplant; you know eggplant is supposed to help a woman get pregnant."

Elizabeth gazed at him for a moment. "Oh, really? So we don't need men? That's good to know because let me tell you, buddy, you guys aren't worth the trouble."

"No, of course, you still need us. I meant it helps make women fertile."

"What witch doctor did you hear that from?"

"I read something about it in *Readers Digest*. Some chemical in eggplant aids fertilization." In reality, Ault made it up twenty seconds ago.

"All right. Since I'm not ready to get pregnant, I'll remember to have a headache the next time you find yourself in the mood, which will probably be tonight."

Frank grinned. He could never win a battle of one-liners with Elizabeth; she always turned the tables. His spaghetti and meatballs had half disappeared while Elizabeth had barely started on her eggplant. He noticed and slowed down. Anthony Sano stood across the room and Frank raised his nearly empty glass of beer as a signal. The waiter nodded and went to fetch another. They ate for a few moments in silence, but Frank knew it was just a matter of time.

"So, what's the latest?" Elizabeth wanted to know. "Any leads on the guy who did it, and why?"

Usually he had to be careful with what he told his wife, but a composite drawing of Anne Brown was being created as they dined. Before he left the station to join Elizabeth for dinner, Frank made sure the police artist was on the job. When he spotted Ray Christian, the young officer who let the "nailed to the wall" detail slip, checking in for his evening shift, Frank shanghaied him from his normal patrol duties. Despite the young cop's mistake with Elizabeth, Frank had taken a liking to Christian, whom he sized up as an able rookie who would develop into a fine cop. The experienced detective knew Christian just had some growing pains to endure and lessons to learn—just like he had when he was a rookie. Frank assigned Christian the job of driving the sketch artist: first to the hospital to work on the sketch with Clare Miller (and the others if possible); then to the Lamar Apartments to get ideas on what Anne Brown looks like from the manager and any residents who could offer help. Frank stressed to the artist that the drawing had to be ready first thing in the morning even if it meant staying up all night to refine it. The drawing would be released to the press early tomorrow. Even though *The Observer* would not have the sketch in time for tomorrow morning's edition, it did not hurt matters if Elizabeth got her scoop and released the news that the suspect was a woman. There was no sense in beating around the bush.

"We're looking for a woman." Frank cut his last meatball in half and ignored the silent staring of his wife. He half-expected her to explode, irked that he had not told her right away. As he took a bite, he looked at her but she continued to say nothing. In a way, Ault enjoyed the moment. Rarely could anyone render Elizabeth Ault speechless. He chewed his food, serenely, and waited. Finally she spoke.

"At what point today did you find out you are looking for a woman . . . sweetheart?" There was a pause before *sweetheart*, as if for a moment she considered calling him something else.

"Oh, let me think . . ." Ault took another bite, taking his time to answer. "This morning."

Elizabeth nodded and sipped her wine. "I see . . . and you waited until now to tell me this little detail."

Ault figured he had trifled with her enough. "We'll release a sketch of the suspect tomorrow morning. Your deadline isn't until ten tonight, so you have plenty of time to get your scoop in to the newsroom that the suspect is a woman."

"I don't get it," she said. "You're telling me that a woman caused all that mayhem? A woman attacked three people who were attacking two innocent victims—the two innocent women who live in the apartment building?"

Now it was Frank's turn to stare. "How do you know that?"

"What? Are you surprised I do my job? I've been doing this for a few years, Frank. I went by the hospital this afternoon and found out two of the victims, the man and the woman with the wrist wounds, had been moved to the sixth-floor psych ward—the place you guys put criminals—and I saw the cops hanging around. The cops wouldn't talk to me, but I knew the patients had to be charged with something or the cops wouldn't be there. Then I went by the apartment building and talked to the manager and a couple of the residents. They told me about the two women who live there. When I got there, you had just left, by the way. What else should I know, Frank?"

He should not have been surprised; this was why his wife was considered by many to be Cincinnati's top reporter. "Yes, the surviving man and the woman with the wrist wounds have been charged with crimes—assault on the two women who live in the apartment building." Ault knew his wife was aware of the laws concerning arrest information. "That is public information that by law has to be released. You know we can't arrest people in secret, so I can tell you that much. The dead man was also identified as an attacker. That's about all I'm going to say right now, Elizabeth."

She ignored his last sentence. "What do you know about the woman you're looking for?"

"Not enough."

"What does she look like? If you're releasing a sketch and description tomorrow, you can tell me that."

She was right. "Caucasian, blonde, probably mid-twenties," he said.

"Do you have a name?"

Frank knew the name, whether real or fictitious, would be released tomorrow with the sketch. "Anne Brown."

"What's her motive?"

"I'm not releasing any more details right now, Elizabeth." He was not going to tell her anything that would not be public information in the morning, and he especially was not going to tell her that it appeared Anne Brown's only motive was to save Clare Miller and Penelope Lindauer.

Chapter 10

Invitation to Anne

Sunday, September 12, 1943

The Cincinnati Observer

Mysterious Woman Suspect in '*Crucifier*' Attacks
by Elizabeth Ault
Observer City Beat Reporter

This reporter has learned that the suspect in the gruesome attacks that took place Friday evening at the Lamar Apartments in the Over the Rhine area of the city is a *female* named Anne Brown. This woman is reported to be in her mid-twenties, approximately 5' 8" tall, with blonde hair and medium build.

Local authorities will release a police artist sketch of the suspect at a press briefing at 10 a.m. this morning. *The Observer* will publish the sketch in a special edition available for purchase at newsstands and from newsboys on the streets by early afternoon.

The suspect is considered armed and dangerous and should not be approached. Anyone with information on the whereabouts of this suspect should call the Cincinnati police or this reporter at the *Observer* newsroom.

To the fugitive, if you read this, turn yourself over to the authorities or call this reporter. Your story will be fairly told.

8:00 a.m. – *Cincinnati Observer* newsroom

The *Observer* newsroom was a large, perfectly square area of many wooden desks and as many never-silent typewriters. Keys constantly clicked and carriages faithfully pinged their warnings when a margin came dangerously near. Telephones rang. Elizabeth Ault sat at her desk among the newsroom bustle. Her story this morning was short, but she had gotten her scoop, front page, and she was satisfied—at least for today. She knew Frank would be furious that she included herself in the contact options for any potential informant or the fugitive, but she had done it before, and in the past it had even worked to the advantage of the police. Although no criminal had ever contacted her, on two occasions an informant called, another time a timid witness, hesitant to speak with police. They felt safer talking to a reporter, particularly a female one, rather than some burly, rough-around-the-edges cop—like her husband. *And this story warranted it; it was going to be huge,* Elizabeth thought. This would be her biggest story because she would make it her biggest. There was a woman out there; a woman who fascinated Elizabeth Ault.

[9:20 a.m. – District 1 Police Headquarters]

"I just got back from the hospital," Frank Ault told Glen Shafer. Ault sat at his desk, Shafer in a chair to the side. "The doctors predict Clare Miller might be released Tuesday, Wednesday at the latest. I spoke with her for a while and I finally got to talk to Penelope Lindauer. Actually, I talked and she blinked once for *yes* and twice for *no* because her jaw is wired shut. I didn't learn much new from her, but what she told me backs up what Clare Miller said. She—Lindauer—has had complications because of her diabetes. The doctors feel it isn't life-threatening, but it looks like she'll be hospitalized for at least another week."

"How about the low-lifes?" a tired Glen Shafer asked.

"No telling how long the man will be hospitalized. The bullet did a lot of damage. Doctor said the woman might be released to the jail infirmary by the end of the week." Now Ault asked a question. "What's the latest from the lab boys?"

"They spent all day yesterday in Anne Brown's apartment," Shafer reported. "Pulled a lot of prints. They were all the same print, not one set of different prints in the entire apartment. Our Miss America is a wallflower it seems—doesn't look like she ever had company. I recruited everyone at the station I could find to help me look at print files. Stayed up all night. When I do hit the sack, I'll be seeing fingerprints in my sleep."

"And . . ." Ault was waiting.

"We don't have a match in our system."

This told Frank Ault that Anne Brown had not committed a crime in Cincinnati: not good news from an investigation standpoint.

"Shit," Ault let out. "That means she's a big flight risk."

"Why do you think that?" Shafer was curious.

"Think about it, Glen. Do you think for a minute that this gal is an amateur? Clare Miller said she nonchalantly walked into the room, pulled out a gun—a gun that had to have a silencer or other people in that rickety old building would have heard the shots—and calmly fired four shots that all hit their target. And do I have to mention what she did to that broad who was one of the attackers? Then to top it off, she calmly called the police."

Shafer felt sheepish. "Alright, I see your point. I haven't slept in thirty-six hours. My brain isn't working."

"And what does it all add up to?—experienced shooter, but no run-ins with the law here?" Ault tested his partner.

Shafer answered quickly this time: "Okay, okay, she is most likely not from Cincinnati."

"Bingo," Ault confirmed. "That means she is a flight risk. Hell, she might already be hundreds of miles away." Ault crumpled a paper coffee cup and threw it on the floor. "What about the wires in her wastebasket?" The wires bothered Ault.

"Nothing much there," Shafer responded. "Standard stuff you can buy in any hardware store. Remember the guy a few years ago that Wiles over in District 3 sent up? The high school chemistry teacher who made bombs he sold to the mob to blow bank safes. What was his name? . . . Delaney, that was it. Some wire they found in his basement helped earn him a nice, long vacation. The guy got thirty years."

"Yeah, I remember," Ault had already thought of the odd Delaney case, odd because it involved an otherwise ordinary high school teacher.

"Maybe we have a gal who works as a manicurist by day and makes bombs to sell to the mob at night," Shafer joked.

"You sent the prints to the FBI in D.C., right?"

"Yeah," Shafer answered. "I told the lab guys to ask the Bureau to expedite."

"Which will probably do nothing to speed them up," Ault commented. "The only thing those guys in Washington expedite now is cases that might concern national security. Standard criminal cases play second fiddle with the war on. The last set of prints we sent took four weeks before we heard back."

"So what's next?" Shafer asked.

Ault knew the options were limited. "We have no place to get started. We have a woman named Anne Brown, which is probably an alias. We don't know where she works or worked in the past. We know of no family, friends, or acquaintances besides the two women at the Lamar Apartments, and they know practically nothing about her that is of any help. Dust off your rabbit's foot because we're going to need some luck. We have to hope the FBI has her prints when they finally get around to running them, or that someone who can give us a lead sees the sketch in the newspaper."

[6:30 p.m. – a coffee shop across the Ohio River from Cincinnati in Newport, Kentucky]

The young woman took a seat at a table near a window. A moment later an elderly waitress wearing a white apron approached.

"Special today is tuna salad, honey."

"That's fine . . . and coffee, unless you have tea," the young woman added.

"I can make some."

"No, don't bother. Coffee is fine."

When the waitress walked away, the young woman turned her attention to the special edition newspaper she brought with her. The sketch looked somewhat like her, but she considered it flawed. Her nose was not that wide, she thought, and the mouth not quite right. Good. And the blonde hair reported in the newspaper would not pose a problem. Her hair was already trimmed, restyled, and now auburn. And with the eyeglasses she now wore she concluded it would be hard, if not impossible, for a bystander to recognize her from the police drawing. *Anne Brown* no longer existed.

The incident Friday night in Clare's apartment was unfortunate and a stroke of bad luck for her. Now things would be more difficult with the police involved. The wise thing would be to move on; however, she had no choice but to remain near Cincinnati until her business was complete.

Changes would have to be made and her time frame moved up.

Chapter 11

Chinese Takeout

Monday, September 13, 1943

The phone rang on Frank Ault's desk. He dropped the ink pen onto the papers in front of him and picked up the receiver.

"Detective Sergeant Ault."

"Frank, I'm at the hospital." It was Elizabeth. *"Why aren't you allowing reporters to speak with any of the victims?"*

"Which victims are you talking about? I have three cases I'm working on."

"Don't play games, Frank. You know which victims I'm talking about."

"I don't want them bothered right now."

"You can't do that, Frank. The police can't restrict press access to a victim. Only the victim decides if he or she will or will not talk to the press. Let me ask Clare Miller if she wants to talk to me. She's listed in fair condition, better than the rest. She can decide. If she says no, I'll turn around and walk out. You can have your watchdog you put outside her room verify."

"Sorry, Elizabeth. No go."

After a pause at the other end, Elizabeth rejoined, *"I know you're mad at me because in the article I invited Anne Brown to call me, but don't try to get even this way."*

"I'm not getting even."

"So may I ask Clare Miller if she wants to talk?"

"Nope, sorry, babe." Frank's normal term of endearment for his wife was *babe;* occasionally he threw out a *honey* or *baby.*

The phone clicked in Ault's ear. It was not the first time Elizabeth had hung up on him. But she was right—he was mad.

At the other end, Elizabeth huffed. This was her story and no one would get in her way, not even her husband.

[that evening]

Cartons of Chinese take-out sat on the dinner table between Frank and Elizabeth. Frank ate with a fork, Elizabeth with chopsticks.

"It's good to have dinner together at home for a change," Elizabeth said.

"Sure is, even if it's take-out."

"I would cook more, but you don't like my cooking."

"I never said that." Frank rolled Chinese noodles onto his fork. "You're a good cook."

"You lie all the time."

Frank said nothing before he put the large roll of noodles into his mouth. Elizabeth continued. "I wonder why men don't cook for their wives. With all the women working in the war plants now, it's only right that men who are still at home share the household chores."

"I cook breakfast," Frank said with his mouth full.

"That's all, and only when you feel like it. You never cook dinner or clean up."

"That's women's work." He knew that would get her going.

She glared. "Why do you love to make me mad?"

Ault smiled. "I don't."

"Baloney! You do it all the time. It must go with your job. You probably aggravate the heck out of your suspects." She pinched a vegetable with her chopsticks then changed the subject. "Anything new on the Anne Brown case you can tell me?"

"Nothing new." This time Ault spoke the truth—the case was stalled. "We're dead in the water unless we get a fingerprint match back from the feds in Washington, or someone recognizes the drawing in the newspapers and comes forward. Or, if Anne Brown turns herself in."

"What are the chances of any of those happening?"

"If she has been booked for a major felony anywhere in the States, the FBI should have her prints on file. Problem is that will be a slow process with the low-priority status the feds will give this case. It might take weeks. Since the war started, criminal cases—even murder cases—play second fiddle to national security cases: suspected espionage, sabotage, that kind of thing."

Elizabeth could hardly believe it. "Are you telling me murder cases are not high priority?"

"It depends on who gets murdered. If someone of note is killed, say, a politician, a celebrity, a rich guy—someone like that, or if it's a multiple homicide, the feds get right on it. Or if the murder takes place during the commission of a federal crime such as a bank robbery or kidnapping across state lines, those cases receive high priority. But this is a local case, and the dead man was a cheap crook and all-around general low-life. The guys in D.C. aren't going to move this case to the forefront and bust their butts trying to find out who did the world a favor when they have a lot on the table. They'll eventually get to it, but it's at the bottom of the stack, I guarantee it."

"So we must depend on someone recognizing the police drawing?"

Frank knew the chances of that were slim. "We have to get real lucky for that to happen. First, we have to assume that the drawing is accurate enough to allow someone to recognize her. Second, we must hope she's still in the area that local newspapers that published the drawing reach. The crime was three days ago. She could be a thousand miles away by now, even out of the country."

Elizabeth thought for a minute. "Then it sounds as if the best chance we have is if Anne Brown turns herself in."

Ault knew she referred to her article and he had held his temper, but now he let go.

"Yes, Elizabeth, turn herself in to us, *the police*, not you! I want you to stop putting invitations in the newspaper offering to talk with criminals. We've had this discussion before."

"I've never had a criminal take me up on it, Frank. You know that. I've had a couple of witnesses or informants telephone me at the paper—people who were afraid to go to the police first. That worked out well for you guys."

"Witnesses and stool pigeons are one thing, Elizabeth. Killers are something different. You suggested that Anne Brown call you!"

"I wrote *'turn yourself over to the authorities or call this reporter.'* I put the police first."

"Oh boy, I feel a whole lot better now."

"Sarcasm doesn't help. What's the matter, Frank? Are you worried I'll trump you and find her before you do?"

Frank took a step back from the war of words and composed himself. He hated arguing with his wife. "Yes, that's exactly what I'm worried about, but it has nothing to do with being *trumped,* or with being a cop. I'm your husband and I love you. I don't want you putting yourself in danger. You don't know what kind of person you're dealing with. She's dangerous, Elizabeth. You've seen the crime scene photos. You've seen what that woman is capable of."

Elizabeth reached across the table and took her husband's hand. "I know you worry about me, darling. But I'm in no danger. I'm not a fool. I've given a lot of thought to what I would do if any criminals on the loose ever call me. I would not meet them in person, at least not while they were on the loose. I would only have a telephone conversation. That's all. And I would encourage them to turn themselves in. I would tell them we can talk on the phone, but if they want to sit down face to face with me to tell their story, that type of meeting has to be held at the police station."

She looked him in the eyes. "There, does that make you feel better?"

"It's still a bad move, Elizabeth, but yes, as a matter of fact it does make me feel a little better," he said. "You'll keep that promise?"

"Of course." She squeezed his hand.

Much later that night, Frank Ault was awakened by his wife who straddled him on the bed. Elizabeth always slept in her undergarments, but now they were gone. She bent forward, kissed her husband then unbuttoned his pajama top. He pulled her to him.

Chapter 12

Clare Returns Home

Tuesday, September 14, 1943

Clare Miller took 30 minutes to walk from the police car to her apartment. Although glad to leave the hospital, Clare did not look forward to going home. The nightmare would still be there; the memories frightening. Detective Ault patiently helped her up the stairs. The limp from childhood always made stairs a challenge and now, to make things worse, she ached all over. The doctor told her it would take some weeks before she completely healed.

Finally on the third floor, Clare noticed the *Off Limits by Order of the Cincinnati Police* sign on Anne Brown's apartment door.

"What will happen to Anne?" she asked Ault as he escorted her down the hallway. He had not told Clare about his suspicions that Anne Brown was more than simply a Good Samaritan who stopped an attack on two innocent women.

Ault downplayed his answer. "We're not sure. The best thing she can do is come in and talk to me. She acted on your behalf, stopping the attack on you and Miss Lindauer. Some might think she went overboard, but the district attorney might consider her actions justified. If he doesn't feel that way, a judge or jury very well might. She needs to come in and let us get this worked out so she can get on with her life. If you ever see her or hear from her, please let me know right away." Ault opened Clare's door for her. Even though furniture had been straightened and floors scrubbed, remnants of bloodstains remained visible here and there. "Yesterday I told the manager you might come home today and I asked him to make sure your place was cleaned. It looks like he did it, at least as much as possible."

Thankful for the cleanup, Clare still dreaded entering. When she did, she avoided looking around and instead made her way to a chair by the window, turned her back to the room, and directed her gaze to the street below. Ault asked if he could do anything else for her. She said no and thanked him.

"Okay then," Ault said. "I'll lock the door behind me. Clare, you are perfectly safe here, and as a precaution, I will have an officer downstairs twenty-four hours a day for as long as I think it necessary.

58

I told him to not let the press bother you. Remember what I told you about the press: more often than not reporters get what you say wrong and cause trouble for you so my advice is to avoid them. I'll stop by tomorrow and check on you. Since it will be hard for you to get downstairs to the phone for awhile, I'll update you on Miss Lindauer's condition when I drop by. I asked the building manager to check on you every day for awhile. If you need anything at all, have him call the station and ask for me. I can have someone pick up and deliver groceries, or whatever you need."

Again Clare thanked him. After the detective walked out and closed the door behind him, Clare glanced at a table in the corner. On it sat the little green hat that she bought Penny for her date.

Clare Miller wept bitterly.

It was not long before fatigue from sitting upright on a wooden chair forced Clare to move to the couch. Some small drops of blood stained the couch—Penny's blood, which Clare could not bear to look at—so she covered the couch with a bed sheet, her condition turning that minor task into a long, daunting chore. When she finally sat back down she was exhausted and slept for several hours. A knock on her door startled her awake.

"Clare, Clare," the voice called from the other side of the door, "are you in there?" It was a woman's voice.

Besides being startled, Clare was foggy from sleep and confused. *Who could that be?* Suddenly she knew.

"Anne!" Clare cried out to the door as loudly as her still swollen jaw would allow. "I'll be right there. Give me a minute." *Anne is home. Things will be all right.*

To rise from the couch and reach the door took Clare a couple of minutes. "I'm coming, Anne."

Clare fumbled with the lock, but at last opened the door. It was not Anne.

"Hello, Clare, my name is Elizabeth Ault. I'm a reporter for the *Observer*. Do you have a minute to talk with me?"

"Um, I don't know . . . the detective told me not to talk to reporters."

"Oh, do you mean Detective Ault? I know he is handling your case. It's okay. He's my husband and he said it was okay if I stopped by." Elizabeth had no trouble telling the lie. She considered it the job of a good reporter to get to the truth, even if it took a fib now and then to do it. When Elizabeth arrived at the Lamar Apartments, she spotted the marked police car out front. She parked around the corner and walked down an alley to the back door of the building. Elizabeth did not encounter the policeman, who must have been somewhere near the front entrance. She made it to the stairwell without being seen.

"I know who you are," Clare said. "I work at the *Observer,* too. But I didn't know you were Detective Ault's wife." The German name *Ault* was not uncommon in Cincinnati. It was not an everyday name like Smith or Jones, but like many people, Clare had come across the name before. There was even Ault Park on the city's east side, renowned for its landscaping and beautiful views. "Come in, Mrs. Ault." Clare felt great relief to have company. She offered Elizabeth a chair, and Clare returned to the couch.

"Thank you," Elizabeth began. "And please call me *Elizabeth.* I hope it is okay if I call you Clare."

"Yes, that's fine, thank you."

"First things first. How are you doing, Clare? I can't even imagine what you've been through."

"I'm not getting around very well. The doctor said it will take some time. But it's Penny I'm worried about. She has always been frail, and they beat her worse than they did me."

"Frank told me the doctors expect Penny to recover fully. I feel very badly about what happened, Clare. It's terrible what some people will do to others." This time Elizabeth told the truth. She felt pity for Clare and her friend. Frank kept his word and yesterday Elizabeth was the first reporter to see the crime scene photographs; ghastly pictures of Clare and Penny before they received treatment, and Elizabeth saw the photos of the other woman, her wrists pinned to the wall with kitchen knives. Elizabeth had seen gruesome crime photos before, but the photos of the impaled woman sickened her. Her sleep last night was erratic; the only positive result of the fitful night was the periods of sleep were not long enough to allow nightmares.

"You said you work at the *Observer?*" Elizabeth asked. She could not recall seeing Clare Miller before, but then the *Observer* had hundreds of employees spread throughout several floors in a large building.

"Yes, I normally work on the fifth floor typing wedding announcements, obituaries, want ads, and a few other things. I also sometimes work in the teletype room."

Elizabeth could not wait any longer. When she knocked on the door, she heard Clare call out *"Anne"* in a welcoming tone. It was more than a surprise; it was a shock. Elizabeth had learned that the suspect, Anne Brown, lived in the Lamar Apartments, so it was not surprising that Clare knew Anne. But Elizabeth, as well as every other reporter at Cantrell's briefing, assumed Anne Brown was an attacker. Why would Clare Miller, one of the victims, call out the name of an attacker and then open the door? Of course there could be another woman named Anne, but Elizabeth's instincts told her otherwise.

"Clare, when I knocked it was obvious you thought I was Anne Brown. . . ."

Clare welcomed the chance to talk to another woman, and Detective Ault had okayed her talking to his wife—Elizabeth said so herself.

Clare told Elizabeth everything.

Chapter 13

The Big Scoop

Wednesday, September 15, 1943

The Cincinnati Observer

'Crucifier' Suspect Saved Women
by Elizabeth Ault
Observer City Beat Reporter

This reporter has uncovered a startling revelation in the case of what is being called the *Crucifier Attacks* that took place this Friday past at the Lamar Apartments in Cincinnati's Over the Rhine neighborhood.

Originally it was thought that the female suspect, Anne Brown, who is still at large and wanted for questioning, took part in the attacks on two female residents of the apartment building.

This reporter has learned that Anne Brown, another resident of the Lamar Apartments, was not one of the attackers, but in fact stepped in and saved the two victims from the real attackers.

The attackers have been identified as Roger Beck, 28; Duane Rudd, 19; and a yet unidentified female who refuses to give authorities her name. Both Beck and Rudd have criminal records for prior thefts. In addition, Beck was convicted of assault in 1938 and served two years at the Ohio Penitentiary in Columbus.

One of the attackers is dead. Roger Beck received two gunshot wounds to the chest and was pronounced dead at the scene. The other two suspects are in police custody at The Christ Hospital recovering from multiple injuries.

Police are pursuing all leads. Anyone with information on the whereabouts of Anne Brown should call the Cincinnati Police or this reporter at the *Observer* city news desk. A police sketch and description of the woman police are seeking are on page 7.

To read an opinion piece concerning this case turn to page 3.

Anne Brown: Villain or Hero?
An opinion
by Elizabeth Ault
Observer City Beat Reporter

A shocking crime occurred Friday last in Cincinnati. One man was killed, another man shot twice and beaten, and three women brutally beaten. One woman was found crucified to an apartment wall with kitchen knives through her wrists.

Those facts alone make this one of the most sensational crimes that I have covered in my five years as a Cincinnati reporter. But the oddities swirling around this case increased twofold when I learned, and revealed to you in this newspaper last Sunday, that the suspect is a woman.

Then, on the front page of this morning's *Observer*, I revealed another new and dramatic twist in the case. I was the first to report that Anne Brown, whom the police are seeking for questioning, was not one of the attackers. In fact, far from it. My sources tell me that Anne Brown saved the two innocent victims, Clare Miller and Penelope Lindauer, from further harm, perhaps even death, at the hands of the true attackers.

This forces us to reflect. Knowing what we now know, what are our emotions? How do we respond?

If nothing else, are we not *intrigued* by Anne Brown? Perhaps if we met her face to face we would be *frightened*. After all, this woman single-handedly stopped three attackers, two of them men. We are *appalled* at the extent of her deeds and what she did to three human beings: killing one man, shooting and leaving another seriously wounded, and crucifying a woman.

Then again maybe we naturally feel *grateful* to her for saving two innocent women from a vicious attack, regardless of the gruesome ends she used.

Intrigued, frightened, appalled, grateful. You'll have to decide for yourself. I find myself feeling all of those emotions.

Who are you, Anne Brown? Where are you?

Anne, if you read this article, I invite you to call me at the *Observer*. Let me tell your story.

It was 8:00 a.m. when Elizabeth walked out of the *Cincinnati Observer* building. She had not been home in nearly 24 hours. She spent most of the afternoon talking to Clare Miller at her apartment, and then it was off to the newsroom to write her story and the opinion piece. She spent the night at her desk thinking about Anne Brown and writing a follow-up story that would appear in tomorrow's edition. All night—writing some, thinking a lot. She could not push Anne Brown to the back of her mind. No story had ever spellbound her like this one. Anne Brown was like no one else—she *had* to be like no one else.

Last night she called home and told Frank she was pulling an all-nighter. It wasn't the first time. And Elizabeth was glad she got the call out of the way before Frank read her articles in that morning's paper.

Again she invited Anne Brown to call her, and in the opinion piece she did not even mention the police. *Frank will be impossible.* But she would deal with him later. Right now she needed a cup of strong coffee and found it across the street at *Stella's,* a small coffee shop frequented by *Observer* employees on breaks, or before or after a shift. Elizabeth found a seat at the counter, ordered the coffee, and thought more about Anne Brown.

Chapter 14

Side Pocket Girls

Thursday, September 23, 1943

Pinky made sure his pool hall was an easy place to spend your money. At *Pinky's Side Pocket,* patrons could drink and play pool. You could also bet on pool. Adding to the attractions, the Side Pocket offered enthusiastic female companionship for a few extra bucks. Almost always there were girls in the Side Pocket who would talk and drink with the men, and play pool. Few of the Side Pocket girls could hit a bank shot on purpose, but the girls knew the men cared little about that. Women know men are simple creatures, and the girls knew if the men standing behind them enjoyed the view when the girls bent over the table that was enough. The courtesans of the Side Pocket appreciated tips for their courtesies; the men of the Side Pocket happily obliged.

Some of the Side Pocket girls were pretty, some not as much, but all were friendly. The girls did not work for Pinky; Pinky was just a nice old man who knew the girls brought in men and he appreciated the girls hanging around. Pinky understood that the girls were the reason his place survived the Depression. The Side Pocket girls received no wages from Pinky, but instead were independent entrepreneurs who came and went as they pleased. The arrangement was mutually advantageous—the girls attracted men to the Side Pocket, and Pinky gave the girls a free place to earn their tips. Pinky demanded nothing from the girls, but still the girls gave him a donation if they used one of the rooms upstairs.

The large pool hall was always busy on weekends and famous for three big parties each year. The Christmas party was mainly just for the girls. They decorated a tree and exchanged gifts. If the regular male customers wished to drop off a present for their favorite girl it was appreciated, but the girls waited until after hours on Christmas Eve (when the men were home with their families) to open their presents together. But at the other two parties customers were invited and encouraged to come: the 4th of July party; and by far the biggest bash of the year, the Halloween party. Everyone looked forward to the Halloween party, which could become quite bawdy. The Side Pocket girls wore costumes, masked their faces, and took great fun in trying to conceal their identities from the men.

A few of the girls were seen often in the Side Pocket, but new girls, and girls who were seen at Pinky's place only rarely, were not uncommon. The same applied to the clientele. Some men stopped in only once and were never seen again; others were regular customers who frequented the pool hall year after year. A number of the regulars came solely to drink, or to play or bet on pool, and enjoying the company of pleasant, nicely powdered females was just an enjoyable diversion. Many men did not need a trip up the stairs to have a good time with the Side Pocket girls. A softness of a cheek, the remarkable swell of breasts and hips, the voice much gentler than their own—all the things that God gave Eve that proves to men that He did indeed love Adam brought men to the Side Pocket. So for many men who frequented Pinky's place, pleasant conversation and the gentle flirtations were enough, and the girls still received a tip for their nice company.

Still, men being men, some sought more robust moments with the Side Pocket girls—those girls, that is, who were willing to oblige (and not all were). For that more vigorous company, a trip up the stairs was necessary, and those men offered a generous tip for the girls' efforts.

And then there was Willy Krause.

Willy liked to drink, play pool, and play with the girls. Willy was a regular at the Side Pocket, and when Willy first started coming around he was popular with the girls. Willy had never worked, but his grandfather (with whom Willy lived) was rich, so Willy always had plenty of cash. Even so, more and more of the girls who had walked up the stairs with Willy avoided the trip a second time. Willy did not fit in with the friendly girls who hung around Pinky's place. Side Pocket girls just wanted to have fun, stay out of trouble, and get by. One day Willy discovered he liked to hit girls, and, as time passed, he hit more and more. A few weeks ago, Pinky called the police on Willy after a girl had to go to the hospital. But Willy paid the hospital bill and tipped the girl generously, so she did not press charges. Yes, Willy was willing to pay extra of his grandfather's money for his fun—sometimes a great deal extra—but since that night the Side Pocket girls all refused to go upstairs with him. Yet Willy still showed up at Pinky's at least once a week to play pool.

Tonight was Thursday night, and for some reason Willy preferred to visit the Side Pocket on Thursdays. When Willy walked in he ordered a beer, as he always did, took a few minutes to find a straight cue stick from one of the racks, then racked up a set of balls on his favorite table. Normally, the pool hall was not busy on Thursday night and that was the case tonight. Maybe that was why Willy liked Thursdays. It was the night before payday for the regulars who had to work for a living (Willy thought people who worked for a living were suckers), and working guys had to wait until after payday on Friday to visit the Side Pocket. In fact, tonight there were more girls than customers, which Willy considered to his advantage since most regular girls avoided him. As Willy looked around, he saw Pinky behind the bar and two men sitting at the bar with two of the Side Pocket girls between them. Only one other man played pool; a thin young man Willy had never seen before stood two tables away. Kathy and Susan, two regular girls, stood at his side. The thin young man seemed to enjoy laughing with Kathy and Susan more than playing pool.

The rest of the girls, a group of four, sat together at a table across the room. They talked and waited. Willy scanned the group and spotted a new girl.

"Any of you intellectual giants want to play a game?" Willy shouted across the room to the group as he chalked his cue stick. The women looked at Willy, disgusted. "How 'bout the new broad?" Willy added loudly.

After a minute's delay, the new girl started to rise, apparently thinking it her duty. Iris, one of the others at the table, grabbed the girl's arm and pulled her back down. Instead, Iris rose and walked toward Willy.

Almost all Side Pocket girls were in their 20s, but Iris was the exception and at 32 was the oldest. And as the oldest, Iris, a spunky red-head, took on sort of a guardian's role with the other girls, especially the newer ones who needed looking after. Iris could certainly show a man a good time if he minded his manners; she would walk up the stairs with a man if she felt like it. But the fiery-tempered Iris suffered no fools, and she loathed Willy Krause.

For his part, Willy hated it when Iris was around. She cramped his style.

"Oh great," Willy commented when Iris reached his table. "I ask for the new bimbo, and I get Mother Goose."

"No one is going upstairs with you, Willy." Iris laid it out. "You can get that out of your head right now. I'll play a game of pool, but that's it. Take it or leave it."

"How about the new floozy if I promise to be good? She's ugly but that's okay, the ugly ones try harder. And if I get drunk enough, I won't remember in the morning what she looked like."

"Forget it. She's a nice girl, and she's a downstairs girl only. And even if she did go upstairs, I wouldn't let her go up there with you."

"You're a real pain in the ass, Iris."

"Better to be a pain in the ass than an asshole. If you want to play pool, shut up and break."

After Willy broke, Kathy, at the pool table with the thin young man, shouted to the other girls, "Hey, ladies, this is Phillip. He just turned twenty-one yesterday and this is his first visit to a bar." Susan, also with Phillip, turned to him. "At least the first legal visit, right, Phillip?"

Phillip smiled. Kathy and Susan kissed him on the cheek. The other girls not with men rose, walked over to Phillip, and one by one gave the young man a hug or a kiss. Phillip blushed, which the girls thought charming so they fussed over him all the more. Willy watched, amused.

"I bet the kid has never even seen a twat," Willy said to Iris.

"You're a real piece of work, Willy," said Iris with contempt. "I bet your mother is proud."

"My parents are dead, and my grandfather stays out of my business as long as I don't get arrested and soil our glorious family name."

"So I guess you blame your grandfather for your being a dirty creep? Easy way out, Willy—blame someone else."

"Fuck you, Iris."

"Keep dreaming, you beady-eyed bastard."

Willy eventually sank the last ball and racked up for a second game. Iris agreed to play again only to keep Willy from bothering the other girls. About half-way through that second game another girl arrived—another new girl Willy did not recognize. The girl walked by, looked at Willy and smiled, then joined the other girls sitting around the table.

"Who's the new slut who just walked in, your daughter?" Willy asked Iris.

"That's Early. She showed up last weekend, just moved here from out of town. If I were you I wouldn't get my hopes up. I haven't warned her about you yet, but I will."

"Early? What does that mean? Early to bed and early to give me a rise?"

"That's real funny, Willy. You ought to try to get on the Amateur Hour. Maybe you can convince Major Bowes to have a contest for *biggest creep.*"

"She's not bad looking. Some of the broads in here look like my German shepherd."

"Is that right?" Iris shot back. "Well, if we look like your dog, then you should feel right at home. You look like something that would drop out of your dog's butt."

Willy, still ignoring Iris's barbs, shouted at Pinky.

"Bring me another beer, you feeble old peckerhead! And bring one for Rita Hayworth here."

"Come get 'em yourself, Willy," Pinky shouted back.

"Iris, go get our beers. Help out the old fucker."

Iris walked to the bar and told Pinky that Willy was buying a round for everyone, to be put on Willy's tab. She grinned, knowing Willy was already on shaky ground at the Side Pocket and would have no choice but to pay. Then she took two beers back to the pool table and handed Willy one.

"Thanks for the beer, Willy." Iris thought about her trick on Willy and started laughing.

"What's the matter with you?" asked Willy.

"Nothing," Iris answered.

Business slowly picked up. Two more men walked in to play pool, and a few minutes after that George arrived, a regular who came in two or three times a month. No one knew much about George other than he enjoyed Iris's company. He spotted Iris and smiled. Iris smiled back.

Willy had to be Willy.

"Hey, there's your fan club, Iris," Willy referred to George. "Looks like you'll make some money tonight. Maybe you can buy that old battle-axe mother of yours a new set of wooden teeth." Many around the Side Pocket knew that Iris's mother was very sick, and that she lived with Iris.

Iris turned and glared at Willy. "I think you have no idea how disgusting of a scumbag you really are." She threw her pool stick on the table, scattering the balls, and walked away to join George at the bar.

Willy gulped down the rest of his beer and looked around. Early was looking at him. When she saw Willy look her way she smiled. Willy motioned for her to join him. Early rose and walked over to Willy's pool table.

"My name is Willy," he said while scanning her from head to foot. She wore a dark brown skirt and a pale yellow sweater with enough open buttons to be inviting.

"I'm Early."

"You're a good-looking broad, Early. You don't fit in around here. Wanna drink?"

"Sure, a brandy would be nice."

"Brandy?" Willy laughed. "That's too classy for this dump. I doubt if that old shithead has any brandy."

"Yes, Pinky has some. I had a glass the last time I came here. Pinky is a very nice man, by the way." She apparently objected to Willy's description of the pool hall owner.

"No kidding?" Willy was surprised, both that Pinky had brandy and that Pinky was not a shithead.

Willy shouted the order at Pinky: another beer for himself, and a brandy.

"I'll go get them," Early offered.

Willy ogled her as she walked away.

Early picked up the drinks at the bar and started back. Willy saw Iris, sitting with George, wave Early over to her table. Even though he could not hear what Iris said, Willy knew it was nothing good about him. When Iris saw Willy watching, she flipped him the finger. Willy sent back to Iris a rude gesture to his groin.

"What did Iris tell you?" Willy asked when Early returned.

"She told me you play rough, and I shouldn't go upstairs with you."

"Do you go upstairs?" Willy was surprised.

She looked at him. "It depends."

"Well, well, imagine that." Willy chuckled. "I pegged you as coming right off Daddy's farm and a downstairs girl only. Some of the bimbos in here think that if they save themselves, Prince Charming will one day ride in on a white horse, sweep them up and pack them off to some goddamn castle."

"Sometimes we farm girls surprise you city boys."

It was Early's shot. When she bent over, her loose sweater sagged in the front allowing Willy an eyeful. He could see she wore no bra. Willy knew that if he could convince this new girl to go upstairs, Iris would butt in and cause a ruckus. But after a few minutes Willy thought he might be in luck. Iris and George left their table and headed up the stairs. When they disappeared, Willy saw his chance.

"If you go upstairs with me, I promise to be good, and I'll give you twice the tip any of the schmucks in here would give you."

Early bit her lip as if she were thinking. "I don't know. Iris said. . . "

Willy quickly thought up a lie and interrupted her. "Look, the only reason Iris doesn't like me is she wanted to take me upstairs one night, but I have high standards and wouldn't go with her."

Early still seemed unsure. Willy upped the ante.

"I'll give you a fifty-buck tip," Willy added quickly, trying to settle the deal. "That's ten times what some of these broads get for a trip upstairs."

"Fifty bucks?" Early seemed doubtful. "Are you sure you have that much?"

Willy pulled a thick roll of bills out of his pocket to show her.

Early wavered. "And you promise no rough stuff?"

"Sure."

"Well . . . okay then."

Willy wasted no time, quickly leading Early toward the stairs. She stopped, remembering her purse she had left at the table with the other girls. While Early went to retrieve the purse, Willy waited impatiently by the bar. Pinky spoke up.

"If there's any trouble, Willy," Pinky warned, "you're out of here for good."

"Yeah, yeah, you and Iris sound like a broken record." Willy was tired of hearing it. "Just go about your business watering down the drinks, you old fart, and don't worry about me. There won't be any trouble."

Two rooms over the pool hall were available to the girls. Sometimes girls with no place else to sleep used the rooms as temporary quarters—sleeping there after Pinky closed for the night. During business hours, the girls who wished to do so could use a room to host a man in private.

When Willy and Early reached the second floor they heard a Benny Goodman record playing behind a shut door, proving that was the room being used by Iris and George. The second door, farther down the hall, stood open. This room, originally used for storage, was more the size of a large living room than a bedroom. But indeed there was a bed, and a sofa, a chair, a table with a lamp and a small gramophone in a wooden box. A few records lay scattered nearby. The table lamp was not on; the light in the room came from a single, naked bulb hanging from the ceiling that flooded the room with a sepia hue. The bedspread looked hastily straightened.

Willy closed and locked the door. Early set her purse on the table and turned to Willy.

"What happens now?" she asked calmly, without expression.

"What happens now?" Willy mocked her. "You take your clothes off. That's what happens now." Willy began undressing.

"Can't we talk first?"

"Talk?" Willy laughed, and then yelled at her. "Do you think I would pay fifty bucks to talk to some whore? Take your clothes off!"

"Just let me powder my nose." Willy was by now down to his underwear, and as Early slowly searched through her purse, Willy's patience left him. He grabbed the front of her sweater and slapped her viciously across the face. As she fell, Willy held onto the sweater, causing it to tear. The blow turned Early around and she fell onto her stomach, her hand still in her purse. Willy again grabbed the sweater, this time the back, to pull her to her feet. All this accomplished was to rip the already torn sweater even more.

"Get up, bitch, and get busy." Willy started to pull down his underwear but never finished. Early sprang to her feet and hit Willy in the head with a hard object she took from her purse. Willy flew backwards and fell on the floor beside the bed, dazed but conscious. It took him a minute to shake the cobwebs. When he finally looked up, she was putting on his shirt. When Early saw that he was lucid, she did not take the time to button the shirt.

"I was going to do this the easy way, Willy," Early said. "But you insist on doing things the hard way."

Willy could see she had something in her right hand. Whatever it was, it was what she used to strike him. Willy smiled and rose to his feet. "My kind of girl," he said. "But we're just getting started. If you like it rough, you've found the right guy."

"I wasn't talking about your perverted idea of a good time."

Willy heard a click. A blade sprang from the object in her hand.

"Hey, what's that? That's a switchblade! What the hell are you doing? Put that away! That's not part of the deal!"

"Sit down, Willy."

"Fuck you! What is this, a shakedown? You think you're going to rob me? That'll be the day when I let some two-bit whore steal from me."

She moved slowly toward him. "What if I'm not after your money?"

Willy progressed from nervous to very nervous, and he stepped back.

"What's wrong with you?" he asked, voice cracking. "Why are you looking at me like that? You're crazy. Where did Pinky get you, from the loony bin?" Willy kept moving, keeping his distance, until the pair now circled the room.

Her voice was not angry, but almost seductive: "You like it rough. I'm ready."

"Put that knife down." Willy tried to act like he was in command, but the words sounded more like pleading. "You're a goddamn crazy woman."

She smiled and held the knife for him to see.

"Jesus Christ." Willy now sweated bullets. "Okay, a hundred bucks if you put that knife down."

"Oh, that's right. I almost forgot. You owe me fifty dollars for my companionship."

"My money is in my pants pocket. Take it and let me get the fuck out of here."

"I haven't earned my fifty dollars yet. I don't want to cheat you."

Willy's nerves were finished. On impulse he picked up a pillow from the nearby bed and rushed toward her, his thought to bowl her over while using the pillow to block any thrusts of the knife. Moving quickly, she slashed the pillow, creating a snowfall of feathers, and spun out of his path. As he stumbled past her out of control, she flicked the knife, slashing his upper arm. Willy fell into the table then onto the floor. At first he was not aware he had been cut, but blood appeared on the floor by his right arm. He placed his left hand over the cut to try and stop the bleeding. When he turned over and looked up, Early stood over him.

"You're not very romantic, Willy." Early looked down at him. "You didn't even put on a record."

She placed her pump on his neck and pressed. Willy gagged for breath and tried to roll away, but quickly lost consciousness.

◊ ◊ ◊

When Willy Krause awoke he was still on the floor. For a moment he thought he had just emerged from a nightmare and felt a brief moment of relief, thinking it was over. But then he felt the pain from his right arm, and when he tried to move he realized his hands were tied behind his back (she used the lamp cord). Then he saw her. It was indeed a nightmare, and his nightmare sat in the chair going through his wallet.

Early noticed him looking at her, and she looked back briefly without expression. Willy's shirt, which she wore, was open and a breast fully exposed. She noticed and closed the shirt. "Sorry, Willy. I should not be so careless with my modesty."

Willy's head pounded. He rambled: "What do you want? . . . Why are you doing this? . . . Look, I'm sorry I hit you . . . I need a doctor."

"You won't bleed to death from that cut. It's not deep enough and there are no significant arteries on that side of your arm." She ignored his other questions and comments, and continued to search his billfold.

"My grandfather is a powerful man. If you let me go right now, I swear I won't tell him about you. He can have you hunted down and very bad things will happen to you, a helluva lot worse than a slap across the face."

Early looked at him, rose, and walked over and stood beside the bed.

"I know all about your grandfather and about you, Willy. I want you to tell your grandfather about me. That's why I'm here. Oh, and about the slap . . ."

Willy heard the switchblade click again and panicked. He screamed for help and rolled away from her. Before he could move again, she put a knee in his back and the knife at his throat. Early told him to get up, and she pulled on his arm as he struggled to his feet. When he was upright, she pushed him onto the bed and ground the knife blade into the cut on his arm, causing him to yelp in pain. She cut off his underwear and placed the blade under his scrotum before leaning over him.

"One question, Willy: are you going to fight?" She put pressure to the blade. A small drop of blood from his scrotum fell onto the bed.

Willy froze in shock, a look of horror on his face.

74

"Good," she said. "Now open wide, Willy."

"No . . . why? . . . What are you going to do?" Blood from Willy's arm began soaking the bedspread.

"Be a good boy, Willy, and open your mouth."

"No way."

Early put the knife blade in his left nostril and sliced the nostril open. Willy let loose with a feral scream as blood gushed. While his mouth was open, Early stuffed his underwear into his mouth.

"There." She was satisfied. "That's better. Now we can talk."

She put the blade back to his scrotum.

"Okay, Willy, I want you to listen very carefully. Will you do that for me?"

Willy tried to speak but could not.

"Good," she said. "Now you have a decision to make. Are you listening carefully? Nod if you're listening."

When Willy did not nod, Early applied more pressure to his scrotum with the knife. Willy grunted and nodded vigorously.

"Thanks. I put an envelope in one of your pants pockets that I want you to give to your grandfather. Do you understand?"

Willy nodded his head yes.

"But you don't have to do it," she added. "You can refuse right now, and I will end any hopes your grandfather has of keeping his family name alive." She again pressed the blade to his scrotum, drawing more blood. "I know you are the last of his direct line, Willy."

Willy tried to spit out the underwear so he could holler for help, but Early stuffed it back in and thumped him on the head with the knife.

"So what is your answer, Willy? Nod your head if you want to have children some day."

Again, Willy nodded enthusiastically.

"So you will deliver the note to your grandfather?"

Another fervent bobbing of the head.

A minute earlier, in the room down the hall, Iris had been entertaining George as a Jimmy Dorsey record, *Tangerine,* played on the turntable. After the song ended, during the silence, Iris thought she heard a strange noise.

"What was that, George?"

"What was what?" George, preoccupied, asked in return.

"That noise. It sounded like someone screamed."

"Some guy downstairs probably won a few bucks in a pool game and let out a whoop."

Iris almost let it pass, but decided to investigate.

"I'll be right back." Wearing only a bra and half-slip, Iris left the room and walked to the top of the stairs. She looked around the pool hall below.

"Pinky," Iris shouted down to the bar. "Where are Early and Willy?"

"They're up there," Pinky shouted back. "I told Willy 'no trouble' or he is out of here for good."

Damn it, Iris thought and rushed down the hall to the other room. She tried the handle but it was locked.

"Early!" Iris shouted as she pounded on the door. "Are you okay?"

From inside the room: "Yes, I'm okay."

"I told you not to trust that bastard," Iris added. "Are you sure you're okay?"

"Yes, Iris, everything is fine."

Iris thought she heard a muffled call for help. Something was wrong.

"Willy," Iris again shouted at the door, "if you hurt her, I'll kill you, you sonuvabitch."

Another muffled sound. Iris had to do something.

"George! George!" Iris shouted down the hall. "Come here quick!"

Seconds later, George stumbled into the hallway, tripping over his pants then hopping to allow them to slide up over his feet.

"What the hell is it, Iris? What's going on?"

"Get over here! Run!" Iris ordered. "Willy Krause is hurting Early. Break down the door so I can kill the rat bastard!"

"What? Are you sure he is hurting her? You know you have an Irish temper, Iris, and fly off the handle."

"Damn it, George. Break down the fucking door!"

George shook his head in disbelief, but he knew Iris, and he knew he had no choice but to try and break down the door. He backed up as far as he could in the narrow hallway and ran into the door with arm and shoulder. The door did not budge and George said, "Damn! That hurt."

"Come on, George, put some steam into it," Iris coaxed. "You can do it." Then she shouted to the door: "I'm coming, Early. Willy, you're going to be one sorry shit-bag when I get in there!"

More muffled sounds from behind the door.

"That creep must have her gagged now, George." Iris was in a panic. "Come on, I have to get in there. Try again."

George lined up again and rushed the door. *Crack!* The wooden doorframe splintered slightly.

"You almost got it, George," Iris encouraged. "Do it again!"

"Iris," George said in pain. "I think I broke my shoulder."

"Use the other one. Come on, hurry up!"

George used the other shoulder for the third assault and this time the doorframe gave way and the door flung open. George fell clumsily into the room and Iris rushed in after him. She saw Willy on the bed, naked, with Early holding a knife between his legs. Something like a rag was stuffed into Willy's mouth, and his hands were behind his back. Blood covered his face and soaked the bed. Willy muttered something, maybe "Help." It took Iris a minute to assess the situation then she spoke quickly.

"Go ahead, Early," Iris said with delight. "Cut his balls off. Do the world a favor."

Early looked at Willy. "It doesn't sound to me like Iris is going to help you very much, Willy," she said.

"Give me that knife, Early," said Iris. "Let me do it." Iris jumped on the bed and reached for the knife. George rushed over, grabbed Iris, and pulled her off the bed.

"What's the matter with you, Iris?" George asked. "Do you want to go to jail?"

"I'm going to cut his nuts off. Let go of me!" Iris flailed and thrashed, but George held her steady.

Early removed the knife from between Willy's legs and got off the bed.

"I'd gladly let you do it, Iris," Early said, "but George is right. Willy would bleed to death before any help arrived, and you would go to prison for murder. He's not worth it. Besides, I need him alive."

Neither Iris nor George thought to ask why Early needed Willy alive.

"Iris, our friend Willy ripped my sweater off. I didn't wear a jacket. Is there a blouse around I can borrow?"

Iris was still focused on Willy. "What? . . . a blouse?" George released his grip on her. "Uh . . . I don't think anyone has an extra blouse." Iris thought for a moment. "Pinky lives here. I can probably get a shirt from him if you want."

"Never mind, I'll use Willy's shirt."

Iris, however, was not finished with Willy. She picked up one of Willy's shoes from the floor and conked him on the head with it as hard as she could. She so enjoyed it that she repeated it again and again. The shoe was not heavy enough to knock Willy out or do any real damage other than to raise a lump and make Willy grunt.

"George, find me something heavy," Iris ordered. "I want to bash the bastard's brains out."

George grabbed her again. As he lifted her away from Willy, Iris managed to swing a leg over and kick Willy hard between the legs. Willy doubled up, rolled off the bed, and thumped loudly on the floor.

While George carried Iris, kicking and screaming, out of the room, Early knelt beside Willy who was obviously in great pain.

"Willy, I'm giving the money in your wallet to Pinky to split among the girls. You don't mind, do you? And Willy, don't forget the envelope for your grandfather. Is there any doubt in your mind that I am a person who would not hesitate to visit you again if you fail to keep your end of the bargain?"

Willy, in a stupor, heard but was not capable of responding.

"Bye for now, Willy."

Early—only a few days ago Anne Brown—brought the hilt of the switchblade (taken from one of the attackers in Clare Miller's apartment) down hard on the side of Willy Krause's jaw, knocking him unconscious.

Chapter 15

The Buckeyes Fall

Saturday, September 25, 1943

Frank and Elizabeth Ault lived in an older frame and brick home in the Clifton Heights neighborhood of northern Cincinnati not far from the college. Frank bought the house two years before he met Elizabeth because he tired of apartments and he got a bargain on the fixer-upper. However, he never got around to fixing it up and his housekeeping was, well . . . less than immaculate. The morning after Elizabeth first spent the night, she told him his housekeeping *is as sloppy as a soup sandwich.* After they became engaged, Elizabeth laid down the law. *Frank, I know you're content to live in squalor but I'm not.* Now, because of Elizabeth's insistence that the house be remodeled, and her good taste in furnishings, Frank Ault lived in the nicest home on the block.

The football game ended.

In its first game of the season, Ohio State lost in Columbus at the hands of the Iowa Pre-Flight squad. Frank Ault and Glen Shafer had listened to the game in Ault's living room.

"Damn!" was Glen Shafer's reaction. Both men were Ohio State fans.

Ault set down his beer and turned the dial on the Philco, searching for another game. He found one and rose from the couch. Shafer slouched in an upholstered wing chair on the other side of the radio.

"Who's playing in this one?" Shafer asked.

"I don't know. You want another beer?"

"Yeah."

Ault walked to the kitchen. When he returned a minute later, Shafer announced, "This is Notre Dame and Pittsburgh. I can't stand those Irish bastards. That Frank Leahy is a cocky son of a bitch. And they think that quarterback of theirs, what's his name? . . . Bertelli—that's it—has a shot at the Heisman. That'll be the day when a wop quarterback at a mick Catholic school wins the Heisman."

"I don't know, Glen, they say the kid is pretty good."

"Fuck him."

Ault laughed at his partner. "You're just pissed because the Buckeyes lost. What did you do, place a bet down at the Rusty Bottom again?"

"Hell, yes," Shafer confirmed. "Ten bucks with the bartender, that bald-headed guy who works the weekends. The fat bastard is a Michigan fan, bets against the Buckeyes every chance he gets."

The men listened to the Notre Dame game for a while but slowly lost interest. The Irish were already ahead three touchdowns in the first half.

"How's things with the wife?" Shafer asked.

"Fine." Ault's answer was short. Like most men, Frank did not like discussing his marital problems. He would never tell his partner that, as of late, he and Elizabeth spent much of their time together arguing over Anne Brown.

But the subject of Anne Brown could not be avoided. Thoughts of the case were never far away for either detective.

"Any scuttlebutt yet on when we might hear something about the prints?" Shafer asked.

"Nope." Ault swigged his beer.

Shafer continued, "I never thought I would get tired of chasing down blondes, but all these false leads are starting to really piss me off. Ever since the sketch was published, that's all I've been doing."

"I'm with you, buddy," Ault said. "I'm spending my share of time in dead alleys, too. I don't think I told you about this one, but a couple of days ago I checked out an anonymous tip about a gal who the caller said looked like the newspaper sketch. Turns out this gal is a cheerleader at UC, and she was at a sorority party with two or three dozen witnesses the night of the shooting. It was probably a prank from one of those pain-in-the-ass fraternity pricks they have on those college campuses."

Both men sat quietly for a few moments, paying more attention to the beer than the radio. Behind them they heard the front door open. Elizabeth walked in with a bag of groceries.

"Wow!" Glen exclaimed. "There's the best-looking grocery delivery boy I've ever seen."

"Hello, boys." Elizabeth said without looking at either man. "How are the Buckeyes doing?"

"We lost," Frank answered. "This is a different game—Notre Dame is ahead of Pittsburgh."

"Hey, Elizabeth," Shafer said. "I just had a brainstorm. Why don't you become the first woman sports reporter and you can take me to the games with you."

"What about my husband, Glen? Are you suggesting I leave him at home?"

"Yes," Shafer answered quickly.

Elizabeth laughed and set the groceries on a wooden chair near the door. She walked over, sat down in her husband's lap, and kissed him on the cheek. "I couldn't leave this good-looking guy behind. I'd just have to take two good-looking guys with me."

"Women sports reporters." Frank Ault said with a grin. "Give me a break."

Elizabeth felt the challenge. "Be careful, Frank. You know what happens when someone tells me women can't do this or that. I make it my mission to prove them wrong, and I always do."

"She's got you there, Frank," Shafer threw in.

"Okay, go for it," Frank replied to Elizabeth. "I won't turn down free tickets to the games." He did not expand on the comment, but now that he thought about it, he silently wished his wife was a sports reporter instead of working the crime beat.

Elizabeth rose, retrieved the sack, and disappeared into the kitchen. She returned in a moment with three beers.

"Here's the last of them," she announced, "unless you want warm ones. I bought some more but they aren't cold." Elizabeth used the bottle opener lying on the coffee table to open the beer bottles. She sat on the couch beside her husband.

"We were just talking about the Anne Brown sketch, Elizabeth," Shafer said. Frank looked at him, trying to send a silent signal to shut up, but his partner ignored him.

"And what did you decide?" Elizabeth asked.

"It's more trouble than it's worth."

"Why is that, Glen?"

"Waste of time. Frank and I have gotten to meet and know about half of the blondes in Cincinnati."

"I would think that might be a pleasant diversion for you, Glen. At least you have an original pick-up line. Let's see, something like, *'Hello, Miss, I'm looking for a blonde killer. Might you be one?'* Not every girl hears that one every day."

Shafer laughed and took another drink. "Seriously," Shafer, now starting to slur his words, addressed his partner. "I have a bad feeling about this one, Frank."

"What do you mean?" Frank asked, and without waiting for a reply added. "We'll get to the bottom of it, Glen. Yeah, it's a tough one, and we don't have much to go on right now, but we've had tough ones before. Even if she has left town, Anne Brown will surface sooner or later."

"I'm not worried we won't find her, Frank. I just have a bad feeling about when we *do* find her."

Frank Ault and his wife stared silently at their guest.

Chapter 16

Hrungnir's Heart

Sunday, September 26, 1943

Adalwulf von Krause begrudgingly invested a little time each day skimming the newspaper in order to keep up with the war, but generally he considered American newspapers a waste of his time. It was the epics he admired: *The Iliad, The Aeneid, The Divine Comedy, Gilgamesh, Paradise Lost*, and his most preferred, the Germanic epics: *Beowulf* and *The Nibelungenlied*. And it was a German language edition of *The Nibelungenlied* that he now sat in his study rereading for the umpteenth time when he heard a knock on the door.

"Breakfast, sir." It was his maid. "Shall I bring it in or leave it in the hall?"

"Bring it in please." Krause had to speak loudly to be heard through the heavy, solid wood door.

The door opened and the elderly maid pushed in a cart. "Good morning," she said.

"Good morning, Viola. Just leave it by the desk, but I will take a cup of coffee now."

She poured the coffee into a Waterford cup from a sterling silver pot and placed it on the desk in front of him. She prepared the coffee with cream but no sugar. The morning's newspaper lay on the cart and she placed it on the desk near the coffee. "Will that be all, Mr. von Krause?"

"Yes, thank you, Viola," Krause said as he closed the book. "How is your granddaughter? You said the other day she was ill."

"She's feeling better now, just a nasty stomach upset, I think. She went back to school Friday."

"Good," Krause said and sipped his coffee.

Viola left the room, closing the door behind her. Krause picked up the newspaper. In an article below the fold, he read about another German setback on the Eastern Front. The German army had evacuated Bryansk, a city 200 miles south of Moscow. But again, a knock interrupted his reading.

"What is it?" Krause called out a bit impatiently.

"It's me."

Krause recognized his grandson's voice. "Come in."

Willy Krause entered. His nose was covered by a white bandage, and he limped noticeably.

"What happened to you?" Krause asked.

"I have a few stitches," Willy answered. "I cut my nose when I fell the other day. Hurt my . . . leg a little too."

"Drunk again?"

"No, sir."

"Where did this happen?"

"In the garage," Willy lied. "I was working on my car."

"Viola told me you came home one night last week without a shirt."

"I, ah . . . a waitress spilled hot coffee on the back of my shirt and I took it off so I wouldn't stain my car seat driving home."

The old man looked at his grandson with suspicion then pointed to a letter on the desk. "There is some mail for you. It is addressed to 'Willy.' You know I disapprove of that nickname. Your name is Wilmar—a noble name you should be proud of."

"Yes, sir."

"If you insist on using that nickname, you could at least spell it the German way, with an *i* on the end."

Willy said nothing as he stared at the floor.

The elder Krause changed the subject. "So, to what do I owe this special occasion? You are rarely out of bed before the afternoon."

"I was given an envelope to give to you," answered Willy. He pulled the envelope out of his shirt pocket and handed it to his grandfather.

Krause took the envelope. "Are you in trouble again?"

"No, sir."

"Who gave it to you?" Krause asked as he opened a desk drawer searching for a letter opener.

"Somebody at the Side Pocket."

Krause exploded. "Side Pocket! I told you to stay out of that place! One of your trips there last summer cost me seven hundred dollars by the time I paid off everybody to keep you out of jail!"

Willy did not say it, but he knew his grandfather would now get his wish. Willy had no intention of ever walking through the doors of the Side Pocket again. The old man found a letter opener and sliced the envelope.

"Who at that sleazy pool hall would send me a letter?" Krause asked indignantly. "You have to be in trouble."

Willy watched his grandfather extract a piece of paper from the envelope. It was a small sheet, folded just once. The message could not have been long, because almost immediately Willy saw the old man's jaw drop, and a stunned look replaced the angry expression of a moment ago. His grandfather stared at the note then looked up at Willy.

"What did the man who gave you this look like?" Krause asked his grandson.

"A woman gave it to me."

"A . . . woman?" Krause seemed to be looking at a place far distant.

"Yes." Willy looked away.

"When did this happen?"

"Thursday night."

"Thursday?" the old man again raised his voice. "And you are just now giving it to me?"

"I thought you were busy."

"Bah!"

For several long minutes Adalwulf von Krause put his thoughts together.

"Tell me about her."

"Her name is Early. She's about my age I guess, kind of reddish hair."

"*Early?* Is that an American name? I've never heard it."

"I don't know," Willy admitted. "I never heard it before either."

"What is she like?"

Willy had no intentions of giving his grandfather details about his meeting with Early. "I don't know, she just said she knew you, handed me the note and asked me to give it to you. Who is she?"

Krause ignored his grandson's question in favor of his own. "She was in the Side Pocket, said she knows me, and knew you are my grandson?"

"Yes."

"Did she say anything else about me, or anything else I need to know?"

"No," Willy replied. "She just made me promise to give you that envelope."

"And there was no trouble?"

"No," Willy lied again.

Normally Krause would have been skeptical of his grandson's last answer, but his thoughts were now deep into other matters.

"Okay, Wilmar. You may go now."

Welcome words to Willy who beelined out and closed the study door.

Adalwulf von Krause looked again at the paper. On it was one hand-written sentence:

I know you hold Hrungnir's Heart.

Krause returned the note to the envelope, rose, and walked to a painting on the wall adjacent to his desk. Krause swung the hinge-mounted painting to the side, revealing a wall safe. He dialed the combination, opened the safe's door, and placed the envelope on a small shelf inside. Krause closed the door, spun the dial, and returned to his chair. He looked at the silver ring on his right ring finger.

Adalwulf von Krause knew his life was about to change.

Chapter 17

Weak Moment at the Rusty Bottom

Monday, September 27, 1943

Many people who worked at the *Observer*, especially reporters, frequented two favorite hangouts. If it were too early in the day for alcohol (though for some it was never too early), *Stella's* across the street from the newspaper headquarters was the place everyone went for coffee and donuts, or a sandwich at lunchtime. Later in the day and at night, the watering hole for the *Observer* gang and many members of the press from other newspapers and radio stations was the *Rusty Bottom Bar* on Fifth Street not far from Fountain Square: the bar's curious name a reference to the corroded keel of the bar owner's fishing boat, which for years sat on the walk in front of the bar until one night it vanished and the mystery never solved. The Rusty Bottom was a good joint, not fancy but familiar. At the Rusty Bottom, the highballs were strong and priced right, and the scuttlebutt always ran thick. Despite the fact that City Hall was not far, politicians avoided the place because they knew to expect an impromptu grilling by at least one of the newshounds sitting on nearby barstools. Everyone knew the press drank at the Rusty Bottom, along with those who did not mind drinking with the press.

In the past, the Rusty Bottom saw Elizabeth Ault infrequently. Once in a while she stopped in for a few minutes after putting a story to bed to mingle with friends and colleagues, but she had never been a true-blue regular. Not, that is, until recently. Now the Rusty Bottom saw more of Elizabeth for several reasons, and all of them revolved around Anne Brown.

Elizabeth had already written six stories about Anne Brown, or was it seven? In fact, she wrote about nothing else unless forced to by her editor. And to Elizabeth, her editor was starting to remind her of her husband, accusing her of being obsessed with Anne Brown.

Frank.

The arguments at home had become commonplace. He would press her to back off the Anne Brown story and she would refuse. *Frank, my career is as important to me as yours is to you. If you want your wife always barefoot and pregnant, you married the wrong girl.*

87

Then he would counter about the danger she might be putting herself in. This was the common theme.

At the Rusty Bottom, Elizabeth could be away from her desk, escape her editor and the arguments at home. Here Elizabeth could think her thoughts—about Anne Brown.

Elizabeth prided herself on her independence, and she had little patience with women who kowtowed to men, regardless of the roles the men played in their lives: husband, boss, friend; it made no difference. She cheered for the women now playing important roles in the war effort. As the men went off to fight, women were needed to build planes, ships, and tanks. Women were now welders, riveters, pipe fitters, and held other jobs that until the war were strictly the domain of men. It was the start of a new era for women, and to Elizabeth it was a sanctioning of women that must continue and expand even after the war ended. When she was born, women could not vote. Women deserved equal opportunities, and although obstacles to that egalitarianism still existed, great gains had been made. Elizabeth would join any fight against attempts to ever again relegate women to second-class citizenship.

Perhaps that ideology invoked the allure and the fascination that gripped her with the Anne Brown story. Surely that must be it. Anne Brown, for good or bad, represented the ultimate shedding of female stereotypes. Elizabeth could not stop thinking about her.

"Another Tom Collins?"

The bartender's soft voice brought Elizabeth back from her thoughts. She looked at her empty glass. "Yes, thanks, Patti."

"Hey, good looking." This time it was a man's voice, and from behind her. When she turned, Glen Shafer stood grinning.

"Hi, Glen," Elizabeth said matter-of-factly. Glen also spent time at the Rusty Bottom. In fact, most of her visits to the bar had been when she, Frank, and Glen had come together. Her husband and Glen had little in common besides their jobs, Elizabeth always thought. Her brawny husband had dark hair and eyes, was cautious around strangers in his personal life, and not inclined to frivolous chat. The sandy-haired, green-eyed Glen Shafer on the other hand was very much the party personality, glib with all and a flirt with the ladies.

"What's cooking?" asked Shafer as he took a seat on the barstool next to Elizabeth. "Where's the poorer half? Is he meeting you here?"

"No, I just beat my deadline and stopped for a drink before heading home. Frank wasn't home when I called. He must still be at the station."

"He was there when I left," Shafer confirmed. "That was three hours ago, but knowing Frank, you're probably right. He's most likely still doing paperwork, or searching the print files. We've been busy this month. There's never a shortage of scumbags, so being in the catch-the-scumbag business keeps us busy. And there was a full moon a couple of nights ago."

"Do you think that is true?" Elizabeth asked. "Are more crimes committed during a full moon?"

"It seems true to me." Shafer said. Patti arrived with Elizabeth's Tom Collins. Shafer ordered Scotch then turned back to Elizabeth. "You heard about the guy who was stabbed three times over by Waterworks Park?"

"Yes, I covered that crime."

"Oh, that's right, I remember reading it. Lucky for us the victim didn't die—we have enough work to do. I hope the guy doesn't kick off and it ends up in our laps in Homicide. Anyway, the reason I mentioned it is that it took place the night of the full moon."

Elizabeth held little interest in Glen Shafer's lunar theories. She had heard the claims before, but the relationship between the full moon and crime, or the full moon's affect on women delivering babies seemed merely a superstition to her. Elizabeth steered the conversation in another direction. Maybe her husband's partner will tell her something her husband would not.

"Anything new on the Anne Brown case?"

Shafer shrugged. The Scotch arrived and Shafer took a drink. "Not anything to brag about. We still haven't heard anything from the FBI about her prints. Those fancy-pants in Washington probably haven't opened the envelope yet. One thing I know, Frank and I are wasting a lot of time following up false leads from people who think they recognize the person in the sketch your paper published."

"I recall you said that the other day at the house, but isn't that pretty much always the case with those sketches?" Elizabeth knew it was, but asked anyway.

"Yeah, some more than others. The Anne Brown case has people talking so we get a lot of calls, most of them anonymous. I scared the bejeezus out of a hairdresser the other day. We got an anonymous call and went to the hair salon where she worked. She looked somewhat like the drawing, blonde hair and all of that. We took her to the station and checked her out and, of course, she wasn't Anne Brown. I think that one was a prank because while we questioned her, she got flustered and mentioned that her teenage brother is always tricking her."

"The brother can get in big trouble for that, right?"

"Yeah, if it could be proved he made the call, which is usually impossible. We wrote in the report what she said, and normally the desk jockeys who process the reports will send a uniform to talk to the brother. But unless he admits doing it, that's the end of it. Unless you're a VIP, you're on a party line, and those calls are practically impossible to trace. And seldom is the caller on the phone long enough to trace the call even if we could trace it. Then, if the caller has half a brain he'll make the call from a phone booth, so there you go. In other words, unless the caller is a total moron—forget it." Shafer took another drink.

Elizabeth could empathize. "It's terrible that people will waste your time. As a reporter, I get false leads. I know how frustrating it is. But at least the police don't have gasoline rationing. That's my biggest problem. Many times the phone just isn't enough, you have to be there, and I don't get enough gas as it is, let alone wasting it on phony tips. Heck, I couldn't afford to waste the gas to come here if it weren't on the way home."

"The newspaper can't get reporters extra rationing?" Shafer asked.

"No, not yet. My paper and some others around the country have made the appeal to the Rationing Board and contacted various congressmen, but it's all stuck in red tape in Washington. Right now the only way we get extra gas is if the story concerns the war effort, and even then we have to fill out a form and send it to the R.B. ahead of time for approval."

"That's screwball," Shafer commented. He noticed Elizabeth's drink was low. "Let me buy you another round."

"No," she shook her head, "this is my second. That's my limit. Thanks anyway. It's been nice talking, Glen, but I'm tired, and it's time to go home and argue with Frank."

"He worries about you, Elizabeth. He worries that one of the criminals you invite to get in touch with you will someday take you up on it."

90

"Frank knows I will talk to them only on the telephone, or if you guys have them in jail."

She settled her tab with Patti; Shafer did the same.

Shafer walked Elizabeth out of the Rusty Bottom. On the way through the door, he placed his hand on her back to guide her, but his hand was too low. She looked at him and he looked back at her. She should have removed his hand, or at the very least moved it up.

She should have . . . but did not.

Across the street from the Rusty Bottom, in a narrow alley perpendicular to the bar, a figure stood hidden in the shadows. The dark figure watched the woman reporter leave the bar with a man. *Interesting.* When the woman arrived she was alone.

The pair walked across the street toward their cars. Suddenly the man took the woman's hand and led her into the alley. He grabbed her and kissed her passionately. As they kissed, the man undid her coat sash, opened the coat, and began unbuttoning her blouse. The woman did not object; she returned the kiss and allowed him to open her blouse, pull down the cups of her bra, and fondle her breasts while they kissed. The dark figure, undetected behind a fire escape merely feet away, could hear the couple breathing heavily. After several minutes, the woman suddenly pulled away.

"We can't, Glen, this isn't right," the shadowed figure heard the woman say.

"Elizabeth, I've always wanted you." The man kissed her again and the woman allowed it for another long moment, but finally she pulled away and began buttoning her blouse. He again reached out for her but this time she moved away, hastily straightened her clothing, and once more told him what they were doing was wrong.

Finally, at her insistence, the two parted: he to his car, she to hers. They drove away in opposite directions.

When the dark figure walked out of the alley, the streetlight revealed the figure of a woman. She crossed the street and entered the Rusty Bottom.

"Brandy, please," the woman told the bartender as she stood at the bar. When Patti delivered the drink, the woman smiled and asked, "Hey, wasn't that Elizabeth Ault, the reporter, I just saw leave here?"

"Yeah, that's her," Patti answered.

91

"Does she come in often?"

"Once in a while, usually with her husband."

"Oh, so that was her husband that was with her?" The woman knew from the conversation in the alley that it was not.

"No, that was her husband's partner, Glen Shafer. Glen and her husband are both cops. Elizabeth and Glen are just friends."

[twenty minutes later]

Frank was home and listening to the radio when Elizabeth arrived.

"Hi, babe," Frank greeted her as he set down his beer and patted the sofa next to him, an invitation for her to sit. "Where you been?"

"I stopped by the Rusty Bottom on my way home," Elizabeth answered. "I'll be right there, Frank. I have to use the bathroom."

Elizabeth walked directly to the bathroom where she brushed her teeth with baking soda. She had wiped away her smeared lipstick in the car. She applied a fresh coat and dabbed perfume to cover any lingering scent of a man before returning to the living room.

"How was your day?" he said as she sat down beside him.

Elizabeth said nothing, staring blankly ahead.

Frank rubbed her back. "What's the matter, babe?"

"I don't want to argue tonight, Frank."

"Me neither."

Elizabeth Ault rose, knelt in front of her husband, and reached for his belt.

Chapter 18

Dancing Fairies

Friday, October 1, 1943

Elizabeth Ault ran through a cold fall rain for nearly a block to the restaurant. It was not raining when she left the house that morning, but the day broke gray and murky and she wisely remembered to take her raincoat with her.

She was meeting Frank at Sano's for lunch, and this time she arrived before her husband. Unlike her husband, she had remembered to call for reservations, a good idea even for lunch at the small, always busy restaurant. Jim Sano seated her at a table for two next to a window near the front door. She ordered coffee and watched the rain. The weather matched her gloomy thoughts. Elizabeth was ashamed and embarrassed about the night at the Rusty Bottom with Glen Shafer. She let Glen fondle and kiss her passionately and she had returned his kiss, at least for awhile, until her wits returned. *What was I thinking? Making out with my husband's partner in some dark, dirty alley!* Elizabeth had considered confessing it all to Frank, but what good would come of that? *No, even though it went no further than the kiss and groping, that was more than bad enough. Frank would be crushed and humiliated, and he would put Glen in the hospital if not worse, God forbid. Frank must never know.*

She had little interest in the coffee, abandoned in front of her, as she stared out the restaurant window. A passing car splashed a man waiting to cross at the corner. Elizabeth could not hear, nor did she care to hear, the words the man shouted at the driver. A few walkers passed the window; those without umbrellas moved more swiftly than those with. An elderly couple entered Sano's and was seated at the last available table. The woman looked at Elizabeth and whispered to her husband. He turned and looked at her, but to Elizabeth's relief they did not bother her.

The rain strengthened. A woman under an umbrella hurried toward the restaurant from the street's other side. She entered, lowered and closed the umbrella, and was greeted by Jim Sano who apologized for the rain, as if the weather was his fault. Sano and the woman stood only a few feet from Elizabeth's table and Elizabeth could not avoid overhearing.

"I'm-a so sorry, we have-a no table for you right-a now."

"That's okay. To be honest I just came in to get out of the rain for a moment."

Sano offered her a chair by the register; she thanked him.

"I will bring-a you a cup of coffee, no charge."

"Please don't go to any trouble."

"I insist-a."

The gracious old Italian walked away. The young woman sat quietly. Elizabeth turned her eyes back to the window. Frank was right: she had become obsessed with Anne Brown. It was making her irrational. Maybe she should recuse herself from the story—turn it over to another reporter. Her thoughts ran uncontrolled; she was mortified about what she had done with Glen Shafer and she was bewildered about why she was so fixated on Anne Brown.

Finally, Elizabeth took a sip of the now tepid coffee and looked at her wristwatch. Frank was 15 minutes late. When she looked up, the woman who had escaped the rain was gazing at her. The woman smiled. Elizabeth quickly looked away. She was in no mood to be bothered for an autograph or frivolous chit-chat. Looking away did not work. The woman rose and approached, bringing her umbrella and coffee with her.

"Hi. You look like the lady who writes the news stories. Are you Elizabeth Ault?"

"Yes," Elizabeth murmured quietly.

"I can't believe it," the woman gasped. "I'm such a fan. I'm studying journalism so I can be a reporter. You're my hero!"

On another day Elizabeth might have felt flattered. Today she was not interested and tried a polite rebuff. "Thanks, and good luck with your studies. I'd like to talk, but I'm waiting for my husband. He'll be here any minute."

"Do you mind if I ask you just a couple of questions before he gets here . . . about being a reporter? I can tell my professor I spoke with you."

Elizabeth hesitated, which she knew was impolite but at that moment did not care. Finally, she halfheartedly motioned to the seat across the table. The woman, a pretty brunette under a brown straw hat, looked to be in her mid-to-late twenties. She wore eyeglasses and a linen coat intended to be the same color as the hat but now was rain-darkened having not benefited from full protection of her umbrella.

"Thanks. This is a real stroke of luck for me," the woman began as she pulled up the chair, "running into you I mean. I've been reading your reports about the woman suspected of that attack at the apartment building. Intriguing. I hope they catch her."

"They will," Elizabeth said without conviction. Anne Brown was the last topic she wanted to discuss with this stranger, and she avoided eye contact hoping the woman would make it brief.

"You wrote that anyone with information could call you. Any new leads?"

"Nothing that I'm aware of—not in the last few days anyway." Elizabeth had had enough. "Look, I'd like to talk but you'll have to excuse me. Like I said, my husband will be here any minute now."

The young woman leaned forward. "Your husband will be late."

Elizabeth looked up. "What do you mean, my husband will be late?"

"He's been delayed."

As Elizabeth looked closely at the woman, the blood drained from the reporter's face like someone had pulled a plug. For a second Elizabeth felt faint, but she stiffened, forcing herself to think.

"Are you? . . . you are . . . Anne Brown." The words came out as a stutter, probably too loud, but no one around them seemed to notice.

The young woman's demeanor remained pleasant and she was calm, much calmer than Elizabeth. "Not any longer, but it is nice to meet you, Elizabeth."

"How do you know my husband will be late?" Elizabeth was frantic. "Did you do something to him?"

"No, of course not. You misjudge me. He has simply encountered a transportation problem."

"He's a cop." Elizabeth stated it like it was a threat.

The young woman looked Elizabeth over before speaking. "You surprise me."

"What do you mean?" Elizabeth's heart raced.

"From your writing, you impressed me as a strong woman—a woman in control. That's not what I see here."

"You swear you did not harm my husband?"

"Yes. Don't you believe me?"

Elizabeth faltered. She had no idea why, but she did believe this woman. With her fear concerning Frank somewhat lessened, Elizabeth calmed a bit—perhaps.

"I think I believe you," was all Elizabeth could say.

One of the Sano sons arrived and topped off the coffee cups. Both women sat silently until he walked away. The former *Anne Brown* was the first to speak.

"I thought you would be a bit more enthusiastic. You wrote in your articles that I could contact you."

"I wrote *call* me. That means on the telephone. Besides, I never thought you'd take me up on it."

Anne Brown smiled and laughed softly. And despite the shock of the meeting, from which Elizabeth had not recovered, she was now determined to revert to her professional reporter mode despite her head swimming. She took a moment to collect her thoughts.

"You don't resemble the police drawing very closely."

"Thank you. Yes, changing hair color, makeup, and putting on a pair of eyeglasses go a long way toward changing a woman's looks. Besides, the nose and mouth in that drawing are all wrong. At least I think so."

"Why did you go to all this trouble to meet like this? You could have called me at the newsroom and arranged to meet somewhere. To meet like this you had to have followed me, right?"

"You're not thinking clearly, Elizabeth. Do you really imagine I would call you to arrange a meeting that you could tell your detective husband about ahead of time? But to answer your second question, *yes,* I have been following you."

"How long have you been following me?"

"Not long, and only when time allowed."

Elizabeth felt a tremble knowing this woman had been stalking her.

"Well," Elizabeth collected her thoughts, "why are we here? Do you want to tell your story?"

No answer.

Elizabeth tried another question. "Do you want to turn yourself in?"

"No."

"Why not? Clare Miller and Penelope Lindauer will testify that you saved their lives. No jury in the country would convict you. It's called justifiable homicide. Why subject yourself to this manhunt?"

As Elizabeth spoke, the young woman gazed out the window.

"Sadly, it looks like our conversation will have to wait. Your husband just now parked across the street."

Elizabeth turned quickly and saw Frank getting out of a car.

"I know you won't tell your husband who I am. I was only a few feet from you in the alley on the night of your indiscretions with your husband's partner, but that is no concern to me. What you need to consider is I am armed and I will have the element of surprise. If you care for your husband, remain silent, at least until I am safely away."

Elizabeth felt like she would vomit.

"Good bye, Elizabeth."

When Frank entered Sano's, he saw a young woman rise from the chair at his wife's table. He thought little of it; it was not uncommon for strangers to recognize and approach his wife. The woman walked toward the door and smiled at him as they passed.

"Sorry I'm late," Frank apologized to Elizabeth as he sat down. "I had to take Glen's car. Some asshole slit one of my tires, and he did it right in front of the station. I can't believe it. The sonuvabitch better hope I don't find him."

Elizabeth, badly shaken, did not respond.

"What's the matter, Elizabeth?" He tried humor. "You look as if you just saw Marley's ghost."

Elizabeth lowered and shook her head. A moment passed as Frank studied his wife and put two and two together.

"Who is that woman you were talking to when I came in? She obviously said something to upset you."

Elizabeth uttered it weakly: "Anne Brown."

Frank Ault rocketed from his chair, which overturned and banged loudly on the floor.

"Frank, she has a gun!" Elizabeth screamed as her husband bolted out the door. Among the restaurant patrons, one woman shrieked; others gasped.

Ault stopped on the sidewalk in front of the restaurant to look both ways, turning fast.

Anne Brown was gone.

"Goddammit!" Ault shouted in frustration then thought silently to himself: *What kind of a creature under God's Heaven is this woman?*

Frank Ault stood in the rain looking back and forth for several minutes then walked back into the restaurant.

Elizabeth was gone.

◊ ◊ ◊

Elizabeth walked through the rain without thought of where she was going. She could not bear facing Frank, so while he was outside looking for Anne Brown she exited out the back door of Sano's, forgetting her coat. She shivered as the rain soaked her clothing, but she walked on.

Her life was coming apart. In her mind she was an adulteress, and she was stunned by her meeting with Anne Brown. Elizabeth shook uncontrollably when she thought of Anne Brown nearby, watching her and Glen Shafer that night outside the Rusty Bottom. And how did Brown know she was meeting Frank at Sano's? How did Brown know that Frank's car was at the station? Had Brown followed them both?

Elizabeth prided herself on being a professional, but when meeting Anne Brown she had been anything but. She had been befuddled and at a loss for words. Now she felt like a fool. A fool because of what she did with Glen Shafer, and a fool because of the way she conducted herself when meeting Anne Brown.

She stopped on a street corner and stood, unconcerned with the cold and the rain that flattened her hair and sent her makeup streaking down her face. Anne Brown said at the restaurant that their conversation would have to wait. Did that mean the woman would again appear out of nowhere when Elizabeth least expected it? A few days ago, all Elizabeth wanted was to talk with Anne Brown. Now she felt terror at the thought of seeing her again.

After a few minutes, a car pulled up and stopped beside her. Frank got out, put his coat over his shaking wife, and gently helped her into the car.

Ten minutes later and three blocks away, the young woman who had sat at Elizabeth's table walked through puddles in a narrow alley. Though the rain continued to tumble steadily, she did not open her umbrella. *They will be looking for a woman under an umbrella.* As she walked, she removed her hat, the brunette wig that covered her dyed auburn hair, eye-glasses, and her dark brown overcoat that covered a light yellow jacket. She tossed the hat, wig, glasses, overcoat, and the umbrella into a large trash container as she passed.

She loved the rain surely always. When she was little, her father told her the splashing raindrops were really dancing fairies. She stopped for a moment and lifted her eyes to the heavens to let the fairies dance on her face, as she did when she was a child.

Chapter 19

Guarding Elizabeth

Saturday, October 2, 1943

The first action Frank Ault took was to protect his wife. Anne Brown had been following Elizabeth and would likely continue to do so if a second meeting was in mind. To ensure Elizabeth's safety, Frank insisted she not be alone on the streets. Whenever he could, he would drop her off and pick her up at the newspaper. If he was not available for routine trips, or any unforeseen ones, such as when she had to be out and about on a story, she was to call the District 1 station and someone would be sent to drive her. The same went for personal errands from home.

The second step: an updated police sketch.

The police artist now sat on the couch, busy. Frank had decided to have the artist come to the house. Elizabeth's unexpected meeting with Anne Brown yesterday had frayed her nerves, and Frank thought a trip to the station might make things worse. Frank stood off to the side, leaning against a wall with a coffee cup in hand. Glen Shafer sat in an armchair against the opposite wall.

The artist drew on a large pad. Elizabeth sat beside him, looking at and referring to the sketch her newspaper published three weeks ago.

"You said the nose is more narrow, Mrs. Ault?" The artist did not look up from his pad and drew as he talked.

"Yes, the nostrils are less flared than in the first sketch."

"And the hair now brunette?"

"Yes, but it might have been a wig. I couldn't tell. A hat covered much of it."

"Anything else?" the drawing man asked.

Elizabeth hesitated, thinking. Frank spoke up.

"She said the woman commented on the newspaper sketch and said the nose *and* the mouth were *off*. Isn't that right, Elizabeth?"

"Yes, she said that." Elizabeth hesitated as she looked at the older sketch. "But I don't remember what was different about the mouth."

Sketch artist: "So you think the mouth in the original sketch is close?"

"I don't know. I guess so." Elizabeth wanted to help and made every effort, but suddenly she grew exceptionally tired of thinking about Anne Brown's nose and mouth, and having Glen Shafer sitting in the room increased her stress, especially after Frank told her Glen might be her occasional bodyguard. She tried to hand off to her husband: "Frank, you saw her."

"Just a glimpse as she walked by. That original sketch left a lot to be desired. I've looked at that sketch until I see it in my sleep, and I didn't recognize her yesterday. I bet Anne Brown did a cartwheel when she saw that sketch in the paper. The UC cheerleader that some guy called in as a prank looked more like the sketch than the real Anne Brown. Plus, in the restaurant she smiled at me as she passed, which distorts the normal shape of the mouth and eyes." The detective knew he hunted a woman not ordinary. "I'm sure she knows that and smiled at me for just that purpose. Almost anyone else in that situation would do everything they could to look away from someone they did not want to recognize them. In reality, what you want to do is look right at that person and smile. A smile gets in the way. It puts your guard down—your mind automatically wants to consider a person smiling at you as a good person, not one for suspicion, and more importantly it distorts facial features. She knows all of that or she would not have smiled. The height and age we published are correct. She is between five-seven and five-eight, and she looks to be in her mid-twenties."

The artist continued to draw, then asked, "What should I do with the hair, Detective, and the glasses? Mrs. Ault said she wore glasses yesterday?"

"Forget the glasses," Ault said immediately. "She's wearing the glasses to fool any concerned citizens who think it's their civic duty to call in about anyone they see on the street who even remotely resembles the sketch. If the face in tomorrow's newspaper has glasses then she'll throw hers away. As for the hair, leave it light-colored like it was in the original sketch. She has already gone from blonde to brunette. It doesn't matter if she wore a wig yesterday. Her hair will be some other color and hairstyle by now." Then Ault added cynically, "She's probably a redhead with Shirley Temple curls today." Ault looked down at his coffee cup, did not want the coffee, and set the cup on a table. "The mouth issue is a wash. Elizabeth doesn't remember, and Brown disguised her mouth by smiling at me. The only change from the original sketch that you should concern yourself with is the nose. Make the change Elizabeth suggested and leave everything else the same."

"Okay," the artist said, "her eye color? This is a black and white sketch but normally if the eyes are blue or green I draw the eyes lighter."

Frank spoke up. "No one seems to be able to put their finger on her eye color. And with the glasses that makes it tougher."

"Hazel," Elizabeth said.

"What?" Frank reacted.

"Hazel . . . her eyes are hazel."

Frank looked at his wife.

The artist thought out loud. "Hazel. That's a light brown."

"Yes," Elizabeth confirmed. "Light brown with some green."

"I'll draw the eyes light then." The man drew for another minute or two. When finished he handed the pad to Elizabeth. "What do you think?"

Frank walked over, stood behind the couch, and looked over Elizabeth's shoulder.

"I guess so," she said, then handed the pad back to her husband.

Frank looked closely. The *Anne Brown* in the sketch had no smile like he saw when she walked by him in Sano's, but as he looked at the face he found himself thinking that she was still smiling at him.

Part II

One generation abandons the enterprises
of another like stranded vessels.
— Henry David Thoreau

Chapter 20

The 11ᵗʰ Olympiad of the Modern Era

Berlin—August 1, 1936

The motorcade wended slowly along the ten-mile route through the heart of Berlin. The caravan of Mercedes, Opel Admirals, and monstrous Horch automobiles, itself over a mile long, transported dignitaries to the opening ceremonies of the summer Olympics. On this blue and beautiful day, tops were down on the convertibles; the hard tops had windows open, the best they could do. In the second car rode the king of Bulgaria. Next in importance behind His Highness came vehicles containing luminaries such as crown princes from Greece, Italy, and Sweden; the highest Olympic officials; and Mussolini's sons. The rest of the long cavalcade consisted of high-ranking German officials and special guests.

No expense had been spared or contingency overlooked regarding security for the illustrious guests. But 40,000 members of the *Sturmabteilung* in brown shirts, and other security forces lining the Via Triumphalis were stationed there today not solely to protect the dignitaries from a hurtful act from a hidden assailant, but also, and chiefly, to protect a rider standing in the first car from adoring and enthusiastic parade watchers who might feel possessed to rush the lead car in their exuberance.

The standing man wore a humble uniform and saluted the brown-shirted Stormtroopers and the masses of cheering people by extending his right arm, with palm down, straight out from his body. When the convoy finally reached the Reichssportfeld, waiting attendants opened the doors of the lead automobiles. The standing man stepped out of his Mercedes and was joined by the king.

Past great phalanxes of uniformed Germans at attention, Adolf Hitler and King Boris, side by side, led the procession of the mighty into the Olympiastadion. The largest stadium on earth, overflowing, erupted with cheers when Hitler entered. The pageant paused when an orchestra, conducted by Richard Strauss and accompanied by a chorus of 3000 Hitler Youth, launched into "Deutschland über alles." Strauss followed the German national anthem with the "Horst Wessel

Lied" and the "Olympic Hymn" while the German chancellor and Bulgarian sovereign resumed making their way to their reserved seats, along with as many of the subsequent foreign dignitaries and Party bigwigs the Führer Box could accommodate. Others from the motorcade, including Karl and Louise Lehmann, were shown to nearby seats.

Lehmann served as press secretary to the German ambassador to the United States, a post he had held since shortly after the 1933 election when Hitler came to power. The Lehmann family (Karl, Louise, and a daughter, Erika, who just two months ago graduated from high school in America) had planned this Olympic holiday for more than a year. They arrived in the German capital three days ago.

Louise Minton met Karl Lehmann in late 1913. Louise's father served as a British diplomat assigned to Berlin before the first war. Karl was an enlisted man serving in the Kaiser's army and for a brief time was assigned duty as one of several German drivers for the British embassy. One day, Louise, the beautiful daughter of the British diplomat, needed a ride through Berlin and Karl Lehmann drew the assignment. After a brief but effective courtship, Louise Minton and Karl Lehmann married in the summer of 1914. On their honeymoon in the Italian Alps, they heard about the assassination of Archduke Ferdinand.

Against the wishes of her parents, and against the advice of the other quickly-packing members of the British contingent in Berlin, Louise elected to stay in Germany during the war. She lived with her husband's parents in Oberschopfheim, a small, rural village in Baden in southwestern Germany. There the young bride felt she would at least be available to her husband during any furloughs.

Their only child was the product of one of those brief, infrequent leaves in 1917.

Karl Lehmann served faithfully on the western front, and a moment's heroism during the Battle of the Somme in 1916 earned him the Iron Cross First Class. Following the war, the Versailles Treaty helped shatter not only the German economy, but also Karl's plans for a soldier's career. With the German military establishment scuttled, Lehmann found himself on the streets, just one in the hordes of unemployed patriots. In 1920, with no prospects in little Oberschopfheim, Karl left his wife and small daughter behind and journeyed the 200 kilometers to Munich where a cousin had located work.

In Munich, Karl found a job as a printer's devil for a small publisher—a humble job for a decorated veteran and former escort to diplomats. He quartered in a flophouse to save money, most of which he sent home to Louise. But the German government's bad fiscal policy during the war and reparations to the Allies after the Treaty caused an inflation rate so fantastic that Karl's wages were rendered practically worthless in just the short time it took the mail to deliver the money home to Oberschopfheim. This, along with the humiliation dealt his homeland with a spiteful and unfair treaty, led Karl, like so many others, to be engulfed in a maelstrom of discontent directed at the Allies and at the Weimar Republic, the democratic wannabe government an increasing number of Germans felt was forced down their throats.

In those early days after the war, one of many small newspapers that Karl Lehmann's employer had as clients was the *Völkischer Beobachter*. The *Beobachter* had its own press, but occasionally contracted out some of its work. That newspaper expounded the views of a small, right-wing fringe organization. In those days, Karl had little time for reading, but over the course of doing business he came to know the man who dropped off and picked up the printing orders for the *Beobachter*. The man's name was Anton Drexler, a short, stout man with bulging eyes. When Herr Drexler learned the young printer's devil was a struggling veteran with a family left behind, Drexler adopted an attitude of friendliness toward him and eventually talked Karl into attending a speech by the new leader of his organization. Drexler told Karl this leader was also a struggling veteran and a man whom Drexler felt had answers to Germany's problems.

In later years, the story of how Karl Lehmann met Adolf Hitler would be often repeated, and it was the centerpiece of conversation at social gatherings. Everyone wanted to know, and no one ever tired of hearing it.

It was early in 1921 at the Zirkus Krone. This was the Munich auditorium that Drexler had told Karl that the organization that sponsored the *Völkischer Beobachter* would hold its first national congress. The movement was called the National Socialist German Workers Party. Karl recognized the name, having set the letters in type many times, although he had paid it little heed. The speech was to begin at eight o'clock that night. Drexler gave Karl a free ticket for admission and told him to look him up after the speech.

At first, Karl Lehmann had little desire to attend a political speech. In those early days, shortly after the Great War, Karl remained a monarchist. Had not Germany's best days been under the Kaiser? Let the Hohenzollerns return from the Netherlands and things could be as they were before the war.

Nonetheless, a family man alone in a strange city has few opportunities for entertainment (at least not a faithful family man such as Karl Lehmann) so he decided to attend Herr Drexler's meeting. Walking through a cold sleet and January wind, Lehmann arrived an hour early to an almost empty auditorium. But the people came. At ten minutes until eight most seats were filled with a line still outside.

The theme of the speech was "Future or Ruin." The speaker was physically not impressive, yet his strong voice and passion won the crowd. Karl later told Louise that some of those around him seemed virtually entranced. In fact, the speaker was forced to stop mid-sentence several times amid spontaneous cheering and clapping that drowned out his words. The man at the podium told of a new and greater Germany rising Phoenix-like from the ashes, and, although Karl would later confess he did not at the time understand many of the programs the man promoted, he agreed with what the speaker claimed had led Germany down the sorry path upon which it now found itself, mainly the "November Criminals"—the German leaders who many felt had betrayed the country by surrendering a war many Germans felt they had not lost, and the spiteful terms of the Versailles Treaty.

After the speech, Karl noticed Herr Drexler, the speaker, and others leaving the stage. Remembering Drexler's invitation, he approached the men. On the floor of the Zirkus Krone, the young Karl Lehmann shook the young Adolf Hitler's hand for the first time. Drexler told Hitler about Karl's service during the war and his work in the publishing business. This seemed to pique Hitler's interest. Hitler and Drexler had business to discuss and, when ready to leave the auditorium, Hitler insisted that Karl Lehmann come along.

Through the cold, dark Munich night the three men walked to Hitler's apartment, which turned out to be a small backroom over a store at Thierschstrasse 41 near the Isar River. The room was no more than a small cell, cold and damp. Louise's husband always enjoyed describing the drab, rundown apartment the future conqueror of Europe occupied when he first met him, and how Hitler had given him his last beer while the future Führer and Drexler went without.

The congenial host who gave up his last beer expressed genuine interest in Karl's war years and his views of current events. Hitler also quizzed him about his work. The men talked for several hours. Later, Louise would hear her husband say that when he left the dingy little room that night his "heart raced with renewed hope for the Fatherland."

So Karl Lehmann joined the infant movement during the earliest days of the struggle, unlike the vast majority of current members who waited until the Party gained power in 1933 and then joined in droves. This gave him status as a Party celebrity. He had earned the *Blutorden,* an honor bestowed only on those who took part in the early street fighting in the 1920s—activity that at the time caused his wife great worry and anxiety.

But 1921 was twelve long, hard years from power. The young Lehmann family continued to struggle. When the Führer went to prison after the ill-fated Beer Hall Putsch of 1923, Karl had no choice but to send Louise and Erika to England to live with his in-laws. There Erika spent her early school years. English grammar overtook her German. Finally, in 1929, Karl brought them back to Germany and the family settled in Munich where Karl now held an important position in the Party propaganda machine under Josef Goebbels.

After Hitler ascended to power in January of 1933, life and fortune would forever change for the Lehmann family. Louise and Erika had taught Karl English, and he was assigned to the German embassy in Washington, D.C., as press secretary to the ambassador. Erika spent the past three years in an American boarding school—the exclusive Blair School for girls in Manassas, Virginia.

Now, the Olympics brought them back to Berlin. Although twice affairs of state had brought Karl back briefly since 1933, this was the Lehmann family's first trip to Germany together in three years.

When the Parade of Athletes began, Karl turned to Louise. "Where is your daughter?" Karl asked. "I have hardly seen her since we got to Berlin. I thought you told me she would meet us here." Karl Lehmann good-naturedly referred to their headstrong child as "your daughter" when talking to his wife.

"*Our* daughter will be along," Louise answered. London born and raised, Louise Lehmann spoke German well, but with a British accent most Germans found charming. "She was fifteen when we went to America, Karl, and has looked forward to this trip for a long time. Let her have some fun. She's somewhere in the stadium with Gretl and Herta."

After the athletes of the various countries had entered and positioned themselves on the stadium floor, Hitler rose and walked to a nearby podium. Into the microphone he welcomed the youth of the world to Berlin and declared the Games open. A runner carried a lighted torch into the stadium—an idea of Hitler's, who a year ago suggested to the Olympic Committee that a torch be lit in Greece, site of the ancient Games, and carried to Berlin by a series of runners. The International Committee initially scoffed at the idea, but later reconsidered.

Nearly an hour after the track and field competitions began, Karl and Louise noticed the bright, corn-colored hair of their daughter as she made her way toward them, squeezing past the spectators in their row.

"Ah, the Prodigal Daughter returns," Karl said as his daughter wedged in between him and her mother. "We thought you had eloped with one of those shot putters from Poland."

"I like the javelin thrower from Iceland," his daughter returned the kidding. "I'm going down on the field to propose in a few minutes, and I stopped by to see if you have my dowry ready, Father."

Karl Lehmann reached into his pocket and pulled out several coins. There was one American dime among the German coins. He handed his daughter the dime.

"I can't spend this here anyway," he said.

"You two," Louise broke in. "You never stop, neither of you."

"Mama, Gretl and Herta asked me to go out with them this evening, after the events."

Karl interrupted. "Erika, that's a question you should ask your father."

"I'd rather ask Mama," Erika said. "You're a party pooper." They had been speaking in German, but she said *party pooper* in English.

Louise laughed. Karl shook his head and looked at his wife. "That is another example of the base foreign slang your daughter learned at that expensive American school that is supposed to be teaching her the genteel ways of womanhood. Instead she talks like a sailor."

"Oh, Karl," Louise smiled. "That expression is not vulgar. You *are* a party pooper." Mother and daughter laughed together, then Louise turned to Erika: "Where will you be going?"

"To a jazz club that has dancing, with an American band here for the Olympics," Erika answered.

"Certainly not!" Karl exclaimed. So far the banter had been light-hearted, but now he was serious. "That music is frowned upon by the Party."

"You can go, Early," her mother assented. "Just don't be out late." The credit for Louise's pet name, *Early,* for her daughter went to her sister's son. In the '20s, when mother and daughter lived with Louise's parents in London, Louise referred to her daughter by both her first and middle names: Erika Marie. But Louise's 3-year-old nephew came up short when pronouncing *Erika Marie,* instead calling her something that sounded like *Early*. And as often happens in families the name stuck, at least with the British side.

Erika did not give her father time for further objections. She rose, kissed both parents, and started away. "I won't be late."

"Louise," Karl protested, "you know she's as wild as a jackal. We really must be stricter."

"We can't keep her wrapped in blankets forever, Karl. It's been three years since the trouble at the first American school. She's eighteen. We have to start relying on her to make the right decisions. And I trust Gretl and Herta."

Chapter 21

Jump and Jive Kitten

Berlin, August 1, 1936 [that evening]

Club Zenzi was a converted warehouse, very large as nightclubs go.

On a typical Saturday, most of the German Jazz Kids arrived at Club Zenzi by nine o'clock. And on a typical Saturday the club could expect between 15 and 20 practiced dancing couples. All of the local jazz aficionados were young, most in their late teens, none beyond their twenties. The rest of the club crowd would be made up of couples who did not dance but enjoyed watching, a few bold, unaccompanied females of various ages, and a great number of young, single males.

But tonight was not a typical Saturday. Today was the first day of the Olympic Games, and the *Jazzjugend* knew the Americans were in town. Restrictions concerning American jazz had been relaxed for the duration of the Games. Street posters warning of the harmful effects of *American Nigger Jazz,* and the new American dance phenomenon called *Swing,* on young German minds had been taken down because the Nazis knew the Americans would send one of the largest contingents of athletes to Berlin, along with a great number of fans and supporters with deep pockets despite the world-wide depression. And the Nazis were grateful to the Americans for not joining the boycott of the Berlin Games when a pitch to do so was made by certain leaders in the international community in protest of the German government's racial policies. Instead the Americans came, and persuaded other nations to come. So now, for the next two weeks at least, things American were acceptable in Germany. Dr. Goebbels even ordered a reporter and a photographer from the *Berliner Morgenpost* to cover this event at Club Zenzi to prove to the world that suspicions of Nazi intolerance were unfounded. The article and photo would appear in the newspaper as soon as they had been cleared by the Reich Propaganda Ministry.

German Jazz Kids cared nothing about propaganda; they cared only that tonight a real jazz band from America would play at Club Zenzi. Also because of the American band, *Spiked Ike and the Jazz Cats,* a small contingent of a newly-formed group of German youths from

112

Hamburg that some called the *Swing Kids* had traveled to Berlin. The first meeting between the Berlin Jazz Kids and Hamburg Swing Kids at Club Zenzi would surely launch a tremendous party all the kids agreed, and it had been the main topic at Zenzi since last winter when Spiked Ike agreed to play the club during the Olympics.

Gretl Braun, Herta Schneider, and Erika Lehmann found a table.

"You'll like this place, Erika," Herta said. "Gretl and I have been here before."

Gretl said, "You mentioned earlier, Erika, that you go to the dance clubs in America. Do they look like this one?"

"The American clubs are all different from each other," Erika answered. "In America the clubs I've been to are smaller than this one, but there are many more of them. Some things are the same: they all have bandstands and dance floors like this one." Then she smiled. "And many men to choose from." The 18-year-old Erika did not tell her slightly older companions (Gretl was 20, Herta 24), that in the States she sneaked away from her dormitory at night to visit the clubs, and then lied about her age when she got there. And no need to tell them about her technique for gaining access to the clubs, with fewer questions about her age: she would approach a single man entering the club, flirt, then accompany him in as if she were his date. Once inside, the man would suddenly discover that she had disappeared into the crowd. Tonight though, Erika needed no ploy. In Germany, there were no age restrictions on beer drinking, and for wine and spirits the legal age at clubs was 18.

Gretl and Herta laughed at Erika's comment about the abundance of men. "I'm a married woman," Herta said to Erika. "I'll leave the men for you and Gretl." Herta Schneider was married to an army officer who was away as much as at home.

"Oh, you say you'll leave the men to us? Are you sure about that, Herta?" Gretl kidded.

"Of course, I'm sure," Herta responded. "I only accompany you, Gretl, because you tell me you don't want to go alone."

"Oh, I see," Gretl would not let up. "So I guess your courtesies to that handsome man at the club down by the Alexanderplatz were for my sake also."

"You always bring that up," Herta accused. "That man just liked to dance."

"Of course, he did," Gretl responded, "especially since you let him put his hand on your breast during the slow dances. Erika, you should have seen where he put his hand. Shameful." Gretl shook her head in mock embarrassment.

"I moved his hand down," Herta asserted.

"Yes, after three dances, or was it four?" Gretl winked at Erika.

Erika grinned.

"You're impossible, Gretl. Erika, don't believe a word. His hand was only on the side of my breast, and I didn't want to be rude."

When Erika and Gretl laughed, Herta realized she had just admitted guilt and laughed with them.

The club was now full to overflowing and the musicians began appearing on the bandstand one at a time to check their instruments. A harried waitress finally showed up to take a drink order. All three women ordered beer.

"Make that four beers, waitress," Gretl told the woman as she started to walk away. "Another person will be joining us."

Gretl turned back to her two friends. "My sister should be here soon."

"I'm glad she agreed to meet us," Herta said. "This will be good for her; she needs to have some fun." Then Herta touched Erika's arm to get her attention. "Gretl's sister and the Führer are an item, Erika."

"An item?" Erika asked. "What do you mean?"

"A romance."

"No!" Erika was surprised.

"It's true," Herta confirmed.

Erika looked at Gretl.

"Yes," Gretl confirmed, then hedged her response. "But I'm not sure even my sister would call it a romance. She met the Führer several years ago, before the election. It has been an on-and-off association, and it has caused her much heartache, I'm afraid." Then Gretl added, "But don't tell her I told you that last part, Erika."

The waitress delivered the beers and Gretl paid. "The next one is on you, Herta."

Herta took a drink. "Hey, the beer is cold."

"That's because of all the Americans in town," Gretl said. "All the clubs and beer houses in Berlin are serving cold beer for the Olympics."

"Do the Americans always drink their beer cold, Erika?" Herta asked.

Erika, who had taken a drink, answered: "Yes, and usually colder than this."

Suddenly Gretl began waving. "There's Eva."

Erika and Herta turned, and Herta joined the waving. A young woman stood near the entrance looking around, not yet aware of the attempts to get her attention. At last, the woman caught sight of her sister and friend waving, smiled, and headed toward them through the crowd.

The pretty young woman approaching (at 24, Eva was the same age as her best friend Herta) looked very much like Gretl but with lighter brown hair; some might call her a blonde, while Gretl's hair was dark brown. But the heart-shaped face, large brown eyes, and the other features betrayed the family bond. In fact, many of Eva and Gretl's mutual acquaintances were forced to use the hair color to tell the sisters apart. When Eva reached the table, she kissed both her sister and Herta.

"Eva," Gretl said, "this is Erika. Her father, Karl Lehmann, is with our embassy in America."

"Ah, yes, I know your father," Eva Braun said to Erika as she sat down. Eva extended her hand across the small table. "You have been in America with your father?"

"Yes," Erika answered as she shook Eva's hand, "for three years."

"I'm jealous, Erika," Eva said. "You'll have to tell me all about America."

Herta now put her hand on Eva's arm. "We told Erika about you and the Führer."

Erika did not wait, "I'm fascinated, Eva, and surprised you can be out like this without an escort."

"It seems I am one of the Reich's secrets, Erika. Other than my family, a few friends, and some people close to him, no one knows."

"A fact that has its advantages at times," Gretl added, afraid the happy mood was changing. "Like tonight, right, Eva? You can get away for an evening and have some fun." A year ago her sister tried to kill herself—her second suicide attempt—because Adolf Hitler had so little time for her. Gretl and Herta worked hard to keep Eva's spirits up.

Eva Braun smiled.

Herta finished her beer and flagged a waitress. The band sat ready to play. Spiked Ike, a short man with a baggy, green suit and New Jersey accent, welcomed everyone to Club Zenzi in English, which few in the crowd understood. Ike asked if someone in the crowd could interpret.

"What is he saying, Erika?" Gretl asked.

"He asked if there is someone here who can translate for him."

No one stepped forward. Among the handful of Americans in the crowd—easily singled out because of their clothes—apparently none spoke German, so Erika's companions encouraged her. She boldly rose and joined Ike on the bandstand.

"What's your name, good looking?" The diminutive Ike looked up at Erika who was three inches taller. Ike held the microphone so the crowd could hear (if not understand) them both.

"Erika."

"Not any longer," Ike said. "From now on you're Blonde Baby. What's your hometown back in the States?" Ike assumed too much because of the American accent she was using when speaking English and because of her clothes.

"I'm German, from Oberschopfheim."

"You're German?" Ike sounded surprised. He turned to the band. "She's one of those Fräuleins you've been dreaming about, cats!" Most members of the band either whistled or whooped. The crowd, not understanding what Ike said, still laughed, if only at the band's response.

"How old are you, doll?" Ike asked, unaware of the difference in legal drinking ages between his country and Germany. "You've got a brick frame, baby, but you don't look old enough to be in this joint." Then before Erika could answer, Ike added, "Never mind, I don't want to know." The band laughed as if they alone knew of some private, inside joke.

"Do you jive, Blonde Baby?" Ike moved on. "And you better jib it in the local lingo; we've left the crowd on Jupiter."

"Yes," Erika responded into the microphone Ike held for her—first in English for Ike, then in German. "I've been to some clubs in America."

Again, Ike swiveled his head to address the band. "Did you hear that, cats? We have a jump and jive kitten here." Turning back to Erika: "I'm changing your name. It's no longer Blonde Baby; it's Fräulein Jump and Jive Kitten." The musicians, still playing along, made loud, strange noises. Then, as if on some cue, they shouted to Erika in unison, "Crazy, baby!"

Ike spoke again: "Well, if you'll be so kind as to help me out, Fräulein Jump and Jive Kitten, I'd like to tell a little story, and then we'll get this hoppin' show on the road."

With Erika translating, Ike repeated his welcome to the crowd and told a funny story about a band member's struggles with the local language; one of the trumpet players was slapped by a Berlin hotel maid when he mistranslated a request. Using an English to German dictionary, the trumpeter meant to ask the maid to leave some extra bed linens, but instead asked her to join him in bed. The German crowd, now understanding thanks to Erika, roared.

Ike thanked Erika, and the crowd applauded as she returned to her table. When she sat down, Gretl, Herta, and Eva laughed and clapped for Erika's time in the spotlight.

Spiked Ike announced the band's first song was a *jump jazz* tune written and recorded by an American musician named Fletcher "Smack" Henderson. When the music began, German couples rushed onto the dance floor. A stampede of teenage boys tripped over themselves running toward Erika's table. They had heard her tell Ike she had been to dance clubs in America. No one asked Erika if she wanted to dance. She had the beer stein to her lips when the first three boys reached the table, and, without speaking, jerked Erika out of her seat (spilling her beer), one on each arm pulling and a boy behind her pushing. They forced her along, running, onto the dance floor. Erika's female companions' laughter stopped when the same fate befell them. Gretl, Herta, and Eva were pulled out of their chairs by German boys and dragged to the dance floor. *These girls are with Jump and Jive Kitten so they must know the American dances.*

The dance floor became grossly overcrowded—not by the 30-or-so couples, but by an overabundance of males looking for dance partners. Not just Erika and her three friends, but all the dancing women became caught up in a comical routine, looking like the metal ball in a pinball machine as they bounced off teenage boys cutting in for a dance.

Ike kept the music coming, the band moving without pause from one fast-paced song to the next. On the floor, Erika especially was given no quarter. The boys quickly saw that she knew what she was doing, even more so than they, so they allowed no respite. She became lost in the gang that formed around her. Eva became another favorite. She lacked Erika's experience in this new style of frenzied dance, but she was a lover of modern American movies, dance, and art, so she was a willing student. Her athleticism innate, Eva adapted quickly to the dizzying spins the boys put her through. Of the four friends' skill

117

level (and therefore popularity among the boys), Gretl was third in line. Herta tried mightily, the kindest that could be said.

A combination of August and substantial body heat quickly converted the warehouse/club into a giant sauna. Several couples took a break after the first song. To her credit, the perspiring Herta lasted through two, and then fought her way back to the table. Gretl tried to follow Herta off the floor, but was grabbed and stayed for one more dance. Eva and Erika remained on the floor, either by choice or from a reluctance to try a breakout through the barrier of males standing guard around them waiting for a chance to cut in. Both Eva's and Erika's clothes became soaked with perspiration. Eva wore a blouse and slacks; Erika a cotton summer dress with a pleated, full skirt.

By the end of the fourth song, enough dancers had sought a break that the hearty remaining ones could at last find some elbow room. Spiked Ike spotted Erika.

"Hey, look, cats," Ike said to the band. "It's Fräulein Jump and Jive Kitten! And she's hip to the moves." Then to Erika, Ike said, "This one's for you, Fräulein Baby." And to the crowd (Ike knew few understood): "This is a little riff we wrote just for our visit to your top cat country. It's called *The Olympic Jump,* and when we say that we ain't talking about the long jump, jitterbugs." To the band: "Okay, cats, time to growl. . . ."

The Jazz Cats, horns blaring and drums pounding, launched into a murderously fast rhythm dance number. The German boy dancing with Erika, Eva and her partner, and the few couples still game did not know the moves required for this frantic tempo. Ike quickly noticed and halted the music. Only the drummer kept playing, keeping a background beat while Ike spoke to the crowd.

"Okay, jitterbugs, I think it's time for Never-Two-Bits Tommy. We call him Never-Two-Bits because he never has two bits in his mouse to pay for his booze; one of us other cats has to always pick up his tab. But he can sure cut the rug. Tommy will put on the skates, play pitch and catch, stoke the coal, and take Jump and Jive Kitten for a crazy ride on the Jazz Cat Express. Let's hope it won't be a one-way trip. She's our Fräulein, Tommy; don't hurt her."

Never-Two-Bits Tommy was a tall, dark-haired, trombone player in his late 20s. Tommy left his place on the bandstand to join Erika on the dance floor.

"You forgot to take your dress off when you took a shower, doll," Tommy kidded her.

Erika looked down and pulled the top of the thin, wet dress away from her skin.

"What moves do you know, baby?" Tommy asked her.

"I've done the Lindy Hop."

"Yeah?" Tommy was surprised. "How 'bout the Coaster, or Jumpin' Joe?"

"Yes."

"No shit?"

"Yes, but the literal translation is *keine Scheiße*."

Tommy laughed and responded, "Crazy. How about the Apache?"

"No, but if you'll lead, I'll follow. I think I can keep up."

Tommy: "I love you. You're looney, baby. Let's get married."

Ike gave the count and the band restarted *The Olympic Jump*. Others on the dance floor, even though they did not understand Ike's introduction of Tommy, somehow knew it was time to make room.

"Hold onto your bloomers, baby," Tommy said. "Here we go."

Never-Two-Bits Tommy and the daughter of the German ambassador's press secretary did not disappoint. Tommy sent Erika airborne several times, somersaulted her over his back, dipped her to the floor and back up while she held on with her spread legs locked around him. He snaked her around his body on her way to the floor before grabbing her hands and pulling her through his open legs and back onto her feet. Too many times Erika's dress rose to a level that would make any father cringe.

The Olympic Jump ended, and the Berlin Jazz Kids and Hamburg Swing Kids applauded loudly for Erika and Tommy. Erika straightened her disheveled dress, wringing wet from the waist up, as best she could.

"There you go, jitterbugs," Ike said to the crowd. "Now that's jumpin'. We're going to take a few minutes to cool our heels and freeze our fingers. We'll be back shortly."

Erika returned to the table, arm in arm with Eva who had stood in the circle around the dance floor during Erika and Tommy's dance.

"Cowards," Eva called Gretl and Herta.

"Look at you two. You look as if you fell in the Neptune Fountain," Herta commented to Eva and Erika, referring to their wet clothes and the famous Berlin landmark.

Earlier that day at the Olympiastadion, Erika had promised her parents she would not stay out late. On the night Erika Lehmann and Eva Braun became friends, Erika broke her promise.

119

Chapter 22

Early to Bed

Berlin—August 2, 1936

Karl and Louise Lehmann returned to their hotel just past 2:00 a.m. following a reception hosted by Josef Goebbels at the Four Seasons for members of the foreign press covering the Games. Karl had been asked to attend personally by the Reich propaganda chief. Karl's ability to speak English kept him busy with the British, American, Australian, and South African reporters—all eager for an interview with a high-echelon Nazi for the folks back home. With Karl Lehmann they could speak directly and not be forced to rely on the sometimes subjective interpretations of a translator.

As the Lehmanns walked through the hotel lobby, they were surprised by a bellman.

"Pardon, Herr Lehmann, there is a message for you at the desk."

"Thank you."

As they turned to walk to the registration deck, Karl told Louise, "Probably the ambassador." The German ambassador to the United States was also in Berlin for the Olympics.

But the message was not from the ambassador.

"What is it, Karl?" Louise asked when she saw concern in her husband's face.

"This is from Herta Schneider. She wants me to come to some nightclub on the Unter den Linden." Karl lowered the note to his side. "I told you we should not have let Erika go to that place, Louise. You said we could trust those two with her."

"Karl, if they could not be trusted, Herta would not have notified us."

"You go on up to the room," he told Louise. "I'll see what this is all about."

"I'm going with you."

Karl did not have time to argue, and he knew it would do little good. When her mind was made up, Louise was as obstinate as their daughter.

The Brownshirt assigned to drive the Lehmanns to and from the reception drove away after he dropped them at the hotel, so Karl asked the desk to summon a taxi. With German efficiency, one arrived in under five minutes, and the Lehmanns got in the backseat. Karl looked again at the note from Herta.

"Driver, do you know of a Club Zenzi on the Unter den Linden?"

"Yes."

"Take us there, please, quickly."

The driver pulled away, and Karl turned to Louise: "I hope she has not hurt someone again."

Louise, the voice of reason in the Lehmann family, also worried yet said nothing.

Karl and Louise Lehmann knew their only child was a prodigy: walking at nine months, speaking complete sentences at two years, playing the piano beautifully by her tenth birthday, a champion at practically any athletic endeavor she cared to try. All this, plus Erika had always been a sweet and loving child to all around her. The child all parents dream of.

Most of the time.

It had shown itself early and caused Karl and Louise great anxiety. Their daughter possessed a dark side, an alcove where something menacing lurked. Many might simply call it a temper, but this temper was different. When Erika's temper surfaced it was never accompanied by a red face, shouts, or tantrums. *If only it were so easy,* Karl and Louise had commented to each other. Erika's temper was like a viper resting in the grass, inclined by nature to bite those who stumbled across it. Thankfully the episodes were rare, in fact years apart (at least the episodes they knew about), but when their daughter's temper reared its head, it was always cruel and someone always got hurt.

The first incident involved a babysitter. Erika was four years old; Karl worked in Munich. Louise and their small daughter stayed behind in Oberschopfheim with Karl's parents. During the winter of 1921 all adult inhabitants of the village were required to register for the census. Louise and Karl's parents were given a date and time to report to the courthouse. It was winter and an influenza epidemic had spread through Baden. Louise Lehmann worried about taking Erika outside in the cold and then standing with her in a crowded courthouse where surely some might be infected with the flu. A teenage girl who lived down the road agreed to watch Erika while the adults in the family went to the courthouse. Little Erika calmly told her mother she did not want to stay with the baby-sitter. There was no crying: no tantrum.

Louise consoled her daughter and assured her that she would not be gone long.

When they returned an hour later, the teenage girl's furious parents sat in the parlor tending to their sobbing daughter who had a two-inch gash on her forehead. Blood spotted the girl's dress. Pieces of a broken ceramic figurine lay on the floor. Four-year-old Erika sat quietly in a corner playing with her dolls, ignoring the shouts and sobs. The babysitter described how Erika picked up the figurine as if to play, then smiled and asked the babysitter to hold her on her lap. While on the teenager's lap, Erika suddenly turned and smashed the figurine against the girl's forehead.

And the boy in England. Their daughter was eleven and now living in London with her mother. Erika was a model student praised by her teachers. There had been no incidents of concern since that day in Oberschopfheim.

Then Karl Lehmann received the letter from his wife.

The boy liked Erika (Louise had written before that the boy had come by the house.) One day at school, the boy teased Erika—as eleven-year-old boys do to eleven-year-old girls they have a crush on—and challenged her to a foot race which he won. More teasing followed. Erika, in turn, challenged the boy to a dangerous climbing contest involving scaling a heavy tile drainage pipe to the roof of the three-story school building.

Erika went first and waved to the boy when she reached the roof. He hesitated, but he had no choice but to attempt the climb. An audience of classmates had gathered and a girl had already made it to the top—a girl who now leaned over the edge of the roof smiling down at him. He would be branded a coward if he backed away. Halfway up the pipe, the boy lost his grip and fell. He was knocked unconscious and suffered a broken collarbone and a broken right arm. Panicked classmates fetched the schoolmaster and the nurse. Louise had written that the schoolmaster told her that as they attended the injured lad, Erika descended the pipe (against the orders of the schoolmaster) and stood over the unconscious boy giggling while the other girls wept and the boys fretted.

One other incident stood out. The Blair School for Girls in Virginia was not the first American school Erika attended after her father was assigned to Washington. Her first American school was a private girls' school in Maryland not far from Annapolis. Hazing of newcomers during the first week of classes was a long-time ritual at the school.

The administration frowned on such antics; nevertheless, over the years the hazing had become such a revered tradition that wealthy alumni objected to attempts by school officials to end the ritual *(We endured hazing and we turned out just fine, let kids be kids)*, so school officials turned their heads.

Like the other new girls, Erika endured the week-long hazing good-naturedly, even allowing herself at one point to be stripped to her underwear, tied to a chair, and covered with flour like the other newcomers. The very white girls were then forced to sing the school song, which they better know by heart or be prepared to endure a spanking on the bare bottom with an old and treasured paddle passed down through school generations for that purpose.

Erika sang the school song and should have been finished like the other girls, but one of the senior girls decided to enhance the fun. With an eyeliner, the girl painted a Hitleresque moustache on the tied-up Erika, and ordered her German classmate to sing "Deutschland uber alles" and give them a few *Heil Hitlers*. Erika refused to sing any more, or *heil* for the crowd's amusement, so the girl pulled down Erika's underpants and paddled her bare bottom with the revered paddle. Other girls later said Erika took the paddling without a whimper and even turned and smiled at the girl wielding the board. This irked the senior who increased the vigor of her strokes. When a welt appeared on Erika's bottom, good judgment finally prevailed among the other girls who insisted the paddling stop.

Two days later, the venerated paddle was missing from a glass trophy case. The next day the senior girl who had shown so much special interest in Erika was also missing. When the girl failed to return to her dorm that night, the police were called and a search mounted. The girl was quickly found tied to a tree deep in the campus wood. She was stripped to her underwear and in shock, her buttocks covered with welts. The paddle, neatly broken in half, lay on the ground beside her. The girl had spent the better part of a day and all night tied to the tree. The welts on her buttocks, large clusters of mosquito bites, and dehydration required a hospital stay of two days.

The girl identified Erika, of course, who calmly admitted to school officials that she was responsible. A simple revenge paddling then releasing the girl might have been dismissed as a case of the senior girl getting what was coming to her, but the severity of the retaliation shocked. Erika had abandoned the gagged and securely bound girl in the woods and gone serenely about her business. The girl's parents pressed charges but Karl Lehmann's diplomatic immunity protected Erika. After an investigation and the testimony of other girls who admitted that Erika's hazing had gone too far, the matter was quietly closed when Karl Lehmann agreed to remove his daughter from the school.

The first psychiatrist found nothing wrong with Erika. Neither did the next one. Only a case of youthful bad judgment and a hot temper, they concluded. So Karl and Louise succeeded in rationalizing these confounding incidents of aggression. The episodes were infrequent—years apart—and Erika such a wonderful, loving daughter that her parents gladly accepted the psychiatrists' findings. But the incidents were never forgotten, especially now, during this cab ride in Berlin.

The driver pulled up directly in front of the Zenzi door where Karl told him to wait. The driver balked, concerned he would run afoul of strict Berlin parking regulations established for the duration of the Games. "I will have to circle the block," the driver said. "Parking on the Unter den Linden is prohibited for the next two weeks."

Karl pulled out his wallet and showed the driver his identification as an honorary *Reichsleiter*—a rank bestowed only on the highest-ranking members of the Nazi Party. Few Reichsleiters were new to the Party, most had been with Hitler from the earliest days.

"I'll wait here, sir," said the driver, no longer concerned with getting a parking citation.

A group of five Stormtroopers milled around on the walk outside the club.

"Why are the Brownshirts here, Karl?" Louise asked as they got out of the taxi.

"I don't know, Louise." Karl was worried. "They are not supposed to be at these places during the Olympics unless ordered. There must have been trouble."

Karl asked to speak to the SA leader. When the man stepped forward, Karl identified himself and asked why they were there. The man told Karl that two hours ago they were ordered there by no less than Werner Fischer, an adjutant to the Führer.

"For what reason?" Karl asked.

"No reason given, Herr Reichsleiter. We were ordered here and told to find Fräulein Braun and offer assistance."

"Gretl Braun?" Karl asked.

"Fräulein Eva Braun."

Louise tightened her grip on her husband's arm. "What is Eva doing here, Karl?"

Karl shook his head indicating he did not know, and then he ordered the men to follow him.

Inside the club, Louise spotted Herta Schneider near the entrance, off to one side, but did not see her daughter. When Herta saw the Lehmanns, she walked briskly toward them.

"Let me talk to her, Karl," Louise said as Herta approached. "You get too upset."

"What is the matter, Herta?" asked Louise.

"You are finally here, Frau Lehmann," Herta said. "I sent the message to your hotel two hours ago."

"We were at a reception," Louise explained, dismissing the young woman's complaint and worry. "Tell me what is wrong. Where is Early—Erika?"

"She left with the band two hours ago," Herta explained. "We told her she should return to her hotel or stay with us, but she left anyway. Gretl and Eva left with her to watch over her. Eva told me to stay here and wait for you."

"So Eva Braun was with you here tonight?" Karl interrupted.

"Yes."

"And she is with our daughter, you say?" Karl made sure.

"Yes, both Eva and Gretl."

"Where did they go?" Louise asked.

"A man in the band said they were going to the Lockerung. I know of it. It's an all-night café just off the Friedrichstrasse."

Karl asked, "The SA men outside—was there any trouble here before our daughter left?"

"No. When Erika refused to leave, Eva telephoned Werner Fischer. He sent the men. Eva was going to have the men take Erika back to your hotel, but she left with the band before the SA arrived. Eva and Gretl did not want her to leave alone so they went with her."

"We have a taxi waiting," Karl added quickly. "Take us to this café."

Outside, Karl gave the Brownshirt leader the name of the café and ordered the men to follow his cab. The Nazis ran across the street to a truck parked in an alley. Two of the men got into the truck's cab; the others jumped into the bed.

Herta gave the cabdriver the name of the café and an approximate location near the Friedrichstrasse. The driver nodded and said he

125

knew the place; Karl told him to step on it. The driver, unconcerned with speed limits with a Reichsleiter in his taxi, sped across Berlin with the Stormtroopers in the slower truck falling behind.

The taxi screeched to a stop in front of the Lockerung Café. Karl hurried in ahead of the others. His daughter was easy to find, everyone's head in the café was turned the same direction watching Erika. Overhead, she walked along a thin rail that served as a safety barrier for the second-floor office landing. On one side of the rail was the landing a few feet below, on the other side a 20-foot drop to the café floor. Erika was barefoot and wearing a man's shirt and rolled up baggy men's pants. A man's fedora sat on her head; a cigarette in her mouth. Eva and Gretl were trying to talk Erika down, but she ignored them and kept up her dangerous balancing act.

Louise caught up with her husband, looked up, and gasped. "Get her down, Karl! . . . Never mind! I'll do it."

"Early, get down now!" Louise shouted as she and Karl made their way to the stairs.

Erika heard her mother and looked. She saw her parents coming up the stairs and jumped from the rail to the second-floor landing four feet below.

"Where is your dress, Early?" Louise asked as she took the cigarette from her daughter's mouth. She handed it to Karl who threw it to the landing floor and crushed it under his shoe.

"I don't know, Mama."

"And your shoes?"

Erika shrugged.

The Braun sisters and Herta joined them at the top of the stairs and overheard.

"Her dress was very wet, Frau Lehmann," Eva answered for Erika. "One of the musicians gave her his clothes at the club. She changed behind the bandstand before we knew what was going on."

"Some strange man gave you his clothes?" asked Karl, his annoyance with his daughter obvious.

Erika nodded.

"For Heaven's sake, Early," Louise said. "And then you decide to get up here and show off, is that it?"

"No, Mama, I was just having fun."

"Fun!" Karl growled. "You'll kill yourself someday having fun. You've been drinking?"

"Yes, Father."

"And too much."

"Perhaps, Father." Erika giggled and hugged him.

"Early, you got up here and walked this rail after drinking," said Louise, the distress in her voice clear. "What were you thinking?"

Erika swayed like a sailor in high seas then hugged her mother.

"Fräuleins," Karl said to the other young women. "I thank you for not abandoning our daughter to her foolishness, but this could have become a very serious matter. You should not have let her drink."

Herta told Karl the band was at fault for the drinks. The band began ordering Erika schnapps and assorted hard liquor drinks, many of which Eva and Gretl hid or diluted while Herta distracted Erika, though it was apparent from Erika's speech and conduct that the tactic fell short.

"Karl," said Louise, "Early is eighteen. We cannot blame others for her mistakes in judgment." Louise turned to the girls, "Thank you, all of you, for your attention to our daughter." Then to her husband: "Let's get her back to the hotel, Karl."

When the group reached the bottom of the stairs, the tardy Stormtroopers suddenly burst through the door, wooden bats in hand, ready to crack the head of anyone Reichsleiter Lehmann thought would look good with a cracked head. Karl told them to lower the bats, and ordered the Brownshirt leader to have a couple of his men escort the Braun sisters and Herta Schneider to their homes. Karl gave the leader cash for taxis so the women would not have to ride in the back of an open truck. Louise asked Gretl that if she happened to find Erika's dress and shoes, to drop them off at the Hotel Kempinski. Heading to the café door, they passed a group of strangely dressed men, surely the American musicians. Erika waved at them. Karl took the fedora from his daughter's head and asked who it belonged to. One of the men held up his hand, the only American wearing a trench coat and obviously the one who gave Erika his clothes. Karl glared and threw the hat at him. Karl Lehmann was not unfamiliar with brawling, a common exercise for a member of the NSDAP in the early twenties, and, for an instant, considered taking the man outside himself, or giving him up to the Brownshirts and letting them do what they did best. *If only the swine were a communist, or it were not during the Olympics.*

As they were about to enter the taxi, Erika stopped. "I forgot to kiss my friends." She turned back to Gretl, Herta, and Eva, who had followed them out, and kissed each on the cheek.

Finally in the taxi, Erika sat between her parents in the backseat, her head leaning on her father's shoulder. As soon as they reached their hotel, it was up the elevator quickly to the two-bedroom suite, where Louise helped her daughter undress and get into bed.

"Good night, Early," Louise Lehmann kissed her daughter's forehead. "My darling."

Erika, nearly asleep, took her mother's hand as if she would never let go. "Good night, Mama. I love you."

Karl waited for his wife outside their daughter's bedroom.

"What are we to do with her?" Karl asked Louise as they walked to their room. "The troubles of the past, and now she lets strange men ply her with liquor, undresses in front of who-knows-how-many of them, then leaves with them to wherever they want to take her. What will become of her, Louise?"

Chapter 23

A Better View for the Führer

Berlin—Monday, August 3, 1936

Unfortunately for Karl and Louise Lehmann, the nuisance caused by the Saturday night escapades of their daughter was not behind them. The telephone call came Monday morning shortly after room service delivered breakfast.

"Who was that, Karl?" Louise asked when her husband hung up.

"It was Goebbels," Karl answered, sitting back down at the table. Karl Lehmann always ate cold-cuts and *Schwarzbrot* for breakfast, his wife and daughter normally oatmeal and eggs. "He asked me to stop by his office today at my convenience. Something about photographs of our daughter." Karl looked at his daughter who sat next to her mother gobbling her food. When Erika heard her father, she stopped chewing.

"What will I see, Liebchen?" Karl gazed at his daughter. Louise also turned toward Erika.

With a mouthful of eggs, Erika looked puzzled. "Um . . . nothing that I know of, Father . . . I mean . . . I don't think there is anything . . . no, don't worry." The food garbled the words, and a piece of scrambled egg fell out of her mouth as she spoke.

Karl Lehmann looked at his wife and threw up his hands.

Karl made short work of breakfast and, unwilling to wait for a Wehrmacht or SA driver, drove himself to the Popular Enlightenment Ministry building on the Wilhelmstrasse. His daughter either did not know or did not remember what the photographs might show. If she had said, he would have believed her. For all the worry she had at times put her parents through, they had never caught her in a lie—she freely admitted to her acts of foolishness or violent behavior, then she would kiss or hug them. She was gifted but exasperating, so unusual compared to the children of people he and Louise knew, and now to add to their angst she was no longer a child, but a young woman.

Arriving at the ministry, Karl identified himself to the SA guards and told them he had come to see the Reich Minister. His status as Reichsleiter got him an immediate escort to Goebbels' secretary. Goebbels, always in a hurry, did not like the delay of waiting for elevators, and since a clubfoot made steps difficult, his office was on the main floor.

The propaganda chief stood outside his office talking to his secretary as Karl Lehmann approached. The two men, longtime Party comrades, exchanged a vigorous handshake. Goebbels led Karl into his office and shut the door.

"How is Louise?" Goebbels asked. The diminutive Goebbels sat down behind a desk so large he looked childlike; Karl sat in a facing chair.

"Fine, and Magda?"

"Wonderful," Goebbels said. "We expect our fourth child sometime this winter."

"Congratulations. I'm sorry Magda missed the reception Saturday. Louise and I are hoping to see her before we return to Washington."

Goebbels nodded. "Is your family enjoying the Games, Karl?"

"Yes, especially our daughter it seems. Louise and I had an unexpected diversion Saturday night when we were forced to reclaim her from the Americans—something you apparently know about."

Goebbels smiled. "She *is* spirited. Always has been as I recall."

"*Spirited* . . . that's a kind word for it."

Goebbels laughed.

Karl asked, "So what is this all about, Josef?"

"I sent a reporter and a photographer to that nightclub to cover the story. With the American musicians coming, a large crowd was expected. As you are well aware, the Party finds such American music is without merit; nevertheless, I decided to allow the event, and I ordered the *Morgenpost* to cover it. We can be accommodating, even if the Jewish world press claims otherwise."

"Yes, Josef, of course," Karl Lehmann was on equal terms with Goebbels, not in position and notoriety, but in standing within the Party and, more importantly, with Adolf Hitler. He could speak freely to Goebbels and was eager to get to the point. "You mentioned on the telephone something about photographs. May I see them, please?"

Goebbels opened a desk drawer and extracted a thick folder of photographs. Inside, he had separated six photos from the others with a clip. He handed the clipped photos to Karl. Three photographs pictured Erika dancing with a man who was obviously an American, her dress in various stages of disarray. In one, her dress straps had fallen from her shoulders, allowing the front of her dress to sag, her breasts barely covered. In another, she was held upside down during a dance move, her underwear exposed. Karl grimaced. In the third photo, Erika danced with Eva Braun. Three more photographs showed Erika with three different men on the dance floor; in each she was in a tight embrace, kissing them on the lips. In two photos she wore her dress; in the third, the man's clothing she was wearing when he and Louise found her at the café.

Karl threw the photos on Goebbels' desk without comment.

"The photographs will be destroyed, Karl," Goebbels promised. "I would not have bothered you with this, but, since Fräulein Braun is in some photographs, I had to show the Führer. He insisted I show you the photos of Erika; he said it is a father's right. The photos will never be seen. The photographer did not know Erika, or Fräulein Braun and her association with the Führer. As you can see from this stack, he simply took many rolls of film, no one was singled out. I have the negatives, and I will decide which photographs are released—none with your daughter or Fräulein Braun, of course."

"Of course," Karl said. "Thank you, Josef. May I have the pictures of my daughter? Louise will want to see them."

"Surely."

Karl gathered the photographs from the desk. Goebbels handed him a large envelope.

Monday, August 17, 1936
"Magda!"

Magda Goebbels, glass of champagne in hand, turned to see Louise Lehmann approaching. Magda stood beside her husband and Leni Riefenstahl at the post-Olympic reception in the penthouse of the Berlin Four Seasons; all those attending had been invited personally by Adolf Hitler.

"Louise!" Magda and Louise hugged and kissed a cheek. The two women, long-time acquaintances through their husbands' Party association, had not seen each other since the Lehmanns arrived in Berlin for the Games.

"Karl tells me congratulations are in order."

"I'm hoping for a boy. Our girls have their father wrapped so tightly around their little fingers I'm not sure he could survive another female."

Louise looked at Magda's husband and laughed. "Is that true, Josef?"

Josef Goebbels smiled. "Have you met Fräulein Riefenstahl, Louise?"

"No."

"Let me introduce you," said Goebbels. "Louise, this is Fräulein Riefenstahl. Leni, this is Frau Lehmann."

Louise, like most in Germany, knew Leni Riefenstahl. A former actress, now filmmaker, Riefenstahl was responsible for *Triumph of the Will*, and had been asked by Hitler to film the Olympics. "Of course I know of your work, Fräulein Riefenstahl," Louise said. "It is a pleasure to meet you. My daughter told me many wonderful things about you."

"Your daughter?" Riefenstahl did not understand.

"Yes, Erika Lehmann. She has been working with you."

Riefenstahl, a statuesque beauty, but a tired-looking one, smiled and became more animated. "Erika, of course. I failed to connect the last names. She has been a great help. It's wonderful having her around, Frau Lehmann. Erika and I went swimming one night in the Olympic pool after the competitions ended for the day. Your daughter is a wonderful swimmer. She might have done well in some of the swimming events."

"Thank you, Fräulein Riefenstahl." Louise was simply glad her daughter had stayed busy and out of trouble since the nightclub calamity on opening day.

Magda asked, "What did you think of last night's closing ceremonies, Louise?"

"Incredible," Louise answered.

Josef Goebbels added, "Yes, I've heard nothing but praise for our organizers. The spotlight cathedral especially impressed the world press from all reports. The Führer is very pleased with the Games. We won by far the most medals—nearly twice what the Americans, who were second, won. The Führer tells me someday every Olympics will be held in Germany."

"When are you returning to America, Louise?" Magda asked.

"My daughter and I leave Wednesday. Karl still has business in Berlin so he'll be here longer, perhaps two more weeks. Erika and I will take our time going back. We're going to spend two days in Paris, then a week with my family in London."

"Where is your daughter, Frau Lehmann?" Riefenstahl asked.

"She is somewhere with her father and Herr Reichskanzler." Like most British, Louise referred to Hitler as Herr Reichskanzler, not Führer. "Earlier I saw them walk out onto the balcony. . . ."

Adolf Hitler stood on the penthouse balcony with Karl and Erika Lehmann. The two men wore business suits, Erika a light-green, chiffon dress. The last two days had been abnormally hot, even for August, and they welcomed the high balcony breeze. The lights of Berlin sparkled below.

"The view has improved since we first met, Karl," Hitler said.

"Yes, I remember your apartment over the store in Munich, mein Führer."

"Back then, trash cans and alley cats made up the view from my window," Hitler recalled.

"Yes, this view is quite different." Karl agreed.

"I think back to those days often, Karl. If the Putsch had worked, I would have been the right age, and had the time to do the things that must be done. Now I am too old."

"No, I disagree; look at what you have accomplished. We now have back the Rhineland; unemployment, a plague three years ago, has practically disappeared—only the lazy are not working; I can go on."

Hitler shrugged and turned his attention to Erika. Hitler enjoyed children, especially the children of his inner circle. "So, Tschapperl, I think you have been enjoying Berlin, yes?" Hitler had seen the photographs from Club Zenzi. *Tschapperl* was the nickname Hitler used for Erika beginning in the late twenties when she was a child. It was a Viennese diminutive meaning *little thing* (although Erika was now the same height as Hitler).

"Oh, you're just like my father, you're both *fuddy-duddies,*" Erika admonished Hitler for his kidding, and then kissed him on the cheek. "But yes, I love the Games, and I spent much of the past two weeks helping Leni Riefenstahl. Eva introduced us. Leni's work is fascinating. I ran errands for her while she and her crew filmed the competitions." Then Erika asked Hitler, "Where is Eva, by the way? I hoped to see her tonight."

"She does not usually attend these events, Tschapperl."

"Why not?"

Karl interrupted to scold his daughter. "That is enough, Erika! That type of thing is none of your business, and you are much too bold with the Führer."

"It's all right, Karl," Hitler assured his old friend, but he did not answer Erika's question.

"I'm going in and find Mama," she said sweetly; again she kissed Hitler and then her father before stepping inside.

Karl shook his head. "My daughter is a handful, mein Führer, and sometimes I think it is her nature to be uncontrollable. You saw the photographs from that nightclub. Louise and I had a long talk with her, but I'm afraid growing into womanhood in the wild culture of America is the worst thing for her. Two years ago, Louise and I considered sending her back here to live with my family and attend a Party Gymnasium. Perhaps we erred in not doing so."

"She is just a healthy German girl, my friend, with a zest for life."

"*Healthy* . . . Josef used the word *spirited.* I thank you both for your kindness."

Hitler laughed. "You and Louise can be proud. I can easily tell she has the best traits of our race. I wish Germany had more like her. Tschapperl—Erika—is strong, talented, and iron-willed. What are your plans for her now that she has finished Gymnasium in America?"

"As long as we are in America, Erika will attend university there. She has been accepted to a prestigious women's college. Everyone tells me it's one of the best American colleges for women. Her classes start next month. Louise would like to see her become a teacher of music or languages. Erika seems to have talent with both. I, on the other hand, suggested she enroll in international studies. She has a year of classes before she has to decide."

"She should honor her father's wishes," said Hitler. "But whatever course she chooses, she will be a credit to the Fatherland, Karl. I'm sure of it."

Adolf Hitler took a drink of his apple tea, Karl Lehmann a sip of his martini.

Hitler asked, "Karl, what is *fuddy-duddies?*"

Chapter 24

Shadow of a Doubt

Cincinnati—Saturday, October 2, 1943

The ushers of the RKO Century Theatre knew to expect Adalwulf von Krause every Saturday evening at five o'clock. The old man would stay for the first movie of the double feature, then walk a block down the street to a favorite café for coffee and strudel. The movie and coffee were a routine tightly embraced, started in New York with the symphony (preferably) or a Broadway show every Saturday night and continued when he moved to Cincinnati with a film as substitute in the absence of the other entertainments. Krause preferred (and insisted on) the privacy offered by the theater's balcony boxes, and he tipped the manager to reserve one for him each Saturday for the five o'clock film. If illness or some other circumstance kept Krause from attending, the manager knew that the next week he would receive his tip for the previous week regardless.

The old man looked out of place in the balcony box of the RKO Century. On the main theater floor below, adult patrons slouched in their seats, children spilled popcorn and argued over candy, and teenage boys fumbled their attempts to place hands on intriguing body parts of girls sitting next to them, but the old man in the balcony sat razor straight in a three-piece suit and tie, holding an expensive teak walking stick with a solid silver snarling wolf's head handle.

Krause, sixty years plus and spry, carried himself like an aristocrat, and indeed he was from a long line. The von Krauses could trace their lineage through five centuries of wealthy Prussian landowners and Teutonic elite. His grandfather had served as an advisor to Otto von Bismarck.

In his younger days, Krause, like most loyal Germans, was a monarchist and in 1909 he received an officer's commission in the Kaiser's army and served until the end of the Great War. During the war, Krause volunteered for front line duty, but never saw battle. Instead, his orders kept him in Berlin where he oversaw the transportation of war matériel to the various fronts.

Directly after the Great War, with the Hohenzollerns exiled to the Netherlands and a democratic government mandated by the victors,

Krause found himself skeptical of the Weimar Republic, abhorring the communists, and firmly opposed to the various ultra-right wing political organizations that sprang up in Germany in the wake of the Versailles humiliations and the collapse of the German economy. He was an opponent of the reactionary groups not because of their ideology—Krause agreed with many of the main principles of the right-wing ideologues—but because he considered them opportunists who put their own agendas ahead of the nation's. To Krause, these men were mongrels with not a person of proper breeding among them. And this was his view even after he heard Hitler speak in 1922 at the Hofbräuhaus in Munich.

In Munich for an unrelated social function, Krause attended the speech at the invitation of a friend who accompanied him. Krause had always considered Hitler just another politician of pedestrian heritage, but he came away that day impressed with some of the plans and programs proposed. Impressed, but unlike his friend Karl who cast his lot with Hitler in the early twenties, Krause bided his time. Only after Hitler came to power in 1933 and Germans went back to work did Krause start to sway. National pride slowly returned. Then when Hitler took back the Rhineland in March of 1936 without a shot fired, Krause was finally convinced. How else but through Providence could this Austrian corporal become Germany's savior?

And it was this same Providence, or perhaps strange fate, that would require Adalwulf von Krause to reside (at least until after the war) in a country now an enemy to his homeland.

Krause's numerous trips to the States started in the 1920s. During the first war, his daughter (Krause's wife died in childbirth) became pregnant out of wedlock and to avoid scandal was sent to stay temporarily with a second cousin living in Cincinnati. There Willy was born. The boy's father, a German soldier, did not survive the war and Krause's daughter never returned to Germany. Krause grew familiar with America as the years passed, and when the Nazis came to power in '33 Krause was approached to help oversee and report back to Germany on the status of various Reich financial assets in America. Eventually his astute financial advice convinced the powers back home that Adalwulf von Krause was someone to be listened to when it came to such matters.

Then fate stepped in.

Willy's mother contracted influenza during a winter epidemic in 1935 and died when Willy was 19. Krause took his grandson back to

Germany, but because of Krause's skillful handling of Reich banking affairs in the States, he was approached by Hjalmar Schacht, the Reich Minister of Economics who served as the banker for the Third Reich. Schacht asked him to move to New York City to manage the Reich's American investments full-time. In America, Krause continued to be a shrewd warden and investor of Reich funds, and by the time the United States entered the war in late 1941, Krause, who had seen the writing on the wall, had wisely converted or transferred much of Germany's financial assets in America back to Europe, to South America, or other select places around the globe—money that, had it remained in American banks, would have been frozen and then confiscated by the United States when it declared war on Germany. Indeed, the Führer himself commended Krause for his astute handling of the Reich's money. Krause kept the letter signed by Adolf Hitler in his study's wall safe.

Overseeing German business affairs in the United States ended when America entered the war, and Krause would have gladly packed up his grandson and returned home, but because of a strange visit in 1939 from a man named Friedrich Haupt, Krause would not be returning to the Fatherland, at least not for the duration. Haupt, a fellow German who was also living in the United States at the time, visited Krause and requested he apply for American citizenship. Krause objected, not being told why he was asked such a thing, but Haupt had a letter confirming that this strange request was sent down from the highest levels. The letter carried the signature and seal of the German ambassador. Krause made a trip to Washington to personally call on the ambassador who confirmed the request, so Krause acquiesced. His papers went through and he was sworn in as a United States citizen in April 1939, less than six months before Hitler invaded Poland. Later, Krause realized that this citizenship request was made so he could remain in the States during the war, a war that some in Berlin must have surely known was coming. Indeed, Haupt eventually reappeared and told Krause that a handful of trusted German patriots were being asked to remain in the United States, all for different purposes. It would be Krause's task to steward the funds for any projects the Fatherland might have in North and South America during the war. Fifteen million dollars was earmarked for Krause—not a huge sum when compared to the dollar amounts of international finance he dealt with before the war, but neither was it a pittance, and more was available if needed. Krause was instructed to liquidate and launder the money, which he did through Swiss banks, and deposit it in his name. He divided the money between various banks both in and outside of the United States. For all intents and purposes, Adalwulf von Krause was now the furtive bank of the Reich in the Western Hemisphere. One Reich operation that von Krause now funded was the Bolivar network, a string of German communication relay substations stretching from Mexico to South America. Krause set up an account in Juárez, just across the border from El Paso, to channel the needed funds to the people in charge of the various communication substations. He ensured no one could trace the money back to him; no one within the Bolivar network even knew the name of their benefactor.

When this new assignment started, Krause lived in New York City, but he never cared much for the city he considered overrun by Jews. So a year later, during the summer of 1940, he sought and received permission from Haupt (who had by now returned to Germany) to move to Cincinnati where his daughter had lived. Krause felt more at home in this city where a substantial number of residents were of German heritage, many only a generation or two removed. Krause sent his request in a letter to an address in Lisbon given him by Haupt in case a need to communicate presented itself. Even though America was not yet at war, letters to and from Germany were beginning to be viewed with suspicion. Portugal was a neutral nation and one of the few locations in Europe where mail from the States could flow freely in and out without raising red flags. Krause eventually received a letter from Haupt granting permission for the move. Krause was told that this would be his final move until the conclusion of the war in Europe. In his letter to Haupt, Krause suggested he might serve the Fatherland as a member of the German-American Bund, which had a significant pre-war membership in Cincinnati, but Haupt issued Krause strict orders that he was to have no ties with the Bund, which the FBI had eyed closely since 1939. No, it was Krause's assignment to lie low, avoid suspicion, and make available the Reich's American assets where needed.

And now, because of this strange fate, and both foreseen and unforeseen events, here he sat: a dignified and proud old man dressed for an opera in the less-than-majestic balcony of an American movie theater.

The movie was an Alfred Hitchcock thriller entitled *Shadow of a Doubt.* Teresa Wright played a small town girl who suspected her mysterious uncle, played by Joseph Cotten, might be a serial killer. The movie unfolded as a cat-and-mouse game between niece and uncle.

"Guten Abend, Herr von Krause."

The words were whispered so closely to his ear the old man felt her warm breath. This, and that she spoke in German startled him and he jerked in his chair. The woman circled around from behind and sat in the chair on his right. Krause, taken unaware, responded in his native tongue: "Sie sind aus Deutschland?" Immediately she lifted a finger to her lips.

"My words were just a whisper," she said softly in English. "We must speak English and be mindful of our words, although I am pleased you prefer to sit alone in the balcony. This is private and good for our purpose," she said pleasantly. "But yes, I am a German, and I am the one who gave the note to your grandson to deliver to you. Let us now enjoy the film."

She said no more, instead directing her attention to the screen. Krause was not sure what to say so he did not. He was not frightened; in fact, he had looked forward to this rendezvous that he knew would come sooner or later after Willy handed over the note. No, Adalwulf von Krause was not afraid, but he was surely very curious. Who is this woman who knows of Hrungnir's Heart?

His glance of her when she sat down beside him in the dark theater was deficient. Krause wanted to turn and look at her, but for a man of his upbringing and background to do so would be bad-mannered. So there they sat—perhaps the world would guess grandfather and granddaughter simply enjoying a Hollywood movie and each other's company. She joined him halfway through the film, so for about an hour they sat without speaking.

"I like Joseph Cotten," were her first words as the credits rolled. "He played a role in *Citizen Kane*. I read in a magazine that he and Orson Welles are best friends."

Krause was surprised at the small talk and unsure how to respond. "I did not know that, Miss," was the only response that came to mind.

The lights in the theater came up, signaling intermission before the second feature. Many of the patrons visited the restrooms or concession counter.

"I believe your normal routine is to stay until the second film begins," she said. "Is that correct?"

"Yes."

Intermission lights and conversation now allowed Krause to get a good look at her without being impolite. Willy was right: she was probably around 25, give or take. She wore a svelte, but conservative blue gabardine dress with pointed collar and matching jacket, her hair pinned up and under a large and fashionable blue felt hat with a silver ribbon and pink paper roses. Her lipstick matched the roses.

"I must say you look very nice, Miss," Krause offered.

"You are to blame for that, dear sir." She looked at him and smiled. "Given the way you dress, I was forced to go shopping." The conversation remained sotto voce, even if the privacy of the balcony box allowed a bit of freedom with words. She added, "We are overdressed for a movie theater in this country, but we would draw even more attention if you accompanied a woman dressed like a seamstress or a war plant worker."

"Americans do not know how to dress properly," he remarked.

"I'm not being critical of your attire, Mr. von Krause. I think you look quite dashing, and I enjoyed shopping. Men know women enjoy shopping, is that not correct?" She smiled and put her hand on his arm. The young woman knew how to charm, and the old Prussian immediately began to enjoy her company.

The theater lights dimmed and the screen brightened as the projector's blue light flickered through cigarette smoke. Brief cartoons starring Bugs Bunny and Betty Boop promoting the buying of war bonds came first. Next was a Three Stooges short titled *They Stooge to Conga*. Larry, Moe, and Curly played fix-it men who stumble across a gang of Nazi spies. Again, the young woman watched dutifully. When the Stooges short ended, the latest Universal newsreel flashed onto the screen. Film of Red Cross nurses caring for G.I.s whose severe wounds brought them back to the States preceded film and news from the Pacific theater and the successful Allied recapture of Lae-Salamaua in New Guinea.

When the second feature began it was time to leave. They exited the theater, and Krause asked the young woman if she cared to dine.

"I would love to."

Instead of taking her to the small café he normally visited after a movie, tonight Krause thought a nice restaurant more fitting. He suggested a favorite restaurant in the upscale Netherlands Hotel. To get to the hotel was a longer walk than to the café, but the weather was pleasant. She took his arm.

"Would it be out of place to ask your name?" Krause inquired as they walked.

"Your grandson knows me as Early, but that is not my real name." She wondered how many facts about the night at the Side Pocket Willy had shared with his grandfather. She suspected not many. The fact that she had been forced to dragoon Willy was regrettable. Erika had planned to simply take him aside and stress to him the importance of delivering the note, but when Willy struck her, she reacted in a way consistent with her nature, and the way in which she was trained.

"Ah, my grandson . . . my life's biggest ongoing disappointment I am afraid." Krause paused and then added, "So, it is obvious you have been following Wilmar and me."

"Of course, Mr. von Krause."

"Well, you have certainly done it skillfully," he praised. "I had no idea."

"The only thing that matters is that we are not being followed now," she replied.

The old man stopped and began to turn to look behind them. She drew his arm tighter to her and kept him walking.

"We are not being followed, Mr. von Krause."

"You know this?"

"Yes."

They waited at an intersection; the light changed; they crossed the street.

"I apologize that our meeting had to be handled this way," she said, "but it's the safest way for us both. I obviously could not request an appointment with you, or come calling at your home. That would not be prudent for our first meeting."

"Yes, I see, of course," he acknowledged.

"I am sure you have questions, Mr. von Krause. Please feel at ease to ask them. I will not answer if it is unwise to do so, but I will not lie to you. If I answer, it will be the truth."

"Thank you." Krause thought for a moment as they walked on. "Do we share the same sentiments toward our homeland?"

"Yes."

"And you are here for a specific purpose?"

"Yes."

"Would it be ill-considered of me to ask of that purpose?"

"Yes."

"Then I will not."

"Thank you."

"Your message was unique," said Krause. "How do you know of Hrungnir's Heart?"

"The ring you wear on your right hand bears it."

Krause was surprised. "How do you know of the Ring?"

"My father wears one."

Krause stopped walking. "Who is your father?"

"Karl Lehmann."

Krause stood thunderstruck, thoughts racing. Then he remembered.

"Erika?"

Chapter 25

Karl's Daughter

[same day]

"Yes, Mr. von Krause. I am Karl's daughter, Erika. And I remember you as one of my father's friends, but I am surprised you remember me. I last saw you during the Olympics. You stopped by our hotel one evening to see my father. My mother and I were just leaving; we crossed paths only briefly."

"I could not forget. Karl and I became close friends. I remember his family, but I didn't recognize you . . . your hair . . . ."

She laughed. "Yes, I've changed my hair color a few times recently, and it has been seven years."

The air had cooled in the early evening so they welcomed their arrival at the hotel. The doorman opened and held the door for the finely-dressed old man and the stylish young woman. Krause tipped the man as they entered.

Erika smiled at the tipping, and when they were out of the doorman's earshot she said softly, "I see you have learned many American customs, Mr. von Krause."

"Yes," Krause answered. "Isn't it ridiculous? Giving a gratuity to someone for doing the job he is paid to do?"

She laughed. Erika knew tipping doormen was an American idiosyncrasy, but offering gratuities had its place in other countries as well. "Surely you gave a token to the robust young ladies who brought your beer at the place you heard a speech with my father many years ago."

Again she surprised Krause. To remain discreet, she spoke without mentioning specifics, but he realized she knew about the Hitler speech he attended with Karl Lehmann at the Hofbräuhaus.

"You astound me, my dear. Please accept my *du*." He was telling the young woman that she had his permission to refer to him by his first name, something the proper Prussian rarely granted.

"Thank you, Adalwulf. And please call me Erika in return."

Krause dined regularly at the hotel's elegant restaurant and the majordomo knew him by name.

143

"Ah, nice to see you this evening, Mr. von Krause," the man greeted. "I see you have a lovely guest tonight."

"Hello, sir (Krause insisted on formality and refused to address the majordomo as *Frederick,* as other patrons did). I did not call in reservations. Is my preferred table available?"

The man looked over a table map on the podium. "Yes, Mr. von Krause. Will it be just the two of you?"

"Yes."

"This way, please."

The majordomo led the way through the elegant dining room of Brazilian rosewood woodwork, snow-white tablecloths, sparkling silverware, and glittering crystal goblets all under a towering two-story ceiling. About half of the tables were occupied by the affluent and tastefully dressed of Cincinnati. Krause's table was situated near a fireplace that did its job: the warmth was appreciated, and the delicate fragrance of fresh amaryllis on the table pleasing. The soothing crackle from burning logs serenaded the diners when a string quartet at the other end of the room paused between numbers.

"Will you allow me to order for you, my dear?" Krause requested after they were seated.

"I would like that, thank you."

When the waiter arrived, Krause ordered dinner and wine. He ignored the ration list and ordered Beef Wellington.

The enjoyable meal lasted a long time and was interlaced with pleasant small talk. Forbidden subjects were avoided, and dinner capped off with a French brandy.

"Thank you for dinner, Adalwulf," Erika said after a sip of brandy. "It was wonderful."

"It was my honor, my dear," Krause said. "I have a bottle of Asbach in my study. I regret I cannot offer you some here." He referred to the famous German brandy from the Rhine region now banned in America.

"That would have been a wonderful treat, Adalwulf, but this is a nice brandy." She took another sip. "I have not enjoyed Asbach in some time. The Asbach winery is not far from the village where I was born."

They lingered over the brandy, but eventually it came time to leave the dining room. The hotel had several private conversation areas in the mezzanine over the lobby. There they ordered coffee, and Adalwulf von Krause learned about his old friend's daughter. In return, Krause mentioned Erika's mother.

"She was beautiful and charming," Krause said of Louise. "I know your father suffered greatly when he lost her. I can remember your mother's face when I look at you."

The old man's comment comparing her to her lost mother struck a heart chord. She reached out, took his hand and squeezed. "Thank you, most dear Adalwulf. I'm afraid at times I was a handful to her and my father while growing up. My father and I grew much closer after my mother died."

Krause continued. He met her father in the early twenties, and he knew Karl learned English from his British wife. Erika interjected that she also helped teach her father English. (She laughed. *"He was stubborn and did not want to learn, but mother forced him to study with me."*) Krause knew even more about the Lehmann family history in the thirties when the small, close-knit family spent almost four years in America. (*"That is when I learned an American accent,"* she smiled.) Krause knew that in the summer of 1933 Hitler asked Karl Lehmann to assume the duties of press secretary to the German ambassador to the United States. The family lived in Washington, D.C. until 1937 when Louise Lehmann was killed in a car accident. Soon after Louise died, Karl sent a personal communiqué to Hitler requesting that he and his daughter be allowed to return to Germany. Hitler immediately accommodated his old friend. And Krause knew that, because of Karl Lehmann's press background, Hitler reassigned his old comrade to the Propaganda Ministry, where he now worked under Goebbels.

Krause knew little about Erika's life after that because he left for America about the time Karl and Erika returned to Germany. Erika filled him in.

"Because I spoke English," she told Krause, "after Father and I returned home, I worked at the Seehaus in Berlin translating foreign radio broadcasts. While at the Seehaus I also learned Russian and practiced my French. Eventually I was asked to attend a meeting with Admiral Canaris." Erika stopped and looked at Krause.

He nodded. She was telling him she was an Abwehr operative.

"I thought as much," he told her. Earlier that evening, Krause deduced that, because of her sophisticated scheme undertaken to meet him, including following him over the course of weeks, she must be a spy. In retrospect, the note she sent through Willy was an act of generosity on her part. It relieved Krause from worry that he had been found out by the American authorities. He did not recognize her, and without the note he might have thought her to be an American agent

145

working undercover if she had showed up tonight out of the blue with claims to be an old friend's daughter. But because of the note, Krause knew someone from the Brotherhood of the Ring sent her, something the FBI or other American authorities would know nothing about.

Krause added, "I thank you for the note. I might have been ill at ease right now without it."

"You are welcome, but I must admit my motives for sending the note were greater than just to identify myself as a comrade. Until I sent the note, I had followed you only on occasion, when time and circumstances allowed. After I sent the note, I followed you closely for several days to see if suddenly your habits changed, or if the places you visited became worrisome."

"Ah, I see. Perhaps I would make a sudden visit to the authorities."

She changed the subject. "So now, Adalwulf, you know about me."

"Thank you. To be sure, you seem very capable at what you do, my dear. Tell me, what do you know of the society your father and I belong to?"

"Unfortunately, Father told me little. When I was younger I questioned him about the engravings. He told me they were symbols from the ancient days of the Germanic tribes and the Vikings."

"Indeed," Krause confirmed.

"May I ask what the ring means to you and my father?"

"Someday you will know." Krause rose and offered her his arm. "I hope you enjoyed dinner. Shall we walk together?"

Erika rose, took his arm, and the two descended the stairs to the lobby. The same doorman held the same door as Krause escorted her outside into a chilly night. They strode the well-lighted street in silence for a short distance. Krause spoke first. With scarcely any other walkers about, he assumed they could talk freely. He knew she would stop him if he were wrong, but he must know why they were together.

"So then, why is it that you sought me out, Erika?"

She did not hesitate. "Before I left home, my father and I spent a few days together. He knew where I was going and why, and he told me if I ever needed help, if I were in trouble in America, I should find you. Father told me that you lived in Cincinnati."

"And you are in trouble?"

"Yes."

"Tell me what you can."

"Circumstances forced me to hastily abandon my work in another city," Erika explained. "I lost some valuable items I wanted to take back to the Fatherland. Also, I lost my radio and code sheets and thereby any way to communicate with the people who could make possible my return home."

Krause thought as they walked. "I see, and there is no way to replace the radio?"

"No. I built a simple receiver out of items that can be easily purchased so I can listen in to certain shortwave broadcasts, but it is impossible to build a transmitter without specific parts that I originally brought with me. I still have in my head information that can be useful to our homeland. Father told me you have contacts in Mexico and Central America that can relay information to Germany. The information is too valuable to trust to a dead letter drop; it is unreliable and the delivery cannot be confirmed. Without my transmitter or code sheets there is only one way I can safely send that information through the air waves. I have a plan, but I need you to supply me with information about your contacts: their frequencies, call signs and codenames, locations. Then, after the information is sent, I need your help getting home."

The old man stopped walking when they were in the shadows under the canvas awning of a closed store. "I will help you, of course. It was wise of your father to send you to me."

"There is something more, Adalwulf. There is risk for you. The authorities are looking for me."

"Yes, but you said your assignment was in another city. The FBI will not know you are in Cincinnati."

"Unfortunately, I got myself involved in some trouble here, in this city, just recently. I stepped in when two women were being assaulted. It was not prudent of me. The local police I'm sure have my fingerprints as does the FBI. They will match them soon if they have not already."

Surely Krause would have read about the attack at the Lamar Apartments—the talk of the town as far as recent crimes; however, if he realized this was the trouble she referred to he did not comment.

"Then we have little time to waste, my dear. Do you have enough money for now? Money will not be one of our problems."

"I have money. I placed some of my money in a bank in Nashville, Tennessee. This was not the city of my assignment, so I retrieved it after I fled. I went to Nashville before I came here."

"Very well," Krause said. "I will supply you with the information you need, and we will find the best way to send you home in a way that is as safe as possible. I will need a few days to think about this and put a plan together. How can I contact you?"

"I will contact you, shall we say, in about a week?"

"Yes, that should be fine," Krause said.

"I know I need not tell you of the importance of telling no one about me or our meeting tonight, not even your grandson."

"Of course," Krause said. "Put your mind at ease; no one will hear of tonight."

"Then I will leave you for now." Erika offered her hand. "Thank you, Adalwulf."

Krause took her hand with a slight Prussian bow.

Erika turned and started away.

"Let me summon a taxi, my dear." Krause called to her. "I will drop you somewhere."

She stopped, but did not turn back to him.

"Good night, Adalwulf. Thank you again for dinner."

Erika Lehmann walked away into the Cincinnati night.

Chapter 26

Annie and the Smith Brothers

Staunton, Virginia—Mary Baldwin College

Friday, April 9, 1937

"Okay, class," said the professor, "we have experienced a few bumps in the road on our journey through Denmark with Hamlet. I am especially disappointed in some of your essays addressing the ambiguity the Priest and the Gravedigger mention concerning Ophelia's death. Nevertheless, we are progressing."

Like most of the English Department faculty at Mary Baldwin, Professor Lynn Bevins taught several subjects, including all of the Shakespeare classes. Thus, since the women-only liberal arts college required all students to complete at least one Shakespeare class, regardless of their major field of study, all undergrads who attended Mary Baldwin had, at one time or another since Bevins' arrival, sat in her classroom.

Bevins immediately drew attention when she arrived on campus in 1929. Unlike her colleagues at the prestigious school—most of them older Ivy Leaguers the students considered stuffy—the 34-year-old Texan brought enthusiasm and a cowgirl accent straight from the Panhandle via the College of Industrial Arts, a women's liberal arts college in Denton, Texas, where she earned all of her degrees. Students liked her because having a little fun in class was not a mortal sin. Yet Bevins could be saddle-leather tough: her students learned quickly that apologies or fabricated excuses for not doing the work were a waste of time.

"Today, let's discuss scene two of the third act," Bevins said as she walked from behind the podium to stand directly in front of the class of 23 freshmen. "Here's our main discussion point: describe the dumb show and *The Murder of Gonzago*. What is the significance of who murders the king in the play-within-the-play for the larger plot?"

No one raised her hand. Several students diverted their eyes hoping to avoid being called upon. One student in the third row, a petite brunette, looked at the girl sitting beside her, a powerfully built blonde, and rolled her eyes. The blonde saw her friend's mockery and

149

grinned. Lynn Bevins observed both and addressed the brunette eye-roller first.

"Miss Drexler, what are your initial thoughts about the dumb show?"

The girl sat up straight. "Umm . . . I, ah . . . I think the dumb show was not dumb. It was smart."

Bevins ignored the snickering from the other students. "You know, Miss Drexler, I never quite thought of it in that way. But it might behoove you to invest more time studying before the final *Hamlet* exam next week."

"Yes, ma'am." Annie Drexler reddened and looked down at her notebook.

The professor turned to the blonde. "Miss Lehmann, why do you think Shakespeare inserted the *Gonzago* play into *Hamlet?*"

"Foreshadowing, perhaps?" answered Erika Lehmann.

Bevins refrained from comment and began her lecture.

When class ended, Annie Drexler and Erika Lehmann spent a few minutes in the hall talking with other girls then left the building to return to their dorm.

"'The dumb show is not dumb; it's smart.'" Erika laughed about her friend's answer when they got outside.

Despite her answer in class, Annie was a top student. "What kind of question was that? I've studied my rear off on that play, but the *dumb show?* How did she come up with that question? I guess you're going to tell me you knew the answer, Miss Perfect-in-Everything?"

Erika laughed again as they strolled by an apple tree so rich with white blossoms it looked like the world's largest cotton ball. Mary Baldwin College, located on rolling hills in the heart of the Shenandoah Valley, offered springtime scenery that could well have leapt from a Monet canvas—the campus a riot of color where trees and flowers exploded with buds, sprigs, and petals in red, white, orange, yellow, and countless hues of green. Four apple trees grew on campus and students were encouraged to partake of the juicy, red pommes. The fruit would be just right for picking when the women returned for classes in September.

Dormitory administrators, when assigning freshman roommates, strove to pair students from diverse backgrounds. That policy paired

Annie Drexler with Erika Lehmann. Annie hailed from southern Missouri, near the boot heel, having grown up literally on the shores of the Mississippi River in Commerce where her family worked hard and made good. And since the Drexler family had wisely invested much of their fortune in real estate, they had so far weathered the Depression, unlike many of their friends and neighbors.

Erika Lehmann, the admittance advisors learned from her application and interview, grew up in Europe reared by a German father and a British mother, spending her elementary school years in England and Germany, then her high school years in the United States after her father became press secretary to the German ambassador in Washington, D.C. Consequently, the diversity-seeking college staff happily assigned the American-as-apple-pie Annie and European Erika to be roommates when they entered as freshmen last fall.

And the two girls differed in other ways.

Petite, raven-haired Annie was 5'3" tall and weighed 103 pounds. Bright blonde Erika stood five inches taller and weighed nearly 140 pounds, her sturdy physique that of a champion swimmer and tennis player: long legs, long arms, wide shoulders. Annie's home in Missouri was an 800-mile train ride away; Erika's parents' home in Arlington, Virginia, across the Potomac River from Washington, only a 3-hour automobile ride.

Even their reasons for attending Mary Baldwin contrasted in almost every way. Annie came to Baldwin because doing so had become a family tradition among the women of her family. Annie's mother and an aunt graduated from Baldwin, and a cousin spent two years here in the early 30s before changing her major to one not offered at Baldwin and transferring. Erika, on the other hand, attended Baldwin because her father refused to consider any co-ed college for his daughter. One evening during her senior year in high school, Erika overheard her father tell her mother: *"Our daughter going off to a college where there are men? . . . Think about it, Louise. God help us . . . and them!"*

Despite all their differences, the two roommates—now best friends—had things in common. Administrators checked the *Exceptionally Gifted* box on both of their confidential student profiles after their first semester, a fact neither Annie nor Erika knew. Both took their studies seriously and enjoyed athletic endeavors. Annie grew up around horses, and the shelves in her proud parents' den back home in Missouri sagged under the weight of first place

151

equestrian competition trophies. Last fall, before winter set in, she took Erika to a local riding stable and taught her friend some of the finer points of horsemanship. Erika, on the other hand, excelled in physically vigorous sports such as swimming, tennis, and, despite her size, gymnastics.

"What classes do you have this afternoon?" asked Erika. Though Erika worked on speaking with an American accent (mostly because the way Americans spoke English amused her), and by and large sounded as American as any girl at Mary Baldwin, occasionally her British accent slipped through.

"Political science and speech class," answered Annie, who aspired to become a radio news announcer. Annie knew it would not be easy breaking into that boys' club, but she was determined.

In return, Annie asked, "How about you?"

"French, and my classical music appreciation course." Erika leaned toward a major in languages and minor in music although she had not yet made up her mind.

"Hey, speaking of music, are we going to try to make it to The Boondoggle tonight? It's Friday." The roommates also shared a love for dancing, especially to the new swing jazz tunes. Unfortunately, the number of jazz clubs in Staunton was zero, the nearest over a hundred miles away in Richmond. But The Boondoggle, a local tavern, had a dance floor and a jukebox with many of the newest hits and was within walking distance, ten blocks from campus.

Erika warned, "You know, if we get caught sneaking out after curfew again, we'll probably be suspended."

"What time are we leaving?"

"The usual. Right after Mrs. Tarkenton finishes dorm check."

Mary Baldwin students could leave campus after dark only if the excursions were pre-approved by their dormitory matron, and, even then, an approved chaperone must go along. Students could study in other dorms or meet to socialize around campus until 9 p.m. when all the women were expected to be back in their home dormitory buildings. There, in their home dorm, they were free to visit with friends and study partners until lights out at 11 p.m. The 9 p.m. dorm curfew was especially enforced on weekends—the evenings most likely to tempt some of the girls to make trips off campus to meet with members of the opposite sex. The only excuse a student had to be out of her home dorm after curfew was if she studied in the school library, which stayed open as long as students studied there, the patient evening library staff sometimes staying on the job through the night until relieved in the morning by the day staff. This happened often during finals week when the last-minute crammers descended on the library to pull their all-nighters. If a student was at the library after curfew, her dorm matron was notified.

Mrs. Tarkenton (no one knew the elderly woman's first name, it seemed) lost her husband in the Spanish American War. With a war widow's pension too paltry to survive on and no family in a position to take her in, she fortuitously secured a position as a dorm matron at the college and was assigned to Memorial Residence Hall. As dorm matron she received no salary, but was assigned sleeping quarters in the building's basement near a bathroom that became her own. She ate free in the campus cafeteria, and this free room and board made it possible to survive on the small government allowance from her husband's war death. Now, in 1937, Mrs. Tarkenton had been at Mary Baldwin longer than any of the faculty (this year, in fact, a granddaughter of one of her first girls entered Baldwin and was assigned to her charge). Mrs. Tarkenton took her responsibilities seriously; it was not easy for any girl to lose her virginity while a resident of Memorial Hall.

At curfew time each and every night, Mrs. Tarkenton began her rounds. She always started on the top floor of the two-story residence hall; that is where she placed the girls who proved to be her biggest problems—on the second floor where the room windows were too high off the ground for a simple escape and re-entry. And to the second floor she had moved Erika Lehmann and Ann Drexler after she caught them climbing into their room through their first-floor window at three o'clock one morning last October.

Mrs. Tarkenton again caught Lehmann and Drexler returning long after curfew one night in January, this time sneaking up the fire escape. They giggled when confronted, the alcohol on their breath obvious. She worried about those two. Both were intelligent and could be charming—qualities that Mrs. Tarkenton valued for finding a suitable, successful husband—but in her mind she knew they were as wild as Tarzan, especially the Lehmann girl. Mrs. Tarkenton worried that those two might let a man get them into trouble in the most awkward way, so she took special precautions. She moved them from the first floor to Room 209 on the second (and farthest room from the stairway). Every night without fail, Mrs. Tarkenton made sure Lehmann and Drexler were in their room at nine, and occasionally returned for a second check around midnight.

When she reached the top floor, Mrs. Tarkenton walked directly to Room 209 and knocked. She heard the voice from inside the room.

"Come in."

The matron recognized the voice of Annie Drexler and opened the door.

"Hello, girls."

In unison, Annie and Erika said, *"Hello, Mrs. Tarkenton."*

Annie lay on her stomach in bed, under the covers, reading a book. Erika sat at the room's study table in a bath-robe perusing a textbook while writing on a sheet of paper.

"Good night, girls."

Again a chorus. *"Good night, Mrs. Tarkenton."*

As soon as Mrs. Tarkenton closed the door, Annie sprang from under the covers fully dressed. Erika, also dressed for an evening out, jettisoned the bathrobe and walked to the closet. From a box on the top shelf, she produced a rope with knots tied every two feet for hand-holds. Annie opened the window; Erika looped one end of the rope around her waist and threw the rest out, then braced herself while Annie climbed down. Erika reeled the rope back and buried it once again in the closet, then climbed out the window, lowered herself to a small ledge and jumped the remaining ten feet to the ground, rolling when she hit.

"I don't know how you do that without breaking a leg," Annie remarked quietly as they hurried into the shadows.

Annie and Erika, both underage, had become familiar customers of The Boondoggle, not making it there every weekend but most. Erika was a journeyman at gaining admittance to clubs and juke-joints; she had been doing it since high school, but her various subterfuges were not needed at the rough-and-tumble Boondoggle where the bartenders did not waste their time worrying about the age of their clientele as long as they paid their tab and took the fights outside.

The usual Friday night bartender was a rotund man with a long, gray beard whom everyone called Fat Prick (a nickname he seemed to take in stride). He recognized Annie and Erika when they approached the bar. When the two girls first started coming in last fall, Fat Prick had his suspicions. Two good-looking young women who always came in alone, never with dates, must be prostitutes, but he had never observed them leaving with men.

"You girls know you're not supposed to sit at the bar," said Fat Prick. "We go through this every time you come in here. Men only at the bar, goddammit."

"Oh, come on, Mr. Prick," Annie said.

Erika tried to stifle a laugh but only partially succeeded. Annie had obviously never heard the word *prick* before coming to The Boondoggle and did not know what it meant. On the girls' first visit to the tavern, Annie thought patrons were calling the bartender Fat Rick. When it became apparent to Erika the name the bartender was actually being called, Erika corrected Annie but did not tell her the name was vulgar because it was so much fun to hear Annie unknowingly call the man the off-color name.

"Yeah," Erika added, "we like to sit at the bar. We're closer to the good-looking bartender." Erika leaned over the bar and patted the man's enormous stomach.

"You girls are full of piss and vinegar, probably underage, too," said Fat Prick, but he did not force them to move. "What ya havin'?"

"Two draws," Erika said. It wasn't necessary to specify a brand of beer. The Boondoggle served only Schlitz on tap. Hamm's and Pabst Blue Ribbon came in bottles. Whiskey and gin completed The Boondoggle's unfussy inventory, and customers drank those straight or mixed the whiskey with RC Cola and the gin with tonic water. A draft beer cost a nickel. As Erika laid down a dime, she told Annie, "You can get the next one. Do you have any cigarettes?"

"No, we smoked the last ones the last time we were in here."

Cigarettes were sold from the bar, and when Fat Prick brought the glasses of beer, Erika asked him for a pack of Camels. Neither girl had matches, but they begged a light from a man sitting two barstools from Annie.

Always crowded on Friday nights, The Boondoggle catered to a country crowd who played mainly that genre of music on the jukebox. Although the tavern served only whites, the color-blind jukebox offered blues by Robert Johnson and Scrapper Blackwell as well as jazz from artists such as Fletcher "Smack" Henderson, Joe "King" Oliver, and Louis "Satchmo" Armstrong.

Several couples now slow-danced to "Mexicali Rose" by Gene Autry. Annie and Erika had taken only one drink when two extremely large men in cowboy hats sitting at the other end of the bar rose and started their way.

"Here come the Smith brothers," Erika said as she took a drag on her cigarette and coughed. Neither girl smoked except when out on an escapade, and both coughed often when they did.

Annie also coughed out some smoke and turned her head to look. "Do you think they're really good luck, Erika?"

"Maybe. The two times we got caught breaking curfew we didn't dance with them that night."

The Smith brothers, Jocko and Zak, were reputed to possess a certain magic and had become local legends around Staunton. The strange story that circulated concerned an Act of God a few years back. As the story went, one day the brothers were working atop a metal manure silo on their father's farm. The silo had only a partial roof with a large opening to allow gases from the fermenting compost to escape. While the brothers labored to repair some wind-damaged sheet metal roof panels, thunderclouds raced in and found the Smith brothers sitting ducks, striking them both with one well-aimed bolt. The lightning strike blew off their shoes, lit their pants on fire, and sent the brothers plummeting 30 feet into the silo, their landing cushioned by a deep pile of fresh, steaming sheep manure—the wet dung not only breaking their fall but also extinguishing their burning pants. Since that day, the brothers, now in their mid-20s, seemed to live a charmed life.

And the myth that now surrounded the Smith brothers appeared especially strong when it came to the ladies, many of whom seemed convinced that dancing with the Smith brothers bestowed good fortune. Lonely, single women sought out the huge Smith brothers (both were heavily-muscled, stocky men over six feet tall) convinced a dance with Jocko or Zak would be the charm that would bring them their true love in short order. Some engaged-to-be-married women around Staunton were so certain that dancing with one of the Smith brothers guaranteed them a happy marriage that they went out of their way to come to The Boondoggle a week or two before they tied the knot to dance with one of the brothers. And married women who had experienced recent turmoil at home were known to undertake a clandestine visit to The Boondoggle to seek out the brothers for a dance. The brothers knew well the legend and did not seem to mind the women seeking them out for ulterior purposes; Jocko and Zak considered it their duty to assist.

"Hello, little ladies," said Jocko. "Good to see you again. Are you ready for some good luck?"

"Yeah," Zak warned. "It's bad luck for you if you don't dance with us." The enormous man took the last swig of beer from the bottle he carried and set the empty on the bar.

Both girls preferred the faster tunes for dancing; nevertheless, they weren't prepared to challenge fate and turn down the Smith brothers. Annie and Erika took the cowboy hats from the men, put them on their own heads, and took to the dance floor. When the slow-tempo song ended, Annie rushed to the jukebox, getting there before someone else could play another leisurely melody. She dropped a penny into the slot, pressed the number, and "Sing, Sing, Sing," the fast-paced swing dance tune by Benny Goodman began. What the Smith brothers lacked in swing dance ability they made up for with enthusiasm. The brothers had perfected one move when it came to dancing to the fast-tempo swing music—a move all their own. Zak lifted Annie off the floor, held her like a newborn, and began yelling at the top of his lungs and twirling in circles; Jocko did the same with Erika. Halfway through shouting and spinning, Jocko handed Erika over to Zak, and Zak traded Annie to his brother, the girls' feet never touching the floor during the exchange. At one point, while Jocko spun Annie, he stopped and threw her at his brother. Zak, his hands full with Erika, watched Annie bounce on the floor. The dizzy-from-spinning Zak dropped Erika on her bottom, then he scooped up the unhurt Annie and spun some more. Erika laughed and jumped into Jocko's arms.

When Benny finished, the girls wanted the Smith brothers for another dance, but the brothers begged off to return to their beers, content that they had bestowed their magic.

Zak chastised Annie and Erika. "You girls shouldn't hog all the good luck."

"Right," Jocko agreed. "There are other women in here that need good luck."

Annie and Erika apologized for being so thoughtless, handed the men their hats, and returned to the bar.

The girls finished their beers and Annie paid Fat Prick for another round. As the bartender set the glasses down, Erika said to Annie, "Take a glance over your left shoulder at who just walked in."

Annie looked over her shoulder and saw Professor Bevins and a man sit down at one of the few empty tables near a far corner of the bar. Annie turned back quickly, hoping not to be seen, "Oh, good gosh, Erika, we're goners now."

"I wonder who that is with her," said Erika nonchalantly. "She's not married, right?"

"Who cares? We're done for."

"He's good-looking. I think our Shakespeare professor has interests in other men besides Hamlet and King Lear."

Annie sneaked another peek and snickered. "You're right, he is good-looking. I wonder if she asks him about any dumb shows when they're alone and he's got something else on his mind."

They both laughed. Bevins remained at the table while the man approached the bar. The Boondoggle had a waitress who showed up for work once in a while when she felt like it. Tonight was not one of those nights and customers picked up their drinks from the bar. The man stopped directly beside Erika and ordered two Pabst Blue Ribbons.

When the man walked off with the beers, Annie suggested: "Let's sneak out the back before she spots us."

"Leave your beer and follow me. Let's go say hello."

"What? Are you crazy? I don't want to get suspended, Erika. I'll never hear the end of it from my parents. Let's sneak the heck out of here while the sneaking is good."

Erika stepped down from the stool.

"Erika, don't do this," her friend pleaded, but Erika started toward Bevins' table. Annie mumbled under her breath, *"Those Smith brothers being good luck is a bunch of crap."* But she would not abandon her friend and got down from the stool.

When the professor saw her two students approaching, a look of amusement appeared on her face. When Erika and Annie stopped at the table, the man stood.

"Hello, Professor Bevins," said Erika.

"Well, hello, Miss Lehmann . . . and Miss Drexler. Fancy seeing you here."

"We were waiting for you. Annie wants to change her answer about the dumb show."

The professor offered a thin smile and Annie blushed. Bevins introduced the man who still stood. "This is my friend, Sam Ulrich. Sam, two of my students, Erika Lehmann and Ann Drexler. Have a seat, ladies." The professor thought it better if these girls, whom she knew were underage and should not be there, stayed with her.

"What brings you two here after curfew?" Bevins asked. "Other than Miss Drexler's Shakespearean motive, of course?"

"We like to dance," Erika answered. "This is the only place we can walk to from campus."

"What does your dormitory matron say about your aspirations for exercise this late at night?"

Neither Erika nor Annie answered so Bevins asked another question. "Haven't you two already been marked down once for staying out after curfew?"

"Twice," Annie answered, her gaze lowered.

"Twice? Sounds as if you're turning late night dancing into an extracurricular activity. If you've been caught twice, that means you've probably done it twenty times. You must like this place. This is my first time here. What can you tell me about it?"

"It's crude, but as Erika said, we can walk here and dance, and we've never had any trouble. It's not bad if you avoid the drunks."

Ulrich laughed and Lynn Bevins grinned at Annie Drexler's review. "Well, I'm from Texas," said Bevins. "Honkytonks feel like home to a Panhandle girl."

Erika and Annie were surprised to hear the professor talk like a normal person.

"Can I get you ladies something to drink?" Ulrich asked. He was unaware of the girls' ages.

Bevins stepped in. "I see they have RC Cola here. Both of you like RC, right?"

Both girls nodded and Ulrich got up and walked to the bar.

"What shall I do about this, ladies?" Bevins asked while her date was away. "Have you been drinking?"

Immediately, and simultaneously, Annie and Erika shook their heads *no*. Ulrich returned carrying two half-empty glasses of beer. "The bartender said these are yours," he said as he set down the glasses. Annie winced.

The professor said, "Looks like the bartender takes good care of you girls." Then she added tongue-in-cheek, "I hope you thank him."

"He's Mr. Prick," said Annie innocently.

Erika fought to remain stoic. Bevins and her date stared at Annie for a moment. "What was that, Miss Drexler?" asked Bevins.

"The people in here call him Fat Prick, but I think that's very rude. So I call him Prick, or Mr. Prick."

Erika lost her battle and burst out laughing.

Annie looked quizzically at Erika. "What's wrong with you?"

Bevins, not sure how to respond to all of this, said, "I laud your devotion to good manners, Miss Drexler."

Another slow-tempo tune began playing and Ulrich asked Lynn Bevins to dance. They walked to the dance floor. A moment later two men, not the Smith brothers, approached the table and asked Annie and Erika to dance.

Erika agreed and Annie said, "We're dead anyway, might as well have a last dance before the execution."

As soon as they reached the dance floor, Annie knew she had made a mistake. Her partner reeked of whiskey and slurred his vulgar words. When he tried to fondle her breast, Annie tried to pull away but he jerked her back. "Let go of me!" she shouted while struggling to free herself from his grip. Suddenly a beer bottle smashed into the back of the man's head and he collapsed to the wood floor amidst the beer and broken glass. Erika stood over him. A woman dancing nearby screamed and ran off the dance floor. Erika grabbed another beer bottle from the closest table and prepared to deliver a second blow if the drunk tried to get up, but he merely lifted his head trying to shake cobwebs.

Fat Prick yelled, "Hey, take it outside, goddammit!"

The drunk's buddy, Erika's dance partner, rushed over, stood over his fallen friend and shouted at Erika, "Damn, woman. What the hell did you do that for?"

Erika kneed him between the legs. He shouted out in pain and crumpled. As he knelt, doubled over, Erika raised the beer bottle but Ulrich arrived just as Erika was about to bring it down on her dance partner's head. The professor's date grabbed Erika and pulled her away. Lynn Bevins rushed over and took Annie's arm.

"Let's get them out of here, Sam."

As the professor hustled her two students out, an angry Fat Prick shouted, "Keep those crazy dames out of here." Then he looked toward the two men still on the floor. "And you guys can get the hell out, too." The drunk that Erika had kneed shouted after her that he planned to get even and rose to his feet to follow her out, but the Smith brothers placed themselves in his path. The man decided quickly that confronting the massive Smith brothers would not be in his best interest and the girls, along with their professor and her date, left without further trouble.

When the four were in Ulrich's car, Bevins turned to her students in the back seat and asked, "What dorm do you live in?"

"Memorial," Erika answered.

"Whoops! Mrs. Tarkenton." Bevins teased. "You two will have your hands full if she catches you coming back this late, but I know you have a plan."

Professor Bevins gave her date instructions on where to drop the girls. When the car came to a stop on the street alongside Memorial Hall, Bevins said, "Good luck with Mrs. Tarkenton."

As Annie slid out of the backseat, she asked, "Are you going to report us?"

"What would you do, Miss Drexler, if you were in my position?"

"Oh, I would definitely give us another chance. No doubt in my mind."

"I see. I should overlook this incident, especially since you assured me you were not drinking. And what would you do, Miss Lehmann?"

"I would report us."

Everyone heard Annie groan.

Bevins sized up the situation. "Ah, we have a conundrum. Perhaps I'll have to flip a coin. Good night, ladies." As Ulrich drove off, Bevins smiled, remembering how often she had sneaked out of her college dorm after curfew.

Erika led Annie up the fire escape to the second-floor fire escape door. The door, normally locked from outside access, Erika had wedged open with a pencil before she and Annie left. They entered the building thrilled to be home free until they turned the corner into their room's hallway and saw Mrs. Tarkenton sitting in a chair outside their door. Erika quickly pushed Annie back around the corner and out of sight. Erika began laughing and cupped her hand over her mouth trying to subdue the sound. Annie rolled her eyes in exasperation and whispered: "Geez, what else can go wrong tonight?"

Erika peeked around the corner. Mrs. Tarkenton sat asleep, her head on her chest, with her false teeth slipped halfway out of her mouth.

"What do we do now?" Annie whispered.

"Stay here. I'll draw Mrs. Tarkenton away from our room so you can get in. Then drop me the rope outside." Erika tiptoed past the sleeping matron and disappeared down the inside stairwell.

In a minute, Annie heard a shout from the first floor: "Hey, what is a man doing in your room?" Annie knew it was Erika disguising her voice and could not suppress a giggle. Unfortunately, the shout failed to rouse the slumbering Mrs. Tarkenton.

Another shout, louder. "Hey, who's that man coming out of your room?"

Mrs. Tarkenton's head bobbed, a leg shifted, and she slowly opened one eye.

Even louder from the stairwell: "Mrs. Tarkenton! Help! There's a man down here and he's not wearing any pants!"

Mrs. Tarkenton sprang from the chair, catching her false teeth as they fell out of her mouth—both moves remarkably spry for a woman her age—and trotted to the stairwell as fast as her legs would take her. "A man! A man with no pants!" Mrs. Tarkenton shrieked. "Lord have mercy! I'm coming, girls! I'm coming!"

As soon as Mrs. Tarkenton disappeared down the stairs, Annie sprinted down the hall to the room, unlocked the door with her key, ran inside, and closed and relocked the door. She rummaged frantically through the closet for the rope Erika kept buried for her, found it, and ran to the window. Erika already waited below. Annie opened the window and flung the rope. Not heavy or strong enough to hold the rope for Erika like Erika did for her, Annie tied the end to the leg of Erika's bed—the closest bed to the window. She went back to the window and nodded at Erika. Using her arms to pull herself along, and her feet to walk up the side of Memorial Hall, Erika climbed through the window within seconds. Annie returned the rope to the closet and both girls went to listen at the door. They heard commotion in the hall. Erika's shouts had roused many of the girls who now milled about the hall asking one another what happened.

The two roommates, and best friends, fell onto Annie's bed laughing.

It was lucky to dance with those Smith brothers after all.

Chapter 27

Wild Bill and the Man from Conowingo

Washington, D.C.—Tuesday, October 5, 1943

Leroy Carr grew up in Conowingo, Maryland, and he was glad to be home, or if not technically home, at least close.

Carr spent the last half of the twenties and all of the thirties in Montana, and he missed the mountains and the wide landscapes of the West, but then again he appreciated the well-defined seasons offered by this region of the East Coast. In Big Sky Country, it was not unusual for winter to barge in uninvited during September, even crashing the parties of summer as early as Labor Day, and refusing to leave until May, with fall and spring brazen flirts that teased for a few days, then fled when the next snow came calling. Here, fall and spring had muscles, rebuffed the winter bully, and set up shop long enough to entertain.

For ten of his sixteen years in Montana, Carr owned a successful law practice in Helena; then in 1935 he accepted a post as the state's assistant attorney general, even though the government job meant less income than from his private practice. In early 1942 the war and William Donovan brought Carr back east for yet another cut in pay. Kay, Carr's wife, kidded him that with a few more *promotions* they would be eligible for the public dole.

Today was one of those comfortable, Chesapeake Bay autumn days of perfect temperature, breeze, and colors: blue sky, and leaves of every other color. Carr made the most of it. Instead of lunch at the office snack shop, he walked to a deli near George Washington University. He ordered a hoagie and a Nehi orange soda. Eating the sandwich as he walked back to the office, Carr turned a corner when a car pulled up and stopped beside him. It was Al Hodge.

"Get in, Leroy," Hodge said from the driver's seat. "Bill is looking for you. They found her fingerprints in Cincinnati."

After a short drive, Hodge let Carr out near the front of the E Street Complex, the cumbersome nickname given the headquarters of the Office of Strategic Services. Carr walked quickly through an area that looked like the lobby of a hotel, passed receptionists and security personnel who knew him, and sprinted up the stairs to a meeting room on the second floor. He knew he would find Bill Donovan there. Everyone knew Donovan preferred to do most of his work in the conference room instead of in his office.

Major General William J. "Wild Bill" Donovan ran the OSS. Where he earned his nickname was one of the many intrigues dealt with by the OSS staff. The name might have come from his football days at Columbia, or from his forays leading a detachment of the New York State Militia into the rugged backcountry of the Mexican border during the Pancho Villa campaigns in 1916; or from his exploits as a soldier in the Great War—no one seemed quite sure and no one asked. Leroy Carr laid his odds that the nickname *Wild Bill* came from Donovan's days on horseback chasing Pancho out west.

Now Wild Bill's efforts concerned Germans and Japanese. Donovan founded the OSS when President Roosevelt and a newly-formed committee of high-ranking military leaders called the Joint Chiefs of Staff asked him to shore up America's lackluster intelligence-gathering efforts. The Brits had their famous SIS/MI-6, and the Germans had their infamous Abwehr. The Americans, on the other hand, had nothing to speak of until Wild Bill rode into Washington. Now Donovan's OSS carried out espionage and sabotage efforts abroad, and maintained a division for counterespionage work at home.

Politically, the counterespionage team was by far the diciest section of the OSS. Dicey because of a man named J. Edgar Hoover. In joint meetings Donovan had had with the White House and the FBI, Hoover had been adamant that his FBI handle all cases of enemy espionage and sabotage occurring in the States. Rarely did Hoover fail to get his way, and the FBI chief's aides commented that he was livid and impossible to deal with for days after Roosevelt and the Joint Chiefs agreed to allow a small counterespionage unit within Donovan's OSS. Bill Donovan was more than happy to remain hands off with sabotage cases; those investigations were myriad and tied up massive manpower. Only certain espionage investigations piqued Donovan's interest, and he chose carefully which ones he would devote OSS manpower to. The agreement with Hoover meant that the OSS would get involved in only a few, very select counterespionage cases; when that happened, the FBI was supposed to back off. Donovan kept his end of the bargain and rarely engaged his OSS in domestic affairs. Nevertheless, when Wild Bill did show interest in a case at home, Hoover's back would arch and a turf war became inevitable.

Leroy Carr headed the OSS counterespionage unit.

When Carr entered the conference room, Donovan sat in his normal spot—a chair at the head of a large, oak table.

"Al told me they found her fingerprints, Bill," Carr remarked before he sat down. Even though Donovan was an Army major general, Carr called him Bill as did most within the OSS family.

"That's right," Donovan confirmed. "At a crime scene in Cincinnati, and a grisly one—apparently a robbery gone bad. She shot two men— one is dead—and stabbed a woman."

"Robbery? Doesn't sound like her," Carr said. "What brought that about?"

"That's foggy; you'll need to find that out."

"How certain are we it's her?"

"The FBI is certain of the fingerprint match," Donovan answered.

"And what about Hoover?"

"He's not happy, of course," Donovan smiled. "I called the president and asked that he remind Hoover of our agreement, and he said he would."

Carr grinned. "What I wouldn't give to be a fly on J. Edgar's wall when he gets that phone call."

Donovan agreed, "Especially since he never got over my request to be notified by the Bureau if ever a match on her prints came through. That's another one I had to go over Hoover's head to get done."

"Do we have any information to lead us to believe she might still be in the Cincinnati area?" Carr asked.

"No, but she had apparently been living in the building where the shooting occurred for a month or more, so she was there for a reason. If she's not still around, we at least want to know why she was there for that long."

"I'll leave right away," Carr said.

"The Army will fly you," Donovan had already ordered the preparations. "Check with Shelley; she'll let you know about the plane, and she's making the arrangements for your hotel in Cincinnati. When you get there, first order of business is to check in with the Army. I know the colonel in charge of war plant security in Cincinnati—James Norquist; he's a good man. I'll give him a call and direct him to make his operation available for help if you need it. I'll have Norquist assign you a car and a driver, and I'm sending Al with you. He can help with some of the legwork."

"Good," Carr was going to make that request. He and Al worked well together.

"The FBI is out of it," Donovan continued, "so the Cincinnati police investigators who sent the prints to the Bureau have not been notified about the match. Telling the local police is your job after you get there. I'll take care of keeping Hoover at bay; you'll have to play footsy with the Cincinnati cops. We can't expect them to walk away from a homicide investigation regardless of the underlying scenario, so you'll have no choice other than to work with the local police if there's a chance she's still in that town."

"Anything else?" Carr asked.

"You know what to do if you find her, Leroy," Donovan said as a reminder.

"I know."

Chapter 28

Flight of the Gooney Bird

Cincinnati—Wednesday, October 6, 1943

Leroy Carr was not happy.

He found out over 24 hours ago that her fingerprints had turned up in Cincinnati, but he was still en route. A lightning storm in the D.C. area rumbled in from the Atlantic yesterday afternoon delaying his departure, and then a heavy fog had settled over Cincinnati early this morning and again forced his plane to wait on the ground in Washington. Yesterday's unseasonal lightning storm was a bolt from the blue to both civilian and military meteorologists, but if Carr had suspected fog would force a second delay today, he would have driven to Baltimore or Philadelphia yesterday and flown out from there.

Carr sat on a metal seat, bumping along at 12,000 feet in an unpressurized and unheated Army transport plane with no view, the windows blocked from the inside by sheet metal cargo racks, knowing he was over West Virginia only because one of the airplane's crew, an Army corporal, told him so.

"My balls have frost-bite," Al Hodge shouted above the din of the engines and rattling metal racks.

"The altitude," Carr answered.

"What?" Hodge couldn't hear.

"The altitude," Carr yelled. "It's this cold because of the altitude."

"No shit," Hodge shouted sarcastically.

An odd turn of events took Leroy Carr from a life as a Montana attorney to the cloak and dagger world of the OSS. Only because of a chance meeting with another lawyer in 1934 was he now in the spy game. That other lawyer was William Donovan.

Carr met Donovan at a gathering of attorneys in New York City there for a legal conference at the Waldorf-Astoria. On the last night of the two-day meeting, both men bellied up to the hotel bar—finding the only two vacant stools. Carr sat down ten minutes before Donovan. The men hit it off. They had things in common other than their occupations. Carr, like Donovan, served in the first war, though nothing as glamorous as Donovan's now-famous escapades. Carr was a doughboy, but he served where asked, fighting in some of the worst battles of the war. Carr still had a small piece of shrapnel in his back, courtesy of a trench mortar during the Second Battle of the Marne in 1918. And another tie between the men, and proof of a small world, surprised them both when in the course of conversation over drinks they discovered that Carr's uncle, Gus Carr, a lieutenant in General Pershing's command in 1916, chased Pancho Villa around New Mexico with Black Jack at the same time Wild Bill did the same with the New York Militia. Carr told Donovan that both his Uncle Gus and his father, George Carr, lay buried in Arlington. Perhaps that said something to Donovan about Leroy Carr's bloodlines, but, for whatever reason, Donovan stayed in touch.

Strange, Carr thought, how life can change over a couple of shots of gin and a quick pour of tonic water.

Carr invited Donovan to Montana in 1935 for hunting and fishing, then again in '37. The two men again crossed paths in '39 when business once more took Carr to New York. This time their bar meeting was pre-arranged. Then, with Donovan overseas, their contacts ended until Donovan surprised Carr with a telephone call one month after Pearl Harbor asking him to come to Washington, *just for a talk.* When Carr arrived, he was floored when Donovan asked him to join him at the COI—the Office of the Coordinator of Information—an intelligence gathering organization founded the previous summer. Carr resisted at first. Yes, it was for the war effort, but Carr reminded Donavan that he had no experience in such matters and would not know where to begin. Donovan seemed unconcerned, telling Carr that he himself had never received any training that was worth the time and effort other than the on-the-job variety. *"After all,"* said Donovan, *"this is new to all of us."* Donovan let the reluctant Montana attorney know that he preferred to surround himself with people he knew and trusted rather than with *trained* strangers.

So to serve his country, Leroy Carr pulled up his Montana stakes and joined Wild Bill Donovan at the COI where necessity forced quick learning. Wars were not for slow studies. In June of 1942, the COI was renamed the Office of Strategic Services.

At mid-afternoon the Army Air Force C-47 *Gooney Bird* finally touched down at Lunken Airfield. An impatient Leroy Carr was out of his seat and making his way toward the hatch while the plane taxied. The plane rolled to a stop, and the Army corporal jumped the four feet from the hatch to the tarmac intending to place a wooden box under the hatch for a step down, but Carr told him not to bother and trailed the soldier out in the same manner, jumping. Al Hodge followed.

Two men in Army uniforms approached. When they were near enough, Carr could see one was a lieutenant, the other a military police sergeant.

"Mr. Carr?" the lieutenant asked as he looked back and forth between the two men just off the airplane. The lieutenant knew only that the men he was sent to meet were from Washington. He did not know they were OSS agents so the title *agent* was not used. Carr preferred it that way.

"I'm Leroy Carr," and motioning to his partner: "This is Al Hodge."

"I'm Lieutenant Hulin," the man said as he stuck out his hand. "This is Sergeant Turner."

Handshakes and nods.

"We have a car waiting," said Hulin. "Where are your bags? We'll take you to your hotel."

"No," Carr replied. "The suitcases are still on the plane. I asked an Army corporal who flew in with us to take them to the hotel. I had hoped to be here last night so we're running late. I'd like to be taken directly to your colonel for a briefing right away."

"Yes, sir, we'll head right to the office then."

Sergeant Turner drove. Carr sat in the front seat, Al Hodge and the lieutenant in the back.

"Have you ever been to Cincinnati, Mr. Carr?" Turner offered small talk.

"No, never been here. Al has."

"Yeah," Al Hodge spoke up from the backseat. The car passed a large park, and downtown Cincinnati appeared ahead. "I was here once before the war, but just for a couple of days."

"Sergeant Turner was born and raised here," Hulin offered. "He knows the town like the back of his hand."

Because of Cincinnati's large number of German immigrants and American-born citizens of German heritage, and because of the pre-war influence of the local German-American Bund, the FBI and the Army both increased its number of local personnel when war was declared. The considerable number of area businesses doing important war work warranted that stepped-up presence. The Army security offices where Leroy Carr and Al Hodge were taken occupied one floor of the ROTC building on the University of Cincinnati campus.

The sergeant parked in a space near the side of the building. The lieutenant led Carr and Hodge through a side door, up steps, and through a large office with many desks, a few empty, most occupied, some with women and some not women. Many of the women wore WAC uniforms but not all; some, obviously civilians, wore dresses. All the men wore Army uniforms of various ranks.

Lieutenant Hulin stopped in front of a desk outside an office with a closed door.

"Is the colonel busy, Vannah?" Hulin asked a smartly-dressed, civilian woman sitting behind the desk.

"Are these the men from Washington?" Vannah wanted to know before she answered.

Carr did not wait to be introduced. "I'm Leroy Carr, Vannah." He extended his hand; she shook it. "This is Al Hodge. Yes, we just flew in from Washington."

"Hello," Vannah said to the two men just before she pushed a button on a desk speaker. A voice came through that speaker.

"Yes?"

"Colonel," Vannah leaned toward the device, "the men from Washington are here."

"Send them in," the voice ordered.

Vannah rose and led the way through the nearby door. Hulin entered the office with the OSS men; the sergeant did not. After they were inside, Vannah smiled at no one in particular, then left, closing the door behind her. A full-bird colonel sat behind a desk. Hulin began the introductions.

"Colonel, this is Mr. Carr and this is Mr. Hodge." Hulin motioned toward each man as he said their names. Carr and Hodge held up their OSS identification as they were introduced.

The colonel stood up and shook hands across the desk. "Colonel James Norquist. Welcome to Cincinnati. Have a seat, gentlemen."

Leroy Carr and Al Hodge sat down on wooden chairs facing Norquist's desk.

"Thank you, Lieutenant," Norquist said to Hulin. "If you'll excuse us, please."

"Yes, sir," Hulin saluted, the colonel returned the gesture, then Hulin ducked out.

"Okay, Agent Carr." Norquist wasted no time with chit chat or niceties, something Leroy Carr appreciated. "I spoke with General Donovan on the telephone yesterday. I understand you are in charge of this mission."

"Yes, Colonel," Carr verified. "If you don't mind, we prefer to forego the 'agent' title—just 'mister' if you would. But again, yes, General Donovan asked me to spearhead things here in Cincinnati and Al will assist. The general told me you would furnish us a driver."

"That will be Sergeant Turner; he's from here," said Norquist, confirming what Carr had assumed, that the MP from Cincinnati would be his driver. "General Donovan gave me a few details yesterday, and he said you would brief me further."

Leroy Carr spent about twenty minutes, probably a little longer, briefing Norquist on the basics of why the OSS wanted to find a suspect in a crime that took place in a rundown apartment building in Cincinnati. Carr was intensely selective about what facts he divulged, omitting details the colonel did not need to know, or should not know. When he finished, Carr cautioned the colonel that the OSS presence in Cincinnati must be treated with utmost discretion. No one should know he and Al Hodge were OSS who did not absolutely need to know.

"We'll have no choice but to work with the local police," Carr told the colonel, "but it's imperative we keep the number of cops we have to let in on this to the bare minimum, and the local FBI office is not to be involved under any circumstances."

"I understand. What's your first order of business?" Norquist asked.

"The Cincinnati police, who sent the prints to the FBI, have not been notified about the match. Al and I will stop there first. The prints were sent to Washington with the name of the local detective in charge of the case. His name is Frank Ault. Do you know him?"

"No," answered Norquist.

"Anyway," Carr picked back up, "I'd like to meet with Ault and whomever else I'll be working with locally right away."

"We have a few empty offices," Norquist said. "I'll have Vannah assign you and Mr. Hodge an office, then Sergeant Turner will take you wherever you want to go." Norquist pressed the buzzer on his desk speaker and in a moment everyone in the room heard Vannah's voice.

"Yes, Colonel?"

"Vannah, please assign Mr. Carr and Mr. Hodge each an office, and send in Sergeant Turner."

"Yes, sir."

Turner entered seconds later.

"Sergeant, Vannah will get these men situated, and then she'll turn them over to you. As I told you this morning, your assignment is to serve as their driver during their stay in Cincinnati."

"Yes, sir, Colonel."

Norquist turned back to Carr. "Mr. Carr, we're at your disposal. We have our orders and we'll help in any way we can."

"Thank you, Colonel."

"Vannah will give you my home phone number in case you need to reach me there. Is there anything else?"

"I'd like to put in a call to the Cincinnati chief of police."

"Vannah will get you the number."

Chapter 29

A Photograph

[same day]

Frank Ault drove away from the Lamar Apartments after dropping off a few groceries and household supplies for Clare Miller. Ault was glad to see Clare felt better, at least physically. Although her facial scars had not fully healed, the swelling was gone, and she moved around better.

Penny Lindauer, now out of the hospital, could not bear to return to the place of the attack, so she returned home to her parents' house in Akron (Ault had the address in case Lindauer had to testify in court). Clare told Ault she had written to Penny, but so far received no answer.

Ault had just turned onto Ninth Street when he received the call from dispatch instructing him to report immediately to headquarters. When he arrived, Glen Schafer was waiting.

"The FBI matched Anne Brown's prints, Frank."

When Shafer said it, Ault was about to throw his hat on the window sill near his desk, an everyday routine. He missed.

"Where's the report?" Ault asked.

"No report," Shafer answered. "Cantrell received a phone call. The Bureau is sending someone over for a face-to-face."

Ault looked at Shafer. Both men knew this meant that there was more to this than a simple felon fingerprint match.

"I'm not surprised," was all Frank Ault said.

When they got to Cantrell's office, he was on the phone with the chief of police. Cantrell motioned for them to sit. When he hung up, he told Ault and Shafer the men they were waiting for were at city hall briefing Chief Weatherly; after that, they would come right over.

Cantrell asked if there was anything new on the Lamar Apartments case he should know before the FBI arrived. The answer was *no,* so as they waited, Ault briefed the major on another case—a murder over the weekend.

"The guy got drunk and beat his buddy to death outside a bar over on Highland Avenue," Ault explained. "We found him yesterday at his girlfriend's apartment. Apparently he thought he'd be hard to

173

find at her place. When we knocked on the door, he answered. Not the sharpest tack in the box. He made a sprint for the fire escape, but Glen ran him down. The guy confessed in the car while we were bringing him in. Told us the guy he killed—evidently a friend—tried to stiff him on a ten dollar bet."

"Ten bucks," Cantrell stated. "That's getting pretty cheap for a life, especially a friend's life, but you still haven't beaten my record. When I was on the streets, I covered a case where a guy robbed a liquor store and killed the clerk—an old man. The guy got away with two dollars and seventy-five cents, all in change . . . oh, and an eighty-cent bottle of wine."

Although the dialogue helped pass the time, the reason the men had gathered hovered like a specter. Patience waned and anticipation waxed as the three policemen waited for the FBI. Finally, Frank Ault could sit no longer. He rose and paced.

"I'm nervous too, Frank," Glen Shafer said. "What do you think we're going to hear?"

"I'm not nervous," Ault scowled, suddenly testy. "I'm just tired of sitting on my ass with this case. Where the hell are those FBI assholes?" Ault carried on. "As far as what we're going to hear, we're going to hear a bunch of bullshit, that's what we're going to hear. The FBI sending people to brief us tells me that they're looking for her too. They'll probably expect us to lay off the case." Ault turned toward Cantrell. "I'm telling you right now, Ed, I'm not turning this over to the goddamn FBI. Even if she skips town, wherever she is when caught by I-don't-give-a-damn-who, I'm going to extradite her."

"Calm down, Frank," Cantrell appealed. "We aren't going to lay off anything—not with an open homicide investigation. But let's see what they have to say before we declare war on the feds."

A few minutes of silent tension followed. On Cantrell's desk was a speaker much like the one James Norquist and Vannah used earlier that day: the devices apparent requirements for people with an office and an aide or secretary. Eventually, and thankfully, Cantrell's office requirement buzzed.

"There are two men from Washington here, Major," announced the female voice.

Surprised, Cantrell, Ault, and Shafer looked at each other, all ready to ask the same question. *Why would the FBI send someone all the way from Washington for a briefing? There were FBI aplenty in Cincinnati.*

174

Cantrell pushed the button. "Thank you, Andrea, send them in."

Two men walked through the door; one carried a folder. Cantrell rose and walked around his desk to shake hands.

"Hello, gentlemen. I'm Ed Cantrell. This is Frank Ault and Glen Shafer, the detectives assigned to the case."

More handshaking as the men produced identification.

"Leroy Carr, Office of Strategic Services," said the man carrying the folder. "This is Al Hodge."

All of the Cincinnati policemen stood silent for a moment. Finally, Ed Cantrell asked the question. "You guys aren't FBI?"

"No," Carr confirmed. "We asked your chief not to tell you on the phone, but to let us do it when we got here. We hope to keep knowledge of our visit to Cincinnati restricted to as few people as possible."

After another silence, Cantrell said, "Have a seat."

Carr and Hodge sat. Even though there were enough chairs for everyone, Frank Ault remained standing.

"Major, Al and I flew in today because, as you now know, the fingerprints your office sent to the FBI about three weeks ago concerning a local crime were matched. The OSS is interested because the fingerprints in your case also match a set of prints found last May in Evansville, Indiana. Also as you know, the prints are those of a female, and I've been informed she was involved in a homicide here in Cincinnati."

"That's right." Cantrell added no details.

"Will you fill us in?" asked Carr.

"I'll ask Detective Ault to do that. It's his case." Cantrell looked toward Ault. "Frank."

Ault shot out the facts like bullets. "Two female Caucasian residents of an apartment building in the Over the Rhine district were attacked in one of the women's apartments on September 10th by two Caucasian males and one Caucasian female. Motive: robbery/rape. The attack was interrupted by another Caucasian female resident of the same building; you have her fingerprints. She used a .32 with a silencer, shot and killed one male attacker, shot and seriously wounded the second male, beat the woman attacker then impaled her to a living room wall using two kitchen knives through the wrists. The woman we're looking for then telephoned the police and reported the crime in order to get help on the way for the two female robbery/attempted rape victims. Then she disappeared. At that time she used the name *Anne Brown,* but we're confident that was an alias. Description: mid-twenties, blonde hair at the time, five feet seven or eight, attractive, no visible distinguishing marks."

As Ault described Anne Brown, Cantrell handed Carr and Hodge a copy of the police artist sketch he had in a desk drawer.

"Anne Brown," Carr said. He stopped for a moment to look over the sketch before continuing. "So you're telling us this Anne Brown saved the two rape victims?"

"No rape occurred. I said attempted rape," Ault corrected with an impatient tone.

"Okay, Detective, attempted rape. But she saved the women—stopped the attack with a silenced handgun?"

"That's right. Now it's your turn."

Carr handed the sketch to Al Hodge, opened his folder, then began with a shocker. "Here is her photograph." Carr took out several copies of a 5 x 7 photograph and started handing them out. None of the Cincinnati policemen expected to see a photograph; Ault walked over and snatched the photo from the OSS agent's hand. The black and white headshot showed a young woman, this time with black hair, smiling directly into the camera, the same smile she directed at him in Jim Sano's restaurant.

When everyone had a copy of the photograph, Carr continued. "That photo is an enlargement of the standard photograph used on identification tags at the U.S. Naval shipyard in Evansville, Indiana. Everyone hired at that facility has their photo taken for their name badge. Your *Anne Brown* was an employee at that shipyard for eight months, from late September of '42 until this past May." Carr gave the Cincinnati policemen a moment to examine the photograph.

"What's her real name?" Ault asked Carr.

"We don't know," answered Carr. "She worked at the shipyard under the name Sarah Klein, but that too is an alias. To eliminate confusion, I suggest for now we refer to her by her latest alias, the one you know her by—Anne Brown. This woman is not an American, but rather German, and she is an operative for German military intelligence—Abwehr. Somehow she broke into the Navy shipyard in Indiana and stole top secret material and photographed several top secret documents. Luckily, we recovered the material and the film, but she escaped. After her escape last June, the FBI found her car. In the trunk was a shortwave transmitter powerful enough to communicate with ships off the East Coast. She had been transmitting intermittently for several months—the FCC picked up the transmissions. Those transmissions used a code similar to the German code called Enigma. Triangulation of the message intercepts, even though they hadn't busted the code, eventually led the FBI to the Evansville area. Found with the radio was a crib sheet with the codes, and dates those codes would be activated—we know the Germans change codes frequently."

Ault interrupted. "That proves she worked for the Germans, but why do you think she's German? She could be an American and a traitor."

"In March '42, a high-level British cryptographer for MI-9, a branch of MI-6, and his secretary-girlfriend disappeared and haven't been seen since. The guy was in charge of communications with the French Resistance. Soon after he disappeared, the Nazis raided several Resistance cells. It was quite a setback for the Resistance. After the episode in Indiana this past summer, I sent that photo you're looking at to MI-6 in London. MI-6 showed that photo to the people in MI-9 who worked alongside the missing cryptographer and secretary. That woman in the photo, the secretary at the Evansville shipyard, is the missing MI-9 secretary. At MI-9, she used the name Margaret Harrison." Carr took out another photograph from his folder and handed it to Ault. "Here is the MI-9 identification badge photograph of Margaret Harrison, the missing secretary."

Ault looked. It was the same woman in the Evansville shipyard photo, the same woman he walked past in Sano's, only with blonde hair. He handed the photo to Glen Shafer.

"Jesus," Shafer shook his head, "this woman's hair changes color more than a chameleon playing hopscotch on a rainbow."

Carr continued as Shafer passed the photo to Cantrell. "I had read the MI-6 reports about the London case and noticed a few similarities to the Evansville case. And after both the FCC and the FBI checked out the transmitter found in her car trunk in Evansville, both said a few of the most critical components, things that could not be purchased here in the States, were German made. She must have brought those parts into the country with her—probably landed by U-boat on the East Coast, like those Nazi saboteurs this past summer."

Everyone in the room was familiar with that case. It had made the newspaper headlines all across the country last year when the FBI apprehended eight German saboteurs who had been delivered by two U-boats to remote East Coast beaches in the middle of the night.

"If she didn't arrive by submarine," Carr added, "she could have come across the Mexican border."

Ault asked, "So what's she doing in Cincinnati?"

"Not sure," Carr admitted. "But when she lost her transmitter, she lost communication. Perhaps she's working her way to the East Coast, but why she remained here in Cincinnati for at least a month—we understand she lived in the apartment building for about a month before the crime—is curious."

"She's been here at least two months because she's still here," Ault said.

Leroy Carr sat up rigidly in his chair. "How do you know?"

"Last Friday she approached my wife in a restaurant. When she saw me coming, she—Anne Brown—got up and left. Elizabeth, my wife, is a well-known reporter. It's not unusual for strangers to approach her, so I didn't think anything of it when I walked in and saw someone at her table. Anne Brown had changed her appearance again but my wife got a good look at her and I got a glimpse. With the disguise, I did not recognize her, and Elizabeth was too scared to warn me until it was too late."

Now it was Carr's turn to pause, excited that she was still in Cincinnati. "You say this happened last Friday?"

"That's what I said."

"And your wife knew who she was?"

"Not at first," Ault answered, "but Anne Brown let her know."

"Why would she approach your wife, especially since your wife is a reporter?"

"My wife is an investigative reporter and in one of her articles suggested Anne Brown call her." Ault tried to say it without cringing; perhaps he succeeded, perhaps not. "But their conversation was cut short when I walked in, so we don't know her motive in seeking out my wife."

"How did Anne Brown know your wife would be at the restaurant?"

"She shadowed Elizabeth, and she slit one of my tires so I would be late."

"Brown knew you were going to meet your wife there?"

"Either that or she just slit my tire as a precaution. My car was parked on the street in front of the station, and the restaurant is not far from here. "

Carr, deep in thought, took a moment. "Whatever is keeping her here is to our advantage, of course. What precautions are you taking to protect your wife?"

"She's never alone on the streets. If she leaves the house, or the newspaper building on a story, someone drives her. A lot of the time it's me. If I can't, then I have someone else drive her."

"A Nazi spy," Glen Shafer said to no one in particular. "I knew something was creepy about this case, but a Nazi spy never entered my mind."

"But that's what she is, and a very dangerous one," Carr warned. "An FBI agent who tried to apprehend her in Evansville is dead, and she killed another man in Indiana."

Cantrell cut in quickly. "She killed an FBI agent?"

"Her accomplice did. Then she killed her accomplice. They escaped our stakeout together then she killed him—knife to the throat. FBI agents witnessed the killing."

Cantrell: "So the accomplice killed an FBI agent to allow them both to escape, then she killed her accomplice?"

"Yes. And she shot the scientist—her mark—for good measure before she left town. Put a round through a leg."

"How did she escape?" Ault asked Carr.

"In a nutshell, it was nighttime and she took a 100-foot swan dive off a bridge into the Ohio River. Her body was never recovered. We now know she survived, thanks to your work."

Now early evening, the sun low, Carr was impatient to see the crime scene and Anne Brown's apartment. Still, he preferred the light of day.

"Gentlemen," said Carr as he stood, "it was a pleasure to meet you and I look forward to working with you. I assure you the OSS has no intentions of interfering with your homicide investigation, but since this involves national security we have to be in charge. I know you understand. Again, we request that as few people as possible know the OSS is interested in this case. There's no need for anyone to know that Al and I are with the OSS. We have alternate I.D.s to use when necessary."

Carr stressed, "Another thing that is very important is that the FBI not be notified. This request comes from the highest levels in Washington, and you are welcome to call my boss, Director Donovan, to verify. As far as the local FBI is concerned, no fingerprint match was found, and we want to keep it that way."

Carr halted for questions, but none were asked.

"Thank you for your time, gentlemen," Carr finished. "I'm eager to take a look at the crime scene, but it will be dark soon. Detective Ault, if I come in tomorrow morning, will you show me around?"

Frank Ault frowned. He had already made up his mind he did not like or trust these men from Washington. "Eight o'clock. Don't be late."

Carr met Ault's unfriendly glare. "I'm never late."

"I don't like it, Major," Frank Ault protested after the OSS men left the office. "Something smells here."

"Yeah, it's damn strange the FBI has been kicked to the curb," Cantrell agreed. "Is that what you're talking about?"

"Right," Ault was glad he was not the only one who smelled a rat. "It's supposed to be the FBI's job to hunt down spies and saboteurs in the States. I'd rather have to work with the FBI. Hoover's guys are a pain in the ass, but at least they're honest pains—what you see is what you get. But these OSS guys are sneaky bastards, and now we have to babysit them. Why would they even get involved with chasing down a spy here in this country? They're supposed to *be* the spies in other countries, aren't they?"

"Frank, I don't know what's behind the scenes here," Cantrell admitted, "and neither do you. I'll talk to the chief tomorrow, and call Washington, as Carr suggested, to see what I can find out. From our end, we'll keep doing what we do—look for a homicide suspect. In any case, let's all keep our mouths shut until we find out what's really going on. It's wartime, and this is a national security issue now. I'll let you know what I find out."

"Holy shit," Glen Shafer blurted out. "I knew this thing would just keep getting weirder."

[the Palace Hotel—one hour later]
Leroy Carr ordered a gin and tonic, Al Hodge a Miller High Life from the tap.

Somewhere near 8:00 p.m. Sergeant Turner dropped them off at their hotel. Both men claimed their suitcases—dropped off at the registration desk by the corporal from the C-47 crew—and took them to their rooms. They agreed to meet at 8:30 in the hotel bar.

"Are you eating?" Carr asked Hodge.

"Damn right. I'm starving. I haven't had anything since breakfast in D.C. this morning."

When the bartender delivered their drinks, the two men asked for menus.

"Well," Carr started out, "give me your impression of the local gendarmes."

"That Ault is an asshole," Hodge minced no words.

"Seems like it, but he has a lot to deal with. That story about our Fräulein chasing down his wife for a chat is interesting to say the least. What do you make of that, Al?"

"I have no clue. Craziest thing I ever heard. What do you think?"

"I don't know what to think," Carr admitted, "but that might be our key. I think I need to get to know Mrs. Ault."

Carr thought the meeting with the Cincinnati police went as well as could be expected. Naturally, Frank Ault would be suspicious of a Johnnie-come-lately who barged in and took over his case. Carr knew he must win Frank Ault's confidence. Leroy Carr, good husband and honest lawyer, was a patriot, his country was at war, and he had a job to do. Deception, subterfuge, and double-crosses were necessary wartime job skills Carr had been forced to hone sharp when he cast his lot with the OSS. Carr knew Winston Churchill was right when he said, *'The truth is so precious she should always be attended by a bodyguard of lies.'* But Carr also knew he had to be careful with Ault. He sized up the hard-boiled detective as no fool, and Carr suspected he would have to work at the top of his game to insure the deceptions he would be sending Ault's direction were convincing. Deceptions like the one today when he told Frank Ault he would not interfere with his investigation.

Chapter 30

Meeting Mrs. Ault

Thursday, October 7, 1943

"How did it go, Frank?" Ed Cantrell was asking about the time Ault had spent with the OSS man, Leroy Carr, earlier that day.

"I took him to the Lamar Apartments," Ault said from the chair in Cantrell's office. "He looked around Anne Brown's apartment then I took him to see Clare Miller. He talked with her for about an hour, then with the building manager for twenty minutes or so."

"Where's Carr now?"

"Glen took him and his partner downstairs to the evidence room. Carr wanted to see the shell casings from the crime, and the wire I found in the wastebasket in Anne Brown's bedroom. He also wanted to see the clothes and other things she left behind in her apartment."

"What's your take on these OSS guys?"

"I don't have a take, Ed," Ault responded. "I spent all morning babysitting them and backtracking on things I did weeks ago, but that's okay if these guys can contribute something. At first I thought they would be a pain in the ass, and I still think that, but I'm willing to put that aside for the country's sake since we're dealing with a German spy. Everybody wants her locked up. If the OSS can help us find her, then I'll work with them. But, for the record, I'm not going to trust them."

"Why do you say that?" Cantrell asked.

"All this secrecy, like keeping things from the FBI. Why don't they want the FBI manpower and resources in on this? The FBI rounded up those eight Nazi saboteurs last summer, not the OSS. I don't get it. Why deal out the FBI?"

"I guess they have their reasons. Did Carr tell you anything about what's next?"

"He wants to talk with Elizabeth," Ault said.

Cantrell nodded. "I figured that would rank pretty high on his list. I know you're probably not crazy about that, Frank, but you had to see it coming. None of us has spoken to Anne Brown, but Elizabeth has, and Anne Brown obviously has some sort of interest in Elizabeth."

Ault said nothing.

Cantrell asked, "How are you going to handle Carr's request to talk to Elizabeth?"

"Carr wanted to come to the house tonight. I said 'no way.' And there's also no way in hell I'm going to bring my wife to the station. He didn't want to meet at a restaurant, so I told him we'll meet at Eden Park."

"When?"

"Tonight. I want to get it over with." Ault looked at his watch. "I need to call Elizabeth."

[that evening]

Leroy Carr arrived at Eden Park several minutes early. He instructed his Army driver to wait, then walked into the park. The OSS man found an abandoned bench near the conservatory and waited. Frank Ault had told Carr he would bring his wife to the conservatory entrance at 7 p.m.

The woman the Cincinnati cops called Anne Brown had dominated Leroy Carr's working hours for the past several months. Wild Bill officially turned the case over to him in June, but Carr's work started even earlier, in April, when the OSS learned the FCC had intercepted suspicious shortwave transmissions and determined they originated in southwestern Indiana. By then the FBI was on the case, so Carr had no choice but to remain in the background, doing what homework he could to put together an OSS file. The work went nowhere until Carr noticed similarities in the modus operandi between the Indiana case and a case file that crossed his desk from the British MI-6: the case of the missing MI-9 cryptographer and his secretary. Carr sent the Evansville shipyard identification photo to MI-6 in London. When the Evansville shipyard secretary, *Sarah Klein,* and the missing MI-9 secretary, *Margaret Harrison,* turned out to be the same person. Carr almost did not believe it himself that such a long-shot paid off.

So when Al Hodge chased Carr down at lunch two days ago in Washington and told him *her* prints had been found in Cincinnati, nothing further needed explaining. The pronoun, *her,* was enough.

And now a second woman had entered the picture—Elizabeth Ault. This morning, while Carr visited the Lamar Apartments with her husband, Carr sent Al Hodge out to gather all the newspaper articles

Elizabeth Ault had written about the case. Carr read them this afternoon. Elizabeth Ault had extended a clear invitation to Anne Brown to call her, no doubts there. The question was why would Anne Brown/Sarah Klein/Margaret Harrison decide to take the offer? There must be a reason, and Carr knew that reason was much more than simply a chance to talk. No, Carr thought, the cunning Abwehr agent cared nothing about chit-chatting with a reporter. Why then risk it? A reason subtle and nefarious propelled Anne Brown to seek out Elizabeth Ault, Carr was sure of it. And Carr felt that reason would be the key to catching her.

At exactly 7 p.m., Carr saw Frank Ault and a woman walking toward him. Carr stood to greet them.

"Hello, Detective Ault," Carr offered his hand. Ault shook it, though not warmly.

"This is Elizabeth," Frank said. "Elizabeth, this is Mr. Carr."

"Call me Leroy, Mrs. Ault. It's nice meeting you."

"Call me Elizabeth, and you can call him Frank whether he likes it or not."

Carr smiled widely. "Okay . . . Elizabeth and Frank—got it. You're right on time, thanks."

"It's a cop thing," Elizabeth said. "The only time Frank's late is when he meets me for dinner."

Carr laughed. "Shall we walk?"

They walked along a flagstone path that took them away from the conservatory and people. The wind and trees conspired to make noise, and the chilly air demanded Elizabeth tighten the sash on her knee-length coat.

When they reached a lonely area, Carr began, "Elizabeth, I'm with the OSS in Washington. It's a new organization that's only been around for a couple of years. Have you heard of the OSS?"

Elizabeth looked at her husband curiously, confirming to Carr what Ault told him earlier: the detective had told his wife nothing.

"Yes," she said. "I've heard of the OSS."

"Good. I'm here because of Anne Brown. At least that is the name you know her by, but I think you probably know that is an alias."

"Yes," Elizabeth said. "She told me that was no longer her name."

"She did?" Carr asked. "At the restaurant where she approached you?"

"Yes. That's the only time I've talked to her." She turned to her husband. "Frank, what is this all about?"

184

"It's okay, Elizabeth," Frank said. "The Anne Brown case has become a national security issue. We are at war, and for our country's sake we have to cooperate. Carr here will fill you in; just answer his questions as best you can."

Elizabeth looked back at Leroy Carr. "National security? Why?"

"Before I explain, Elizabeth, let me get some housekeeping out of the way. As Frank said, this is now classified a national security case, which means anything I tell you about the case legally obligates you under the 1918 Sedition Act to keep that information confidential under penalty of law. From now on, anything I say to you about this case is top secret. I have to stress this to you, not because I or anyone questions your patriotism, but because of your job as a reporter. You cannot talk or write about anything I tell you about the Anne Brown case without clearing it with me from now on. And I have to ask you, do you understand that legal obligation?"

"Yes."

"Thanks, Elizabeth," Carr made sure he smiled when he thanked her. He wanted to be as unintimidating as possible; he needed her on his side.

Carr now answered her question. "The Anne Brown case made the national security list when the fingerprints Frank sent to the FBI in Washington matched prints in a national security case from last spring in Indiana. I'll make a long story short. Anne Brown is a German spy. She escaped when the FBI moved in on her in Indiana, and dropped from sight until your husband found her fingerprints at that apartment building crime scene here in Cincinnati last month."

Elizabeth looked at her husband, then back at Carr. "A German spy? You're joking." Elizabeth felt silly as soon as she said it. The news surprised her, but she knew Carr was not kidding.

From an inside coat pocket, Carr pulled and handed her the two photographs her husband had seen yesterday. "The woman with black hair broke into a U.S. Naval facility in Evansville, Indiana, and stole top secret material. The blonde woman kidnapped a high-level cryptographer for the British Secret Service in London. The Brits think she somehow smuggled him into Nazi-occupied France or Germany to extract information."

Elizabeth looked at the pictures: both were of Anne Brown.

Carr continued, "In Evansville, she killed a man and wounded another, although not on the same night as she did here in Cincinnati. In Evansville she spread out the shootings over two nights. Her partner in Evansville killed an FBI agent during their escape—a partner she later killed, by the way. In Indiana, she used the name Sarah Klein, colored her hair black, and posed as a Jew. I only mention that because it's now evident that her mission in Evansville involved seducing a Jewish scientist involved in top secret work for the Navy, and from him gather what information she could. But she didn't stop there; she broke into the facility. We're not sure how she did it. The place was well guarded, but she pulled it off. Oh, and by the way, when she knew she was leaving Evansville, she broke into the scientist's house in the middle of the night, knocked out an FBI agent stationed at the house as a guard, then shot the scientist in the leg as a going away present. Our Anne Brown is clever and ruthless, Elizabeth."

The walking brought them to one of several redwood benches scattered throughout the park. Carr suggested they sit, and then returned to the subject. "Frank said yesterday your conversation with Brown at the restaurant was cut short when he arrived. Can you tell me exactly what she said?"

"It wasn't a lot," Elizabeth conceded. "She told me Frank would be late, and I was worried she had done something to him. When I asked her, she told me she did not hurt him."

Frank interjected, "Like I told you yesterday, Brown slit one of my tires to give her more time to talk with Elizabeth, but I was at the station so I took another car. She delayed me about 15 minutes, no more."

"That's bold—to slit your tire at the police station," said Carr, "but I'm not surprised. Small potatoes when you consider the moves this woman has made so far. Please go on, Elizabeth. Did she mention anything about why she sought you out? I read your articles where you offered to meet with her. Did she give you any indication at all about what she wanted to talk about? "

"No, but I think she was about to when Frank showed up."

"Why do you think that?" Carr asked.

"She saw Frank pull up outside and said our conversation would have to wait."

"Meaning she might seek you out again?"

"Maybe."

That was the best news Leroy Carr had heard since he officially opened the case in June.

"Elizabeth, I must ask you something I think Frank knows I will ask." Carr looked at them both. "We need your help to catch her. You might give us the only chance we'll have. I won't kid you; there might be some danger; Frank knows that. Don't give me an answer tonight. Go home and talk it over. Even though Frank is a detective, this has to be a husband and wife decision."

Frank knew it was coming; Carr was right about that. He knew it as soon as Carr asked him for this meeting with his wife earlier that day. If it were not wartime, Ault would have refused to involve Elizabeth. But he reluctantly admitted to himself that he agreed with Carr: Elizabeth offered the best chance to force Anne Brown to the surface. Regardless, Frank Ault despised Carr for asking because he knew his wife would say *yes*.

Later, back in his hotel room, Leroy Carr made his nightly telephone call home. Kay had grown stoic about his sometimes lengthy absences since he joined Bill Donovan at the OSS. Although he had traveled a great deal since he went to work at the E Street Complex, Carr was never a fan of the road, so perhaps his wife had less trouble than he adapting to the trips. Kay did not ask, but Carr repeated what he told her the night before—he had no way of knowing how long he would be in Cincinnati.

After he hung up, Carr turned on the radio and sat back on the bed with one of the many folders of information he brought to Cincinnati. He opened it and read for the umpteenth time the FCC reports on the shortwave transmissions from Evansville. At the time of the transmissions, the German Enigma code had not yet been deciphered, but in August the British finally cracked the latest Enigma called Shark. At Bletchley Park, not far from London, the Brits had assembled their country's best mathematical minds—mostly college math professors shanghaied from Oxford and a few other select universities. There, at Bletchley, the best minds in England built a new electronic contraption they called Colossus. The cumbersome apparatus took up a large room with its panels, tubes, wires, relays, and assorted gadgets, but Colossus could compute the mathematics of numbers and code in a fraction of the time it took the English math professors. So by working together, the crazy contrivance and the Limey eggheads broke the unbreakable. They broke the German Enigma.

Now, finally, Leroy Carr was able to read what she had transmitted from Indiana, and it was not information he would share with the Cincinnati police.

And he knew more.

In her Evansville transmissions, now deciphered (the cipher key out of reach of the FBI), she used a code name, and that was the official OSS file name Carr gave the case. *Lorelei.*

Carr took yet another folder from his valise, this one containing three photographs. One photo was from a German newspaper article published in the fall of 1937. The caption read:

    Fräulein Erika Lehmann accepts the first place
    medal in distance swimming from Deputy Director
    Rudolf Hess at *The Party Day Aryan Maids Games*

The grainy photo pictured a smiling, teenaged version of the woman in the Evansville Shipyard I.D. photo and the British MI-9 I.D. standing on a podium and bending over while Rudolf Hess placed a lanyard around her neck. The second photograph, even older, was taken in 1935 at a Washington, D.C., gala hosted by Vice President John Nance Garner. In a large group of people surrounding the vice president, Carr had underlined three names: Karl Lehmann, Secretary to the German Ambassador; Louise Lehmann, wife of Mr. Lehmann; Erika Lehman, daughter of Karl and Louise Lehmann. The third photograph, taken in 1938 at a dinner for the American press hosted by Joseph Goebbels in Berlin, listed Erika Lehmann as an interpreter and showed her in another large group photograph posed with German luminaries such as Goebbels and Reinhard Heydrich, as well as several well-known American reporters including William Shirer and Edward R. Murrow.

Leroy Carr had lied when he told the Cincinnati police he did not know her real name, one of those lies necessitated in wartime.

Erika Lehmann, *Lorelei,* the ghost that was *Anne Brown,* had for several months occupied most of Carr's efforts. Now she was real. If he could find her, any deceptions or sacrifices from here on would be worth it, and for a much more important reason than simply catching an enemy spy.

That reason Leroy Carr would zealously shield from Frank Ault and the Cincinnati police.

Chapter 31

Rhine River Brandy and a Hot Bath

Saturday, October 9, 1943

Adalwulf von Krause spent the first week of October preoccupied with thoughts of Karl Lehmann's daughter. His maid and his grandson, Willy, saw little of him. Other than a mid-week trip downtown, and his daily late-morning walks, Krause had spent nearly all his time behind the closed door of his study, thinking and planning. Karl's daughter asked for his help and he would give it, willingly. They were countrymen at war (he had learned his old friend's daughter was an Abwehr operative on the run, fighting for their homeland) and it was his duty to the Fatherland. That alone was reason aplenty to help her, but what's more, the friendship with her father, a brother of the Ring, bound Krause by honor to aid Erika Lehmann.

He looked forward to the commitment. The delightful dinner last Saturday with a charming companion restored vigor. Life had become tedious. Yes, Krause funded the Bolivar Network, but two years ago he had arranged a self-sustaining annuity through a bank in Paraguay and nothing more needed his attention. Since then, to wait had been Krause's only chore: wait for a communiqué from Lisbon with another assignment from Freidrich Haupt that never came, wait for the Führer to win the war so he could return home, wait for Viola to bring his morning coffee and newspaper.

Now he had a task, a call to serve, and he welcomed it. Krause had thought a great deal about what she told him: about the FBI hunting her in Cincinnati and the local trouble she had gotten involved in. He now knew about that trouble. On his desk lay a *Cincinnati Observer* folded to a page displaying a police artist sketch of a woman wanted for questioning in an attack that took place in the Over the Rhine neighborhood last month. Krause opened a desk drawer, put the newspaper in it, and closed the drawer. That did not matter; it had nothing to do with his task.

Krause could give Erika the contact information she requested— no problems there—and he had devised a plan to help her return to Germany, but when would he see her again? When they parted seven days ago, she told him she would contact him "in about a week." For the past couple of days, as the week happened by, Krause almost expected her to reappear out of nowhere during his morning walk.

Now it was Saturday, and Krause, filled with anticipation, stepped out of the taxi at the RKO Century Theater. This would be it. *She will join me in my box as she did last week.*

The lights dimmed, the movie began, and Adalwulf von Krause fidgeted in his seat. The combination of an expected rendezvous and a movie that held no interest for Krause, *Lassie Come Home,* made him restless. Only in America, Krause thought, could a dog become a leading box office movie star. That and the fact the other main players were children, a boy named Roddy McDowell and a ten-year-old girl named Elizabeth Taylor, ended any appeal the movie might have had for the Prussian aristocrat who believed children should be neither seen nor heard except perhaps at a music recital, and only then if the music were that of the German classical composers.

Anytime Krause heard the slightest sound from behind the box curtain he stiffened, but when the movie and the newsreels ended he still sat alone. After the show, Krause walked to the nearby café—his custom. Since she had not appeared, he felt no need to walk the several blocks to the Netherlands Hotel where he took her to dine last week.

Krause finished his strudel and coffee, paid the bill, and left disappointed but not overly concerned; after all, there was no preset rendezvous date or time. On the street, he hailed a taxi and got in the back seat. The driver twisted his neck to check for oncoming traffic as the cab crept forward. When he turned back to pull out into the street, he suddenly slammed on the brakes and hammered on the horn.

She stood in the headlights of the rocking cab.

"Holy Mary!" exclaimed the cabbie. He rolled down the window and stuck out his head.

"Lady," he shouted, "what's the matter with you? You wanna get yourself killed?"

"Wait, driver," Krause ordered. "She is with me."

Krause opened the door. Erika walked around and slid in beside him. Knowing the driver could hear, Krause was discreet.

"I'm glad you could make it, my dear."

"Sorry I'm late, Grandpapa," she leaned over and kissed Krause on the cheek. "Have you given the driver our address?"

"No," Krause turned to do so, but she stopped him with her hand on his arm.

"Driver, 73 Raritan Drive, please," she said.

What the driver heard was an address about four blocks from Adalwulf von Krause's home.

Krause glanced at her, confused. She returned the glance, smiled, and said softly, "I'm looking forward to the special brandy you mentioned."

Because of the driver, they said little during the ride. Krause lived in a fashionable area of town known as Price Hill, his home one of several large, Victorian mansions standing sentinel atop one of Cincinnati's highest overviews. Price Hill was for the upper crust. When the driver turned onto Raritan, the taxi's headlights lit a tunnel of large sycamores and evergreens along the cobblestone street. Close to the address, the driver slowed, trying to read house numbers.

"This is fine, driver," Erika said. "You can pull over here."

The driver stopped the car. Krause paid the fare, and they exited the cab.

Once on the sidewalk and the cab gone, she told him: "It would not be wise to have the driver drop us at your home." They began walking, and in a short time arrived at a large mansion with two turrets and many pointed arches easily seen in the moonlight. A porch light made it easy for Krause to find the door key. He stepped aside to follow Erika into the entrance hall.

"Your coat, my dear." Krause acted as butler and helped her off with it.

"Is anyone home, Adalwulf?" She was thinking of Willy.

"Viola, my maid and cook. She is a widow and quarters here, but is fast asleep I am sure. She retires very early. My grandson is not here. I noticed his car is gone, which is normally the case on a Saturday evening."

Erika nodded. She felt she could trust Adalwulf von Krause because she had followed him at random times, including tonight, and especially because her father told her Krause could be trusted. Besides, Erika knew that Krause would implicate himself if he divulged anything about her to others. So she had no doubts that Krause had kept her secret, even from Willy. Willy would not know she was a German spy on the run, so the prospect of encountering Willy again did not concern or bother her, but she imagined it might Willy. Good that Willy was not home.

"Please, let me show you to my study," Krause said.

He ushered her through several rooms, each with antique furniture (mostly pine), pricey art, and expensive figurines on tables and shelves. Each room had a fireplace with the marble mantelpieces of various hues, and an exquisite clock—grandfather or cuckoo. Bright burgundy, and rust Persian and Caucasian rugs covered some areas of the highly polished hardwood floors. In the parlor sat a Blüthner grand piano, its black enamel shining. Erika commented on the German-made piano considered masterpieces of craftsmanship.

"Adalwulf, a Blüthner? I did not know there were any in this country."

Krause paused to show her, pleased that she was impressed. "There are indeed, but only a handful. A few American virtuosos became interested when a Blüthner was brought across on the *Hindenburg* in 1936. I don't know if you are aware that the first music to ever be broadcast from the air was played on the *Hindenburg's* Blüthner. I purchased this one from the estate of a maestro in New York. Do you play, my dear?"

"Yes."

"Wonderful," Krause said before they moved on. "No one has touched it other than Viola to clean and polish. You must play for me before you leave."

They entered a study that occupied a corner of the north wing. Krause closed the door behind them.

"We can talk freely here, my dear. Viola's quarters are on the far end of the house and these walls do not have ears. When Viola or Wilmar knocks on my study door, I must shout before they can hear me tell them to enter. We need not worry."

A massive cherry wood desk dominated the décor; a dark red brocaded settee with matching side chair faced the fireplace. A large, freestanding world globe occupied one corner. Heavy drapes, now closed, covered the two windows. Three paintings hung. Erika recognized one, a portrait of a young, dark-haired woman.

"I see you have *Nanna,*" Erika commented, referring to the name of the woman in the painting.

This time Krause was impressed. Not many her age, he thought, would recognize a painting by Anselm Feuerbach, a 19th-century German neoclassical artist. Krause joined her in looking at the painting. "I am afraid it is not the original. You are familiar with this painting, my dear?"

"Yes, but I won't pretend to be an expert," she explained. "I commented only because I have seen the original."

"Have you?" Krause's curiosity piqued. "Where was that?"

"In the Berghof, Eva—a friend of mine—pointed it out to me."

Krause hesitated in awe. "Wonderful. I did not know the Führer owned the original. Fascinating." Krause offered her a seat on the settee. "I remember your father made regular visits to the Obersalzberg before the war. Does he still?"

"Not as frequently," she answered after she sat. "The war keeps him in Berlin. Before I left for this country, over a year ago now, I was there on a brief holiday and Father joined me."

Krause walked to a small cabinet. "Of course, your father and the Führer are old friends. I wish I had joined the Party sooner, in the early days, like your father. Karl tried to persuade me, but I resisted— stupid of me. Not until we retook the Rhineland did I finally join."

From the cabinet, Krause took a half-full bottle of brandy, poured two snifters, and brought one to Erika.

"Asbach, my dear."

"Thank you."

"Let us drink to your father." Krause and Erika saluted with the glasses and sipped. She thanked him for the toast.

"Are you comfortable?" Krause remained standing. Despite the cool autumn night, and the silent fireplaces, the house was comfortably warm.

"Yes, very comfortable."

"I have a steam boiler in the basement that is sufficient for all but the coldest days when Viola will make use of the fireplaces." Krause sat in the side chair. A few more minutes of chat followed, then Krause rose and walked to the painting Erika referred to when they entered the room. Krause opened the safe behind *Nanna* and took out an envelope. "I have the information you requested." He handed her the envelope. "And I have a plan to get you home."

It took Krause half an hour to explain the details of his plan to return Erika to Germany. Occasionally she asked a question; he answered. When finished, he took a ring sizer from his suit pocket and handed it to her. Erika used it to verify her ring size, and he wrote down the information.

"I know a local jeweler," Krause said, "a skilled craftsman from Leipzig. I went to see him a few days ago. He can create the Ring within a few days. I will visit him Monday morning and give him the commission. We should have the Ring within the week."

Erika told Krause she would contact him in some fashion near the end of the week to see where the preparations stood. With serious business finished, he poured them both a second Asbach, finishing the bottle. He remembered his earlier request.

"I would be honored if you played for me, Erika."

They left the study for the parlor.

"I haven't played since I left Germany, Adalwulf," she said as she adjusted the bench and lifted the fallboard. "Be patient with me."

After a few moments to check her memory and test the tuning, she played Schumann's *Fantasy* in C Major. Krause listened, rapt, and remembered happy days at the Prussian State Opera House in Berlin and at the Wagner festivals in Bayreuth. When Erika finished, Krause said "Brava!" and thanked her wholeheartedly. Earlier he had considered offering her an invitation to stay the night; now he did.

"I have four extra bedrooms, never used," he added after the invitation. She thought for a moment and, to his surprise and pleasure, accepted. Krause showed Erika upstairs and pointed out the bedrooms and a nearby bathroom. She chose the corner bedroom.

"This is the guest wing," Krause said. "You will not be disturbed. Wilmar and I have rooms on the far side of the house, and Viola's quarters are off the kitchen. There are items such as combs and brushes in the bathroom cabinet, linens and I'm sure a robe or two. Please feel free to make use of anything you find. In the morning, I will let Viola know you are with us and your decision about breakfast can be made then. Viola is a skilled cook and she will be happy to prepare anything you wish." Krause gave the necessary Prussian bow. "I am very pleased you are my guest. I will leave you now, Fräulein."

Erika came forward and for the second time that night, kissed him on the cheek.

"Thank you, dear Adalwulf. Good night."

"Good night."

Twenty minutes later, Erika sat back in a hot bath, leaning her head on the edge of the tub. The spartan place where she now lived after leaving the Lamar Apartments offered only a small, often dirty shower, shared with others, with only tepid or sometimes cold water. So tonight she very much enjoyed the large, cast iron bathtub and steaming water. The abundant hot water and the two snifters of

Asbach relaxed her. And no one stood outside the door impatient for their turn.

Erika thought about Adalwulf's plan to help her return to Germany. She thought of Elizabeth Ault and how the next meeting—and there must be a next meeting—would be dangerous and much more difficult now that she was being guarded (she had three times watched Elizabeth leave the newspaper and seen the chaperon; twice it was her husband). Then she thought of home: her father and the war. Erika thought of the almost daily newspaper reports of large, Allied bombing raids raining death and destruction on her homeland, raids more intense now than when she left Germany over a year ago. She thought about her mortal enemy, Heinrich Himmler, and things happening in Germany she did not understand. *What will I be going back to?*

Even so, she was tired of the always present strain and danger of living secretly among enemies, trying to fit in as one of them. The worry about making a mistake, perhaps forgetting which lie had been told, had hung over her for more than a year like a bleak, threatening cloud. Erika Lehmann embraced the thought of home.

[the next morning]

Adalwulf von Krause rose at precisely 6:30 a.m.—the usual time. He dressed and went downstairs to find Viola who was already busy in the kitchen, kneading her dough for that day's bread. Guests were few and far between at the Krause home, so the need rare for formal breakfast in the dining room. His grandson could never be counted on, many days dragging in from a night of drinking and troublemaking too late for breakfast, so Krause normally ate the morning meal alone in his study. Consequently, Krause surprised Viola with news of a guest in the house, a young woman (this increased Viola's surprise). Krause told Viola that if their guest did not come down for breakfast by eight, he would knock on the young woman's door.

Krause checked outside for his grandson's car, still not there, and returned to the kitchen where he took his coffee and scanned the newspaper until a few minutes past eight, when he walked up to Erika's room. He knocked gently.

"My dear," Krause said to the slightly ajar door, "are you awake?"

"Yes, Adalwulf," he heard plainly. "Come in."

195

He hesitated. Perhaps entering would not be polite. He heard her repeat.

"Come in, Adalwulf, please."

As Krause slowly opened the door, he saw first the empty four-post bed, covers askew. He stepped in. Erika stood in front of a full-length mirror, naked, brushing her hair. Krause froze, shocked. She turned to him.

"It's all right, Adalwulf." She smiled and continued to brush her hair. "I don't mind. I hope this pleases you."

Krause was at a loss.

Erika realized her very proper host was embarrassed and uncomfortable. She reached for a nearby robe.

"Forgive me, Adalwulf," she apologized as she slid on the robe. "I did the wrong thing."

"No . . . my dear, ah . . . I thank you. About breakfast . . .," Krause said.

"Give me fifteen minutes, Adalwulf. I'll be right down."

Breakfast was served in the formal dining room, Erika and her host alone at a large, linen-covered table with a dozen chairs. Erika Lehmann's hearty appetite pleased Viola, who considered it an insult if someone left something on a plate.

"Your biscuits are wonderful, Viola," Erika praised. "Everything is delicious."

The old cook smiled and refreshed Erika's coffee.

Erika turned to Krause. "I thought I would see Willy by now."

He frowned. "It is not unusual for Wilmar to stay out all night. I try to be patient with him for my late wife's and daughter's sake, but he often tests that patience."

Erika sympathized with Krause; he had no idea about the extent of his grandson's flaws.

Once breakfast ended, Viola cleared the table and disappeared into the kitchen. Erika reminded Krause that she would contact him later that week.

"I must go now, Adalwulf."

"I will telephone for a taxi."

"No. I will walk. There is a gasoline station only two miles away. I will call for a taxi from the phone booth there."

"You know best, my dear." Krause escorted Erika to the entrance hall and retrieved her coat from a closet near the front door. She thanked him for everything. As he helped her with the coat, they heard a car.

"That will be Wilmar," Krause said. "I will have him drop you."

Krause opened the door and they stepped out onto the porch. Willy and his hangover dragged themselves out of his cream-color Cadillac convertible; he stumbled toward the steps holding his throbbing head. His nose still bandaged and his head down, Willy was unaware of his grandfather and the woman he knew as Early watching from the porch.

"Fuck me!" They heard Willy say, commenting to himself about his pounding headache. Erika noticed the elder Krause shaking his head in displeasure.

Willy finally reached the steps and, with his head still down, climbed as if he scaled Pikes Peak. When he finally reached the summit his grandfather spoke.

"Wilmar," Krause said, "I want you to drive our guest wherever she wants to go."

Willy, startled at his grandfather's voice, looked up with bloodshot eyes at his grandfather and the woman next to him.

"Good morning, Wilmar," Erika said.

"Aaaaaaaggghh!!!" Willy screamed and jerked violently backward. This motion sent him recoiling against the porch rail; he flipped backwards over the rail and fell face first into a thorny shrub. "Aaaaaaaggghh!!!" again, this time from the thorns. "Aaaaaaaggghh!!!" a third time for emphasis.

"I think it best I walk, Adalwulf."

Chapter 32

The Plan

Sunday, October 10, 1943

A bright streak of sunlight bounced off a mirror and into her eyes when Elizabeth sat up in bed, causing her to scoot over. Her undergarments lay on the floor—where Frank always threw them—so she drew the sheet up and looked down at her sleeping husband. He certainly was not movie star handsome, but rugged and virile. Elizabeth supposed that is what attracted her to him when they met. Frank was a man's man, hard-muscled and tough. She reached over and ran her fingers through his hair.

After lighting an Old Gold cigarette from a pack on the bedside table, Elizabeth sat back against the headboard. She quit smoking three years ago, but went back to it Thursday night after Leroy Carr told her Anne Brown was a German spy.

Elizabeth let Frank know on Friday, the day after the Eden Park meeting, that she would cooperate with the OSS. *Frank, we have to do it, you know that. We're at war. The world is fighting for survival from Hitler, and this is one of his spies. What type of people would we be if we refused?*

Frank did not like the danger Leroy Carr planned for his wife, but admitted to her that she was right. Yesterday he called Carr into his office and quizzed the OSS man about his plan. Frank objected to a few details, and the two men hashed and rehashed until it was settled. At a meeting scheduled for this afternoon, the select few who had to know would be told the plan. Frank still refused to take Elizabeth into the station, so the meeting would be held in an empty suite at Leroy Carr's hotel. Carr's partner, Al Hodge, would meet everyone in the hotel lobby with the suite number when they arrived.

Frank stirred. Elizabeth smashed the cigarette into an ashtray and started to lie down next to him, but changed her mind, rose, picked up her bra and underpants and took them to the clothes hamper in the bathroom down the hall. When she returned, Frank was awake and looking at her.

"Good morning," he said with a scratchy voice. "Hey, I like watching a naked lady walk around the room."

"A naked lady? That doesn't sound like you're very particular. Do naked women walk around for you often?"

"All the time."

"Oh? Well, maybe I'll start doing it for other men."

"Come here," Frank ordered.

"Calm down over there, tiger. I have to take a bath." She pulled fresh undergarments from a dresser drawer.

"Come on. Come over here for a second."

"Aren't you tired from last night?"

"Yeah. I'm tired. I just want to tell you a secret, but you have to come here to get it. I'll give you a scoop."

"Scoop? Is that what you call it now?" Still naked and holding her undergarments, Elizabeth walked to the side of the bed, just out of Frank's reach, teasing. He tried to grab her but she stepped back, laughing.

"Clare Miller has been cleared by the doctors to return to work this week," Elizabeth said out of the blue.

"Don't change the subject."

"Did you know that?" she asked.

"Yeah, I knew that. How did you know it?"

"I went by and checked on her a few days ago—one of those days Officer Christian drove me because you were in court. How about Penelope Lindauer? Do you know how she's doing?"

"She's still at her parents' house in Akron. I think she's healing okay, at least physically."

"Is she having other problems?"

"I talked to her father about a week ago," said Frank. "He told me she doesn't want to leave her room—sits in a dark bedroom all day."

"Poor woman." Elizabeth shook her head and walked back to the dresser to gather some makeup.

Frank sensed his hope of a rematch of last night's lovemaking was on hold until a later time so he sat up on the edge of the bed.

That afternoon, during the drive to Carr's hotel, Frank made several unnecessary turns and glanced often in his rear view mirror. Arriving at the Palace Hotel on 6th and Vine, he parked the Plymouth in the loading zone near the front entrance. Elizabeth stepped out. She had not driven since the day Anne Brown sat down with her at Sano's restaurant.

Frank showed his identification to a doorman. He told the man he was there on police business and the car would remain parked in front. Al Hodge waited in the lobby.

"Hello, Detective Ault," greeted Hodge, then he turned to Elizabeth. "And, of course, you must be Mrs. Ault. Nice to meet you, ma'am. I'm Al Hodge."

"Hello."

"Detective, everyone has arrived. I'll take you up."

Hodge led them to the elevator and asked the boy for the seventh floor. After a rather long, silent walk through the seventh-floor hall, Hodge stopped at a door and used a key. When they entered, Leroy Carr, Ed Cantrell, and Glen Shafer rose to greet Elizabeth.

After the greeting, Shafer said, "Before you got here, Frank, I was telling Carr that the taxpayers are treating him right. He's got some great digs." The large suite was beautifully appointed.

"Unfortunately," Carr corrected, "our rooms—Al's and mine—are not like this one. I rented this for the meeting. We would have a heck of a time squeezing in one of our rooms." Carr pointed to a coffee pot sitting on a corner table, kept warm by a Bunsen burner, cups alongside, and asked Elizabeth if he could get her a cup then he invited the men to help themselves. Carr and Shafer already held a cup, neither of the Aults wanted coffee.

"Let's get down to business," Frank suggested.

"Good idea." Carr set his coffee cup in its saucer on an end table beside his chair. He addressed the group. "Detective Ault and I met and have agreed on what we think is our best chance of bringing our German lady-friend to the surface. I know everyone here knows this, but by law, I have to inform you that this case has been tagged as national security, and is covered by the Sedition Act. No one besides the six people in this room is to know of anything we discuss here today. For example, Major Cantrell, you cannot even brief your Chief of Police about anything we discuss here today."

Cantrell looked annoyed. "Yes, I understand all that, Mr. Carr. We all understand it; you told us that in my office."

Carr knew the three cops would be irked by the reminder. "I realize that, Major, but I'm also obligated under the Sedition Act to say what I just said."

"Fair enough," Cantrell granted.

Carr: "Here is what we want to try. First, we all have to keep in mind this German is obviously highly-trained, clever, cunning: pick your own adjectives. Unless we are very careful, she will smell a trap not a mile away, but five or six miles away. And, of course, the reason we had to ask for Elizabeth's help is that whatever we do, it revolves around her. Anne Brown obviously had a reason to seek out Elizabeth. Of course that reason has nothing to do with turning herself in, or accepting Elizabeth's invitation to tell her story. It would be nice to know what the real reason is, but we don't know, and probably won't find out until we catch her. But regardless, right now Anne Brown's interest in Elizabeth is the only card we have to play."

The men looked at Elizabeth. She had steeled herself for this meeting and displayed no reaction, determined not to be what she felt most of them expected—a frightened female.

Carr continued: "Something we cannot do is publish the Evansville shipyard photograph in the local newspapers. I know that is very tempting, but we can't do it for a couple of important reasons. One, the local FBI will see it and send it to Washington where it will be quickly matched from the Bureau's Evansville case. We don't want the FBI involved; we've already discussed that. And two, Anne Brown will also see it. She'll know where the photograph came from, and realize we have her tagged. We want her to continue thinking she is being sought solely for questioning in the apartment attacks."

"What we want to do is this," Carr said next, "we want Elizabeth to write another newspaper article about the case. We know Anne Brown was still in Cincinnati as recently as October first when she approached Elizabeth. If she is still here, we can assume she will read the article; she obviously read the others. Whether another article will do anything to entice Brown to again get in touch with Elizabeth is debatable, but I think we all agree it is better to be hands-on than to sit back and twiddle our thumbs hoping and waiting."

Now Carr turned to the reporter. "Elizabeth, you'll write the article. You're the professional. Please let me check it, as we agreed, before it's published. You know there are many things we cannot say, but that aside, what you write is your call. Just one important point: inviting Anne Brown to contact you again might, on the surface, sound logical, but she'll smell that as a trap immediately. You must not suggest another meeting even though that is what we want so we can move in for the capture."

When he began talking about a newspaper article, Carr entered a realm where Elizabeth was the expert. She commented quickly: "Then I'll need something new—a scoop or a new angle. If there is no substance, no real reason for the article, she'll probably see through that too. I have an idea on a piece I considered doing but backed off."

The men waited as she took five seconds.

"I can write about meeting her. That would definitely be a new angle."

Most of them thought her idea was as good as any other; they waited for Leroy Carr's reaction.

"I think you've got something there," Carr said eventually. "Gentlemen?" Carr asked for their thoughts for diplomacy's sake. Frank nodded, and the other men fell in line.

"Okay," Carr went back to Elizabeth, "we need to get the article in your newspaper as soon as possible. When can you get that done?"

"Give me one day," she decided. "I'll have it ready tomorrow, and it can appear in Tuesday morning's paper. I'll let Frank know when it's ready, and he can call you so you can look it over before I send it to my editor."

"Thanks, Elizabeth. Gentlemen, we have one other major consideration to deal with: what to do about Elizabeth's bodyguard. After Anne Brown approached his wife, you know that Detective Ault ordered a bodyguard for Elizabeth when she's in public, as any of us would have done for our wife. We'll leave the bodyguard in place. Anne Brown followed Elizabeth on occasion before the first meeting. If there is to be a second meeting, Brown will follow her again and maybe has already done so. If she has already followed Elizabeth at any time since the first meeting, she has seen that Frank or another policeman has been with her. If we suddenly pull the bodyguard, Anne Brown will know why. She'll know it's a set up."

"Then how is she going to get to Elizabeth so we can move in?" Shafer asked.

"If Anne Brown still wants to meet, Elizabeth will probably receive a note or telephone call with instructions on when and where, and to come alone. Then Brown will have the place staked out, looking for a double-cross."

Carr ended with a warning. "Whatever pans out, if Anne Brown wants to get to Elizabeth, that woman will find a way. Believe me. We have to be very careful."

Chapter 33

Late Night Telephone Calls

Wednesday, October 13, 1943

10:15 p.m.—*Observer* newsroom

The reaction was immediate and ample to Elizabeth's front page revelation in Tuesday's *Observer* that the fugitive from the sensational Over the Rhine crime in September—Anne Brown—had approached her in a restaurant. Within an hour after the newspaper hit the streets Tuesday morning, the first edition sold out and *Observer* presses fired up to get the second edition on the streets by lunchtime. WLW radio called the *Observer* newsroom seeking her editor's permission to interview Elizabeth on the air later that day. Two other radio stations followed with the same request.

In the article, Elizabeth stuck to the facts: nothing was changed, nothing embellished. She did not attempt to pass herself off as a heroine; instead, she wrote candidly about her anxiety (*perhaps it was fear,* she wrote) when Anne Brown identified herself. Elizabeth admitted to her readers that she disappointed herself with her unprofessional behavior. And staying true to what happened that day, Elizabeth revealed that the surprise meeting was cut short before the fugitive offered any reason for it. At Leroy Carr's behest, Elizabeth did not extend another invitation to meet, and she left out only two facts: that Anne Brown was a German spy, and the name of the restaurant.

No one predicted the degree of the reaction, the intensity of the firestorm, not even Elizabeth. The curious had to know, and were not too shy to ask:

—*Why did the Over the Rhine Crucifier do what she did? Why did she crucify that woman?*
—*What could she have wanted to talk to you about, Elizabeth?*
—*Who is she really? What is she like?*
—*Where is she now?*
—*Are you telling us everything?*

Elizabeth went from being a well-known local reporter on Monday, whom strangers occasionally approached seeking a handshake or a brief chat, to on Tuesday being pursued like an escapee from a chain gang. And the vastly stepped-up attention came not only from the public *(If your newspaper sketch is accurate, I think I saw her in Sears last week, seriously . . . You must have been frightened out of your mind, poor dear)* and fellow journalists *(What's your next move, Elizabeth? . . . Are you willing to meet with her again? . . . What does your cop husband say about all this?)*, but from friends and relatives as well who called to express their concern and curiosity. Tuesday evening at home, the only time the telephone did not ring was when Elizabeth was on it. She spent a half hour reassuring her worried mother alone. Mother would not be dissuaded from her worries, or from hanging up, until Elizabeth put Frank on the phone to calm her. Later, at eleven o'clock, after several more calls from family, friends, and acquaintances, Elizabeth finally left the receiver off the hook.

Today had brought more of the same, and for the first time since she met Anne Brown at Sano's, Elizabeth was glad she had a driver/bodyguard (today Frank had to testify in court, so he sent Ray Christian, the young patrolman she met the night of the Lamar Apartments crime). Yes, glad she had a chaperone, not because of Anne Brown, but because of the onslaught of people running up to her when she was out. Carr wanted her out and about, keeping her normal routine; that was part of the plan. Yet the public hubbub, and interviews with radio stations and other Cincinnati and northern Kentucky newspapers, denied her a typical day and almost made her miss her own deadline for a short, 250-word follow-up piece about the public reaction to her meeting Anne Brown story—an easy assignment given her by a merciful editor who recognized she had not had time to cover any other news since her big splash Tuesday morning.

Nevertheless, she managed to make her 10:00 p.m. deadline, if only by minutes, and was now ready to go home. She threw some paperclips and carbon paper in a desk drawer and slammed it shut. Her husband sat by her desk, waiting.

"That's it, Frank. Let's go," she said and grabbed her jacket. "I don't know about you, but I'm ready for a nightcap."

"Do you want to try the Rusty Bottom?" he asked.

"No way. I've answered enough questions for today. Let's go home."

When the Aults wanted a drink, they usually went to a bar or restaurant. Other than a few of Frank's beers in the refrigerator, seldom was there alcohol at the house, so Frank pulled over at a liquor store on the way home. Elizabeth's preferred cocktail was a Tom Collins, but he was no good at making them, and he knew she would drink a much simpler whiskey and cola if it wasn't too strong. For Frank, whiskey had to be made in Kentucky and called Bourbon. "Give me a fifth of Heaven Hill," he told the clerk. He wasn't sure if they had any cola at home so he bought a six-pack of Royal Crown.

When they arrived home, the telephone was, of course, ringing.

"It's for you," Frank said without picking it up. Elizabeth lifted the receiver; it was her mother.

"Yes, Mom," Frank heard his wife say, ". . . I couldn't answer the phone earlier, Mom, Frank and I just walked in the door . . . No, I have not been murdered . . . Okay, Mom, I'll be careful . . . Yes, Frank or another policeman is always with me when I'm out . . . Thanks, Mom, I love you too. Tell Dad I love him . . . Okay, Mom, good night. . . ."

Elizabeth left the receiver off then collapsed on the sofa. Frank went to the kitchen to pour the drinks. He made Elizabeth her whiskey and cola and poured himself a straight whiskey on the rocks.

"I hope it's a double," Elizabeth said wearily when Frank handed her the drink. She rested the glass on her right thigh, as if too exhausted to lift it. "What do you think are the chances this is going to work, Frank?"

"You mean as far as Anne Brown trying to contact you again?"

"Yes."

"I don't think that article Tuesday will make any difference one way or the other." He took a sip. "All it has done is create a giant headache for you, and I told Carr that today—he came by the station. The key will be Brown's reason for contacting you. If that reason is still there, and still important to her, she might contact you, but it won't be easy for her now that you're under police protection. Like Carr said at the meeting, she'll have to get a message to you. She can't just show up like she did at Sano's."

"What will happen to her if you catch her?" Elizabeth had never asked it before, and she was not sure why.

"Since she's a woman, they might electrocute her instead of hang her."

She looked at him. "Not just prison forever?"

"In wartime, spies are executed almost without exception, and to top it off she has aggravating circumstances. Her partner killed an FBI agent in Indiana, and she killed an American here in Cincinnati. Yeah, the guy was a low-life and we're better off without him, but I think betting on a life sentence in her case is definitely a sucker's bet."

Frank Ault did not tell his wife, and he had not told Leroy Carr, that if he ever saw Anne Brown again, the German spy would not have to worry about her eventual sentence. Ault would shoot to kill.

[across town]

Meanwhile, on Price Hill, another telephone rang. Willy Krause ignored it for several rings as he listened to Doris Day sing *Day after Day* on the radio. Willy knew that the singer, Doris von Kappelhoff, adopted her stage name from that song. He knew it because he had heard his grandfather grumble after finding out the popular young singer had changed her *proud German name. Too many Germans in America are doing that, Wilmar.*

The song ended, yet the telephone kept ringing. Willy knew his grandfather and Viola were probably asleep by now.

"Jesus Christ!" Willy got up and walked to the phone in the next room.

Yesterday the doctor removed the stitches from Willy's nose. The scar would be permanent, and the rest of his face was still marred from the fall into the thorny bush. *I'll show that Side Pocket whore a thing or two if we ever cross paths again.* After she left the house that day, Willy asked his grandfather who the woman was, but was told it was none of his affair.

"Yeah!" Willy rudely shouted when he picked up the phone.

A voice with a heavy German accent came through the phone. *"Hallo, ist Herr von Krause there, please . . . Adalwulf von Krause, please."*

"Man, do you know what time it is?" Willy was not sure himself and looked at the cuckoo clock on the wall. It was nearly eleven. "He's in bed. Who the hell is this?"

"I'm calling for Adalwulf von Krause, please. He expects my call."

"Call back tomorrow."

"Herr von Krause waits for my call. My name ist Ostermann."

"Hold on." Willy banged the receiver down on the table. *If the old man jumps me I'm going to find this moron and kick his ass.* Willy went upstairs and knocked on his grandfather's bedroom door. It took two knockings.

"Yes." Willy heard through the door.

"Grandfather, some guy named Ostermann is on the phone insisting to talk with you. He says you are waiting for his call. I told him you were asleep. . . ."

"It is fine, Wilmar," his grandfather interrupted. "Tell him to hold. I will take it in my study." Adalwulf rose and put on his robe. Willy went back downstairs and again told the caller to wait. Eventually Willy heard his grandfather pick up the telephone.

"Wilmar, are you there?" Krause asked from the phone in his study."

"Yes, sir," Willy confirmed.

"You may hang up now, thank you."

"Yes, sir." But Willy did not hang up. He pushed down the receive button to make a click, then let up and held the phone to his ear.

"Hello," Adalwulf said into the phone.

"Hallo, Herr von Krause, this ist Ostermann. I vould not have called at such a late hour, but you insisted I call as soon as it ist ready, and you said regardless of the hour of day."

"Yes, yes, Herr Ostermann, that is fine. So it is ready?"

"Yes, Herr von Krause. I just finished."

"Splendid, I will call on you in the morning."

"Very well."

Adalwulf von Krause and the caller hung up, and a moment later so did Willy.

Chapter 34

For the Fatherland

Thursday, October 14, 1943

Adalwulf von Krause stepped out of a taxi on East 13th Street and entered a small shop with heavy bars over the large store window and a sliding metal barricade (now open) that secured the entrance door after hours. Inside, the dim lighting and musty air reminded Krause of his wine cellar. Two small counters on either side of the shop displayed rings, bracelets, necklaces, and other pieces of jewelry in silver and gold, some with stones, some without, and men's and women's watches. A few finely crafted clocks hung on the wall behind one of the counters. Toward the back, a small, elderly bald man wearing spectacles with a jeweler's eyepiece attached to the right lens worked at a table inspecting the diamonds and emeralds in a gold broach he held under the light of a small desk lamp. When the old man heard someone enter, he flipped up the hinged eye piece like a welder flips up his helmet when finished with his fire and looked up. He saw Krause and rose with considerable effort. Krause knew the old man was crippled.

"I will come back there, Herr Ostermann." Krause walked toward the old man.

"Herr von Krause, gut morning," greeted the stooped man in a combination of German and English words with the same thick German accent Krause heard on the telephone last night.

"Good morning, Herr Ostermann. Are we alone?"

"Ja, ja."

"May I see it, please?"

Ostermann turned around and limped through a doorway, pushing aside a curtain to enter an office/storage area at the rear of the shop. He retrieved a ring box from a safe and returned to Krause.

"All ist in order," Ostermann said, handing Krause the box.

From an inside coat pocket, Krause took out a pair of eye glasses and put them on. He opened the box, took out the silver ring, and turned it around several times, inspecting.

"This is a size seven?" asked Krause.

"Ja, as you ordered."

As Krause examined the ring, Ostermann said, "I know of za Ring des Erschlagenen, Herr von Krause, und . . . how do you say *die Legenden?* . . . za legends und za curse over zose who are not vorthy to vear za Ring. Za Ring ist not to be taken lightly. Are you sure vhat vee do ist proper?"

Krause did not answer until satisfied with the ring. "Yes, Herr Ostermann, all is proper. The person who will receive this Ring is valiant and deserving, I assure you. Just make sure you tell no one about the Ring, or about me. Do you understand?"

"Of course, Herr von Krause."

"I will pay you now," said Krause. He handed Ostermann an envelope from a breast pocket. "In the envelope is double the amount you quoted me Monday when I visited you. I want you to destroy all receipts and records concerning this order."

"Ja, Herr von Krause."

Krause returned the ring to its box, then the box went into a coat pocket. He turned to leave, but stopped when he reached the door and looked back at Ostermann. Krause knew that before the war Ostermann had been a member of Cincinnati's German-American Bund and was still a Nazi sympathizer. Krause made sure the old jeweler from Leipzig knew the importance of keeping his mouth shut, and that what he did was for the Fatherland.

"Für das Vaterland, Herr Ostermann."

The old man appeared suddenly energized and straightened from his stoop. "Für das Vaterland."

Willy Krause sat in his parked car a block away and watched his grandfather exit the place he entered several minutes earlier. His grandfather had been acting strangely—*secretive* might be the word— since Willy had given him the note from Early, *that Side Pocket slut.* Then Willy came home last Sunday morning and there she was, standing on the porch with his grandfather. Viola told him later that she had spent the night at the house! *What is happening? Is that whore trying to extort money from Grandfather?* After surreptitiously listening in on his grandfather's mysterious telephone call late last night from someone named Ostermann, Willy's curiosity got the best of him. His grandfather told Ostermann he would call on him this morning, so when the taxi pulled up to the house Willy was ready.

Willy let the cab drive away, and then he rushed out, jumped in his car and followed the taxi. He had never secretly followed anyone before, and Willy was proud of himself for fooling the cabdriver—*the dumb shithead.*

After his grandfather's taxi pulled away, Willy moved his car to the next block and parked in front of the shop. The sign over the door read:

Nikolaus Ostermann
Fine Handcrafted Jewelry
Gold and Silversmith
Watchmaker and Repair
Engraving

When Willy entered, he saw an old man sitting at a table. The old man eyed Willy and stood slowly.

"May I help you, young man?" When the old man spoke, Willy recognized the heavy accent from the telephone call.

"Yeah, my grandfather was just in here. What did he get?"

The old man was suspicious. "Your Großvater?" Ostermann could not say the word *grandfather* without sounding silly to an American ear, so he used the German.

"Yeah, Adalwulf von Krause. He just left here. What did he get?"

The old man said nothing. Willy drew his wallet from his back pants pocket and showed the old man his driver license. "See, I'm Willy—Wilmar—von Krause."

The old man looked at the license but still offered no answers. Willy tried to think of a different approach.

"Look," Willy said, "I want to get my grandfather something nice for his birthday. I was driving by and saw him come out of your store. I'm looking to buy something from you, but I don't want to buy something he just bought."

Nikolaus Ostermann was no one's fool. That, and he had not felt comfortable reproducing the Ring in the first place. He was certainly not about to answer questions about it when it was his duty not to— he had given his oath in the name of the Fatherland. Besides, this young man is *ein Großmaul,* a big mouth. Probably the same one he spoke to on the telephone last night.

"Your Großvater did not purchase; I repair a vatch."

"You repaired a watch?"

"Ja."

"You called my grandfather at eleven o'clock at night to tell him his watch was fixed?"

"Ja."

Willy knew the man was covering up. "You're full of shit. My grandfather would never tell you to call him and get him out of bed just to let him know his watch was fixed. I want to know what he got here, you old fuck."

Ostermann let loose with several expletives in German and ordered Willy to get out. Willy cursed him in return, but decided questioning the stubborn Ostermann a waste of time. On his way to the door, Willy pushed a small display of earrings off a counter and onto the floor, breaking the display and scattering the jewelry.

Determined to find out what was going on even if it meant confronting his grandfather, Willy returned to the house. He assumed the taxi had already delivered his grandfather home, but Willy's knock on the study door went unanswered. Viola was sweeping near the entryway and Willy inquired about his grandfather. Viola told him that the master of the house had not yet returned. Willy stood thinking while Viola walked away to another room. Going into the study when the old man was not there was strictly forbidden, but Willy returned to the study door, turned the knob, walked in and closed the door behind him.

He looked around on his grandfather's desk: the only papers a few small household bills. He started opening drawers but found nothing that might satisfy his curiosity. Willy was about to leave—the last thing he wanted was for his grandfather to discover him snooping—but suddenly was drawn back to the right top drawer. He again opened the drawer and this time looked more closely at the newspaper that was folded open to a sketch of the Over the Rhine Crucifier. Willy had heard people talk of the attacks, but he spent little time reading newspapers and had not seen the sketch.

Willy took out the newspaper and looked closely at the woman's face before his own paled.

[that afternoon]

Unless there was a press conference, a breaking news story, or some other important reason to start her day earlier, Elizabeth Ault reported for work each day shortly after lunch. She would check in with her editor, do whatever traveling around town was required to cover that day's assignment, then report back to her desk to work up the story for her 10 p.m. deadline. If all went well, sometimes she could leave for the day as early at 5 or 6 p.m. On the other hand, sometimes it was 10:30 before she walked out of the *Observer* building after barely meeting her deadline, and she even pulled an occasional all-nighter if something was fresh in her mind and she sought to get a running start on the next day's work.

Elizabeth, ready to leave the house, hoped today would be one of those easier days after two days of the frenzy that surrounded her after she revealed on Tuesday that she had met the Over the Rhine Crucifier. She heard the knock and looked at her watch. *One o'clock, at least cops are punctual—when they're on the job, anyway.* Frank, still tied up in court testifying, could not drive her again today, but he promised to send a substitute. Yesterday the substitute was Officer Christian. When Elizabeth opened the inside door, she was surprised. It was not Officer Christian.

"Glen," said Elizabeth through the locked screen door.

"Hi, Elizabeth, Frank asked me to drive you to work today. It's Christian's day off."

"Oh, I see. I'll grab my jacket." She disappeared for a moment, then came outside and locked the door. Nervous (it was her first time alone with Glen Shafer since that night at the Rusty Bottom), Elizabeth did her best to make small talk as they walked to Shafer's car. "I don't know if I need a jacket, it's so nice out, but better to be safe than sorry."

"Good idea," Glen said, also trying to appear at ease. "You don't need it right now, but after the sun goes down it's a different story this time of year."

When weather comments dried up, an awkward silence settled over them for the first few blocks of the drive. Elizabeth lit a cigarette, rolled her window halfway down, blew smoke, and stared out the window.

Eventually, Shafer thought of something to talk about. "We finally identified the woman who was nailed to the wall. Cantrell will release the information to the press this afternoon."

Terms used for the woman's impaling varied. While the press preferred the more sensational *crucified*, other words Elizabeth had heard were *pinned*, *stuck*, and the word used most frequently by the police: *nailed*.

"Oh?" He had her attention.

"Yeah," Shafer said. "Her name is Harriett Rosten. After a couple of weeks, a woman figured out her sister was missing and reported it. A few days after that, a desk sergeant in Missing Persons noticed the description similarities between the missing sister and our Jane Doe while he was checking through some case files. The guy was on his toes. Missing Persons checked it out and sure enough."

Elizabeth always carried a pen and small note pad. "Harriett Rosten. Is that *r-o-s-t-e-n?*" she asked while writing.

"Yeah."

"What's her story?"

"Don't know yet. She's at the county jail. Frank went there this morning to question her. Now that we know who she is, maybe she'll start talking. He'll fill me in after he gets out of court this afternoon. The gal hasn't been convicted of any crimes, at least not around here. That's why we had no print record. Crowley, the Missing Persons desk sergeant who identified her, told us the sister who reported her missing is a real piece of work herself. Crowley said the woman came in half drunk and cussing while filling out the missing persons report. He said he almost threw her in jail. Maybe he should have. The sisters could have held a family reunion in County. Sounds to me like being a good-for-nothing runs in the family. I've seen it before: an entire family of crumbs."

"Thanks for the heads-up, Glen."

"No problem, Elizabeth." Silence returned. Shafer made a right turn, then a left, and pulled to a stop in front of the *Cincinnati Observer* building.

"Thanks for the ride, Glen." Elizabeth reached for the door handle.

"Elizabeth." He said her name to stop her. It did. "I want to apologize for that night at the Rusty Bottom."

She stopped him by lifting her left hand. "Don't apologize, Glen. It's every bit as much my fault."

"No, hear me out, please," said Shafer. "It was a dumb thing on my part, and I don't want it to ruin our friendship. I've felt bad about it ever since. Then I got to thinking how much I respect Frank, and that made it worse . . . a lot worse. Don't get me wrong. Everything I said that night is true—about always wanting you, I mean. But I still want to kick my own rear end for pulling you into that alley."

She looked at him for the first time since getting into the car. "Glen, I love Frank." She left it at that, unwilling to open up to Glen

213

Shafer about her own regrets about that night. She opened the car door. "I also hope we remain friends. Thanks again for the ride." She got out quickly, closed the car door, and walked into the *Observer*.

A line of people waited for the elevator so she took the stairs. Elizabeth knew a clearing-of-the-air with Glen Shafer was inevitable; avoiding eye contact with him when they crossed paths was awkward and ridiculous. She was relieved it was done. He had to add the part about always wanting her—she could have done without that: it made her uncomfortable hearing it again. Bluntly telling Shafer that she loved Frank made her feel better. Elizabeth knew she would never forget betraying her husband, but she was still sure confessing to Frank was the wrong thing to do. It had to stop where it was now, with the coming to terms with Glen. Maybe now she and Glen could repair their friendship, then again maybe not, but at least he knew where she stood.

At least once each day, Elizabeth checked in at the *Observer* mailroom. The mailroom girl saw her coming down the corridor and had Elizabeth's mail and messages waiting.

"Here it is, Elizabeth."

"Thanks, Kelli." Elizabeth thumbed through and found two handwritten messages: one from her editor telling her to check in with him about that day's assignment before two o'clock that afternoon because he had to leave early, and the other from Frank reminding her he should be done with court by three. *If you can get off early, I'll buy dinner for the prettiest reporter I ever married,* he wrote. The note was in his handwriting. Instead of calling in the message to the newsroom, he had dropped it off himself or had it delivered to the mailroom. She knew why. Frank Ault would never dictate any private sentiments to a stranger over the telephone.

Elizabeth had received a few letters every day since her Anne Brown meeting story, and today there were three. She took her mail and walked up one more flight of stairs to the newsroom and stopped to put a nickel in the coffee donation cup. A handwritten sign by the pot said: *Out of coffee ration for the month, this is Postum.* Elizabeth had actually grown to like the wheat and molasses beverage that many Americans now used as a coffee substitute. She poured a paper cupful, added a touch of evaporated milk from a can with Elsie the cow's picture on it, and then took the Postum to her desk.

The first envelope showed the stamped return address of the downtown Cincinnati library, the letter a request for Elizabeth to speak at a November luncheon. The other letters showed hand-written return addresses. The first one she opened was a flattering letter from a female reader who wrote that she admired Elizabeth's stories and her commitment to female causes. The second letter read:

Meet me at Union Terminal Friday. Arrive at noon in front of Gate 5 inside the terminal. Leave from your home. Take a taxi. After you arrive at the terminal do not have the taxi wait. You'll look nice in a red hat, so wear a red hat and carry a Bible. Come alone. Wait until I contact you. I like the heart-shaped gold pendant with garnets you wore that rainy day we met at Sano's.

Two hours later, the letter from Anne Brown lay on police Major Ed Cantrell's desk surrounded by Frank Ault, Glen Shafer, Leroy Carr, and Al Hodge. One notable absentee: Elizabeth. As soon as she read the note from Anne Brown, she called Frank. He informed Cantrell and Shafer. Cantrell called Leroy Carr. They decided not to bring Elizabeth into the station. The German spy might be watching and smell the trap if she saw a police car pick up Elizabeth and whisk her away to police headquarters soon after reporting to work on the day the spy knew Elizabeth would receive the letter. And so that no policemen were seen going into the *Observer*, young Officer Christian, wearing some hastily gathered, ill-fitting workman's clothes borrowed from a janitor's locker at the District 1 station, entered the newspaper building by way of an alley delivery dock to pick up the letter from Elizabeth. Frank would go over the plan for Friday with Elizabeth later.

The note from Anne Brown had been hastily studied by all the men. First checked was the envelope's return address, which turned out to be an empty lot near Washington Park.

Leroy Carr led off. "Notice the envelope stamp. It's a canceled stamp, but if you look closely you'll see it went through the post office two weeks ago. She took that stamp off another envelope and glued it on to make it look as if the post office delivered the letter. The markings next to the stamp that are always present alongside a canceled stamp have been drawn on. Anne Brown delivered this note to the newspaper mailroom herself."

"Why go to all that trouble?" Shafer asked. "She used a fake return address. Why not just mail it?"

"Two reasons: first, she wanted control over when Elizabeth read the note. There are no guarantees the post office will deliver a letter on a certain day, even a letter going just across town. Anne Brown wanted Elizabeth to read the letter in time, but not any earlier than necessary. The meeting is tomorrow, and to Brown, Elizabeth is an unknown factor. If Elizabeth received the letter yesterday and decided to let her husband know, it would give the police two days to plan for the capture instead of just one. And Brown couldn't afford to have the message arrive Friday afternoon—too late then. So she delivered it herself to control all that. The other reason she went to all the bother to make it look like official U.S. mail is sometimes nosey mailroom people will open and read other people's interoffice messages, but they won't open U.S. mail because they know that's a felony."

Ault said, "That would take a lot of balls to walk into a newspaper that has published a drawing of you, even if you could change your appearance as she's been doing."

"Yeah," Al Hodge agreed, "but she's got the balls, at least figuratively speaking."

Shafer noted: "Of course the red hat is for easy identification in a crowd, but what's the Bible for, and the stuff about the necklace Elizabeth wore when they met? Why the chit chat in the note? What's she trying to do, impress Elizabeth that she's smooth?"

Carr answered, "Nothing is chit chat. There are no wasted words in the note. Every word means something. Elizabeth did not name the restaurant in her article about their meeting. Anne Brown wrote about the necklace and named the restaurant to prove to Elizabeth the note is from her and not some crackpot or prankster. And as you said, the red hat is so she can spot Elizabeth in a crowd from afar. We all know Brown will be somewhere in the background tomorrow and leery of a trap. She won't be sitting in front of Gate 5 reading a book when Elizabeth gets there. The Bible is there as a back-up sign in case of coincidence; another woman could show up in a red hat and be similar in appearance to Elizabeth, at least from a distance. It's not impossible; things like that can happen."

"I don't like the part in the note about Elizabeth not having the taxi wait," said Ault. "That sounds to me like Brown might have plans to take her someplace else. I'm not going to let that happen."

"No," Carr said. "I agree; we can't let that happen. Frank, when you brief Elizabeth, tell her to go nowhere other than Gate 5 and don't leave Union Terminal under any circumstances. We'll make the arrest as soon as Elizabeth is approached."

Ault said, "I want a cop driving the taxi in case Brown tries to double-shuffle us and get to Elizabeth before she gets to the train station." He turned to Cantrell. "Chuck Warzyniak."

Cantrell nodded, and Carr insisted: "It must be someone who hasn't been driving Elizabeth or been seen with her in the last month. We know Brown has followed Elizabeth on occasion. If Brown recognizes the taxi driver as a cop it will blow everything."

"Already a step ahead of you, Carr," said Ault. "Warzyniak fits that bill."

"And, Frank," Carr added, "you know you can't hang around the terminal tomorrow. Brown will recognize you in a heartbeat regardless of what you're wearing."

"Bullshit, Carr!" Frank leapt from his chair. "I'm there. No discussion!"

"Keep your shirt on, Frank," Cantrell said.

"To hell with that, Cantrell! There's no goddamn way that I'm not going to be there!" Ault looked at Carr. "Carr, go fuck yourself, and you too, Hodge!"

"Frank, if you'll let me finish . . ." Cantrell turned to Leroy Carr: "Carr, we know you're in charge, but you can't expect Frank to stay away. This is his wife we're putting in danger. There has to be some type of disguise or concealment we can come up with for Frank. We'll take care of that. Now, what's your plan for tomorrow?"

Chapter 35

Gate 5

Friday, October 15, 1943

Last night, despite her husband's offer, Elizabeth did not dine out. She did not own a red hat, and by the time Frank explained to her the plan for capturing Anne Brown, and add to that the time it took Elizabeth to rush out, find a store still open, and buy a red hat (she chose a straw weave hat with a turned-up brim that did not have to be pinned to her hair) there was no time left for a restaurant. Dinner, at home, was canned chicken noodle soup and a grilled cheese sandwich that they split down the middle at 9:15 p.m. Luckily, she did not have to take time to find a store to buy a Bible (she had one at home) or the soup and half-sandwich would have been eaten even later.

Anne Brown's note specified Union Terminal for the meeting. The train station was always a hub of activity, especially now with the war. Scores of out-of-town soldiers, sailors, and Marines passed through daily on their way to other places. Adding to the crowd, military men and women who lived in Cincinnati were dropped off, or picked up, by family members there for sad goodbyes to sons, husbands, and fathers shipping out, or happy greetings to those coming home on brief leaves. Add to those totals the everyday civilian travelers to create a shoulder-to-shoulder setting for Elizabeth's meeting with the German spy. Good for the spy; not so good for her husband and the others whose job was to watch out for her.

Last night Frank told Elizabeth the taxi would pick her up at 11:20 a.m. and the driver would be a police officer in disguise. Frank chose Chuck Warzyniak, a veteran detective assigned to Vice. Frank's description of him to Elizabeth: *He's short and wide, dark hair, a tough Polack who isn't afraid to kick some rear ends when he has to.* Frank said Warzyniak would not be told specifics—only that his assignment was a brief, one-day undercover job, and his number one order: protect Elizabeth no matter what.

The Yellow Cab arrived on time. Elizabeth, her red hat, and her Bible were ready. Frank left the house at 7:30 that morning, his usual time. Before he left, he promised Elizabeth he would be near Gate 5, watching her every second.

You won't see me Elizabeth, but I'll be there. So will Glen, some other officers working undercover both inside and outside the terminal, and Carr and his OSS buddy. We'll all be there watching out for you. I want to capture Brown as much as anyone else, but I'm looking out for you first, everything else comes second. Don't worry. Just play it like we talked about and everything will be okay. Just watch your step as soon as you leave the house. Remember what I said about the taxi. Anne Brown told you in the note to leave from the house in a taxi. We have to consider everything, including that she might send her own taxi early to pick you up and take you somewhere else. Warzyniak will keep the front passenger window closed when he pulls up in front of the house. He'll watch for you. When he sees you coming, he'll roll down the front passenger window so you can ask him the question I told you to ask. If that window doesn't go down, or you don't hear the right answer to the question, run as fast as you can back to the house. Christian will be watching and he knows his number one job is to protect you. I told Christian if he sees you turn around and head back to the house to run out there and arrest the driver.

Ray Christian now stood at the edge of the living room window. Curtains drawn, he peered out at the cab through a slit. Frank had sneaked Christian in the house via the back door before dawn. Elizabeth walked to the front door, put her hand on the knob, then stopped, took a deep breath and exhaled. "Wish me luck," she said to Christian just before opening the door and stepping out.

The taxi had stopped on the street, directly in front of the house. Elizabeth stayed on the walkway that divided the front yard. She saw the front passenger window go down, a relief. The driver was a stocky man with black hair, bushy eyebrows, and a five-o'clock shadow. Elizabeth leaned over and spoke through the open window.

"Where did you get your cauliflower ear?" she asked.

"Your husband gave it to me," the driver answered.

Again relieved, Elizabeth got into the back.

"Hello, Elizabeth," the driver said as he stepped on the gas. "I'm Chuck Warzyniak."

"Hi."

"It's true," said Warzyniak.

"What's true?"

"That pain-in-the-ass husband of yours gave me this cauliflower ear. I finished second to that sonuvabitch two years in a row in the police boxing tournament. Excuse my French. But I like Frank; we get along good. He's my kind of cop."

"Why's that?"

"Why's what? Why do I like Frank?"

"No, why is he your kind of cop?"

"He'll conk the head of a guy who needs his head conked and ask questions later."

"Oh, really?" Elizabeth had suspected as much.

"Yeah. Good cop." To Chuck Warzyniak, the willingness and ability to conk heads were necessary skills all good policemen should hone. "How do you like my hat?" Warzyniak said as he made a right turn onto McMillan Street.

"I like it," Elizabeth assured him. He wore a gray cotton Greek fisherman's hat.

"Frank told me to not shave this morning and to look like a cabbie, so at the cab garage I took the guy's hat when I took his cab," Warzyniak broke out in loud laughter and made another turn. "I'll give him back his cab, but I'm keeping the hat." More laughter.

"Nice touch," Elizabeth surprised herself when she smiled at the gregarious policeman's banter. Earlier that morning, she worried that on this drive to meet Anne Brown, she would squirm in her seat, or much worse: lose her nerve.

Elizabeth noticed Warzyniak looking at her in the rearview mirror. He asked, "You're that reporter broad, right?"

"Yes, I'm the reporter broad."

"How did Frank ever latch onto a classy dame like you? Do you have poor eyesight?"

"Yes, very poor eyesight."

She thought his eyesight question was a joke, but apparently not. Her attempt to joke with him went over his head. Warzyniak nodded, and said seriously: "I knew a good looking broad like you had to have something wrong with you to be forced to settle for Frank. Sorry to hear it."

The train station was not far, and after another turn they drove past the Union Terminal fountain and pool. The terminal building loomed ahead. Warzyniak pulled over and stopped in the area marked for taxis near the main entrance.

"Get out first, and then don't forget to pay me," Warzyniak reminded.

"Right," said Elizabeth. Frank had told her the same. Her husband also told her to not watch the taxi drive away. Frank said no one watches a taxi drive away unless they know someone in it. *She might be looking for that,* Frank had warned. Elizabeth got out and paid while standing at the front passenger window. Warzyniak gave her change, and told her, "Tell Frank I said he got lucky when he beat me in the tournament and I want a rematch. And tell him I said he's a bum." He drove away laughing. Elizabeth turned her back to avoid watching the cab pull away, squared her shoulders, and, under a red straw hat and carrying a Bible, walked into Union Terminal at a quarter to twelve.

Before Union Terminal was built, passengers used five separate railway terminals, three of which flooded regularly, all in various stages of disrepair. But Union Terminal changed all that, consolidating all the railway companies in one location. When the new terminal opened in 1933, Cincinnati went overnight (after four years of construction) from being known as having some of the worst railroad facilities in the nation to what many argued were the best—and most beautiful. Travelers found themselves either speechless or muttering *"Wow!"* the first time they stood looking up at the multicolored rotunda ceiling ten stories overhead. Besides marveling at the enormously high ceiling, visitors admired the walls of limestone and shining glass, and the colorful mosaic tiles underfoot. Eye catching fluorescent signs pointed the way to coffee shops, restaurants, and stores.

Elizabeth had been inside the terminal many times. She admired the avant-garde design, and her first visit several years ago had been simply to admire the Art Deco architecture and Maxfield Keck wall murals—said to be the largest collection of non-religious murals under one roof anywhere in the world. Since then she had returned to take occasional train trips herself, to greet or send off others, or to shop at one of the many stores; a few times she and Frank had come together to dine in one of several restaurants. Today, however, murals, shops, and restaurants were not on Elizabeth Ault's mind.

With the metal chairs and wooden benches full of travelers waiting to travel, and others there to greet or say goodbye, many people were forced to stand. Crowds of various sizes huddled everywhere, like football squads calling a play. A small group of Marines stood over here; over there, at the Baltimore & Ohio Railway ticket counter, a larger cluster of people, both military and civilian, waited to have their tickets checked.

Elizabeth began the walk down the main concourse to Gate 5. At the first gate she approached, the Norfolk and Western gate, travelers from Pittsburgh and other points along the way had just disembarked. Elizabeth wove her way through the mob and was jostled several times. Then she walked past, in order, the Chesapeake and Ohio gate, the L&N gate, and the Pennsylvania Railway gate. Each area had its crowds.

Southern Railway typically used Gate 5. When Elizabeth got there all the benches were full. Military men filled half the seats (Elizabeth did notice a few women in uniforms sprinkled about); the rest filled with civilians. She found a place to stand against a wall between a cigarette vending machine and a trash can. Three large posters hung over the cigarette machine. The largest poster pictured men in uniforms crowded onto a loading platform waiting to board a train and read: MILLIONS OF TROOPS ARE ON THE MOVE . . . IS *YOUR* TRIP NECESSARY? The other posters advertised cigarettes. On one a photograph of Ernie Pyle bore the caption: A FIRST HAND REPORT FROM A FIRST HAND REPORTER, then Ernie was quoted: *"IT'S CHESTERFIELD ON EVERY FRONT I'VE COVERED . . . WITH OUR BOYS AND ALLIES, CHESTERFIELD IS ALWAYS THE FAVORITE."* Another poster promoted Kool menthol cigarettes: THEY WILL CLEAR YOUR HEAD AND PREVENT COLDS.

Elizabeth wanted to be familiar with her surroundings and looked around the Gate 5 area. She saw an old man with a gray beard pushing a hotdog cart. Sitting people talked with others, read newspapers or magazines, or slept. Besides the considerable number of fighting men, the civilians reflected every age group and life's circumstance: grandmothers, grandfathers, moms, dads, brothers, sisters, the poor and the well-to-do—all were there waiting for trains. A group of three Orthodox Jews in traditional black dress sat near the back, their long, curly side strands falling from beneath black hats. Elizabeth saw a Marine lacking an arm. Several Negro porters in black uniforms with small, black box hats cocked to the side of their heads loaded luggage onto dollies. Like Elizabeth, some people stood, others walked—some in one direction, some a different way. She looked for her husband, Glen Shafer, or Leroy Carr, the three men she knew among the several Frank told her would be undercover. She saw no one she knew.

Of course, she looked for Anne Brown even though Elizabeth did not expect to see her until the exact moment Anne Brown was ready to be seen. She had not recognized Anne Brown that day at Sano's even when the woman sat directly across a small table; Brown had to let her know. Even Frank, an experienced detective, walked on by her.

Two Army privates, talking and laughing loudly, jolted Elizabeth from her pondering when they stopped at the cigarette machine next to her. One of them dropped a coin into the slot and noisily pulled a handle. A pack of Lucky Strikes fell to the tray.

Elizabeth pulled a crumpled pack of Old Golds with only one cigarette left from her purse and put the cigarette to her lips. She wedged the Bible under her arm to free both hands for the search through her purse for matches but found none. Instead of returning the cigarette to the pack, she impatiently threw it and the empty pack into the trash can.

Her wristwatch pointed to ten minutes after twelve. The note did not stipulate when Anne Brown would meet her; it simply ordered Elizabeth to arrive by noon and wait. Remembering how befuddled and frantic she felt at Sano's, Elizabeth determined this meeting would be different. And she thought she had conducted herself well so far, remaining more or less calm, even joking with Chuck Warzyniak during the ride to the terminal. But now . . . she did not want her nerves to get a foothold and decided if she moved about it might help. She walked around the Gate 5 area for a few minutes. Maybe she spotted Leroy Carr in an Army officer's uniform sitting on a bench reading a newspaper but wasn't sure; she quickly diverted her eyes, and the man's cap and newspaper kept her from a clear view of his face. A call-to-board the 1245 to Cleveland came through the loudspeaker. This cleared spaces on some benches, so Elizabeth sat down in the front row, facing the boarding gate. She placed her purse on the bench beside her and held the Bible in her lap where it could be easily seen. If that Army officer was Leroy Carr, he was seven or eight rows back and several benches to her left.

She saw no signs of Frank or Glen, but Frank warned her not to expect it. Last night he told her: *Anne Brown has apparently followed me, and she might have seen Glen driving you yesterday. Glen and I will have to be more careful than Carr and Hodge. She's never seen them.*

Frank did not know, as Elizabeth did, that there was no "might" when it came to Anne Brown having seen Glen Shafer. There was that night outside the Rusty Bottom.

12:40. A sailor sat down on the bench a few feet away and set his duffle bag on the floor between his legs. He pulled a pack of Pall Malls from a pants pocket and lit one.

"Do you have a spare smoke, sailor?" Elizabeth asked.

"Sure do." He shook another cigarette from the pack as he scooted himself and the duffle bag closer. He extended the pack to Elizabeth.

"Thanks." She pulled the half-exposed cigarette out. "I need a light." He was ready and struck a match.

"Where you headed?" the sailor asked with a Southern accent as he held the fire to the cigarette. When the end of the cigarette glowed orange, he shook the match dead and threw it to the floor. He looked very young, probably still in his teens.

"I live here," Elizabeth answered. "I'm meeting someone arriving."

"Oh, okay," he said. "I'm from Augusta. That's in the great state of Georgia. I just finished a week's leave at home after radar school. Now I'm shipping out to the Pacific. I'm on a tin can that's waiting for us in San Francisco. It was great to see my folks and Sally Jo."

Elizabeth knew a *tin can* was a ship, a Navy destroyer. "Is Sally Jo your girl?"

"You bet. We'll get married when I get back . . . at least I hope so. Haven't asked her yet, but I'm going to as soon as I get home. Hope she says 'yes.'"

"She'll say 'yes,'" Elizabeth promised and hoped she was right. "Send her a letter and tell her you want to marry her when you get home."

"Yeah? That's okay to do that? Propose in a letter?"

"Yes, if you can't be together it is, especially now, with the war. But do it with a letter. A woman would rather get a letter than a phone call. That way she has proof." Elizabeth smiled at the boy.

"Okay, thanks. I should have asked her before I left so we could get married before I shipped out. That way she'd get my benefits . . . and be waiting for me when I get back from the war." For the next 20 minutes the sailor talked of Sally Jo, his parents and two sisters, but mostly of Sally Jo. Elizabeth tried to be attentive, yet sometimes found herself distracted with her own concerns of the moment. Nevertheless, she made sure to occasionally smile pleasantly and nod at the boy as he continued on with stories of home.

At 1:00 the loudspeaker blared: *"BOARDING WILL NOW BEGIN AT GATE 5 FOR THE 135 TO SAINT LOUIS, KANSAS CITY, DENVER, SALT LAKE CITY, AND SAN FRANCISCO."*

"Hey, that's mine," said the sailor. He rose and swung his duffle bag over his shoulder. "It was nice to meet you, ma'am."

"Very nice meeting you," Elizabeth said. "God bless you, and good luck with Sally Jo. She'll wait for you," Elizabeth assured him. Again she hoped she was right; she hoped Sally Jo would wait.

The boy's smile was wide. He walked away, disappearing forever to some unknown fate—a fate resting in the hands of the Japanese and Sally Jo—through Gate 5. He never told Elizabeth his name, nor did he ask for hers.

1:15. Elizabeth wanted another cigarette and left the bench for the cigarette machine. As she walked, she glanced toward where the man she thought might be Leroy Carr sat earlier; he was no longer there.

Before the war, cigarettes cost a dime a pack. After Pearl Harbor a pack shot up to twenty cents in the stores and a quarter from a vending machine—good old American supply and demand. The fighting boys had to be taken care of first and no one complained about that, but that big demand put limits on the tobacco earmarked for civilian sales and the price skyrocketed. Elizabeth dropped a quarter into the slot and pulled the Old Gold handle. Nothing came out, and only then did she notice the empty Old Gold dispenser. *Great.* She dropped in another quarter and pulled the Chesterfield knob. A pack fell to the tray and she looked up at Ernie Pyle. *I hope this makes you happy.* Still she needed a light, and asked for one from a middle-aged lady she saw smoking nearby. When Elizabeth returned to the benches to wait, a harried mother trying to keep a rambunctious toddler in tow had taken her seat, but she found another spot two benches away, also in the front.

1:30. Since Elizabeth arrived at Gate 5, regardless if she stood, walked, or sat, she often swiveled her head looking for Anne Brown, hoping she might at least avoid the shock of seeing the spy standing next to her without warning. Every time Elizabeth saw a woman who looked to be anywhere near mid-twenties she looked closely, paying no attention to clothes, eyeglasses, make-up, or hair color, but gazing only at the face, hoping she might recognize her. *How long is this going to go on? Where is she? I've done okay until now. Calm down . . . calm down . . .*

At 1:50 the waiting began taking its toll. Elizabeth suddenly felt angry. Angry at Anne Brown. First, there had been her fixation with Brown after the Lamar Apartments attack. Next, the surprise meeting at Sano's where Elizabeth panicked and embarrassed herself in front of Brown and in front of Frank. But all that was before Elizabeth learned who Anne Brown really was—an enemy spy. Then, since that day at Sano's, she had been chaperoned when out in public like a school kid on a field trip. And now this: sitting in a train depot in a silly red hat waiting, waiting, and waiting some more. Since the night of the attack, Elizabeth felt her life had been dominated by and under the complete control of Anne Brown and it now made her mad.

2:05. By now Elizabeth had watched hosts of people walk through Gate 5, either watching their backs as they passed through the gate on their way to the departure platform, or looking at their faces as they arrived in Cincinnati. She had arrived at Gate 5 over two hours ago and still no sign of Anne Brown. Elizabeth looked to the left. A man and a woman carrying a baby approached and walked on by. She looked to the right. An Army sergeant walked past, and a heavy woman with a limp came from the direction of Gate 4. Elizabeth turned her head back to face front. Suddenly she turned to again look at the heavy woman with a limp. The woman walked toward her, about 50 feet away. The limping woman looked at Elizabeth and smiled.

The woman was Clare Miller.

Chapter 36

Mexican Loco

Ciudad Juárez, Mexico—[same day]

They played Mexican Loco in an office above the *La tintorería Sol* dry cleaning business on Avenida 16 de Septiembre, three blocks from Calle Mariscal.

Alfredo Kohler Plácido enthusiastically threw down two pairs—jacks and eights. He knew he had won. Playing poker with Alfredo were José, Paco, and Luís, only four players in all, so the pots never amounted to much with the low stakes. Still, winning money from friends was much more agreeable than losing, never mind the amount, and Alfredo grinned with satisfaction as he shoveled the money toward him.

"Qué barbaridad!" José exclaimed as the money moved away. "The third pot in a row for the mestizo." José worked at the dry cleaners and played during his lunchtime. Paco and Luís were friends who stopped in for the weekly afternoon card game. Alfredo worked at the cleaners too; his father and mother owned the business.

Alfredo laughed and took a bite of a mango. When he won, his friends tried to get his goat by referring to him as a half-breed, a *mestizo,* but he didn't care. On the contrary, to Alfredo his dual nationality was a matter of pride. Alfredo's father, a German from Frankfurt, came to Mexico unemployed in 1923, found work and a wife (Alfredo's mother, Marisol Plácido, was originally from Torreón) and ended up staying.

Gustav Kohler took his wife, son and daughter to visit family in Frankfurt in 1937 when Alfredo was 13 years old, his sister 10. In Germany, Alfredo learned a great deal about the German side of his family, and he had fond memories of the trip and of his father's homeland. Especially well-remembered was the 11-day voyage each way across the Atlantic—Alfredo had never been in a boat larger than a canoe, and certainly never on an ocean. He found he loved the sea and now dreamed of someday working on a merchant ship. And he remembered vividly a beautiful, 14-year-old blonde, blue-eyed second cousin named Ute who led him into the woods one day during a family picnic and treated him to a very long and exciting kiss on the lips—his first, at least his first very long and exciting one. Now out of school, Alfredo would soon be on his own, and he hoped to take another trip to Europe someday when the war was over. He sometimes wondered how Ute, who would be 20 now, fared with the war going on around her.

Alfredo's father allowed the young men to gather in this upstairs room once a week to play cards as long as they did not disturb anything. Not only his father's office, the room also served as a storage area—shelves lined two walls piled high with detergents, solvents, brushes, rags and assorted linens, boxes, and bags. His father's desk sat in a front corner near the only window to the avenue below. Next to the desk was a table supporting a cumbersome machine that looked like something a mad scientist had created by mating a radio with a large, heavy, and complicated typewriter. Alfredo's friends had asked about this machine and he answered honestly with what little he knew: *It is something my father brought in and set up about four years ago, something to do with business.*

Rarely did Alfredo see his father use this piece of equipment, perhaps no more than a dozen times over the four years, but he had seen the odd contraption, without anyone controlling it, start humming, clicking and clattering. Keys pounded out letters onto long, thin strips of paper fed from a spool inside the machine, the letters forming strange words not in Spanish. Alfredo had learned some German from his father and a bit of English in school, and he thought the words were not in any of those languages either. The strange words appeared on their own, as if an invisible ghost had pulled up a chair and sat typing a letter to home in some unknown spirit language. And even though the peculiar gadget stayed quiet most of the time—sometimes hibernating for months—his father fussed over it: cleaning it inside and out, making sure the paper spool was full, and replacing the ink ribbon twice monthly regardless of whether the machine had printed anything. As far as Alfredo knew, his father's strange machine had now sat dormant for at least three months, maybe four. Nevertheless, Alfredo knew exactly what to do if he saw the machine working when his father was not in the room: find his father immediately. Normally, this was not a problem. His father spent most of his time downstairs, where he was now, working alongside Alfredo's mother and sister in the laundry.

"It's your deal, Paco," Luís said. Everyone tossed two pesos to the middle of the table. Paco shuffled the deck and had just offered José the cut when suddenly Gustav Kohler's strange machine started making noise.

Chapter 37

Servicemen's Discount

Cincinnati—[same day]

Union Terminal

Never before in her life could Elizabeth Ault remember her jaw dropping from surprise as it did when she saw Clare Miller walking toward her in Union Terminal. *No, it can't be.* Elizabeth tried to concentrate. Could Clare be here to meet someone arriving? Was her appearance here today just one of those strange coincidences that sometimes happen? If so, and the spy was somehow watching, what would happen to the meeting? Would Anne Brown leave?

"Clare?" Elizabeth knew it was Clare Miller so she did not intend to raise the inflection at the end of the syllable and say the name like a question. It just came out that way.

"Yes, it's me. Hi, Mrs. Ault—Elizabeth, I mean. You said to call you Elizabeth."

Elizabeth nodded but had not yet made up her mind on which words to use.

"May I sit down?" asked Clare. "It's been a long walk."

"I'm sorry. Yes, please sit." Elizabeth moved her purse and Clare sat beside her.

"Whew, that's better. I was starting to think I wouldn't make it. That's a long walk."

"Clare," Elizabeth decided on her words and talked quickly, "I can't explain why, but I need to know what you are doing here. Are you meeting someone? If you are and this is the gate, I think it best that we not sit together."

Clare looked surprised. "Anne told me you'd be expecting me."

It was not easy, but Elizabeth stopped her jaw from dropping a second time. "Anne Brown told you I would be expecting you? You've talked to Anne Brown?"

"Yes. This morning she got on the bus I take to work. I was glad to see she's okay. I've been worried about her. She asked me to give you this." Clare reached into her purse and removed a sealed envelope with *for Elizabeth* written and underlined on the front.

230

"Anne Brown got on your bus this morning and asked you to come here—told you I'd be here—and asked you to give me this?"

"Yes," Clare answered. "Anne told me she wanted to get all this behind her but she was scared. She said she set up a meeting with you here at Gate 5 today at two o'clock, but she was having second thoughts about coming herself and was afraid. Then she asked me to come and give you the envelope, and told me she would call you and tell you I was coming with the note. I'm a little worried because I've been gone from work longer than my lunch break, but I figured since it was for you that you would clear it for me if my boss at the newspaper is mad."

Elizabeth remembered that Clare worked as a typist and teletype operator at the *Observer*. She needed to think. Should she open the envelope now, or wait and give it to Frank? What about fingerprints? But they already had Anne Brown's fingerprints. No, fingerprints should not matter. Elizabeth opened the envelope and read the note. Clare watched Elizabeth blush. Elizabeth folded the paper, put it back in the envelope, and then sat back farther on the bench to think. Clare waited for a long moment, not asking about the note.

Eventually, Clare saw Elizabeth put the Bible she held on her lap into her purse, then turn and look at her, the envelope still in her hand.

"Clare, I'm going to take off my hat. When I do, some men will come quickly. One of them is my husband. You know him, and I don't want you to be frightened by the others, okay?"

Instantly, Clare looked very worried. "Men? . . . your husband? . . . What? . . . W-w-why?" she stuttered.

"Don't be afraid, Clare. Everything will be okay."

Elizabeth removed the red straw hat. This started an immediate rush toward her by the three Orthodox Jews, the hot dog vendor, an Army officer (Elizabeth was right), a Negro porter, and a woman dressed as a Southern Railways employee who had been checking tickets as people walked through Gate 5. The Negro porter and the woman surprised even Elizabeth.

Clare Miller panicked, tried rising to her feet, lost balance, and dropped to her knees—painfully. Quickly, Elizabeth knelt beside her. Sure that Clare did not know Anne Brown's true colors, Elizabeth remembered that any reference to spying was taboo. "It's okay, Clare. Anne shot two men and these people are here to protect me. It has nothing to do with you, believe me."

[District 1 police station: 6:15 p.m.—three hours later]

Elizabeth sat in a chair by her husband's desk waiting for him to return from the interrogation room where he and Leroy Carr had taken Clare Miller. Elizabeth had insisted on staying with Clare on the ride to headquarters. She felt sorry for Clare who was obviously terrified, and just as obviously an innocent pawn in Anne Brown's game.

Elizabeth's feelings about the day were mixed. She felt a tinge of relief that she had been spared seeing and dealing with Anne Brown again, but at the same time there was disappointment—the spy must be captured. And the note Clare delivered: had Elizabeth made a mistake that tipped off Anne Brown? What would happen now? Was hope of catching her lost?

Elizabeth could thank Anne Brown for one thing. Since the day Brown approached her and involved her directly in the case, Elizabeth had learned a great deal about her husband's day-to-day work as a cop, something she knew little about before that rainy day at Sano's. She had been in this room before but only for brief moments now and then, occasionally stopping by his desk to say hello if she was at the station for a press conference (if he happened to be in and not on the streets, the latter being common). Getting Frank to open up and talk at home about his job was a waste of time: easier to chew glass and walk on tacks than to get Frank Ault to talk about his day. All this added up to Elizabeth knowing little about her husband's work setting and daily routine. But over the course of the past two weeks, and after sitting for hours today at his desk, watching and listening, she learned—despite the phantom of Anne Brown looming over her life.

In some ways the room was not unlike the *Observer* newsroom, though on a smaller scale. Twenty or so scuffed wooden desks (about half as many as her newsroom) with scuffed wooden chairs on a scuffed wooden floor. Like the newsroom, a telephone or two always rang somewhere in the room and people walked, sat, and stood. But here, instead of the room divided by departments called *City, Feature,* or *Sports,* the two departments were called *Homicide* and *Vice.* On different floors were *Burglary/Robbery, Bunco, Assault* and other departments. A detective two desks away questioned a bleached-blonde prostitute in a purple dress who looked to be about Elizabeth's age. That the detective and the woman knew each other was obvious.

232

Elizabeth overheard the woman ask the detective about his children and he asked her the same question.

"Where did you get those nylons, Bernice?" Elizabeth also overheard the detective ask the woman. "They look new."

"Been saving them, Earl," the prostitute answered then popped her chewing gum. "Why, do you like them?" She hiked her dress up past her underpants to show more of the stockings.

"They're real nice, Bernice. You can pull your dress down now. I asked because I hope you're not getting them from the black market. The fine for black market purchases is more than the fine for your line of work."

"Thanks for the warning. You got a smoke?"

The detective opened a drawer, took out a pack of Viceroys and a book of matches and laid them in front of her.

"Thanks."

"So how's business, Bernice?"

"Never been better. Servicemen everywhere and they all got money. Sometimes there ain't enough hours in the night to take care of them all and I have to ask friends to help out. I offer a servicemen's discount. It's my part for the war effort." Bernice saluted with her left hand.

"That's real red, white, and blue of you, Bernice." While she smoked he filled out paperwork, then he waved over a uniformed officer from the Sergeants Desk, which was actually a long, high judge's bench at the far end of the room. "Okay, Bernice, you know how this works. Unfortunately it won't be just a one-nighter this time. Since this is Friday, you'll stay with us until Monday morning. You can't see the judge and pay your fine until then."

"Fuck! I forgot about that! Shit!" She paused, and then came up with a plan. "Earl, let me go and I'll make it worth your while."

"Sorry, Bernice, no can do." The detective handed the paperwork to the uniformed cop. "Officer Harmon here will take you to the floozy tank. You know, Bernice, we're going to have to put your name on one of those cots down there."

"Shit! Earl. I don't want to be here all weekend. I've got too many customers depending on me. I'll lose them to my competition."

"Just doing my job, Bernice. You do your job and I do mine." As Officer Harmon led Bernice away the detective reminded the woman: "Remember what I told you about the black market and those nylons, Bernice. Don't get caught." The uniform and Bernice disappeared through the door just before Glen Shafer entered and walked over to Elizabeth. He still wore the black pants and white shirt from his Orthodox Jew disguise. The beard, wig, black hat, and black tie were gone.

"Elizabeth," said Glen. "Frank sent me to take you home. He said there's no need for you to wait around here."

"How's Clare Miller?"

"She's doing okay. Questioning was rough at first. She was hysterical but we got her calmed down eventually. Carr and Frank have been with her the entire time. Frank came out to tell me to take you home."

"I think I'll wait for Frank. Clare's not in trouble, right? I mean, she obviously was duped."

"I don't think she's in trouble, but that's for Carr to decide. He's in charge." Shafer paused, then added in a lower voice. "Look, I understand if you don't want me driving you home. It was Frank's idea. I can get someone else."

"It's not that, Glen, honestly. That's over. I would have no problem with you taking me home. But I'll wait for Frank, and I want to make sure Clare is okay."

Shafer did not argue. "Alright, I'll tell Frank you want to wait."

"Thanks, Glen."

It took another hour, but Frank finally appeared. He went to the Sergeants Desk, handed the sergeant on duty some papers and spoke to the man for a moment. Ault wore the same clothes he left the house in that morning. The hot dog vender clothes, apron, eyeglasses, beard, and hat were gone. As he walked toward her, Elizabeth smiled at him.

Frank said, "Hi."

"Hi." She rushed into his arms. "I love you, Frank."

He hugged her. "I love you, babe. You did a great job today. I'm proud of you."

"Thanks, but I didn't do much, and it didn't take much courage. I knew you were there looking out for me."

"It took courage."

"How's Clare? She's not in trouble is she, Frank? She's not going to be held here overnight, right?"

"No. I told her I would take her home so you and I will do that. Clare knows nothing about Anne Brown being a spy, and we didn't tell her. Let's be careful we don't talk about that in the car."

The interrogation room was on the second floor, one floor below Homicide. When they got there, Clare sat on a bench outside the room. Leroy Carr, no longer an Army officer, and Al Hodge stood nearby. When Clare saw Elizabeth approaching, she rose and hobbled to her, tears misting. Elizabeth and Clare hugged in silence.

No one discussed the day's events. Elizabeth walked with Clare as Frank went on ahead to move the car close. Frank's unmarked Plymouth was a two-door so Elizabeth had Clare sit in the front where getting in and out was easier. She helped Clare get in, then walked around to Frank's side and got into the back.

They had driven less than a block before Clare asked about Anne Brown. "Is Anne going to talk to you, Elizabeth? Is that what the note was about?"

Frank interrupted. "We can't talk about that, Clare. Sorry, but all of that is part of a homicide investigation."

"But Anne saved Penny and me so she shouldn't be in too much trouble. You still think that don't you, Detective Ault?"

"She should come in and talk to us so we can get this case laid to rest. I've always said that. Clare, I doubt if Anne Brown will contact you again but if she does I want you to call me immediately. I understand how you feel about her. She saved you and Penny so you feel loyalty and feel that you owe her, but you have to call me right away if you hear from her again, understand?"

"Yes," Clare said meekly.

During the rest of the ride little was said. At one point, Clare mentioned Penny and how she would like to see her again. When they arrived at the Lamar Apartments, both Frank and Elizabeth helped Clare up to her apartment.

To be back in the car and finally alone with her husband was an enormous relief for Elizabeth. It was almost 8:00 p.m. and neither of them had eaten since yesterday.

"I'm starving," Frank said as he turned the key and pulled the headlight knob.

"Me too." She almost made a joke that he should have eaten some of his hot dogs at the train station and brought her one, but she was mentally exhausted and not in the mood for humor. Seeing Frank with a beard and apron and Glen Shafer disguised as an Orthodox Jew at any other time would cause her to fall on the floor laughing, but not today. She made only one comment about the disguises. "I spotted Leroy Carr not long after I got to Gate 5."

"Yeah, Carr and his partner didn't need to go to all the trouble with beards and all the crap that me and Glen did. They're unknown to Brown. They just borrowed a couple of Army uniforms from some men at the college ROTC office they work out of." Frank put the car in gear and drove away from the Lamar Apartments. "That's where the colored guy and woman came from. He's an Army recruiter, works down in the Negro section of town, came highly recommended. The woman is a WAC at the ROTC office. The other two guys dressed like Orthodox Jews with Glen are our guys. I don't think you know them. They work Bunco."

"What did you tell Clare Miller about Carr and his partner?"

"I didn't tell her anything. Carr told her some bull about being investigators for the State of Ohio. He even pulled out an I.D. to that effect. That guy has more phony I.D.s than a bus load of teenage boys in a striptease club. Where do you want to eat?"

"I don't care, just some place quick. I don't want to sit in a restaurant for an hour or more. We haven't had chili in awhile. How about the Chili Shack?"

"Okay," Frank responded. "Sounds good to me."

Elizabeth wanted to know. "Frank, what are your thoughts about the note?"

When Elizabeth opened the note at Union Terminal there were two words: *I'm disappointed.*

He answered, "She either knew for sure that you tipped me, which I doubt, or she suspected you would tip me and this was a test."

"A test?

"Maybe."

"Something else, Frank" said Elizabeth. "Clare told me that Anne Brown asked her to meet me at the terminal at two o'clock. Why would she tell Clare two o'clock when her note to me said noon?"

"Probably to give herself plenty of time to check things out."

"So you think she was there today?"

"At some point, sure."

Chapter 38

Chasing Geese

Saturday, October 16, 1943

Elizabeth always reported in at the *Observer* newsroom on Saturday. Sunday morning's paper was the week's most widely read, and unless she had a scoop during the week that could not wait, she preferred that her most important stories appear in the Sunday edition. And even if no Saturday night deadline loomed for the Sunday paper, Elizabeth still stopped in, if only briefly, to check messages and keep up on that day's newsroom scuttlebutt. This was the case today.

The note from the *Observer's* teletype room lay on top of her mail and messages waiting for her in the mailroom when she arrived at 1:30 p.m.

Message sent per authorized employee Elizabeth Ault: sd, Fuller
15 OCT 43: 1244 HOURS: 4583 KHz: 50baud/450 Hz: ITA2
Cincinnati Observer radio teletype Model 15, Teletype Corp., Skokie,
Illinois

Elizabeth recognized this type of note. The *Cincinnati Observer* gave its top reporters clearance to send messages to other newspapers through the paper's teletype machines and Elizabeth was one of those designated reporters. The *Observer* had three such machines—two connected to land lines and one radio teletype that sent messages by shortwave. Elizabeth had sent many communiqués to other newspapers around the country, and she knew this note came from one of the *Observer's* teletype operators to notify her that her message had been successfully sent.

But this message baffled. The last time Elizabeth had sent a teletype message was over a week ago when she sent one to the *Pittsburgh Post-Gazette* seeking details about a story it published concerning an inmate on the Pennsylvania State Penitentiary death row who just recently admitted to committing an unsolved murder in Cincinnati several years ago. But Elizabeth had received the confirmation note for that transmission the next day.

She looked again at the note. It said the message had been sent yesterday at 12:44 p.m. At 12:44 yesterday Elizabeth and her red hat both sat in Union Terminal waiting for Anne Brown.

Elizabeth picked up the telephone and called Frank.

Five hours later Elizabeth was on her way to District 1 police headquarters. When Frank received her phone call, he told her to not leave the newsroom. *I'll be right there, Elizabeth.* He brought Officer Christian with him. Frank took the teletype confirmation note but left Christian, ordering the young policeman to stay with Elizabeth until he called.

Frank's call finally came and Christian drove Elizabeth to headquarters. Frank, waiting outside, led her to Major Cantrell's office. There were no surprises as far as who was already in the office when she walked in: Cantrell, Leroy Carr, Al Hodge, and Glen Shafer. The men rose and Frank Ault pulled up a chair for his wife.

"Elizabeth," Cantrell said as everyone returned to their seats, "we think we now know what yesterday was all about. I'll let Mr. Carr here explain."

Carr began: "The first thing we did this afternoon, Elizabeth, after Frank brought us together to look over the teletype transmission note, was to locate the *Observer* teletype operator who sent you that note. Her name is Lea Fuller. Miss Fuller told us she has transmitted messages for you in the past."

"Yes," Elizabeth answered. "That's right. Lea has sent messages for me before and then sent me a confirmation."

"And Miss Fuller said sometimes you don't bring the messages to the teletype room yourself, but ask a copyboy or someone else, like an intern or student reporter to deliver them."

"Yes, that's pretty standard. Most reporters and editors use copyboys or anyone else who might be available at the time to deliver messages around the building."

Carr nodded. "Elizabeth, I feel as if I should apologize to you and everyone in this room. I'm in charge of this case and the responsibility falls on me. I allowed us to be made fools of. While we were all at Union Terminal yesterday, Anne Brown was at your newspaper sending a message over the radio teletype. Lea Fuller told us a student reporter, a female, brought her a message to transmit that was supposedly from you. I showed Miss Fuller the Evansville shipyard photograph and, of course, I don't have to tell you who the student reporter turned out to be. Different hairstyle and color, wearing glasses—all of that, but Lea Fuller had no doubt she was the woman in the photo."

"Anne Brown sent a message over our—the *Observer's*—radio teletype? To whom?" Elizabeth asked.

"We don't know. Normally the teletype operator would receive a confirmation from the person or newspaper that the message had been sent to letting them know the message had come through, but Miss Fuller never received a confirmation. Instructions on the message—again, supposedly from you—said to change the transmitting frequency from the normal band used to send communiqués to other newspapers. There is no way for us to know who was tuned to the frequency Anne Brown specified. Miss Fuller didn't question the change. She told us that occasionally the *Observer* teletype operators send messages using other frequencies and we confirmed that with Fuller's supervisor. We already have our people back in Washington working. They'll be able to take the frequency used and check it against atmospheric conditions yesterday afternoon when the message went out, and give us a likely radius of the miles the message could have covered without becoming garbled. But that's all we'll get—a radius from Cincinnati in all directions. We won't know a location."

Elizabeth knew the teletype operators were required to keep a copy of all messages sent. "What did the message say?"

Carr answered, "Obviously Anne Brown could not send a message encrypted in a German intelligence or military code. The words were in English." Carr handed Elizabeth a piece of paper.

JEHANNE
WINE AND HENRY POEM
BELATED FORAY ACUMEN IMPENDING

"Al has already sent that message to our headquarters in Washington to see if they can make anything of it."

Hodge added, speaking to everyone, "They'll work on it night and day."

Elizabeth continued to look at the note. "Wine and Henry poem" she said. "What could that mean?"

"No idea," Carr admitted. "Before you arrived, Elizabeth, I told everyone here that from my experience with German transmissions, the first line before the break usually identifies who the message is being sent to. If the message takes a relay to reach the intended recipient, which in this case is almost a certainty considering distances, Anne Brown wants that message to ultimately get into the hands of someone or someplace called *Jehanne*. The second line normally identifies who sent the message, so something in that second line tells *Jehanne* who the sender is—our Anne Brown. Then usually the message itself is the third line and beyond if there are more than three lines."

"I know Jehanne is French—a female name," Elizabeth stated.

"Right." Carr agreed. "It's the equivalent of *Jean* or *Jeanne* in English I think."

"Yes," Elizabeth confirmed. "Or *Joan*. Jehanne was Joan of Arc's real first name."

Leroy Carr flinched and hesitated.

Frank butted in and addressed the group. "Last night Elizabeth asked me if Anne Brown was at the terminal watching and I said 'yes,' and I told her the meeting might have been some kind of a test. I didn't feel very sure I was right, but that was the only thing I could come up with. Now we know Brown was never at Union Terminal and never had any intentions of showing up. The entire circus yesterday was nothing but a set up to get all of us out of the way so Brown could waltz into the *Observer* and transmit a message. Carr told us at the briefing the first day he got to town that Anne Brown, or whatever name she used in Evansville, lost her radio when she escaped. That's why this scheme with the radio teletype. Most of the radio teletypes are in possession of the military, only a limited number are available for civilian use and most of those are at large newspapers or a few large radio stations around the country. That's what you said about the civilian teletypes earlier, right, Carr?"

"That's right."

"Then I couldn't figure why Brown sent Clare Miller to the terminal," Frank admitted. "Why not just let us sit with our thumbs up our asses at Gate 5 for hours until we finally called it quits? Now I know the answer. Brown sent Clare Miller in her place for the same reason she sent us—to get Clare out of the way. She knew Clare occasionally worked in the *Observer* teletype room and Brown couldn't risk Clare being in there when she walked in. So Brown told Elizabeth to be at Gate 5 at noon and wait, and told Clare two o'clock. That would get everyone out of her way for at least two or three hours."

"I think that about sums it up," said Carr. "And that might be the reason Anne Brown was living in the Lamar Apartments in the first place. Maybe Brown had already identified Clare Miller as a civilian radio teletype operator and had moved into the apartments to get to know Miller, gain her confidence, then trick Miller into sending a message. But all that changed when Miller was attacked. Brown stopped the attack, maybe for her own selfish reasons—she didn't want Miller to be killed. But in any case Brown was forced to flee and hide and that forced a change in her plans. Elizabeth started writing those articles offering to meet with Brown and maybe that's what shifted Brown's focus to Elizabeth. Clearly Brown knows about civilian newspaper radio teletypes in this country. She would assume that Elizabeth, as one of the *Observer's* top reporters, would be authorized to have teletype messages transmitted from her newspaper's machines."

Frank shook his head in anger. "The goddamn fox sent us on a wild goose chase so she could steal into the henhouse and screw the chickens."

Despite Frank Ault's incorrect and bristly version of the old saw, no one laughed.

Chapter 39

Star of David

Evansville, Indiana— Friday, January 8, 1943

Forced to duck underneath a sagging utility wire heavy with icicles, Joe Mayer stepped from the warmth of Building 11 into a ruthless blast of river wind that swayed the wire and clinked the icicles. A light snow had begun falling, and even the snowflakes suffered from the blistering attack—the wind taking delight in swirling the light flakes about, refusing them rest on the still dry concrete. Someone in Building 11 said it was 14 degrees; bad enough, but the 30 mile-per-hour wind made Mayer think they must have meant minus 14.

The wind and the river. Mayer became acquainted with both last March after the government assigned him to Evansville and gave him an office less than a hundred yards from the Ohio River. Mayer, a scientist, knew the accord between air and river had to do with the temperature difference between the land and the water causing thermal updrafts. Still, the phenomenon surprised Mayer when he encountered it firsthand in Evansville; some days he left his house, a mere three miles away, in practically no wind, only to get to work and struggle to open his car door, or be forced to grip the door hard when the wind tried vigorously to help him open it. This tight bond between wind and water many times served fine purposes: sailboats sailed, and the river breezes brought welcome respite from the heavy heat of a southern Indiana summer. But now, in January, the wind was a callous and pitiless brute.

Mayer made the right decision this morning when he chose the heavy wool greatcoat that Sarah gave him for his birthday last month over the lambskin jacket he usually wore. He fixed the top button and pulled the collar up, gripping the front tight to his neck with one hand, and holding his hat with the other as he walked.

Born and reared in Indianapolis, Mayer graduated as valedictorian of his high school. That accomplishment earned him scholarship offers from several prominent universities. His passion was chemistry. His goal had been to attend Harvard, but restrictions on the number of Jewish students allowed to enroll at the Ivy League school dashed any dreams he had of becoming a Harvard man.

242

Ultimately, the University of Notre Dame came through with the best scholarship. Notre Dame had a respected chemistry department, so Mayer packed his bags and traveled the 150 miles from his parents' house in Indianapolis to South Bend. There he quickly became the top student in the chemistry program: the Jewish whiz kid at the Catholic university.

It took Joe Mayer only five years to earn both his bachelor's and master's degrees. He chose metallurgy as his field, and published a well-received paper on the process of sintering nickel alloys. Mayer postponed work on his doctorate when Bethlehem Steel came calling with a lucrative job offer. He spent three years at the company with most of his work devoted to alloy development. Mayer quickly proved he was someone to be listened to in the company's research labs. Joe Mayer planned on happily spending the rest of his life in Pennsylvania finding ways to make car fenders lighter but stronger, and water heaters more rust resistant. But in 1936 he was contacted by the U.S. government and coaxed away from Bethlehem Steel with an offer to lead his own research team at a military research facility in New London, Connecticut, and there he stayed until the Japanese entered the picture.

Shortly after Pearl Harbor, Mayer attempted to join the Army and serve as an infantryman like his father in the first war. The government quickly nixed that idea: a respected research scientist like Joe Mayer could better serve the war effort by improving metal alloys for tanks, aircraft, and submarines. Mayer spent six months assigned to a government research project at the Massachusetts Institute of Technology in Cambridge, where he worked with scientists from nearby Harvard—the school that 13 years earlier had too many Jews. Mayer contributed greatly to a project that developed an unconventional metal anodizing procedure. When the project was completed, the Navy decided to use the process in its most recent high priority project: the building of a massive fleet of shore landing craft.

A project of immense proportion. Thousands of "Elsies," a play on the letters *l.c.* for landing craft, were needed—boats of various sizes and purposes. Evansville, Indiana, was chosen as one of the locations to build the radically new, and the largest, shore landing ship. The goliath craft now being constructed on the banks of the Ohio River (in a surprising place like southwestern Indiana—700 miles from the nearest ocean) was called the Landing Ship-Tank, or LST. LSTs were engineering marvels: longer than a football field, they could cross the ocean; beach themselves on an enemy shore; disgorge dozens of tanks, heavy trucks, halftracks and jeeps; then successfully retract from the beach and return to sea. Because these amazing craft required more engineering skill and know-how than any destroyer or battleship, the United States assigned its top ship building masterminds to the LST project. Joe Mayer considered it no small honor, and a great responsibility, to be included.

When his assignment to Evansville came through, at first it surprised Mayer that such huge, ocean-going ships were being constructed in the midst of the cornfields of the Midwest, but he quickly realized the astuteness of such a choice. Hundreds of miles from the Atlantic coast and 2000 miles from the Pacific, what shipyard was safer from enemy attack? After launching on the Ohio River, these ships simply made their way downriver to the Mississippi, then south to the Gulf of Mexico.

Mayer nodded to the Quonset hut compound guard and stepped through a gate in the security fence that surrounded a grouping of huts where engineers, project managers, design personnel, and scientists like Mayer worked; then he walked out into the shipyard proper. The massive jungle of concrete and steel never stopped astonishing Mayer: a garden of war with acres of crossing and twisting iron foliage casting lunatic images under the drab winter sky. He walked through an alienesque landscape of belching smoke and fire.

This jungle had taken root almost overnight. The Japanese planted the seeds on December 7, 1941. To Mayer, the scene served as testimony to the times. Innumerable tons of I-beams, rebar, and steel plating formed narrow metal canyons for trucks and forklifts. Ahead he saw the silhouette of one of seven immense sea craft under construction. Workers scurried around massive hulls. Scaffolding six stories high latticed the sides of the enormous ships. Workers who could not find access via the scaffolds hung like spiders from cables. The constant loud banging and pinging of people working with metal played a cacophonic symphony.

Overhead, several enormous cranes stretched their cantilevered limbs high into the gunmetal sky. Mounted on moving gantries, the cranes rolled along between the ships on train-like tracks rooted in four-foot-thick reinforced concrete. When the gargantuan cranes moved, they struck Mayer as looking like giant dinosaurs trudging their way through a dense primordial landscape. But in this jungle the rain was not water, but fire. Throughout this steel forest, thousands of welders—mostly women—worked nonstop high overhead, sending a constant shower of orange-hot sparks downward. The mist of this orange-hot rain, veins of bluish-gray smoke, whiffed slowly upward, like fleeing ghosts.

Heaven for a research metallurgist like Joseph Mayer.

He walked by a small group of women wearing heavy dungarees, some with welders' shields flipped up from their faces. The women stood next to a tall stack of rebar that blocked some of the wind, and they huddled around an oil fire in a discarded 55-gallon drum. Other drum fires burned here and there. Mayer saw one inside the open bow doors of an LST under construction where, again, workers circled to warm.

Joe Mayer did not always take lunch; often, when a problem needed a quick fix he skipped it altogether to continue working, or he might eat a sandwich brought in from the shipyard canteen while working. But on Fridays he took Sarah to lunch, and today was Friday.

They first met last fall, on Halloween in fact, at the launching of the first LST. A huge crowd gathered that afternoon at the christening celebration, and as Sarah walked by the food tent Mayer stood under, she was jostled and spilt lemonade on him. Embarrassed, she apologized profusely. He knew he should say it was not a big deal, so he said that. They talked for a few minutes and he learned she was a secretary at the shipyard. One thing led to another, and now, although he never much cared to drink it, Joe Mayer was very thankful to whoever invented lemonade.

Normally Sarah worked in Building 23, another of the Quonset huts in the same compound with Mayer's Building 11. However, a secretary in the administration building had been out sick since Wednesday, and Sarah had been temporarily transferred to cover for the woman until she returned. As Mayer neared the administration building, he saw Sarah watching for him from a window near the door. By the time he reached the steps, she was there to greet him.

"Thanks for the weather, Joe," she joked.

"Hey, I love it. I'm nice and snug in my new coat."

Sarah smiled as they started walking to Mayer's car. "I should have kept it for myself." She wore a black, Navy pea coat over a gray dress; a white ribbon held her jet hair.

"I've never seen that coat on you," Mayer commented.

"One of the LST sailors gave it to me a few weeks ago. This is the first time I've worn it. It's warmer than my other coat."

"A sailor gave you his coat?"

She looked at him and grinned.

"Why didn't you get his Dixie cup, too?" She was hatless, and he referred to the white sailors cap worn by Navy enlisted men.

"I did, but I didn't bring it because it's too big, and I'd lose it in the wind."

"What other articles of clothing did you get off him?" Mayer cracked.

"Wouldn't you like to know?" she countered.

They walked quickly to Mayer's car parked in a secured area not far from one of the shipyard exit gates. Getting in was a relief. Even though the temperature in the car was the same as outside, being out of the wind made it feel much warmer. Mayer started the 1940 Lincoln and turned the heater on high, but changed his mind and shut the heater off when air as cold as they just walked through blew through the vents.

"I'll let the engine warm up first." Mayer's breath steamed when he talked. He drove to the exit where a Navy Shore Patrolman, his face chapped red from trips in and out of the cold wind, emerged from the guard shack and manually moved aside a white wooden barricade. Mayer guided the Lincoln under the sign, *U.S. Navy Auxiliary Shipyard at Evansville,* before pulling out onto Ohio Street.

"How's work going in the administration building?" Mayer asked.

"Fine," Sarah answered. "I'm doing the same things I normally do in Building 23: type, sort mail, file, that sort of thing."

"Any idea when the lady you're filling in for will be back?" Mayer tried the heater again, its air starting to warm slightly so he let it run. The light snow still had not stuck. The streets were dry, and the windshield clear, all thanks to the blustering wind.

"Someday next week if all goes well. One of the supervisors called to see how she's doing. She's got the flu."

"That was my guess. The newspaper said several cases have been reported lately."

"The supervisor told her to stay home until she's over it, and she'll have to be cleared by the shipyard doctor before she is allowed to return. I guess they do that with anything contagious."

"Right," Mayer confirmed. "The bosses don't want an epidemic to sweep through the shipyard and have a mass of people off work. They especially try to keep an eye on that sort of thing with people who work inside, in tight quarters with others."

"So, where is this place you're taking me?"

"It's a kosher market and deli—great sandwiches. I've gone there several times and have gotten to know the owners—real nice couple. Mrs. Kweskin, the wife, is always giving me the third degree about if I'm dating anyone. I figured I better take you by."

"Oh, so you're ashamed of me, and have to be prodded to take me there."

Mayer laughed.

Just as the heater realized its goal of making the car comfortably warm, they arrived. Mayer found a parking space a half-block away. Because of the cold, Sarah spared Mayer the gentlemanly task of circling the Lincoln and opening her door. She got out with him and they walked briskly to the market. At least here, farther from the river, the wind was not as stout. When Mayer opened the Kweskin Delicatessen door, a brass bell jingled a welcome to the warmth inside.

"Hey, it's Joe," said a husky man in a white apron standing behind a counter. Several men standing together toward the back turned to look. A woman slicing rye bread, also in an apron, put down her knife when she saw Sarah.

"Hello, Mr. Kweskin," Mayer greeted.

Kweskin smiled. "Hi, Joe. Who do we have here?"

Mayer turned to Sarah. "Sarah, this is Mr. and Mrs. Kweskin. They own the deli." Then to the Kweskins: "This is Sarah Klein."

Sarah said, "Hello, it's nice meeting you."

Mrs. Kweskin wasted no time. "Klein? Is that the *Jewish* Klein?"

"Yes," answered Sarah.

Mrs. Kweskin looked at Joe. "It's about time you found a nice Jewish girl."

"I'm not sure how nice she is," Mayer joked. Sarah punched his arm.

"We haven't seen you before, Sarah," said Mrs. Kweskin. "You're not from around here?"

"No, ma'am. We moved around quite a bit while I was growing up. Like many others, I came to Evansville because of the war jobs. I work at the shipyard. That's where I met Joe."

Mrs. Kweskin approached and sent several more questions Sarah's way.

Mr. Kweskin interrupted his wife's questioning of Sarah. "If you'll put the interrogation on hold for just a minute, I'll get Joe and Sarah's order." He turned to Joe. "The rye bread just got here from Louisville

247

right before you and Sarah walked in, Joe. It's still warm. They set the box near the engine housing inside the Greyhound."

"Okay," Joe said, then turned to Sarah. "Sounds like we want something on the rye bread."

"The corned beef looks wonderful," Sarah said to Mr. Kweskin. "I'll have that on rye, with mustard, please."

"What to drink, Sarah?" Kweskin asked.

Sarah looked quickly at the soft drinks in the cooler. "Orange Crush, please."

When Sarah finished ordering, Mayer said: "I'll have the pepper beef on rye, with mustard, and a Double Cola."

"Coming up."

The market had no customer tables or chairs, but Mrs. Kweskin offered her husband's desk at the back of the store so Sarah could sit. Sarah commented that the thick sandwich could feed two, but neither she nor Mayer left anything uneaten. As a token of welcome to Sarah, Mrs. Kweskin brought them a slice of Halvah, a popular candy available only at Kweskins. Locals called it *Halavah,* inserting an extra syllable.

Finished, Mayer and Sarah thanked the Kweskins and walked under the jingling bell back into the cold. On their way back to the car, Mayer detoured them into Goldman's where he picked out a small gold pendant on a delicate gold chain.

"Will you wear this now?" Mayer asked her. "I'd like to put it on you."

Sarah looked at the pendant, then at Joe and smiled. She opened her coat and turned her back to him. He placed the jewelry around her neck and fastened the clasp.

"How does it look?" she asked as she turned around.

"Looks good. Do you like it, Sarah?"

"I love it," Erika Lehmann declared about the Star of David hanging from the chain.

Chapter 40

Live by the Slain

Cincinnati—Sunday, October 17, 1943

The Holy Cross fathers built Immaculata Church before the Civil War to serve the German Roman Catholics of Cincinnati's Mount Adams neighborhood. Erected near the Ohio River atop the city's highest hill, the church offers its congregation a breathtaking view of the river below and Kentucky beyond.

Reared a German Lutheran, Adalwulf von Krause had not attended Sunday services in years; nevertheless, at a quarter to ten the taxi dropped him on the corner of Pavilion and Guido streets behind Immaculata. Krause walked to the front of the church and, in another of his expensive three-piece suits—this one gray with matching felt bowler—entered alongside parishioners arriving for the ten o'clock Mass. He chose a middle pew, took a seat at the end, and placed his hat and walking stick beside him on the bench.

The pews filled quickly. Many of the faithful were already on knees and sending supplications to the Queen of Heaven as they moved fingers from bead to bead. *A strange lot, these Catholics,* thought Krause. He had to admit, however, that Catholics built the most striking churches, using skilled stonemasons and sculptors for their altars and statues of marble. And in the past, in other Roman churches (perhaps he had been there for a wedding or funeral) Krause had admired beautiful paintings and murals. At Immaculata, all of these were there. Below the large altar painting of the Immaculate Conception, Krause noticed a painted scroll; the words, in German, translated to: *Oh Mary, conceived without sin, pray for the conversion of this country.*

"Good morning, Adalwulf."

"Good morning, my dear." Krause stood and stepped into the aisle so Erika Lehmann could sit on his inside. She sat down and lowered the kneeler. Krause returned to his seat and moved his hat and cane out of her way.

Viola had called him to the telephone yesterday afternoon.

"Hello, von Krause here."

"Hello Adalwulf, this is Karl's daughter. Do we have something to meet about?"

"Yes."

"Will you attend ten o'clock Mass with me tomorrow morning at Immaculata Church on Guido Street?"

"Yes."

"Then I will see you there. Good-bye, Adalwulf."

The phone call lasted less than half a minute. Now she knelt beside him in a conservative, navy blue cotton dress with a white lace veil covering her shoulders and hair. That hair, no longer tinged with red, was now dark brown. She wore rather frumpy-looking eyeglasses with pillow-shaped lenses and heavy metal frames the same color as her hair.

After the bell rang giving notice of the processional, the choir began singing "Faith of Our Fathers," from the loft over the rear pews. Erika made the sign of the cross and rose to her feet as did everyone else. Krause hesitated, then rose to stand beside her, thinking it gentlemanly. From the sacristy, a priest in a white robe covered by an ornate green and white chasuble followed three altar boys in black cassocks and white surplices. Two of the boys held lit candles; the third carried the cross. When the processional reached the front of the altar, the priest and company paused, their backs to the congregation, and waited patiently as the choir finished.

"In nomine Patris, et Filii, et Spiritus Sancti."

Krause watched Erika Lehmann and the Immaculata parishioners cross themselves. A young family of five arrived late: father, mother carrying an infant, a girl perhaps seven or eight, and a boy toddler. From the other end of the pew, the family squeezed in beside Erika. From the start, the toddler was a handful: squirming, standing in the pew jabbering at those behind, jumping up and down, and, at one point, ducking under the pew ahead and crawling under the skirt of a woman in that row. His mother, busy with the baby, and his father, on the other side of his wife and too far away to help had to depend on their young daughter who fought a losing battle with her brother.

The priest spoke his confession. *Confiteor Deo omnipotenti. . . ."*

"Mother," the little girl whispered, "Hermie has ants in his pants again." Then she turned to her brother. "Hermie, I'm going to spank your butt if you don't sit down and be good." Ignoring the threat, Hermie tried to pick up the heavy wooden kneeler but lost his grip, causing it to bang loudly on the floor. The girl reached for the boy but he saw and fled, trying to run out of the pew in front of Erika. Erika caught the boy and lifted him up, then looked over at his mother and smiled. The mother smiled back weakly with a tired, grateful expression.

The sister whispered to Erika, "You can spank his butt if you want."

The priest stepped up to the altar and kissed it. *"Oramus te. Domine, per merita Sanctorum . . ."* He lit the incense and swung the thurible about the altar. The smoke drifted upward, like prayers to Heaven.

"Is your name Herman?" Erika asked the toddler softly. He did not answer, but neither did he fight her, seeming content to look at her.

The sister overheard and whispered, "Yes, his name is Herman, but we call him Hermie."

"You like your mischief, don't you, Hermie?" asked Erika in a whisper.

After the *Gloria,* the congregation sat. Erika placed Hermie on her lap. When time came for the Gospel reading—Matthew 9:1-8—everyone rose then returned to their seats for the sermon. The priest emphasized the necessity of sacrifice:

"Something has to be sacrificed, something has to die, for something else to live. It is true that we, as God's children, live by what we slay. We slay animals to nourish our bodies. Our boys are now fighting in foreign lands slaying the enemy so we can live free, and some of them—too many of them—are slain by that enemy, their deaths offered as a sacrifice for our freedom here on earth. And the greatest sacrifice of them all is God's own innocent Son, slain for our sins so we can be redeemed and live in Heaven with his Father."

When his sermon ended, the priest initiated the Credo and the people joined in. The Mass of the Faithful began and the congregation returned to the kneelers. Erika convinced Hermie to kneel beside her; Krause remained seated.

"Hoc est enim corpus meum." The priest placed the Host on the paten, genuflected, then raised the consecrated Host high for all to see.

With the bread and wine now Body and Blood and the Canon prayed, the faithful rose from their knees and in unison recited the *Pater Noster: "Our Father, Who art in Heaven . . ."* Krause could hear Erika reciting the prayer beside him.

251

After the *Pater Noster* and the *Agnus Dei,* the choir began singing Mozart's "Ave verum corpus" as the communicants began filling the aisles. Krause remained seated while Erika and the family filed past him.

"Hermie, you go with your papa and mama now," Erika said to the child, but he raised his hands over his head indicating he wanted her to carry him. Erika picked up Hermie and joined the family for the walk toward the altar. When she reached the communion rail, Erika knelt with Hermie in her arms. An altar boy held the paten under Erika's chin and the priest laid the Body of Christ on Erika's tongue.

"*Corpus Domini nostri Jesu Christi custodiat animam tuam in vitam aeternam. Amen.*"

Hermie reached for the paten but Erika pulled his arm back. The priest smiled and made the Sign of the Cross in the air over the child's head.

After the pious who came forward had received Holy Communion and returned to the pews, the priest attended to the remaining Eucharist then led the congregation in the *Salve Regina.* The blessing was given and all crossed themselves. The choir sang "Immaculate Mary" as the priest and altar boys left the altar, then the parishioners started filing out. When Erika turned Hermie over to his father, both parents thanked Erika for her help.

"He's never been this good in church," said the mother.

Hermie's sister piped up: "You should have spanked his butt anyway."

On the way out, Erika dipped a finger in the Holy Water font and crossed herself.

Cold earlier, the clear sky allowed the sun to warm Cincinnati to a pleasant fall day.

"Is there somewhere you would prefer to talk, Erika?" Krause said when they had left the church.

"We have such a nice view, Adalwulf. Shall we just walk?"

[Newport, Kentucky—later that day]

The night of trouble at the Lamar Apartments had forced Erika Lehmann to make an abrupt and unexpected departure, and to find a new place to sleep. Publicity from that night made a prolonged stay at a hotel a bad idea. At a hotel, too many people had to be dealt with daily: desk clerks, bellhops, maids, people in the halls and lobby, the elevator boy (she had learned that American elevator boys make it a point of honor to snoop about guests). No, a hotel was not wise.

So here she sat in a cramped, 18-foot trailer, one among many in a trailer park hastily constructed for war plant workers on the outskirts of Newport, Kentucky, across the Ohio River from Cincinnati. The trailer had few amenities: no bathroom, no kitchen to speak of, and no running water. When necessary, Erika walked 50 yards down the road to the toilet/bathhouse. If she ate at home, the meal was cold or heated on a Bunsen burner, and she toted water from one of the well spigots near the bathhouse. Spartan, but the trailer park nevertheless had its advantages. The turnover of residents was high, and everyone here was new to the area having moved in for the war jobs. Both were to her advantage. People here had little time or inclination to be nosey about their neighbors. To them, she was probably just another Rosie the Riveter who had come here from somewhere else.

The Ring Adalwulf had given her was off her finger and Erika studied it over a small table that pulled down from the trailer wall. The Ring was solid silver with a black stone, heavy and sturdy but humble in material worth. On either side of the stone were engravings. On one side were three interlocking triangles, the Viking symbol called Hrungnir's Heart or the Valknot—the Knot of the Slain. The engraving on the other side of the stone symbolized Gungnir—Odin's spear, also known as the Spear of Valhalla. This symbol consisted of an X with a small square transecting the two larger lines.

Erika Lehmann now knew the legends surrounding the Ring of the Slain. Krause told her the Ring was reserved for a secret society whose members' final goal in life was to die a noble death, and if this death proved violent even the better. *"For it was sent down from the men of the North, my dear, that the ultimate goal in life is to die bravely in battle with one's enemies,"* Krause had said. He went on to explain that men who wore the Ring believed that those who died for their principles defending family and homeland, merited the supreme award: a place in Valhalla—the Hall of the Slain—where the slain warrior would be taken by one of Odin's beautiful warrior daughters—the Valkyries. The notion was one of days long past, and of a pagan culture, but Krause added that there were Christian members of the Ring of the Slain Society who believed the Ring's creed was reinforced by the Christ himself when he stated his manifest in

253

John 15:13: *Greater love has no man than this, that he lay down his life for his friends.*

And Krause told Erika of the curse connected to the Ring. Anyone aware of the tenets of the Ring, but not believing, who placed the Ring on his finger was fated to die an ignoble death and be passed over by Brunhild and her sisters. And anyone who stole the Ring, or who gained possession of one by surreptitious means, would suffer that same doom. Only if the thief or fraud atoned for his act by returning the Ring to its rightful owner could the anathema be removed.

But in truth, Erika Lehman had little opinion about the tenets of the Ring. She believed in the nobility of those willing to sacrifice all, so saying *"Yes"* to Adalwulf when he asked her if she believed in the Ring's canon was truthful. But she had much to do and little time for such legends, and no time to ponder the veracity of a curse. Her need for the Ring was more pragmatic.

She placed the Ring back on the ring finger of her right hand: *"It has to be worn on the right hand, Fräulein Erika, regardless if the Society member is right or left handed."* For Erika, this piece of jewelry was a calling card. It would help her get home. Krause revealed there were four other members of the Ring Society in the United States, and one owned an oceangoing freighter company headquartered in New York City. *"You can mention my name, my dear, but first show him the Ring. Without the Ring you will not be trusted. He will probably ask you questions about the legends and the Ring creed to make sure you are one of us."* The plan—to get her on a freighter bound for neutral Portugal. Once there, she would take over. It would be a simple matter of reporting to the German embassy in Lisbon. Erika's first Abwehr assignment in 1940 had been in Lisbon and she was familiar with that city.

Still, Erika could not leave until she completed her mission, and to do that she must spend a night with Elizabeth Ault.

Chapter 41

Four Breakfasts

Monday, October 18, 1943

The Cricket restaurant in the Palace Hotel, Cincinnati

Leroy Carr and Al Hodge met in the hotel restaurant for breakfast every day at 7:00 a.m. to go over that day's plans. Today, the anxious Hodge already had his coffee when Carr sat down. A few minutes earlier, Hodge received a crucial phone call from OSS headquarters in Washington.

A familiar waitress walked up with a coffee cup and pot. She set the cup in front of Carr and poured. "What can I get you today, gentlemen? We're out of breakfast meat for this month."

"Eggs sunny side up, biscuits and gravy," Hodge answered.

"I'll take mine scrambled, Lily," said Carr. "And hash browns."

"Toast or biscuits?" Lily asked Carr. He ordered toast. When Lily walked away Hodge got straight to the point.

"Just before I came downstairs I got a call from the E Street Complex about the message," Hodge said. Saturday, Hodge sent the OSS cryptanalysts in D.C. a copy of the message Anne Brown sent Friday over the Cincinnati *Observer* teletype. "They agree with you that *Jehanne* is probably the Abwehr transmitting station in Domremy, France."

Carr nodded. After Saturday's meeting about the transmission with the Cincinnati cops and Elizabeth Ault, Carr told Hodge that when Elizabeth Ault mentioned that the French name *Jehanne* was Joan of Arc's real name, Carr immediately thought of the French town Domremy la Pucelle. Two years ago, the Germans built a powerful shortwave transmitting station in Domremy—Joan's hometown. Eisenhower forbade bombing of the transmitting station from the air because it was located near a church and school in the revered pilgrimage town—exactly the reason the Germans chose Domremy. "Anything else, Al?"

"Got to hand it to those eggheads in Crypto," Hodge continued. "We know her codename is *Lorelei*, and the Crypto boys guess the

255

'*Henry poem*' reference in the second line refers to the German poem *Lorelei* by Heinrich Heine."

Carr interrupted. "'*Henry poem*' tells the Domremy Abwehr station Lorelei is sending the message."

"Right."

"What about the word '*wine*' in that second line?"

"They aren't sure about that word," Hodge said. "Crypto thinks it might be the word that identifies her mission codename. As for the third line—the message itself—since she had to send it in English, without encrypting it, Crypto thinks the words '*Belated Foray Acumen Impending*' are just synonyms of the actual words used to disguise the message from the *Observer* teletype operator. Crypto says her message to Abwehr is: '*Delayed Invasion Information Forthcoming.*'"

Carr stopped. Everyone who read a newspaper or watched the movie newsreels knew a massive buildup of troops and matériel was already underway in England for the invasion across the Channel. The most important secret of the war: when and where the invasion would take place. If the Germans found out either or both it would be a disaster of monumental scope for the Allies. If the Nazis could find out when, and especially where, the invasion would take place they could build up their defenses and most assuredly repel it and drastically change the tide of the war.

"Christ!" Hodge exclaimed. "Could that woman have information about the invasion?"

Lily returned and set the plates in front of the two men. Leroy Carr looked at his scrambled eggs but no longer felt hungry.

[the Ault home—same time]
If the Aults ate breakfast at home, the duty of cook fell on Frank for three good reasons: he enjoyed cooking breakfast, it was the only meal he knew how to cook, and he had no intention of learning to cook anything else. And when Frank cooked, breakfast was always the same: eggs over medium, hash browns, sausage links, toast and coffee. Because of their conflicting work schedules, the Aults did not prepare meals at home every day, and Frank cooked breakfast only once, maybe twice a week so their ration of eggs, pork and coffee usually held up for the month.

The links looked done. Frank used a towel to grasp the handle of the cast iron skillet then dumped the sausages onto a plate next to the stove.

"Just one egg for me, Frank," said Elizabeth. She stood looking out the kitchen window in a pink silk robe, cigarette in one hand and coffee cup in the other.

"Okay." Frank, in boxer shorts and T-shirt, scooped more Crisco and cracked four eggs into the skillet—three for him. Before the war Frank had always fried the eggs in butter, but now no one wanted to use their small butter ration for cooking. Lard was also rationed, so everyone used Crisco.

The Aults had talked about Anne Brown all weekend, saying everything that could be said multiple times so now both Frank and Elizabeth avoided broaching the subject again while the eggs sizzled. Frank's home police radio crackled. A female voice put out a call for Car 21. Car 21 answered and was informed about a domestic disturbance and given an address. Elizabeth heard someone say *ROGER.*

"Car 21," Frank said. "I think that's Houchen and Ruble. They'll love that call." Frank grinned slyly. "Those domestic calls are a pain in the rear. Usually some drunk beating his wife. Not always though, once in a while it's the wife beating the crap out of the kids, maybe beating the husband, too."

"Do we have to listen to that right now?" asked Elizabeth.

Frank reached over and flipped off the radio then flipped over the eggs. "Do you know what story you'll be working on today?"

"Unless my editor assigns me something else when I check in this afternoon, I'm going to do an opinion piece about the dismissal of charges against the city councilman charged with graft."

"The guy you exposed a couple of months ago?"

"Yes. His lawyer has made a case that the charges be dropped for lack of evidence, and I heard through the grapevine the judge is likely to do it. The guy was caught red-handed. It looks to me to be a good old case of having friends in high places."

"That happens, no doubt about it," Frank agreed. "But if the guy gets away with it now, he'll pay for it next election. Especially with the war on, the voters will have no tolerance for that stuff. They'll bounce him out on his butt come election day." Frank scooped Elizabeth's egg onto a plate, added hash browns from a skillet on a back burner, sausages and toast, and took her plate to the table. She waited while Frank filled his plate.

Elizabeth returned Frank's inquiry about the day ahead. "Do you know what you'll be working on today, Frank?"

"I've got a couple cases that need some follow-up," he said as he sat down. "I don't have court today, so unless something happens, I'll be here at one o'clock to drive you to the paper."

"Alright. I just hope. . . ." She stopped abruptly.

Frank looked at her. "What, babe?"

Elizabeth hesitated and shook her head.

"What is it?" Frank insisted.

Again, she paused, but finally said, "I hope I can have a day where I don't have to deal with something to do with Anne Brown. I don't want to go to a meeting about Anne Brown, write about Anne Brown, or answer questions from people on the street about Anne Brown. If I could have that for just one day it would make me a happy woman."

Frank tried to lift his wife's spirits. "Maybe you need to wear my hot dog vendor beard when you leave the house."

Elizabeth did not laugh.

[home of Adalwulf von Krause—same time]

"Thank you, Viola," said Krause.

Viola set the tray table down and moved the tray to Krause's desk. She filled his coffee cup and left. Krause laid down the newspaper and pulled the tray to him. On one plate, a poached egg rested on a slice of heavy, dark bread. A smaller plate offered a slice of white cheese. As Krause cut his first slice of egg and bread he heard a knock and his grandson's voice.

"Grandfather," Willy yelled from the other side of the heavy door, "may I come in?"

"Yes, come in." Krause, too, had to shout.

Willy walked in carrying a newspaper; he stopped and stood in front of the desk. His face showed evidence of the two times Willy had encountered *Early*. The scarred nose from the night at the Side Pocket, and small puncture wounds not yet totally healed from the fall off the porch into the thorny scrub.

"Good morning, Wilmar."

"Good morning, Grandfather. May I talk to you?"

Krause motioned for Willy to sit. "Have you eaten?" Krause asked before taking a bite of egg and bread.

"No, sir. Viola is fixing it now." Willy laid his newspaper on the desk folded to the sketch of Anne Brown. Willy first saw the sketch that day in his grandfather's study but was not about to own up to nosing through his grandfather's desk, so he went out and found his own copy. "Grandfather, I saw this at a newsstand. This looks like the woman from the Side Pocket that gave me the message to give you; the woman that was here at the house that day. I'm pretty sure it's her."

Silent, Krause gave the newspaper a fleeting glance without picking it up then quickly turned his attention back to his breakfast.

Willy expected a comment, but when none came he continued. "That woman in the drawing is the one who killed a man last month and attacked another guy and a woman down in Over the Rhine. She looks like Early from the Side Pocket. We need to call the cops, Grandfather."

Krause put down his fork and knife, patted his lips with his napkin, and locked eyes with his grandson.

"I want you to listen to me very carefully, Wilmar," Krause said sternly. "You do not know if the women are the same. I want you to forget all about this. Do you understand?"

"Grandfather, I'm almost positive that's her. She's dangerous and she's been here in our house. I'm worried about you. She might come back to rob you or even hurt you. I didn't tell you this because I didn't want you to worry, but that woman can't control herself. I was minding my own business that night at the Side Pocket and she pulled a knife on me for no reason. I'm going to call the cops—at least they can check her out."

"You will not call the police!" Krause raised his voice then lowered it and tried to explain. "Wilmar, there are important things I cannot tell you at this time, but you do not have to worry about her causing me harm. She is not the woman of that newspaper drawing; I can assure you of that. You must trust me for now." Krause paused to consider how much he would tell his grandson then continued. "The woman you met is the daughter of an old friend of mine. She was in Cincinnati for a time and decided to find me and send her father's regards. That is all, Wilmar. She has now left and is no longer in Cincinnati." Krause hoped the last part were true.

"And this daughter of a friend worked at the Side Pocket?"

"It is not my affair what children of friends do with their time or with their lives."

"Why did she go to all the trouble to send you a note through me, Grandfather? Why not just telephone or stop by the house?"

Krause was not going to tell him about Erika identifying herself with the reference to Hrungnir's Heart. "I don't know, Wilmar. I didn't ask her."

Willy said no more. Because he had found the newspaper in the study desk folded open to the sketch, Willy felt sure his grandfather knew Early was the woman in the newspaper. The old man's reaction surprised him. *Why is he protecting her?*

"Wilmar," Krause added when Willy rose to leave, "this request is very important. You will do as I ask?"

"Yes, Grandfather."

When Willy left, Krause sat back in his chair. He hoped his grandson could be trusted to keep his word but lacked confidence in that hope. Notifying the police would result in disaster for them all: Erika, himself, even for Willy. Willy would lose everything if his grandfather were identified and arrested for helping an enemy spy: the house, his inheritance, everything would be gone. Perhaps he should have appealed to his grandson's sense of greed and told him as much, but then he would have had to explain too much, so he told his grandson the lie that she was not the woman in the sketch. Willy knew nothing about his grandfather's ongoing association with the Fatherland. To Willy, his grandfather was simply a successful, retired banker.

Karl's daughter had told Krause she would leave Cincinnati *after I complete a few tasks, Adalwulf.* She did not say how long those tasks might take. If she were still in Cincinnati Krause felt he must warn her about Willy implicating her in the Over the Rhine incident, and therefore she should leave town quickly. But how? Krause had no way to contact her and with their business concluded no prospects of seeing her again. Erika had the Ring and he hoped she was on her way to New York City.

[Newport, Kentucky—same time]

Unless circumstances kept her out very late at night, Erika Lehmann rose at 5:30 every morning to begin 90 minutes of calisthenics: sit-ups, push-ups, deep knee bends, stretching, along with various weight-lifting exercises—the weight provided by a cinderblock. She had been introduced to using weight with exercise at Quenzsee. Erika had always been naturally strong, and she found out quickly using weight with her exercises made her even stronger, and she liked the toned feeling the weight exercises gave her muscles. Always done inside and in private, she kept the pace of her workouts brisk. When finished she would be drenched with sweat.

Erika had just returned to her trailer from the bathhouse. Showering after the morning exercises worked well in the trailer park because the community showers were less crowded in the mornings.

As Erika combed her hair she heard a knock. That would be Danny, a young man who recently moved into the trailer next to hers. Danny, from a small town 40 miles east of Cincinnati, was 4-F because of a heart murmur so ineligible for military service. He moved into the trailer park when he found a job at a Cincinnati company that made linings for Army helmets. In peacetime Danny might have commuted to a job in Cincinnati, but with the war, 80 miles a day, six days a week, was much too far for his ration of gas.

Danny drove an old pickup truck and had twice given Erika a lift into Cincinnati. In Evansville, Erika drove her own car but that was before she was discovered by the FBI. It was not wise for a fugitive to drive a car: too many ways to get pulled over. Erika had false I.D.s but best not to use them whenever it could be avoided. This was especially true now in her case. If she were behind the wheel and pulled over because of a dead taillight, or if some motorcycle cop thought she were driving five miles over the 35 miles-per-hour national wartime speed limit, that policeman looking at her through the driver's window would have studied the newspaper sketch of Anne Brown.

So Danny and his pickup proved expedient. She would have Danny drop her downtown and from there she took a taxi or rode a bus. Now, every time Danny headed across the river he asked her if she needed a ride.

"Early," Erika heard Danny call from outside. "I'm heading into work. Do you need a ride over?"

She put on her eyeglasses and opened the door. "No thanks, Danny. I'm off work today."

Danny looked disappointed. "Okay, see you later."

She smiled at him. "Yes, thanks again, and have a good day at work."

Erika closed the door, removed the glasses, and plucked an apple from a bowl of several. She needed a bigger breakfast after the workout, but without a kitchen and with no restaurant within walking distance, an apple or pear was usual breakfast fare. Erika sat at the table and opened a folder containing many pages of notes compiled over the past weeks, and other papers with handmade charts and drawings.

When Erika lost her transmitter in Evansville, she lost direct communication with Abwehr. The radio school in Potsdam had taught her ways to assemble shortwave receivers and transmitters. Building a receiver was a simple task using common radio parts and hardware anyone could purchase in America without raising suspicion. The small receiver she built in her bedroom at the Lamar Apartments she kept hidden under a blanket in the trailer's only closet. She would bring it out and listen when needed.

A transmitter, however, was a much different story. A transmitter powerful enough to reach a U-boat off the East Coast or the northernmost Bolivar relay station in Mexico was much bigger, heavier, and more complicated than a simple receiver. Erika had assembled her Evansville transmitter after she arrived in America 14 months ago, but she brought the crystals and other critical transmitter parts with her—the parts that she could not gather in America during wartime without raising suspicion. Anyone wishing to acquire those parts would have to appear before the Federal Communications Commission and make a case for the need.

So with her transmitter gone (she had kept it behind a false panel in the deep trunk of her 1936 Ford, the car she abandoned when she escaped Evansville) Erika's only means to contact Berlin was through a dead letter drop sent through the Bolivar Network, and many disadvantages lie there. The surreptitious route through Bolivar was sluggish to say the least. A letter had to make its way through various addresses in Central and South America: arriving at one point, then getting mailed or sometimes hand-delivered by a courier on burro-back to the next point along the network. Then, if the letter happened to be lucky enough to reach Uruguay, it would be loaded onto a slow-moving South American freighter that happened to be carrying mail. All this added up to an odyssey of months before someone in Berlin read the communiqué. And, unlike her radio transmissions where confirmation of reception was sent back immediately, Erika would never know if her letter through Bolivar found its destination. Her information was much too important to trust to such a system.

However, Erika knew Bolivar also had a string of shortwave transmission substations for transmitting encrypted messages using Morse code and the German Enigma code (the most secure means to relay a message). Bolivar also had radio and land teletypes that used standard Baudot ITA2 teletype code to relay messages. The shortwave encrypted messages, and the teletype ITA2 messages followed basically the same Bolivar route as a letter but a transmitted message reached Berlin that same day. In Evansville, Erika used her transmitter to communicate with U-boats off the East Coast. The U-boats relayed her messages to Berlin. With her transmitter gone, that left the Bolivar radio teletype system her best option to re-establish communication with Berlin.

When Erika arrived in Cincinnati, she did not have the Bolivar transmitter or radio teletype contact frequencies. This is where Adalwulf von Krause came in. Before she left Germany on her mission to America, Erika's father had told her about his friend. *Adalwulf can help you a great deal, Liebchen, if things don't go according to plan.* Her father told her about the Brotherhood of the Ring of the Slain, and of Adalwulf's ties to the Bolivar Network. Because of Heinrich Himmler, things in Evansville certainly did not go according to plan so Erika took her father's advice and made her way to Cincinnati to call upon Adalwulf, who gave her the Bolivar teletype hookup information she needed. She knew American newspapers had teletypes and she used Adalwulf's information for the first time Friday when she sent the rudimentary message to Juarez from the *Cincinnati Observer.*

Erika saw the *Observer* teletype operator keep a copy of the message. Sent in English and disguised only by the use of synonyms, she knew her message would be easily and quickly deciphered by the Americans, but that message simply informed Berlin that she was still active and important intelligence would follow. Bolivar's job was to get that message to the Abwehr communication station in Domremy, France. Then Abwehr personnel in Domremy would send the message on to Berlin. Erika knew in this case she would receive no confirmation. When the Bolivar agent in Juarez saw that the message came from an American newspaper teletype, he would know not to send back a confirmation. Still, the teletype transmission was a far more reliable option than a dead letter drop.

Erika bit into the apple and referred to one of her charts:

Ø0		Ø1		Ø2		Ø3		Ø4		Ø5		Ø6		Ø7	
*NUL		E	3	*LF		A	—	*SP		S	'	I	8	U	7
Ø8		Ø9		ØA		ØB		ØC		ØD		ØE		ØF	
CR		D	*ENQ	R	4	J	*BEL	N	,	F	!	C	:	K	(
10		11		12		13		14		15		16		17	
T	5	Z	+	L	)	W	2	H	£	Y	6	P	Ø	Q	1
18		19		1A		1B		1C		1D		1E		1F	
0	9	B	?	G	&	*FIGS		M	.	X	/	V	;	*LTRS	
Letters				Figures						*Control Chars.					

Using the chart, Erika began writing. This next communiqué, which she would have to convert to the American ITA2 teletype code and send herself, was much longer and more detailed than Friday's message. This message was what kept her in Cincinnati for the past two months at considerable risk. If she succeeded in sending it, and it reached Berlin, after that it did not matter what happened to her.

And if by chance she remained free, she could use the Ring to get home.

Chapter 42

Sleeping in Shoes

Wednesday, October 20, 1943

Leroy Carr had just returned to Cincinnati from Washington. Back in his hotel room after a very long two days, he threw his briefcase on the bed and looked at his wristwatch—9:28 p.m. Long past suppertime, yet food was the last thing on his mind. He might have been hungry; in fact, he had to be hungry, he skipped breakfast and a pimento cheese sandwich from an E Street Complex vending machine around noon was all he had eaten today, but any hunger pains were overcome by fatigue. Carr removed his overcoat and suit jacket, throwing both over the back of a chair. He loosened his tie, picked up the telephone, and dialed Al Hodge's room.

"I'm back," Carr announced.

"How'd it go?" Hodge asked from the other end.

"As expected—lots of meetings."

"Do you want to meet for a drink?"

"No, I'm bushed," answered Carr. "Just come down to my room, I'll fill you in, then I'm hitting the sack."

"Be right down."

Carr hung up. Since arriving in Cincinnati two weeks ago, he had called Bill Donovan twice each week with telephone updates on the Lorelei case. But on Monday, after Carr told Donovan about the teletype message, Wild Bill requested a face-to-face. So Carr boarded another Army C-47 *Gooney Bird* early Tuesday morning—not the same one that brought him and Hodge to Cincinnati, but one just as cold and noisy. After four hours of rattling and shaking his way back to D.C., he met with Wild Bill for several hours yesterday at the E Street Complex; then Donovan invited him and Kay to dinner at his home. After dinner, Kay and Ruth Donovan moved to the living room and chatted in front of the fire. Carr and Donovan retired to Donovan's library where they talked into the wee hours. This morning, after three hours of sleep, Carr again reported to E Street, this time to convene with OSS cryptographers and the agency's German Military Intelligence experts. Adding to the meeting marathon, Carr suggested to Donovan that the FCC triangulation people be brought in so Carr also had to brief them.

265

Put in charge of the FCC crew that would set up around Cincinnati was Stanley Mullen who had intercepted Lorelei's transmissions last spring and correctly identified Evansville as the signal origin. It was late afternoon before the C-47 pulled up its wheels. Now, half frozen from the flight and dog-tired, Carr planned to forego a late supper and call it a day.

Hodge knocked and Carr let him in.

"I'm going to make this short and sweet, Al. I'm beat. We'll talk more tomorrow at breakfast," Carr said as Hodge leaned against the desk. "I met with Bill all day yesterday, first at the Complex and then at his house last night. Today I met with our cryptographers and Abwehr specialists, also some FCC triangulation people. I want the FCC keeping an extra eye on any shortwave transmissions coming out of this area, including radio teletype transmissions, so I asked Bill for permission to brief them and bring them in."

"Boy, it won't be easy for the FCC to sort through all of the teletype traffic, Leroy. Regular shortwave transmitters are regulated and it's easy to spot their footprints on the air. But every Tom, Dick, and Harry newspaper and radio station has teletypes."

"Right, but not all have radio teletypes. Many have just land line teletypes and she won't use one of those—too easy to trace where the message was sent. Since the war began, usually only the largest newspapers and radio stations have been allowed to purchase and use radio teletypes."

"Okay," Hodge yielded. "So what's the plan? Do the FCC eggheads think they can triangulate a transmission from a radio teletype fast enough to give us a location while the transmission is still being sent? Once she has completed the message, she'll be out of there faster than the old man in the last pew at church."

"Maybe. They said they can try. It all depends on how long the message takes to send." Carr knew his partner's doubts were well-grounded. *Triangulation* was a method to locate the source of a shortwave transmission. When it could be established that at least three separate monitoring stations, located in a triangular pattern surrounding the transmission area, had received the same suspicious signal, triangulation of the signal could determine within a certain distance the transmission's origin point. The strength of the signal received at each station would vary and the FCC mathematicians would do the computations. During peacetime, the FCC used triangulation to locate unlicensed radio stations. Since Pearl Harbor the technique was needed for finding those who used the airwaves for sinister purposes. "The FCC will bring monitoring stations to Cincinnati and set them up just outside town. The closer they are to the transmission, the better chance they have of giving us a pin-point."

"Do you still think she'll send another transmission? It's been almost a week, and if she's figured out we know about the first one, she'll know we'll have that newspaper's teletypes staked out."

Carr had asked Colonel Norquist to station one of his men outside the *Observer* teletype room and a guard had been there 24 hours a day since they found out about the teletype message Lorelei had sent. "She'll send another message, Al. I have no doubts about it, but it won't be sent from the *Observer.* I had to put Norquist's guard there because that's a by-the-book security precaution, but she's too smart to attempt to use the same teletype location twice."

"So what's next?" Hodge asked.

"We need to sit down again with the Cincy cops and fill them in without any great detail."

"Oh, that will be fun. I get to listen to that smart-ass Ault again. You know, Leroy, I can't figure out how those two ever hooked up . . . Ault and his wife, I mean. She's a classy, good-looking dish. What did she ever see in that guy? It's like that fairy tale, what's the name? . . . oh, yeah, 'Beauty and the Asshole.'"

Carr, too weary to laugh, said seriously: "Of course the best thing would be to catch Lorelei before she sends another message. The reference she made to having information about the invasion has everyone on edge, including Donovan. He's worried FDR might change his mind and bring the FBI back in. But I told Bill all we can do right now is prepare for the next message and hope she is still in Cincinnati when she sends it. Then we have to hope the message is a long one and the FCC guys are at the top of their game and triangulate the transmission location. Maybe, if it's our lucky day, we can move in and snag her before the entire message is sent, and the military can undertake damage control depending on what's in the message. That's probably the best-case scenario we're going to get. From now on we better sleep in our shoes, ready to jump up and run if the FCC calls us in the middle of the night." He only half-joked about sleeping in his shoes. Leroy Carr knew anyone hoping to catch Lorelei would need some luck, and be ready to move quickly.

Chapter 43

No Gridiron for the Bearcats

Thursday, October 21, 1943

Before the war, Elizabeth and Frank Ault's favorite place of escape, even if just briefly, was the car. Short drives during the week and long on Sunday. In the car, no telephones rang and no one knocked on doors. For the shorter weekday drives they usually stayed in town and ended up parked atop one of the many hills that made up the Queen City—enjoying the view before heading home. On Sunday, they often made a day of it. One week they might head up Highway 42 to Columbus and dine there before returning home. Maybe the next week they might cross into Kentucky and drive the two hours to the Daniel Boone National Forest for a picnic in the woods beside one of the fast-moving brooks falling out of the mountains.

The Japanese canceled those simple diversions. Gas rationing changed car trips to walks. And for the Aults, busy schedules over the past year reduced regular walks to infrequent until in September Anne Brown ended the walks altogether. Now, after a light dinner at home, Frank and Elizabeth took their first leisure walk in nearly two months.

"Does your brother have any idea where he's headed?" asked Frank as they strolled the college campus three blocks from their house. At dinner, Elizabeth informed Frank that her mother had called that day with news that Elizabeth's Marine brother had shipped out of the Aleutian Islands.

"No, they won't tell him."

"Yeah, that's standard procedure." Frank knew his wife was worried and he tried to reassure her. "During a war, the military always keeps the troops in the dark about where they're going until the last minute. Makes it hard on the families not knowing but it adds security for the troops. Things have been looking up lately out there in the Pacific. I read the other day in your newspaper that we got a foothold on a couple more islands in the Solomons that the Japs use for airfields."

Elizabeth nodded and took her husband's arm. In the twilight, the sky, clear earlier that day, planned a change—clouds now met and

268

moved fast. A nippy breeze couldn't make up its mind which way to blow a half-yellow, half-red leaf. As the Aults approached, the leaf bounced across the brick walkway then turned and scooted back across. Two young women carrying books followed the leaf across the bricks.

"Did you have many boyfriends when you went to college here?" Frank asked his wife.

She looked at him suspiciously but couldn't help but grin. "I guess so, one or two."

"One or two, huh?"

"I don't know. Maybe two or three."

"We better stop there." Frank decided.

Elizabeth laughed.

Frank said, "You never talked about 'em. Who were they?"

"Why, Frank? Do you want to arrest them?"

"Just curious."

"Curious about what? If I slept with them?"

"Okay."

"I think I'll keep you wondering. At least till you tell me more about those two women you almost married."

"Let's drop it," Frank suggested.

"That's what I thought."

They walked on in no hurry. Overtaking them from behind, five robust young men in letterman jackets talked about football as they passed the slower-walking Aults. As with many college teams across the nation, many of the University of Cincinnati players had traded football helmets for the Army variety, leaving athletic departments two choices: cancel the season, or field a team made up of students granted exemptions from military service. The Bearcat powers-that-be chose the cancel option, but Frank remembered reading in the *Observer* sports pages that some of the remaining UC players continued to practice hoping the war would end before the '44 season.

"I met with Carr today." Frank blurted out.

Elizabeth released his arm and stopped walking. For a moment she considered telling him she did not want to hear about Leroy Carr or anything he said but changed her mind. She intended to see the Anne Brown odyssey through. She took back his arm.

"And?"

"His boss in Washington had him fly back there for a sit-down. Carr was there Tuesday and Wednesday."

"So what's that got to do with us? Is there a new plan?"

"In a nut shell," Frank summed up, "Carr's plan is to sit on our butts until Anne Brown makes a move. Carr believes she'll send another message, but we don't know if she's still in Cincinnati. According to him, all we can do is try to be ready if she's still around here so we can react if she surfaces."

"So Carr thinks she might be gone?"

"He doesn't know, Elizabeth. No one knows." Frank stopped walking and turned to his wife. "Elizabeth, I told Carr this afternoon that as of today you are out of all of this. I don't want you involved. It's dangerous, I worry about you, and I've had it with Carr and his bull."

Elizabeth looked at him. "What if Anne Brown telephones, or writes me again?"

"Carr asked me that. I reminded him that no one can force you to take part in this. I told him I'd share any new developments with him since the welfare of the country is a factor, but I can't handle you being in danger. I've had it with Carr. Technically he's still in charge of the case, but I'm back to treating it like any other homicide. Carr's way isn't working. If Brown is still in Cincinnati, I have just as good a chance to apprehend her by going about it as a routine homicide investigation. Carr and his OSS buddy have crapped out so far. It can't get any worse. And with my way, my wife isn't in danger."

Newport, Kentucky—later that evening

Danny had just showered after an exhausting 14-hour shift and as he walked slowly, tiredly, back to his trailer from the bathhouse, Early stepped out of her trailer with a trash can.

"Oh, hi, Danny," she said when she saw him.

"Hi, Early." Seeing Early made Danny feel a bit less tired. He tried to think of something else to say, but words to girls never came easy. He had stuttered up until high school, and Danny had always been smaller and younger looking than the other boys. Even now, at 21, at 5 feet 5 inches, with sandy hair and freckles he looked 17. His shyness, small stature, and young look affected his success with the girls back home. Most girls liked Danny in the platonic gist; he was the proverbial harmless nice guy. Back home, Danny had lots of friends who were girls, but so far no girlfriends.

By the time he thought of something to say to Early (he would volunteer to empty her trash) she had already walked by and was nearly to the trash bin. He stopped outside the door to his trailer and watched her dump the trash, but was embarrassed when she turned and saw him staring. She smiled and returned to her trailer.

Inside, Danny thought about dinner. He had found a used icebox at a flea market. Small, it held only a 25-pound block of ice, but luckily ice was not rationed (frozen water seemed to be one of the few things still plentiful nowadays). An ice truck serviced the trailer park three times a week so there was always ice to keep a small amount of food cool. When Danny looked inside the ice box, he saw only a half-full quart bottle of milk, two eggs, and a tin of peanut butter. No bread. He could boil the eggs but his old Bunsen burner wasn't working well. He stuck a spoon in the peanut butter and poured himself a glass of milk. With the milk and peanut butter, he sat down at a small card table where a pencil and a Big Chief writing tablet waited. Danny shoveled a heaping spoonful of peanut butter into his mouth and began a letter to home. Even though home was only 40 miles away, because of gas rationing he made it back only once a month. And because his trailer had no phone, Danny wrote a couple of letters each week to his parents and little sister. Just as he flipped up the red Big Chief cover to begin writing, a knock surprised him. No one had knocked on his door since he arrived at the trailer park two weeks ago. He rose and answered the door.

"Hi, again." It was Early.

"Hi . . . ah, hi," Danny said it twice, had no idea why, and blushed.

"May I come in?" she asked.

"Oh, sure. Sorry." He held open the door. "Come on in."

Early stepped into the trailer and he closed the door. She wore men's clothing: blue denim pants and a red plaid, long-sleeved lumberjack shirt. No hat covered the brunette hair. Danny, two or three inches shorter, looked up at her.

"I don't have much of anything to offer you," Danny apologized. "Would you like a glass of milk?"

Instead of answering, she scanned the one-room trailer for a moment then gazed at Danny with a wild, predatory look that made him nervous. He wished he could come up with something good to say.

"Ah . . . milk," he said, almost stuttering. "I'll get milk. . . ."

Early put a finger on his lips to shush him, then put her arms around his neck and her body against his. When she pressed her lips to his, Danny faltered backward one step until a wall stopped him, their lips staying locked. The wall allowed Early to press into him. She drew her lips back and said, "Open your mouth a little." Danny obeyed and Early started over. She unbuttoned his shirt while they kissed, then pulled back and helped him shrug out of it. Danny's trailer was even smaller than hers and it had no bed. She led him to the couch where Danny slept and gently pushed him down. She turned her back to him as she slowly undressed, occasionally turning her head to smile at him. When she got down to her underpants, she turned to face him and teased him for a moment by fluffing her hair and touching her breasts before unbuttoning her underpants. When she was totally naked, she straddled Danny's lap.

"Now you know my secret," Early breathed into his ear. "I'm really a blonde."

Danny couldn't speak. Early took his hands, placed them on her breasts, and kissed him again. She sat back and loosened his belt. Once she pulled his pants and underwear down to his knees, she could see Danny was very ready. She helped him out of his shoes, socks, and pants until they were both naked, then she again straddled his lap.

Danny was no longer tired.

Chapter 44

Newsroom Huddle

Friday, October 29, 1943

Cincinnati Observer **newsroom**

"What's the latest with the fire chief, Larry?"

Otis Kapperman, city news editor at the *Cincinnati Observer,* was asking city beat reporter Larry Liniger about Cincinnati's fire chief whose recent ill health had fueled speculation he might retire. Every day, Kapperman—bald, with a thick gray handlebar mustache that made him look like a singer in a turn-of-the-century barbershop quartet—gathered his reporters in the early afternoon to check on stories in the works and to hand out new assignments. Seated in Kapperman's office, in addition to Liniger, were two other city beat reporters: Clarence Holcomb and Elizabeth Ault. The other member of the city beat team, Bud Becht, was out covering a story.

"No change, Otis," Larry answered. "He's decided to play Mr. Tight-Lip. The chief told me he's feeling fine but he's tired of reading his health report in the newspaper. He's stalling. I'm looking for him to announce his retirement soon. One of my contacts at City Hall told me the district chiefs are tripping over each other positioning themselves for a run at the job. I guess some heavy-duty ass-kissing is being directed at the mayor. I'm putting together background info on the top candidates so I'll have it ready when I need it."

"How about you, Clarence?" Kapperman asked. "Has the mayor convinced the City Council to vote in his storm drain bond issue?"

"I think so," Holcomb answered. "It's slated for a vote next Tuesday. At least it's on the docket."

"They'll probably postpone the vote again, but make sure you're at City Hall Tuesday. A storm drainage bond issue is boring as hell, but a lot of people are interested because of the floods last spring. This afternoon, Clarence, I want you to head over to the Army recruiting station on Broadway. We haven't done a recruiting story this month so it's about time. Get a few interviews with some of the recruiters and the men enlisting. Look for a new angle. Maybe find some guy who's enlisting that has an unusual story—maybe an older guy with a

273

family—or see if they signed up a married gal for the WAC who hasn't shipped out yet and get her story. Something out of the ordinary. Have it ready for Sunday's paper."

Holcomb nodded. "Okay."

Kapperman turned to Elizabeth Ault and asked the question he had asked her every day for weeks. "What's cookin' with the Crucifier?" Liniger and Holcomb also looked at her. Everyone in Cincinnati, it seemed, was still interested in the sensational case. Of course her editor and colleagues knew nothing about Anne Brown's spying. And no one at the newspaper knew about that Friday two weeks ago at Union Terminal, or that the teletype message Anne Brown sent from the *Observer* in Elizabeth's name was not really from Elizabeth (Leroy Carr had insisted she tell no one at the newspaper that the message was not from her). Kapperman and everyone else at the *Observer* knew only that Anne Brown was tied to the Over the Rhine attacks.

Elizabeth answered, "Nothing new."

"What's your take, Elizabeth?" Kapperman asked. "Will they ever find that woman? With Frank on the case you must have some idea of any progress." Like most newspaper editors, especially the good ones, Kapperman never thought of a question he was afraid to ask.

"I don't know, Otis." Elizabeth played the part she had been asked by Frank and the OSS to play: unknowing and elusive when answering questions about Anne Brown. "Seems to me that since she saved those two women she'd come forward, answer questions, and then move on with her life. Some people think she went overboard while saving the women, but just as many or even more think she's a hero. Even the district attorney says it would be hard to convict her of anything other than perhaps owning a gun with a silencer. But for some reason she won't come forward, so if I were her I'd be long gone by now. That's just my opinion. But until something breaks, I've covered all the bases. I've reported the facts several times and written opinion pieces. I did the story about her approaching me in the restaurant then I followed that up with a story about the reaction to *that* story. I don't know what I can write that won't be old news until something happens—either new information is uncovered or they catch her." Elizabeth knew a lot of things she *could* write but never would.

Her editor agreed. "Yeah, we don't want to rehash old news. But that's a helluva story, sold a lot of newspapers and you scooped much of it. Let's hope something breaks soon. What's the latest on your favorite city councilman?"

"Odds are he'll squirm his way out of the graft charge," Elizabeth predicted. "I'm keeping an eye on it."

"When will I see something from you on that?"

"I'm working on an opinion piece for Sunday."

Kapperman nodded. "Okay, gentlemen and lady. Keep up the good work. Check in before you leave for the day or before I leave. I'm here till deadline at ten tonight."

On the way back through the newsroom, Elizabeth stopped and poured a cup of Postum before returning to her desk. From a file in a desk drawer, she took out the opinion piece she started earlier concerning the recent travails of the crooked city councilman. It was a rough draft, but Elizabeth always did her writing on the typewriter, never by longhand unlike some of her colleagues who used a pencil for the rough drafts before switching to a typewriter. Elizabeth would type away, not worrying about grammatical mistakes or spelling, then pull the paper and proofread, making notes for the next draft. Otis Kapperman liked to kid Elizabeth that she single-handedly saved the companies that manufacture typewriter ribbons from the Great Depression.

Elizabeth scribbled her corrections and alterations where needed then rolled a clean sheet of paper into the carriage of her Underwood for her next draft. She had begun punching keys when Larry Liniger shouted at her from three desks away.

"Phone, Elizabeth!" Liniger held up the receiver.

Elizabeth pushed back her chair, rose, and walked over to Liniger's desk. "Sorry, Larry, probably someone I asked to call me about an interview but they asked for the newsroom instead of my desk."

Elizabeth accepted the receiver from Liniger and put it to her ear. "Hello, Elizabeth Ault speaking."

"Hello, Elizabeth. It's Anne. How are you?"

Chapter 45

Stella serves a cold Coca-Cola

[same day]

" . . . *Elizabeth, are you there? . . . Elizabeth?*" Anne Brown was on the telephone.

"Yes, I'm here," Elizabeth finally responded. She looked down at Larry Liniger who sat three feet away, typing. "I'm not at my desk."

"*I know. I chose not to call your desk in case your husband and his friends had made arrangements to listen in. I will not keep you. Please listen carefully. Are you listening, Elizabeth?*"

"Yes."

"*Go across the street to Stella's Café. Sit down in the café, order something, and wait. Any questions?*"

Elizabeth hesitated.

"*Elizabeth?*"

Elizabeth answered, "I understand."

"*You must do this right now, Elizabeth. I expect you to be seated in the café within five minutes. You do not have time to make a phone call and wait for your husband.*"

The phone clicked.

Elizabeth placed the receiver on the cradle and Liniger looked up.

"That was short and sweet," Liniger commented.

"Yeah . . ." Elizabeth, trying to remain calm, needed a quick cover-up. "Just a . . . someone confirming a scheduled interview like I thought. Thanks, Larry."

Not bothering with her coat and hat, Elizabeth walked briskly out of the newsroom. As she descended the stairs, thoughts and questions raced. *Should I call Frank as soon as I get there? No, she might already be there or somehow be watching. I'll wait as she said. Maybe I can grab her and yell for help, or overpower her myself and have someone call Frank. If she isn't there, what then? How long should I wait? ten minutes? twenty? an hour?*

Elizabeth left the building half-walking half-running and darted into the street forcing a delivery truck driver to lock his brakes and skid to a noisy stop. Elizabeth jumped back, her heart pounding. She ignored the angry, shouting driver and hurried across while he was stopped.

When Elizabeth walked into the café, Stella, a middle-aged woman who always wore a flowered apron and her hair in a bun, stood at the cash register making change for a man paying his bill. "Hello, sweetie," said Stella when she saw Elizabeth.

"Hello, Stella." Elizabeth kept her head on a swivel, looking at the customers, but other than the man paying his bill, there were only three: a man sat at the counter smoking a pipe, and an elderly couple occupied one of the tables. No Anne Brown. Elizabeth sat at a small table near a wall.

Stella moved behind the counter and asked Elizabeth, "Coffee, sweetie?"

"No, a Coca-Cola, Stella," Elizabeth answered.

Stella delivered a cold six-and-a-half-ounce bottle of Coca Cola and a glass with ice. As Stella set down the drink, Elizabeth realized she had no money. Besides leaving her coat and hat in the newsroom, she had left her purse in one of her desk drawers.

"Special today is chicken salad. Comes with potato chips," Stella announced.

"No thanks, Stella, not right now. I forgot my purse in the newsroom. Can I give you the nickel later?"

"Yes, that's fine. Don't worry about it. Just remind me the next time you're in."

"Thank you."

Stella returned to her station behind the counter. The telephone beside the cash register rang. Stella made her way over and answered.

"Yes, she's here . . . hold on." Stella lowered the receiver and looked at Elizabeth. "It's for you."

Of course it could be only one person. Elizabeth rose, walked to the register, and took the phone. Stella began counting money as Elizabeth talked.

"Yes."

"Elizabeth?"

"Yes."

"Go into the ladies' restroom. Behind the sink is an envelope taped to the porcelain. Reach around the sink from underneath and you will feel it. Once you have the envelope you may leave. Open it when you are alone. Good-bye, Elizabeth."

At the other end, Anne Brown hung up. Elizabeth handed the telephone back to Stella. She had been in the café restroom before and knew it was single occupancy: one sink, one water closet. Elizabeth walked to the rear of the café and knocked on the closed door, turned the knob, and walked in. The white porcelain sink, bolted to the wall, rested on a thick china pedestal rising from the floor. She bent over and felt around the back of the pedestal but touched nothing other than slick, cool china. She knelt for a better reach and finally felt paper up high. Her first pull failed to release the securely taped envelope; Elizabeth had to use both hands to free it.

The sealed, plain white envelope showed no markings. Elizabeth debated whether to open it now or wait. She folded the loose tape around the envelope and put it in her pants pocket before walking out of the restroom to rejoin her Coca-Cola.

On impulse, Elizabeth took the knife from the silverware rolled into a napkin and sliced the envelope flap. The one page, hand-printed note, had a small key taped to its corner.

Dearest Elizabeth, I had hoped your offers to meet were sincere but I see they were not. I thought you were a woman of strength and purpose. Sadly, I was mistaken. What I have seen is a weak and frightened woman. If by chance my original thoughts about you are correct, be in the Rusty Bottom Bar tomorrow, Saturday, at 4:00 p.m. Wear a long coat and comfortable walking shoes. Do not wear a hat. Order a drink and sit at the bar. Sip the drink lightly. You will not want alcohol making you sluggish. I will call you with further instructions. Do not forget the key.

I promise you two things, Elizabeth.

I have many safeguards planned for your journey to meet me. If you betray me I promise you I will know it. You will never see me tomorrow and never hear from me again. If you were sincere about meeting me, this chance is your last. Perhaps you will find a way to capture me yourself or discover a clue that can help your husband later. My second promise is that you are in no danger from me unless you force me to defend myself.

Elizabeth folded the paper and returned it to the envelope. If Anne Brown's goal was to humiliate her, she had succeeded. Yes, Brown had cause to accuse Elizabeth of being weak and frightened after the meeting in Sano's. Caught off guard and downcast about the incident with Glen Shafer, she reacted badly. Then to add insult to injury:

Perhaps you will find a way to capture me yourself or discover a clue that can help your husband later.

Elizabeth regarded the note as an insult, a taunt daring her to show her mettle. She left Stella's and returned to the *Observer* newsroom. The next couple of hours were spent at her desk acting busy when someone approached, hoping she wouldn't be bothered, fiddling with papers she cared nothing about, all the time thinking. Elizabeth did not doubt Anne Brown's promise that if Elizabeth were under surveillance the spy would know. So far Anne Brown had always stayed a step ahead. Besides, Frank had already told Leroy Carr that Elizabeth would no longer be involved, and even if she could change his mind he would never allow it without her being watched and protected. Anne Brown would know, somehow, and that would be the end of it. If she did not tell Frank and she decided to sneak away to meet Anne Brown she would have no protection. Obviously, she should let Frank deal with this. That would be the logical thing. More than once Elizabeth picked up the telephone to call Frank, then stopped and put back the receiver.

She opened the envelope, reread the note, and examined the key—all markings had been filed off. Elizabeth glanced at the wall clock: 4:03 p.m.

She knew that at this time tomorrow she would be at the Rusty Bottom.

Chapter 46

A Welcome Back

[same day]

Elizabeth dialed Frank's direct number at District 1.

"Detective Sergeant Ault."

"Hi, Frank. I'm done for the day."

"You're getting off early. Did they run out of trees over there at the paper?"

Elizabeth ignored the quip. "I want to go out to eat, Frank. When will you be done?"

"I can probably be out of here in an hour. Where do you want to go?"

"Sano's."

A moment's silence at the other end.

"Sano's? I thought you didn't want to go back there."

"I changed my mind. If I make a reservation for seven o'clock will that work for you? If you pick me up in about an hour that will give us time to go home first so I can freshen up."

"Okay, if that's what you want."

Jim Sano warmly welcomed the Aults, much to Elizabeth's relief. She had felt uncertain how they would be greeted after the tumult of the Anne Brown meeting. When Frank arrived that day and Elizabeth told him the woman who just left her table was Anne Brown, Elizabeth alarmed the other customers when she shouted after Frank that the woman had a gun as he charged out the door. But Giacomo *Jim* Sano had grown up around guns with many friends and even relatives active in the Naples *La Cosa Nostra*. He had told Frank this when the two chatted once while Frank waited for Elizabeth. Jim Sano worried little about someone with a gun as long as it was not pointed at him or somebody in his family. The old Italian even expressed disappointment that Elizabeth did not name his restaurant in her article about the meeting.

"That-a would-a been a nice advertise."

After Sano seated the Aults and walked away, Elizabeth remarked about her uncertainties. "One reason I was hesitant to come back here is because I wasn't sure they would want me back. You'll remember I shouted to you that Anne Brown had a gun and I know it alarmed the other customers."

Frank downplayed her concern. "I'm sure some of the customers were startled, but guns don't scare the Sanos. Jim keeps a gun on a shelf under the register."

"How do you know that?"

"I saw it. One day I needed to look up a phone number. Jim keeps the phone book under the cash register. I helped myself and there it was. It wouldn't be smart to rob this place. I'd lay odds that cash register gun isn't the only gun around here."

"You know how I feel about guns," she said. "I think there are too many around."

"Nothing wrong with people having guns," he countered, "as long as the right people have them. The problems happen when bad people have guns and good people don't."

Growing up, Elizabeth had fired her father's and brother's hunting rifles, and once she fired Frank's handgun during a picnic in the woods. Guns did not scare her, yet she never understood the American fascination. However, she did not wish to get into a lengthy debate— not tonight. The subject was dropped when Anthony Sano brought over menus and took their drink orders.

"Anything new with the Anne Brown case?" asked Elizabeth.

Frank was surprised at her question. Since the Union Terminal debacle, his wife had tried to avoid the subject of Anne Brown. "Not really. I told you a few days ago that Carr had the FCC bring in some fancy radiowave monitoring equipment. They have these things set up outside town so they can monitor any shortwave radio signals coming out of the area. If Brown is still around and sends another message, they might be able to find out where it's coming from while it's being broadcast. That's the latest." Anthony returned with Frank's beer and Elizabeth's wine; he said he would come back shortly to take their dinner orders. "How was your day?" Frank asked.

"Fine," she said.

"Babe, it's a big relief for me that you're out of all of this—you don't know how much of a relief. I don't think she's going to send you any more notes, but if she does just turn them over to me. That's all you need to do."

281

Elizabeth drank her wine and said nothing. She wanted to enjoy the evening with her husband, and tonight might be their last pleasurable time together for a while. And it wasn't solely because of the meeting tomorrow with Anne Brown that caused her to think that way. Elizabeth had decided that, before she left tomorrow to meet with Anne Brown, she would tell Frank about her mistake with another man.

Part III

**Saturday, October 30
and
Sunday, October 31, 1943**

Die Lorelei *(The Lorelei)*
Heinrich Heine (1797-1856)

Ich weiß nicht, was soll es
bedeuten,
Daß ich so traurig bin;
Ein Märchen aus alten Zeiten,
Das kommt mir nicht aus dem
Sinn.

Die Luft ist kühl und es dunkelt,
Und ruhig fließt der Rhein;
Der Gipfel des Berges funkelt,
Im Abendsonnenschein.

Die schönste Jungfrau sitzet
Dort oben wunderbar,
Ihr gold'nes Geschmeide blitzet,
Sie kämmt ihr goldenes Haar.

Sie kämmt es mit goldenem
Kamme,
Und singt ein Lied dabei;
Das hat eine wundersame,
Gewaltige Melodei.

Den Schiffer im kleinen Schiffe,
Ergreift es mit wildem Weh;
Er schaut nicht die Felsenriffe,
Er schaut nur hinauf in die Höh'.

Ich glaube, die Wellen
verschlingen
Am Ende Schiffer und Kahn,
Und das hat mit ihrem Singen,
Die Lorelei getan.

Translation by Mark Twain:

I cannot divine what it meaneth,
This haunting nameless pain:
A tale of the bygone ages
Keeps brooding through my brain:

The loveliest maiden is sitting
High-throned in yon blue air,
Her golden jewels are shining,
She combs her golden hair;

The doomed in his drifting shallop,
Is tranced with the sad sweet tone,
He sees not the yawing breakers,
He sees but the maid alone:

The faint air cools in the gloaming,
And peaceful flows the Rhine,
The thirsty summits are drinking
The sunset's flooding wine;

She combs with a comb that is
golden,
And sings a weird refrain
That steeps in a deadly
enchantment
The listener's ravished brain:

The pitiless billows engulf him!-
So perish sailor and bark;
And this, with her baleful singing,
Is the Lorelei's gruesome work.

Chapter 47

Sensible Shoes

Cincinnati—Saturday, October 30, 1943

9:10 a.m.—the Ault home

Frank had cooked one of his big breakfasts and now noticed his wife poking around on her plate.

"Not hungry?" Frank asked as he shoved a sausage into his mouth.

"No, not very," Elizabeth answered. "I didn't sleep well . . . drifted in and out."

He swallowed. "Something bothering you, honey?"

She shook her head no.

Frank said, "I have to go into the station for a while, but how about tonight I take you to Grandpa Floyd's Chili Shack for some chili and a beer? We haven't had chili in a couple of weeks."

Elizabeth laid down her fork and looked at her husband.

"Frank. . . ."

Frank waited. When she didn't continue he said, "Okay, babe, what is it? What's bothering you?"

"Frank, I met a man; I did not have an affair, Frank," she added quickly. "He kissed me and I let him do it. That's all that happened. It was a one-time thing—I haven't seen him since and I'll never do it again. I love you, Frank. I made a mistake and I am truly sorry."

Frank stood without scooting back his chair, causing the table to partially lift with him then bang back to the floor. Both cups of coffee overturned. "Who is he?"

"Frank, it was a mistake and I am sorry. It won't happen again!"

"Who the fuck is he?" Frank shouted. He never used that word in Elizabeth's presence but he forgot himself.

"His name is John." Her face was crimson.

"John! . . . John what?"

"He's from out of town. He's gone. I'll never see him again and I don't ever want to see him again. Frank, you have every right to be mad. . . ."

Frank didn't let her finish. "Where were you when this happened?"

285

"Downtown."

"Why did you do it, Elizabeth?"

"Oh, Frank. I don't know why . . . I guess it was a weak moment. We had been having problems—arguing a lot about Anne Brown—but that's not an excuse for me, and it's not your fault. It's my fault."

"You're not telling me everything. What else?"

"What??? I told you I didn't have an affair, Frank. I'm telling the truth. I didn't sleep with the guy!"

"Don't bullshit me! I've lived with you long enough to know when you aren't telling me the whole story. What are you leaving out?"

Elizabeth was panicky. He knew she was holding back. *I can't tell him it was Glen, both for Glen's sake and especially for Frank's sake.* "Frank . . . he felt my breasts. There, I hope you're happy!" Elizabeth rose and marched out of the kitchen. From the bedroom, she heard the front door slam, Frank's car start, and tires squeal. She ran back to the kitchen where they kept an address book by the phone. She thumbed through and dialed a number. It took several rings.

"Hello." Glen Shafer sounded as if he had just awakened.

"Glen, it's Elizabeth."

"Elizabeth?" Shafer sounded surprised.

"Glen, I just told Frank about the mistake I made with you. . . ."

Shafer interrupted. *"Holy God, Elizabeth. . . ."*

"Let me finish. I didn't tell him it was you. I was afraid of what Frank would do, and I don't want anyone blamed but me. I made up a name and told Frank the guy is from out of town. I'm just telling you in case Frank talks about it when he sees you."

"Knowing Frank, I doubt that he'll talk about it, but I'm glad you told me, Elizabeth. Do you want me to tell him it was me? You shouldn't take all the blame."

"No, no, no! Glen, that's the worst thing you can do. All that will do is make everything much worse. Knowing it was you will just hurt Frank even more. Promise me you won't do that!" Elizabeth feared Frank might seriously harm Glen, and doing so might ruin Frank. "Promise me, Glen. If you care about Frank and me you won't tell him."

"Okay, Elizabeth."

"Keep that promise, Glen." Elizabeth hung up and dropped into the nearest chair.

[3:00 p.m.]
Never a great user of makeup, Elizabeth looked into the bathroom mirror and applied mascara. For work and any average day, her makeup included mascara, rouge, and a light gloss of lipstick. For a formal social function such as a charity ball (attended infrequently because getting Frank to go was like parting the Red Sea), or an occasional symphony, she spent more time on her makeup.

Frank had not returned. She must be at the Rusty Bottom by 4:00. If Frank returned before she left, she would tell him she had to go in to work: something she normally did on Saturday, if just briefly. Getting away was not the problem—dealing with marital problems was. The confession gave her a measure of relief. Right after the incident, she felt like an adulteress. Clearing the air with Glen eased some of that feeling, but still she felt like a cheat for hiding it from Frank. Now it was over. Elizabeth felt horrible for hurting her husband, and she realized it might take time for him to trust her again, but for today, at least, mending things with Frank would have to move to a back burner. When she finished with the mascara, Elizabeth ran a brush through her hair, straightened her top (she decided against a skirt in favor of slacks), and walked back to the bedroom.

She sat on the bed and slipped on the most sensible pair of walking shoes she owned, then stood and put on her long coat but no hat: all by orders of Anne Brown. Elizabeth did not know Brown's motive for this meeting, but the reporter knew she was not going on an interview. Before she left the bedroom, Elizabeth laid a piece of paper—a carefully prepared note for Frank—on the bed. On her way out the bedroom door she stopped suddenly, turned back, went to the dresser and opened the second drawer. Elizabeth rummaged through Frank's T-shirts and found it. She took out his spare gun, a Smith & Wesson .38 snub-nose revolver, looked at it for a moment, checked that it was loaded then put it in her purse. She went back to the piece of paper and added another sentence at the bottom.

From the kitchen, she dialed Frank's number.

"Detective Sergeant Ault."

"Frank, I'm going out for a while and I left you a note in the bedroom. I love you, Frank." She hung up quickly, not giving him time to respond or question. Then she left the house for a waiting taxi.

287

[3:50 p.m.—Rusty Bottom Bar]

Elizabeth took a seat at the bar.

"Hi, Elizabeth," greeted the bartender.

"Hi, Melvin. Just a club soda for now." If she were forced to walk far, alcohol was what she wanted least.

Melvin delivered the club soda and told Elizabeth there was no charge.

"Thanks, Melvin. I might get a phone call."

"Okay."

Melvin moved down the bar and Elizabeth, nervous about what lay ahead, sipped the soda. Clarence Holcomb, one of her *Observer* city beat colleagues, sat with his wife at a booth. When Clarence shouted a greeting, Elizabeth turned and waved.

Melvin answered the ringing phone at exactly 4:15, laid down the receiver and nodded at Elizabeth. She rose and walked around the end of the bar where the phone sat on a counter.

"Yes?"

"Hi." Anne Brown sounded chipper.

"Yes!" Elizabeth knew she sounded impatient but didn't care.

"You have the key?"

"Yes, I have it."

"Walk to the Negro YWCA on Eighth and Cutter. I'm sure you know of it." She paused.

"Yes, I know where it is."

"Take this route: walk west on Fifth Street to Elm, then north to Eighth, then west to Cutter Street. Repeat that, please."

"West on Fifth to Elm, north to Eighth, west to the YWCA."

"Very good, Elizabeth. Do not deviate from that route. When you get to the YWCA, go inside. At the rear of the first floor hallway you will see a series of small wall lockers. Your key will open locker number 17. Inside you will find an envelope with further instructions. Again, that's locker 17. Any questions?"

"No."

"Leave now and walk quickly."

Elizabeth heard the click. She laid a dime tip on the bar, left what remained of the drink, and walked out of the Rusty Bottom.

Cincinnati had two YWCAs, one on 9th and Walnut—the white YWCA, and the Negro YWCA on 8th and Cutter streets. The 8th and Cutter YWCA, Elizabeth's destination, was approximately ten blocks west of the Rusty Bottom. She cut though Fountain Square, her presence shooing a flock of strutting pigeons skyward. Heading west on 5th Street for two blocks before turning right on Elm, Elizabeth walked briskly and kept an eye out, wondering if she were being watched at that exact moment. Anne Brown had not given her a set time to reach the YWCA: *walk quickly* was the instruction. She did not need her coat for the sunny and 62-degree day and considered taking it off and carrying it, but the coat was among the instructions so she left it on. When she reached 7th Street, traffic held her up before she could cross, then on to 8th and then left to Cutter.

There was more than one entrance into the building so Elizabeth picked one. This YWCA had no official designation setting it apart from the YWCA on Walnut other than a handwritten sign taped to the door: *Coloreds Welcome.* Inside, Elizabeth saw two hallways heading in different directions. Down one hall stood a group of five young women, apparently friends, laughing and cutting up. The group included two Caucasian women. She approached the group.

"Can someone tell me where the lockers are?" Elizabeth asked the group in general. "I was told they are down a hallway."

"What is the locker number?" asked one of the white women.

"Seventeen."

Apparently the woman did not know the location of 17, so she looked at the group. One of the Negro women said, "All the way down the other hall, ma'am."

"Thank you." Elizabeth backtracked and located locker 17. She touched around in her purse until she felt the key under Frank's gun and opened the locker. Inside rested a white, unmarked envelope like the one she yesterday pulled from the back of Stella's restroom sink. Elizabeth opened the envelope; inside was another note and another key. This key, bigger than the YWCA locker key, also had the markings filed off.

> Near the northeast corner of 5th and Race Street is a small drug store called Schwenck's. On the curb in front of that store is a telephone booth. I will call you there at exactly 5:00.

Anne Brown wanted Elizabeth to basically return to where she had started—5th and Race was only a block and a half from the Rusty Bottom. She looked at her wristwatch. It was 4:42. Elizabeth had walked vigorously for about 20 minutes to get to the YWCA, and then she used some extra time finding the locker. She shoved the note and key back in the envelope then into her purse. She would have to hurry to make it to the phone booth in 18 minutes.

Elizabeth walked back the same way she came as swiftly as she could without breaking into a run. It seemed even warmer now. Perspiration beaded on her forehead and, ignoring orders, Elizabeth removed her coat as she walked.

[4:45 p.m.—the Ault home]
Frank parked on the street. He unlocked the front door and entered the house. He had spent most of his day in a daze. He believed her about not having an affair, but just kissing another man and allowing him to fondle her still shocked and hurt. *Why did Elizabeth do it?* He had asked himself over and over. And where was she going when she called? She hung up before he could ask.

Frank walked into the bedroom to look for the note Elizabeth promised and saw it right away on the bed.

Frank, yesterday I received a phone call and note from Anne Brown. I have left to meet her today. I must be at a certain place at a certain time and she said she would call me there. I'm doing this for two reasons: for our country, she needs to be stopped, and also because I feel this is the only way I can put an end to her controlling my life. I decided to do it this way because I think she will know of any attempts to guard or watch me. My plan is to try and get a phone call to you with a location when I meet her and I will try to keep her there until you come. Please stay home and by the phone. I will call you there. I don't know how I will pull this off, or even if I can, but I will try. I will be careful, darling.

I love you, Elizabeth

I took the gun.

[5:00 p.m.—5th Street]

Her watch said 5:00 when Elizabeth was still half a block from Schwenk's Drug Store. She could see the phone booth and that the door was folded open. When Elizabeth reached the corner directly across the street she heard the phone ring, but before she could cross she had to let a city bus pass. As soon as the bus no longer blocked her view, she saw an old man walk into the booth and answer the phone. Elizabeth ran across the street and shouted at the old man.

"Sir, that's for me!"

"They hung up," the old man said as he backed out of the booth and handed Elizabeth the receiver.

She entered the booth and put the receiver to her ear. "Shit!" she said out loud when she heard the dial tone. The old man looked at her and walked off. Elizabeth hung up. *What do I do now?*

A few seconds later the telephone rang again. Elizabeth jerked the receiver off the hook. "That was just a man on the street. I didn't get here in time and he heard the phone ringing and answered. . . ."

"*I know, Elizabeth. I saw.*"

"You saw?"

"*Yes, I saw you walk by earlier on your way to the YWCA and I see you now. Turn and look up to the fifth floor of the hotel across the street.*"

Across 5th Street was the Netherlands Hotel. Elizabeth looked up, counted floors, and scanned windows. She spotted Anne Brown, with a telephone to her ear, looking down at her from an open window.

"*Come on up, Elizabeth. Room 511. Don't knock. The key in the YWCA envelope fits the door. Room 511, got that?*"

"Yes."

Click.

Elizabeth looked again at the window. Anne Brown was gone.

291

Chapter 48

Room 511

5:08 p.m.—The Netherlands Hotel

The doorman greeted Elizabeth.

Opened in 1931, the swanky Netherlands Hotel was the place most visiting celebrities and the rich and powerful quartered when travels brought them to town. The hotel also served as a gathering place for local blood that was blue, and a venue for society events. The chic hotel restaurant offered cuisine prepared by top chefs seduced to come to Cincinnati from New York City and Philadelphia by hotel ownership with deep pockets, and waiters who made everything perfect for those who could afford to pay the bill after dessert. Elizabeth and Frank Ault dined here on their anniversaries and a few other special occasions.

Once inside the lobby, Elizabeth walked directly to the elevator. She did not like the meeting location—a hotel room. She would feel safer in a public place, preferably a busy public place, but she had no control at this point and was determined to see this through.

"Floor?" asked a teenaged elevator boy in a green and gold uniform topped off by a matching bellhop cap.

"Five, please." After the door closed, Elizabeth considered moving the gun to her coat pocket but decided to leave it in her purse.

"Nice day today," the boy said as he pushed a button, his back to Elizabeth. A soft clank was followed by a gentle whirl as the elevator started upward.

"Yes," said Elizabeth, submerged in her own thoughts.

She watched the arrow over the elevator door sweep the face of a dial, first passing the Roman numeral II then III. As the arrow crossed IV the compartment slowed. When the elevator reached the 5th floor, it went slightly past, stopped, and then settled back down. The door opened.

"Fifth floor," the boy announced.

"Which way to 511?" she asked.

"At the end of this hallway make a right, ma'am."

She stepped off and the door closed behind her. Following the boy's directions, in a moment Elizabeth stood outside room 511. Habit nearly forced her to knock, and she had in fact raised her hand to the knocker, but then remembered the instructions. She took the key from her purse, inserted and then turned it and heard the bolt click. Elizabeth opened the door a few inches, then stopped and took a deep breath.

[5:10 p.m.—the Ault home]

With only one hope to talk to Elizabeth—that being a possible phone call from her to the home phone—Frank could not leave. Immediately after reading Elizabeth's note, he called Ed Cantrell at his home and Glen Shafer (still at the station). They both rushed over and now stood in Frank Ault's living room. Both men had read Elizabeth's note.

"We'll have to work out of here," Frank said.

"I'll call the station and tell them we're setting up a command post at your house," said Cantrell. "I won't tell them the specifics, but I want to make sure that if anything comes through headquarters concerning Elizabeth or Anne Brown they relay it to us immediately."

Frank nodded and Cantrell used Frank's home police radio to contact headquarters, leaving the Ault's telephone line open.

"Why do you think Elizabeth is doing this, Frank?" a worried Glen Shafer asked.

"Christ, Glen," Frank was beside himself. "I know she felt embarrassed about the way she handled herself when Brown approached her at Sano's. And I think she feels she let us down. I think she even feels she let down her country and her Marine brother, even though he doesn't know anything about any of this shit. Elizabeth's a strong woman and she can't live with any of that. And I think Anne Brown knows that and is playing her for some goddamn reason. I'm telling you, Glen, if that woman hurts Elizabeth I'll find and kill her if it takes the rest of my life."

Cantrell, now off the radio, said, "Everything is set up at headquarters. If anything comes in about Elizabeth or the case they'll relay everything to us here until I tell them differently. I told them to radio your RCA here at the house, Frank—not call the phone."

When a car screeched to a stop outside, Frank went to the window. Leroy Carr and Al Hodge stepped out of a Jeep driven by an Army sergeant.

"It's Carr and Hodge," Frank said. "Cantrell, what are those pricks doing here?"

"I called Carr before I left to come over here," Cantrell answered. "Frank, whether you like it or not, Carr is still in charge and it's not up to you, me, or anyone else to cut them out. With any national security case we're required to work with the government. It's the law, and all of us have sworn to uphold the law, Frank."

"That's all I need right now," Frank complained. "I'm sitting at home on my ass while my wife is out, God only knows where, with a trigger-happy Nazi, and now I have to deal with Charlie Chan and his number one son."

[Same time—The Netherlands Hotel]

Elizabeth pushed open the door and looked into room 511 before entering. From the hallway, she saw no one.

"Hello," she called loudly. No answer. A laughing couple with a young child came out of the next room and headed in the direction of the elevator. Elizabeth took one step into 511 and tried again.

"Hello . . . Anne?"

Nothing.

She left the door open and took two steps into the room. "Hello?"

Besides the large bed, Elizabeth saw a small couch, a chifforobe, and a desk with an upholstered chair. On the desk was a telephone. In the corner a Philco sat on a highly polished, wooden table. The room was large and well-appointed, but not a multi-roomed suite so Elizabeth could see that nobody was there. Then she spotted the door to the bathroom. She walked to the closed door, listened but heard nothing. She had to know for sure. Gently, and nervously, Elizabeth opened the door.

Anne Brown was not in room 511. Other than some clothes on the foot of the bed, the room looked unused: the bedspread unruffled, the linens in the bathroom fresh. Elizabeth stood for a moment, thinking. This was the right room; the key had worked. She walked to the window and looked out. The phone booth across the street confirmed this was the window from which Anne Brown had looked down at her. Elizabeth walked back to the door, looked into the hall, saw no one and closed and locked the door using the chain. Apparently Anne Brown planned on letting her stew for a while, possibly to ensure

Elizabeth was not followed, or perhaps merely to play a cruel game of nerves. But at least now, with the chain latched, when Brown came back she would have to knock. Elizabeth felt a small measure of relief knowing Brown could not walk in and surprise her.

Elizabeth eyed the telephone. There was no way Anne Brown could be watching her at this moment. She rushed to the phone and picked it up to dial Frank. No dial tone. She pounded the cradle then saw the wire had been ripped out of the wall. She dropped the dead receiver to the desk then reeled in the phone line to look at the frayed end.

Disheartened, Elizabeth threw down the wire and realized she would have to wait. She couldn't leave the room to make a call and risk being gone when Brown returned. Elizabeth set her purse on the desk, loosened her coat sash, took off the coat and laid it on the bed. That's when the clothes again caught her attention. She walked to the foot of the bed to look more closely and immediately noticed a piece of paper sticking out from under a skirt atop the neatly stacked clothing. Elizabeth pulled out the paper:

> Elizabeth, thank you for keeping your end of the arrangement to this point. You might have noticed that I disconnected the telephone. If you tried to use it I am sure it was just to reassure your husband that you are well. I have no objection to such a call but a hotel room phone would be an unwise choice as a call can be easily traced through the hotel switchboard.
>
> I bought you some clothes. I hope you like them. We are close to the same height and I am usually accurate at judging women's clothing sizes. Please change into all of these clothes. When you walked by the hotel on your way to the YWCA I saw that you are wearing pants so you do not have a slip to worry about. You may wear your underpants but not your bra. Take it off. Shoes are in the closet. I guessed at your shoe size but nevertheless I bought a few sizes. There is a tube of lipstick under the clothes. That is the only makeup change necessary. When you leave the room, your long coat will cover the new clothes. Remove your wedding ring and put it in your purse. Leave the clothes you are wearing now and your purse in the room. I will not be returning to the room. You have a key. Put it

295

in your coat pocket and you can return for your things before hotel checkout time tomorrow.

At exactly 6:00 p.m. a taxi will pick you up in front of the hotel. Make sure you get in the correct taxi. Ask the driver if he has come to pick up Elizabeth. He will know where to take you. The driver has been paid and tipped well.

I believe you have so far kept our bargain, meaning you are alone. If you told your husband ahead of time, I doubt he would have agreed to let you proceed unwatched. If you were being watched I would know by now so I commend your courage. I will keep my promise that you are in no danger as long as you do not betray me. If you dress quickly you might find a moment to call Frank from the phone booth across the street. I do not mind. You can assure him you are all right.

An important thing to remember: my name is now Early.

Chapter 49

Frank Gets a Call

5:40 p.m.—the Ault home

Frank Ault and four other men in shirtsleeves milled about Ault's living room. All had by now removed their suit jackets revealing each wore a shoulder holster with firearm. The telephone, on an extra-long cord, had been moved from the kitchen and now sat on a lamp table. In the corner, on another lamp table, were Frank's home police radio and two U.S. Army walkie-talkies Leroy Carr and Al Hodge brought with them. The walkie-talkies linked the OSS men to the FCC watchdogs Carr brought to Cincinnati to monitor shortwave radio traffic. If the FCC men intercepted any suspicious transmissions emanating from the immediate area, orders were to work frantically to triangulate the intercepts and pinpoint the transmission origin location. Then the FCC would radio Carr and Hodge on the walkie-talkies. The radios had not left Carr's and Hodge's sights in a week, even taking them along to the toilet. Plenty of spare batteries were always on hand. If the FCC called with a location, that call would trigger a mad race by the OSS men. Carr had promised Ed Cantrell that, if such a call came, he would notify Cantrell immediately, but since then Carr had had second thoughts. He knew notifying Cantrell would be the same as notifying Frank Ault. Carr had not had to deal with Ault in over a week and had not missed him. He had sized up Ault as a competent detective, but overly obstinate and hot-headed. Those qualities could derail Carr's top secret OSS mission—a mission the Cincinnati police knew nothing about. Carr could order Cantrell to take Ault off the case—it was within his power—and he had made up his mind to do just that if he encountered any more problems with the detective.

Now Carr's plan to cut Frank Ault out of the case was out the proverbial window. That afternoon, Elizabeth Ault opened that window and tossed Carr's plan out. Carr thought the German spy might be done with the reporter after using Elizabeth's name to send the transmission from the newspaper radio teletype, but this second contact made it obvious that Lorelei had more plans for Elizabeth, leaving Leroy Carr no choice but to continue to work with her

297

stubborn husband. Thus the five men familiar with the case—Carr and Hodge from the OSS and Cincinnati cops Ault, Shafer, and Cantrell—were back together.

All five were on edge.

"How in the devil is Elizabeth going to make a phone call with Anne Brown there?" Al Hodge asked the others. When around the Cincinnati policemen, Hodge and Carr both referred to the German spy codenamed *Lorelei* as Anne Brown, the name familiar to the cops.

"It's not going to happen," answered an equally doubtful Glen Shafer. "We need some other ideas besides sitting here with our thumbs up our asses."

Cantrell frowned. "I'm sure we're all ears if you have those ideas, Glen."

"What about Carr there?" Shafer glared at the OSS man. "He's supposed to be in charge and know everything."

Leroy Carr, lost in his thoughts, did not respond to Shafer's sarcasm.

Frank Ault, too, had been thinking and seemed distracted and distant, but he spoke up.

"Elizabeth will find a way."

[5:43 p.m.—Room 511]

Elizabeth changed quickly into the clothes left by Anne Brown and now stood looking into a full-length mirror attached to the back of the chifforobe door.

I look like a French prostitute from the movies.

The bright red skirt was too short. Elizabeth knew when she sat down the tops of the thigh-high, black cotton hose and the garters that held them would be visible. She had removed her bra as ordered. The sleeveless, off-the-shoulder, white peasant girl top revealed a shameless amount of cleavage. The thin fabric embarrassed Elizabeth because it revealed the outline of her nipples. The shiny, bright red lipstick seemed mere window dressing in the transformation from professional reporter to tart.

She hurried. The taxi would pick her up in front of the hotel in a few minutes and she wanted enough time to call Frank. She went to the closet. Inside were three pairs of shoes, all red pumps of various sizes. Elizabeth quickly picked size 7 and leaned against the wall to slip them on.

Thankful that Anne Brown allowed her the long coat to cover the embarrassing outfit, Elizabeth donned it and tightened the sash. When she had entered the room, she laid the key on the desk. Now she dropped it into her right coat pocket along with the gun from her purse. She also took the money from her purse and stuffed it in the left coat pocket, then returned to the mirror. Elizabeth could see the pocket bulge from the weight and size of the gun, but no outline. She assured herself no one would know she carried a gun.

Elizabeth looked at her wedding ring and hesitated, then pulled the ring off her finger and placed it in her purse. Leaving her clothes and purse behind, Elizabeth walked out of room 511, made sure the door locked behind her, and, getting used to her new shoes, hurried to the elevator.

[5:54 p.m.—the Ault home]

None of the other men had commented on Frank's prophecy that Elizabeth would find a way to call, instead chalking up his remark to a husband's wishful thinking during dire straits.

"Carr, what in God's name could Anne Brown still want with Elizabeth?" Ed Cantrell asked. "You said after the *Observer* transmission that Brown wouldn't use the same location twice."

Carr had taken a seat in a wing chair. "She won't use the same location."

Cantrell kept looking at Carr. "So, why is Elizabeth still in the mix?"

Carr shrugged, unwilling to reveal his thoughts. Frank Ault glowered at Carr, suspecting the OSS man was holding back.

"Carr, you mother!" Ault roared. "If you know something, tell me or I'm going to beat you till your dog won't recognize your smell!" Ault started toward Carr; Carr stood; Cantrell and Shafer rushed to restrain Frank. Even with two men to drag, the bull-like detective continued toward Carr. Shafer finally managed to trip his partner and the three men fell into and overturned the lamp table where the telephone sat. The men and the telephone crashed to the floor. The room became as silent as a vault as every man looked at the telephone with its receiver off the cradle.

[same time—the phone booth across the street from the Netherlands Hotel]

Elizabeth dropped a nickel into the slot and dialed her home phone number as quickly as the dial would turn. As she waited for the connection, she saw a taxi pull up in front of the hotel. Then she heard the busy signal. Elizabeth couldn't believe it. *Who is Frank talking to?*

[same time—the Ault home]

"Get off me, goddammit!" Ault shouted. Cantrell and Shafer immediately released their grips. Ault sprang toward the telephone and quickly placed the receiver back on its cradle.

[the phone booth]

When Elizabeth hung up, her nickel dropped into the coin tray. She retrieved it and tried again. This time she heard her home telephone ring; she breathed in relief.

"*Hello!*" Elizabeth heard her husband shout from the other end.

"Frank, thank God. I just called and the phone was busy. I don't have much time. . . ."

"*Where are you? Is she there?*" Frank shouted.

"No, Frank. Let me talk. I have only a minute. I still haven't met with Anne Brown. I'm calling from a phone booth across the street from the Netherlands Hotel. She's having a taxi pick me up in a couple of minutes—at six o'clock. One just pulled up in front of the hotel. It's a Checker cab and it might be the one. The driver is supposed to know my name. I know this isn't much. I'll try to call again if I can. I have to go, Frank. I love you."

Elizabeth hung up.

[the Ault home]

"Elizabeth! . . ." Frank yelled into the telephone. He heard the phone go dead and slammed the receiver down as he turned to the others. "She's across the street from the Netherlands Hotel. A cab is picking her up at six. I'm outta here!" Ault bellowed. "Glen, stay here in case she calls again, then radio me." Ault snatched his jacket from the back of the couch.

"Frank, it's six o'clock now," said Cantrell. "The Netherlands is at least ten minutes away even under siren."

"If I miss her, I'll radio you here. Then call the cab companies. She said a Checker cab had pulled up so try Checker first, but call them all if you have to and find out which car and driver was sent to the Netherlands Hotel to pick up a woman named Elizabeth. She said the driver would know her name."

"Okay," Cantrell said. "And I'll call dispatch and tell them to notify all of our cars to be on the lookout for any cabs carrying a lone female, and if they spot one to pull it over and identify the passenger."

"Good!" Ault called as he raced out the door. Leroy Carr and Al Hodge grabbed the walkie-talkies and followed.

Outside, as they ran, Carr directed Hodge to follow, so Hodge got in alongside Sergeant Turner who had waited at the Jeep. Ault jumped into his Plymouth and Carr climbed in on the passenger side.

"What are you doing?" Ault yelled as he turned the key and revved the engine.

"What do you think I'm doing? We all want the same thing, Ault—your wife safe and Lorelei—Brown—behind bars. You can drive or you can ask me more goddamn questions."

With no time to argue, Frank Ault turned on the siren, floored the accelerator, popped the clutch, and burned rubber.

[6:00 p.m.—on the street in front of the Netherlands Hotel]
Elizabeth left the telephone booth and started across the street toward the taxi that moments ago had stopped in front of the hotel. The driver's window was down and Elizabeth addressed him from the traffic side of the cab.

"Are you here to pick up someone in particular?" Elizabeth asked the cabbie.

"Yeah."

"What's the name of the person?"

"Why? What's it to ya?" the surly driver asked.

"I might be the person."

"What's yer name, lady?"

"No, you tell me who you are here to pickup."

301

The driver looked at her impatiently. "I was told to pick up Elizabeth."

"I'm Elizabeth."

"Get in, lady. I just finished a twelve-hour shift and was punching out when they sent me down here. I'm bushed and wanna get this over with. It's a good tip or I'd a told my dispatcher to stick it."

Elizabeth circled and entered the cab from the right rear door. The cab pulled out into Fifth Street. From the information she gave Frank over the telephone, Elizabeth knew her husband could find out which taxi picked her up and question the driver to find out where he dropped her.

The driver turned right at the next block, Vine Street, and crossed 4th Street. The heavyset driver wore wire-rimmed glasses and a cabbie hat. He looked to be mid-40s.

"Where are we going?" Elizabeth asked.

"We're already there, lady." The driver pulled over and parked in front of a curbside newsstand.

Elizabeth looked out through the glass. "What do you mean, we're there?"

"Just what I said. My dispatcher told me to pick up a woman named *Elizabeth* in front of the Netherlands Hotel at six sharp then drop her off at the newsstand on the corner of Fourth and Vine. Lady, right there is the newsstand at Fourth and Vine. You must have a big problem with walking to have to be driven around the block."

Elizabeth ignored the acerbic remark. "You're sure this is the place?"

"Lady, I got supper waitin' for me. My dispatcher said this is the place and that the fare is paid for. Whataya wanna do? If you wanna go someplace else that's fine by me but it'll cost ya extra."

"No . . . if this is the place. . . ."

Elizabeth exited the cab and the driver sped away. She looked around undecided about what to do until she heard a man yelling her name from across the street.

"Elizabeth!"

She turned toward the voice. A young man waved at her and stepped out of an old pickup truck, the original gray paint losing the battle with rust. The man looked for oncoming traffic, and then dashed across the street.

"Elizabeth?" he repeated, this time a question.

"Yes."

"Hi, I'm Danny. Early asked me to pick you up. She told me a cab would drop you off at the newsstand at six or a little after and that you'd be wearing a long coat and no hat. I knew it was you."

"And . . . you're supposed to take me somewhere?"

"Yeah, sure." Danny seemed confused by the question.

"Where?"

Danny chuckled. "Early said you would ask, but it's a surprise. She made me promise. Are you ready?"

Elizabeth nodded and walked across the street with Danny. He opened the passenger door for her and she climbed in.

"Early said you two have been friends for a long time. When did you meet?" asked Danny as he started the truck.

Elizabeth began to suspect that Danny, like Clare Miller, was simply a dupe for Anne Brown and not an ally. "Oh, quite a while back," she answered.

Danny shifted into first gear, grinding the old gear box, and stuck his head out to check for traffic. As he pulled away, Elizabeth realized the information she had given Frank about the taxi was now worthless.

This is why Anne Brown let me call Frank.

Chapter 50

Huck Finn

By 6:19 p.m., in the growing twilight, Frank Ault and Leroy Carr had twice driven around a two-block area surrounding the Netherlands Hotel. Ault left his siren on knowing if Elizabeth's taxi driver were still within earshot he would have to pull over. But no cab and no Elizabeth. A few minutes ago, Carr had used his walkie-talkie to radio Al Hodge in the trailing Jeep, instructing him to increase the search area by two more blocks, but Hodge also came away empty. After his second pass, Ault pulled over in front of the hotel entrance and switched off the siren. He radioed Ed Cantrell. Ault knew he had to be careful about what he said over the air because the conversation would be heard by every Cincinnati cop near a radio.

"Car 11 calling Cantrell. OVER," Ault said into the microphone. The radio squawked.

"*Cantrell here. OVER.*"

"No sign of her, Ed. OVER."

Cantrell came back. "*I already called the cab company. Confirmative that it is Checker Cab and we've identified the driver. Driver is expected back at the company garage shortly. A patrol car has been dispatched to the cab garage and an officer will stay with the cab driver until you arrive.*"

"ROGER that, I'm on my way. Is that it? OVER."

"*I'm leaving Glen here and I'm going back to the station to monitor things from there. OVER.*"

"ROGER, OUT."

Ault turned the siren back on.

[same time—room 505, The Netherlands Hotel]
Erika Lehmann switched off the radio she used to monitor the police frequency. She knew that when Elizabeth called her husband she would tell him about the taxi. Making love with Danny was now paying off. She had been with him three times now, being gentle with him the first time since it was his first, not so gentle the other two times. Erika enjoyed her time with Danny; she found it pleasant. But more

304

importantly Danny would now do anything she asked, although she realized that by using Danny tonight, she could not safely return to the trailer park. Last night Erika cleared the trailer of all possible links to her, packed a small suitcase with her papers and a few clothes, and found a ride across the river with a trailer park Rosie the Riveter reporting for her graveyard shift. She spent last night in a fleabag hotel a block from the bus station.

Erika had rented two rooms at the Netherlands for this one day. If Elizabeth mentioned room 511 on the telephone, her detective husband would inspect that room and ask at the desk about the person who rented it. If Erika were still at the hotel using her room, that could be disastrous. To thwart this, she reserved each room under a different name, on different days, making sure she dealt with a different desk clerk each time.

She heard the siren and watched Frank Ault drive past. He circled the hotel and stopped briefly out front, but he did not leave his car before driving away. Apparently Elizabeth had not mentioned the room, so Erika's precautions were wasted, but better to be safe.

Erika pulled up her red skirt and adjusted the garters holding the black cotton hose. She looked into the mirror and adjusted the white, peasant girl top. She rolled on a coat of the bright red lipstick and ran her fingers through her hair. Erika had ordered Elizabeth to wear no hat so when the reporter walked past the hotel on her way to the YWCA, Erika could make sure Elizabeth's hairstyle was the same as usual—it was—and it was the same hairstyle and color Erika now saw in the mirror. She slipped on the red pumps and reached for her long coat. Into a large shoulder bag went her other clothes and the radio.

When on an assignment, Erika Lehmann never used an elevator if stairs were an option. An elevator held her captive for a moment with no way out, and she never knew who might be standing there when the door opened. Erika walked out of room 505 and passed room 511 three doors down on her way to the stairwell at the end of the hall.

[6:30 p.m.—Danny's truck]
Danny had turned a half-dozen times since he picked up Elizabeth at the newsstand, and they were now many blocks from the Netherlands Hotel, sitting at a stoplight on Central Avenue.

"How long have you known Early?" Elizabeth asked. Elizabeth Ault had not become Cincinnati's most famous reporter without learning how to deal with human nature. And she was a skilled questioner. If this guy were an unwitting pawn of Anne Brown, Elizabeth knew her question would be taken as chit chat and not avoided.

"About three weeks," Danny said and smiled.

"Where did you meet her?"

"I moved into the war worker trailer park where she lives."

Elizabeth felt more and more confident that Danny was innocent of everything except gullibility. She tried to sound friendly while pumping him for information. "Oh? That new war worker trailer park out by the airport?"

Danny looked at her incredulously: she should know where her friend, Early, lives. "No, it's across the river in Newport."

"That's right. What's wrong with me? Early told me that, but we're both so busy I haven't visited her there yet. When we get together it's always here in town."

The light turned green and Danny shifted from neutral back to low; the gears of the old truck once again objected to being jolted from their slumber, the grinding sounded like an impatient growl. To be able to give Frank an accurate description, Elizabeth took a good look at Danny. His light sandy hair stuck out from under a floppy straw hat pushed back on his forehead. The hat, his freckled face and denim overalls gave him a Huck Finn look.

Elizabeth continued. "So you and Early are friends or just neighbors?"

"She's my girl," Danny beamed.

Elizabeth looked at him but remained silent. Now she knew what motivated the eager Danny.

[6:35 p.m.—Checker Cab garage]

Frank Ault and Leroy Carr got out of the car and double-timed it to the Checker Cab dispatcher's office. The cab driver had returned ready to punch out for the day, but was intercepted by a Cincinnati patrolman sent to do just that. The cabdriver, dispatcher, and the patrolman were all in the office when Ault and Carr walked in. Ault identified himself and State Police Investigator Leroy Carr to the dispatcher and cabdriver, then excused the patrolman to return to his duties. The dispatcher gave his name and introduced the driver. Ault wasted no time and began interrogating the man who drove Elizabeth.

"So you picked up a woman named Elizabeth in front of the Netherlands Hotel about six o'clock?"

"Yeah," the cabdriver acknowledged, slumped in his chair, his plump fingers locked together and resting on his broad belly. "Can we hurry this up? I want to get out of here, not sit and yak with you guys." The man was as boorish as he had been with Elizabeth. But he no longer was talking to Frank Ault's polite wife.

"If you know what's good for you," Ault warned, "you'll watch your goddamn attitude or I'll drag you down to headquarters. I can keep your fat ass there a long time."

Suddenly the driver's posture improved and his outlook changed. "Yes, sir. I picked her up just like you said."

"And dropped her off where . . . *exactly?*" Ault put emphasis on the last word. He knew the cab ride could not have been a long one since the man returned so quickly.

"I dropped her off on the corner of Fourth and Vine."

Ault thought for a second. "Fourth and Vine? That's just around the block from the hotel."

The dispatcher broke in. "I can confirm that the woman who paid for the ride specified the corner of Fourth and Vine. She told me to have the driver drop off the passenger in front of the newsstand on that corner."

"I'll get to you in a minute, Sherlock." Ault was out of patience and he wanted to get this over; he didn't want to be away from his car radio any longer than necessary in case Glen Shafer called. Ault turned back to the driver. "Did the passenger, Elizabeth, say anything during the ride?"

The driver took a second. "When I pulled over, she asked if I was sure this was the right place and I said I was sure. I asked her if she wanted to go someplace else, but she said *no* and got out."

"Was there someone waiting for her? Another woman maybe?"

"I didn't see nobody but I wasn't lookin' neither. Soon as she got out I drove off and came back to the garage."

Ault now turned his attention to the dispatcher. "You talked about the woman who paid for the fare. Tell me about that. When did she come in?"

The elderly dispatcher answered, "She came in this afternoon, around one o'clock or so. I had just finished my sandwich."

"What color was her hair?"

"Uh, brown I think. Yeah, dark brown. I'm not sure how old. . . ."

Ault interrupted. "That's all I asked about—the hair." He knew any additional information about Anne Brown's appearance would prove a waste of time, as would his question about hair color if she wore a wig. Ault turned to Leroy Carr. "Do you have anything you want to ask?"

Carr addressed the dispatcher. "Did the woman who came in this afternoon give any special instructions besides what you've already told us? Did she have a note for the driver to give Elizabeth?"

"No, just what I already said."

The cabdriver confirmed he had received no note.

Back in the car, Ault radioed Shafer to ask if Elizabeth had called, but no. Leroy Carr used his walkie-talkie to call Al Hodge and tell him to drive around the Fourth and Vine area and keep a sharp eye, but both Carr and Ault knew they were probably wasting Hodge's time.

After he disconnected from Hodge, Carr said, "Since Brown did not send Elizabeth another note, Brown would have had to be waiting for Elizabeth at Fourth and Vine when the taxi arrived."

"I know that, Carr," Ault said. Ault realized the OSS man's question to the dispatcher was a good one, one he should have asked, but Ault was in no mood to pay a compliment. "With no instructions, Elizabeth would not know where to go next, so somebody had to be waiting. Question now is: did they walk to someplace close by? Brown wouldn't have Elizabeth walking long in the open because Brown has to know we're looking for Elizabeth—or did Brown, or an accomplice, have a car? Do you think there's any chance Brown isn't in this alone?"

Carr thought. "Hard to say. I don't know who it might be. As you know, the Bund was here before the war but only a small handful of those guys could be labeled hard-line fascist supporters. She's normally a loner, but she's great at making people unknowing collaborators. She did that in Evansville."

"I'm going to drive around for a while hoping I get lucky," Ault said. "If I go back to the house I'll go stir-crazy. If you don't want to tag along, you're free to get out any time you want, Carr. You can radio your buddy to pick you up."

Leroy Carr knew his best chance of staying near the action was to stay near Elizabeth's husband.

"Let's go," Carr said.

[7:02 p.m.—Danny's truck]

"We're almost there," Danny announced happily. It was now dark, and he held his left arm just outside his window so he could read his wristwatch as they passed a streetlight.

"Where?" asked Elizabeth.

"At the party. Early told me to drive around if I had to and not get you there before seven. It's seven and here we are."

Danny drove the truck into an alley where a few cars already parked. He found room to pull over just past a large trash bin. Elizabeth twisted in her seat, looking each way including turning to look behind, trying to see. She wasn't sure what she looked for.

"Where are we? What do you mean a *party?*" Elizabeth asked.

"Oops! I shouldn't have said that. Never mind what I said. But where we're going is just down the alley," Danny assured her. "After Early asked me to bring you here, I drove by yesterday to make sure I knew where it was."

"What kind of party? Who's at the party?"

"It's the party Early said you'd like . . . some friends of hers are there, I reckon . . . not sure. I think I'm not supposed to say that with the surprise and all. I hope I didn't spill the beans."

Danny got out of the truck and Elizabeth followed. With the sun gone, the temperature had dropped considerably. Elizabeth's coat now served its intended purpose instead of merely covering the skimpy outfit. He led her down the alley until they came to three steps rising to an alleyway door. A rusted sign over the door, made readable by a street light at the end of the alley, read *Pinky's Side Pocket.*

Chapter 51

Rye Whiskey

7:05 p.m.

Elizabeth stood outside the alley door to Pinky's Side Pocket expecting Danny to lead her inside. When he did not, she asked, "Are we going in?"

"Not me," Danny answered. "Early said the party is only for girls until eight o'clock, and she's gonna meet me later at the trailer park. She told me to drop you off here. I'll probably just have a beer somewhere and go on home and wait for her."

Elizabeth suspected the boy would never see his *girl* again. She knew Anne Brown would never use a dupe who, if caught, could lead authorities to her hiding place. Obviously, the Newport trailer park had seen the last of *Early,* but still it was information she could tell Frank. Maybe questioning Danny and searching Brown's trailer could lead to a clue if the spy weren't caught tonight. *As long as I survive to tell Frank.* Elizabeth shuddered when that thought flashed through her mind, a fear that until then she had refused to consider.

Determined to remain composed, she said to Danny, "Well, I guess that's it then."

"Have fun, ya hear? Tell Early I'll see her later. Bye, Elizabeth . . . Adios, as they say down Mexico way." Danny turned and started back to his truck.

Elizabeth watched him walk away.

She walked up the three steps feeling like the condemned ascending the gallows, praying silently that God grant her strength. The windowless, heavy metal door took effort to open, the rusty hinges groaned for want of oil. When she opened the door Elizabeth immediately heard music. Inside, a short, dark corridor led Elizabeth to a large, open area with pool tables and round, sit-down tables and chairs. On the far wall she saw the bar. Beyond the bar, stairs led to somewhere. Light bulbs in green metal fixtures suspended on wires from the 12-foot ceiling lit the green felt of the pool tables. Danny was right: except for an old man behind the bar, Elizabeth saw only women, a dozen or so. They meandered about talking and laughing, most carried drinks, some smoked. Two played pool while a few

310

others watched and encouraged. In front of a jukebox, two women danced together to Tex Ritter's *Rye Whiskey*. Several stood at the bar, talking.

Every woman wore a red skirt, white peasant blouse, black stockings, and red pumps.

Elizabeth stood just inside the dark corridor, unsure what to do. She quickly scanned the faces within her view. She did not see anyone who she thought was Anne Brown, but not all the women faced her direction. One woman by the bar noticed Elizabeth and walked over.

"Hi, I'm Kathy." Kathy was a long-legged, busty brunette. She switched her drink to her left hand and stuck out her right. Elizabeth shook it.

"I'm Elizabeth . . . I, ah . . . somebody invited me here. . . ."

"Elizabeth!" Kathy sounded excited. "You're Early's friend, right?"

"Ah, yes."

"She told us you were coming. Do you have your costume?"

"Costume?" asked Elizabeth.

"Yeah, your costume. We're all wearing the same costume this year for the Halloween party. Iris got us all masks. We'll wear masks and fool the men. It will be a riot. Early said she would get you a costume."

Elizabeth had forgotten about Halloween. *The outfit was a costume.* "Yes, I have it on."

"Great," Kathy said. "Let's see it."

As Elizabeth removed her coat, Kathy turned and shouted over the music: "Ladies! Elizabeth is here—Early's friend."

The women waved or hollered a greeting; two started over from the bar. Kathy looked Elizabeth over and gave a wolf's whistle. "You look great. I'll take your coat and put it in Pinky's office. There's a coat rack in there."

For a second, Elizabeth hesitated to give up her coat. She had hoped to keep it, and therefore the gun, near her, but she realized zeal to hang on to her coat would look suspicious, especially to Anne Brown. She surrendered it to Kathy.

When the other two women arrived, Kathy quickly introduced them then left to stash Elizabeth's coat. While being greeted by the other women, Elizabeth watched where Kathy went with her coat. One of the women was Iris, a red head, the other, auburn-haired Susan.

"Any friend of Early's is a friend of ours," Iris stated.

"Is . . . Early here?" Elizabeth asked. She almost slipped and said *Anne.*

"No," Iris answered. "She said she might be a little late. Let's sit down."

Iris chose a table and the three women sat. Elizabeth felt a degree of relief. If this were to be the venue for her meeting with Anne Brown—*Early*—at least it was a public place with others around.

"Your costume is cute," commented Susan, who wore the same outfit.

"Thanks," Elizabeth said. "Yours is too. And nice lipstick."

The other women laughed. Everyone at the table wore bright red lipstick.

"What do you want to drink, Elizabeth?" Iris asked.

Iris did not have a drink. Elizabeth noticed Susan's glass of beer and said: "A beer, thanks."

Iris left to get the beer. Suddenly the music volume dropped considerably. Iris returned with Kathy and two glasses of beer. (Elizabeth had seen Kathy take her coat through a door next to the stairs.)

"I told Pinky to turn down the music," Iris remarked as she set a glass in front of Elizabeth and took a sip from the other.

"Good idea," Susan said. "We don't need it that loud, and now we can talk without shouting."

"Thanks for getting the beer," Elizabeth said. "How much do I owe you? I have some money in my coat."

Iris shook her head. "No, Pinky doesn't charge girls for drinks at the Halloween party if they wear a costume."

Kathy laughed. "Yeah, showing our boobs like this, Pinky will make plenty off the guys. They'll hang around and drink all night." Iris and Susan grinned. Elizabeth used her left hand to raise the front of her top and reduce the amount of cleavage exposed, but the adjustment didn't last as the top of the off-the-shoulder blouse slid back to rest just above her nipples.

"I take it Pinky is the man behind the bar?" Elizabeth asked, again pulling up her blouse. Again it slid down.

"Yeah, that's him," Iris answered while watching Elizabeth struggle for modesty.

Two young men walked in and stood looking around the room.

At the table, Susan saw them first. "Look, its Delmar and Mickey." Then she leaned over to Elizabeth. "Those guys are cousins and come in a lot. Delmar's a good guy and a good tipper. Mickey, the bigger one, is okay. He never gets out of line with us girls, but he wants to fight any guy who beats him in pool."

Pinky also recognized the men and bellowed across the room. "You boys can't come in till eight. Party is just for the ladies till then. There's a sign on the door."

"There's no sign on the door, Pinky," remarked one of the men, also shouting. He was the smaller of the two, Delmar.

"Yeah, there's no damn sign, Pinky," the younger, bigger cousin yelled.

Pinky looked around behind the bar and found the sign. "Here it is!" shouted the old man, happy he found his handwritten sign. He made the men an offer: "Put it on the door. There should be some magnets on the door to stick it up with unless some asshole cabbaged them again. Come back after eight and your first beer will be on the house." It seemed an agreeable offer, so the men walked over to Pinky then walked out with the sign.

"What are their last names?" Elizabeth asked. She sought any information she could give Frank, including who was at Pinky's that night in case he wanted to question them. So she wouldn't appear to be interrogating, she added, "I think I might know one of them."

"Umm, I don't know," admitted Susan. "They have the same last name. Something like 'Whiskey' I think."

Kathy snorted. "It's not 'Whiskey'. . . it's 'Wilson' or 'Williams'— something like that."

"You two have taken them both upstairs," Iris interjected. "You don't know their last name?"

"What is this? An exam?" Susan asked, and she and Kathy laughed.

"If it is, next time let me know ahead of time and I'll do my homework," said Kathy, still laughing.

"Upstairs?" Elizabeth asked the group.

"There are two rooms upstairs Pinky lets us use if we want," Iris answered. "What has Early told you about the Side Pocket?"

"Nothing," Elizabeth answered truthfully.

Iris leaned her head toward Elizabeth. "Not all girls go upstairs. And no girls go up there with any man they don't like. And if they go upstairs, it still doesn't mean the girl will go all the way. The men know the rules before any of us go up with them, Elizabeth, so if you want to go upstairs with a guy you don't have to do anything you don't want to do."

Not sure how to respond, Elizabeth nodded. "Okay, thanks."

"Early got rid of one of the guys who didn't follow the rules," Iris continued.

"Willy the dirt bag," Kathy added.

Elizabeth: "Willy?"

The others deferred to Iris to tell the story. "He was a guy who used to come in here every Thursday night. At first he was okay, and then one night he beat up Rita so bad she had to go to the hospital. Pinky called the cops but Willy's rich grandfather paid everybody off to keep Willy out of jail. Anyway, Willy kept coming around, but of course the girls stopped going upstairs with him."

Susan grinned. "Until the night he talked Early into going upstairs. Dumbest thing Willy ever did." Susan and Kathy chuckled.

Iris picked up again, delighted to tell the story. "Early went upstairs with Willy. He hit her and tore her sweater. Bad move, Willy. To make a long story short: Early had a knife in her purse and sliced Willy up pretty good—almost cut his balls off. She would have if it had been up to me." All three women smiled, clinked their beer glasses together, and took a drink as if saluting Early.

"Early's our hero," Susan said earnestly.

"That's right," Kathy concurred. "We haven't seen that sonuvabitch Willy since." All three women again raised their glasses.

Iris looked at Elizabeth. "Now you know what I meant when I told you any friend of Early's is a friend of ours."

When Elizabeth heard Iris talk about Early using a knife on the man, the notion occurred to her that the man was lucky he wasn't dead, or crucified to a wall.

One of the women near the bar dropped a coin into the jukebox and a fast-paced bluegrass fiddle tune began. Three women danced together this time.

"Your face looks familiar, Elizabeth," Iris commented. "Are you sure you haven't been here before?"

"No, I've never been here. I'm sure."

"Are you from here?" asked Kathy.

"Yes," Elizabeth answered. To change the subject of a conversation, the reporter knew the best tactic was to ask a question on a different topic. "So this is the Halloween party tonight. Does Pinky do this every year?"

"Yeah," Susan answered happily. "This is my first and I'm excited."

"It's my second," said Kathy. "You'll have fun, Elizabeth."

Iris finished the round-robin. "It's a day early this year because Halloween is tomorrow and the place is closed on Sunday. I've been to several, but I missed last year because my mother was sick and I stayed home with her. I've been coming around here for four or five years. Not often the first couple of years, but more after that."

"Especially more after George started coming in," Kathy kidded Iris.

"Shut up, Kathy," Iris said, but couldn't help grinning. "Besides, look who's talking. The first night Digger showed up it took him about 15 minutes to get you upstairs."

"I was just showing him the place," Kathy claimed.

Susan snickered. "Yeah, and we know what place you showed him."

Elizabeth acted out a laugh with the rest of them. She wanted to fit in so she could find out anything that might help Frank.

"And all the girls wear the same costumes every year?" asked Elizabeth to be friendly.

"No," Iris answered. "We always wear costumes with masks. It's fun to make the regular guys try and guess who we are. But this is the first year we have all worn the exact same thing. That was Early's idea."

"Nobody is wearing a mask," Elizabeth pointed out.

"They're in Pinky's office. I'll hand them out before the men start coming in at eight."

Elizabeth nodded. She had to find out what Anne Brown wanted with her. *Why am I in her plans?* It was a question that had burned in her mind ever since the day at Sano's. Both Frank and Leroy Carr thought it was all about the teletype message from the *Observer,* but now here she sat in a pool hall dressed like a strumpet.

Elizabeth set up her next question. "Early didn't tell me how long she has been coming here. How long have you known her?"

"Not long," answered Iris. "She came in once before the thing with Willy. After that happened I didn't think we'd see her again, but she showed up a couple weeks ago asking about the Halloween party. I guess Early saw the sign by the bar about the party when she was here last month. She told me she loves costume parties."

"Yes," Elizabeth said. "She always liked costume parties. Hey, is there a phone around here? I might have to make a call."

"There's a phone in Pinky's office," Kathy answered. "You can use it. Pinky doesn't care. Do you need to make it now?"

"No, not now." Elizabeth didn't know what Anne Brown had up her sleeve. For all she knew, the pool hall might be just another diversion, the clothes another test of her willingness to cooperate, and she might end up somewhere else before finally meeting the spy. Elizabeth knew for her to get a telephone call to Frank under the clever spy's nose would take something near a miracle or a titanic piece of luck, but calling him again now, before meeting with Brown, seemed useless and might ruin everything if Brown found out.

Iris stood. "I'll get us another round."

As Iris walked away, Susan said to Elizabeth, "I can't wait to find out who Early's bringing tonight to meet you."

"What did you say?" asked Elizabeth.

Kathy butted in. "Dammit, Susan. That's supposed to be a surprise."

Susan: "Oh, shit."

"What do you mean?" Elizabeth insisted on an answer. "Early is bringing someone? Who?"

"We don't know," Kathy answered while giving Susan a look of disapproval. "But since Walter Winchell here broadcast the news, Early invited you to the party so she could introduce you to some guy she knows. I think Early's playing matchmaker [Susan giggled]. But don't tell Iris we said anything; she'll be pissed off. She's Irish and can throw a damn fit like you never saw. She promised Early we'd keep it a secret."

Chapter 52

Pool Shark

7:45 p.m.—the Ault home

"What's the latest?" asked an impatient Glen Shafer.

Frank Ault and Leroy Carr had just walked through the front door. After a fruitless, hour-long drive around downtown, Ault decided to return home in case Elizabeth somehow found a way to call again. Carr radioed Al Hodge, instructing him to head to District 1 headquarters and hang around Ed Cantrell's office in case a call came in to the station.

"The cabbie took Elizabeth one block and dropped her off," Ault answered his partner.

Shafer frowned. "One block! Where?"

"Fourth and Vine. Dropped her off in front of a newsstand."

"What the hell! Where'd she go then?"

"Goddammit, Glen. If I knew that, you think I'd be standing here?"

Carr chimed in. "Anne Brown must have had a car and waited for her. The cab was a diversion or a precaution so Brown could avoid picking up Elizabeth in front of the hotel."

"Maybe there was another taxi waiting on Vine," Shafer suggested.

"Unlikely," Carr responded. "The cab driver had no note or instructions from Brown to give Elizabeth. Elizabeth knew about the cab at the hotel—she told Frank about it on the phone, and the cabbie told us Elizabeth approached his cab, which makes sense. Brown could rely on Elizabeth to find the cab. But Brown isn't going to rely on a second cab driver to get out of his cab and find Elizabeth, which is what would have had to happen with a second cab."

"Carr's right," said Ault. "Brown would never leave that in the hands of a cab driver. But whoever met Elizabeth had to know what she looked like, and knew she would be getting out of a cab at that corner at a certain time."

"*Whoever met Elizabeth?*" Shafer questioned. "You mean Anne Brown."

"Probably."

"*Probably?* What do you mean 'probably,' Frank?"

317

"Jesus, Glen, you sound like a damn parrot."

The comment angered Shafer. "Damn it, Frank. You're not the only one here who cares about Elizabeth."

Ault looked at his normally light-hearted partner. "Sorry, Glen. I know you're worried. Carr and I talked about it. It would be risky for Brown to wait on the street. Safer to have an accomplice or some sucker she's playing for a fool pick up Elizabeth. But who knows? Brown's got a lot of nerve and it could have been her."

Shafer asked, "So you think Brown has a car, or a partner with one?"

Ault answered, "Looks like the only thing that fits."

"A partner . . ." Shafer paused for a moment. "Who the hell could that be?"

Carr now spoke up. "We talked about that, too. As Frank said, it doesn't necessarily mean the partner is a co-conspirator. Brown's a pro at getting innocent people to do her bidding. It could be someone she made friends with who has no idea who she is and what is really going on. She's done it many times before. She fooled a lot of people in Indiana and in London."

"So what's our plan now, for Christ's sake?" asked Shafer.

No one answered.

[7:50 p.m.—Pinky's Side Pocket]

Elizabeth saw the woman at the bar.

She wore a short red skirt and white peasant blouse like every other woman in the Side Pocket, and stood waiting for Pinky to bring her a drink. It might be Brown, but Elizabeth could not be sure from the side view. Then, as if the woman sensed Elizabeth's gaze, she turned and their eyes met. Anne Brown, now *Early,* smiled and waved.

Iris saw Elizabeth looking and turned her head the same direction. "There's Early," Iris told Kathy and Susan. "It's about time."

Again, Early smiled and waved. Slow-moving Pinky finally handed Early a beer and she walked over, bent and kissed Elizabeth on the cheek, then circled the table and kissed and hugged each woman. Early pulled up a chair from the adjacent table and wedged in between Elizabeth and Kathy. She gave Elizabeth an excited hug and took her arm.

"I'm so excited!" Early exclaimed. "I've been looking forward to this party for a month."

"Me, too," Susan said. "It's my first one here."

Iris looked at the clock over the bar. "It's almost eight. Men will start coming in soon. I better hand out the masks."

"I'll help," Susan volunteered.

"Me, too," said Kathy.

As soon as the three women left, Elizabeth turned to Early. "I know who you are."

"Of course you do. Fingerprints at the apartment. It was only a matter of time. Bad luck for me—that night those people attacked Clare and Penny."

"And especially bad luck for them." Elizabeth talked quickly. Iris, Kathy, and Susan, masks in hand, walked around the room giving them out. "You stepped in and saved Clare and her friend . . . why?"

Early did not answer.

Elizabeth continued. "What is this about tonight? I know we haven't gone through all this for an interview."

Early again ignored the question and sipped her beer.

Elizabeth demanded, "I want some answers. If I don't get them I'm walking out of here right now. You won't stop me in front of all these people. I'll shout to everyone in here that you're a Nazi spy."

Early looked at her, amused. "I don't think you will. That would be against your nature. A heightened sense of curiosity is one reason you succeed as a reporter. And besides, you think you're on a grand mission for God and country. No, you won't leave and you won't tell anyone here about me. You'll do everything I tell you to do tonight. Tonight is the only chance you'll get to quiet the storm of your own thoughts concerning me." Early looked into Elizabeth's eyes. "Am I right?"

Elizabeth felt her face flush.

"I can see that I am," said Early. "Before the others return, I want to tell you that at ten o'clock a man will walk in. I will introduce you. I want you to flirt with him and make him feel comfortable. Do you understand?"

"Susan said something about that before you arrived. No, I don't understand! Who is he? I'm not going to do it! I'm married."

"Who he is doesn't matter. And let me remind you that you were just as married that night in the alley outside the Rusty Bottom. You didn't have any trouble being friendly with your husband's partner that night."

"I thought you might try to hold that over my head. I told my husband all about that. You can't blackmail me."

"I have no intentions of blackmailing you, Elizabeth. I never had those intentions."

"So why do I have to flirt with some guy? Why don't you do it?"

"Just do as I say, Elizabeth. It will be worth your time and effort if you want your questions answered. Trust me."

"Trust you," Elizabeth said incredulously. "That will be the day."

"Okay, Elizabeth, I'll make you a deal. You cooperate until eleven o'clock, and then we'll go in Pinky's office and you can make another phone call to your husband to let him know you're all right. If you wish you can tell him where you are so he can rush here and rescue his poor little wife. You can be safe in your bed by midnight. Of course, I will not remain here waiting for your husband. I will leave and our night together will be over. Or you can stay and finish what you started six weeks ago when you wrote that newspaper opinion article about me. It will be your choice. Is that agreeable to you?"

Elizabeth looked at her but did not answer.

Early said, "I take that as a *yes.*"

With masks handed out, Iris, Kathy, and Susan returned and Iris handed both Elizabeth and Early a mask. They were black, Venetian-style masks that covered the top half of the face, leaving the mouth and chin unconcealed.

"Let's put them on," Iris suggested. "It's almost eight."

[8:30 p.m.]

When Pinky opened the Side Pocket to men at 8:00, the pool hall filled within minutes. The men brought with them abundant noise, abundant cigarette smoke, and abundant enthusiasm for Side Pocket girls.

Almost all of the girls immediately busied themselves with the men: playing pool, sitting at tables, talking at the bar. One girl danced with a man near the jukebox. Kathy and Susan had already broken the rack of balls in their second pool game with two men. Iris, Early, and Elizabeth remained at the table.

"Is George coming tonight, Iris?" asked Early.

"Maybe, but it will be real late. He has a family thing today out of town—something at his sister's house. She lives somewhere mid-state. George said it's a four-hour bus ride, but if he gets back in time he'll come by."

Early turned to Elizabeth. "George has a thing for Iris."

"He's married," said Iris. "His wife and him split up about two or three times a year, but always get back together. To me, he's just a guy who's a good tipper."

Elizabeth wondered if Iris were being truthful with herself that her feelings for the man were strictly business. While Iris talked, a man walked over and tried to identify the three masked women.

"Hi, Iris," he said with a grin. "I know that's you because of the red hair." He looked at Elizabeth and Early. "Not sure about these two. Who are they?"

"Nuh-uh, Harold," said Iris. "You have to guess."

"Rachel and Nina."

"Yeah, you're right." Iris misled the man. "How did you know?"

"I know all the girls."

"Well, I guess you do." Iris giggled.

"Can I buy you a drink, Iris?"

"Sure."

After Iris rose and walked off with the man, Early commented, "Men are a barrel of laughs, aren't they, Elizabeth? Little boys their entire lives."

"You might be right."

The conversation stopped when Delmar, one of the two men who had come in early, walked up.

"My cousin and I have a table if you want to play." Delmar was thin, probably mid-20s, with a Clark Gable moustache and a well-worn Cincinnati Reds cap.

"Thanks," Early said. "Side Pocket girls never turn down a game of pool." Then to Elizabeth: "Right, honey?"

"What girl would turn down a game of pool?" Elizabeth answered, trying to sound enthusiastic.

They followed Delmar to the pool table where he introduced the other man—Mickey.

"We know who you are," said Early.

"Oh, okay, I couldn't tell which ones you are with the masks and all," Delmar replied. "So I guess we know each other. Which girls are you . . . what're your names?"

Elizabeth spoke up. "You don't know us. We're pretty new here. We know who you are because the other girls pointed you out when you came in before eight o'clock. My name is Elizabeth."

Early looked at Elizabeth. "We aren't supposed to tell our names. You forgot."

"You're right, sorry." Elizabeth was not sorry.

"Well," Early said to the men, "since my girlfriend let the cat out of the bag, my name is Early."

The men nodded and decided Elizabeth would team with Mickey and Delmar with Early. While Early and Elizabeth chose a cue stick, Mickey, a tall man with a crooked nose whose black beard was longer than the hair on his hatless head, racked the balls and broke. None of the balls dropped on the break for Mickey, and Delmar missed his first shot.

"You're up, Lizzie," Mickey announced. "You've got an easy shot on the 3 ball in the corner."

"No one said what game we're playing," Elizabeth said. "But since you pointed out the shot on the 3, I assume we're playing 8 ball?"

The men looked at each another. "Yeah."

"Then I think I'll save the 3 for my next shot." Elizabeth circled the table, lined up the 6 ball, and sank it with a thud in a side pocket. The cue ball rolled back to line up with the 3 ball and Elizabeth quickly deposited the 3 in the corner. Next she made the 2 disappear into another corner, and the 5 in the adjacent side pocket. Finally, when she was faced with an almost impossible shot, she tapped the cue ball lightly to send it to a spot on the felt where a shot at one of the striped balls would be difficult for Early.

Elizabeth looked at Early. "Years of playing at home with my brother when we were growing up."

"What other surprises do you have?" Early bent over the table, winked at Delmar who strained to look down her top, and missed her shot. "Oh, pooh! Sorry, Delmar."

Mickey sank one solid-colored ball then missed his next shot. Delmar finally sank one of the stripes. When it was Elizabeth's turn, she eliminated the rest of the solid balls and won the game by sinking the 8 ball in the pocket she called. The men stared at Elizabeth, open mouthed, not sure of what to say. Finally, Mickey chortled and declared to Delmar, "We win! You owe us a buck! Pay up!"

Delmar paid, but insisted that his cousin and he change partners after each game. As a consequence, for over an hour the cousins handed the dollar bill back and forth, the money going to the man teamed with Elizabeth.

Near the end of the sixth game, Elizabeth, teamed with Delmar, bent over the table to line up a shot on the 8 ball to win the game. Suddenly she felt a hand squeeze her bottom. Surprised, she jerked as she attempted the shot and completely missed contact with the cue ball.

Behind her Mickey laughed and bellowed, "Now I know how to get her to miss!"

"Hey, cut that out," Delmar complained. "Do that when she's your partner. Besides, she didn't make contact with the cue ball so she hasn't missed. She gets another try."

Well aware of the rules of the game, Elizabeth had already retaken her sights. Again, as she was about to strike the cue ball, Mickey grabbed her bottom. This time Mickey's strategy failed; Elizabeth ignored his hand, took a gentle stroke with her stick, and quietly sank the 8 ball.

Elizabeth had made up her mind. She would do anything to capture the enemy spy, even if it required letting a man put his hands on her.

Chapter 53

Tempers Flare

9:50 p.m.—Pinky's Side Pocket

"Boys, it's time for a break," Early announced. She and Elizabeth had played pool with Delmar and Mickey for over an hour, and a small crowd of men and a few Side Pocket girls had formed around the table to watch and be impressed by Elizabeth's skill. "I'm sure there are plenty of other partners available if you want to keep playing."

The men did not object. "Okay," Delmar said quickly, glad to get rid of Elizabeth so he and his cousin could win some money from other players instead of trading the same dollar back and forth as Elizabeth switched partners. Delmar and Mickey tipped Early and Elizabeth each a dollar for their company, and the two women left to find a place to sit. Iris, Kathy, and Susan, still busy, had moved on to other men. Their original table now taken by customers, Early spotted two seats that opened up at the bar when a man and a Side Pocket girl got up to go upstairs.

"I'm going to frame this," said Elizabeth after they sat, referring to the dollar bill. "And put a note underneath *'For services rendered at the Side Pocket.'* I'd stash it in my bra, but thanks to you I'm not wearing one."

Early looked at Elizabeth. "Wow, a joke. I don't believe it. What am I seeing here? Miss Jittery Reporter finally calming down?" Elizabeth said nothing and Early added: "Your husband might wonder what you did to earn it, especially now that you've told him about the night in the alley outside the Rusty Bottom." Early saw daggers in Elizabeth's eyes. "I'm joking . . . and you have a better place to keep it than in a bra." Early took her dollar, lifted her skirt, and secured the bill under a garter. "That's where a Side Pocket girl keeps her money."

When Elizabeth did not do the same, Early grabbed the dollar from her, lifted Elizabeth's skirt, folded the bill and placed it under Elizabeth's garter. "There, now you're officially a Side Pocket girl. You know, Elizabeth, you could make a lot of money here, and I'm not talking about taking men upstairs. You could do it with pool." Then she grinned. "You wouldn't need to go upstairs, unless you wanted to, of course."

"Very funny."

Pinky brought two beers. Elizabeth looked at the clock behind the bar—almost ten. "I want to know about this flirting you want me to do with the man you said is coming in at ten. What is your definition of *flirting?* You don't mean. . . ."

"No, we don't have time for that. Just be friendly . . . act as if it's your first date with Frank." Early grinned again. "Unless you took Frank to bed on the first date. In that case, tone it down just a little."

"You're a barrel of laughs. But you said if I cooperate I can call Frank at eleven, right?"

"That's right." Early swiveled her stool to face the crowd.

For the past hour, Elizabeth had tried to think of something she could say on the phone that might be a clue telling Frank she was at the Side Pocket. She realized Early would surely stand next to her during the call. So far she had thought of nothing that might serve as a clandestine tip for her husband.

"There he is, Elizabeth, by the door. The man in the brown jacket."

Elizabeth turned. He stood looking around the crowded pool hall. Early waved, which got his attention. The man smiled and walked their way. Elizabeth turned back to the bar. Pinky stood nearby and Elizabeth ordered whiskey. Pinky poured a shot.

"Hi, Jim!" Elizabeth heard Early say.

"Early, is that you? I can't tell with the mask."

"It's me. Tonight's our Halloween party."

"Nice costumes."

"Thanks. Jim, this is Elizabeth, the girl I told you about. Elizabeth, this is Jim."

Elizabeth downed half the shot of whiskey before she turned.

"Hi, Elizabeth." He was handsome, perhaps late 20s, blond, clean shaven, and nicely dressed.

"Hi."

Early asked, "What are you drinking, Jim?"

"A beer—High Life if they have it."

Early waved Pinky over, ordered the beer and Jim paid. With no empty seats at the bar and no open tables, Early looked around the room. "There are three chairs at Kathy's table—she won't mind."

Early led the way through the crowded pool hall.

"Kathy, do you mind if we join you?" asked Early.

"Heck no, have a seat." Kathy introduced the man at the table. "This is Digger."

325

"Hi, Digger. My name is Early. This is Elizabeth and Jim."

After the hello, Jim put a cigarette in his lips and offered everybody one. Only Elizabeth accepted. Jim lit Elizabeth's first, then his own with a golden lighter.

Small talk bounced around the table for the next half hour when Kathy and Digger left for upstairs. Iris and a man named Leo joined them for a few minutes but left when a pool table became available. Elizabeth wondered what became of Harold, the man Iris left the table with earlier, but she did not ask. When Iris and Leo left, Early saw Elizabeth looking at her wristwatch.

"Jim, Elizabeth needs to make a phone call," announced Early, "and I have to show her to the phone. Will you excuse us for a few minutes?"

"Of course."

"We won't be long, and when we get back we'll leave."

"Okay."

Elizabeth followed Early to the bar where Early told Pinky they needed to make a telephone call. She then led Elizabeth into Pinky's office and closed the door.

"You told that guy we would leave with him when we got back," Elizabeth said dourly. "You didn't say anything to me about leaving here."

"Oh, come now, Elizabeth. Do you think I went to all this trouble so you and I could stay here all night playing pool and drinking beer?"

"No . . . but where are we going?" Elizabeth realized any attempt to give Frank a clue to her whereabouts was now useless.

"We'll talk about that later. Let's call Frank."

[11:03 p.m.—the Ault home]

No one sat.

Frank Ault, Glen Shafer, Leroy Carr and now Chuck Warzyniak (Frank's friend and former boxing adversary—the cop who drove Elizabeth to Union Terminal) stood in the living room. Frank called Warzyniak at home and asked him to come, bringing together the two toughest cops on the Force. Because Carr had little choice (Warzyniak knocked on Ault's door before Carr knew Ault had called him), Carr agreed to bring Warzyniak into the case and he filled in the tough Vice cop on some of the details when Warzyniak arrived an hour ago. Ed

Cantrell and Al Hodge still waited at Headquarters in case a call came in there.

"Frank, will you stop pacing for a minute?" an agitated Glen Shafer asked. "You're driving us all nuts."

Four hours had elapsed since Elizabeth called and with each minute the tension in the room heightened. For the past two hours, Frank had paced like a caged, belligerent panther, snapping at every comment, any patience long ago petered out.

"Fuck you, Shafer! You can get the fuck out if you don't like it."

Shafer had had enough and stepped toward Frank with cocked fists. Frank quickly delivered a crashing right, sending Shafer flying backward and to the floor, blood running from the corner of his mouth.

"Get up!" yelled Frank, ready to hand out more of the same. Warzyniak and Carr rushed over and took hold of Frank's arms.

"Calm down, buddy," Warzyniak entreated. "You'll hurt the poor guy."

"Let go of me!" Frank jerked his arms from the men's grasp and walked away.

Carr tried to help Ault's downed partner. "Get away," groaned Shafer, dazed and bleary-eyed.

The phone rang and Ault sprinted across the room, nearly bowling over Leroy Carr.

"Hello!" The others watched Ault as he listened for a brief moment. "Olivia, I can't talk now. I have to keep this line open. Hang up, now, please." Ault banged down the receiver. "Jesus Christ, that was Elizabeth's mother."

The gregarious Chuck Warzyniak laughed and poked fun, trying to lighten the gloom. "Does your mother-in-law call you at eleven o'clock every night? What if you and the little lady are doing the no-pants dance?"

"She calls whenever she wants," Ault answered. "She's as hard-headed as her daughter."

The phone rang again. Ault jerked the receiver off the cradle. "Yes?"

"Frank, it's me."

"Elizabeth! Are you all right?" The other men moved toward Ault, hoping in vain to hear Elizabeth.

"Yes, Frank. I'm fine."

"Where are you? Have you seen Anne Brown yet?"

327

"She's standing beside me."

"Jesus . . . but you're okay? Are you sure? Can she hear what I say?"

There was a second's pause. *"Yes, Detective Ault. I can hear you."*

"Goddamn you! If you hurt her I'll tear you to shreds! Let her go!"

"I'm not forcing her to stay. We have a deal. I'll give the phone back to your wife and, if she wishes to do so, she can tell you where she is and you can come get her. Of course, I will not wait for you to arrive, but Elizabeth will be here."

In a moment Frank heard his wife's voice again. *"Frank, I'm okay."*

"Elizabeth, where are you, tell me . . . don't do this!"

"Frank, I know asking you not to worry is ridiculous, so I won't. Good-bye, Frank. I'll see you soon."

"ELIZABETH!" Then he heard the dial tone.

Chapter 54

The Drive

11:20 p.m.

Early told Elizabeth to leave the mask and take her coat. A minute later the two women and Jim stepped into the alley outside Pinky's Side Pocket. Elizabeth could not afford to be seen checking to make sure the gun was still in her coat pocket, but she could tell from the weight that it was there.

Jim laughed. "It's nice to see your face, Elizabeth."

Early said, "Jim, I don't want to leave my car here. Elizabeth and I will follow you."

"Well . . . okay." Jim was looking forward to the women's company during the drive.

"If we get separated, don't worry. I know the way," Early assured him.

Both cars were parked on the street near the end of the alley. Early led Elizabeth to a light-colored Cadillac convertible. "You're driving," Early told her. Jim got into a dark sedan a half-block away.

"What do you think?" Early asked when they were inside the car. "Pretty snazzy, huh?" She handed Elizabeth the key and flipped on a dashboard light so Elizabeth could see the instruments.

"This is your car?"

"A friend lent it to me for the night. It's a 1941, the last year your country made cars. Too bad it's not warmer; we could put the top down."

"I haven't driven one of these."

"It's easy."

"Where's the shifter? And there's no clutch pedal."

"You don't shift. This car has the new transmission that shifts for you. Start the engine and I'll show you."

Elizabeth fired the engine and Early showed her how to engage the Hydramatic transmission. "That's all you have to do as far as shifting. Let's go."

Elizabeth guided the Cadillac out into the street. Jim, waiting in his car, pulled out in front of them. Elizabeth pulled the Cadillac close enough to Jim's car to read the Kentucky license plate, which she memorized, repeating it in her head several times.

After five or six turns, the caravan approached the Cincinnati Bridge. Called simply the Suspension Bridge by locals, it spanned the Ohio River connecting Cincinnati to Covington, Kentucky.

Elizabeth asked, "We're leaving the city?"

"Yes, we have a bit of a drive ahead."

Elizabeth's heart sank. *How far are we going from Cincinnati, and from Frank?* Traveling out of town with the German was a scenario she had not considered.

When they were on the bridge and over the river, Early looked to the sky. "There's a new moon tonight, so no moonlight. You're lucky you don't have to drive at night with headlight dimming shrouds, Elizabeth, like they do in England because of the blackout. I was there in late '41 and early '42. At night you could barely see where you were driving. The shrouds allow about as much light as someone walking in front of the car with a flashlight. If you drive over twenty miles an hour you'll run off the road or crash into something. At least here you're permitted full headlights."

"How many people did you kill in England?"

Ignoring the question, Early again looked skyward through her passenger window. "Clouds were moving in earlier. I don't see any stars, so the clouds must be hanging around. Hopefully we won't get rain."

They crossed the bridge and drove into Covington. Jim's car, about a hundred yards ahead, disappeared when a large truck pulled between their cars, blocking Elizabeth's view. The truck slowed to turn and Elizabeth was forced to stop. When the truck moved out of the way she saw Jim's car down the road, pulled over, waiting.

"Elizabeth, are you pleased with your husband?" Early asked out of the blue.

"Yes, I'm very happy with my husband, but I really don't want to chit chat if you don't mind." Elizabeth stepped on the gas to close the distance between the two cars, reaching 40 miles per hour—5 miles per hour over the wartime speed limit.

"Don't speed. If Jim sees us falling behind, he'll slow down. Besides, I know the way. We don't want to get pulled over for speeding."

"Speak for yourself. *You* don't want to get pulled over. I'm not opposed to it."

"You should be. I won't let a policeman take me before we finish what we've started."

"And what is that, exactly?"

Again, Early did not answer. "How did you and Frank meet?"

Elizabeth sighed. "We met when I covered a crime he was investigating about five years ago."

"But you have no children. Is it your career? Or perhaps he is not a good lover?"

"Look, it's none of your business, and why does any of this matter? And how do you even know I have no children?"

"If you'll answer my questions, I'll answer yours."

Elizabeth glanced at her. Early looked straight ahead. Still in Covington, a street light cast a yellow hue across the German's face. "If I answer your questions, then you'll answer any question I ask you?" queried Elizabeth.

"Any personal questions, yes." Early lit a cigarette and offered Elizabeth one.

"No, thanks. How do I know you'll tell the truth?"

Early took a drag and exhaled. "How do I know *you* will?"

"I changed my mind about the cigarette."

Early took another from the pack, put it to her mouth, lit it, and handed the cigarette to Elizabeth. Elizabeth took a drag, rolled down her window a couple of inches and blew the smoke toward the gap.

Elizabeth answered her question. "We have no children because I'm not ready. Frank and I have talked a great deal about it. I'm thirty, so I have a few more years. Maybe in a couple of years."

"What do you do to keep from becoming pregnant?"

"Probably the same thing you do with Danny."

Now Early looked at her. "What did Danny tell you?"

"He said you are his *girl.* He's at home waiting for you, by the way."

"I enjoyed Danny. It's unfortunate I won't see him again."

"Where will you go after tonight?"

"That's not a personal question, Elizabeth."

Having crossed Covington from north to south, they left the streetlights and traffic behind for the dark loneliness of a country highway.

"You have a brother fighting the Japanese?" asked Early.

"Yes. How do you know these things about me?"

"I went to the city library and found and read all your past newspaper columns and articles. Reporters not only reveal things about others, but they reveal a great deal about themselves when they write; much more than they realize, I think. Soon after your country entered the war, you wrote a column about men going off to fight and mentioned your brother. Also, that's how I found out you are childless. About a year ago, you wrote an opinion piece about a child murderer. You mentioned you have no children of your own but can imagine the devastation of losing one, especially to violence. I assume you have not had a child in the past year."

Elizabeth remembered both columns. A sharp turn forced her to slow, warned by the glow of brake lights from Jim's car. "Okay, my turn. What's your real name?"

"Erika Lehmann. Erika with a *k,* not a *c.*"

"Are you sure?"

"I'm sure."

"How about your family?" Elizabeth thought it prudent to learn everything she could about the German spy, even if just frivolous personal information—bearing in mind the woman might lie about everything.

"I have no siblings. My mother died in 1937. She was British and my grandparents on her side are still living. And I have other family members in England and Germany."

"You're not married, then?"

"No." Erika took the last drag and tossed the butt out of her partly open window.

"Your mother is British, yet you are on the side of England's enemy."

"Germany is the country of my birth. Was your husband born in this country?"

"Yes."

"Yet his last name is German. Tell me, would he fight for the United States or Germany?"

Elizabeth had to concede her point, but not verbally. Instead, she went back to asking about Erika's family. "Then your father is German, I assume."

"Yes."

"How old are you?"

"Twenty-five."

Elizabeth did the math. "Twenty-five. You were born during the first war. How did that happen? England and Germany were enemies in that war, too."

"My parents met in Berlin before the war. They were on their honeymoon when the war broke out. My mother remained in Germany for the duration."

Now well out of the city, oncoming headlights became increasingly infrequent. Ahead, faraway lightning occasionally sparkled behind heavy clouds, the barely audible thunder coming several seconds after the flash. With windows slightly open to pull out cigarette smoke, chilly air fluttered in, but with her coat Elizabeth was comfortable. Neither woman suggested the car's heater be turned on.

Elizabeth asked, "How can you in good conscience fight for a man like Hitler who wants to rule the world and mistreats his own people? Everyone has read about German Jews being rounded up and sent off to work camps. Even worse if some of the rumors are accurate."

Erika laughed, "Americans are like a broken record. I knew we would get to that. I think a debate about ideologies takes us away from the area we agreed to discuss . . . but I will answer. First, Hitler has never made the statement he wants to take over the world. If you read his book you'll see he seeks safe living space in countries to the east of Germany for Germans who already live there—many have been mistreated over the years. He does not want to rule the world. He simply wants Germany to serve as a positive example for the world, a model to emulate so everyone can live in peace."

"So to gain living space for Germans you attack, destroy, and enslave others?"

"No nation has ever survived without a sense of purpose and destiny. You Americans have short memories. The only difference between my country and yours is a direction on a map. Your country expanded to the west, attacked, killed or displaced peoples who lived on the land for centuries. You use a grand name for it: Manifest Destiny. Germany does the same to the east and we are cruel warmongers. You concentrated your Indian tribes on reservations and claimed it was for their own good, and now do the same to Japanese Americans. My country concentrates Jews and we are evil slave masters."

"What about the reports of atrocities in Poland and Russia?"

"Propaganda. Of course our enemies accuse us of the most horrendous acts. My countrymen would never purposely kill non-combatants . . . and the Führer would never allow it."

"How do you know he wouldn't allow it? I'll bet you've never met him."

"I have spoken with him many times."

Elizabeth looked Erika's way while keeping an eye on the road. "You have spoken to Adolf Hitler about his ideology?"

"Our conversations were mostly of a casual nature."

"If he won't allow innocent people to die, what about the Blitz on London, your mother's country? Thousands of innocents died."

"Germany did not seek war with England. England declared war on us, and even after that the Führer twice offered England peace before any bombing began. Mr. Churchill refused both offers. And the Allies are quick to forget that the British bombed Mönchengladbach and Gelsenkirchen—German cities—in the spring of 1940 before the London Blitz. What would you do if American cities were being bombed, sit back and do nothing? And must I remind you that both England and your country still bomb heavily-populated German cities almost daily? In Hamburg just this past summer, your newspapers and magazines reported that over 40,000 civilians died because of your bombs—many more thousands than in London."

Neither woman spoke for a long moment until Erika continued. "I will admit that in my opinion there are a few petty, malicious men with positions of power in my country. My trust in the Führer's judgment has wavered concerning his choices of advisors and appointments of certain men to high offices within the Reich, yet I believe he would never allow innocent people to be taken away and murdered. Our camps serve the same purpose as your camps for Japanese Americans."

"I have always thought our internment of Japanese Americans is wrong," admitted Elizabeth. "I wrote a column and expressed those feelings. But the action is guided by the thought that they might feel pressure to take sides with their ancestral homeland. The German Jews don't have a homeland they might be tempted to support other than Germany. Why such fear of the Jews?"

"I don't know."

The answer surprised Elizabeth. "You don't know?"

"I know what we have been told. The powerful and influential Berlin Jews sabotaged our war efforts in the first war; the Jews want to subvert from within; they started both wars, and all the rest. I never understood it, but I serve my country, not a man. I have grown to disagree with the Führer's sentiments toward the Jewish people. Many German soldiers in the first war were Jewish. My father told me some of the men who fought alongside him in the first war were Jews and they fought bravely. I feel we should have welcomed the Jews in Germany to fight alongside us, as fellow patriots, in this war. It's the Bolsheviks that are Germany's real enemy. You'll find out one day they are your country's enemy also. Perhaps we should fight on the same side—Germany and the United States."

They drove toward the lightning, or perhaps the lightning drove toward them: flashing clouds grew brighter and thunder louder as the car traveled south.

"So, where are we going? I assume we will arrive sooner or later and I'll know then. I would think it shouldn't be a big secret by now."

"We're going to Jim's house."

"Why? Truthfully."

"I must make a telephone call."

"A telephone call?"

"Yes."

"What do you mean? This Jim guy invited you to his house to make a telephone call? Who is he?"

"No, no. Jim knows nothing about the call. He thinks we're going there because you and I are on a double date with him and a friend. You're with Jim. I'll be with his friend who waits at the house. Jim's simply a means to an end. He's not an evil enemy agent like me, if that's what you're thinking. He knows nothing about who I am. We'll make our telephone call after we arrive."

"Why do you need me to make a telephone call?"

"It's transatlantic."

As a news reporter registered by the War Department, Elizabeth had called the BBC several times for war news updates, and she had clearance for transatlantic calls through a Philadelphia switchboard that routed calls through a switchboard in Bermuda, all overseen by the U.S. military.

Elizabeth applied the brakes, steered the car to the shoulder, and stopped. "If you think I will help you send information to the enemy, you might as well shoot me right now." She gripped the steering wheel.

"It's a personal telephone call to my grandfather in London. The call involves no information concerning the war or your country. As I said, it's personal."

"You're lying."

"Am I?"

"Now I know why you wanted to talk about *personal* things. You thought I might feel differently about you and help you with this phone call if I knew some things about you as a person. Well, you're wrong."

Elizabeth opened the door to get out of the car, but Erika grabbed her arm. Elizabeth tried to pull away, but could not break the German's grip. Elizabeth attacked, trying to push Erika's head into the car window to stun her, but Erika easily knocked Elizabeth's hands away and violently shoved her back to her side of the car, the side of Elizabeth's hip banged the steering wheel and sounded the horn. Elizabeth was 5' 8", close in height to the German, and had never been frail or weak, but she was astonished at Erika's strength. Elizabeth settled back into her seat.

"You said at the pool hall I could leave if I wanted to."

"I knew you wouldn't. You've come too far, and I was right when I judged you as being strong enough to go through this. You won't give up now. That's why I picked you."

"What do you mean, you picked me?"

"My original plan was to use Clare to help me send the teletype message. After doing some research to find out the names of a few radio teletype operators, I thought Clare might be a good choice. That's why I moved into her apartment building. But then all that changed the night of the attack. I knew Clare would not be returning to work any time soon, and time was ticking away. And even if it had worked out with Clare for the teletype message, I still had the problem of finding someone to help with the transatlantic call. Clare couldn't help me there. I read your articles and you became my Plan B. After more research, I learned that some important reporters like you are authorized to not only request messages be transmitted by the radio teletypes, but are also authorized to place transatlantic telephone calls without prior clearance."

"I see—with me you could kill two birds with one stone."

"If you want to put it that way. By the way, to ease your mind about the teletype message I sent in your name, it was simply a notification that I am still alive."

336

"Oh, I feel so much better," Elizabeth said sarcastically. "I'm not helping you make that telephone call."

"It is a personal phone call, nothing more. I believe my father will soon be in danger. A call to Germany would, of course, never be put through by your transatlantic switchboards. I have a Lisbon contact I trust, but telephone calls to Lisbon have to be approved ahead of time and paperwork filed. You, on the other hand, have high-priority status for phone calls to London. If I can alert my grandfather, he can relay the information to my Lisbon friend by courier. He served as a chargé d' affaires for the British government and has the necessary connections."

"Forget it."

Erika hesitated. "If you help me, I'll turn myself in at the end of the night. You can take me to your husband."

Chapter 55

In the Mood

Kentucky—Isolated backwoods road about 50 miles south of Cincinnati

Sunday, October 31, 1943—12:40 a.m.

Following Jim's car, Elizabeth had turned off the paved road onto a gravel one ten minutes ago. After another turnoff, the Cadillac now bumped its way up a rough, at times steep, dirt road becoming muddy from a light rain. Elizabeth found the windshield wiper switch. The no-longer-distant lightning cracked and the wind now fought with the trees.

Elizabeth had little faith in Erika's promise to turn herself in if she helped her make a personal phone call, but she knew the German was right about one thing. Elizabeth had come too far to walk away now.

"Why are we coming all the way down here to make a telephone call?" asked Elizabeth. "We could have called from anywhere in Cincinnati."

"These guys have a private line. We won't have the delays that usually go along with a party line."

"You couldn't find a private line in Cincinnati?"

"What's the matter, Elizabeth? Don't you like the countryside?"

After a 15-minute drive through Kentucky woods, and nearly to the top of a hill, Elizabeth saw a small house ahead when lightning flashed.

"We're here," Erika announced. Jim stopped his car near the front of the house and got out; Elizabeth parked alongside. Before Elizabeth could do so, Erika reached over, shut off the engine, and took the key. Jim joined them as they exited the car and they walked toward the house where a second man, having heard the cars, now stood on a covered porch.

"Hi, Early," greeted the waiting man as the three hustled to the porch to escape the cold, blowing drizzle.

"Hi, Merle." Erika smiled and kissed him on the lips.

Jim introduced Elizabeth to Merle and the four went inside. The house was clean and simple. In the living room sat a blue and gray

338

tweed sofa, a wingchair with a slipcover that did not match the sofa, and a coffee table. An Emerson radio and a telephone sat on a small corner table. A wall-mounted bookshelf holding a few books and what looked like information manuals hung over a small propane space heater. A clock with a white face and brass frame hung beside the shelf. On one side of the room, part of the kitchen could be seen through an open door; on the far wall was a closed door.

"Let me take your coats, ladies," said Jim. He helped them out of their coats and hung them on a coat stand near the door. As Jim took her coat, Elizabeth thought of Frank's gun.

"Hey, you two are dressed alike," commented Merle.

Erika said, "We just came from a Halloween party at the pool hall. All the Side Pocket girls are wearing the same costume tonight."

"I love it. Have a seat, girls," Merle said. "Champagne?" Merle had dark hair and a moustache. He was probably a bit older than Jim, maybe early 30s, and not as good looking.

"Champagne!" exclaimed Erika as she and Elizabeth found a seat on the sofa. "Sure."

As Merle left for the kitchen, Jim sat down beside Elizabeth. "It's great you two could make it tonight."

"We've been looking forward to it all week. Right, Elizabeth?"

"On pins and needles."

"That's the first time I've been in that pool hall," said Jim. "Looks like a fun joint."

"Oh?" Elizabeth was a bit surprised. "I guess I assumed you and Merle met Early at the Side Pocket."

Erika had to smile; she knew Elizabeth was attempting to gather information from the men. "No," Erika piped in. "I met Merle at a diner in Covington. I accidentally spilled my coffee on him. Totally embarrassing for me, but Merle was very nice about it. He later introduced me to Jim when I told him I had a girlfriend and we like to double date."

"How long have you two been going to the pool hall?" Jim asked.

Early: "Just a couple of months for me."

Elizabeth: "Not long at all."

A loud *pop* was heard coming from the kitchen then *"Ouch . . . damn!"*

Jim laughed and hollered, "Hey, don't hurt yourself, buddy! You need some help out there?"

"No, I got it!" Merle called back.

"We don't open many champagne bottles out here," Jim said to the women, chuckling. "The cork probably hit him in the nose."

Lightning lit the two windows and loud thunder followed almost immediately. The rain suddenly increased and streaked down the side window. The front window, protected by the porch, stayed dry. Merle returned carrying a metal oven tray with four ordinary water glasses half-filled with champagne.

Merle smiled sheepishly. "The darn cork ricocheted off the ceiling and hit me in the head." He set the tray on the coffee table and handed out the drinks. "Sorry we don't have fancy glasses, but the champagne is supposed to be the good stuff—from France, pre war. I bought it at a big liquor store in Louisville the other day."

"I'm impressed," said Erika.

With not enough room on the sofa for four, Merle sat in the chair and said, "Drink up, ladies. We have plenty. The liquor store had only one bottle of this, but I bought a second bottle the guy said was just as good. We've got beer and whiskey, too, if any of that suits your fancy."

"Gee!" Erika exclaimed. "With all of that, Elizabeth and I can't be held responsible for our actions tonight."

"That's what we're hoping for, right, Jim?"

"You betcha." The men and Erika laughed; Jim proposed a toast: "Here's to the French, they can't fight, but people say they make good booze." Everyone lifted their glasses.

"Hey, that *is* good," said Erika.

Elizabeth took a second drink and finished the glass. "I'd like another."

"Atta girl," Jim said. "I'll get it." He carried her glass to the kitchen.

"How long have you guys lived out here?" Elizabeth asked Merle.

"We don't live here. This place belongs to our club. I live just this side of Louisville, and Jim lives in Frankfort. We come here on weekends."

Erika rose quickly and sat on Merle's lap.

"A club?" Elizabeth asked.

Before Merle could answer, Erika kissed him, shutting him up. Jim returned, saw the two kissing, and sat down with Elizabeth. This time their thighs touched. Jim handed her the glass and put his arm on the back of the sofa, his hand on her shoulder. As he moved in to kiss her, Elizabeth quickly put the glass to her lips, took a drink, and asked, "Do you have a bathroom?"

"Sure, through that door, first room on the left."

Erika overheard and broke lips with Merle. "I need the ladies room, too. I'll follow you, Elizabeth."

Both women rose and left the room. Erika closed the door behind them. They now stood in a hallway with four more closed doors, two on each side. At the end of the hall was a window with no curtains. Erika opened the first door on the left and looked in. "Here you are."

Elizabeth entered the bathroom; Erika followed her and shut the door.

"I'm not sleeping with that guy!" Elizabeth said sternly. "Let's make the phone call to your grandfather. I want to get out of here."

"Keep your voice down, Elizabeth. You don't have to sleep with him. Just go back out there and give me about thirty minutes. Then we'll make the call."

"Why do we have to wait thirty minutes?"

"The telephone is in the living room. We can't let them listen in."

"What are you going to do?" Elizabeth felt panic. "You're not going to kill them, are you?"

"No! Elizabeth, I am not going to kill them."

"Yes you are!"

"You have to talk quieter, Elizabeth. They'll hear you." Erika turned on the faucet to drown out the conversation. "I am not going to kill them. Think about it: if I were going to do that I would have already done it. Look." Erika reached down into a shoe and pulled out a small, white paper packet. "This is a barbiturate called Nembutal. Have you heard of it?"

"I know about Nembutal. Doctors use it in hospitals to anesthetize patients for surgery."

"That's right. I'll slip some into their drinks when I get the opportunity. The dosage I'll give them will knock them out for about three hours. You don't have to worry; I know how to use it. They won't be harmed. They might wake up with a headache, nothing more."

Elizabeth looked at the packet. "Who are these guys, really?"

"I told you, when I met Merle I found out he has a private phone line."

"Yeah, right. You spilled coffee on him. That's original. Somehow you knew and you wanted to meet him."

"Okay, you got me on that one." Early smiled slightly. "But men are so gullible, spilling your drink on them is a quick way to strike up a conversation. It never fails. It's worked for me before."

"I bet."

341

"Give me thirty minutes, Elizabeth. I'll find a way by then, I promise."

"You're making a lot of promises." Elizabeth paused to gather her thoughts. "So if I go back out there and let the guy paw me for a half hour, then help you call your grandfather in London, you promise you won't kill them, and you promise to turn yourself in."

"That's right."

"And you promised me the telephone call is to your *British* grandfather who worked for the *British* government, and the call is only to get a warning to your father, not passing along war secrets."

"Yes."

"And you said I can listen to what you say to make sure?"

"Yes."

"And you'll turn yourself in if I do all of that?"

"You already asked me that question. My answer is still yes."

Elizabeth stared at her, unsure and doubting anything the German promised, and having second thoughts about agreeing to help her make a transatlantic telephone call in the first place. That alone might constitute treason on her part even if it were merely a call to a British family member and no secrets divulged. And what if it were all a trick and the spy started giving information over the phone that sounded like secrets? Elizabeth knew she would have to try and stop her.

Erika continued. "Here's the plan. When we go back to the living room, the first thing you need to do is ease up on the alcohol. Take small sips. You must stay lucid. Next, we must get the men to finish the drinks they have now. When their glasses are empty, I'll offer to refill them. When I return from the kitchen, I'll propose a toast. Don't let Jim kiss you after he takes a drink—it takes twice as much of the drug to knock out a man as it does a woman, so just a small amount transferred by a kiss, especially with the amount of alcohol you've been drinking, might make you groggy. After the toast, take Jim to the bedroom. That will save us dragging them in there."

"Take him to the bedroom? No thank you!"

"Nembutal acts fast, Elizabeth. All you have to do is keep your underpants on for 15 or 20 minutes after he drinks, and the guy will be out. Any questions?"

Elizabeth shook her head.

"So," Erika said, "do you really need to use the bathroom?"

"No."

"I didn't think so. Now let's get back out there. I want to get this over with as much as you do."

When the women returned to the living room, the lights were low. Their drinks, now topped off, waited for them on the coffee table.

"There they are," Merle announced cheerfully, "the two E's—Early and Elizabeth."

"Yes, here we are," Erika said as she picked up one of the two glasses and again sat on Merle's lap. When Elizabeth returned to the sofa, Jim leaned toward the table, picked up her drink, scooted close, and handed it to her.

Merle set his half-full glass on the floor and put his arms around Erika. She put an arm around his neck and held her glass in the other hand. Jim put his drink on the table and placed an arm around Elizabeth's shoulder and the other on her stomach. Elizabeth tried to spark small talk to kill some of the 30 minutes. She looked at the window. "Looks like the rain's getting harder."

"Yeah, looks like it," Jim agreed without looking at the window. He leaned her back on the sofa and kissed her neck.

Elizabeth looked at Erika who glanced back at her. Merle had a hand on Erika's thigh. She turned to Merle, smiled, and kissed him. Jim, still kissing Elizabeth's neck, pulled her blouse up past her navel. She felt his hand on her skin. "Early told me you were a doll," he whispered in her ear, "but you're even more than I expected." He kissed her lips. Elizabeth knew she must act willing, but when Jim moved his hand up to her breast she felt perspiration bead on her forehead, stimulated not by passion but by alcohol. The spy was right, Elizabeth had drunk too much: two beers and a shot of whiskey at the Side Pocket, and, after they arrived here, nerves prompted her to drink the first two glasses of champagne too quickly. It was more alcohol than she normally drank in a week or more. The high anxiety of this night kept her wits intact, but she felt nauseous and had a headache. After a few minutes of Jim's petting, she broke lip contact and sat up on the edge of the sofa.

Elizabeth fanned herself and made sure she sounded pleasant. "Whew! It's getting hot in here." She looked at the other couple. In the chair, Erika and Merle kissed, his hand invisible under the front of Erika's skirt, her legs spread to allow Merle access. Erika now had a drink in each hand, taking a sip from hers then putting Merle's glass to his lips so he would drink. Elizabeth saw that Merle's glass was almost empty and then she looked at Jim's still half-filled glass on the coffee table.

"Do you want a drink?" she asked Jim.

Jim sat up with her. "Champagne's not my cup of tea. There are rooms in the back. What do you say we get some privacy?"

Erika overheard Jim and stopped kissing Merle. "How about some music, Merle? Side Pocket girls love to dance, right, Elizabeth?"

"Right! Great idea!" Headache or no, this time Elizabeth did not have to feign enthusiasm.

Merle appeared reluctant to remove his hand from under Erika's skirt, and Jim seemed much less keen about dancing than about getting his hand on the inside of Elizabeth's thigh. Erika ignored the men's weak enthusiasm for dancing and rose from Merle's lap.

"Do you get the Cincinnati radio stations down here?" Erika asked as she crossed the room.

Merle said, "Some of them."

"On Saturday nights, WLW plays big band and swing jazz," said Erika. With her back to the men, she bent over much farther than necessary to turn on the radio and adjust the dial. "Let's see." She spun the knob through static and a few country and bluegrass music stations. Suddenly, the smooth sound of the Glenn Miller Orchestra playing *In the Mood* filled the room. "There, that's it."

Erika walked to Elizabeth and took her hand. "Elizabeth and I will show you wallflowers how it's done." She led Elizabeth toward the radio and away from the men. Erika took the lead for a close-body slow dance despite the quick pace of *In the Mood*.

Erika drew Elizabeth close and spoke into her ear. "If you don't get your guy to finish his drink, we're going to be here until next weekend."

"He doesn't like champagne."

"When the song ends, hand him his drink and sit on his lap. I'll use the toast then. With you on his lap, he'll drink up, trust me. I'll take it from there. With the toast over, it'll be up to you to get Jim to finish the drink with the Nembutal. Make sure he drinks it all, Elizabeth. And remember what I told you—don't kiss the guy after I come back from the kitchen and he drinks. Then take him to a bedroom before he passes out so he'll be out of our way."

"What are you gals talking about?" Merle asked over the music. "Something naughty we hope."

"Oh, very naughty," answered Erika. She stopped dancing, looked at both men, smiled and winked, then kissed Elizabeth passionately on the lips. Elizabeth flushed crimson and her body shook. After the very long kiss, Erika again smiled at the men, now watching with dropped jaws as the song ended.

Elizabeth returned to the sofa. Still shaken, she either could not bring herself to sit on Jim's lap, or forgot the instructions.

"Damn!" Jim exclaimed. "That was something. I've never seen women kiss like that before."

"Did you like it?" Erika asked, still standing. Both men nodded enthusiastically.

Erika picked up her drink and placed herself back on Merle's lap. "Let's have a toast."

Merle held his drink; Jim picked up both his and Elizabeth's and handed hers to her.

Erika raised her glass. "To Glenn Miller and to the fun I think we're in for tonight when we finish drinking." Erika and Elizabeth sipped; both men eagerly drained their glasses. Merle spilled part of his on his shirt.

Erika rose from Merle's lap. "You men need a refill," she said, looking at the glasses. "Elizabeth and I still have some, but gentlemen don't let ladies drink alone. I'll get you one more, then the real party will start. Sound okay to you, Elizabeth?"

Elizabeth nodded.

"I'll get them." Merle started to rise. "The first bottle is empty. I'll open the other one."

Erika put her hand on his shoulder to keep him seated. "That's okay. I don't mind. I like opening champagne bottles. Besides, I don't want you to hurt yourself, big guy."

Jim laughed. Erika took Merle's glass and walked over to get Jim's.

"Jim, do you want something else? I heard you say champagne isn't your drink."

With his attention devoted to Elizabeth, Jim only half heard Erika and said, "Huh?"

"You said you don't care for champagne," Erika repeated, taking his glass. "Do you want something else?"

Distracted, Jim said, "Uh . . . I don't care, Early. Whatever you bring is fine."

Erika laughed and headed to the kitchen. The storm had lessened. Lighting had moved east, taking thunder with it, the rain now a sprinkle. From the radio, the Tommy Dorsey Band played and Frank Sinatra sang *I'll Be Seeing You*. Merle waited impatiently, but quietly, for Erika to return while Jim caressed Elizabeth's hips. The *pop* from the kitchen finally sounded, but another long minute passed before Erika returned. When she did, she handed each man his glass. "Drink up, boys. Elizabeth and I are getting eager."

Merle took a robust drink, emptying half his glass.

Erika smiled and took Merle's hand. "Show me the way, mister. You can bring your drink with you." Merle jumped out of his chair and led her toward the hall door. "Just a minute, Merle. Let me get my coat. My cigarettes are in it." She retrieved her coat from the rack and rejoined Merle. "Elizabeth, don't do anything I wouldn't do." Merle opened the door and Erika passed through. As he closed the door behind them, Erika laughed and added, "Never mind."

"Okay," Jim said. "We're finally alone." He took the drink from Elizabeth and set both glasses on the coffee table. She watched closely which drink belonged to him. Jim moved in for a kiss, his hand going immediately on her breast.

"Let's finish our drinks first."

"I've got a better idea: let's use the other bedroom."

Elizabeth reached for the drinks and handed Jim's to him. She said "Cheers," and took a drink. *Make sure he drinks all of it, Elizabeth.*

Jim took a tiny sip and set his glass down. "You know what? I think I will have something else. A beer sounds good. Can I get you something?"

Elizabeth felt blood drain from her face. She shook her head no. Jim got up and walked to the kitchen, taking his champagne with him and pouring it into the sink.

Chapter 56

A Halloween Gag

Kentucky—isolated house in backwoods

1:30 a.m.

Jim returned from the kitchen with a bottle of beer, taking a drink as he walked, and rejoined Elizabeth on the sofa.

"Could I have another cigarette?" Elizabeth asked, stalling for time. Jim set down his beer, pulled a pack from his shirt pocket, handed her one, held the lighter, then placed the pack and lighter on the coffee table.

What am I going to do now? After Merle is out, Erika will come looking for me. When she sees Jim wide awake and finds out he did not drink the drugged champagne everything will change; she'll take matters into her own hands. Elizabeth had seen photos of what the German was capable of, and when Erika left the room with Merle she insisted on taking her coat. *She has a gun and will shoot Jim. Then she'll say it was my fault for not doing my part.* Elizabeth could hear Erika's voice in her mind: *"I gave you a chance to do this the easy way, Elizabeth. You left me no choice."*

Elizabeth detested Jim's fondling, but she wanted no one harmed, or worse. She realized Jim was merely some guy who thought he was on a blind date with a willing pool hall girl. Practically every man Elizabeth ever dated had impatient hands, many on the first date, including Frank. Jim and Merle were just two unlucky guys who, through no fault of their own, had fallen in the way of that fearsome woman, and Elizabeth feared Jim might pay a fearful price. And, if Erika killed Jim, what might happen to Merle?

And what about her? Elizabeth remembered the evening in Eden Park, the first time she met Leroy Carr. Carr told her that in Evansville the German killed her last partner. *Am I her partner now?* Elizabeth doubted Erika would harm her before they completed the phone call. The German needed her help. Clearly, Erika must have spent weeks planning, organizing, and putting into motion the elaborate scheme that brought them to this remote house in the Kentucky backwoods— all for a telephone call. Erika could not make that call without

Elizabeth's help. But after the call, she would be in danger, too. Elizabeth knew she must think of something fast.

Elizabeth never really believed the spy's promise to turn herself in; rather, she held to her hope of finding a way to call Frank secretly, or take any opportunity to get the jump on the German and hold her at bay with Frank's gun, then asking someone else to call.

Jim pulled her close. Elizabeth knew he had sipped the drugged champagne and remembered the warning to not let him kiss her. She kept the cigarette in her lips. Jim brushed back her hair and kissed her cheek and ear, his hand moving under her skirt. Elizabeth kept her legs closed; Jim, undeterred, pushed up the front of her skirt and fumbled to unfasten a button of her underpants.

She looked at the telephone near the radio. Erika was out of the room, but calling Frank now was not a safe option. She couldn't risk being discovered. She needed a minute to think.

Elizabeth Ault opened her legs.

"You're teasing me, Merle," Erika said. She sat beside Merle on the edge of a bed in a cramped room big enough for a single bed and a small lamp table, nothing more. The lamp was lit.

"What do you mean?"

"You get me all worked up in the living room, then get me in here and sip that champagne like you want it to last till Christmas. That's cruel. Finish that drink." Erika rose, faced Merle, and pulled her blouse off over her head. Like every earnest Side Pocket girl, she wore no bra. Erika unfastened her belt, slipped her skirt to the floor, and stepped out of it. She stood in front of Merle in underpants, cotton hose and garters.

Merle turned up his glass and chugged the last of the champagne.

Erika knew the faster she got his heart to beat and blood to flow, the faster the drug would work. She moved Merle's legs apart, stood between them, and began unbuttoning her underpants.

Elizabeth had considered letting Jim in on what was happening, tell him who Erika really was, and enlist his help. They could go to the bedroom where Jim could pretend to be unconscious. When Erika entered to check, as she surely would, Elizabeth would be waiting with the gun. She would hold Erika at bay and Jim could call Frank. It sounded like a good plan, but two unknown variables forced Elizabeth to decide against it—Jim and Erika. Elizabeth knew nothing about Jim's true character. She would be placing everyone's lives in his hands. What if he panicked? And Erika. What if she entered the bedroom with her gun in hand? That night at the Lamar Apartments, *Anne Brown* fired four shots, all hitting their mark. Elizabeth knew how to fire Frank's gun, but realized her chances in a shootout with the trained enemy agent ranged from miniscule to zero.

The only choice left, the only plan she could think of to get a jump on the spy and, if her worst fears proved right, save the men: Elizabeth would have to get Jim into the bedroom and knock him out herself. Frank had given her instructions on self defense, and Elizabeth remembered him telling her the most likely way a woman of average strength could knock out a male attacker.

Hitting an attacker over the head, Elizabeth, is not an efficient way to knock him out. Most people believe that, but to knock a guy out by hitting him on the head requires a very heavy object and a blow delivered with great force; otherwise, it usually just dazes the guy for a few seconds at best and causes a lot of blood. Boxers don't knock out opponents by hitting them on the top of the head. They hit them in the jaw. A hard blow to the jaw causes a sudden jarring to the brain. Grab something hard, babe, and the heavier the better but not so heavy that it's difficult for you to swing, and hit him in the jaw.

If she could not find a suitable object in the bedroom, she would have to hit Jim with the gun. Both men would be unconscious; that's what Erika said she wanted. Why should the spy care how one of them got there? After knocking out Jim, Elizabeth could hide the gun under a pillow and wait. The blow might not keep Jim out for long; Elizabeth would have to explain to Erika what happened. Erika could tie up Jim—she was probably an expert at that, too. There would be no need to harm him further. While restraining Jim, Erika would have to set down her gun and that would give Elizabeth her chance to get the drop on her. If the spy entered the room without a gun, Elizabeth would pull her gun right away.

Jim fondled her and kissed her shoulders. Elizabeth's cigarette, now short, had to be discarded. She moved to the edge of the sofa and ground the butt in the ashtray, her movement having no effect on Jim's hand. Elizabeth took his hand, moved it away, and stood.

"Jim, I think I'll take you up on that bedroom offer now," Elizabeth said as she pulled the front of her skirt down.

Jim rose and took her hand.

"Let me get my coat," she said. Since she had borrowed cigarettes, she could not use Erika's reason for taking her coat. "My hair comb for afterwards. I hate for anyone to see me with messy hair, even in private." She smiled at him and added, "And I have a feeling you're going to mess up my hair, aren't you?"

"I'll do my darnedest!" He released her hand. "I'll get your coat."

Elizabeth wanted to carry the coat so she could place it where she thought best, but Jim beat her to it.

"Do you want me to just get your brush?"

"NO! Um . . . no, just bring the coat, please."

Jim shrugged. "Okay." He paused, as if he momentarily lost his train of thought. "I feel a little funny . . . too much of that champagne, I guess. I don't drink much booze, just a beer once in a while."

Elizabeth thought the Nembutal might be taking effect, but, since Erika told her to make sure he drained the glass, she doubted his tiny sip could put him under; and, indeed, in a moment he seemed to shake it off. Jim took her hand and led her through the door to the back area of the house. The first door to the left was the bathroom Elizabeth had been inside earlier. Jim and Merle, because they stayed in the house every weekend, each had a bedroom. Jim stopped in front of the first door on the right. "This is Merle's room," he said, and with a sly grin knocked on the door. "Merle, what are you doing in there?" he yelled.

"He's busy right now, Jim," they heard Erika say. "And just about ready to do the same thing you'll be doing in a few minutes, right, Elizabeth?"

Elizabeth raised her voice and said, "Yes."

Jim laughed and led Elizabeth down the short hall to the second door on the right, across the hall from the fourth door.

"Here we are," he said as he opened the door to the dark room. "Don't expect fancy, and it's small, but we keep things clean here. I'll turn on the light." Jim entered and switched on a small lamp with a blue shade and a weak bulb. On the wooden lamp table sat a thin metal ashtray and a small, windup alarm clock. A gray metal wastebasket sat beside the table. The single bed barely fit into the tiny room, pushed against one wall with both the brass headboard and footboard touching the walls at either end. That left a floor area about five feet wide. Nothing hung on the walls; there was no window, closet, or rug on the wooden floor. When Elizabeth first joined the *Observer* staff, her editor gave her a road trip assignment to write a feature article about a Kentucky monastery that served as an Underground Railroad sanctuary for escaped slaves before and during the Civil War. One of the brothers gave her a tour. Jim's bedroom reminded her of a monk's cell.

"There's not really a place for a coat," said Jim, still holding it.

Elizabeth took it from him. "I'll put it here on the floor." She folded it and laid it in front of the lamp table, close to the bed, with the pocket holding the gun on top.

Jim closed the door and started to undress.

"Can we take it slow?" asked Elizabeth. "I have more fun that way."

"Sure." Yet he kept undressing until he was naked, throwing his clothes on the floor in the only available corner, by the lamp table. "I'd sure like to see you take yours off."

Elizabeth hesitated, blushing.

"Can I help you?" Jim took hold of the bottom of her blouse. Elizabeth again wavered, but finally raised her arms. Jim pulled the blouse over her head and off. He undid her belt and pushed her skirt down off her hips and to the floor. "You're a knockout, Elizabeth."

If he only knew.

Nothing on the lamp table would be heavy enough to strike him unconscious. She had to get him on the bed and the light out. From there she could reach down for the gun. Elizabeth put her hands on Jim's sides, turned him, and guided him backwards to bed. He sat on the edge and reached for her buttons, but Elizabeth, determined her underpants would stay on, gently pushed him back on the bed. She sat down beside him and was about to reach for the lamp switch when Jim grabbed her, pulled her to him, and, laughing, rolled her across him to the side of the bed against the wall. He leaned his body against hers and attempted to kiss her on the lips. Wedged between the wall and Jim's body, Elizabeth could barely move. Instead of letting him kiss her mouth, Elizabeth put a hand on his head and guided his face to her breast. She closed her eyes and gritted her teeth. He divided his time between her breasts for what, to Elizabeth, seemed an hour but was only a couple of minutes. When Jim moved his mouth from her breasts and began kissing down her stomach, Elizabeth knew she could not let things progress.

"Can we turn the light off, Jim?"

351

He lifted his head. "Yeah, if you want."

"I'll do it." She would turn off the lamp and make sure she stayed on the outside of the bed this time where she could reach the gun in the dark.

"That's okay; I got it." Instead of simply rolling over and reaching for the lamp from the bed, Jim sprang to his feet. "Oops, I think I stepped on your comb. I'll lay your coat on my clothes so it won't get dirty." Before Elizabeth could object, Jim had picked up her coat—by the wrong end.

The gun fell out of the pocket and thudded onto the floor. Elizabeth sat up, saw the gun, and looked at Jim, her thoughts racing as fast as her heart.

Jim stood silent for a moment looking down at the gun then picked it up. "What's this all about, Elizabeth? Why do you have a gun?"

"Ssshh! Jim, speak softly." Elizabeth wasn't sure where to begin, but she saw no alternative now other than enlisting Jim's help. "Listen to me. Early is not a pool hall girl, and neither am I. She's a German spy."

"A German spy? What are you talking about?"

"Just listen, please. You're in danger, Jim, and probably so is Merle if you don't do as I say. She's a killer, and I'm sure she also has a gun in her coat." Elizabeth saw him look at her with skepticism and amusement. "You must believe me, Jim. She's killed people, but I don't think that's her plan tonight. When she went into the kitchen, she drugged your and Merle's champagne. I was supposed to get you to drink it. Merle is probably already out."

"Come on, Elizabeth. What is this? A Halloween gag? You guys are playing around for Halloween, right? All the girls at the Side Pocket dressed alike with masks, pretending they're somebody else. Who are you, General MacArthur?"

"I'm a reporter for the *Cincinnati Observer.*"

Jim chuckled. "Let's get back to bed."

"Damn it, Jim. You better believe me, or you'll find out the hard way. Give me the gun. You need to lie on the bed and act like you're unconscious. She's going to come in here any minute now and check to make sure you're out. I'll pull the gun on her at the first opportunity and keep her covered while you call my husband; he's a Cincinnati detective."

"What? Now you're married?"

"Yes, I'm married. Give me the gun, Jim."

"You're pulling my leg. I'm going to check on Merle. I'll get to the bottom of this." Jim reached down for his pants, but before he could put them on, the door opened.

Erika Lehmann stood leaning relaxed against the door frame, her right arm concealed behind her back. She was naked save for her stockings and garters.

"Hi, kids!"

Chapter 57

Elizabeth Shocks Erika

Kentucky—isolated house in the backwoods

2:10 a.m.

For a brief moment, Elizabeth was absolutely sure she was dreaming. The surreal scene before her could not be happening. In the dream, she found herself sitting on a bed, nearly naked, in a strange man's bedroom. The man stood naked four feet from her, holding one of Frank's guns. Then the dream Muse, not satisfied Elizabeth's dream play was sufficiently bizarre, brought in another ethereal character: a female Nazi killer, also naked but for stockings exactly like those Elizabeth wore in the dream, stood in the doorway concealing a gun behind her back.

This has got to be a nightmare. In a minute, I'm going to wake up next to Frank and this will all be over.

But the thought fled as fast as it arrived, and she was forced to accept what was happening was real. Elizabeth looked at Jim and suspected he might be thinking the same, sure that he was in some weird dream. He stood drop-jawed with a stupefied look on his face, staring at the naked woman in the doorway.

"Elizabeth, I'm shocked! You got him naked. I'm surprised at you." Erika looked between Jim's legs and gasped. "My, my, my, and I can see you got him wound up. Elizabeth, you could hang one of your hats down there."

Jim held the gun backwards by the barrel in one hand and his pants that he never got the chance to put on in the other; he moved the pants to cover his groin.

Erika turned her eyes to Elizabeth. "And look at you! When we were at the Side Pocket, I began to think Jim would be lucky if he got to hold your hand. I can see I was very wrong." Erika smiled. "You know, Elizabeth, you're a very naughty lady and I'm going to have to keep a closer eye on you. But I'm happy to see you at least kept your underpants on. Frank would be very upset with me for bringing you here if he found out those came off, too."

Jim finally emerged from his trance. "What in the Sam Hill is going on here?"

Elizabeth moved quickly to the edge of the bed, trying to remain calm. "Jim, look at me." He turned his head and she talked quickly, pleading, "Put that gun down, Jim. Drop the gun to the floor, right now." He remained frozen. "Jim! Drop the gun! Do it now!"

Jim looked back at Erika. She gazed back at him expressionless, still leaning against the doorframe; her right hand remained behind her back. He grew uneasy, thinking this might not be some crazy game the women played. "Where's Merle?" he asked. "I want to see Merle."

Erika said nothing and continued to stare him down, now with a darker mien, making him more nervous. He looked down at the revolver in his hand.

"Don't do it, Jim!" shouted Elizabeth. She sprang from the bed and placed herself in front of Jim, facing Erika.

The darkness left Erika's face. "Not just beautiful, but truly valiant—willing to sacrifice herself for a stranger. I knew I was right about you, Elizabeth. Now step aside."

"Don't do it. Please!"

Behind Elizabeth, Jim yelled, "Holy God!" and threw the gun on the floor at Erika's feet.

Elizabeth felt a small relief that Jim had given up the gun because she felt he had no chance against Erika, but she was not sure that was enough to save him. "There . . . there's the gun! No need to do anything now. We can tie him up."

Behind her Jim said, "What???"

"Shut up!" Elizabeth told him without turning. To Erika she pleaded, "I'll do anything you say if you don't kill anybody . . . anything. You have my word and I've kept my word so far. I sneaked away from Frank as you asked. I've gone along with everything you've wanted. I tried to get Jim to drink the champagne but he poured it out."

"I know. I listened at your door."

"Then you know I keep my word."

"Move, Elizabeth."

Elizabeth felt she might vomit, and she fought back tears. What she said next surprised even her. "Erika, if you love me, you won't do it."

For the first time, Elizabeth thought she saw a candid look on the German's face. Everything up to now had been acting, a veneer to

355

cover real thoughts and intentions. But now Erika looked truly shocked and perplexed.

"What did you say?" Erika asked sternly.

Elizabeth hesitated, wondering if she had just made the mistake of her life. After a painfully long silence, Elizabeth lowered her head and said softly, "I think you care for me. If you do, you'll do as I ask."

Another stillness followed, this one not as long. "Which one is it, Elizabeth?" Erika's voice now friendly. "Do I love you, or care for you? Those are different levels of emotion, aren't they?"

Elizabeth didn't respond except to raise her head and look at Erika, her eyes glassed with tears she would not let fall.

Erika Lehmann brought her right hand out from behind her back and let it fall to her side. She held nothing in it. Frank's revolver lay at her feet.

Humiliation washed over Elizabeth, both for what she had said and for falling for Erika's bluff. She looked at the gun and considered rushing for it.

Erika saw her looking and knew what Elizabeth was thinking. "Okay, Elizabeth, I'll accept your offer. You gave me your word you will do anything I ask if I don't kill anyone. What I want you to do is pick up your gun and put it back in your coat pocket."

Again Erika had made a fool of her. *How does she know it's my gun? She said she listened at the door, that's how. She heard Jim ask me about it. But how does she know where I kept it? Of course, she knew my coat pocket is the only place the gun could have been.*

She now realized why Erika did not bother to bring to the room her gun, which must surely be in her coat as well. Elizabeth walked toward Erika and picked up Frank's gun. "I don't suppose it's still loaded." Elizabeth opened the cartridge cylinder to look. "The Side Pocket?" She felt foolish for thinking she could conceal a gun from this woman who had been steps ahead of everybody all along.

"I checked your coat before I went to the bar for a drink. If you want your bullets, you'll find them in a crumpled piece of paper at the bottom of Pinky's office wastebasket—if you get there before he empties it."

Jim, knowing he faced no loaded gun, charged the women. Erika pushed Elizabeth out of the way and ducked to the side. Jim ran directly toward the door where Erika had stood and his momentum carried him past the doorway. He grabbed the doorjamb as he stumbled by to pull himself back into the room for a second try. From inside the room, Erika slammed the door on his hand. Jim shouted in pain. Erika flung the door open and kicked him hard between the legs. In the doorway, he crumpled to the floor, bent over in agony. Quickly, Erika placed both hands on Jim's head and, with her body weight behind the shove, violently thrust the side of his head into the doorframe, knocking him unconscious.

Seeing Elizabeth was on her hands and knees on the floor, Erika walked over and knelt beside her.

"I'm going to be sick," Elizabeth muttered weakly.

Erika rose and walked out the bedroom door, stepping over Jim in the hallway. Elizabeth crawled to the wastebasket and vomited. Erika returned with a wet towel, knelt, and placed the cold towel to Elizabeth's neck. She vomited again, mostly dry heaves since she had nothing left in her stomach to evacuate. Elizabeth had not eaten since picking at her food during breakfast when she told Frank about her indiscretion with another man. That breakfast seemed an eternity ago.

When Elizabeth felt she had finished vomiting, Erika helped her up and guided her to the bed. "Lie down for a few minutes," Erika said.

"I'd rather sit."

"Do you want me to see if there is any stomach medicine in the bathroom or Seven Up in the kitchen?"

"I just want to get dressed."

"I brought you some clothes. They're in the trunk of the car. I'll put on my shoes and get them. Wait here." Erika disappeared into the hall.

Elizabeth rose slowly from the bed, stepped through the doorway and knelt beside Jim, searching for a pulse. He was breathing, and she found the pulse. She went down the hall and opened the door to Merle's room. Merle lay on the bed unconscious, fully clothed except for his shoes. His shirt was unbuttoned and Elizabeth could see his chest slowly rising and falling.

Erika returned with an olive-drab canvas bag that looked like a small Army duffle bag. She saw Elizabeth standing in Merle's door.

"The rain started again," Erika said. She had put on her shoes to go outside but not her coat; her wet skin glistened. "Do you mind getting me a towel from the bathroom?" She saw Elizabeth glance again at Merle. "He's alive, Elizabeth. I told you I keep my promises."

Elizabeth crossed the hallway to the bathroom and found a towel. When she reentered the hall, Erika was kneeling beside Jim, the canvas bag on the floor beside her. Elizabeth watched her extract a

357

hypodermic needle, pull off the needle cap, and inject a substance into Jim's buttock.

"What's that?" Elizabeth asked.

"Nembutal—the same thing I put in the drinks. The bump on the head won't keep him out for the time we need." Erika threw the empty needle into the bedroom. I'm going to tie their hands and feet as a precaution. They both should still be sleeping when we leave. I'll cut the ropes before we go."

Erika pulled a spool of rope from the bag and a switchblade knife. She cut the rope and bound Jim's hands and feet, then, taking the bag with her, walked into Merle's room. As she cut the rope for Merle, Erika said, "I took this knife from one of the men who attacked Clare and Penny. There's a small detail for the article you'll write about this night: *The Night I Captured a German Spy.* You'll be the most famous female reporter on the planet, Elizabeth. That's what you've always wanted, isn't it?" Not expecting an answer, Erika finished with Merle and walked out of the room. "Of course, you may need to adjust a few details for Frank's sake."

Elizabeth confronted her. "Don't you think I'm humiliated enough by everything that's happened tonight? Why do you want to add to it?"

Erika halted and looked at her. Elizabeth recognized the look in Erika's eyes, a look she had seen before from people she had questioned who wanted to confide their thoughts but were hesitant. If that were the German's intentions, she stifled the impulse. Instead, she tenderly brushed aside Elizabeth's hair, kissed her cheek and said, "I'm sorry, Elizabeth. I've grown too hard. Forgive me."

Elizabeth, expecting another glib retort, was thunderstruck. Erika took the towel from her and led the way back to the living room. She set the bag in the chair, removed her shoes, garters and hose, and dried herself with the towel. From the bag, Erika took two sets of clothing wrapped in brown paper and laid them on the sofa. "Take off your hose, Elizabeth, and your underpants. I knew you wouldn't want to wear that ridiculous outfit any longer than necessary, and neither do I, so I brought these clothes. Take either package. I think we wear the same size."

Although the two women stood about the same height, Erika had wider shoulders and was more muscular, therefore heavier. Elizabeth could see the sinew definition of her legs and arms. Her powerful beauty reminded Elizabeth of a champion thoroughbred.

"Why should I change underpants?"

"You'll never want to wear them again. I noticed some of your buttons are undone. They will remind you of being forced to let a man other than your husband touch you. You might as well throw them away now. I brought everything you'll need."

She was right about the underpants. Elizabeth sat on the sofa, removed the garters and hose, and then stood and removed the underpants. Erika ignored Elizabeth's nakedness and both women began dressing. "I wasn't sure of your bra size so I didn't bring you one," Erika said, "but I put a man's T-shirt in the package. It's a small size and should work for you in place of a bra. In my line of work you have to be prepared to improvise, Elizabeth." She looked at Elizabeth and smiled.

"You've proved you think of everything, I have to give you that."

"Not always. Sometimes there are surprises—like your remark to me in the bedroom."

Elizabeth blushed. "I don't want to talk about that."

Erika dropped the topic and continued. "And I thought you brave, but still it surprised me when you stepped between Jim and me. You didn't know I wasn't holding a gun."

"Don't give me more credit than I deserve. Yes, I thought you had a gun, but I reasoned you wouldn't harm me, at least not till after the telephone call. You've gone through too much trouble to set all this up. After the call, all bets are off, right? I know you won't turn yourself in. You know what's likely to happen to an enemy agent, especially one who has stolen secrets and killed."

"The gallows," said Erika. Conversation paused while they continued to dress. "Maybe it's not so bad to die, Elizabeth, if you die the right way."

"What do you mean?"

"Historically, some cultures have considered dying with courage and honor the greatest goal of life—the Vikings, for instance. That's why the armies of other lands feared the Vikings so; the Vikings' beliefs made them fierce warriors." Erika looked down at her right hand and the ring Adalwulf gave her. Elizabeth noticed her looking.

"What is that ring on your finger?"

"It's a silver ring with an onyx stone a friend gave me. It's called the Ring of the Slain." Erika looked at Elizabeth and raised her right hand so Elizabeth could inspect. Elizabeth took her hand.

"What are these symbols next to the stone?"

359

"Norse symbols. This one (Erika pointed) is called *Gungnir*. That's the name of a spear. It seems all mystical swords or spears have names, like King Arthur's *Excalibur*. *Gungnir* is Odin's spear, sometimes called the Spear of Valhalla, or the Spear of Heaven."

"And the other symbol?" Elizabeth was looking at three interlocking triangles.

Hrungnir's Heart . . . to honor those who die valiantly—also known as the Valknot, or the Knot of the Slain, binding together all who die bravely and with honor, even if they were enemies in life."

Elizabeth released her hand. "You sound as if you're a believer."

"Do I?" Erika paused. "What are your beliefs, Elizabeth?"

"My family is Scot Catholic."

"Ah, I was right. I thought you had the Celtic look. I'm Catholic, too."

They were almost finished dressing. "Catholic? So you're not a Nazi?"

"I am a member of the Party."

"I thought Nazis didn't believe in God."

"More propaganda, Elizabeth. Only recently have some members, not all, of the Schutzstaffel—you know it as the SS—begun to renounce Christian ties. And I am not SS. My greatest enemy commands the SS."

Elizabeth paused to think while they finished dressing. "Are you referring to Himmler? He is your enemy?"

Erika did not respond; instead, she looked Elizabeth over from head to foot. "Hey, I like your outfit." Both women were again dressed alike, this time in dark gray slacks, gray long-sleeved men's shirts, and black socks. Even their hair color nearly match, Erika's dyed shade close to Elizabeth's natural brunette. "What size shoes do you wear?"

"Seven."

"I guessed you wore something close to that."

Of four pairs of shoes in the canvas bag, Erika had brought her own size and, like the pumps at the hotel, three sizes for Elizabeth. Erika found Elizabeth's size and handed her the shoes. They were highly polished, black leather women's lace-up shoes with soft, pebbled soles for good traction.

"I hope you like them," Erika said. "At least they're not heels. These are more practical, like men's shoes. Men wear much more comfortable and more practical shoes than we women, don't you think?"

"Yes. The shoes we're expected to wear are ridiculous. High heels supposedly make our calves look prettier so men will look at our legs."

"Exactly . . . like those pumps. Sorry about those." Erika moved the bag to the floor, sat in the chair, and laced her shoes. She stood up and turned around as if modeling for Elizabeth. "Well, give me an opinion."

"We look like Rosie the Riveters without the scarves, not that that's a bad thing. The Rosies will make things better for women in this country."

Erika laughed. "Elizabeth, you sound like me. Maybe we're related. Shall we make our telephone call now?"

Chapter 58

Peg Gets a Call from Beth

Kentucky—isolated house in the backwoods

2:45 a.m.

The black telephone that sat alongside the radio on a living room side table was one of the older model *candlestick* phones with the earpiece on a cord and the voice horn above the dial. Elizabeth picked up the earpiece, pressed the cradle rapidly three times then lifted the rest of the phone so she could speak into the horn.

"To expedite a transatlantic call, I have to first call the *Observer,*" she told Erika as she waited for a local operator. "One of the newspaper's switchboard operators has to call a transatlantic operator in Philadelphia and give the Philadelphia operator codes and information. I cannot call directly myself; reporters aren't given the codes. It's a safeguard."

Erika offered no comment because she already knew about these safeguards for wartime transatlantic calls. Those safeguards were what forced her to enlist Elizabeth's aid.

Elizabeth's attention suddenly focused on the telephone. "Hello, yes, Operator, I want to place a collect call to the *Cincinnati Observer* newspaper switchboard. The number is Baker 21793, and my name is Elizabeth Ault . . . that's right, Cincinnati."

While waiting for the operator to pull wires from various sockets on her panel and push them into others, Elizabeth turned again to Erika. "I don't know who's working our switchboard tonight. . . ." Elizabeth stopped, interrupted by the operator. "Yes, thank you, Operator." After a pause, Elizabeth said, "This is Elizabeth Ault, newsroom reporter. To whom am I speaking? . . . Hello, Carol, is Peg working tonight? . . . Great, will you put me over to her, please? . . . Thanks." Since Elizabeth did not know Carol, she was relieved Peg was on duty. "Hi Peg, it's Beth Ault . . . yes, Beth. It's nice to talk to you again, it's been weeks . . . Fine, how are you? . . . Glad to hear it. Peg, I'm working on a story and I need to call London. It's mid-morning over there and that's when I was told to call . . . Yes, I'll hold."

She turned to Erika. "When I get through to Philadelphia, the operator there will ask for this telephone number; then she'll call back after she connects with Bermuda—another safeguard. Philadelphia and Bermuda log the phone numbers of all transatlantic calls sent from the U.S. Write down the London number. I'll need that when I talk to the Bermuda operator."

Erika had the number and name ready and pulled a slip of paper from her bag. She walked over and laid the paper on the table.

After a two-minute delay, Elizabeth spoke to the Philadelphia operator. "Yes, that's correct, London . . . Elizabeth Ault, *Cincinnati Observer,* authorization number OH52577." Obviously responding to a request, Elizabeth looked at the telephone dial. "Locust 88160. It's a Kentucky number . . . yes, I understand. I'll be waiting at that number. Thank you." Elizabeth hung up and returned the phone to the table.

"How long a wait?" Erika asked.

"I don't know. It's always different. It probably won't take long to get connected to Bermuda, especially at this hour. The phone traffic will be lighter than if we were calling later, say in the afternoon. It's the connection to London from Bermuda that might require a long wait. One time I was put through in twenty minutes; another time I waited nearly two hours."

The women moved to the sofa and sat at opposite ends. Thunder, not heard in an hour, grumbled. Erika remarked, "It looks like another front might be moving our way."

The telephone rang.

"That was fast," Elizabeth commented as she rose. "Bermuda normally takes at least ten or fifteen minutes." She lifted the phone and put the ear piece to her ear. "Hello . . . yes, this is Elizabeth Ault . . . I'm a reporter for the *Cincinnati Observer* newspaper, Cincinnati, Ohio . . . Yes, I've been a reporter there for five years, and I've made previous calls to England; my authorization number is OH52577." A lengthy pause followed, as if someone at the other end went about the business of verifying Elizabeth's information. Finally, Erika heard her say, "This call is to London." A half-minute later, Elizabeth picked up the paper Erika had laid on the table, read the number aloud, and said, "Person to person, Mr. Louis Richard Minton . . . Reason: American newspaper interview." Elizabeth listened for half a minute, then said, "Did Philadelphia give you my telephone number?" Elizabeth listened and looked at the phone dial again. "Yes, that's it. I'll be waiting at that number. Thank you." She hung up and returned to the sofa. "Now we wait."

[3:00 a.m.—*Cincinnati Observer* switchboard room]
Cincinnati Observer assistant night editor, Clete Ingram, walked into the switchboard room every hour on the hour during the graveyard shift. It was Ingram's job to check incoming calls and decide if any information received was newsworthy enough to wake a reporter at home to pursue a story that could not wait until morning. If a switchboard operator received a call she knew Ingram would want to know about immediately, she could summon him by pressing a button that sounded a buzzer in the newsroom.

"Anything cooking, girls?" During the day, eight operators worked the long switchboard; for graveyard, only three. As Ingram approached the console, each woman handed him a clipboard with a description of calls received that hour and Ingram detached the paper. When he got to Peg, she handed him her clipboard and said, "Not much there, Mr. Ingram. I put a call through to the transatlantic switchboard in Philly for Elizabeth Ault. Other than that, just the usual. A call came in about five minutes ago about a minor fire over on Sycamore, but the caller said the Fire Department already had it contained. I knew you'd be by any minute and it didn't sound like an emergency that couldn't wait till you got here."

"Elizabeth is making a transatlantic phone call?" He read the report. "To London?"

"Yeah, it's morning over there. That's when she had to call for a story she's working on."

Ingram returned his attention to the clipboard and shrugged. "Well, okay."

Peg laughed and added, "I almost fell over when she told me it was *Beth* Ault calling."

Everyone around the newspaper was well aware Elizabeth Ault disliked the common short versions of her name.

"What? You're kidding," Ingram chuckled. "I made the mistake of calling her that twice. The first time she politely corrected me. The second time I thought she might put rat poison in my coffee. She must have had one too many at the Rusty Bottom."

"She called long distance from Kentucky."

"Okay, she was drunk when she left the Rusty Bottom, made a wrong turn, ended up going over the bridge and called from a bar in Covington." Ingram chuckled.

Peg laughed. "You might be right because she also forgot we ran into each other a couple of days ago."

"What do you mean?"

"She said on the phone she was glad to talk to me, that it had been weeks since we last talked. She worked late a couple of nights ago and we ran into each other in the ladies room as she was leaving. We talked for a good ten minutes."

"There you go—too much time tonight at the Rusty Bottom." Clete Ingram grinned, detached the hourly report from Peg's clipboard, and left the room.

[same time—house in Kentucky backwoods]

Erika walked back into the living room. She had left to check on Jim and Merle. "They're still out. Merle is snoring." She returned to the sofa.

"Elizabeth, tell me more about your husband and married life. Are you happy?"

"Yes, I am happy. I've never regretted marrying Frank."

"He is kind?"

"Yes. He can be very sweet. At times, Frank can be a little rough around the edges, but I'm no jewel to live with. I know I can be overly stubborn and uncompromising at times."

"He has never hit you?"

"No, absolutely not."

"So, he did not hit you when you told him about that night outside the bar?"

"No. Frank would never hit me. He got mad and left the house. What I did was very wrong and he was hurt. It's something a wife, or a husband, should never do."

"But you find yourself attracted to Glen?"

Elizabeth was surprised. "How do you know Glen's name?"

"You said his name in the alley that night outside the Rusty Bottom. And after the two of you drove away, I went into the bar and struck up a conversation with the bartender. I told her I was a fan of yours and asked if the man you left with was your husband, which I

365

knew he wasn't, of course, from your conversation in the alley. The bartender told me the man's name and said he is your husband's partner."

"No, I am not attracted to Glen. He's a friend. And I won't make excuses—it was stupid of me."

"So when your husband found out, he confronted Glen, I'm sure."

"I didn't tell Frank it was Glen."

"Oh?"

"I was afraid of what Frank might do. I told him the man was from out of town."

"I see. I think that was wise for Glen's sake. Your husband looks much stronger."

"Frank is strong, and tough."

"Do you enjoy making love to him?"

"Yes, I do." After a brief silence, Elizabeth asked, "Do you enjoy making love?"

"I used to, not so much anymore."

"Why is that?"

"I don't know."

"Danny?"

Erika smiled. "It was nice with Danny. He was so innocent. I'm sure I was his first."

"Do you want to marry someday?"

"When I was a little girl I dreamed of marrying. I think all little girls do, don't you think? Standing at the altar in a grand white dress beside their loving prince. Of course I had that dream, but I'm not sure marriage is in my future."

Elizabeth changed the subject. "Tell me about this phone call. You said I can listen, so I will know the details soon. Why do you think your father is in danger?"

"I have a powerful enemy. I told you earlier."

"Himmler?"

"Yes."

Elizabeth's interview mode kicked in. "Why does he want to hurt your father?"

"Himmler never forgets a slight and will bide his time until he feels the time for retribution is right. He holds grudges against both my father and me for past snubs—real or imagined. Himmler sent a man to follow me to this country with orders to murder me because he knew he dare not plot against the daughter of Hitler's close friend

366

while I was in Germany. If I were killed here in America, my father would never know how it happened. The man Himmler sent is the one you think I murdered in Evansville. But it was self-defense."

"Your partner?"

"He was never my partner."

"I still don't understand why your father is in danger."

"I know how Himmler's tainted mind works; he is not a man who leaves loose ends. Because of my father's friendship with the Führer, Himmler would never risk me surviving, returning to Germany, and telling my father of his plot against me. Himmler will reason that if I ever return, with my father gone he can eliminate me without risk."

"Your father is a close friend of Adolf Hitler?"

"They met in the early twenties. My father has been with him from the beginning. Himmler has also been with Hitler from the start, but my father is a war veteran like Hitler and they have a special bond. Himmler never served in the military and he has always been jealous that Hitler holds my father in such high esteem."

"You're not going to turn yourself in after this phone call, are you?"

Erika looked at Elizabeth but said nothing.

"Am I right?" Elizabeth hunted for an answer.

"I promised you if you helped me reach my grandfather in London so a warning can be sent to my father, I will turn myself over to your husband at the end of the night. If my phone call is successful, I will keep my promise. If not, I'll have no choice but to try to get home to warn my father."

Elizabeth wanted to believe her, but could not. All she could wish for now was that the things she said to Peg warned her that something was wrong, but that hope was pitifully small. Her hints were so terribly obscure, forced to be so by Erika's presence.

"What's your father's name?" Elizabeth asked.

"Karl . . . with a *K*, like my name, not a *C* as you Americans normally spell it."

"And you said in the car that your mother is gone?"

"She died in an automobile accident here in America. We lived here for four years. I finished high school in this country and a year of college."

"So that's why you speak English like an American. Where did you attend college in the States?"

"In Virginia. I made a great friend there, my roommate, her name was Ann."

"As in *Brown?*"

"Yes, but she spelled *Anne* without the *e*. I added the *e* when I signed the rental papers at the Lamar Apartments." Erika smiled. "A little European flair I didn't have to worry about anyone picking up on. I've thought often of Ann, and wondered what happened to her. She wanted to be a radio newscaster. She was like you, Elizabeth, unafraid to invade men's territory."

The thunder grew louder.

"Looks like you were right about that second front," Elizabeth commented.

[3:20 a.m.—Cincinnati, home of city news editor Otis Kapperman]
After eleven or twelve rings, Geraldine Kapperman awoke and answered the telephone. She knew the call was for her husband. Middle-of-the-night telephone calls to the Kapperman home always came from the newsroom and always concerned breaking news that could not wait until morning. She reached for the phone on the lamp table between her and her husband's twin beds.

"Hello."

"This is Clete, Mrs. Kapperman. I'm sorry to wake you, but can I speak to Otis?"

"Hold on. I'll wake him." She lowered the receiver and turned on the lamp. "Otis! . . . Otis!" No response. She rose from her bed and shook her husband. "Otis, wake up!"

Kapperman grunted and turned away.

"Otis!" she yelled louder and shook harder.

"What is it, Geraldine?" Kapperman scratched out.

"You know what it is. It's the newsroom! Here's the phone."

Kapperman rolled onto his back and fumbled for the phone. "Yeah."

"Otis, this is Clete. Sorry to bother you. I was wondering, do you have Elizabeth Ault working on a story having to do with London, or someone in London?"

"No. Why?"

"She called here about a half hour ago and initiated a transatlantic call to London."

"Why?"

"I don't know why. That's why I'm calling you."

"Where did she call from?" Kapperman asked, still half asleep. "Is she in the newsroom?"

"No. It was a long distance collect call. Peg said the operator told her the call was from Kentucky. That's all Peg knows. The Kentucky operator didn't name a town."

Kapperman scratched his stomach. "Clete, you know how Ault is. That woman doesn't clear half the things she works on with me, so why the worry?"

"I don't know. Peg told me Elizabeth said some funny things."

"Like what?"

"She identified herself as Beth Ault and said she was glad to talk to Peg—that it had been a long time. But Peg said she and Elizabeth had a friendly conversation just two days ago. Peg and I laughed about it and I joked that Elizabeth stayed too long at the Rusty Bottom. But the more I thought about it, the call just sounded weird—not like Elizabeth. That's why I called. Sorry I bothered you, Otis. Go back to sleep. You can ask her about it Monday."

"Yeah, I will."

"Again, sorry I woke you."

"That's okay, Clete. Forget it."

Kapperman reached over, hung up the phone, and rolled over to go back to sleep. He lay there for five minutes and then sat up on the edge of the bed.

[same time—house in Kentucky backwoods]

"Why did you choose that pool hall?" asked Elizabeth, still on the sofa with Erika waiting for the phone to ring. "If it was because you needed a public place to meet Jim, there are dozens of bars you could have chosen where you wouldn't have needed to go through all that trouble with costumes and a hotel room just so I could change clothes."

Erika smiled. "I can see why you're a successful reporter. You think before you ask a question. You presented me with a unique problem, Elizabeth, something I've not been forced to deal with before. Your photograph is in the newspaper several times a week. I couldn't risk you being recognized. You never know what can happen and that problem I wanted to avoid. When I found out about the Side

Pocket's Halloween party, I knew I had gotten lucky. The masks got my attention. I knew you wouldn't be wearing the mask until eight and the Side Pocket girls would see your face, but I wasn't overly concerned about them recognizing you. If they did, they had no reason to fret that something was wrong. However, at eight, when the public was allowed in, if some married man who knew he shouldn't be there in the first place recognized you he might cause a stir—worried his name might end up in the newspaper. Or someone who knows you and your husband, maybe even an off-duty policeman friend of Frank's looking for a friendly Side Pocket girl, could arrive while we waited for Jim. Any friend or acquaintance would be shocked to see you working as a Side Pocket girl. He would surely approach you and pry—perhaps even call Frank. Your mask resolved all of those concerns. And I recommended those outfits to Iris—no place to conceal a gun. If you brought a gun, you would be forced to leave it in your coat."

"And you weren't worried that Jim or Merle would recognize me. They live too far away to be *Observer* readers."

"Very good, Elizabeth. Perhaps you should become a detective like your husband . . . or a spy."

[3:30 a.m.—Cincinnati, the Ault home]

Every ashtray overflowed in the Ault living room, and coffee stains decorated the coffee table and the upholstered chair where Chuck Warzyniak had toppled his mug when he dozed off for a moment around 3:00 a.m. On one end of the sofa, Glen Shafer sat holding an ice bag to his swollen jaw; Leroy Carr occupied the other end. Frank still paced.

Carr had just radioed Stanley Mullen, the FCC supervisor in charge of the three triangulation stations set up just outside the city. Every half hour Carr radioed Mullen for a report, but nothing out of the ordinary was happening on the airwaves. Ed Cantrell had called from headquarters four times over Frank's RCA to check for any news; there was none. The telephone had not rung since Elizabeth and Anne Brown called shortly after 11:00 p.m., the call too brief to trace.

Shafer, tired of sitting, rose and walked around the room.

The telephone rang. Frank picked up the receiver before that first ring stopped resonating.

"Hello!"

Carr and Warzyniak rose from their seats.

"Who is this again?" Frank asked loudly. "Kapperman? Yeah, I remember you . . . No! She's not here. Why are you calling?" The room was silent for one minute as Frank listened, then interrupted. "Alright, alright, I've heard enough. You did the right thing calling. Where are you? . . . Give me your address." Frank scribbled on a small pad. "Be standing on the street in front of your house in five minutes. I don't care if you're in a bathrobe. I'll pick you up and take you to the newspaper so we can talk to your people."

Frank slammed the receiver and talked quickly. "About a half hour ago, Elizabeth called the *Observer* switchboard from somewhere in Kentucky to place a transatlantic telephone call. Glen, you and Chuck stay here. Glen, you answer the phone if it rings. If we get a lead on her whereabouts, I'll let you know. Let's go, Carr."

[3:35 a.m.—house in Kentucky backwoods]

"Why did you cause all that tension in the bedroom with Jim?" Elizabeth asked. "You knew my gun wasn't loaded—why hold your hand behind your back and act as if you had a gun? Was it because you wanted to see what Jim would do?"

"I wanted to see what *you* would do."

[3:37 a.m.—Cincinnati]

Otis Kapperman managed to throw on a shirt and pants and make it to the street in front of his house in time to hear a police siren. He stood under a streetlight so he would be easily seen. The sound of the siren came from his right and he turned in time to watch a dark-colored Plymouth fishtail around the corner. Kapperman had to jump back to avoid being hit as the car screeched to a stop at the curb. He saw two men inside the car and recognized the driver as Elizabeth Ault's husband.

"Get in the back, Kapperman. Hurry up!" Frank Ault shouted from his rolled-down window.

371

After the scariest car ride of Otis Kapperman's life—he feared they would all die before they reached the *Observer*—Frank Ault slammed on the brakes, skidded on smoking tires, and finally stopped near the front entrance.

The three men hustled past the security guard and up one flight of steps with the middle-aged Kapperman falling behind. "Come on, Kapperman," Frank ordered. "Get the lead out." When they reached the second floor, Kapperman led them to the switchboard room where he pushed the button to summon Clete Ingram from the newsroom.

When Frank saw three women wearing operator headsets, he chose not to wait for Ingram. He held up his badge. "Police. Who took the call from Elizabeth Ault?" A woman raised her hand. Frank turned to her. "I'm Detective Sergeant Frank Ault, Cincinnati Police. I'm Elizabeth's husband." The two other women turned their heads, wanting to see what Elizabeth Ault's husband looked like. "What's your name?"

"Peg Mehringer."

"I know about the transatlantic phone call, Peg. What I need from you is anything you can tell me about where Elizabeth called from."

"It was long distance; the operator told me *Kentucky*, but that's all. Elizabeth didn't tell me anything about where she was calling from. Is she okay?"

"Kentucky? That's all you know?" asked Frank, the annoyance apparent in his voice. "You don't ask where an expensive phone call like that is being made from?"

Otis Kapperman spoke up as Clete Ingram walked into the room. "She's not supposed to ask, Detective—all overseas calls are transferred to the transatlantic switchboard in Philadelphia. Philadelphia takes over from there. That's the way it's been done since the war started. All overseas calls from anywhere in the country have to go through the Philadelphia transatlantic switchboard. Philadelphia then routes the call through a switchboard in Bermuda. Both the Philadelphia and Bermuda switchboards are monitored 24 hours a day by our military. Elizabeth would have to give her name, an authorization number, and the phone number she called from to both switchboards."

"Call Philadelphia and get the phone number," Frank told Kapperman.

"The military won't give Otis or me the number," Ingram said. "The newspaper will receive the bill from the phone company next month and the number won't even appear on the bill, not even if the call originates from the newsroom—just Xs in place of the numbers. You'll need to talk to them, Detective, and convince them it's a police emergency. Even then, you might have to get the local police to contact them."

"Just get the Philadelphia people on the phone." Frank said sharply.

Carr interjected, "If it's military we're dealing with, let me talk to them, Frank. If someone starts carping about red tape, I'll wake up General Donovan in Washington if I have to. He'll make them snap to. After I get the telephone number, your people can find out where it came from."

[3:55 a.m.—house in Kentucky backwoods]
"Elizabeth, your remark in the bedroom about love, why did you say that?"

"Erika, I said I don't want to talk about it. Please, can we forget I said that?"

"That's only the second time you've called me by my real name. The first time was when you made that remark in the bedroom."

"Erika, please." Elizabeth wanted desperately to change the subject. "Tell me more about your grandfather in England. Does he know you are a spy for Germany, and that you're here in the United States?"

"He knows neither. Was it the kiss, Elizabeth?"

Elizabeth turned her head so Erika would not see her blush.

"The kiss, Elizabeth? It bothered you?"

Elizabeth sighed and surrendered to Erika's persistence. "It was the way you kissed me more than anything else. I felt there was more behind it than merely entertainment for the men. Then the way you looked at me after the kiss. . . ."

"Yes, go on, please."

"That's all."

Erika saw Elizabeth's discomfort. After a long pause, Erika said, "Elizabeth, I have been with a woman, but for a particular purpose during a mission. I kissed you simply to excite the men and move our plan along."

Instead of being embarrassed for being wrong, Elizabeth felt relieved the subject was put to rest.

Erika continued, "Perhaps this is the reason I don't enjoy lovemaking as much now. For me, it's become merely another skill."

The telephone rang.

Chapter 59

Her Real Voice

Kentucky—backwoods house

3:55 a.m.

Elizabeth glanced at the wall clock as she rose from the sofa. "Just over an hour to be put through to London—not bad."

Erika followed her to the ringing telephone. "We're calling almost two hours later than I had hoped," Erika said. "It's ten o'clock in London. I hope I haven't missed him."

Elizabeth picked up the telephone and lifted the ear piece. "Hello. . . . Yes, Elizabeth Ault, OH52577, *Cincinnati Observer* . . . yes, person to person to Mr. Louis Richard Minton . . . that's correct." Elizabeth kept the earpiece tight to her ear but lowered the phone. She turned to Erika and nodded. "The operator established the connection and is putting us through." After another pause, Elizabeth spoke again into the phone. "Thank you, Operator."

In a moment, Elizabeth heard ringing at the other end. Someone picked up after three rings. Elizabeth heard a woman say *Ello.* The operator, still on the line to establish person to person, responded to the voice.

"Operator 881 calling from Bermuda. I have a person-to-person transatlantic call from the United States for Louis Richard Minton from Elizabeth Ault."

"From the United States? Elizabeth All?" The woman at the other end mispronounced Elizabeth's last name in a heavy Cockney accent. Elizabeth then heard the woman tell the operator, *"Sorry dearie, the guvnah's not at home. He and the lady are out and about, on their morning walk, they are."*

The operator spoke to Elizabeth. *"United States, the person you are calling is not at this number."*

Elizabeth said, "Operator, hold one moment, please." She lowered the phone and said to Erika, "A woman answered. Your grandparents are not at home."

Erika winced. "Tell the operator to go ahead and put it through. The woman must be Maggie, the cook and housekeeper. She's been with my grandparents for as long as I can remember."

Elizabeth raised the horn to her mouth. "Operator, please put the call through to the person who answered."

"Very well," the operator responded. *"United States, you are connected."*

"Thank you, Operator," said Elizabeth. She heard the operator click off the line, her job finished.

"Hello," Elizabeth said.

"Ello, who's calling?"

"My name is Elizabeth Ault, but I'm calling for a friend. Here she is." Elizabeth handed the telephone to Erika.

"Hello, is this Maggie?" Erika's British accent surprised Elizabeth. "Maggie, this is Erika—Early—Louise's daughter. How are you, Maggie?" Elizabeth saw Erika smile widely. "Yes, it's really me . . . Yes, I'm in America . . . It's a long story, Maggie. Do you have any idea how long my grandfather will be out?"

Lightning lit the window near the phone, the accompanying thunder louder than before.

"Look, Maggie, I don't have much time, and I have a very important message for Grandfather that I will count on you to give him. You'll need a pencil and paper."

Erika looked at Elizabeth while waiting on Maggie.

Elizabeth said, "A British accent?"

"I learned English in England as a child. You're hearing my real voice. My American accent is practiced, helped by the years I went to school here."

Maggie came back on the line.

"Crackers, Maggie. You know my father is in Germany. I need Grandfather to send a message to him by diplomatic courier through a person in Lisbon . . . no, not Leyland in Lancashire—Lisbon, Portugal. Maggie, write this:

—message for Karl Lehmann K A R L L E H M A N N (Erika spelled the name)

—diplomatic courier to Lisbon, that's L I S B O N

—address message to Catia Nuria Montolongo at the Heritage Av Liberdade Hotel (Erika again patiently spelled the words)

—message from Lorelei L O R E L E I . . . it doesn't matter who that is, Maggie, just please write that down. . . .

"Okay, Maggie, here's the message. This will sound a bit daft, but my father will understand. Write down: 'Rooster sent a dragon to Vinland to early' . . . no, that's all. 'Rooster sent a dragon to Vinland to early' . . . yes, that's right. And Maggie, spell both of those *to's* with just one *o* in each, and my nickname with a lower-case *e.*"

There was a pause while Maggie told Erika something that excited her. "Aces, Maggie! I'll hold."

Erika turned to Elizabeth. "Maggie looked out the window and caught a glimpse of my grandparents down the block, walking home."

"What does that message mean?" demanded Elizabeth. "It's code!"

"Yes, it's code. Catia Montolongo is a Portuguese courier for the German Embassy in Lisbon. The German Embassy pays for a room at a Lisbon hotel so she can stop at the desk twice daily and check for messages from people like me. Catia will take the message to my embassy's chargé d'affaires, and he will ensure it reaches my father. But I can't send a message to my father that reads *Himmler sent an assassin to America to kill me*, now can I? That's what it means. Himmler was once a chicken farmer and my father, who hates Himmler, likes to refer to him as *Rooster* in private. *Early* is me, of course, a name my mother called me. *Dragon* was slang used by my father's regiment during the first war for *sniper*. *Vinland* is a German codename for America. The German Embassy people will know what Vinland means but they won't be able to decipher the rest, and with my father's standing in the Reich they dare not hesitate to forward him the message. I'm confident my father will understand the message, and he'll know how to proceed from there. You can rest your mind, Elizabeth. The message has no war secrets."

"I assume you're *Lorelei.*"

"That's my codename used by German Military Intelligence—the organization I work for. My father will know I sent the message and therefore survived Himmler's plot."

"You're in the German army?"

"Navy."

"What is your rank?"

"I have a special rank called Sonderführer, used for . . ." Erika stopped mid-sentence; her attention returned to the telephone.

"Yes it's me," Erika laughed. "How are you Granddad? . . . Yes, Maggie is right, I'm here among the Yanks (more laughing). Is Grandmum there?" A second's pause. "Hello from America, Grandmum." Erika again laughed with delight. "How are you, darling? .

. . Yes, I'm chipper. How is Babs? . . . That's wonderful, Grandmum. When is she due? . . . An April baby, I predict a boy; he'll arrive just in time for the daffodils in your side garden to bloom. Did Jeffrey make it into the RAF? I know that was his goal . . . Ha, he settled for one of Montgomery's tanks, eh? Say, Grandmum, I'd love to chat forever, my darling, but I'm pressed for time. May I have another word with Granddad? I love you."

Erika waited to hear her grandfather's voice then talked quickly. "Granddad, I've given the information to Maggie, but I'd like to go over it with you. I believe my father could be in danger. I want to warn him and I know you can send a message through diplomatic courier to Lisbon. I know you're wondering why I think he's in danger, but it's a long story and I have no time to explain. Please just trust me. I don't want to use the Red Cross. You know better than anyone that sending a message through the Red Cross is unreliable, and if it gets through it can take weeks if not months. This way, my father will have the message in hand within hours after your courier arrives in Lisbon. If the courier is on an airplane by this afternoon, my father can be reading the message in Berlin before the day's end. Mama would want you to do this, Granddad."

A lengthy silence, at least a full minute, as Erika listened. Suddenly she dropped the phone heavily onto the table, bent over as if in pain and dropped to her knees.

Elizabeth knelt beside her. "What is it? What's wrong?" When she heard Erika's barely audible groan, Elizabeth stood and picked up the phone.

"Hello, Mr. Minton. My name is Elizabeth Ault. You don't know me, but I'm a friend of your granddaughter. What has happened?"

"Who is this again?"

"Elizabeth Ault, a friend of Erika's."

After an awkward silence, he said, *"Erika's father was killed in a sailing accident three months ago."*

"How . . . how do you know? Forgive me, sir, but are you sure?"

"Reich Radio released the news in Germany, and it was reported in German newspapers; Hitler attended the service. We monitor all German radio broadcasts, of course. A former colleague at the embassy was aware my late daughter was married to Lehmann. He forwarded me the report. It's dreadful news for Erika. She and her father grew especially close after Louise died. We thought Erika knew. We thought she was in Germany. Put her back on the line, please."

"Erika, your grandfather wants to talk to you."

Still on her hands and knees, Erika did not respond.

"Please, Erika, talk to your grandfather."

Erika rose slowly and took the phone. Without listening, she said, "I love you, Granddad. Good-bye." She hung up and bent slightly so she could rest her hands on the table, her head down.

Elizabeth stood beside Erika and put an arm around her waist. "I'm sorry, Erika." Elizabeth saw a tear tap the table like one of the raindrops tapped the nearby window.

"It was not an accident. My father was an expert sailor but quit boating when the war started. He told me he would feel guilty boating while our men died in the field."

An empty darkness fell over her face.

"Himmler had my father murdered."

Chapter 60

Chester and the Davenport

Kentucky—house in the backwoods

4:25 a.m.

Erika violently jerked the telephone cord from the wall and broke away from Elizabeth. She crossed the living room, picked up her bag, and walked briskly toward the door to the hall. Elizabeth followed. Erika stopped at Merle's door and looked in; Elizabeth did the same. Merle was still sedated and bound. So was Jim, still face down and naked on the hallway floor. Erika opened the fourth hallway door and stepped in with Elizabeth right behind. Unlike the bedrooms, this larger room had a window and a long metal table with two metal chairs. But the dominant feature of the room was a large cluster of sophisticated radio transmitters, receivers, keypads, and other assorted equipment coupled together. The room was a shortwave radio shack.

"What is this?" asked Elizabeth, stammering out the words. She wasn't sure why she asked; she knew what she was looking at.

"What does it look like, Elizabeth?" Erika sat in one of the chairs and dug through her bag.

"You . . . you lied."

"What about?" Erika found what she looked for and pulled from the bag a folder and several pencils tied together with a string.

"You promised if I helped you call London to warn your father, you wouldn't relay secrets and you'd turn yourself in after the call."

"You didn't listen carefully, Elizabeth. Yes, I promised I would not relay secrets in the telephone call, and I didn't. But I never told you the telephone call was the only thing I had to do tonight. And as far as turning myself in, I said I would do that at the end of the night if the call was successful. The night is not over, as you can see by looking out the window, and the call did not succeed."

"So you won't turn yourself in?"

"No, I was clear about my promise. The call can't warn my father, can it? I will return to Germany—I have business there with a pig." Erika removed several pages from the folder, placed them on the table, and began writing. "I don't want to hurt you, Elizabeth. Please sit down. When I finish here, we'll go our separate ways. You can take Jim's car."

A lightning strike, followed by thunder so deafening it shook the window panes, lit the woods behind the house. Through the window, in the luminance of the lightning, Elizabeth saw a tall radio antenna tower on a nearby hill. She rushed toward the radio equipment and began frantically pulling wires and cords. Erika grabbed her, lifted her away, and, like a wrestler, twisted and took Elizabeth to the floor.

"Let's not do it the hard way," Erika said grimly.

Elizabeth ignored her and continued to struggle, trying in vain to push Erika off. Finally, Erika locked onto Elizabeth's left hand and twisted it palm out until it would turn no farther without breaking. Elizabeth shouted in pain. Erika flipped Elizabeth over onto her stomach and sat on her back. Keeping Elizabeth's hand twisted with one hand, Erika managed to reach her bag. She pulled out the rope and laid it on the floor beside her. Then she pulled Elizabeth's right hand behind her back and crossed Elizabeth's hands to tie them. Elizabeth tried to break Erika's grip but could not.

"Stop struggling, Elizabeth! You'll only get hurt."

Erika quickly tied Elizabeth's hands behind her back. When she pulled the last knot tight, Elizabeth winced. "If that's too tight let me know."

It was too tight, but Elizabeth said, "Go to hell."

Erika rolled Elizabeth onto her back. "You continue to surprise me. Imagine Elizabeth Ault saying such a thing. Your loyal readers would be shocked." Erika brought her face within inches of Elizabeth's face. "If you were right and I wanted you, I could take advantage of this situation."

Before, such banter from the German had been lighthearted and spoken with a twinkle of mischief; now her eyes were dark and cruel. The woman who hung up the telephone had changed mightily from the woman joyful to hear her grandfather's voice.

Erika stood, helped Elizabeth stand, then put her in the second chair. Erika tied Elizabeth's bound hands to one of the metal uprights on the chair's backrest. Erika dragged the chair with Elizabeth in it to the side, farther away from the equipment where she would work. Erika disappeared from the room for a moment; she returned with a handgun, which she laid on the radio table.

"Is that the gun you used in Clare's apartment?" asked Elizabeth.

"That's right, but I took the silencer off. No need for it tonight. Don't use a silencer if you don't need it, Elizabeth. A silencer diminishes the projectile speed."

Frank was right about the silencer, Elizabeth thought.

Erika began reconnecting the wires and cords Elizabeth had yanked out. Unfortunately for Elizabeth, she had not damaged any of the equipment and it took Erika only a minute to return the radio to working order.

[4:30 a.m.—District 1 Police Headquarters, Cincinnati]

In his office, Ed Cantrell, telephone to his ear, wrote on a notepad. Frank Ault sat in a chair opposite Cantrell and fumed. An hour had passed since Frank learned about Elizabeth's phone call and still he had no address. Leroy Carr had to awaken William Donovan in Washington after all, and solicit the general's help to persuade a reluctant military switchboard supervisor in Philadelphia to hand over the telephone number Elizabeth called from. Then Frank turned the number over to Ed Cantrell who woke the necessary person at Bell to get an address. The Bell contact had finally called back, and Cantrell talked on the phone with him now.

Cantrell hung up and took a large map from a desk drawer. Frank, Leroy Carr, and Al Hodge gathered around. Cantrell unfolded the map and spread it out on his desk. "The location Elizabeth called from is in Grant County, Kentucky." Cantrell looked, then pointed. "The Bell guy said the phone location is west of Dry Ridge off of State Road 467, but the road doesn't have a name—not even a rural-route number for postal delivery. Dry Ridge looks to be about an hour down Highway 25. The Bell guy said he can get exact directions after the main Bell office opens up at eight o'clock."

"What? That's it!" Frank shouted. "How in hell are we supposed to find it? Wait till eight? Fuck that, Cantrell."

Leroy Carr said, "Hold on a minute." He turned to his partner. "Al, check your list."

Hodge pulled a folded sheet of paper from an inside suit pocket, opened it and looked it over. In a moment he said, "Here's one in Grant County, Kentucky."

"Here's what?" asked Frank.

"A shortwave transmitter," answered Hodge. He turned to Carr. "It's an amateur HAM radio club, Leroy. Location is latitude 38 degrees, 40 minutes, 44.166 seconds. Longitude minus 84 degrees, 41 minutes, 11.0184 seconds."

Frank said, "I thought the government shut down all the amateur HAMs for the duration."

"It did," Carr confirmed. "But some amateur clubs were given Civilian Defense status and are used as relay or monitoring stations if needed. The Civilian Defense HAM volunteers can't transmit without authorization, and to get Civilian Defense status the members of the HAM club have to agree that someone will be on hand day and night to answer a phone in case they're alerted, then the club is given a direct telephone line so a call isn't listened to by someone on a party line. That's got to be it. That's where Elizabeth made her call. Why a phone call to England was made makes no sense, but obviously Anne Brown needed Elizabeth's help to do it. We all had wondered these past weeks why Brown pursued your wife, Frank. Now we know—the transatlantic call. But access to a transmitter was Brown's ultimate goal all along."

Frank banged his fist on Cantrell's desk. "And now she doesn't need Elizabeth anymore!"

"I'll call Colonel Norquist, our local military liaison. With those coordinates, his people can plot the exact location on a map."

"How long will that take?" Frank asked impatiently.

"I don't know. I'll have to get him out of bed and to his office, then he'll have to call in someone who can plot coordinates."

"Jesus, Carr, sounds like another hour at least."

"Unless you have a better idea—"

Cantrell interjected, "If it's a registered transmitter, the local police or sheriff's office should know about it. I know our police chief's office has to keep a list of any HAMs in Cincinnati, operational or not, because of a mandate that took effect after Pearl Harbor. If it's out in the boonies, the county sheriff will have jurisdiction." Cantrell picked up the receiver and dialed the desk sergeant. "Sergeant, this is Cantrell in Homicide. Put me through to the Grant County, Kentucky, sheriff's department immediately. And I want to talk to the sheriff, not a deputy. He's probably at home this time of night. Whoever answers the phone, tell them it's a police emergency and have them put me through directly to his house or give us his home telephone number. Call me back." Cantrell returned the receiver to its cradle.

Leroy Carr was less than enthused about notifying anyone outside the circle, but he realized time was now the key. "We only want directions," Carr told Cantrell. "We can't chance sending some local good-old-boys to the scene. If Brown is there, they won't stand a chance. All we'll do is get them killed, and she'll be gone when we get there."

"I wasn't planning on sending them to the scene, Carr," Cantrell responded. "But I'll need to tell the sheriff something. He'll know something big is up when he gets an emergency phone call from the Cincinnati police at 4:40 in the morning."

Frank said, "Ed's right. If he doesn't tell the locals something, they'll go barging in for sure. Ed, tell them there's a possible hostage situation and ask them to set up a roadblock somewhere along the way, but not close—that will make them feel included. Make sure they know they cannot be spotted from the location. And no sirens or lights as they drive there or while they sit and wait for us."

Carr added, "Tell them the case is under federal jurisdiction and U.S. marshals are en route to meet up with them. Al and I have marshal I.D.s."

While they waited uneasily for the desk sergeant to call back, Frank cursed the situation. "Goddammit! What in the hell was that London phone call all about? If it weren't for that, Elizabeth wouldn't be involved."

"It might have been a call to Brown's handler," reasoned Carr. "A transatlantic phone call to Germany wouldn't be possible without getting it cleared several days in advance, and the call would be monitored. But Abwehr might have an underground handler stationed in London to circumvent that."

"Elizabeth would never agree to help an enemy agent make a transatlantic phone call to another agent. She'd die first." Frank turned to Cantrell. "I'm going to set out, Ed. Radio me when you get the directions."

"Right," said Cantrell.

Frank ran out the door with Leroy Carr and Al Hodge on his heels.

[same time—Kentucky backwoods HAM clubhouse]

Erika had positioned Elizabeth's chair about ten feet away and to her right. Elizabeth watched Erika write numbers, refer to several sheets of paper in front of her, then write more numbers. While watching, Elizabeth fidgeted with the ropes, trying to undo, but she was too well bound to loosen them.

"What are the secrets?" Elizabeth asked.

"Just one secret. Your country and its allies are in the process of a massive troop and matériel build-up in England for the inevitable invasion of France. It's just a matter of time until that happens. Knowing *where* you will invade is the biggest secret of the war."

"And you know that secret?"

"I don't know where you'll invade, but I know where you won't."

"Where is that?"

"Many of our generals think you'll choose the shortest route across the English Channel and invade at the Pas-de-Calais so you can capture the docks for a place to unload your heavy equipment: tanks, halftracks, trucks, artillery. But because of things I learned during my mission in Evansville, I believe you won't invade at Calais. Just as we know about your build-up in England, your generals know a large portion of our western army waits in and near Calais for its defense. An invasion there would be extremely costly for the Allies, if not fail outright. Yet our forces sit in that pas and could not be of immediate help if the invasion comes somewhere else, which I think it will."

"Because to invade at Calais will prove too costly to the Allies?"

"No, because over the past 19 months your country has been constructing a massive armada of large ships specially designed to transport your heavy equipment and unload it without the need for a dock. The ships can run aground on any sandy beach. Doors on the bow open and vehicles drive directly from the ship onto the beach."

"I know what you're talking about—LSTs. They build them in Pittsburgh and I watched one sail down the Ohio River."

"Yes, the ships themselves are not a secret. Your country builds them at many shipyards around the country. Before I came to Cincinnati, I was at the largest LST shipyard. We know about your LSTs. Your country used them against us in North Africa and Sicily, yet those battles are over and your country continues to build them by the hundreds. Your country would not do this if Allied plans were to capture a docking port—like Calais. No, you will invade beaches somewhere in France. I have draft specifications about your ships that our naval engineers can use to find out which French beaches have the necessary gradients needed by these ships. From that, they can identify which beaches in France are likely invasion points and free up some of our troops that now waste their time at the Pas-de-Calais."

Elizabeth challenged her: "So now you must kill me. You wouldn't tell me this information and let me go. You know I'll tell everything you've just told me. But of course, killing me after I helped you with the call to London was in your plans all along. And I'm sure Jim and Merle are doomed, too. You just kept them alive because if you killed them before the phone call you knew I wouldn't help you."

Erika, still writing, said, "I tell you because your FCC will intercept my message and your OSS in Washington will decipher it quickly. It causes me no concern that you will tell what you know. I no longer have my naval codes. I am forced to use a common transmission code called Baudot that is not unlike your teletype codes. Your people in Washington will read what's in my message before you eat lunch today, Elizabeth."

"If we can break your code, why bother sending the message?"

Erika stopped what she was doing and looked at her. "Should I not send it? This is still critical information my country must have, and it will cause your generals great alarm. What would you do, Elizabeth?"

Elizabeth paused. "I would send it, but I would never work for the Nazis."

"The Democratic Party controls your White House; does your Marine brother fight for the Democrats, or for his country?"

Elizabeth did not answer.

"It's the same with me, Elizabeth."

Erika finished writing, put the headset on, spent several seconds adjusting dials on the transmitter then began tapping on a keypad.

[4:40 a.m.—Dry Ridge, Kentucky]

Chester Poindexter always slept sitting up on his living room davenport. Although the davenport converted into a bed, Poindexter never bothered with that. Now 44 and never married, there was no one around to care where he slept. Instead, his life's partner was insomnia, so Poindexter stuck with what helped him drop off: a light left on, a radio, and a tumbler or two of Old Crow. Poindexter never considered moving the radio to the bedroom once he found he could sleep sitting on the davenport. During the winter, with no blanket (a blanket made him feel as if he were in bed and kept sleep at bay), the cold would shiver him awake; he solved that problem by keeping the living room space heater set on High during cold weather. He used to smoke a cigar with his end-of-the-day whiskey, but twice he had dozed off and almost burned up the davenport with him on it, so now he always finished the cigar before he poured the Old Crow.

The telephone sat on a table near the davenport, but Poindexter's snoring and the radio, still on, muffled the rings. It took 25 rings before he stirred. Poindexter, still in his pants and undershirt, finally opened his eyes and reached for the phone.

"Poindexter here," he said before he coughed.

"Sheriff Poindexter, this is Major Ed Cantrell, Cincinnati Police. Sorry to bother you at this hour, Sheriff. Your deputy on duty at your jail, a Deputy Roby, gave me your number. We have an emergency."

"What is it?" Poindexter moved to the edge of the davenport.

"We have reason to believe there is an ongoing hostage situation in your county. Cincinnati police and U.S. marshals are on their way as we speak. I'm requesting that you set up a roadblock until they arrive."

"Roadblock? Where?"

"I need your help with that. We know the hostage is being held in a building that has a shortwave radio transmitter and I understand there is an amateur HAM radio club in Grant County. I'm sure because of Civilian Defense requirements that you're aware of the transmitter."

Poindexter stood and scratched his buttocks while he thought. "Yeah, those HAM boys have a club a couple of miles off Clark's Creek Road."

"Is that the only one in your county?"

"The only one registered with me."

"That must be it. Sheriff, I need detailed directions so I can radio the men who are already underway. Right now, they're driving south on Highway 25."

Poindexter was still groggy from sleep. "Ah . . . tell them to take 467 west off the Dixie Highway. That turnoff is just before they get to town."

"Before they reach Dry Ridge?" Cantrell knew the Dixie Highway was Highway 25.

"That's right. Then take 467 for about a mile to a fork in the road. Take the right fork; that's Warsaw Road."

"Got it."

"Once they're on Warsaw, it's about five or six miles to Clarks Creek Road. It's a gravel road on the left. About a mile and a half, maybe two miles down Clarks Creek there's a sign with an arrow that says *HAM Club of Grant County*. The clubhouse sits up on a hill another mile or so up a dirt road."

Cantrell quickly reviewed the directions with Poindexter then said, *"Sheriff, it's critically important that the suspect not be alerted that we're coming. Where do you plan to set up your roadblock?"*

Poindexter took a moment. "I'll set up on Clarks Creek Road at the base of the road to the club."

"Anyone in the club building able to see you from there?"

"No. And there's no other way out. They would have to come that way."

"Okay, Sheriff. Again, I can't stress enough the importance of not tipping the suspect. Please don't use sirens or lights."

"Okay, Major. You said *suspect*. Is there only one?"

"We're not sure, but whoever is there will be armed and dangerous."

"How many hostages?"

"We don't know that either. Sheriff, this is a federal case and they have jurisdiction. If anything goes wrong, innocent people could be killed."

"Major, we small town boys aren't as smart as you big city boys, but we're not stupid. I'll set up the roadblock."

Chapter 61

The Heavens Play a Role

Kentucky—Highway 25

4:55 a.m.

With few motorists on the roads, Frank Ault strained the engine and tires of the '41 Plymouth as he sped through Covington, Kentucky, weaving past an occasional car or truck pulled to the shoulder, warned off the road by the blaring siren and a flashing light placed on the dashboard. Frank glanced at the speedometer.

"Going about 80," he told Leroy Carr and Chuck Warzyniak. "We should be there in about 35 or 40 minutes." Frank had stopped by the house and picked up Warzyniak after leaving headquarters. Each man carried a handgun, and Frank always carried two rifles in the trunk of the Plymouth; he grabbed a third rifle from his gun case at home. Frank wanted at least two men at the house, so to replace Warzyniak he instructed Glen Shafer to radio Ed Cantrell and have him awaken Officer Christian.

"I don't see your partner, Carr," Frank said after a quick glance in the rearview mirror. Al Hodge and his Army driver followed but had fallen behind.

"They can't keep up in that Jeep. I'll radio him the directions." Carr got on his walkie-talkie, contacted Hodge, and read him the directions Ed Cantrell had radioed to the Plymouth two minutes ago. Carr said *Over and Out* to Hodge, then turned to Frank: "I'm going to radio Mullen, my FCC man, and have him redirect his receivers south toward Grant County."

When they left the Covington city limits and hit open highway, Frank saw lightning flash in the distance. He pressed the accelerator pedal to the floor, pushing the needle to 100.

[same time—backwoods house]

Adalwulf had given Erika the shortwave frequency information she needed to transmit her message to the Bolivar substation in Juárez,

389

Mexico. The HAM frequency differed from the frequency used to send her earlier message via the newspaper radio teletype—the message Erika tricked the *Observer* teletype operator into sending.

But transmitting to Juárez was Erika's second choice. Bolivar would have to relay the message through several substations and errors could occur—one coded word left out, or changed ever so slightly, could negate the entire message. Erika preferred to transmit to a U-boat patrolling off the East Coast as she had done during her Evansville mission. She realized her odds of connecting with a U-boat were slim—the Oberkomando der Wehrmacht, the German High Command, changed the naval frequencies almost daily as they did the Enigma codes, but she wanted to try. Erika turned the transmitter dials to 80 meters, 3.550 megahertz, the last frequency she had used in Evansville. She knew the frequencies had been changed many times since she last transmitted, but perhaps the OKW had come full circle to that frequency over the course of time. Wishing for luck, she tapped in letters on the keypad and repeated three times:

QQVD QQVD QQVD

For those letters, Erika used international Morse code, not the Baudot code she used to encode her message. The Morse code letters were a simple recognition signal used by the Kriegsmarine, the German Navy, to alert German warships that a coded message would follow. She waited for the confirmation *KXK KXK* from a U-boat but it did not come. She tried again.

[5:00 a.m.—Kentucky, Highway 25]
Leroy Carr said what was on his mind.
"Frank, we have to take Anne Brown alive."
"Why?"
"It's critical that we find out what she knows. Tell me you understand that."
Frank did not answer.

[5:10 a.m.—backwoods house]
Time dictated that Erika Lehmann abandon her hope of reaching a U-boat. She established a connection with Juárez at 40 meters, 7.100

megahertz and began tapping the keypad when lightning struck. Through the curtainless window, the bolt lit the room in eerie blue, complemented by an eardrum-rattling boom. The lightning killed her connection. She spun one dial over to 160 meters and another dial to 1.900 megahertz.

"Having trouble?" Elizabeth asked.

"Yes, you'll be happy to know."

"That's a shame."

Elizabeth watched Erika continue to fine-tune the dial. Finally, Erika began tapping again.

[5:10 a.m.—roadblock on Clarks Creek Road, eight miles west of Dry Ridge, Kentucky]

One car could easily block the narrow gravel road bordered on one side by a thick forest and the other by a deep ditch with a running creek, but Chester Poindexter had two. He stood behind the cars wearing a coat protected by a rain slicker. Three other uniformed men, also in rain gear, stood next to Poindexter.

"What the hell, Chester?" said one of the men. "What's your take on all this?"

"I told you what I know, Purvis," Poindexter answered. "There might be a hostage situation at the radio club and the feds are on the way. Let's all get in my car. My goddamn socks are wetter than a catfish's ass."

[5:15 a.m.—Highway 25]

When rain slickened the highway a few miles back, Frank was forced to slow to 60 when the Plymouth almost slid off the road near Crittenden. The necessity to slow evoked a curse from the driver.

"Damn the rain!"

Chuck Warzyniak tried to reassure his friend. "We'll get there, old buddy. Elizabeth will be okay. Just from that time you had me drive her to Union Terminal I could tell she's a heady gal. Hey, I wouldn't mind driving a cab for some extra dough after I retire from the Force. I kind of liked that. And I never gave the cabbie his hat back so I already have the uniform." Warzyniak laughed by himself.

"There's a mileage sign coming up," said Carr, ignoring Warzyniak.

"What's it say?" asked Frank.

Carr squinted through the rain-splashed windshield as the car zoomed by. "It said *Spencer, two miles.*" With his flashlight, Carr checked the map and the directions. "That means the turnoff at Dry Ridge is about six or seven miles ahead . . . then we've got another seven or eight to that radio club. We won't be able to go this speed on those gravel and dirt roads, but if they're not too much of a mess from the rain, we should be there in about 15 or 20 minutes."

[5:25 a.m.—backwoods house]

Twice the storm had broken Erika's connection and now she keyed her message for the third time.

"What will you do if you don't get the message sent?" Elizabeth asked, her hands numb from the ropes.

Erika ignored the question and continued to tap her coded message, concentrating on the sheets and the keypad.

[same time—roadblock on Clarks Creek Road]

Rain pelted the fogged windows of Chester Poindexter's sheriff's car. Inside, three of the four men smoked. Purvis Delaney had bummed a Lucky Strike from Ray Cummins and both lit up. Poindexter puffed on one of his huge cigars. The fourth man, the newest recruit to the Grant County Sheriff's Department, 21-year-old Billy Holcomb, coughed in the backseat.

"What's the matter back there, Billy?" Purvis asked. He sat in the front with the sheriff. "Got a cold?"

Billy Holcomb coughed again. "It's the smoke."

Purvis and Ray laughed.

"How long are we supposed to wait here, Chester?" Ray Cummins asked. "When are the government boys supposed to get here?"

Poindexter looked at his watch. "I don't know. They called almost an hour ago. They want us to wait here. Those city boys don't trust us." He paused to puff on his cigar two more times then said, "Ray, you stay down here. Angle your Ford so it blocks the road. I'll drive on up there with Purvis and Billy. We'll see what's going on."

Chapter 62

Remember, It's Just a Gal

Kentucky backwoods muddy road

5:35 a.m.

Chester Poindexter struggled.

Twice the sheriff got stuck in rain-filled ruts in the dirt road leading up the hill to the HAM radio clubhouse. Both times he was forced to shift multiple times into reverse, then back to first, to rock the car and free the tire. Finally, only half-way to the clubhouse, he shut off the headlights and the engine.

"We'll hoof it from here, boys," Poindexter told Purvis and Billy. "It's only a half mile or so from here, and this ol' road's gettin' worse. We don't want to get our asses stuck and can't get out, and we don't want to drive right up to the place anyhow. We've got to sneak up there and take a look-see around without being spotted if the fella who called me was right and there's some criminal doings up there."

The three men got out of the car. In the trunk, Poindexter always carried a double-barrel, twelve-gauge shotgun and a Winchester rifle he used for deer hunting. He gave the shotgun and a few extra shells to Purvis, and the rifle and cartridges to Billy.

"Keep the barrels down, boys, so you keep the rain out."

[5:40 a.m.—State Road 467, west of Dry Ridge, Kentucky]

"Okay, Frank," Carr said as he shined a flashlight on the paper with the directions. "There's a fork in the road coming up any time; take it to the right. We want Warsaw Road."

"There it is," Frank said almost immediately and turned the steering wheel. "What time is it?"

Carr checked his watch. "Twenty to six."

"It doesn't start getting light this time of year until about seven. We'll have to find the damn place in the dark. I'll have to shut off the headlights on that dirt road that leads to the place and it's probably muddier than hell. How far away are we?"

"Maybe seven miles if the sheriff Cantrell talked to is accurate."

Frank switched off the siren and the flashing light on the dashboard.

[5:45 a.m.—in the woods, 100 yards from the radio clubhouse]

In a steady rain under a flashing and banging sky, the sheriff and his two deputies double-timed it up the road on foot as fast as the mud and their energy allowed. They trotted in the less muddy moss and underbrush next to the road. Poindexter fell behind the two younger, fitter deputies but caught up when they stopped to wait for him.

"There it is, Chester," said Purvis in a low voice. Through the trees, they saw lights from the radio clubhouse. Two cars sat parked in front.

"Okay . . ." Poindexter said huffing and puffing, the knees of his trousers soiled from a stumble along the way. "Okay," he said a second time once he caught his breath. "Let's be careful, boys. We can't go busting in there. We want to take a quiet look-see. Purvis, you go around the house to the left. Billy, you to the right. We can't go check the front with that porch light burning. Just check the side windows and in the back. Look inside but be careful—don't let anybody see you. It's dark out here, and light in there, so no one inside will see you unless you put your face right up to the glass. Be smart. I'll move up closer. I'll wait for you in front of the house, as close as I can get without being in the open. Don't do anything else till you report back to me, ya hear?"

Purvis said, "Got it, Chester."

Billy said, "Yes, sir, Sheriff."

"Okay, boys, go ahead now. And watch yourselves."

The three men gingerly made their way toward the clubhouse. Purvis with the shotgun. Billy with the rifle.

[5:47 a.m.—Warsaw Road, about six mile west of Dry Ridge]

The Plymouth sped along the snaking country road. Frank sped up on straight stretches and slowed, begrudgingly, for curves. Leroy Carr signed off from a radio call with Stanley Mullen, the FCC triangulation expert he brought to Cincinnati.

"That was Mullen," said Carr. "He refocused the triangulation stations to this direction, and said someone is currently transmitting from the area but the atmospheric conditions are breaking it up. That means Anne Brown is still there."

"Thank God!" said Frank. He forced himself to hope that if Brown's plans included harming Elizabeth, the spy would wait until she was ready to leave.

"Right," Carr agreed. "With storm interference it will take her longer."

Chuck Warzyniak spoke from the backseat. "And that's good for us—the United States—that her signal is breaking up, right, Carr?"

"Depends. The effect of atmospheric conditions on radio waves is unpredictable—in a storm especially. A signal transmitted during a storm might come across as nothing but static or garble to a receiver 50 miles away, but the same signal might work its way through the storm, bounce around the atmosphere, and be picked up clearly a thousand miles away or farther."

"There it is, Frank!" Leroy Carr shouted. "Clarks Creek Road. You just passed it."

Frank slammed on the brakes. "Dammit, Carr! Let me know before I get there!"

"Ault, I'm looking for goddamn signs in the dark just like you are."

Frank jockeyed the Plymouth forward and back three times before he managed to turn the car around. He spun the rear tires, drove back, and turned onto the gravel road.

[5:50 a.m.—outside the radio clubhouse]
Staying under cover of the forest, Purvis Delaney and Billy Holcomb split up and slowly worked their way to the sides of the clubhouse. As ordered, Purvis approached the left side and looked into the living room window; he saw no one so he crept to the next window.

On the opposite side of the house, Billy peered cautiously into the kitchen window and saw no one. That window being the only one on the right side of the house, Billy made his way toward the back.

Purvis crept to the second window on his side and raised his head from a ducked position to look inside. Rain streaks on the window forced him to draw nearer than he wished. Two women sat in chairs: one across the room, facing him with her arms behind her back;

another woman, with her side toward the window, sat at a table with radio equipment. Lightning flashed and Purvis ducked so as not to be seen, then he headed to the back of the house. As he stepped around the corner, he saw Billy peering into the only window at the back of the house. Billy flinched, startled by a moving shadow. When he saw the shadow was Purvis, Billy waved him over.

"There's a guy on the floor, Purvis," Billy whispered. "He's tied up."

Purvis looked into the hallway window. "Lord Almighty." Purvis also whispered. "Bucknekked, too. Ass shining like two new silver dollars."

"Is he dead?"

"I don't know. Might be. Let's get away from the window." The two deputies stepped back into the trees.

"Did you see anyone else in other rooms?" Purvis asked quietly.

"No."

"I saw two women. Looks like one might be tied to a chair. Let's get back and tell Chester."

[5:57 a.m.—roadblock on Clarks Creek Road]

Occasional lightning flashed but the rain diminished. As Frank straightened the wheel after steering around a bend, he saw a car parked ahead, blocking the road. A man, apparently noticing the Plymouth's headlights, got out of the car.

"There's the sheriff," announced Carr. "And he's parked at the base of a dirt road. That's got to be the road to the HAM club."

Frank pulled within a few feet of the standing man, stopped, and everyone got out. Frank looked for other officers but saw none.

"Sheriff, I'm Frank Ault, Cincinnati Police." Frank held up his I.D. and talked quickly. "It's just you out here?"

"I'm not the sheriff. I'm Deputy Cummins. The sheriff already went up to check on the situation."

"What?" Frank grabbed the deputy and jerked him around. "How long ago?"

"About a half hour! He took two deputies with him. Get your hands off me!"

"Jesus Christ!" Frank, still gripping the deputy's jacket, violently shoved him backwards, slamming him against the side of his car.

Carr interjected angrily, "Deputy, your sheriff was told to wait. This case is under federal jurisdiction."

Frank didn't wait for the deputy to reply to Carr. He released his grip and said, "Get that fucking car out of our way. Now!"

Quickly, the deputy got in and moved the car. Frank, Carr, and Warzyniak loaded into the Plymouth and sped up the dirt road, the car fishtailing in the mud.

[6:00 a.m.—inside the radio room]

Elizabeth had taken heart. She noticed a silhouette of a man standing near the window when the lightning flashed a few minutes ago. Maybe her hints to Peg had worked. She knew the silhouette did not belong to Frank; he would never wear a cowboy hat. But the man of the silhouette had to be someone Frank brought with him. Elizabeth felt sure Erika, who did not face the window, was unaware.

"How much longer?" Elizabeth asked.

"Not long if the storm doesn't knock me off again."

[6:05 a.m.—in the woods, 40 yards from the front of the clubhouse]

Purvis and Billy found Chester Poindexter.

"What did you see, boys?" Poindexter asked.

Purvis did the talking. "There's a guy lying in a hallway tied up and nekked as a jaybird."

"Nekked?"

"As a goddamn jaybird. He wasn't moving. Might be dead."

"Dead? What else?"

"I saw two women in the radio room. One's using the radio; the other's in a chair and I think she's tied up."

"What else?"

"That's all, Chester. That's all we seen."

"Nobody else?" Poindexter looked at both men in the darkness.

"Nope," Purvis answered.

Billy said, "That's all I seen, Sheriff. Just the nekked man."

Poindexter thought for a moment. "The woman using the radio must be the one the federal boys are after if she's the only one in there not tied up. Somebody had to do the tying. Holy moly, those federal boys think the Grant County Sheriff's Department can't handle a woman."

"We can get the drop on her, Chester," said Purvis. "What can a woman do against three trained lawmen?"

"Are there any other doors? On the sides or in back?"

"No door on my side," Purvis answered. "And none in the back."

"No door on my side," Billy parroted.

"Okay, boys, listen careful now. Purvis, you go back to that window where you saw the woman on the radio—she's got to be the one we're after. Check to make sure she's still in there. If she is, come back to the front corner of the house so I can see you in the porch light. Stay down, and wave your hat a couple of times if she's still in the room. Billy, you git yourself to the other corner where you can see Purvis signal. If Purvis waves his hat, Billy you go on back to the rear and make sure she don't hightail it out the back window. Purvis, you go back and cover that side window where she's at. I'll give you boys one minute to get in position, then I'll go in the front door. If it's unlocked, I'll do my best to sneak in on her. If the door's locked, I'll holler *Po-lease* and bust in the door. You'll hear me, Purvis. As soon as you hear me holler *Po-lease,* you break the window and keep her covered till I get back there so she don't try to use the other woman as a shield. Any questions so far?"

Neither man spoke.

"Purvis, if she isn't still in there, leave your hat on and both you two come back here so I can rethink it. Got all that, boys?"

Both men said *Yeah.*

"What's this gal look like, Purvis?"

"Uh . . . medium build, couldn't tell her age. Dark hair, and it looked to me she's wearing men's duds."

"Men's duds? Are you sure it's a gal?"

"Yeah, I'm sure, Chester."

"What color duds?"

"Uh . . . gray I think."

"Did you hear that, Billy? Dark-haired woman in gray men's duds."

"I heard it."

"Okay, boys," Poindexter added. "Remember, it's just a gal. Don't be too rough on her. We don't want those federal boys thinking we're hard on women here in Grant County."

Chapter 63

To Save the Sheriff

Kentucky backwoods—outside the radio clubhouse

6:10 a.m.

Billy Holcomb, in position at the right corner of the house, watched and waited. Chester Poindexter, hidden among the trees in front, did the same. Purvis Delaney appeared at the left corner, knelt and waved his hat—the agreed signal that the woman they were after was still in the radio room. Poindexter watched both men disappear: Billy to guard the back, Purvis to wait near the radio room window.

Poindexter waited for what he thought was a minute then started trotting, hunched down, toward the front door.

[same time—inside the house]
Erika removed the headset, but left the transmitter switched on as she waited for the letters VVXV to be sent back—confirmation her transmission had been received. She picked up her gun, stood, and put the gun inside her belt behind her back. Erika grabbed up her papers and in a moment they were on fire in the metal waste basket. From a pants pocket she took out the switchblade, clicked it open, and looked at Elizabeth.

◊

Chester Poindexter crept onto the porch. When a loose board groaned under a footstep, Poindexter stopped and grimaced. He tried the doorknob. *Locked!*

◊

Erika and Elizabeth did not hear the faint groaning of the porch board over the crackle of radio static. Erika cut the ropes binding Elizabeth.

"You're on your own now, Elizabeth. Jim's car keys are probably in his pants."

400

◊

Purvis crouched under the radio room window, waiting. Suddenly he heard a loud crash as the front door came off its hinges and the sheriff scream *Po-lease!* Purvis rose up and used the shotgun barrel to smash the window pane. Inside, one woman still sat in a chair, but now the other woman stood behind her holding a knife.

◊

Erika and Elizabeth heard the crash at the front door and the shattering of the room window. Both now looked down the twin barrels of a shotgun.

"Hold it right there!" the shadow aiming the shotgun through the window yelled. "Get your hands up! Now! Both of you!"

As Erika and Elizabeth raised their hands, they heard loud footsteps in the hall. A man wearing a uniform ran up to the doorway, stopped, and pointed a revolver at Erika.

"Drop the knife!" he ordered. "I'm Sheriff Chester Poindexter of the Grant County Sheriff's Department and you're up Shit Creek, little lady."

Erika acted as if she were about to drop the knife, but instead snapped her arm and threw it. The blade sank into Poindexter's chest. He screamed and fell back into the hall on top of Jim.

Still standing behind Elizabeth, Erika tipped over the chair, dumping Elizabeth onto the floor and away from the line of fire of the shotgun. Erika dived under the radio table.

Outside the window, Purvis had hesitated, stunned as he watched the knife fell the sheriff. Finally, he turned the shotgun toward the table the knife-throwing woman dived under and pulled the trigger.

[same time—road leading to clubhouse]
The Plymouth's tires kept spinning in mud, making progress up the clubhouse road agonizingly slow. Then suddenly Frank saw a car ahead.

"It's another sheriff's car and it's blocking the goddamn road. The sonuvabitch must have gotten stuck. How much farther is it, Carr?"

401

"Cantrell's instructions say about a mile up this road. We've only gone half of that at best. Either the sheriff got stuck, or he stopped here and they walked the rest of the way to avoid the car being seen."

"How many deputies did that knucklehead at the roadblock say the sheriff took with him?"

"Two." Warzyniak answered before Carr.

Frank stopped the Plymouth behind the sheriff's car and shut off the engine. The men hustled out of the car and dug the rifles and three flashlights from the trunk. As Frank closed the trunk lid, they heard a booming gun blast.

[same time—inside the house]

The shotgun blast exploded much of the radio equipment, sending debris flying up into the air and down onto Elizabeth. Poindexter had dropped his gun when the knife struck him; it lay on the floor near the doorway. Elizabeth watched Poindexter climb to his feet in the hallway and stagger toward the living room.

Erika suddenly rolled out from under the table and fired two shots at the window, aiming a few inches above the shotgun barrel still jutting into the room. Elizabeth heard a scream and watched the barrel disappear into the darkness. Quickly, she picked up the sheriff's revolver so Erika would not have another gun and fled the room.

"Elizabeth!" Erika screamed. "Don't go out there!"

Just as Elizabeth reached the end of the hall, she saw the sheriff stagger out the front door. She raced across the living room and began yelling "*Frank!*" thinking he must be outside.

◊

Billy had been watching through the hall window at the back of the house when Poindexter fell into the hallway with a knife sticking in him. He heard the shotgun blast, then seconds later two gunshots and a scream. He ran to the left side of the house and saw Purvis lying motionless on the ground under the window. He ran toward the front of the house and stopped after he turned the corner. Billy saw the sheriff staggering onto the porch and, chasing him with a gun, the woman Purvis had described as having dark hair and wearing gray men's clothing. Billy panicked, aimed his rifle and fired, hoping to save the sheriff.

◊

After Erika shouted her warning to Elizabeth, she jumped up and ran after her. Erika caught up to Elizabeth just as she reached the porch. Erika reached out with her left hand and grabbed Elizabeth's left shoulder to pull her back into the safety of the house. A shot rang out and Elizabeth's blood sprayed out the back of her shirt and splattered Erika's shirt and face.

Chapter 64

A Honeymoon by the Sea

Kentucky—backwoods HAM radio clubhouse

6:25 a.m.

The bullet spun Elizabeth and she fell into Erika's arms. Erika pulled her into the house and laid her on the floor. Elizabeth's blood sprinkled Erika's face and shirt, and Erika knew she too was hit. She looked and saw the area around a hole in her shirtsleeve growing wet from her own blood. After passing through Elizabeth, the bullet struck Erika in the arm. The arm still functioned, so Erika knew the bullet must have missed her bicep.

Elizabeth's wide, shock-filled eyes gazed at the ceiling. Erika ripped open Elizabeth's shirt, popping buttons, and rent the bloody T-shirt to expose the wound. Blood bubbled from a hole about three inches down and two inches outside her right nipple.

Erika looked for something to staunch the blood. She yanked the doily from the coffee table; Elizabeth's half-full glass of champagne crashed and broke on the floor, and the ashtray scattered butts and ashes. Erika knew Elizabeth would also have a hole in her back because the bullet had passed through. She quickly folded the doily, laid it across the wound in Elizabeth's chest, and lifted Elizabeth's upper body a few inches off the floor and found the exit wound. She wrapped the doily around Elizabeth and used her left hand to apply pressure to the exit wound and her right to press hard on the bleeding hole in front.

"Don't talk, Elizabeth. Just stay focused on my voice. I will guess your anniversary. Let's see. I bet you're a June bride, and you and Frank went somewhere by an ocean for your honeymoon."

Elizabeth looked at Erika, but with distant eyes. She coughed and blood showed on her lips.

Erika heard footsteps on the porch and turned her head to see a young deputy standing in the doorway holding a rifle.

"She needs help!" Erika shouted.

The young deputy looked frightened, and stammered, "I . . . I'm sorry. She was going to shoot the sheriff." He saw the look on Erika's face change from concern to fury.

Erika sprang and drove her body into the shocked deputy like a linebacker making a tackle, driving them both across and off the porch. They fell together onto the gravel at the base of the three porch steps—Erika on top, Billy still holding the rifle. The deputy grunted loudly when his back hit the ground. He tried to free the rifle, perhaps intending to strike her, but Erika's body pinned it against his. She swung her elbow violently into the side of his face. Dazed from Erika's blow and from having the wind knocked out of him when he fell on his back with Erika on top, Billy lost his grip on the weapon. Erika stood with the rifle and brought the butt down hard into his face with a hideous crunch. She ducked and looked around, expecting others to rush in or start shooting, but no one did. The only other person she saw was the sheriff. He sat groaning, leaning against a tree at the edge of the clearing.

Erika heard Elizabeth cough, sprinted back to her, and again applied pressure to her bleeding wounds.

[6:35 a.m.—woods near the clubhouse]
Frank Ault kept his flashlight pointed toward the ground in front of him and sprinted the entire way up the muddy road after hearing the first gunshot, his adrenaline leaving Leroy Carr and Chuck Warzyniak behind. When he saw a light through the trees, he shut off the flashlight but started shouting *Elizabeth!* as loud as he could even though he knew an officer should never give away his position if a possible gunfight loomed. But he ignored the rule and continued to shout her name as he ran toward the light.

[6:36 a.m.—inside the clubhouse]
Erika knew she shouldn't have left Elizabeth. Blood flowed freely whenever pressure was released and Elizabeth lost more blood in the seconds it took Erika to attack the deputy. Her rage and violent responses had vexed her since childhood. Since the deputy with the rifle was apparently the last man outside, Erika now regretted not

staying with Elizabeth and having the deputy summon help. After he called for help, Erika could have fought him then and escaped when she heard help arriving.

"Elizabeth, you're going to be okay. Stay with me, Elizabeth."

Erika heard a voice in the distance. In a few seconds she heard it again—a man shouting Elizabeth's name. The second time he sounded closer. *It must be Frank,* she thought. Erika doubted anyone except Elizabeth's husband would foolishly herald his presence to a gun battle, and surely he would have heard the shots.

Erika felt relief that help was coming for Elizabeth. Now she must consider her own circumstances. She knew Frank would be forced to reconnoiter, and be concerned about barging in the house and putting Elizabeth at risk if she were a hostage. Erika decided to carry Elizabeth to the porch and lay her where Frank would see his wife right away. *A policeman will know how to attend to a wound and Frank will surely have other men with him who can lend a hand.* With help assured for Elizabeth, Erika could escape out the back window at the last minute and disappear into the forest. She removed the doily and checked the wound.

[6:38 a.m.—woods near the clubhouse]

Frank Ault finally broke out of the heavy woods and now saw the clubhouse clearly. He slowed to look around then stopped when he reached the last tree before the clearing. In the porch light, he saw a motionless man lying on his back on the ground a few feet from two parked cars. Ault heard a groan, turned, and saw another man at the edge of the clearing, sitting on the ground with his back to a tree.

He wanted to run inside the house but knew he had to be cautious in case Elizabeth was held at gunpoint. Frank knew a dozen reasons he should not do it, but he again shouted, "Elizabeth!" praying for a response.

In a moment he saw Anne Brown walk out the door and stand on the porch carrying Elizabeth in her arms.

"Hurry, Frank!"

Chapter 65

A Long Lost Family Member

Kentucky—backwoods HAM radio clubhouse

6:39 a.m.

Erika knew she must carry Elizabeth onto the porch if she were to get immediate help; otherwise, Frank might think her call from inside the house a trick. Once she knew Frank saw his wife on the porch, Erika carried Elizabeth back into the house for the better lighting. Elizabeth's wounds, especially the chest wound, still bled badly. Realizing she was the only person who could explain Elizabeth's injury so she could receive proper care quickly, Erika abandoned her plan of ducking out the back. She would stay with Elizabeth.

◊

Frank saw Erika carry Elizabeth onto the porch, call his name, then take Elizabeth back inside. The edge of the clearing where he stood was 40 yards from the front door. He sprinted toward the house, rifle ready.

◊

In the living room, Erika laid Elizabeth farther from the doorway, away from the pool of blood, and resumed applying pressure to her wounds. Elizabeth closed her eyes. Erika's own injury throbbed, but she had no time to rip the sleeve and check the damage.

◊

On a dead run, Frank Ault jumped from the ground onto the porch and ran in the door. He saw Erika kneeling over Elizabeth.

"Get away from her! Goddamn you!"

Ault rushed toward Erika and swung the rifle butt at her chest to knock her away from Elizabeth, but Erika quickly leaned to one side and avoided the rifle. She jumped to her feet and Frank connected with a lightning left hook aimed at her right jaw. Erika reacted fast enough to spin her head so the blow merely glanced; still, the detective's powerful fist staggered her and sent her sprawling ten feet away. It took Erika a moment to regain her wits and when she looked at Elizabeth, Frank knelt beside her checking her wound, the rifle on the floor beside him. Ault looked at Erika, furious, and pounced. Erika rolled away and Ault missed landing on top of her, but he managed to grab her ankle. She tried to kick away but Ault was too strong and he pulled her back. With both of them on the floor, Erika pulled her gun from behind her back and swung it at Ault's head, aiming behind his ear so if he jerked back she would still strike a blow to his jaw. But the former boxer saw the motion and moved his head toward her, not away, and Erika's forearm hit the side of his face instead of the gun. He knocked her hand away and tried to grab the gun as he maneuvered his body on top of her, but Erika jerked her hand and gun away before he got a grip. Ault drew his right arm back to deliver a knockout blow, but before he could swing he felt the gun barrel on his left temple.

Erika's finger tightened on the trigger, but she stopped.

Ault looked at her for a moment. "You forgot to pull the trigger." As Erika held her gun to his head, Ault patiently drew his revolver from his shoulder holster and put the barrel under her chin.

Cincinnati Homicide Detective Sergeant Frank Ault and German Abwehrabteilung Sonderführer Erika Lehmann stared into each other's eyes as they held loaded and cocked guns to each other's head.

"The only reason you're still alive is because Elizabeth loves you." Erika withdrew her gun from his temple and laid it on the floor. With his free hand, Frank picked up her gun a second before Leroy Carr and Chuck Warzyniak stomped into the house pointing rifles.

Ault used his finger to flip over the safety on Erika's .32 Beretta and threw her gun to Warzyniak. He then dragged Erika to her feet. "Chuck, keep her covered."

Frank rushed back to Elizabeth. Warzyniak put the Beretta in his jacket pocket and stepped forward with his rifle trained on Erika. With his left hand, the burly Warzyniak grabbed her shirt and pushed her back and down onto the sofa. "Don't move!" Warzyniak ordered.

Erika looked at the third man. He stood looking at her strangely, almost with admiration or wonder. The man approached and cuffed Erika's hands while Warzyniak kept her covered.

"Chuck!" Frank shouted. "Give me a hand."

Carr took over guarding Erika.

"The bullet passed through her, Frank," Erika said.

"Shut up!" Warzyniak ordered as he helped Frank with Elizabeth.

Frank looked up. His concern for his wife outweighed his hatred of the person who put her in danger. "Let her talk, Chuck." Then to Erika: "What can you tell me?"

"She has another wound on her back where the bullet exited. What's her pulse?"

"I don't know, goddammit . . . it's high, over a hundred."

"I think the bullet at least grazed her right lung because she coughed up blood. But I think she has a chance if you get her to a hospital very soon. If the bullet severed an artery, she would be dead by now. Her pulse is high because she's lost a lot of blood. That's your main concern right now."

Frank handed Warzyniak his car keys. "Chuck, I don't care if you have to push that sheriff's car over a cliff to get it out of the way, get my car up here!"

"Right." Warzyniak ran out the door.

Frank looked at Erika. "Who shot her?"

"The bullet came from the rifle of that deputy lying in front of the porch."

"Jesus Christ!"

"Mistaken identity. I'm sure he thought Elizabeth was me."

Frank glared at Erika as he pressed the doily on Elizabeth's wound.

"Your wife is very brave, Frank."

"You don't need to tell me that."

Leroy Carr asked Erika, "What happened to the grunting guy sitting outside under the tree?"

"He identified himself as the sheriff," Erika said without answering the question.

Carr asked another. "A deputy stationed on the road at the bottom of the hill told us the sheriff and two deputies came up here. Where's the other deputy?"

"Outside . . . he might be dead. He fired a shotgun into the room Elizabeth was in at the time. I couldn't let him do it again. There are two sedated men in rooms behind that door." (She nodded toward the hallway door.)

[6:45 a.m.—roadblock on Clarks Creek Road]
The storm had moved off, and Deputy Ray Cummins was standing outside his squad car when a pickup truck pulled up and stopped.

A half hour ago, Cummins heard faraway gunshots. He could not abandon the roadblock because of direct orders from the sheriff to remain *"no matter what,"* so he followed procedure and radioed for backup. Cummins shined his flashlight into the cab of the pickup truck. The passenger wore a deputy's uniform; the driver, a heavyset man with a long gray beard, wore bib overalls. A hunting rifle and a shotgun hung on a rack across the truck cab's rear window.

"Dadgum!" Cummins exclaimed. "What took you so long, Junior?"

The deputy answered, "I had to get Mutt to come in and cover the jail, Ray. I brung my Uncle Eugene. He was a military po-leaseman in 1918."

"Okay. Listen up, Junior. The sheriff, Purvis, and Billy drove up to that radio club over an hour ago. Then some smart-ass po-lease boys from Cincinnati showed up and took off up the road. I heard gunshots but Chester ain't radioed. You take over the roadblock, Junior. Use your uncle's pickup and block the radio club road after I git on it; it don't matter if you can't block Clarks Creek. I'm going up there and check things out. Anybody comes back down that road, y'all stop 'em, ya hear?"

"We'll stop 'em, won't we, Uncle Eugene?"

"Ya goddamn right we will," said Uncle Eugene.

[6:55 a.m.—Chester Poindexter's squad car, halfway up the road to the radio clubhouse]
The muscle-bound Chuck Warzyniak ran much faster down the road than he had running up it. He now stood shining his flashlight into the sheriff's car blocking Ault's Plymouth. Surprised to find the keys in the ignition, Warzyniak jumped in, started the engine, and steered the car into a ditch where it nearly flipped over. He climbed out and had just opened the Plymouth's driver door to get in when he saw headlights approaching. He closed the door, shut off his flashlight and, still holding the rifle, used the Plymouth for cover.

A car stopped behind the Plymouth and a man got out. Looking into headlights, Warzyniak could see only the outline of the man.

"Cincinnati Police!" Warzyniak shouted. "That's far enough. I've got a rifle aimed at your balls. Get your hands up! Who the fuck are you?"

The shadow raised its hands. "I'm Deputy Cummins, Grant County Sheriff's Department."

"Stand your hillbilly ass in front of your car, in the headlights, where I can get a look at you!"

As the man moved to the front of his car, Warzyniak saw another set of headlights coming up the road.

"Who the hell is coming now?" Warzyniak asked Cummins. "Let me guess. It's your cousin, Cow Pie Magoo."

[7:04 a.m.—radio clubhouse]

Outside the clubhouse, the sky began to lighten with the twilight that precedes dawn. Inside, Frank continued to apply pressure to Elizabeth's wounds and took her pulse every few minutes. She was still unconscious.

"What's her pulse, Frank?" Erika asked.

Frank wanted to bark at her to shut up, but he answered, "About 110."

"Her heart is racing because it doesn't have enough blood to furnish her body," said Erika.

"I know that, dammit."

Erika looked at the man in the chair. He had pulled the chair Merle had used directly in front of her, but left the coffee table between them. His rifle lay across his lap. He had said nothing since handcuffing her, but sat staring.

"I assume you're with the FBI," she said.

"No."

"No? Not FBI?"

"My name is Leroy Carr. I'm in charge of counterespionage for the Office of Strategic Services, Erika."

She was surprised he knew her name and surprised at the absence of the FBI.

Outside, a car horn blared in the distance, louder with each honk.

"That sounds like my car horn," Frank shouted. "Thank God."

Carr said, "I'll go outside." He rose and signaled Erika to do the same. Carr got behind her and firmly held the handcuffs with one hand

411

and the rifle with the other as they walked onto the porch. Two cars and a Jeep drove out of the forest and skidded to a stop in the gravel. Erika and Carr watched Chuck Warzyniak step quickly out of Ault's Plymouth, a uniformed deputy emerge from a Grant County squad car, and Al Hodge and Sergeant Turner get out of the Jeep. The deputy saw Billy sprawled at the bottom of the porch steps, rushed over, and knelt beside him. Hodge told the sergeant to remain at the Jeep and ran with Warzyniak onto the porch.

"This guy says he's with you," Warzyniak told Carr, pointing to Hodge. Then he pointed at Cummins at the bottom of the steps. "I came across that yahoo on the road. I figure the yahoo can tend to the local guys this broad fucked up while we get Elizabeth to a hospital."

Without waiting for Carr to comment, Warzyniak ran into the house to help Frank get Elizabeth into the Plymouth.

Al Hodge looked at Erika.

Carr said, "It's her, Al."

Like Carr when he first saw Erika, Hodge gazed at her oddly, as if he had suddenly found a long-lost family member. Then he turned to Carr and apologized.

"Sorry, Leroy. We took a wrong turn in the storm and that damned Jeep only does 50 at best. What's happening?"

Suddenly Frank Ault shouted, "Get out of the way, Carr!"

Carr moved himself and Erika from in front of the door as Frank carried Elizabeth out of the house. Warzyniak had walked ahead and waited at the bottom of the porch steps.

"Chuck," Frank shouted, even though Warzyniak was only fifteen feet away. "Get a cartridge from that deputy's rifle, the one who shot Elizabeth. See what type of round he used."

Warzyniak picked up Billy's rifle, ejected a round, and turned it over in his hand. "It's a .30-30 Winchester, full metal jacket." Warzyniak put the cartridge in his pocket and trotted to the Plymouth to open the door. At the bottom of the porch steps, Frank impatiently asked Cummins for directions to the nearest hospital.

Carr, with Erika in tow and Hodge beside him, followed Ault to the Plymouth. Carr gave Hodge instructions as they walked. "I want you to take over the scene, Al. She's done damage here: a downed sheriff and two of his deputies. The sheriff is over there under the tree (Carr pointed with the rifle). The other deputy, who may be dead, is somewhere around the building. Miss Lehmann here told me there are two sedated men inside the house. I didn't check because I wasn't

412

going to let her out of my sight, but I'm sure we can rely on her. Keep them here unless they need medical attention. If they must be taken to a hospital, you remain here, but tell the deputy who just arrived that the sedated men are to be kept under guard and not allowed to leave the hospital until federal authorities arrive. Leave the local deputy in charge of the casualties; he can radio for help. You and the sergeant assist him with the injured until help arrives, but as soon as the downed officers are taken away, no one goes inside the clubhouse—no local police or anybody else."

"You don't want the sergeant to drive you and her out of here?"

"No. We have to secure this site and you'll need him. Post the sergeant under arms at the front door while you check on the sedated guys. When they awake question them—see what you can find out. I'll go with Ault to the hospital. My radio is still in his car; I'll radio you as soon as I can."

"Got it," said Hodge.

At the Plymouth, Frank told Warzyniak to drive then he carefully placed Elizabeth in the back seat and got in beside her. That left Carr no option other than to crowd Erika into the back seat with the Ault's while he sat up front. When the doors closed, Warzyniak turned the key and sped down the muddy road as fast as he could safely drive on the bumpy road with Elizabeth as precious cargo, doing his best to steer around potholes.

Frank said, "Chuck, that deputy said the nearest hospital is in Williamstown, south of Dry Ridge. He told me we don't have to go back through Dry Ridge to get there. He said instead of heading back on Clarks Creek Road the way we came in, take it the other direction to Fords Mill Road then turn left. That will take us to State Road 36 and into Williamstown."

"Okay, I got it—head farther down Clarks Creek to Fords Mill, then left to 36."

Suddenly, Warzyniak slammed on the brakes to avoid crashing into a pickup truck blocking the base of the clubhouse road.

"Jesus Christ!" Ault bellowed in the back seat. "What now?!"

In the Plymouth's headlights, Warzyniak saw two men ducked behind the truck aiming weapons. He rolled down his window.

"Cincinnati Police!" Warzyniak held his badge out the window. "Get that truck out of the way!"

"I'm a Grant County sheriff's deputy!" one of the men yelled. "Get out of the car! Now!"

"We have a critically injured woman we're taking to a hospital in Williamstown!" Warzyniak yelled back. "Your sheriff and two deputies are down and need assistance. Get that goddamn truck out of my way and go help them!"

"I said get out of the car!"

The man beside the deputy yelled, "You heard what he said! Get out of that goddamn car before I let loose with my scattergun. You'll wish you dun what he said if I give you a taste of Fat Fannie here!"

Chuck Warzyniak stepped out of the car and, holding his I.D. in front of him in the headlights, walked toward the men. As Warzyniak neared, they stood. Warzyniak hit Junior in the jaw with a short right cross, then said hello to Uncle Eugene's chin with a left uppercut. Both men dropped like stones, unconscious. Warzyniak grabbed their shirt collars, one in each hand, and dragged them out of the way. He put the truck in neutral and pushed it several feet, then jumped back in the Plymouth and sped down Clarks Creek Road.

"I really pulled my punches, Frank," Warzyniak said. "They won't be out long."

[Cincinnati—same time, the Ault home]
Glen Shafer used Frank Ault's home police radio to talk with Ed Cantrell. He had radioed Cantrell every half hour after Frank had stopped back at the house to pick up Chuck Warzyniak.

"You've got to find a way to get in touch with Frank, Ed." Shafer said into the radio. "OVER."

"Glen, I have no way to do that. When I radioed Frank the directions to the transmitter, he was in range. Now he's not. If Frank wants to reach us, he'll have to use a telephone until he's back in range. If he calls here, you'll be the first to know. If he calls you, radio me right away. OUT."

Chapter 66

Blood of the Reich

Williamstown, Kentucky

7:50 a.m.

Besides a modest emergency room, the tiny hospital in Williamstown consisted of two wards: one with eight beds, the other with four. Of the five remaining rooms, one served as an operating room for the minor surgeries the underequipped staff could handle, two rooms were used to store supplies and equipment, another reserved for those impatient to be born, and the last room was used for those waiting patiently for the undertaker.

When Frank Ault carried Elizabeth into the emergency room, two persons were on duty: an elderly nurse and a young intern just graduated from the University of Louisville College of Medicine. Chuck Warzyniak held the door for Frank. Leroy Carr, with Erika Lehmann, followed. The nurse watched them enter and rose from behind a desk.

"This woman has suffered a gunshot wound!" Frank shouted as he rushed toward the nurse. When he spotted a gurney, he laid Elizabeth on it.

The nurse shouted, "Doctor! Emergency!" A young man wearing a white lab coat with a stethoscope around his neck trotted into the room from a corridor. The doctor rushed to the gurney and Frank filled him in.

"The bullet entered there (Frank pointed to a half-inch hole amid the blood that covered most of Elizabeth's chest and stomach) and exited out her back. The bullet was sterile from heat as it left the barrel, and it was jacketed so there should be no fragments. But she's lost a lot of blood."

The doctor said, "I can see that. Help me roll her onto her side so I can check the other wound." Frank helped the doctor gently roll Elizabeth onto her left side. The one-inch hole in her back had torn edges. "Okay, lay her back down. Let's get her to the operating room."

Frank rolled the gurney and everyone followed.

The nurse objected. "Only one family member can go back with her. Is anyone related?"

415

"I'm her husband, nurse. I'm also a Cincinnati police officer. Every man here is law enforcement, and we have a prisoner we will not let out of our sight." Chuck Warzyniak and Leroy Carr flashed I.D.s.

"Oh, my," the nurse said. "And a victim with a gunshot wound. I'll have to call the sheriff."

Leroy Carr took over talking while Frank rolled the gurney around a corner. "We just saw the sheriff and several of his deputies. They'll arrive shortly." Carr did not tell the nurse that the sheriff and at least two of his men would arrive needing gurneys.

The doctor led the way into the operating room. Although the white walls could stand a fresh coat of paint, everything looked clean and in place, the green and white speckled linoleum freshly waxed. After everyone filed in, Carr put Erika in a chair and stood beside her. Warzyniak guarded the only door. Frank hovered over Elizabeth while the doctor listened to her heart and the nurse checked her blood pressure.

"65 over 40, doctor," the nurse said.

"Pulse is 120," the doctor said. "This woman needs a tube thoracostomy, but we have to get some blood into her first, and right away. What's her blood type?"

"AB negative," answered Frank. He knew a thoracostomy was a chest tube.

The doctor winced. "We have only positive blood on hand, mostly O and some A. Since the war started, blood is hard to come by for small hospitals like this one." He asked Frank, "What's your blood type?"

Frank hated his answer. "O positive."

"Does anyone here have negative-antigen blood?" the doctor asked as he looked around the room. "In an emergency, we can substitute other blood types for AB negative as long as the blood is negative."

Warzyniak said, "O positive."

Carr said, "A positive."

"God!" Frank shouted, his dependable iron nerves about finished. "What's your blood type, Doctor, and the nurse?"

The young doctor shook his head *no.*

"Doctor, my blood is negative."

The doctor looked at the handcuffed woman sitting in the chair.

"Is it AB?" the doctor asked her.

"No, B negative."

"That will do for now." The doctor's attention had focused on Elizabeth, but now he noticed the blood-covered shirt, hands, and splattered face of the handcuffed woman. "Are you injured?"

"The same bullet passed through my left arm, but I think the injury is minor. Most of the blood you see on me is hers."

"You're willing to transfuse to this woman?"

Everyone in the room looked at Erika Lehmann.

"Yes."

"Nurse," the doctor said.

The old nurse knew what to do. "There's another gurney down the hall," she said. "Will someone bring it in, please?" She opened the door of a wall cabinet and began extracting supplies while Chuck Warzyniak hustled to fetch the gurney.

"Somebody take those handcuffs off her so she can remove her shirt," the doctor ordered. Then he turned to the nurse, referring to Erika: "We'll use the right arm since the left is injured. I'll check her injured arm after we get the transfusion underway."

Warzyniak rolled in the gurney and retook his position guarding the door. Leroy Carr removed the cuff from Erika's left wrist to allow her to remove her shirt. In her T-shirt, Erika lay down on the gurney and Carr locked the loose cuff around a gurney rail. Carr helped Ault position the gurney so Erika's right side, the side bound to the gurney by the handcuffs, was near Elizabeth.

Frank watched the doctor locate the big vein on the inside of Erika's right elbow and Elizabeth's left, and then pierce their flesh with a number 15 needle. When the needles were secured with tape, and tubes and accessories connected, the doctor nodded to the nurse.

In a moment, Frank Ault watched the blood of a Nazi begin flowing into Elizabeth's veins.

Chapter 67

The Longest Night

8:20 a.m.—Williamstown, Kentucky—hospital

After the transfusion, the doctor ordered the men and their prisoner from the operating room.

Leroy Carr wheeled Erika's gurney to the vacant room used as the hospital's morgue and kept her under guard with Chuck Warzyniak. Frank Ault looked for a telephone.

Because the Grant County Hospital owned none of the new X-ray equipment used in most of the large hospitals, the young doctor decided to install a chest tube based on the firmness of Elizabeth's right chest and armpit area and her rapid, shallow breathing. The nurse cleaned Elizabeth's chest and right side then placed sterile towels around the bullet entry wound. Using the hospital's last vial of Novacain, the gloved doctor stuck the needle into several spots to numb the tissues. With a scalpel he cut a one-inch incision. The nurse handed him a stout clamp holding a dime-sized, red-rubber hose. The doctor shoved it hard through the cut and underlying fat and muscle, and over Elizabeth's fifth rib until it popped through the chest wall pleura. He snaked the tube four inches deeper and upward, then clamped it. He hooked the red tube to a clear tube leading to an underwater collection bottle sitting on a metal tray on the floor and then loosened the clamp. Blood and water poured into the collection bottle. The doctor sewed the red tube to Elizabeth's skin with a heavy silk suture. Slowly, the rate of fluids escaping diminished from a pour to a drip. Elizabeth, still unconscious, began coughing as her collapsed right lung started to expand.

[8:30 a.m.—Cincinnati, the Ault home]

During the night, all communications from the Ault home had been conducted over the police radio in case Elizabeth phoned. So when the telephone rang, Glen Shafer jumped. He knew the caller had to be Elizabeth—or Frank with news.

"Hello!" Shafer did not realize he shouted.

"Collect call from Kentucky for Mr. Glen Shafer."

"Yes! Yes! Operator. Put it through."

"Glen, it's me."

"Frank! What's going on? Where are you? Where's Elizabeth?"

"I'm in Williamstown, Kentucky. I've got Elizabeth."

Shafer nearly dropped to his knees in thanks. "Merciful God in Heaven."

"She's been shot, Glen."

Shafer staggered. "My God! How bad is it?"

"She took a .30-30 to her chest. I don't know how much damage yet. I'm at the hospital now. She's in the operating room."

Shafer suddenly exploded, "I hope you killed that bitch!"

"Anne Brown didn't shoot Elizabeth. A local sheriff's deputy mistook her for Brown. Glen, I want you to find Steve Hagan and drive him down here."

"Jesus, Frank. The coroner?"

"You're forgetting that before he became coroner, Hagan was the best gunshot trauma doctor around. Find him and bring him down here as fast as you can—use the siren. Grant County Hospital: it's right off 25, and you'll see signs. You can't miss it. The hospital is just before you enter Williamstown. Tell Steve that Elizabeth has been shot in the right side of the chest and the bullet exited her back. Tell him she coughed up blood, lost a lot of blood, and that's all I know right now."

"Holy Jesus. Okay."

"Don't worry about calling Cantrell. I'll call him after we hang up. Get moving and find Hagan. He's probably at home; his address and home telephone number are in the address book in the kitchen—on the counter where we normally keep the phone. Christian's still there, right?"

"Yeah."

"Bring him with you. I'll tell Cantrell to send a paddy wagon to transport Brown back to Cincinnati."

"So you got Brown?"

"Yeah, we got her. Christian can drive your car back while you and Carr go with Brown in the paddy wagon. I'll stay here with Elizabeth, and keep Chuck down here for now."

"Okay, I'll pick up Hagan and be there pronto, Frank."

Ault hung up the phone on the nurse's desk and looked out the glass emergency room doors. Morning had finally ended the longest night of his life. He said a silent prayer that it was not his wife's last.

419

[8:50 a.m.—Williamstown, Kentucky—hospital]

Two Grant County Sheriff's Department squad cars carrying Chester Poindexter and his two injured deputies screeched to a stop in front of the emergency room doors. Purvis Delaney, shot at the window by Erika, was alive.

[11:30 a.m.]

Glen Shafer and Ray Christian, along with Leroy Carr and Chuck Warzyniak, guarded Erika Lehmann (Carr had finally told Frank her real name an hour ago). Al Hodge was also now at the hospital, relieved by an Army lieutenant, a sergeant, and two privates from Fort Knox summoned by Leroy Carr to take over at the HAM clubhouse. When Hodge arrived, he found Carr and told him the sedated men had come to. One of the men had a large goose egg on his head, but neither needed to be brought to the hospital. Hodge had instructed the lieutenant to keep the men at the clubhouse until notified.

The day-shift doctor and nurse had arrived at 8:00 a.m. The elderly nurse and young doctor who tended Elizabeth stayed on duty past their shifts to help a local doctor and two extra nurses called in to care for the sheriff and deputies.

Frank Ault stood waiting outside the busy operating room. An hour ago, a nurse brought him a chair, but he had yet to sit. Finally, Dr. Steve Hagan walked out of the operating room, pushed down the white cloth surgical mask that covered his mouth and chin, and joined Ault.

"It's crowded in there, Frank." Then Hagan smiled. "Elizabeth will pull through."

Frank Ault, the toughest cop on the Force, suddenly felt weak. Nineteen hours ago he had read the note Elizabeth left on the bed telling him she had gone on her own to meet Erika Lehmann—19 hours of anxiety, fear, anger, and other torments he had been forced to fight off in order to function with a clear head. Now, those words from Steve Hagan finished him off like no opponent in the boxing ring ever could.

Ault stumbled backwards and collapsed into the chair.

Hagan continued. "There's no X-ray equipment here, but the bullet had to have grazed the right lung or Elizabeth would not have coughed blood. I've found no fresh blood in her mouth or throat since I arrived, so I don't think she suffered any severe pulmonary injury. It was the grazed lung and not a significant artery that was the culprit for all that blood loss. She still has some fluid buildup in her chest cavity but the chest tube will drain that. We'll probably have to leave the tube in for a few days. That young intern and the nurse did a good job, Frank. For a guy who doesn't have his license yet, he did a helluva job."

"He's not a doctor?" Frank asked.

"He doesn't have the paper for his wall yet, but for a young kid who never saw a gunshot wound before today, let alone treat one, he did a bang-up job, especially with what he has to work with around here. He's 28, and he's earning his bones today. He's still back there working. Two tube thoracostomies in one day; he had to put one in that sheriff with the knife wound."

"How are those guys?"

"They'll heal. The sheriff got lucky. The blade penetrated his chest high enough to miss the heart and lungs, but an inch higher and it would have severed the subclavian vein and then it's *Goodnight Irene*. But as it is, Elizabeth's chest wound is more severe than his. One deputy got his skull grazed by one bullet and a second bullet blew off a chunk of his ear. The other deputy got the worst of it as far as recovery time is concerned. Somebody smashed his face in: broken mandible and missing teeth."

"So what's next? Is Elizabeth awake?"

"I sedated her to lessen the coughing until we get her back to Christ where we can give her proper care. I haven't sewed the exit wound yet. I patched it for now. I'll get an ambulance down here."

"She can be moved today?"

"Yeah. I want to get her back to Cincinnati for an X-ray. Plus, she's going to need more blood because of that chest tube drainage and they don't have her brand down here. It's just a little over an hour ride and an ambulance from Christ will be as well equipped to monitor her as this hospital."

"So she'll fully recover, Steve?"

"Elizabeth is strong and healthy. We'll have to keep a close eye for infection, but with a jacketed bullet our chances of avoiding that are a lot better, and I see no evidence of clothing material accompanying the projectile into the wound. The transfusion was the key. That's what staved off disaster. They pumped two-and-a-half pints out of that woman handcuffed to the gurney before they stabilized Elizabeth. The nurse told me that the woman insisted they keep transfusing until Elizabeth got what she needed. The intern finally shut down the tube because he feared losing the donor. Who is she anyway?"

Ault took a long moment. "She's my suspect in the Over the Rhine attacks last month."

"No! That *Crucifier* case? The one I was on the scene of at that apartment building?"

"Yeah," Ault said wearily.

Steve Hagan shook his head. "She's a strange one."

"Why do you say that?"

"After we got Elizabeth taken care of, I checked the woman's arm. The same bullet that struck Elizabeth went through her arm—under the skin and back out. It missed the bicep but left two very messy holes. When I checked her, she had her eyes closed. I spoke to her; she didn't respond, so I assumed she had passed out like someone of her body weight normally would with two-and-half pints of their blood just pumped out of them. It's the last day of the month and the hospital ran out of its monthly war allotment of Novocain, so I decided to stitch her arm while she was out. When I finished she said *Thank you, Doctor* with her eyes still closed. She was awake the entire time. That had to hurt like hell."

Twenty minutes later, a Cincinnati Police paddy wagon arrived. When Deputy Cummins saw the wagon, he tried to take custody of Erika, but Leroy Carr produced his faux U.S. marshal identification. That, and Chuck Warzyniak telling Cummins he better clear out of the way unless he wanted to join his buddies in the operating room, convinced the deputy to back off. A weak Erika Lehmann, hands and feet shackled, was loaded into the wagon. Leroy Carr, Glen Shafer, and two men of the paddy wagon crew got in the back with her. Another officer joined the driver in the cab. Erika was driven quietly away from the Grant County Hospital. Al Hodge and his driver followed in the Jeep, and Officer Christian drove Shafer's car.

The ambulance arrived an hour later, but Steve Hagan delayed Elizabeth's departure for three more hours until he was satisfied she was ready. A few minutes before 4:00 p.m., Elizabeth, with her husband and Hagan in the ambulance with her, was on her way to The Christ Hospital. Hagan did not want the siren, preferring a calmer ride for Elizabeth. Chuck Warzyniak followed in Ault's Plymouth.

Before he left the Grant County Hospital, Frank Ault found the exhausted intern and nurse and thanked them heartily. As he rode away in the ambulance, Ault realized he never learned their names.

Part IV

All war is deception.
— Sun Tzu

Chapter 68

Lumpi's Christmas Tree

Cincinnati—Monday, November 1, 1943

The Christ Hospital

A prelude to winter days to come swept down from the Great Lakes during the night. From the window of Elizabeth's private, fourth-floor room, Frank Ault watched people wearing winter coats getting into and out of cars in the hospital parking lot, the mid-afternoon sky battleship gray.

Glen Shafer left ten minutes ago. Shafer was not allowed to see Elizabeth on doctor's orders, but the two detectives spoke in the hall. Shafer had a one-inch cut on his lower lip and a large blue and yellow bruise on the side of his chin from where Ault hit him. Frank apologized; Shafer shrugged it off.

Frank had spent the night in a chair beside Elizabeth's bed mostly awake from worry, occasionally dozing from exhaustion. He had last slept Friday night. For Elizabeth's part, Thursday was the last night she slept soundly. Friday night, after she received Erika's note at the *Observer*, sleep was fitful and Saturday there was none. Sunday evening she awoke disorientated after the sedative wore off, but then she quickly fell into a deep sleep. That was 18 hours ago.

"Frank." Her voice sounded frail and scratchy. Ault spun from the window and rushed to her bedside.

"Elizabeth." He clasped her left hand.

She smiled faintly and tears welled. "Where am I?"

"Christ Hospital. You'll be fine, Elizabeth."

A long pause followed, words unnecessary, Elizabeth content to have Frank hold her hand.

In time, Frank said gently, "I haven't called your mother yet. She doesn't know anything about this. I know that's not right, but the doctors said no visitors until after you wake and they examine you. And you know how your mom gets; I thought it would be hard on her

427

to be down here and not allowed to see you. I'll call her when the doctors clear you for visitors."

Elizabeth nodded slowly.

Frank knew she would want to know about her injury. "The bullet grazed your lung, but that's taken care of. . . ."

Elizabeth interrupted. "What happened to her, Frank?" she asked weakly.

Frank hesitated. "Forget about her. Just think about getting better."

"Is she alive?"

"We've got her locked up at District 1. We didn't want to put her in County—one of the few things Carr and I have agreed on since this whole thing started. She's under twenty-four-hour watch by our men, and by U.S. marshals and MPs Carr brought in." Frank tried a small joke to lighten her spirits. "They're real U.S. marshals, not guys with phony credentials like Carr." He smiled; Elizabeth did not. Frank kissed her cheek.

[same time—District 1 Police Station]

The long-term criminal housing facility for the Cincinnati area was the Hamilton County Jail. For short-term or overnight holding, most Cincinnati police stations had a small number of cells. At District 1, police headquarters, the cell block in the bowels of the building (called the *Hole* by police staff) included the drunk tank, the floozy tank—both with multiple cots—and four single-person cells.

By Monday afternoon, all District 1 detainees had been moved to the county jail or holding cells in other district stations around Cincinnati.

All except one.

The Hole had been evacuated to hold Erika Lehmann. As Frank had told Elizabeth, now guarding the cell block, besides Cincinnati police jailors, were U.S. marshals and Army military policemen from Fort Knox, Kentucky. The regular jailors and the extra men brought in, including the U.S. marshals, knew little about the prisoner other than her status as *a high-priority prisoner of the United States government.*

Erika lay on a bunk bolted to a red brick wall in one of the single person cells. She wore denim Cincinnati jail dungarees, and a light blue cotton button-down shirt. Her shoes had been replaced by

428

slippers. A heavy bandage covered her upper left arm. Three of the cell walls were brick, the only view through the bars into the cell block corridor where a uniformed MP wearing a white helmet stood, and a man in a suit sat. Both men faced her. Erika could hear voices of men farther down the passageway.

With a heavy heart, Erika recalled happy childhood times with her parents, especially of Christmas in Oberschopfheim. Each year Erika's task was to make a new crowning ornament for the tree, usually from paper or cloth. She worked on her creation for weeks. On Christmas Eve, never earlier, her father took her into the forest where she selected the tree. After her father set it up near the fireplace, everyone did their part to decorate, her father lifting her so Erika could reach the upper branches. Lumpi, Erika's pet dachshund, always caused her mother consternation when he sought to use the tree for more practical purposes. After they lit the candles, the small family feasted on a traditional German Christmas Eve dinner of Weihnachtskarpfen—Christmas carp—prepared by her British mother who could not resist serving it with figgy pudding. After dinner, her father always concocted some errand that required leaving the house, and the errand always required Erika's help. By the time they returned, the Christkind had magically visited. Her mother rang a bell, signaling that Erika and her father could enter and look at the gifts.

Erika Lehmann turned toward the wall and cried for her dead parents—but silently, refusing to let the guards hear and think she cried for herself.

Chapter 69

One of a Kind

Wednesday, November 3, 1943

District 1 Police Headquarters

Except for 20 minutes each morning when she was taken to a shower room, Erika Lehmann had not been outside her cell since being locked up. When she arrived Sunday, she was strip-searched twice: first by a Cincinnati police matron, and an hour later by two Army WACs. After donning her jail garb the second time, Erika was lined up against a wall where an Army first lieutenant took dozens of facial photographs from every conceivable angle. She had not yet been interrogated, which surprised her, and no one had come calling at her cell other than the guards who escorted her to the shower, a guard who brought meals, and the Army nurse who dressed Erika's injured arm each day. During the nurse's visits, the cell door was left open and two MPs crowded into the small room; other men stationed themselves outside in the corridor.

An hour ago, Erika was brought shackled to the District 1 interrogation room, leg irons limiting her to tiny steps. When she entered, one MP removed the leg irons but not the handcuffs. The room was drab and spartan: white-washed plaster walls, a wooden floor painted black, and a rectangular metal table with one wooden chair at each end and two on each side. Erika was placed in one of the end chairs, alone in the windowless room, the guards stationed outside the door. Knowing she was not truly alone, Erika gazed at the large mirror built into one of the side walls. She had seen similar mirrors in the debriefing rooms at Abwehr headquarters on the Tirpitz-Ufer in Berlin.

Erika had always known that if she were captured, odds against her escape were astronomical. She was not the first Nazi agent captured in America, and they had all been guarded to a degree nearing the absurd. Last year, a 20-man platoon of MPs had been assigned to deliver one of the eight captured German saboteurs to a courthouse hearing. Erika saw the photographs in the newspapers.

But, of course, she knew the extreme security and precautions would be the same in Germany with any captured Allied spy or saboteur.

She heard the doorknob turn. In walked the man who had told her at the HAM clubhouse he worked for the OSS. Erika had not seen him since being placed in her cell Sunday. When Leroy Carr saw the handcuffs, he asked the MP who opened the door to remove them.

"Good morning, Erika." He sounded cheerful as he sat at the opposite end of the table. "I'm sorry, may I call you *Erika?*"

"I suppose so, Mr. Carr," Erika answered. The MP removed the cuffs, walked out, and closed the door.

"Feel free to call me Leroy."

"I rather prefer *Mr. Carr.*"

He smiled. "Your British accent is still with you."

"I don't see a reason to speak in my mimicked American accent, do you?"

"I suppose not. I don't know why I was surprised to hear the accent Sunday. I know your mother was British and you learned English from her, of course. I found the information about your parents from our embassy registration lists. Your father was the press secretary at the German embassy in Washington for several years in the 1930s."

"I will switch to German if you prefer."

Carr chuckled. "No. English would be better. My Deutsch is shaky, to say the least. If you have a two-year-old cousin back in Germany, I might be able to converse with him."

"He's five."

"Well, I'd be in trouble then."

Carr opened his briefcase and pulled out a folder. "I just returned to Cincinnati yesterday evening. After your capture, I was summoned to Washington for a conference with my boss. That's why you haven't seen me until now. I'll get to the point. Some parts of your transmitted message were garbled because of the storm, but what got through we've decoded. You caused quite a stir at the Pentagon."

"Ah, the Pentagon," said Erika. "I read about that—last winter, I believe. There were photographs in *Look* magazine, or was it *Life?* The Pentagon is a new building for your generals."

"That's right. It's not quite a year old. And as I said, you're already giving them fits."

"Sorry."

"Erika, I don't want to play games. I know you won't answer any questions about your message and you don't need to. You couldn't send it in Enigma or other naval codes because you didn't have an Enigma machine, and you lost your naval code crib sheets in Evansville; the FBI found them behind a false panel in the trunk, or should I say the *boot,* of your car. The code you were forced to use allowed us an easy decipher, so I don't have to sit here and attempt to wrest that information out of you. I would like to know, of course, to whom and where the message was initially intended. The final destination was Domremy, France; I know that from the text of your *Observer* radio teletype message two weeks ago. *Jehanne*—Joan of Arc's name. Domremy is her hometown, and Abwehr installed a large transmission station there because your Admiral Canaris knew the Allies wouldn't bomb a pilgrimage town. And I know the *Observer* teletype message was simply a notice of more information to come, and that information you transmitted from the Kentucky HAM club last weekend. But your teletype message, like your message sent over the HAM transmitter, first had to go somewhere else and be relayed. That's what I want to know."

While Erika watched Carr open his folder, she asked, "Will you tell me how Elizabeth Ault is faring?"

"She's going to be okay. Unfortunately, I haven't visited the hospital yet because I've been out of town, but I'm going this afternoon. In fact, Elizabeth, indirectly, is why I'm here today. We now know the reason you involved Elizabeth was for her help with the transatlantic telephone call. The phone number you called from was recorded by a Philadelphia operator. That's how we found you."

"How did you find out about the phone call that night?"

"From people at the newspaper. Elizabeth dropped a few clues with the *Observer* switchboard operator that caused people there to think something might be wrong."

"Clues?"

"She identified herself as Beth Ault, a name Elizabeth apparently hates and everyone at the newspaper seems to know that, and she said something to the switchboard girl about not having seen her in a long time when they'd talked just recently."

Erika thought for a moment, and then smiled.

Carr continued. "Regrettably, for me, the London number was not recorded by the Bermuda relay operator because Elizabeth has a United States issued authorization number for such calls. By the way, of course you knew that ahead of time, and I commend you for your research. So as it stands, I don't know to whom you placed the call or why. That's what I want to know today."

"Elizabeth hasn't told you?"

"The doctors haven't cleared her for questioning, or even visitors, yet. But you're right: as soon as we're allowed to speak with Elizabeth we'll know to whom it was placed. You may as well tell me now, Erika. I answered your questions; now you answer mine. Who relays your transmissions? And who was on the other end in London?"

"About the transmissions, of course I will not tell you. And the other, the telephone call, you must wait to ask Elizabeth."

Leroy Carr shut the folder and rose quickly. "You're not making it easier on yourself." He walked out the door, then turned and walked through an adjacent door, entering the observation room. Inside, Al Hodge waited. Hodge was the only person Carr allowed to observe his questioning of the German spy.

"That was short and sweet, Leroy, but good acting job. I'll send your name to those Academy Awards people out in Hollywood. Do you think she'll realize those questions were a set up?"

"No, I don't think so. She knew we'd break that Baudot code quickly; that's why I told her we did. If I had gone in there demanding to know what was in the message, she would know something was fishy. But she can't be aware we already know that her transmission was relayed by Germany's Central America network. By the way, good work on that, Al. When you told me the FCC monitoring station in Tucson picked up the relay in the wee hours Sunday morning coming out of northern Mexico, it all made sense. She knows we have monitoring stations in the Border States, but we can't triangulate for an exact fix. The FCC stations north of the border, and our Navy ships in the Gulf and Pacific are spread too far apart to triangulate a fixed point in Mexico. She knows that, so my question will appear legitimate."

Hodge said, "I think you were right when you told Donovan we won't get anything out of her. Do you think Wild Bill will consider more extreme persuasion tactics?"

Through the one-way mirror, Carr and Hodge watched two MPs, supervised by a U.S. marshal, begin shackling Erika. Another MP, holding a rifle, watched at the door.

"Torture isn't going to pry any information out of Erika Lehmann. If the decision is made to try torture, the only purpose it will serve is as a final exam, so to speak." Carr paused as the MPs finished putting on her restraints. "Everything with her from here on will be cat and mouse. Let's just make sure we remain the cat."

Both men watched the MPs and marshal escort Erika from the interrogation room.

"Just think of what it would be like to have her on our side." Carr said earnestly. That was Leroy Carr's secret mission: if Erika Lehmann were captured, he must test her mettle and, if she passed the test, find out if she could be persuaded to work for the OSS. She passed the brief, initial test today. If she had given up information readily, the OSS would not want her. Giving up information now implies she would do the same in the future if caught by America's enemies. If she failed the testing at any point, she would be handed over to the Justice Department and surely hanged.

Carr thought about his next step. He would offer her a deal: give up information and avoid the gallows. Carr would show her false documents from the Attorney General offering her a life sentence in exchange for her cooperation; Carr might even go as low as 20 years. That's how two of the eight saboteurs escaped the hangman last year: the two who cooperated received prison sentences; the other six were hanged and buried in a Potter's Field. She will know that; it was reported in the newspapers. But in her case, if she accepts the phony deal, she will hang. No court would give a moment's thought to a prison term for Erika Lehmann. Spying in wartime was by itself a capital offense, and her case carried the severest aggravating circumstance. The bumbling saboteurs had caused no damage, but with her an FBI agent was killed trying to capture her in Indiana. Even though she did not kill him, the law would hold her responsible at sentencing.

"I'll keep testing her, Al. But I'm telling you now she'll never give up information, so I know we're going to want her, but I also think she'll never flip on her country. Then we face the problem: what do we do with her? I guess we'll have no choice but to hand her over to the Justice Department. What a shame to destroy an asset like her."

Carr paused to light a cigarette and offer Hodge one.

"That admiral at Abwehr is one lucky Nazi bastard."

Chapter 70

Elizabeth Surprises Leroy

[same day]

2:30 p.m.—The Christ Hospital

Leroy Carr had lied to Erika when he told her the doctors had not yet cleared Elizabeth for visitors. A limited number of visitors were allowed to see her Tuesday morning. The problem was her husband. Tuesday afternoon, with Carr still out of town, Al Hodge had driven to the hospital to question Elizabeth about the HAM radio transmission and London telephone call. But Frank Ault sent Hodge packing, telling him no one would question Elizabeth until the chest tube was removed and she felt stronger. Hodge found the doctor on duty, produced his marshal I.D., and inquired about the chest tube. The doctor told Hodge the tube might come out Wednesday.

It was now Wednesday.

After stepping off the hospital elevator, Hodge led Carr down fourth-floor corridors. Once in the corridor of Elizabeth's room, they saw Glen Shafer talking to a group of people in a waiting area. When Shafer noticed the OSS men approaching, he broke away from the group and walked toward them.

Shafer, his mood much improved from Saturday night, joked pleasantly. "We knew you guys would pop up today."

"How's Elizabeth?" Carr asked.

"She's stronger. They took out that chest tube this morning. That alone perked her up." Shafer knew why Carr and Hodge were there. "As far as questioning her, you'll have to talk to Frank. He's in the room, and so are Elizabeth's parents."

"Who are all these people?" asked Hodge, referring to the group.

"A few friends of the family and coworkers from the newspaper. Word spread fast that Elizabeth is in the hospital. These people don't know the details, not even that she was shot—only her parents know that, and Frank swore them to secrecy. Frank decided to keep the nature of the injury a secret. He wants things to return to normal for Elizabeth, and if it gets out that she was shot, there will be another

435

circus to deal with like the one following her story about being approached by the *Crucifier*—only this time it'll be worse."

"That's smart," commented Carr. "What's Frank telling everybody about the injury?"

"Elizabeth was in Louisville visiting an old friend from college and suffered broken ribs and a collapsed lung in a car accident riding as a passenger in the friend's car. The friend suffered only a few cuts and bruises."

"Good, we'll stay with that. What about the doctors and nurses who know about the gunshot?"

"Cantrell was here this morning. After he visited Elizabeth, and Frank told us his plan, we spoke with the hospital administrator. Hospital policy already requires no medical details about a patient be released to the public, but the hospital director said he would bring in members of the staff who treated Elizabeth and make it clear that the Cincinnati police made a special request for privacy in Elizabeth's case."

"Okay. As we leave, Al and I will go see that director as U.S. marshals and tell him the same request comes from the government."

Shafer nodded and led them away from the waiting area and toward Elizabeth's room. "I'll tell Frank you're out here." He opened the door and stepped inside.

Hodge asked Carr, "How much you wanna bet that asshole doesn't let us in the room?"

"I think he will if he feels Elizabeth is up to it. You heard what Shafer said: Ault wants things back to normal. He knows we're not going away until we talk to Elizabeth."

The door to Elizabeth's room opened and Frank Ault walked out into the hallway, impatience on his face. "You've got five minutes, Carr. I'll be timing you so you better get to the point fast. And if I think Elizabeth is getting upset you're out of there. Got it?"

"Eventually, I'll need more time than that, Frank. But I don't want to tax Elizabeth. I appreciate the five minutes today."

Carr saw Ault's *I-think-you're-full-of-crap* look—a look he had seen before—but the detective did not comment.

"Give me a minute to get Elizabeth's parents out of the room. When they walk out, you come in."

It took longer than a minute, but eventually a couple who looked to be in their 50s walked out of the room. Carr and Hodge entered. Ault and Shafer stood at the far side of the bed—the bed inclined so

Elizabeth sat up slightly. A sheet covered her, and an I.V. ended in her left hand. Carr walked to the near side of the bed; Hodge hung back a few feet.

"Elizabeth, I hear you're feeling stronger every day," Carr said cheerfully. "That's the best news I've gotten in a long time."

She spoke slowly. "Thank you."

"Have the doctors mentioned when you might go home?"

Frank interrupted. "Get to the point, Carr. You're on the clock."

"Don't be rude, Frank," said Elizabeth. Then to Carr: "Doctor Hagan told Frank maybe Sunday if all goes well."

"That's wonderful. We'll pray that all goes well."

Elizabeth nodded her thanks this time.

"Elizabeth, sometime after you're released, I'd like to sit down with you and go over all the things that happened last weekend, but today I'll ask only a couple of questions."

"That's fine."

"I asked a United States marshal to question the Grant County sheriff injured at the scene. The marshal drove down and spoke with him yesterday morning—by the way, the sheriff is in a Lexington, Kentucky hospital and will be okay. The sheriff told the marshal you were in the radio room with Erika." Carr paused so she could confirm.

"Yes."

"We deciphered parts of Erika's message, but the storm garbled some of the transmission. Did she say anything about the message, offer comment before or after she sent it? Anything at all? Something that seemed insignificant at the time might help us."

"She told me everything in the message."

"She told you everything?" Carr wanted to make sure he heard her correctly.

"Yes. She said she knew the Allied invasion would not come at Calais, but somewhere else in France—on sandy beaches because of LSTs. She said she had information about beach grades best suited to LSTs."

Carr stopped. Everything Elizabeth said they had already deciphered from the transmission except the part about beach grades. That part must have been transmitted during one of the lightning strikes, but the FCC's failure to pick it up did not mean that part of the transmission did not get through in another direction. He had to let Bill Donovan know immediately. Donovan would relay the information to the White House, and on to Eisenhower in London. Carr

437

wanted to hear more from Elizabeth about the transmission, but he saw Frank Ault frown and point to his watch. Carr moved on.

"We know now why Erika involved you, Elizabeth. The transatlantic telephone call. Were you allowed to stay in the room once Erika began talking to London?"

"Yes."

"Who did she call, and what did you hear her say?"

Elizabeth took a moment. "I'll tell you everything I know or heard her say that has to do with secrets or our nation's interests, Mr. Carr, such as the information I just gave you about her transmission message. But the London telephone call had nothing to do with our country. I won't talk about that."

Chapter 71

Try Gasoline

Friday, November 5, 1943

District 1 Police Headquarters

Frank Ault sat behind his desk for the first time in six days. He arrived at noon—a half hour ago—and worked quickly so he could return to the hospital. He finished an outline of the sequence of events during the past weekend, stood and ripped the paper from the Underwood's carriage and headed for Ed Cantrell's office. When he walked in, Cantrell asked about Elizabeth.

"She gets a little stronger every day," Ault responded. "Yesterday afternoon the nurse got her up and walked her around the room for a few minutes; then she sat in a chair awhile. If she keeps improving, Steve Hagan thinks he might release her Sunday."

"Great," said Cantrell. "When I was there last night I could see the improvement from Wednesday."

"Here's a brief outline of last weekend, Ed," Ault said as he laid the paper on Cantrell's desk. "I know you want the full report, but that's all I have time for now. I'll do the full report after Elizabeth goes home and I get back to work. Unless some complications with Elizabeth crop up, I'll be back on duty Monday."

"No hurry on the report, Frank." Cantrell picked up the paper and filed it in a desk drawer. "Carr put a hold on all reports."

"Carr doesn't want me to write a report? That can't be right."

"It's right. For now anyway."

"That's horse shit. What about the Lamar Apartments homicide? If I don't file a report, that case stays open forever."

Cantrell shrugged. "We can't file any reports until Carr okays them, so I recommend not wasting your time typing one up until we see what Carr wants in it. I have a feeling our official report will be something Carr cooks up. Chief Weatherly knows all about it. He told me what I've told you a dozen times: we have to do what the feds ask when the case has been designated wartime national security. It's federal law. Orders from Carr mean orders from the top—from Washington. I've phoned William Donovan three times since the first

439

day Carr showed up in my office, and Donovan always backs Carr. Donovan was appointed by FDR—can't get much higher than that. To go over Carr's head, I'll have to telephone God and ask him to tell Roosevelt to tell Donovan to tell Carr the Cincinnati police want to do things differently. If you have God's phone number, Frank, I'll give him a ring."

Cantrell took a drink of coffee and lit a cigarette. "That's the way it is, Frank, and there's nothing you, me, or the chief can do about it. Now, I have some good news. Weatherly plans to recommend you to the mayor for a Police Valor Star. The citation can't mention anything about a spy, of course; the mayor's not even aware of this spy business. Weatherly told me he has to figure out how to word it— probably have to be awarded for rescuing a hostage from a dangerous felon, something like that. But there you go, my friend. Congratulations. You deserve it."

"I don't deserve it. I didn't capture her; she surrendered."

"What do you mean? Warzyniak told me when he arrived, you had fought her to the floor, taken her gun away, and were holding your gun to her head."

"She had her gun to my head before I pulled mine out of my holster, but she didn't shoot so I called her hand and drew mine. She told me the only reason I was alive is because Elizabeth loves me, then she laid down her gun. She had the opportunity to blow my brains out and escape, but passed on it." Ault could not resist adding sardonically, "All that would have been in the report Carr doesn't want me to write."

"She told you she didn't kill you because your wife loves you?"

"Yeah."

Cantrell sat looking at Ault, mouth slightly open, cigarette dangling.

Ault added, "And another thing, Lehmann could have left long before I arrived on the scene. Escaped clean. But she stayed to tend to Elizabeth."

Cantrell was puzzled and looked it.

"Before I leave," said Ault. "I'm going down to the Hole and ask her a few questions about the Lamar case."

"She's not down there, Frank. At nine o'clock this morning, Leroy Carr arrived with a gang of U.S. marshals and Army MPs. He had paperwork—official, legitimate paperwork this time; Weatherly checked it out—signed by a Supreme Court justice and a congressman ordering the release of the prisoner to Carr. They loaded her into an

Army paddy wagon and took her away. The damn caravan of Jeeps looked like a funeral procession for some general."

Frank stood abruptly. "Why didn't you tell me, Ed?"

"I just did, dammit."

"Where did they take her?"

"Carr wouldn't say. You ought to be happy. You've been carping for weeks that you wanted to get the Anne Brown case settled because of Elizabeth. Now it's settled and she can't bother Elizabeth any more. *Anne Brown's* gone for good."

[10:00 p.m.—the Ault home]

Frank Ault, Glen Shafer, and Chuck Warzyniak sat in the Aults' living room. Frank had spent every night this week sleeping in a chair in Elizabeth's hospital room. Earlier that evening, Elizabeth had insisted Frank go home tonight: *"Frank, you need to get a decent night's sleep and you're not going to get it in that chair."* Frank objected, but Elizabeth told him if he stayed at the hospital another night, she would sit up all night in the other chair. Frank knew his stubborn wife would do exactly that, so tonight he would sleep at home for the first time since last Friday—one week ago.

Shafer and Warzyniak had been visiting Elizabeth when Frank left the hospital, and they asked him to join them for a nightcap. When Frank refused to go to a bar with his wife in the hospital, they agreed to meet at Frank's house. Shafer said he would stop at a liquor store on the way.

"You better clean up this joint before the little lady gets home, Frank," commented Warzyniak. "It looks like a band of retarded gypsies camped out in your living room."

Shafer laughed.

During the week, Frank had come home for only a few minutes now and then to pick up items for Elizabeth and to shower and shave. The mess Warzyniak commented on was put there during the long night last weekend. Dried coffee stained the tables and the arm of an upholstered wing chair; cigarette butts and ground-in ashes from an accidentally overturned ashtray adorned the rug. A lamp table leaned from a broken leg. The table's ceramic lamp, now sitting on the floor, was cracked and its shade ripped, damaged when Frank fell into the table when he went after Leroy Carr. Shafer and Ed Cantrell grabbed him, and Frank went down when Shafer tripped him.

"I'll clean up tomorrow in case Elizabeth comes home Sunday," Frank said before he took a drink of Bourbon. "I'll go somewhere and get another lamp. Do you guys know how to get coffee stains out of upholstery?"

"Uh . . ." said Shafer, clueless.

Warzyniak said, "Try gasoline."

"Gasoline!" exclaimed Frank. "That will stink up the whole house. Are you sure that works?"

"It works for cleaning paint brushes," Warzyniak answered.

"Yeah, out in the garage, numb-nuts."

"I clean my brushes in the kitchen sink," said Warzyniak. "But if the chair won't fit in your sink, clean it in the garage, ass-wipe."

"Good idea. I never thought of that. All I need to do is leave the chair in the garage until the gasoline smell wears off. That should only take a year and a half." Frank looked at Shafer and shook his head before telling Warzyniak, "I want to see the inside of your house, jerk-off. When I come over I'll bring a gas mask and make sure I don't light a cigarette."

All three men enjoyed the good-natured exchange. It was the first time in a week Frank had allowed himself to look forward to Elizabeth's and his life returning to normal. Elizabeth was doing well with her recovery, better than he had expected. Frank had seen too many times the catastrophic trauma a bullet can inflict on a human body. God had answered Frank's prayers and he was thankful.

Warzyniak stood. "I need another beer." He walked to the kitchen. As he walked back into the living room, he said, "I heard they came in and packed off the Nazi this morning. Brother, there's a weird and creepy broad—took out half of the sheriff's department of Cornpone County."

"Chuck, you know you can't tell anybody she's a Nazi spy," warned Shafer.

"Yeah. I know. Where did they take her, Frank?"

"Cantrell asked but Carr wouldn't say."

"So Carr, that OSS guy, packed her off?"

Frank nodded. When Cantrell told him this morning that Carr took her away, at first he felt angry, but Cantrell was right: with Erika Lehmann gone, things could return to normal. And Ault had no doubt that justice would be meted out; a wartime spy responsible for the damage she had caused in Evansville, in Cincinnati, and now in Kentucky, had no prayer of avoiding the noose.

"Why wasn't the FBI around?" asked Warzyniak.

"That's the million-dollar question, Chuck. But Glen's right. We have to keep all this stuff under our hats."

"I know. Cantrell bent my ear for twenty minutes Monday about saying nothing to nobody about Nazis or the OSS. I'm just talking to you guys."

All three men sat silent for a moment. Frank took another drink.

Warzyniak said, "I almost shit my drawers in that podunk hospital when the Nazi volunteered to give Elizabeth blood. Why do you think she did that, Frank?"

"I don't know, Chuck. I don't know a lot of things. This afternoon I told Cantrell she could have bailed out before any of us got there and been long gone, but she stayed to help Elizabeth. She could have put a bullet in my head and didn't do that, either."

"Come again? You took the gun away from her. I was there."

"She laid her gun down before you got there and I picked it up. I didn't capture her. She surrendered."

All of this was also news to Shafer. Both men looked at Frank. He did not mention Elizabeth's refusal to tell Leroy Carr about the London call. On the surface, Elizabeth's refusal appeared as if she were protecting Erika Lehmann. Frank had decided to hold off talking to Elizabeth about it while she was in the hospital.

Warzyniak finally broke the silence. "Like I said, that Nazi is one weird and creepy broad."

Chapter 72

A Personal Item for Elizabeth

Monday, November 8, 1943

The Christ Hospital

Elizabeth did not go home Sunday.

Doctor Hagan, in charge of Elizabeth's care, was called out of town Sunday on his own family emergency and could not be reached. Without Hagan's okay, another doctor could not sign her release papers. Elizabeth was disappointed; she wanted to go home and told Frank that the hospital could not keep her if she insisted on leaving. This time Frank refused to yield: Elizabeth would not leave the hospital without Steve Hagan's okay. It was one of the few times Frank got his way, and Elizabeth now smiled remembering the pleased expression on his face yesterday when she relented.

Frank. Until this past week, I never realized how lucky I am. She had picked a man who was tough and courageous. Yes, Frank was rough around the edges and sometimes vulgar and impatient when dealing with others, but never with her. Nothing but kindness. And when it came to protecting her, he was a lion.

Steve Hagan, back in town this morning, arrived at the hospital shortly before lunchtime. After examining Elizabeth, he signed her release papers and instructed her on what she could and could not do for the next several days. He said he would stop by the house on Wednesday. *("But if any bleeding or swelling occurs before then, call an ambulance or have Frank drive you to the hospital right away, Elizabeth.")* That was an hour ago.

Cookie—the nurse and Frank's friend from the old neighborhood—now helped Elizabeth finish dressing. Frank had gone down to move the car to the entrance.

"Thanks, Cookie," Elizabeth said as the nurse helped her with her shoes. "This is the first time someone has dressed me since I was three." Elizabeth almost joked that Frank only helped her *undress,* but thought it inappropriate. She knew Cookie through Frank, but not well.

"Frank will need to help you for a few days."

444

"Yes, but I can't let him pick out my clothes. Nothing will match. I'll look like a billboard."

Cookie laughed.

Elizabeth asked, "Do you have any funny or embarrassing stories from high school you can tell me about Frank?"

"Oh, let's see," Cookie took a moment as she finished with the shoes. "Did he ever tell you about the time he spilled his lunch tray on a teacher in the cafeteria?"

"No."

"I think it was ninth grade. Chili went all over the front of Mr. Rudy's pants. It was an accident, but Mr. Rudy thought Frank did it on purpose and got mad when students laughed. Mr. Rudy marched Frank to the principal's office. Frank got suspended for a day because of an accident."

"Knowing Frank, are you sure it was an accident?"

Cookie laughed again. "You've got a point."

Cookie walked to a white dresser and from the bottom drawer removed a bag. "I was on duty when they brought you in last week. Since you were unconscious, I put your personal things in this bag."

On Sunday, a Netherlands Hotel maid had found Elizabeth's clothes and purse (her wedding ring inside) left behind in the room. The desk manager found Elizabeth's drivers license in her purse. He checked the telephone book for a home number, but a long column of *Aults* listed no *Elizabeth.* (Even if the manager had known her husband's name, he would not have found a number; police phone numbers were unlisted.) Finally, the manager recognized Elizabeth's name and called the *Observer.* His call was sent to the newsroom. Monday, Otis Kapperman got in touch with Frank and later that day Frank retrieved Elizabeth's things. Elizabeth knew the only personal item she would have had on her when she arrived at the hospital was her wristwatch.

"Here are your watch and ring," Cookie said, handing the bag to Elizabeth.

"Watch and ring?" Elizabeth had left her wedding ring, the only ring she wore that day, in her purse at the Netherlands Hotel as ordered by Erika in the note left with the Side Pocket clothes. Her wedding ring was in her purse when Frank brought it to the hospital Tuesday. "I wasn't wearing any ring."

"It was on your right middle finger when they brought you in, Elizabeth."

Elizabeth looked in the bag. Beside her watch was a rolled-up tissue. She took out the tissue and laid the bag with the watch on the bed.

In the tissue was the ring Erika showed her in the clubhouse living room while they waited for the operator to call back. Elizabeth discarded the tissue and looked at the ring. Erika had called it the Ring of the Slain. *Erika must have placed it on my finger when I was unconscious.*

Dried blood coated most of the ring—Elizabeth's and Erika's mingled blood.

Chapter 73

Lorelei

> Lor•e•lei \ lōr-ĕ-lī *noun* [German] : a siren of Germanic lore whose singing lures Rhine River boatmen to destruction on a reef
> —*Merriam-Webster's Collegiate Dictionary, 10th Edition*

Brandenburg, Germany

June 1942

The primary German training academy for the art of espionage and the science of sabotage was located at Quenzsee in Brandenburg, not far from Berlin. The buildings resided on a lavish old estate that included a lake, a large park, and beautiful gardens. A high fence topped with barbed wire encircled the grounds, belying the serene setting. Machine gun toting guards patrolled both sides of the fence, leashed and muzzled German shepherd attack dogs at their side.

The motto at Quenzsee was *Fetch the Devil from Hell.* The goal of the school: to train agents to carry out that mission.

Quenzsee was a second home to Abwehrabteilung agents. After finishing preliminary indoctrination at another facility in Tegel, all Abwehr agent wannabes reported to Quenzsee for their core training. Here they underwent a grueling, ten-week training period all had to successfully complete before being considered for advanced training that would require eight more weeks. In addition, the elite few eventually chosen for covert assignments returned to Quenzsee before each mission for further training and to acquire any special skills needed for the specific assignment.

However, the vast majority of recruits who passed through Quenzsee would never see duty as an Abwehr spy or saboteur. Even though prospective agents were carefully selected and screened (all were recruited; volunteers were never accepted), six of seven washed out during the initial Quenzsee training. Of those left, only one of nine would eventually see duty as an *asset*—the Abwehr euphemism for secret agent.

With a few exceptions. Specialized cram courses gave amateur saboteurs—usually malcontents from enemy countries—a few needed skills in explosives before being dispatched back home. These traitor missions rarely succeeded; most ended with the fumbling amateurs blowing themselves up or being apprehended and summarily executed before any damage was done, none of which distressed their former instructors at Quenzsee. *("If nothing is tried, nothing is gained. They were not Germans, after all.")*

The preparation of bona fide, professional German agents was handled much differently. Training was extensive and no stone unturned when it came to processing a candidate. The few elites who measured up as full-fledged Abwehr agents demonstrated exceptional skill levels in both espionage and sabotage.

The espionage section at Quenzsee taught trainees international Morse code and the use of shortwave transmitters (later they would learn how to build their own transmitter at a school in Potsdam). Trainees became well-versed in microphotographing documents and coding and decoding messages, along with knowledge of the chemistry of secret inks. Burglary skills were taught including gaining access through locked doors and windows without leaving evidence of entry, lock picking, and safe cracking. For specific countries, satisfactory language skills entailed much more than just proper speech. Regional dialects, mannerisms, and idioms they practiced repeatedly; syntax, grammar, and accents had to be flawless. Would be agents attended classes on the country to be infiltrated. Knowledge of the target country's history and geography was meticulously tested; skill in map-making demanded.

Quenzsee's second branch, the sabotage section, instructed trainees in the use of explosives and fire bombs. (Advanced candidates learned how to make bombs from ordinary materials that could be purchased at hardware or agricultural stores.)

All trainees fired an assortment of pistols and rifles for a minimum of one hour each day with pistol marksmanship especially stressed. Before they left the school, agents could make homemade silencers from readily available materials. Effective use of blackmail was an included course. Hand-to-hand combat was practiced every day, and silent killing methods studied.

◊ ◊ ◊

Near the Quenzsee lake, Erika Lehmann stood third in a line of eight young women. In front of the women stood a 12-feet-high chain-link fence topped with three strands of barbed wire, the fence part of the Quenzsee obstacle course. A heavily muscled male instructor in a white T-shirt and navy blue short pants stood near the fence. Quenzsee's *Fetch the Devil from Hell* logo—a swastika engulfed in flames through which a very Aryan-looking secret agent ran dragging a devil—could be seen above the left breast of the man's shirt.

The women wore navy blue shorts similar to the man's. They also displayed the Quenzsee insignia on their white shirts but in a different location. Because the women's' shirts were the sleeveless and open-neck athletic *Bluse*, the swastika and flames were displayed between breasts.

These eight women had worked areas of the obstacle course for most of the afternoon. In addition to the chain-link fence now in front of them, the course included a 20-feet-high brick wall that had to be scaled using a rope and grappling hook, a descent from a three-storey tower using a cast iron rain gutter downspout, a belly-crawl under a set of barbed wire obstacles, and a three-kilometer run around the lake to be completed in (for women) less than eleven minutes. Several swimming tests were part of required Quenzsee training including a timed sprint across the lake, a marathon swim around the lake, diving and retrieving objects from the bottom, and remaining submerged for designated time intervals. The swimming tests were scheduled for the next morning.

Erika Lehmann was a celebrity to the other women in the line. They were plebe agents—*Anlernling;* none had ever gone on a mission. But the blonde *Sonderführer* in line with them now trained for her third assignment. The two dagger insignias above the burning Quenzsee swastika confirmed that she had successfully completed two covert missions. Of course, the others knew nothing of the particulars of these assignments. They did not even know the Sonderführer's real name. Agents and trainees at Quenzsee went by code names. The other women, and even the Quenzsee instructor standing by the fence, knew Erika Lehmann only by her Abwehr code name *Lorelei.*

The muscleman barked at the women: "As you know, twenty seconds maximum to touch ground on the other side."

"You! First in line! Get ready! . . . Go!" He clicked a stopwatch.

449

The woman at the front of the line ran toward the fence, stopped, and then started climbing. When she reached the top, she gingerly negotiated the barbed wire then lowered herself down the other side.

"Twenty-nine seconds! Terrible!," he shouted, then added sarcastically, "The only way you would not have been spotted is if you were breaking into the asylum for the blind. Get back to the end of the line."

"Next! Go!"

The second woman ran to the obstacle, and, like the first woman, stopped and then started the climb. She ascended the fence faster than the first woman, but at the zenith she cut the inside of her left leg on the barbed wire. On the ground, the instructor showed no sympathy for her injury.

"Twenty seconds. But look at the drops of blood on the ground!" he shouted in the woman's face, veins bulging on his forehead. "A trail easily followed! You've just blown your mission, idiot! And probably gotten yourself and anyone with you killed!"

The woman stood rigid, blood running down her leg, as the instructor continued his rebuke. One name directed at the woman was the German equivalent of the English *shit-heel* among other even more vulgar monikers. Whether from the pain of her injury or the reprimand, or both, tears welled in the woman's eyes.

Don't let him see you cry! Erika thought as she watched the woman being castigated. She hated it when a female trainee cried in front of an instructor. "Don't let anyone see you cry," Erika said to the others behind her. "Crying makes you look silly and weak. Just try again."

When the instructor thought the woman suitably harangued, he sent her, still bleeding, to the back of the line. Like the first trainee whose time was too slow, she would have to try again.

Now Erika stood at the front of the line. When the instructor saw who was next, he paused.

"Fräuleins, pay close attention." Then to Erika he shouted: "Go!"

Erika sprinted to the fence but instead of stopping, jumped high up the fence to save some climbing. She shot up the chain-link portion, grabbed the highest strand of barbed wire between two barbs, flipped herself over the top then free-fell to the ground. The instructor clicked his stopwatch.

"Nine seconds!"

The other women applauded until a sharp look from the instructor halted them.

"That, Fräuleins, is an acceptable effort." The stern man could not find it in himself to embellish the compliment further even though he knew the word "acceptable" failed to do *Lorelei* justice. Twenty seconds was the required time for a female to clear the fence, fourteen seconds for a male. In all his time at Quenzsee, he had seen only four *men*, among hundreds of men, scale the fence in less time than this young woman.

When the last woman had scaled the fence, and the instructor satisfied that the ones who failed to make the required time had been cursed sufficiently, he released the women. He reminded them of dinner in one hour, followed by the mandatory swimming practice scheduled after the meal (purposely forcing the recruits to swim with full stomachs). Then their last foreign language classroom session of the day. The instructor added that a movie of the Führer's latest speech to the Reichstag would be shown before lights out at 2200.

With the obstacle course over for the day, the female trainees walked sluggishly toward their billets, their only goal to collapse on their beds for the hour until mess. The Sonderführer, *Lorelei,* the one with the two daggers on her chest, stayed behind. She plucked a Quenzsee swimsuit from a rucksack, changed into it inside a boathouse on the lake's shore, and began crossing the half-kilometer wide lake—a full-out front crawl across, a butterfly back. She calculated the free hour would allow at least three complete crossings.

After the evening meal and mandatory swimming practice (Erika served as an additional swimming instructor for both the men and women), the last training activity of the Quenzsee day was language instruction. The sign over Erika's classroom read *American English* (there was a separate room for the British version). Speaking German was strictly forbidden in the classroom. Ernest Kappe, Abwehr's specialist on America, was one of the Quenzsee instructors for American English. Before the war, Kappe had worked as a journalist in New York City for four years. Lieutenant Richter and Wolfgang Blaum, two Abwehr supervisors sent to Quenzsee to supervise Erika's training along with Kappe, were the only personnel at Quenzsee who knew *Lorelei's* real identity.

Kappe stood at the front of the room and welcomed eight men and two women as they found their seats. Fifteen minutes were spent reviewing the previous day's work and *Hausaufgaben* (homework) collected. Yesterday's homework assignment involved writing a paper, in informal American prose, describing sights that might be seen while taking a bus ride in New York City. Here again Erika Lehmann served more as an instructor than as a student, and Kappe handed her some of the papers to speed the evaluations.

In the first of her classmates' papers, Erika found some spelling errors, but not any a poor American speller might not make so she thought it acceptable. The second paper contained a dangerous error: all the nouns were capitalized including *Bus* and *Seat* as in *bus seat*. Erika noted on the paper that, unlike German, not all English nouns are capitalized. When Erika finished looking over the essays, she handed them to Kappe who offered further comments then handed the papers back to be corrected and resubmitted by the authors.

All of the recruits in the room spoke English well; but passing for native speakers was their goal, and that demanded much more than simply being well-versed in a language. The remainder of the class time was spent working on accents, with Kappe and Erika listening closely for any hint of German inflections. Erika estimated that half the men might succeed in passing themselves off as Americans, but the other half still had work to do. The only other woman in the class, a woman around 30 with the code name *Hippolyta*, was improving. Hippolyta had been one of the women in line with Erika at the obstacle course earlier that day, and Erika remembered her scaling the fence in 21 seconds, only one second from passing. Hippolyta had commented that she would make the time tomorrow and Erika did not doubt that she might. She was a strong, big-boned woman in trim shape.

Hippolyta was working on a New York accent; the easiest American accent for a German to master in Erika's opinion. (Erika thought a Midwestern accent was the toughest for a German to mimic.) Hippolyta's New York accent had improved over the past few weeks, but Erika still noticed occasional syntactical slips. The woman used the words *also* and *still* too often and sometimes in the wrong place in a sentence. The German equivalents to those words, *auch* and *noch,* were used more frequently by Germans in everyday speech, especially by Bavarians, and Erika concluded Hippolyta most probably hailed from there. Regardless, her mistakes were enough to tell Erika the woman should not leave for America too soon.

After class, Kappe asked Erika to stay. This was not unusual considering Kappe's responsibility to help prepare Erika for her mission. During these post-classroom sessions, none of the mission particulars were discussed. Those top secret deliberations were limited to a soundproof security room in another part of the building. Topics after class included innocuous subjects such as things that had changed in the United States since Erika and her father left after her mother's death in 1937. Perhaps one night Kappe might show her magazines with current American hairstyles, another night catalogs with the latest fashions. Tonight Kappe handed Erika a long list of popular American dance music and several phonograph albums to listen to on the record player he had issued for her room. These subjects were addressed in a morning class designed especially to cover American culture, but Kappe, always the fussy teacher, gave Erika an opportunity to study ahead. When he finished, they left for the mess hall where Hitler's speech would be shown.

Before lights-out each night, trainees and Quenzsee staff were treated to 90 minutes of organized recreation, normally in the mess hall. An opera recording might be played, a Propaganda Ministry motion picture might be shown (Erika recognized some films her father helped produce), or a special speaker brought in. Erika's father had spoken here several times; Göring had spoken once, and Hess had been a regular guest speaker before his baffling flight to Scotland.

Tonight's treat was a film of the Führer's recent speech before the Reichstag. After everyone was seated and the Führer's speech given its proper introduction with sufficient accolades from August Pampe, Kommandant of Quenzsee, the lights were dimmed and the film rolled.

Hitler spoke for just over an hour on the war in the East and the many sacrifices the German people must ready themselves for to achieve final victory. Here he was not the ranting, fist-shaking Hitler of the British newsreels Erika had watched during her last assignment in London. On the screen a subdued Hitler stood with his hands behind his back, moving slowly through his speech choosing words carefully. Hitler had always been a powerful orator; his ability to bewitch the masses from a podium legendary. That ability had not abandoned him; Erika looked around the room at faces frozen in attention.

Curiously, Erika found herself critiquing the Führer's grammar, the lower Bavarian dialect evident from the abundant use of little modifiers such as *denn, ja, noch,* and Hitler's favorite adverbs *besonders* (especially) and *damals* (then).

I've been spending too much time in language classes, Erika mused silently.

At the conclusion of the Führer's speech, everyone stood and applauded then the mess hall slowly emptied. Tired bodies gladly homed in on bunks back in the barracks. Most trainees quartered in basic-training style—several two-level bunk beds in a large barracks room. Men billeted in a barracks behind the main chateau, the lesser number of women occupied a similar but smaller barracks closer to the lake.

Experienced agents quartered in the same buildings as the *Anlerlinge* (raw recruits), but these agents, the ones with the dagger(s) embroidered above the Quenzsee devil, were given individual rooms. These rooms were small, the size of a jail cell, and sparsely furnished: a cot, a small table with one wooden chair, and a hanging wall picture of the Führer. Each room had one small window—a summer necessity.

Back in her room, Erika disrobed and looked through the stack of music records. Ernest Kappe included music by Cole Porter, Glenn Miller, Bing Crosby, and Hoagy Carmichael among others. Erika was familiar with the names, either recalling them from her years in the United States or from her more recent visit to England. Some of the music had been written years ago but was apparently still popular— Herr Kappe would not make the mistake of giving her outdated material to study. Erika noticed Carmichael's *Georgia on My Mind* and *Stardust* in the stack. She remembered both tunes were popular in the mid-30s when she lived in America.

On Erika's table sat a stack of folders containing briefs, maps, and engineering data concerning shipbuilding and metallurgy. Next to the folders, occupying the rest of the small table, sat a record player. Erika placed an Artie Shaw record on the turntable. As the band played, the sultry Kay Grainger sang a popular Cole Porter tune.

Below, in the bunkhouse with open windows, seven exhausted German women lay on their cots serenaded by music filtering down from the room overhead—the room of their idol, Lorelei.

¶ *When they Begin the Beguine*
It brings back the sound of music so tender.
It brings back a night of tropical splendor,
It brings back a memory evergreen. ¶

Chapter 74

Hot Dogs and Beans

Fort Knox, Kentucky—Tuesday, November 9, 1943

Fort Knox, by automobile about 150 miles southwest of Cincinnati, became home to the 7th Cavalry Brigade (Mechanized) in 1936 when the 13th Calvary Regiment joined the already-on-base 1st Calvary Regiment and both units traded horses for tanks. Also in 1936, construction got underway on the Treasury Department's U.S. Bullion Depository.

The shockingly quick successes of *Blitzkrieg* in Poland, the Low Countries, and France early in the war forced the War Department to re-evaluate America's mechanized warfare capability and create a counterpart to the German Panzer divisions. Thus, the Armored Force, headquartered at Fort Knox, was born in July 1940. Now at its training peak, the Armored Force School operated two shifts per day to satisfy the Army's demand for qualified tankers and artillerymen.

The Fort Knox stockade, built to house 280, seldom held more than half that many inmates. Occasionally a serious offender served a lengthy sentence: a deserter, a thief, a soldier who was told *no* by a local girl but did not back off quickly enough. But most incarcerations were brief: a private who got drunk on leave and reported back to base a few hours late could count on a night behind bars; a sergeant involved in a Louisville tavern brawl might expect to spend a night or two in the stockade, unless the fight was with a Marine or a sailor who made a crack about *dogfaces,* then Sarge received an official reprimand but an unofficial pat on the back before returning to his men without any stockade time.

Leroy Carr had asked that Erika Lehmann be housed in the small, six-cell officers' section of the stockade for three reasons: one, this windowless section was separated from the stockade proper by a thick brick wall and a heavy metal door; two, currently no officers were incarcerated so privacy assured; three, there was a small shower room across the corridor from Erika's cell. Guards would not be forced to clear men out of the large, enlisted men's gang shower for Erika.

When the stockade was built in the '30s, the thought apparently escaped the designers that a woman might someday be imprisoned there. Besides the showering facilities separated solely based on rank and not gender, Erika's cell had, in addition to the toilet, a tin urinal that emptied into a floor drain.

Logistics at the Fort Knox Stockade suited Leroy Carr much better than those at the Cincinnati police jail. In Cincinnati, if Carr sought to speak with Erika privately, the process of shackling her and the slow, guarded walk to the interrogation room consumed time and put her under the stares of all eyes along the way. Carr liked neither the time the walk consumed nor having her the object of curiosity. Human nature assured that, sooner or later, someone among the few at the District 1 police station who knew the truth about her would slip under the weight of constant quizzing from colleagues. Best to take her away from where the nosey saw her every day. And at the stockade, for privacy no move was necessary. Carr could simply pull up a chair in the locked-down corridor outside Erika's cell and talk to her through the bars, coming and going as he pleased.

Carr passed several MPs until he stood at the heavy metal door to the officers' cell block. The staff sergeant in charge of the door recognized Carr but still waited to see his credentials. Now, finally, Carr could use his unfeigned OSS identification. The sergeant opened the door.

Inside the small cell block, Carr spoke to the young MP stationed in front of Erika's cell. The soldier's orders: stand outside the prisoner's cell and never take his eyes off her. "Thank you, Corporal. Please wait outside the cell block door."

"Yes, sir." The soldier left.

Carr pulled up the chair he had instructed to be left in the corridor. Inside the cell, Erika was on the floor doing sit-ups, her back to Carr and the corridor.

"Good morning," said Carr.

"Any snow about?" she asked in her British accent as she continued to exercise.

"Still cold, but no snow so far. Predictions are for it to warm up by the weekend. Maybe even get back to some fall temperatures."

"I enjoy the snow."

"My wife likes snow, too. I don't care much for it although I got used to it living in Montana for sixteen years. If three or four inches of snow falls in this part of the country, they think they've really got something. Four inches in Montana is considered a dusting."

"I understand. I've spent quite a lot of time in the Alps." She did another sit-up.

"I hope your arrangements here are suitable. Any problems I can help with?"

"No, I don't believe so. I think some of your guards become a bit embarrassed when they watch me use the loo. The same when they watch me shower. Then again, others among them don't mind too terribly, I think."

"I'm sorry about that, Erika. I'll see what I can do." Carr had no intention of changing the *never-eyes-off* order. He had given that order. *Never-eyes-off* was an important tool used to intensify the test: pressure by humiliation.

Carr came to the point for the day. "Yesterday, I drove back to Cincinnati and spent a few hours speaking with a couple of young men. One drove Elizabeth to the pool hall for the meeting with you . . . a Daniel Offerman."

"Ah, Danny," said Erika. "Lovely young man."

"He told me you two were quite close."

"Yes, very good friends. Danny knew nothing about any of this, by the way. I can assure you he's totally innocent, Mr. Carr. I told Danny that Elizabeth was an old friend. As far as Danny knew he was merely doing me a favor by picking her up and taking her to a party."

"Then I spoke with a young man named Wilmar von Krause." Carr paused to see if she reacted to the name, but she never hesitated in her sit-ups. "He owns the car you drove to Grant County."

Erika stopped at the top of a sit-up and turned to face Carr. "Really? Sounds like a chipper German name, although I've found that many people in Cincinnati have German surnames. But perhaps I would not have blagged his motorcar if I had known he had such a fine name."

"'Blagged'—I assume that means *stole*, right?"

"Yes, sorry. You say he is a young man?"

"Yes. So you don't know this man? His car keys were in your coat pocket."

"No. I don't know him, but if I had known he was a young man, perhaps I would have shagged him and not have needed to *steal* his motorcar. Young men would let a woman borrow their motorcar for a shagging, I should think. But the chap you refer to left the keys in the toggle—if he is the one who parked it near the pub. So I didn't have to shag him, did I now? I hope you told him that leaving keys in the toggle is bad form."

Carr moved on. "I hope you've reconsidered my offer."

"Your offer to spare me the noose for life in prison if I betray my country?"

Carr lied convincingly, "The Attorney General informed my boss, General Donovan, that he would consider a twenty-year sentence instead of life in exchange for full cooperation. You never know what can happen after the war, Erika. Relationships between countries often improve quickly and gestures made to show good will. You might serve only half of that, or even less. You might return to Germany still a young woman."

Erika resumed her sit-ups.

"You need to think hard on it." Carr stood. "How's the food?"

"Brilliant. Last night I dined on hot dogs cut up and cooked in beans. It really was quite good. I enjoyed it, truly."

"Good. Do you have any requests? Is there anything you need?"

"I would like a priest to hear my confession so I can take Holy Communion."

He looked at her for a moment, surprised. "That's not a problem. I'll take care of that."

"Good day, Mr. Carr."

Carr left the stockade with the non-answers he expected and hoped for, but he still feared she would be lost. Passing the test, as she had done so far, was no use to the OSS unless she agreed in the end to come over. Refusing to turn would ensure wartime justice for spies—a rope. The only accomplishment today was clearing up the loose end concerning the Cadillac. The license plate was traced; the car was registered to a man who called the Cincinnati police at noon Sunday to report it stolen. Yesterday, Carr questioned the man and showed him a picture of Erika taken by an Army photographer at the Cincinnati police station after her capture. The young man stated he did not recognize her. He had mistakenly left his keys in the ignition outside a bar Saturday. When asked why he didn't report the car as stolen until noon the next day, the man said he left the bar late that night through an alley door, accompanied by a prostitute who had approached him in the bar. Because the prostitute worried about her customer's ability to drive after so many drinks, they rode a bus to a seedy hotel. When he woke the next morning, the prostitute and his money were gone. By the time he made it back to where he had parked his now-missing car, it was noon. Nothing the man said conflicted with Erika's answers, and his willingness to admit the embarrassing details led Carr to believe he told the truth. Carr moved the notes about Daniel Offerman and Wilmar von Krause to the back of his folder after he got into his car.

After Carr left, Erika got up from the floor and sat on her bunk as the corporal retook his position. She was relieved had Willy kept his nerve. Though she had devised the plan concerning Willy and his car with the FBI in mind, her scheme apparently worked nevertheless. Two nights before her meeting with Elizabeth at the Side Pocket, Erika called on Adalwulf at his home and informed him she would need a car that weekend. She did not want to steal a car because the owner would most likely report it stolen within minutes and the police would have an eye out right away. Adalwulf agreed to her plan to borrow Willy's car. Willy was not home so they waited. When he returned, Adalwulf called him into the study. Willy saw Erika, turned pale, and bolted out the study door. Adalwulf finally got Willy back in the study and ordered him to sit and listen.

Erika knew the authorities would quickly trace the car's ownership after she abandoned it. What happened to Willy after that was of no concern to her, yet she thought of Adalwulf. To protect Adalwulf, Erika would not take Willy's car without his knowledge and willingness to cooperate. The FBI had her photograph from the Evansville shipyard and might show it to Willy, so he must be let in on the scheme. If Willy was kept in the dark, and unaware of the importance of not linking her to his grandfather, he might think that protecting his grandfather required telling the authorities the woman in the photo had come to the house. That would result in Adalwulf being investigated, exposed, and imprisoned. So Erika coached Willy on the story about the bar and prostitute and stressed the importance of including these embarrassing details.

Then she gave Willy his instructions for Saturday: that afternoon, no later than two o'clock, Willy must park his car on Main Street near Fountain Square, leave the keys under the front seat and walk away. At noon Sunday, Willy should call the police and report the car stolen, thus protecting both himself and his grandfather but allowing Erika the time she needed. After calling the police, Willy simply needed to stick to the story. Of course, Erika did not tell Willy she was a German spy, but she emphasized that if he faltered it would mean disaster for him and his grandfather.

Adalwulf von Krause knew his grandson's priorities. After Erika finished explaining the plan, Adalwulf assured Willy that if anything happened to the Cadillac, he would buy Willy another car. Then Adalwulf added the clincher: he told Willy, "Wilmar, if I am arrested, the government will seize our fortune and you will be forced to find a job."

Those last three words quickly convinced Willy to go along.

Chapter 75

Bless Me Father

Fort Knox, Kentucky—Friday, November 12, 1943

He spoke broken English with a heavy Russian accent.

"Hallo, I am Father Prokip Motyka, I am sent to you to hear the confession," said the man through the cell bars. He wore a dark, bushy beard and the epitrachelion stole of an Eastern Orthodox priest.

"Thank you, Father," said Erika Lehmann.

"I must to say, my child, I come from Ukraine and the English not so very good."

"Father, I see you are Orthodox. I was baptized Roman."

"Yes, but I must to serve to our military men of to all Christian fates, this is to including to the Roman and to the Protestant."

"I see."

"I hear the confession in the English, my child. But must you very slow to speak so I understand."

Erika gazed at the priest for a moment, then knelt at the bars and began to pray silently. The priest pulled up the chair and sat near her in the corridor.

When Erika finished her silent prayer, she began: "Blagoslovi menia, otets, ia sogreshila. Poslednii raz byla na ispovedi mesiats nazad."

Chapter 76

A Bond

Cincinnati—Saturday, November 13, 1943

The Ault Home

"You made short work of that, babe. I'll cook you another egg," Frank offered. Elizabeth had just finished one of his big breakfasts.

"No, I've been eating like a pig and sitting on my rear since I came home from the hospital. If I keep this up, none of my clothes will fit."

"That's okay. You need to gain weight; you're too thin. I'd love it if you were pleasingly plump," Frank shoveled a forkful of hash browns into his mouth. After chewing and swallowing, he added, "And don't worry about exercise. When Steve gives you a clean bill of health, I'll give you plenty of exercise."

Elizabeth smiled. "I look forward to that."

Frank returned to duty after Elizabeth came home Monday. When he was at home, he pampered her: helping her dress, bathe, even comb her hair because Dr. Hagan ordered Elizabeth not to raise her right arm above her shoulder for at least two weeks. Frank brought in take-out meals unless Elizabeth's mother cooked dinner. While Frank was at work, Elizabeth's mother stayed with her.

"Frank, yesterday I told my mother she didn't need to come and sit with me all day."

"Your mother is happy to do it."

"I know. But I'm doing fine."

Frank shook his head. "I feel better knowing your mom is here while I'm at work, Elizabeth. Let's have her come for at least another week."

Elizabeth yielded quickly. She knew she would lose this debate, and not only with Frank. Her mother was a stubborn worrier. Mom would show up anyway.

"Yesterday, Doctor Hagan told us you can take me for a drive Sunday. Let's do that, Frank. The walls are closing in on me."

"Okay, where do you want to go?"

"Why don't we drive down to Grant County?"

Frank looked at her. "Why there?"

"I want to see the place during the day."

"'The place.' Are you talking about that HAM clubhouse?"

"Yes."

"Why, Elizabeth?"

"I just want to see it in daylight, Frank. Don't you?"

"The place is blocked off. Carr's MPs are there. No one is allowed up that dirt road."

"They won't keep you out. You can tell them you're on police business."

"Carr ordered the MPs to let no one up that road, including police. Not even the local sheriff's people are allowed on the road going up to that clubhouse. But even if we could see the place, there are other reasons we don't want to go there. Steve said we can go for a *short* drive; that's not a short drive, and that dirt road is rougher than an alligator's back. You don't need jostling right now."

"So you still see Carr?"

"I saw him Tuesday after he questioned the guy whose car she stole. Carr asked me if he could talk to you; I told him maybe next week. Then he stopped by the station Thursday to talk briefly with Cantrell, but I didn't see him that day."

"So Carr must not have taken her too far if he is still showing up in Cincinnati."

"He has an Army plane at his disposal. Maybe he flies in."

Earlier that week, Elizabeth had told her husband everything about the long night two weeks ago: all of her conversations with Erika and all the humiliating details concerning Jim. She left nothing out. Elizabeth told Frank everything she refused to tell Leroy Carr at the hospital—the London telephone call was to Erika's grandfather to get a warning to her father. And she told Frank the news about Erika's father being killed.

As she related the details, Frank had occasional comments and questions on all except the details about Jim, where he remained silent. Then Frank told her everything about Erika's surrender: Erika staying with Elizabeth, Erika sparing him for Elizabeth's sake, and the blood transfusion. Elizabeth had not commented until now.

"Why do you think she did all that, Frank? All the things you told me about a few nights ago?"

"I don't know. But I do know it never should have come to that. I don't feel sorry for her or thankful to her, Elizabeth, and neither should you. If it weren't for her, you wouldn't have been in Grant County, and you wouldn't have been shot."

"I don't feel sorry for her, Frank. But I am grateful she didn't shoot you."

Elizabeth could not help but feel gratitude. Erika spared her husband, and saved Elizabeth's life with the blood transfusion. Other than that gratitude, Elizabeth was unsure what she felt regarding Erika Lehmann, other than bewilderment.

[Fort Knox, Kentucky—that evening]
Leroy Carr and Al Hodge sat at a small table inside the Officers Club. Both men billeted on base in quarters reserved for lower-ranking officers—the only quarters with vacancies. A hotel on the southern outskirts of Louisville was less than an hour's drive, but Carr preferred to stay as close to Erika Lehmann as possible. Carr placed Hodge in charge of putting together a detailed timeline of events that took place at the HAM clubhouse the night of the transmission. This included questioning the two sedated men. Hodge had ordered MPs to deliver the men to Fort Knox, where they were still being held. Hodge had just given Carr his final report on the men's interrogation.

"Unless you can think of a reason we need to keep holding them, Leroy, I'm going to release those guys. I'm convinced they're just two chumps who thought they were going to get lucky with a couple of pool hall girls. Lehmann targeted them because they're amateur HAMs with access to a transmitter. Those guys are scared out of their wits, and they're clueless about the London telephone call and the transmission; they spent most of the night in the Land of Oz." Earlier in the week, Hodge had briefed Carr on how the man, Jim, told him about picking up *Early* and Elizabeth at a Cincinnati pool hall. Hodge made a trip to the pool hall, questioned the owner, and located a couple of the girls who were at the pool hall that night. They corroborated his story.

"Okay, send them on their way tomorrow." Carr sipped his gin and tonic.

"I've verified their home and work addresses. They think I'm a U.S. marshal. I'll tell them that until further notice they're under orders from the Justice Department to call the base commandant's office if a home or work address changes."

"Good work, Al."

"How did it go with Lehmann today?" Hodge swigged his beer and took some popcorn from a small paper bowl.

"She gave me some information."

Hodge stared at Carr for a moment. "No way."

"I asked her how she came up with the alias *Early*. Apparently it was a pet name her mother called her."

Hodge shook his head. "Smart-ass! You had me suckered for a minute. When will that pain-in-the-ass cop let you talk to his wife?"

"Next week."

"Why don't you get a 7.6C injunction, Leroy?" Hodge referred to a writ authorized by the Sedition Act that would force a United States citizen to submit to questioning in any case designated national security.

"Next week is fine, Al. I doubt if she knows anything about Lehmann we don't already know, and Elizabeth told us what she knows about the transmission. I have to find out about that London call, but I don't want to go barging in with a 7.6C—not at this point, anyway. Bill called this afternoon; he wants a face-to-face update. I'm flying back to D.C. Monday morning and returning Tuesday. Before I leave, I'll call Ault and ask for a meeting with Elizabeth on Wednesday. If he still refuses, then I'll use a 7.6C."

"That's sure a baffler—why Elizabeth clammed up about that London call, I mean."

Carr agreed. "Yep. It's a baffler, and it's very interesting."

"What do you mean?"

"The first time I interrogated Lehmann she asked about Elizabeth right off the bat—you heard her. Then on Thursday I spoke with Cantrell and got Ault's story about what went on in the clubhouse before I arrived. Ault told Cantrell that Lehmann could have escaped but stayed to help Elizabeth. Then, Lehmann could have shot him but didn't because he was Elizabeth's husband. And I was there at the Williamstown hospital when Lehmann volunteered to give Elizabeth blood; she told the nurse to keep transfusing until Elizabeth got what she needed. Add all that to Elizabeth's refusal to talk about Lehmann's London call. There's some sort of bizarre rapport or bond between our Fräulein and our Mrs. Ault." Carr took another sip of gin. "And that might be something that works to our favor, because I don't think either one of them realizes their relationship."

465

Chapter 77

A Strange Kettle of Fish

Washington, D.C.—Monday, November 15, 1943

The Office of Strategic Services, E Street Complex

For the past 90 minutes, Leroy Carr had sat alone with William Donovan in the large E Street Complex conference room briefing Donovan on the almost daily Fort Knox interrogations of Erika Lehmann.

"So the FBI report from the Evansville case is correct: she speaks Russian?" asked Donovan.

"Yes," said Carr. "She asked for a priest to say confession. I asked Pete Szekely from the Russian Division to fly to Fort Knox. He posed as an Eastern Orthodox priest—fake beard, vestments, broken English, the whole nine yards. Pete told me she spoke her entire confession in Russian and she's fluent."

"Did she reveal anything in the confession we can use?"

"No, she confessed to hurting people and having lustful thoughts. She offered no names about either."

"Hurting people? You mean killing people?"

"We know she's killed two people. Two criminals: the man in Evansville who shot the FBI agent, and one of the men in Cincinnati who attacked those women in the apartment building. But that last killing occurred over two months ago. She told Pete her last confession was a month ago—she must have already confessed to that killing."

"A pious Nazi." Donovan shook his head. "But it looks like you had her pegged, Leroy. She sounds perfect. Exactly what we need: a female with her innate abilities who speaks Russian and won't sing to save her neck—won't double-cross the country she works for. Your report confirms she's anti-Communist from the way she decried the president and Churchill lining up with Stalin."

"Yeah, putting a Nazi and a Communist in the same room is like throwing a mongoose in a bucket with a cobra. But you nailed my main problem on the head: she'll never come over during the war. Can we hold her for the duration? Once the war ends, she wouldn't need to

466

betray Germany. You and I discussed how the Russians are sure to make a play for control of Poland and Germany during any Allied post-war negotiations. If the Reds get their claws into Germany after the surrender, she can help Germany by working for us. After the war, the Allies won't allow Germany—if there's a Germany left—to undertake covert operations, at least not for a long time. If she wants to protect Germany from the Reds, the only outlet available to her will be through us or the British. . . ."

Donovan interrupted. "The Brits, there's another problem. You can bet your house MI-6 will want her to work for them after the war as badly as we do. We captured her; I've got to make sure we stay in control. I don't want MI-6 to even know we have her—at least not until I'm ready to tell them. If this works out and she goes to work for us after the war, we gotta make sure any and all records concerning her traipsing around the States are destroyed. She never existed as far as any records go."

"That's going to be a big job, Bill. The FBI has its records, the Embassy Department has records of the family when they were here in the '30s, then there's the personnel records at that shipyard in Indiana, and now we have that Cincinnati crime."

"Well, no sense in worrying about that now. We'll cross that bridge if we ever come to it."

"Right," Carr agreed. "Anyway, what I'm suggesting is we keep her under wraps until the war is over. After the war, I feel we'll stand a good chance of persuading her to work for us—if for no other reason than she'd be working against the Communists for Germany's sake."

"Can't do it, Leroy. The White House isn't going to let us keep a German spy—especially one who has caused so much mayhem—locked up in secret for the duration simply because Bill Donovan and Leroy Carr *hope* she'll spy against the Russians someday down the road. The Russians are our allies at the moment, and nobody knows how long this war will last."

"So if I don't get her to turn on Germany, we'll have to surrender her to the FBI and the Department of Justice?"

"We'll have no choice, Leroy. And we don't have much time." Donovan paused to mull over the many things Carr told him in his long report. "That apparent bond between Lorelei and that detective's wife you told me about is a strange kettle of fish."

Carr did not respond.

"Anything there you can use?" asked Donovan.

"I'll have to try. That's the only card I have left."

"You've got to pull something out of her—and soon. Something legitimate; it can't turn out to be false intel she's fed us. I'll need something solid within a couple of weeks to convince FDR she's some use to the United States alive, or we'll have to give her up, Leroy."

"You know they'll hang her, Bill."

"I know. Get me something, Leroy. By the end of the month."

Chapter 78

Leroy Plays his Last Card

Fort Knox, Kentucky—Wednesday, November 17, 1943

8:00 a.m.

"How was breakfast, Erika?" asked Leroy Carr as he pulled up the chair outside the cell.

"Very good," Erika answered. "I haven't seen you in a few days, Mr. Carr."

"I was called back to Washington—just returned yesterday evening. Did the priest make it by last week?"

"Yes, thank you."

"The base head chaplain told me he had to send a Ukrainian priest," Carr lied. "Apparently, the Roman Catholic chaplain was not available. But the chaplain said from now on the Roman Catholic priest who normally calls on the stockade will give you Holy Communion on Sunday mornings."

"I had never confessed in Russian before."

"Oh? So he asked that you speak in Russian?"

"No, he struggled with English, so I spoke Russian."

"I see. I read in the FBI report from Evansville that you spoke in Russian during a telephone call they monitored. How many languages do you speak, Erika?"

"German, English, French, and Russian are the languages I feel comfortable using. I know some Danish and Slav but do not consider myself well-versed."

"Impressive, to say the least. Where did you learn French and Russian?"

"It doesn't matter, Mr. Carr, does it now?" Besides English, Erika learned French from her mother's side of the family; her mother and both grandparents spoke it well. She also took French in college. After Erika and her father returned to Germany in 1937, Erika worked at the Seehaus in Berlin translating English and French foreign radio broadcasts into German. There, while mingling with fellow Seehaus translators fluent in other tongues, she became well-versed in Russian and to a rudimentary degree Danish and Slovak. The Seehaus was her first paying job and she worked there while completing her university studies in Berlin. She eventually left the Seehaus (against her father's wishes) when Abwehr came calling. *My background in Germany is not something to tell the enemy,* she thought. "I picked up languages here and there. It seems I have a flair for learning languages. I don't know why."

"Erika, I need to know about that telephone call to London."

"Whatever Elizabeth told you I'm sure will be the truth."

"Yes, Elizabeth told me about the call, but I must hear it from you. I don't want you to hang, Erika. I need some cooperation, or I'm not going to be able to help you. Time is running out."

Erika did not respond. If Elizabeth had told Carr about the London call, he would ask detailed questions. She knew her grandparents faced no legal trouble stemming from her call; they knew nothing of her work. When she was in London on assignment in '42 she did not visit her grandparents to protect them from any knowledge that she was in England in case she was captured. She longed to visit her grandparents while in London. Twice she watched them on their morning walk—she hidden and they never knowing. But Erika was glad Carr did not know the details. Her grandfather, a British patriot and man of sterling reputation, would be embarrassed to be questioned about his granddaughter, and both he and her grandmother would be shocked to learn she was a German spy. Erika would have never called them if she had any other reliable way to get a message to her father. *And now Elizabeth won't tell the OSS about the call. Why?*

[2:15 p.m.—the Ault home]

"Hello, Elizabeth," greeted Carr after Frank Ault let him in. "Ed Cantrell tells me you're doing great."

Elizabeth sat on the sofa dressed in brown slacks and a pale yellow blouse. "I think he's right. I certainly can't complain. Dr. Hagan visits twice weekly and tells me things look fine, and Frank waits on me hand and foot. I'm enjoying that. Please have a seat."

Carr sat in an armchair that did not match the décor. He did not remember it being there during the long night two weekends ago. "Nice chair."

"It's new. It was here when I came home from the hospital. Frank won't tell me what happened to the chair that matched the sofa. But when I came home, the living room reeked of gasoline and that chair sat there."

"Well," said Carr. "I don't smell gasoline now."

"We kept the windows open for two days. Ice wouldn't have melted in the living room."

Carr smiled. "I appreciate your talking to me, Elizabeth. I'd like to re-create that Saturday night. Please tell me, step-by-step, the sequence of events with every detail you remember. But first, how did Erika Lehmann get in touch with you?" Carr extracted a large note pad and pen from his attaché case.

"She called the newsroom Friday afternoon, the day before I met with her, and told me there was an envelope taped to the back of the lavatory basin in Stella's Café. Stella's is across the street from the *Observer*." Elizabeth handed Carr the note.

"I've seen that place," said Carr as he scanned the note.

"As instructed in the note," Elizabeth said, "I went to the Rusty Bottom—that's a bar off Fifth and Main—at four o'clock Saturday afternoon. She called me at the bar a few minutes after four."

For the next 40 minutes, Elizabeth related the story: her walk to the YWCA to retrieve the Netherlands Hotel room key, her walk back to the hotel, the phone booth call from Erika, the hotel room and change of clothes, the phone call to Frank (Carr told her he heard and remembered her call), her rides in the cab and with Danny, the encounter with Erika and Jim at the Side Pocket, the drive to Grant County and conversation along the way, the radio transmission, the shotgun through the window, the knife and the sheriff—everything until the deputy's rifle shot ended her memory of the night. Carr often stopped her to ask questions, which she answered to the best of her knowledge. Elizabeth, however, offered no information about the London call or any details about her forced intimacies with Jim. She had told Frank about Jim; only her husband deserved to know.

As she talked, Carr wrote. Frank remained silent, doing his best to look stoic but impatient to get Carr satisfied and on his way.

"About that London call, Elizabeth. I'll ask you again about that."

"I'm sorry, Mr. Carr. I promised you in the hospital that call had nothing to do with our country's interests."

It was the answer Carr expected. He would have to pressure her. He put the note pad back in his case, stood, and first offered praise.

"Elizabeth, the clues you left with the *Observer* switchboard operator were very clever. The situation you were in—Erika listening to every word—made it difficult to say the least, and coming up with clues that tipped your colleagues at the newspaper without being obvious to Erika was an exceptional piece of work. Frank told us you'd find a way."

Elizabeth looked at Frank. It made her happy that Frank had that much confidence in her.

"Well, I won't keep you any longer. I'll call if I have other questions." Carr pulled two cards from a jacket pocket. "If you change your mind about the phone call, Elizabeth, or think of anything else you want to tell me, please call this number. You'll reach a woman named Vannah; she's the aide to Colonel James Norquist. His office is here in town—at the university. Colonel Norquist will relay your message to me."

"You're not in town?" Elizabeth could not help asking.

"No."

"May I ask about Erika? Frank said she was injured by the same bullet."

"She sustained a nasty flesh wound to her upper left arm, but that's the least of her problems," Carr said somberly.

"Of course. Do you think she has any chance of avoiding the death penalty, Mr. Carr?"

"That's already over with, Elizabeth. Things move quickly in wartime. A military tribunal tried her last week. The trial didn't take long with her record. She's scheduled to hang on November 23rd— next Tuesday."

[one hour later]

As Leroy Carr drove back to Fort Knox, he knew he had confirmed the bond between the two women. Elizabeth looked soundly shocked and downcast when he invented the tale of Erika's fate. And he had no doubt about the bond from Erika's end: she allowed herself to be captured because of Elizabeth. This morning Carr did his best to strengthen that bond. Erika would know Elizabeth did not tell him about the London call because of the general question he posed. Erika now knew Elizabeth protected her.

When Elizabeth calls (Carr knew she would) he would get the information about the London call. He lied about the military tribunal and execution next week to pressure her and force her to talk. Perhaps the London call held the key to something he could use to save Erika. Leroy Carr knew this was the last card he'd be dealt, and Elizabeth Ault was the dealer.

[same time—the Ault home]
"I want to see her, Frank."

Frank had felt it coming. Once Carr left, Elizabeth sat like a statue of dismay. "Honey, there's nothing you can do, and seeing her is just going to put you down in the dumps. You don't need that right now; you've got a lot of healing still ahead of you. Look, I think I know how you feel, and even I've got mixed emotions. When she involved you in all of this and I found out she's a spy, I would have lined up early for a front row seat to the hanging if I didn't get the chance to shoot her myself. I don't feel that way anymore. I still hate her for almost getting you killed; but now, if it was up to me, I'd keep her in prison till the war ends then deport her back to Germany. Except I don't have that power and there's nothing you can do for her, either. People who become spies know if they're captured, even in peacetime, they face execution. During wartime, it's guaranteed unless they turn traitor and sing. Even then many still hang or are shot. Our enemies executed our spies, usually after torture."

"I must see her before Tuesday."

Chapter 79

A Crowded Mess

Fort Knox, Kentucky—Thursday, November 18, 1943

7:20 a.m.

Wartime overcrowding at Fort Knox forced soldiers to report for breakfast in staggered, half-hour shifts that began at 0530. The 0700 mess was the morning's last. Leroy Carr and Al Hodge, their breakfast finished, sat at one table among many tables sipping coffee in the crowded mess hall. Carr had just briefed Hodge on the ploy he used yesterday with Elizabeth.

"When do you think she'll call?" asked Hodge.

"Soon."

As if responding to a prompt, a private first class appeared at the cafeteria entrance and scanned the enormous room. Though the bustling mess hall was half the size of a football field, the PFC located Carr and Hodge quickly—the only men in suits—and approached.

"Sir, a message." The private handed Carr a sealed envelope.

"Good morning, Private Dodson," said Carr. Dodson and another private, Knaebel, had been assigned to aid Carr and Hodge: driving them around base, running errands, delivering messages.

"Good morning, sirs."

Hodge, in the middle of a swallow, raised his coffee cup to acknowledge the private.

Carr opened the envelope and read the message. "That will be all, Private, thank you."

"Yes, sir."

"Elizabeth?" asked Hodge as the soldier walked away.

"Yep."

"She didn't waste any time."

"The Colonel and Vannah arrive at the office at seven o'clock. Their phone must have been ringing when they walked in the door. That's good."

Hodge finished his coffee and rose with his food tray, expecting to leave so Carr could return Elizabeth's phone call.

"No hurry, Al," Carr said. "Have another cup."

Elizabeth would have to wait. Carr still had groundwork to lay, which included telling Erika Lehmann the truth.

[9:45 a.m.—stockade]

"It's about 45 now and might reach 55 today," Carr said after he dismissed the guard. Erika always asked about the weather so he got it out of the way as he pulled the chair nearer the cell bars.

"It has warmed. I'm sure the trees look beautiful."

"Yes, very colorful. That's another big change from Montana. Out there, most of the leaves have dropped by early October."

Erika stood near the bars when Carr arrived. She noticed he was not carrying his attaché case.

"Erika, in our line of work we often misrepresent the truth. Let's face it; we need to lie skillfully to do our jobs. I lie to you and you lie to me. Now I'll tell you everything I deceived you about before I tell you the truth."

Erika leaned on the bars. Carr saw her doubtful smile.

He continued. "All those things I told you pertaining to evading execution by cooperating were false. There was never an offer from the Attorney General. If you force me to turn you over to the Justice Department there will be no deal in your case. Execution is guaranteed and that will take place soon. Justice for spies moves swiftly in wartime, as you know. Pretty much everything I've told you or done concerning you to this point has been a sham. I issued the never-eyes-off order for the guards. The Russian priest who heard your confession was a man I sent from the OSS Russian division."

Now expressionless, she continued to look at him through the bars.

"Everything was a test. You passed the test. If you would have given me any information, I would have walked away and surrendered you to the FBI. After the FBI finished with you, they would turn you over to the Justice Department."

Carr waited for a comment, but she had none. "Now I'll tell you the truth. General Donovan and I want you to work for the OSS. I don't want you to be executed. Someone with your abilities can offer great service to the United States."

"I will never work against my country."

475

"I'm glad you said that—again. If you betrayed your country, we couldn't trust you. I'm not asking you to turn traitor. But your country will lose this war; it's inevitable. A country the size of Germany, with its limited resources, cannot win a two-front war against enemies with the manpower and resources of the United States and Russia. It's only a matter of time, Erika. I know you realize that."

She said nothing.

Carr said, "We won't ask you to work against Germany. I'll transfer you to the stockade at Fort Dix, New Jersey, for the duration. After the war, you'll enter OSS training. We want you in our Russian Division."

Erika left the bars and sat on her bunk facing him. "So this is why I haven't seen the FBI. They would never agree to this course. Your General Donovan must have great influence."

"He does. And we know from the FBI reports that the man who killed the FBI agent in Evansville was also trying to kill you. We know you weren't responsible for the agent's death or we could not and would not make you this offer."

"And the man posing as a priest was to confirm I speak Russian." Her words a statement, not a question. "I must commend you on the priest, Mr. Carr. I asked for a priest and you found a way to use that against me. Clever."

She paused to think before continuing. "Your offer is intriguing, Mr. Carr, because I am not forced to decide if I believe you. If I decline, I die. If I accept and you're lying, I die. And I certainly would have no qualms about working against the Bolsheviks. But there has to be something else, am I right?"

"General Donavan must have something he can take to President Roosevelt that will convince him to allow us to implement our plan. The president is not going to grant clemency solely because you promise to work for us after the war. I need your cooperation now; you've got to give me something, some information. Think this over carefully, Erika. Help me save you."

"I'm afraid I must decline your offer."

Carr was taken aback. He had planned to give her time to think it over, and before she answered bring in Elizabeth Ault to make an appeal to reason. Erika's immediate answer caught him off guard. "After the war, Stalin will do everything in his power to turn Germany into a Communist vassal. After your country capitulates, the Allies will scuttle the German military complex; you'll have no Abwehr to work for. If you turn down this offer, you're ensuring yourself the gallows and turning down an opportunity to help your country after the war."

"Ensuring myself the gallows, yes. Helping my country after the war, perhaps. But in the meantime turn traitor to save my life."

Carr's frustration began to show. "Do you realize what's going on in the country you'll be sacrificing your life for? We have reports of widespread atrocities: entire villages in Poland and Russia wiped from the map, civilians executed; forced labor camps where prisoners are worked until they die of exhaustion; rumors of wholesale executions of Jews."

"I refuse to believe Allied propaganda, Mr. Carr. Our propaganda ministry issues reports of atrocities by the Allies. Do you believe those stories?"

[11:30 a.m.]
Carr and Hodge had been issued an office cubicle in the base administration building (the only office space available on the overcrowded Army base). But the din of shouting WACs rushing past the cubicle, frantic in their duties to process that day's mountain of wartime paperwork, quickly convinced Carr to set up a makeshift office in his quarters. OSS headquarters at Fort Knox was now Leroy Carr's bedroom. Carr had the bed taken away to accommodate a small desk, two chairs, and a file cabinet. The metal file cabinet that stored highly confidential government briefs sat next to the wooden dresser that stored Carr's socks and underwear. He slept on the sofa in the tiny living room.

Private Knaebel, the other private assigned to Carr and Hodge, had just left after delivering a message—another note from Colonel Norquist's office in Cincinnati that Elizabeth Ault was trying to reach Carr.

Hodge sat with Carr in the bedroom headquarters. "That's the third time she's called this morning, Leroy."

"I still plan to call Elizabeth because I want to find out what that London telephone call was about. But Lehmann's mind is made up. I could tell the thought of working against the communists piqued her interest, and I had hoped that if she wavered, Elizabeth might play a role in persuading her, but no one is going to change Lehmann's mind. After I told her I needed something from her to take to Donovan, she

477

turned me down before I got the chance to give her time to think it over. We don't have a prayer of saving her."

[12:10 p.m.—Cincinnati, the Ault home]
"Hello."

"Hello. This is Leroy Carr. I'm returning Elizabeth's call."

"Hold on, please." Elizabeth's mother lowered the receiver and turned to her daughter. "He said his name is Leroy Carr."

Elizabeth rose from the kitchen table and took the receiver with her left hand. "Hello."

"Hello, Elizabeth. It's Leroy Carr. I received your message."

"Thanks for calling, Mr. Carr."

"I wish you'd call me Leroy. You make me feel even older when you call me Mr. Carr."

"Sorry. Force of habit, I guess."

"What can I do for you, Elizabeth?"

"I want to see Erika. I know there's nothing I can do for her, but I must see her."

"Why?"

A pause. "I'm not sure why."

"I'm afraid I can't allow you to see her. I'm sorry."

"I've done everything you asked of me and more. Now I'm asking you. Please let me see her."

"I'd like to, Elizabeth, but I can't. Anyone who sees her before the execution must have an important reason, such as key information. But I don't want to discuss this any further on the phone. Tell you what: I've got business to tie up in Cincinnati and will be there today from about four to six. If you want me to, I'll stop by your house."

"Yes. Thank you."

"Okay, I'll see you later this afternoon."

"Thank you again. I'll be waiting."

"Goodbye, Elizabeth."

"Goodbye."

On the other end, Carr hung up, then looked at Al Hodge and nodded. "You're driving."

◊ ◊ ◊

478

[7:30 p.m.—the Ault home]

Carr had no other business in Cincinnati and waited until nearly five o'clock before leaving Fort Knox. He wanted Elizabeth Ault to stew for awhile, and if she grew worried he might not show, all the better. Purposely very late, Leroy Carr finally knocked on the Aults' front door.

Frank answered the knock. "What's the matter, Carr? Haven't you figured out how to wind your watch?"

Carr apologized as he and Hodge walked through the door. "Sorry, Frank. Running behind. My scheduled stops took longer than expected. I'm sure Elizabeth told you *she* called *me.* This stop was unexpected."

"Yeah, she told me."

Elizabeth walked into the living room from the hall. "Hello."

Carr and Hodge greeted Elizabeth and everyone took a seat: Frank and Elizabeth on the sofa, the OSS men in chairs.

"Would you like coffee?" asked Elizabeth.

"None for me," said Hodge. "But thanks anyway."

"Me neither," Carr said. "As I told Frank, we're running way behind. I apologize for being late."

"Have you reconsidered allowing me to see Erika, Mr. Carr?" Elizabeth still used his surname. "I hope you have."

"As I said on the phone, Elizabeth, that won't be allowed unless you can tell us something new."

Frank stepped in. "What's that got to do with it, Carr? Why would Elizabeth's seeing her for a few minutes depend on if you get new information? Elizabeth told you everything she knows."

"Except about that London telephone call. You surprise me, Frank. You sound as if you *want* Elizabeth to see her. Do you?"

Frank hesitated. "I didn't, but if it will allow closure for Elizabeth, then I do."

"If I tell you about the call, you'll let me see her?" asked Elizabeth.

"I'm sure I can swing it," Carr answered.

Frank glared at Carr but remained silent. It was obvious to him that Elizabeth was being played. In his line of work, Frank had used the same *quid pro quo* tactic hundreds of times. But Elizabeth felt she had to see Erika Lehmann one final time, and if information about the call to Erika's grandfather would accomplish that, Frank felt Elizabeth should decide.

Elizabeth said, "Mr. Carr, I'll tell you about the call, but, as I've already told you, it had nothing to do with secrets or our country's

479

interests. If it did, I would have told you, of course. I'm afraid you're going to be disappointed. If you are disappointed, you'll still let me see her?"

"Yes, Elizabeth. You have my word."

"Erika called her grandfather. He's a highly-respected, former British diplomat. By the way, he knows nothing of Erika's work as a German spy. . . ."

Carr interrupted. "The call was to London, so he's her grandfather on her mother's side, of course. We know her mother was British."

"That's right."

Carr reached down into his attaché case, withdrew a folder and shuffled through some papers until he found what he looked for. "Louis Richard Minton?"

"Yes, that's him."

"Go on." Carr stroked his chin.

"Erika believed her father was in danger and she asked her grandfather to relay a message of warning through a contact in Lisbon. That was the purpose of the call—to warn her father."

"We know about her father. He was press secretary for the German embassy in Washington during the mid-30s, but he was killed last summer." Carr quickly found another folder. "Here it is . . . Karl Lehmann, killed in a boating accident last July. The British learned about it from a German newspaper. Hitler and nearly the entire Nazi hierarchy attended the service—Goebbels, Göring, Himmler, Bormann. Erika didn't know her father had died?" As soon as Carr asked the question, he realized that, of course, Erika could not know. She lacked any means to communicate with Germany since losing her transmitter in Evansville.

"No, she did not know. And he did not die in a boating accident."

"How do you know that?"

"Erika said her father was murdered by Himmler. Himmler is her mortal enemy; he even sent a man to Evansville to kill her. Erika told me her father was an old friend of Hitler, and Himmler had her father murdered because of old grudges, and because her father would be an enemy too powerful for Himmler to overcome if she survived and made it back to Germany to tell her father about Himmler's plot against her."

Leroy Carr was a master at disguising thoughts and feelings, but he felt himself turning pale. He adjusted himself in the chair to give himself a moment to fight the feeling. "So that's what the warning was about?"

"That's right."

Carr glanced at Hodge who had an astonished look on his face. The silence lasted so long Elizabeth looked at Frank to see if he had something to say. Frank picked up on her silent message.

"That's it, Carr. She's told you everything. I expect you to keep your word and let Elizabeth see her."

After another pause, Carr said slowly, "I'll keep my word."

Chapter 80

A Lady Yank

The outskirts of London, England—Friday, November 19, 1943

7:30 a.m. London time

"Put down the newspaper, Louis, and finish your porridge. The doctor says you need your oats at least four times weekly."

"Bah!" exclaimed the old gentleman to his wife. "Tell him to eat that swill. The man should be hanged for quackery. I'm as healthy as an Epsom Derby steed, Marie. Have Maggie bring me two eggs and beans, would you, my dear?"

"We don't have eggs. I gave our ration to the Saint Paul's Shelter."

Louis Minton dropped the newspaper to look at his wife across the table. He could not complain; she had done the right thing. He lifted the paper and said, "The Russians have retaken Kiev."

"That's wonderful news."

"Kiev has suffered under the Nazi thumb since '41. Even though the Ukrainians don't live well under the Soviets either, they have to be happy to get rid of the Germans. There have been reports of random executions by the Nazis in and around Kiev for two years now."

The telephone rang in another room.

"Who could that be at this early hour?" Marie asked.

Her husband shrugged and continued to read.

Maggie appeared at the dining room doorway. "It's for you, guvnah; a lady Yank calling from America."

Louis Minton again dropped the newspaper and looked at his wife; he rose quickly and walked to the phone.

"Yes." He said into the receiver.

"Mr. Minton?"

"Yes, this is Minton."

"Mr. Minton, my name is Elizabeth Ault. I spoke with you briefly three weeks ago. I'm Erika's friend here in the United States."

◊ ◊ ◊

[3:45 p.m.—Fort Knox, Kentucky]

Leroy Carr answered the knock at his door.

"What is it, Leroy?" asked Al Hodge as he walked in. "Private Knaebel told me it was urgent."

"Twenty minutes ago I got a call from Donovan. This morning Elizabeth Ault called Erika Lehmann's grandfather in London. She called at seven-thirty London time, which means she stayed up to call in the middle of the night in Cincinnati. Elizabeth told him everything: Erika is a German spy, Erika thinks Himmler ordered her father murdered, the OSS has his granddaughter locked up—everything."

"Damn! Even the part you made up about the execution happening next Tuesday?"

"That, too. Her grandfather, who is well connected, went straight to the Imperial General Staff; they notified MI-6. All hell has broken loose. Donovan is livid. He didn't want the Brits to know we had her—not yet, anyway."

"So now what?"

"I don't know, but Donovan said to keep our plans intact until further notice—that means bringing Elizabeth Ault down here to try and get some information out of Lehmann."

Chapter 81

Personalized Meatballs

Cincinnati—Saturday, November 20, 1943

10:10 a.m.—the Ault home

With her mother in the bathroom, Elizabeth picked up the ringing telephone.

"Hello."

"Good morning, Elizabeth. Leroy Carr here." The call was not person-to-person, so the operator put the call through directly. Carr always called direct, putting the charges on his government expense account so the person he called would not know his location.

"Good morning."

"Elizabeth, I wish you would have called me before you called Erika's grandfather."

"I'm sorry." Elizabeth was not sorry.

"I've scheduled you to see Erika on Monday. I assume Frank will be coming with you?"

"Yes."

"Al Hodge will come to your house Monday at six a.m. to pick up you and Frank."

"Monday at six o'clock a.m." Elizabeth confirmed. She knew she would not forget but wrote it down anyway.

"That's right. You won't need to bring anything. There will be no overnight stay. Al will take you back to your house later that day."

"I understand. Will Erika know I'm coming?"

"No. I'll see you Monday, Elizabeth."

"Yes, Monday."

Click.

[6:30 p.m.—Sano's Italian Restaurant]

"I bet it frosted Carr when he found out you called her grandfather yesterday," Frank said with a mischievous grin.

484

"I think it did," responded Elizabeth as Anthony Sano set two cups of pasta fagioli soup on their table. When rationing began in 1942, pasta fagioli and minestrone made the cut as the wartime soups because neither contained meat.

"Do you know what you're going to say to her?"

"That's all I've thought about since Mr. Carr called this morning. I don't know, Frank." Other than one short drive last Sunday and a trip to the hospital Tuesday for a follow-up X-ray, Elizabeth had been homebound. She had looked forward to this dinner all week, and was determined not to fixate on the Monday meeting and ruin the evening for both her and Frank. Elizabeth took her husband's hand across the table and smiled. "How was your day?"

"Mostly just paperwork—not very exciting, but sometimes boring is okay," he said as he dipped soup. "Although I had a pleasant excursion to court for the sentencing of Duane Rudd and Harriett Rosten."

Elizabeth's eyes widened. Rudd and Rosten were the surviving attackers of Clare Miller and Penny Lindauer. "You told me you couldn't close the case because Leroy Carr wouldn't let you file a report."

"That's the Anne Brown *homicide* case. Carr can't stop me from processing the assault cases against Rudd and Rosten; those cases aren't designated national security. Normally, I wouldn't be involved in their cases because they didn't kill anybody, but I asked Cantrell to bend Chief Weatherly's ear and get permission for me to take over. "

"You can bend mine now, Frank, because I'm all ears."

"Neither scumbag wanted anything to do with a trial. Given the viciousness of the crime and two victims to testify, Rudd and Rosten knew they'd crash and burn if a jury got involved. Duane Rudd would most likely get twenty-to-life; Harriett Rosten would probably get ten-to-twelve."

"So they took a deal?"

"Yeah, but get this, babe. The D.A. was ready to offer Rudd eight-to-twelve, and Rosten two-to-five. I objected (silent translation: Frank caused a shouting and door-slamming scene at the district attorney's office, warning the D.A. that if he offered the criminals those light sentences Frank would have every cop on the force campaigning against him in next year's election). I asked the D.A. to let me bargain with Rudd and Rosten, using his offers as the lowest I would go. He said okay. I offered Rudd twenty-to-thirty, and Rosten eight-to-twelve.

I told each of them that was the best offer they'd get and they both went for it."

"Wow! That's not much less than what you said a jury would give them."

"Right."

Elizabeth could tell he was pleased. "The woman should have gotten the same sentence as the man, though."

Frank shook his head. "Women typically get lighter sentences, but in this case the fact that this was her first offense weighed more heavily than her sex. As you know, I've never agreed with leniency for first-time offenders. I guarantee this wasn't her first crime—God knows what someone who would take part in an attack that cruel has done in the past—but this was her first arrest. You're right; she should get the same sentence for the same crime, but in our court system it's not going to happen."

Elizabeth sipped her wine, then said, "I spoke with Clare Miller today."

"Yeah?"

"I called that apartment building to ask how she's doing, and the manager told me she moved out a couple of weeks ago."

"Right. I knew that because I asked her to keep her address current with the station in case I needed to talk to her. You were in the hospital when she moved and I forgot to tell you."

Elizabeth nodded. "I didn't want to bother her at work, but the manager didn't know where she moved to so I called the *Observer* and talked to her there. She's doing okay with work."

"Good."

"Clare said Penny Lindauer is coming back to Cincinnati. Penny didn't want to return to the Lamar Apartments, but since Clare found a new place, Penny is going to move in with Clare and share the rent."

Frank finished his beer and signaled Anthony for another. "Sounds like a good plan. Clare's new apartment is off Kinsey Avenue and it's a nicer building. I know the rent must be higher."

Anthony delivered a plate of mushroom and cheese raviolis for Elizabeth and Frank's spaghetti and meatballs.

Elizabeth kidded. "They're never out of your meatballs, are they, Frank? Ration Board be darned. Let me see those meatballs—are your initials carved into them?"

Frank grinned. "They are, but you can't see the letters because they're covered with sauce."

They ate in silence for a minute.

"Since we're being picked up so early Monday does that mean we have a long way to go?" Elizabeth asked.

"Maybe. But with Carr, who knows? Nothing is ever as it seems on the surface with that guy. He might want us to think she's far away when she's right outside Cincinnati. Or she could be 500 miles from here and Hodge will take us to the airfield. I know the Army flies those guys anywhere they want to go."

Frank twisted his fork in the spaghetti and continued, his detective instincts taking over.

"Carr gets his MPs from Fort Knox and she might be there. That's about a four-hour drive now with the wartime speed limit, and it would make a lot of sense to keep her on an Army base: no snoopy reporters—present company excepted, of course (he smiled), and more guards then he could ever use. By the way, after you called me at the station this morning and told me about Monday, I called Steve Hagan and asked him about your traveling. He said it's okay. So I'm not worried about the travel; I'm worried that seeing her will upset you."

"I know I will be sad—visiting someone who is to be executed the next day. The whole situation is sad. I don't know what to think of her. The fact that she's a Nazi and has been spying against us makes me sick, but. . . ."

Frank waited for her to finish.

"Never mind," she shrugged. "Like I said, the entire situation is sad."

Chapter 82

A Murder of Crows

Monday, November 22, 1943

5:50 a.m.—the Ault home

Elizabeth sat at her dressing table and adjusted the small mirror. She rolled on lipstick and heard Frank shout from the living room.

"Elizabeth, Hodge is out front. I'll tell him we'll be out in a minute."

She finished, clicked on the cap then dropped the tube into her makeup case. From the top drawer, she pulled out her small jewelry box, took out the Ring of the Slain, and slid it on her right middle finger.

[10:35 a.m.—Fort Knox, Kentucky]
The Aults sat alone in an administration building conference room waiting for Leroy Carr.

"You were right about Fort Knox," said Elizabeth.

"Where the heck is Carr? We've been sitting here for half an hour." Because he was speaking to Elizabeth, Frank used *heck* instead of another word he deemed better.

"I wonder if he'll bring her in here," she asked.

"Not likely. She's either in the stockade or in some special holding cell. I know the Army has trailers with cells they can move by truck. My guess is Carr will take you to her. And expect to go by yourself, babe. I doubt that Carr will let me tag along."

In another minute or so, the door opened and Leroy Carr walked in. He offered no greeting as he took a seat. "I'm going to be blunt. Erika Lehmann has not been tried and she is not scheduled to be hanged Tuesday."

"Goddammit, Carr!" Frank exclaimed. "I knew we couldn't trust you."

"Frank, please," said Elizabeth.

"What I told you is not true only as far as the timeframe is concerned," Carr cautioned. "Erika *will* be put to death within a matter of weeks after I surrender her to the Department of Justice."

"Why, then, did you tell us *Tuesday?*" asked Elizabeth.

"Elizabeth, there is a bond between you and Erika. I think it's a strong bond and perhaps stronger than you're willing to admit, even to yourself. You're not here today because you told me about the London call. I brought you here because I'm hoping you can help me save Erika's life."

For the next 20 minutes, Carr expounded his plan: to save Erika by offering her a job working for the United States after the war. He needed only some tidbit of classified information from Erika he could use to convince the powers in Washington to spare her the gallows.

And that was Elizabeth's job: to persuade Erika to surrender that information so Carr could save her.

[11:50 a.m.]

Erika lay on her bunk, eyes closed, when she heard the cell block door open and Leroy Carr excuse the guard posted outside her cell. *He's late today.* Carr normally called on her much earlier. Her eyes still closed, she heard the guard leave and the heavy door bang shut.

"Hello, Erika."

Erika's eyes shot open and she raised her head. Elizabeth Ault stood alone on the other side of the bars.

Carr waited outside the cell block door. Al Hodge stayed behind with Frank in the administration building. Carr was surprised when the buzzer sounded after only 20 minutes. The buzzer signaled the cell block door sergeant that the person inside the block was ready for the door to be opened. The sergeant looked at Carr. Carr nodded, the sergeant opened the door, and Elizabeth stepped out.

"Erika longs to see the sky and trees so I promised we would go outside."

"I can't let her go outside, Elizabeth." Carr had the cell block bugged. The conversation between the two women would be recorded on audio wire, which Carr would listen to later. "Did you mention the offer?"

"No. She asked about my health and the rest was chit chat. She talked about the changing of the leaves and how she would like to stand in the rain. I told her it wasn't raining but the trees are beautiful. Mr. Carr, she didn't ask to be taken outside; I offered. If I can't keep a promise about something as simple as going outside, why would she trust my advice about your offer?"

Carr hesitated, then exhaled impatiently. "Alright, we'll do it, Elizabeth. But it's not *simple;* it will take me some time to set up." Carr turned to Private Dodson who stood nearby. "Private, take Mrs. Ault back to the administration building or to the mess hall if she's hungry. Keep your walkie-talkie with you and I'll call when I'm ready."

"Yes, sir."

Elizabeth added, "Outside, I want to be left alone with Erika so we can speak privately. I think that way Erika would be more receptive to my suggestions about your offer."

Elizabeth was not interested in lunch so Private Dodson drove her to the administration building. She expected to rejoin Frank but instead was ushered to a different room where she sat alone for two hours. Finally, Private Dodson opened the door.

"Mr. Carr is ready, ma'am."

The drive on a dirt road to a remote area of the base lasted thirty minutes. The open Jeep and cool autumn breeze caused Elizabeth to tug her coat tight. Dodson pulled over and stopped near an Army paddy wagon parked at the edge of a glade. Spread out among the surrounding trees were four more open Jeeps with armed MPs. Two metal chairs in the middle of the glade looked comically out of place. Carr and three MPs stood next to the paddy wagon. Carr approached as Elizabeth got out of the Jeep.

"Okay, Elizabeth. Here's how we'll do this. Erika will remain shackled. The guards will take her to a chair and cuff her to it. Then you can join her. Sit in the other chair. The chairs are five feet apart and you are not to move your chair or touch her. The guards will remain in the background so you can speak privately. When you're finished, stand up. That's the signal that the conversation is over."

"I understand."

Carr nodded to the MPs near the paddy wagon. One opened the rear door, and two climbed in. In a moment, Erika was helped to the ground. The foot shackles limited her to twelve-inch steps and her wrists were cuffed to her sides, bound to a chain circling her waist. She wore a stockade-issued men's jacket. Erika saw Elizabeth and smiled.

The guards took Erika on the slow walk to the middle of the meadow and cuffed her to a chair.

Carr said, "Go ahead, Elizabeth."

Elizabeth walked through the meadow's yellow grasses. As Elizabeth neared, Erika said, "You made me keep my promise after all."

"Which promise?" said Elizabeth as she sat.

"To surrender to your husband."

"Yes, I guess I did. I bet you didn't know I planned all along to get shot so you'd stay with me till Frank arrived."

Erika swiveled her shoulders and head to take in the scenery. Fat white clouds crossed the sapphire sky and a murder of crows whirled by; trees crowding the meadow yielded gaudy leaves to the breeze that kicked them playfully about. She closed her eyes and breathed deeply, savoring the brisk air. "Thank you for this, Elizabeth."

"Frank told me what you did—saving me and sparing him. Thank you very much for that, Erika."

Erika took another deep breath and, with her eyes still closed, said, "I noticed you're wearing the Ring. You have slim fingers, Elizabeth. I wore it on my ring finger, but it fit your middle finger better."

Elizabeth looked down at her right hand. "Why did you give it to me?"

"I knew it would be taken from me after my surrender and whoever took it off my finger would be cursed. I wanted you to have it. You are worthy to wear the Ring. Remember, those who wear the Ring must face death valiantly and be willing to sacrifice for a cause they feel is just or to protect others."

"As you protected and sacrificed for me? So you are a believer."

Erika responded with, "My father believed; that's enough for me." Then she added: "When you wear the Ring, it should always be on your right hand."

After a moment of silence, Elizabeth said, "Erika, my original reason for coming was to say goodbye because Mr. Carr told me you were to be executed Tuesday."

Erika looked at her. "He told you Tuesday?"

"Yes."

After a moment to think, Erika said, "If he told you that, it means he wanted you to come all along, and soon."

"Yes, he did. He admitted that this morning."

"Yet he would not let you visit me unless you could be of some service to him. Mr. Carr does the same thing for his country that I do for mine. He's using you for his purposes as I used you. What does he want you to do, Elizabeth? Find out information I won't tell him—convince me to save my life by becoming a traitor?"

"I don't want you to die, Erika. I'll be honest with you; I completely abhor your link to the Nazis but I feel that link was forged more by circumstance than by choice. I believe that if given an option you would have chosen a different path—different principles to risk your life for. I'm not saying you're wrong to be loyal to Germany; no one can be faulted for loyalty to the country of their birth. That's why I believe your stubborn refusal to accept the reports of Nazi abuse is fueled by your allegiance to your country and not out of support for Hitler's ideology."

"I will not betray my country to save my life."

"You don't have to. The OSS wants you to work against the Communists after the war. Mr. Carr claims you would actually be helping Germany, and, after thinking about it, I see his point."

"What if we do not lose the war?"

"I knew you would say that, and I thought about that since I spoke with Mr. Carr this morning. For the sake of argument, let's say Germany doesn't lose outright but negotiates some type of pact with the Allies that allows Germany to avoid total surrender. Then what have you lost by agreeing to the OSS offer now? You've lost nothing."

"And, to secure this arrangement, Mr. Carr must gain top secret information from me now, and he sends you to persuade me because of our . . . should I say *friendship?* I would never ask you to betray your country, Elizabeth. I would not have asked for your help with that transatlantic telephone call if doing so would compromise your duty to your country."

"I believe that. And, yes, Mr. Carr hopes I will persuade you to cooperate so you'll live, but I know you won't give him top secret information to save yourself. I'm here with news Mr. Carr doesn't know about. . . ."

Erika interrupted quickly. "Stop." Suddenly Erika grinned widely. "If you're going to tell me something you don't want Mr. Carr to know, you must smile very wide as you speak, as I'm doing."

"Why?"

"Were you told, as I was, to not move your chair?"

"Yes."

"Those men in Jeeps watching us through binoculars are reading our lips. The one on my side is reading your lips and the one on your side is reading mine. If you smile broadly as you speak, lip reading will be difficult."

Elizabeth looked.

"Don't look at them, just smile broadly."

Elizabeth forced an exaggerated smile. "Last week, I called your grandfather in London—I had memorized his telephone number. I told your grandfather everything—that you're a German spy, that you think Himmler ordered your father killed, and that you had been captured. Mr. Carr knows about my phone call, but he doesn't know your grandfather has called me twice since then. You didn't tell me your grandfather had been knighted, Erika."

Elizabeth concentrated on keeping a ridiculously wide smile as she continued. "As we speak, your grandfather and other men are on their way to Washington. They're flying from London to meet with the man who heads the OSS. Your grandfather is arriving unannounced. He told me it's important that you are not moved from here until he can talk to the people in Washington tomorrow. We need to stall for a day, Erika. Let me tell Mr. Carr you will consider cooperating, but you need a day to think it over."

Chapter 83

A Loving Child

Wednesday, November 24, 1943

The Ault home

Now early afternoon, close to the appointed time, Elizabeth peered out the living room window for the fifth time then glanced again at the wall clock: three minutes until one. He should arrive any minute.

It was nearly midnight Monday when Al Hodge dropped the Aults at their house after the day at Fort Knox. Unbeknownst to Elizabeth, her plot to have Erika stall Leroy Carr to ensure she would not be moved turned out to be unneeded. At two o'clock Tuesday afternoon, William Donovan called Carr to tell him all plans concerning Erika Lehmann were on hold until further notice. Carr and Hodge were to sit tight at Fort Knox and await Donovan's next telephone call.

Yesterday, Frank went in to work and Elizabeth spent the day wondering what was happening at Fort Knox and in Washington. Finally, at 9:30 last night, Erika's grandfather called from his hotel in D.C. He would fly to Cincinnati first thing this morning, and he asked Elizabeth for permission to call on her at one o'clock.

The sixth time Elizabeth looked out the window she saw two U.S. Army staff cars slow down and park on the street. Two men emerged from the back doors of the lead car. The driver and a passenger in the front seat remained in the car as did the men in the second car.

Elizabeth opened the front door and stepped outside to greet the two men.

"Hello, I'm Elizabeth Ault."

"Hello, and good day, madam. I am Louis Minton, Erika's grandfather." He was tall, probably six feet, and in his mid-to-late 60s. He wore a brown Crombie coat and bowler hat. In his left hand he held a cane he did not need. Elizabeth extended her hand. He took it and said, "It is wonderful to meet you, my dear. Let me introduce Mr. Thomas." No first name or organization affiliation for *Mr. Thomas* was offered.

"Madam," the man said as he extended his hand. Also tall, close in height to Erika's grandfather, Elizabeth guessed Mr. Thomas to be in his late-30s. Hatless with coal-black hair, he had a jagged, two-inch scar starting on his cheek and ending near his left eye.

Elizabeth shook his hand. "Please come in, gentlemen."

Inside, Erika's grandfather removed his hat to reveal a full head of silver hair. "Let me take your coats." Elizabeth hung the coats and bowler on the rack near the door. "Please have a seat. May I get you something? Coffee, perhaps?" Both men politely declined. "My husband is a police detective. He called about thirty minutes ago to say he is delayed. But he'll be on his way here soon."

Both men wore suits, Louis Minton's three-piece and brown, a shade darker than his coat. A silk tie with a perfect Windsor knot at the top disappeared at the bottom under a vest on which a gold watch chain dangled. His highly-polished brown shoes looked hand-made and expensive. Mr. Thomas wore a two-piece navy blue suit; his shiny black shoes looked military issue.

"You have a lovely home, Mrs. Ault," said Minton. Neither man would sit before Elizabeth did.

She sat on the sofa. "Thank you. And please call me Elizabeth."

Minton sat in the new wing chair, Mr. Thomas in the wooden chair.

"Thank you for agreeing to see me, Elizabeth," said Minton. "How is your injury?"

"I'm doing well. I'm hoping to return to the newspaper where I work in two weeks."

"That's a brilliant report. During our telephone talks you told me of my granddaughter's efforts on your behalf after you were wounded. Her compassion towards you was the lone good news after you informed me about Erika's . . . shall I say, *unsavory* efforts on behalf of our mutual enemy and of her present predicament."

Elizabeth nodded.

Minton said, "Erika has always been of a different sort, Elizabeth, but my wife and I never for an instant thought. . . ." He stopped mid-sentence then continued. "She was always headstrong, and as a child, Erika's temper led her to react with violence too quickly if she felt some individual had wronged her or a friend or family member. But she was also a loving child and enormously talented in many areas. Our hopes for her were exceedingly high . . . and now it has come to this."

The front door opened and Frank walked in. The men stood and Elizabeth introduced them. Frank shook hands and joined Elizabeth on the sofa.

Elizabeth asked, "When is the last time you saw Erika, Sir Louis?"

"Shortly before the war, in the spring of '39. After that, her grandmother and I received two notes Erika sent our way through our embassy in Lisbon. The last note arrived in the spring of 1940. After that, we heard nothing until the telephone rang just over a fortnight ago. My wife and I thought Erika was in Germany."

"Sir, how close are you to Erika? If you don't mind me asking."

"At one time, my wife and I were very close to her, and other family members in England were close to her as well. Louise, our daughter—Erika's mother—brought Erika to live with us for a few years in the '20s when Karl struggled to earn a living in Germany. After they rejoined Karl, Louise brought Erika to visit three or four times a year until they left for America in 1933. After Louise died in 1937, and Karl and Erika returned to Germany, Erika visited us in London at least twice yearly until this war began."

"Sir Louis, I want to tell you that I believe Erika was formed by the times and circumstances that boiled up around her. Not that she is without blame—we all have choices to make—but I think she chose to support the Nazis out of allegiance to her father and to her country. I told her as much when I saw her Monday. And I truly feel Erika believes the reports of Nazi abuses are purely propaganda on our part. She has been away from Germany on missions for most of the war. How can she know what is going on unless she trusts the news reports?—which she does not. I must agree with you about Erika's cavalier approach to using violence as a means to an end, but I believe your granddaughter is at heart a good person, Sir Louis. I hope you can save her."

"Thank you very much for your kind judgement of Erika, Elizabeth."

Frank inserted a typical *Frank Ault* comment: "Nothing wrong with violence if it's used on the right people; she just has to learn who the right people are."

Elizabeth ignored her husband's comment. "Can you save her?" she asked Minton.

"I don't know. From the reports I read yesterday in Washington concerning her . . . *activities* in this country, the Americans have every right to subject her to wartime justice. Erika's fate lies in the hands of your country first, and then in Erika's hands."

"Erika's hands?" asked Elizabeth.

"Yes. That is why I asked to see you today, my dear. As my granddaughter's friend—her only friend in this country, I'm quite sure—I hope you'll agree to accompany me to see Erika over the course of the next few days. I'm told the auto trip takes four hours each way. I know you are still recovering and an eight-hour journey each day will be quite tiring. I will overnight in this city and the American Army has agreed to fly us to Fort Knox. The air journey takes thirty minutes and the Army will pick you up here and drive you to the air-pad and return you home, of course."

Elizabeth said *Yes.* Frank decided not to waste his breath objecting.

Minton continued. "Yesterday in Washington, Mr. Thomas made your government a proposal on behalf of the British government." He turned to his countryman. "Mr. Thomas. . . ."

"Yes." Mr. Thomas responded. "I cannot discuss certain details, you understand, but if Washington accepts I will present the proposal to Miss Lehmann." His voice was raspy and low-pitched; Elizabeth thought his accent more Scottish than British but the gravelly voice made it difficult to tell. "If all parties agree, Miss Lehmann will be taken to England where she'll begin training for a mission."

"A mission . . . now? I mean—during the war?" Elizabeth asked.

"Yes, madam," Mr. Thomas answered. "Sir Louis has been briefed on this proposal and he will fill you in on the elements you'll need to know."

All three men saw worry on Elizabeth's face.

"I can only assume the mission concerns Germany, Mr. Thomas." Elizabeth waited for a confirmation, but Mr. Thomas remained pokerfaced. She finished her thought, anyway. "I'm sorry to say this, but I can tell you now that you'll be wasting your time. Erika will never agree to take part in a mission against Germany."

Mr. Thomas did not respond, but Minton said, "Only Washington I worry about, Elizabeth. I think we can count on my granddaughter accepting this particular mission."

Chapter 84

Reunion

Thursday, November 25, 1943

8:10 a.m.

The olive-drab Army staff car sped across the Lunken Airfield tarmac toward a twin-engine airplane the same color. In the cockpit, the pilot and co-pilot warmed the engines, the spinning propellers a blur. Louis Minton and two other men waited near the plane.

Elizabeth Ault rode alone in the backseat of the staff car. An Army sergeant sat in the front passenger seat next to a private behind the wheel. The private stopped near the three waiting men; one of the two men Elizabeth did not know opened her door. The deep-throated growl of the engines and scream of the propellers made conversation on the tarmac impossible, so the four hustled up the steps and into the plane. The last man in closed and secured the hatch, sealing out the November chill and some of the engine noise.

Other than the pilots, no one else was aboard the ten-passenger airplane. The low ceiling of the fuselage forced Elizabeth and the men to hunch over as they sidestepped down the plane's narrow aisle. Elizabeth and Louis Minton chose seats together on the right side of the aisle, the two men spread out on the left side. On the forward bulkhead a sign read *Lockheed L-10 Electra.* Elizabeth could not avoid thinking that the first airplane ride of her life would be in the make and model of aircraft Amelia Earhart had been flying when she disappeared in 1937. She pulled the lap harness tight.

Inside the plane, the cacophony from the engines was not as loud as on the tarmac; still, Louis Minton was forced to speak loudly. "Mr. Thomas drove on to Fort Knox yesterday. These men are my aides. That's Robert Smythe (he pointed, the man saw and waved at Elizabeth) and that's James Devon. Devon sat in front of them and did not see Minton's gesture. "Elizabeth, it got past me that today is a big holiday in your country. Of course, I have heard of your Thanksgiving, but I did not realize your holiday was today until I overheard the staff at the hotel discussing it yesterday. I hope this trip doesn't impose too greatly, my dear."

"No. Frank and I will celebrate when we can this year," said Elizabeth, her voice barely heard above the engines.

When the plane began to taxi, Elizabeth clasped Louis Minton's hand. The Electra slowly made its way to the runway where it stopped to await take-off clearance. Suddenly the engines roared, the plane jerked forward and began picking up speed. Elizabeth braced herself and squeezed the hand of Erika Lehmann's grandfather as the wheels left the earth.

[same time—Fort Knox]

Victor Knight walked with four men outside the main Fort Knox administration building. Knight was the man introduced as *Mr. Thomas* yesterday at Elizabeth Ault's home. Whenever possible, Knight preferred to hold confidential discussions outdoors. All the men walking with him were fellow Britons who accompanied him from England: two were members of the British Admiralty; the other two men, like Knight, were members of SOE, the British Special Operations Executive. All five men served in the British military. Knight and one other SOE man held British Army officer rank; their other SOE colleague and both members of the Admiralty were British naval officers. None of the men were in uniform; all wore suits under their greatcoats.

"I received a call this morning that the Americans will arrive by mid-day," said Knight, "and they've agreed to meet at fourteen hundred."

"Any last minute adjustments, Victor?" asked a short, middle-aged man with a graying goatee—one of the members of the Admiralty.

Knight shook his head. "No, I just want to remind all that the Americans must believe our sole purpose is simply to create chaos within the Nazi hierarchy by liquidating a select few of Himmler's top lieutenants. They must not be told the additional objective that we're considering since Lehmann entered the picture. Understood?"

All the men either answered *yes* or signaled as much by nodding.

Knight continued. "And Sir Louis must continue to believe that the mission is simply to meddle in Himmler's business and make his life complicated. Sir Louis knows nothing about liquidations or the possible additional objective of our endeavor."

"Can the American woman be trusted?" the other man from the Admiralty asked.

"We don't have to trust her. I allowed Sir Louis to brief her after I left them yesterday. She won't know anything more than he does."

"And the German—Lehmann?" the same man asked.

"She won't care why the mission is being offered to her—if it gets that far today. All that will matter to her is the opportunity for revenge."

[10:25 a.m.]

An hour ago, Erika Lehmann was brought shackled and blindfolded from her cell. She heard a door open and in a moment her blindfold came off. She was in a small, windowless room—empty except for the chair she sat in. Leroy Carr and an MP stood next to her.

"Remove her shackles, please," Carr said to the MP. For the sake of international decorum, Carr had decided to have the restraints removed while Erika met with her grandfather. The guard went to work while Carr spoke to Erika. "Your grandfather and Elizabeth Ault are in a room down the hall. You have thirty minutes."

Three more MPs waited outside the door and the entourage escorted Erika down the hall. She felt tentative. How would her grandfather receive her now that he knew she was a German spy? But when the door to the room opened and her grandfather stood, Erika left apprehension behind and rushed into his arms.

"Granddad!"

An MP closed the door and they were alone. Erika hugged and kissed her grandfather several times. He hugged her. Elizabeth Ault stood to the side and she also received a kiss before the trio sat down. Erika noticed the three-foot-square mirror on one wall. Fifteen minutes of banter followed. Erika asked about her grandmother and other family members in England. Louis Minton avoided talking about Erika's service for the enemy and her present predicament, answering his granddaughter's questions as if they enjoyed a pleasant holiday family reunion. He said he would telephone his wife that night with the news that he had seen Erika. Elizabeth remained silent. Eventually, as time wound down, Minton addressed the crucial topic.

"Erika, I have brought men with me who have made a proposition to the Americans. Tuesday they met in Washington, and they'll meet again this afternoon here on this base. The proposition, if accepted by the Americans, will allow you to return to England to begin training for a mission where you can work against the man you think had your father killed."

"Himmler." Erika said somberly. It was not a question.

"Yes. Himmler and his minions. How sure are you, Erika, that Himmler is responsible for Karl's death?"

"I'm absolutely sure, Granddad."

"Will you accept this proposal if indeed the Americans consent?"

Erika looked at the mirror and said to her grandfather, "When you ring Grandmum tonight, give her my love."

Victor Knight and Leroy Carr stared at Erika from the other side of the one-way glass.

[2:00 p.m.]

Eleven men sat around the conference table.

Representing the United States were Joseph K. Timmerman, a White House staff member; Brigadier General Harold Kenney of G2—the Army's intelligence branch; and a four-man contingent from the OSS: William Donovan; Allen Dulles, coordinator of OSS European operations who worked out of the OSS office in Berne, Switzerland; Leroy Carr, and Al Hodge. Duty forced all to miss Thanksgiving with family.

From Great Britain: Victor Knight and his four walking partners.

Timmerman welcomed the men from England, then asked Knight to recap the proposal they had all heard Tuesday in Washington.

"Delighted," said Knight as he rose. "The mission we propose entails inserting a small band of highly-trained personnel behind enemy lines to create chaos among the SS High Command—to throw a monkey wrench at Himmler I think you Yanks might say—by eliminating important members of the SS, SD, and Gestapo. Work on this mission began a year ago, but plans were shelved because we felt we lacked a trump card. When Sir Louis notified the Imperial Staff last week about Mrs. Ault's telephone call, and we found out you Americans had captured Erika Lehmann, SOE scrambled to get the mission back on the table. Because Himmler sent an assassin to your country to kill Lehmann, and since she thinks Himmler ordered her father's murder, we think she'll be receptive. Lehmann can be the missing cog that gives the mission a better chance for success. She can function easily within Germany or its occupied territories. To the Nazis, she would be beyond suspicion—a hero returning from America after finding a way, with no transmitter of her own, to send important information."

General Kenney argued, "And when Himmler finds out she's back, he'll eliminate her immediately to save his hide. Her father was a friend of Hitler as I understand. Surely Himmler will worry about that."

"Lehmann must act as if she does not suspect her father's death was anything but accidental. And Himmler has no way to know what transpired in your city of Evansville. For all Himmler knows, his assassin got icy feet and fled immediately to South America without attempting his mission."

Donovan waded in. "I want to hear again that this is a *loan*. If we allow Lehmann to work with the SOE on this mission, the OSS will be kept abreast of her every move, and she returns to us immediately after the mission or at the end of the war, whichever comes first, either to work for us or, if not, be subject to our courts. There can be no compromise in this matter and I want to make sure there is no misunderstanding."

"Yes, General," Knight assured. "Mr. Churchill is prepared to make a personal guarantee to your president."

After a brief pause, Timmerman asked if there were any more questions.

Allen Dulles had one. "How much of the mission plan has Sir Louis been told?"

"Only that it involves working against the SS. Liquidation was not mentioned. I allowed him to brief the Ault woman so that will be all she knows."

Timmerman again waited, but this time his fellow countrymen seemed satisfied.

"Thank you, Mr. Knight. I think your recap confirms what we heard on Tuesday and we've all had a couple of days to think over your proposal. If you and your colleagues will excuse us now, we'll give you our decision shortly."

The British contingent left the room.

"Gentlemen," said Timmerman, "the president is en route to Tehran for a conference with Churchill and Stalin. Tuesday evening, I sent the president a top-secret communiqué with the details of the

British proposal. I received his reply yesterday afternoon. President Roosevelt believes the final decision should lie with this committee and he will support that decision. But I assure you, gentlemen, the president looks favorably on the proposal. He feels we have little to lose. If Lehmann double crosses the British, it's egg on their faces, not ours, and the president knows a favor given the British now can mean money in the bank for us later if we find ourselves in a position similar to the British—of being forced to ask them for . . . how can I put it? . . . a *sensitive* request in the intelligence field. The president believes in tit for tat, gentlemen. It has served him well in the past. Shall we vote?"

Obviously, Timmerman was attempting to sway the committee, but Wild Bill Donovan was not a man who caved to political pressure.

"I want to hear everyone's opinion before any vote. Timmerman, we know where you stand. General Kenney?"

"I think the whole idea is harebrained. The German will double-shuffle the Limeys first chance she gets and turn their entire team over to the Gestapo."

"Allen?" Donovan was looking at Dulles, not Hodge.

"The British are certainly assuming a great deal of risk," commented Dulles. "But I want to hear from Leroy and Al before giving my thoughts. They know her better than anyone here."

Al Hodge said, "A month ago I would have agreed with General Kenney, but now I think it might be worth taking a chance on her."

Donovan: "Leroy?"

"She can be trusted in some areas."

"Explain."

"Lehmann won't double cross her British mission partners once they're in the field. She would consider that bad form, or a transgression against some ancient warrior code she's mentioned a couple of times—the creed of a secret society to which her father belonged. Unless, of course, the Brits double cross her first, then they better make sure she doesn't survive or God help them. As far as her handlers at SOE, if they want dead Nazis, I'm sure they can count on that, but it might not be the ones they want. Once the Brits let Lehmann loose on the mainland, they'll have no control over which Nazis she goes after. It won't matter to Lehmann whose name is on some list. If she gets back inside the Reich, Lehmann will go straight after anyone involved in her father's murder and cut their throats. Then she'll go after Himmler."

"That sounds like a *yes* vote," Donovan said.

503

"Yes," said Carr. "That's my vote. Knight and his buddies don't have a clue what they're getting themselves into with Lehmann; she'll have them pulling their hair out. But she'll be Himmler's worst nightmare, and that's what counts."

Donovan concluded, "The British get the headaches while we sit back and watch. This will be a good test mission. If she survives, we get her back and we can decide then what we want to do with her. General Kenney, I think you're going to be outvoted. Now it's up to Lehmann."

Chapter 85

Flying with the Red Baron's Ace

Fort Knox, Kentucky—Friday, November 26, 1943

10:45 a.m.

Louis Minton had just stepped out, summoned to a meeting by Leroy Carr. Erika Lehmann and Elizabeth Ault sat alone in the same room as yesterday.

"Your blonde roots are showing," said Elizabeth.

"Good. I despise coloring my hair," Erika replied. "My grandfather told me you had never flown until yesterday."

Earlier, Elizabeth had taken the third plane ride of her life: two yesterday, one today so far.

"That's right," Elizabeth answered. "Have you flown?"

"Yes. In the Führer's plane from Berlin to Bavaria for holidays on the Obersalzberg, and Hermann Göring took me up in his open cockpit biplane once before the war. He flew in Baron von Richthofen's squadron in the first war, you know."

"Göring flew with the Red Baron?"

"Yes. He was one of Richthofen's aces. Göring was a national hero."

Elizabeth shook her head. "Amazing some of the things you've told me."

"What do you think of flying, Elizabeth?"

"It wasn't so bad the *second* time." Elizabeth emphasized the adjective and both women laughed. "And it's not as noisy when the plane is airborne."

"The noise doesn't have the ground to reverberate off."

"Ah . . . makes sense. I've had quite a few new experiences since meeting you that day at Sano's restaurant: dressing like a vamp and going on a date while my husband waits at home, getting shot, flying, and being strip-searched, twice."

"Strip-searched? . . . Yes, of course. The Americans would not allow us to be alone otherwise."

"Your grandfather apologized when he found out. They hadn't told him, but I reassured him I took it in stride. I've lost much of my modesty lately, Erika. That's to your credit or blame, you decide which."

"Who searched you?"

"Two Army WACs. After I stripped, they searched me, and MPs outside the room searched my clothes. Men don't know how to fold clothes, that's for sure."

"Did you tell Frank?"

Elizabeth shook her head no. "So far I've told Frank everything except that. I think for Leroy Carr's sake I'll wait until he's back in Washington, or wherever it is he goes."

Erika laughed.

"Erika, the offer from the English to work against the people who killed your father—I know you're going to take their offer . . . won't you?"

"There has been no offer, Elizabeth, other than the one from the Americans that would require me to betray my country. No one other than my grandfather and you has spoken to me about the British offer. Perhaps the Americans won't agree."

"But if they do, you'll accept? Tell me you'll accept, Erika."

"It will depend on the offer. If I'm allowed to avenge my father and not asked to betray my country . . . perhaps."

"Avenge your father. That means working against Himmler's operation, right?"

Erika did not answer.

[1:40 p.m.]

Ten minutes after MPs removed Erika's and Elizabeth's lunch trays, Louis Minton returned to the room.

"That was a long meeting, Granddad."

"They will be coming for you shortly, Erika. I was told no details, but the Americans have come to a decision."

Elizabeth said, "That's good news, I'm sure . . . wouldn't you agree, Sir Louis?"

Minton's demeanor left it unclear of his outlook. "They did a bang-up job of not revealing if their decision was favorable from our standpoint."

The three sat in silence for a few moments then Al Hodge and two MPs walked in.

"Sir Louis," said Hodge, "we're ready for Erika now. MPs in the hall will drive you and Mrs. Ault to the plane."

"I wish to remain and see my granddaughter after the conference, Mr. Hodge."

"I would like that, too." said Elizabeth.

"I'm sorry. That will be all for today. We'll get you both back to Cincinnati."

"Then I will return tomorrow morning," Minton said as he rose.

"Sir, I'm not sure that will be allowed. I will call you tonight at your hotel. After my call, please inform Mrs. Ault about what's on the agenda for tomorrow."

Minton paused and stared at Hodge. "Very well. If I have no consideration in the matter we must do as you say. I will expect that telephone call, Mr. Hodge."

"Yes, sir. Thank you for your cooperation."

Minton turned to Erika. She rose to hug and kiss him.

"Good-bye, my darling," Erika said.

"Good-bye until tomorrow," said Minton, ignoring Hodge.

"Yes, of course, until tomorrow." Erika turned to Elizabeth and the women embraced. Erika whispered in Elizabeth's ear, "Regardless of what is decided, I doubt I'll see you again."

Erika Lehmann kissed Elizabeth Ault's cheek, and said, "Good-bye, my dear friend."

Chapter 86

Cheeky

Fort Knox—[same day]

2:10 p.m.

Al Hodge and the MPs escorted Erika, still unrestrained, into the large conference room. The MPs were dismissed to wait outside the door. She recognized only Leroy Carr and Al Hodge among the eleven men around the table. No one rose from his seat when their enemy entered, and no greetings or cordial introductions offered. Carr identified, in a voice almost mechanical, the other Americans. (*So he's the famous Wild Bill*, Erika thought when Carr identified Donovan.) After Carr finished, Victor Knight, sitting on the other side of the table, identified himself as Mr. Thomas and introduced the four other Britons by last name with a *Mister* in front (Mr. White, Mr. Jones, and Mr. Waters) with no ranks or affiliations attached. Erika knew the names were aliases.

Carr motioned for her to sit in the empty chair at one end of the oval table. Donovan sat at the other end. Wild Bill took charge of the meeting and wasted no words.

"We will refer to you today as Miss Lehmann," Donovan announced. "We have learned a great deal about you from your grandfather over the past few days, and we won't waste time rehashing your biography. First, Mr. Thomas wants to ask you a question and you will answer promptly. Mr. Thomas...."

Mr. Thomas, gazing at Erika, asked, "Man sagt, dass Herr Himmler Deinen Vater auf eine lange Bootsfahrt mitgenommen hat. Stimmt das?"

Erika glared at him and did not answer.

"Answer the question," Donovan ordered without emotion. The men in the room who did not speak German had been told the translation beforehand.

"Shall I answer in German or English, General Donovan?"

"Both."

Erika looked at Mr. Thomas. "Verpiss dich! Fuck off!"

Most of the men around the table reacted with frowns and murmurs. Leroy Carr stifled a smile.

"You're quite cheeky, aren't you?" Thomas asked.

"Shall I answer. . . ."

"Don't be an arse!"

Donovan stepped in. "Miss Lehmann, I think it wise on your part to avoid being so flippant. You're in an extremely tenuous position."

"His question was insulting and absurd. Should I have been shocked? Should I rant? Or should I laugh like a fool at his insult hoping to endear myself to your group and save my life?"

"We'll move on," said Donovan. "On the thirtieth of this month— that's next Tuesday—I will turn you over to the FBI. You'll be tried before a United States military tribunal for wartime espionage and for the murder of an FBI agent in Evansville, Indiana."

"I did not. . . ."

Donovan held up his hand. "Be silent. We know you didn't kill the agent, but that won't matter in the eyes of the military court. You'll hang, simple as that. Now I'll give Mr. Thomas the floor again. You will make no comments and ask no questions until you're permitted to do so. Do you understand?"

"Yes, General."

Donovan looked at Thomas, who leaned forward and rested his forearms on the table.

"Thank you, General. Miss Lehmann, I'm quite confident your grandfather told you why my associates and I accompanied him from London. The United States government has graciously allowed the British government to make a proposal. Your grandfather knows none of the details, which I will review now. If you accept, the British government will take you into custody and transport you to a secret and heavily guarded compound in England to begin training for a special mission. You'll live under many harsh restrictions; you will not be free. The training will be grueling, and you must pass every test. *If* you complete training, only then will we decide what to do with you. You have no guarantee we won't change our minds about using you at any point along the way—even if you successfully complete training. If we decide not to use you, for any reason, you'll be returned to the custody of the United States and to the fate you deserve. If you refuse this proposal, my associates and I fly back to England and leave you to that same doom."

Thomas moved around in his chair and continued, "Now, Miss Lehmann, the mission: to assemble a crack team of specialists and insert the team behind enemy lines on mainland Europe. The goal being to disrupt operations of the SS, SD, and Gestapo by liquidating certain key members of those organizations, with special emphasis on the SD. You and Himmler are enemies. Is that correct? You may answer."

"Yes. Himmler is my enemy."

"Therefore, this mission should be of great interest to you since Himmler controls all of those organizations I mentioned and they supply him his power base. Now for the details."

Thomas looked down at the papers spread out before him and began reading the details in bullet form.

"The moment you step foot on English soil you'll be placed under arrest for espionage against the United Kingdom, and for the kidnapping/disappearance of MI-9 supervisor Henry Wiltshire in March 1942."

Donovan interjected, "Per the agreement between my government and our British allies concerning this arrangement, you'll also remain under arrest by the United States government, which can cancel your involvement at any time and bring you back to this country."

"Yes, thank you, General," said Thomas before returning to his list.

"As I already mentioned, you'll be taken to a remote and heavily guarded compound where you and your prospective British team members will train. Unlike them, you'll receive no furloughs, nor will you billet in the same quarters as the other team members. You will be placed in a cell each night at lights-out and returned to the cell during the day when not engaged in training. During training, you'll never leave the sight of guards who will be under orders to shoot to kill if you attempt escape.

Per the agreement, Mr. Carr or another OSS representative may visit the compound whenever the OSS wishes, and the OSS will be kept informed of your every step along the way during training and the subsequent mission if you make it that far.

If all goes well, and I repeat, *if all goes well,* in deference to your grandfather's past service and admirable reputation in England, after training you'll be allowed a brief meeting with him and Lady Minton before departing on the mission. This meeting, if it indeed takes place, will be held at a separate military facility and you'll be under guard, of course.

During the mission, when you are in the field, if any team member suspects a double cross or a problem developing on your part, he will have authority to put a bullet in the back of your head. That team member won't be asked later to justify killing you. An impulse or a whim on his part will be an acceptable reason.

If you survive the mission, and regardless of its outcome, upon its completion you will be immediately returned to the custody of the United States."

Thomas turned to Donovan. "General."

Donovan said, "At that time you'll be subject to justice by a military tribunal, unless the United States government agrees to some other arrangement concerning you."

Erika knew Donovan referred to spying on the Soviet Union for the United States.

"Now you may ask questions, Miss Lehmann," said Thomas.

"How many members in the team?" Erika asked.

"Six to nine, depending on how many complete training," answered Thomas.

"That's too many. Three, no more than four."

Leroy Carr hid another grin.

Thomas frowned. "That decision is not yours to make. Any other questions?"

"Since you speak German, Mr. Thomas, I assume you'll be on the team, perhaps the leader in the field?"

"That's correct. All British team members will speak German and French as fluently as native speakers."

"Both German and French? And pass as native speakers? I doubt it, Mr. Thomas. The question you asked me in German was an accurate translation, but too accurate. A native German would not say, as you said: 'It is said that Himmler took your father for a long boat ride.' He would say: 'I've heard that Himmler. . . .' The correct would be 'Ich habe gehort' not 'Man sagt.'"

The other men looked at Thomas.

Erika continued. "You have a Scottish accent and did an acceptable job of suppressing it when you spoke German, but a Scottish accent is not difficult to suppress. I assume the other team members will be English. An English accent is the hardest accent to curb—I speak from experience. Have your team work on speaking German with a lisp, a slight stutter, or some other speech impediment, perhaps one caused by a throat injury suffered in battle. Speech abnormalities help camouflage syntactic errors and accent slips—and your men will make many, I assure you. That's one reason a smaller team than you propose would be wise—fewer people to make mistakes. That your team members can somehow pass as native Germans is what's important. Don't concern yourself with the team speaking French. France is an occupied country; your team will not be suspected as long as everyone can pass as German. If they speak French, they should speak it with a German accent and not try to disguise themselves as French. Make it as simple for them as possible. Your men should carry German-to-French dictionaries like the German troops do. That will be convincing."

Men on both sides of the table looked around at one another.

"We will consider that," said Thomas, now positive Erika Lehmann was the one who might give the mission hope.

"Please do, if you want to survive." After a pause, Erika continued. "Himmler is a traitor to Germany. Because of a personal grudge, he sent an assassin to this country to murder me while I was on an important mission, ignoring the best interests of his country. That's treason. I will gladly work against a traitor. But I must be assured, in front of the Americans, that further conditions for my involvement such as revealing information that has nothing to do with the mission will not be required of me."

"Correct."

Erika glanced around the table at the faces staring at her. She took some time doing it.

"I will accept your proposal, Mr. Thomas, and your conditions . . . if you accept mine. You have my word I will not attempt to escape in England, and I will do what I can to help and protect the team in the field as long as you keep your promise that the mission will target only the SS, SD, and Gestapo. Now for my conditions: I must be allowed to avenge my father. This is all-important to me. I would think this should be acceptable to you since the Gestapo will be involved. In addition, I want to make it clear that I will not work against any branch of the Wehrmacht: neither the Army, Navy, Air Force nor the German High Command. Nor will I work against German civilian industry. If once in the field I find the team's efforts are directed against any of those, I will consider our agreement breached and my promise to the team void."

"You're bold for a woman with the hangman breathing down her neck, Miss Lehmann," Thomas said.

Erika locked eyes with Leroy Carr for a moment before finishing.

"You have my promises and my conditions, gentlemen. If anything I have said is not acceptable, now is the time for General Donovan to turn me over to the FBI."

[8:10 p.m.—Cincinnati, Netherlands Hotel]
"There he is, Frank."

Elizabeth spotted Louis Minton at a table near the fireplace with his back to the restaurant entrance. Elizabeth told the majordomo she found who she was looking for and he escorted her and Frank, weaving around tables, to where Minton sat.

"Hello, Sir Louis."

He turned and rose. "Hello, Elizabeth. And hello, Frank."

Frank said hello and shook Minton's hand.

"Have a seat, please," Minton said, motioning to the chairs. Elizabeth and Frank sat down to place settings of ornate tea cups and saucers, plates of fresh fruits, and white linen napkins folded to look like stars on Old Glory.

The Netherlands Hotel was, by now, a key venue in Elizabeth's life. She and Frank dined here on special occasions. It was here, in room 511, Elizabeth became a Side Pocket girl. And, although she would never know it, Elizabeth now sat at the table where Adalwulf von Krause and Erika dined the night they met at the RKO Century Theater.

Minton continued. "You disappointed me when you told me earlier you had already eaten; I had hoped you'd dine with me. But I took the liberty of ordering tea and scones and fruit." The scones were in a basket at the center of the table next to jars of blueberry jam and honey, the tea in a sterling silver pot.

"Thank you, Sir Louis," said Elizabeth. "This is very thoughtful." Impatient to hear what Erika's grandfather had learned from Al Hodge's phone call, Elizabeth held little interest in tea and scones, but she knew the English considered an invitation to tea a compliment. She reached for the teapot, but Minton insisted on pouring and filled her and Frank's cups. Frank looked down at the tea with a *where's-the-beer* expression but minded his manners.

Minton came to the point immediately. "The news Mr. Hodge had for me on the telephone an hour ago was mixed, I'm afraid. The good news for us, Elizabeth, is the Americans agreed to the proposition from my country—or at least they agreed to some form of the original proposition, I should say—and Erika accepted."

Elizabeth sighed in relief. "That's wonderful news. Can we see Erika tomorrow?"

"I'm afraid that is the bad news. Mr. Hodge said Erika has already departed Fort Knox with Mr. Carr and Mr. Thomas."

"She's already gone?"

"I'm afraid so, my dear."

Frank said, "Well, that's good news any way you look at it. Erika's getting another chance and Carr is gone."

"So, I guess I'll never see her again," Elizabeth said to both men. "Erika was right. When we parted, she whispered that no matter what the decision, she and I would not see each other again."

The table talk went silent for a moment before Elizabeth went on.

"Sir Louis, I'm sure you'll see your granddaughter again in England."

"Mr. Hodge told me that if things go well with Erika in England, her grandmother and I will be allowed to visit her briefly before she leaves on her mission. But Mr. Hodge had no idea when that might be. He said it could be months. He also asked me to tell you he will call on you and Frank tomorrow before he returns to Washington. He has papers for both of you to sign. I was asked to sign this morning. The paper is our promise to not reveal what we know; if we do, we can expect to be arrested and prosecuted. I was asked to sign two agreements: one from my country and another from yours."

Frank shrugged. "Sure, we'll sign the papers. But if they're worried about us talking about that mission, they don't have much to worry about. How much do we know? Something about working against the SS. What's that going to tell somebody? Nothing."

"I agree," Minton responded. "Still, I'm sure they will ask you to sign."

"I'm very relieved things worked out as we prayed, Sir Louis," said Elizabeth. "I was so hoping to see her again—at least once more— but I'm happy she's no longer in that stockade and that you'll get to see her before her mission. Then, after the war, I hope she returns to you to live in England if that's allowed, or at least visits you often. You and your family are all she has left. Please give her my love."

Frank stopped chewing on a scone and looked at Elizabeth—the word *love* surprised him.

"I will, my dear. And thank you for all you've done for my granddaughter. You saved her, Elizabeth. If you had not called me in London because you were concerned about Erika's welfare—and certainly no one could blame you if you weren't—I'm afraid. . . ." He stopped.

Elizabeth put her hand on his. For a few minutes they talked over tea and scones and fruit, with Frank eating most of the scones. All knew the dangers of a mission behind German lines; all knew Erika might not survive; but they avoided talking about it. Instead, the conversation focused on the relief they felt because of Erika's temporary reprieve.

Finally, Elizabeth sensed it was time to part. "We'll leave you now, Sir Louis. You have our address and telephone number. May I count on hearing from you occasionally?"

"Of course. And if ever you and Frank are in London, our home is yours."

"Thank you." Elizabeth rose, then Frank and Minton stood.

Frank extended his hand. "It was nice meeting you, sir. I wish you the best. So long."

"Thank you, Frank. Farewell."

Elizabeth said good-bye and kissed Minton on the cheek. As she and Frank walked out of the restaurant she looked back. Erika's grandfather had sat back down. When they reached the restaurant entrance, Elizabeth stopped suddenly. "I'll be right back, Frank." He waited while she returned to the table. Frank watched Elizabeth speak with Minton, put something in his hand, and walk away.

Chapter 87

The Specter of Eggplant

Cincinnati—Saturday, April 8, 1944

Frank and Elizabeth sat at a booth in Grandpa Floyd's Chili Shack, a small diner two blocks from the University of Cincinnati campus. Grandpa Floyd's served some of the best chili in a city famous for chili, and it helped during a time of gas rationing that the Chili Shack was within walking distance for UC students and the Aults. For the past couple of years, whenever Frank and Elizabeth ate out, most of the time they went to either Sano's or nearby Grandpa Floyd's.

Using his spoon, Frank fished around in his bowl of chili. "You need to be a Navy frogman to find the meat in the chili nowadays."

Elizabeth smiled and shook her head. "What is it with you and meat? Sometimes I think I married a tyrannosaurus."

Frank shrugged and continued his search.

Elizabeth said, "As soon as the war is over and rationing ends, I'm going to buy you a side of beef and let you eat until you pass out."

"Sounds great, thanks."

Elizabeth laughed. Not until February did she feel fully recovered from the gunshot wound. Now, in April, her and Frank's life together had returned to normal—at least as normal as a world war allowed.

"Mother received a V-mail from my brother this morning," said Elizabeth.

Frank looked up from his chili. "Oh, yeah? How's he doing?"

"Okay. He's now somewhere in the South Pacific but can't say where."

"God bless him. Your brother is a real hero, Elizabeth. All the guys in the service are heroes. You and your family can be very proud of him. I'm proud he's my brother-in-law."

Elizabeth nodded. "Today is a big day for news. Sir Louis called this afternoon."

"No kidding? What did he have to say?"

"He and Erika's grandmother were taken somewhere in England to visit Erika yesterday. He told me the meeting was brief, but that Erika looks fit."

"*Fit?* I take it that means healthy."

"I guess. He said her hair was back to her natural blonde and cut short."

"Short? Like a man's?"

"No, Erika told him it was a hairdo popular among German women since the start of the war."

"So, I guess she's about ready to leave on the mission?"

"Sir Louis didn't know; Erika couldn't say."

"Anything else?"

"The connection was bad and we didn't talk long, but he said he gave her the Ring." Elizabeth had told Frank about the Ring and her giving it to Sir Louis at the Netherlands Hotel to return to Erika. "More and more static kept interrupting, so he said he would send a letter to fill me in on the rest."

"Well," Frank said thoughtfully. "I never thought I'd say this, but I wish her luck."

They ate chili. Frank drank beer and Elizabeth Coca-Cola.

"I have one more bit of news, Frank."

"Wow, it is a big day for news. What is it?"

"Do you remember a few months ago when we were at Sano's? I had eggplant and you told me eggplant helps women get pregnant?"

Frank laughed. "Yeah, I remember. I got you on that one, babe." He laughed again.

"You were right, Frank."

Chapter 88

The Bridge

Evansville, Indiana – Saturday, June 5, 1943

Twilight waned as Erika Lehmann drove her car into the crowded Trocadero parking lot. The multitude of cars forced her to park farther away from the nightclub's entrance than preferred, but she expected as much. Having been to this nightclub several times, she knew the parking lot, like the club, would be crowded on a Saturday night.

Out of her car, she locked the door then looked at her wristwatch. She walked through the lot checking as best she could in the semidarkness for anything out of the ordinary. *It will be a miracle if the FBI isn't waiting.* She would have handled the rendezvous much differently, but unfortunately she had little say. She did succeed in getting the location changed to this nightclub. It was a small compromise on his part, but because of the crowd and the location, it would be better for her than the remote country tavern he preferred.

Erika was there to meet Axel Ryker. Ryker was an extremely unpleasant surprise three weeks ago when he broke into her apartment. Unpleasant and painful. The bull-like Ryker had given her the first true beating of her life. Now she was forced to meet with him: the purpose, an exchange. He had taken from her the top secret material she stole from the Evansville Naval Shipyard and now he was demanding money for its return. Erika knew Ryker had no intention of keeping the bargain. As soon as he had the money he would kill her. She had procured Ryker's money from her handlers at the Abwehr, who transferred the funds from a Swiss account to a bank she specified in Nashville, Tennessee. But, like Ryker, she did not intend to keep the bargain, and in fact had already given the money away. Now she would have to take her chances with Ryker. It was a gamble, and probably unwise on her part to have returned to Evansville to face him, but if he had the materials he stole from her with him, maybe her mission could be salvaged. Before she passed through the Trocadero doorway, she stopped, bent over on the pretext of checking her shoe strap, and felt through her pant leg one last time to make sure the dagger taped upside-down to her lower leg was secure.

Inside the Trocadero, many people stood near the bar around seats that were taken. In the dining area more of the same—all tables were occupied, and the dance floor full. It took Erika a moment to find Ryker, whom she finally spotted sitting at a small, two person table along a wall near the far side of the dining area. She worked her way through the crowd trying to keep an eye out for men who might be FBI, but many men wore suits at the nicer nightclubs and she knew the Americans were expert at blending in during stakeouts, regardless of the attire or social status of the clientele.

Ryker saw her approaching. He did not rise. A drink sat before him and another on the table in front of the empty seat. Without a greeting from either of them she sat down.

"I took the liberty of ordering you a drink, Sonderführer," Ryker said in heavily accented English.

"Don't call me that in here," she admonished him sternly while leaning forward so she did not have to say it loudly.

Ryker seemed unconcerned. "I doubt if we will be heard above this clamor," he countered, referring to the boisterous conversations all around and the band music.

Axel Ryker was German but born and raised in Lithuania, so Russian was his native tongue. This gave Ryker the perfect cover in America. To anyone who needed to know, he told them he was forced out of the Soviet Union in the 1930s during one of Stalin's collectivization purges—a lie, and best of all untraceable.

"I think you are known to enjoy a brandy," Ryker motioned toward the drink in front of her. "The selections of brandies here are limited. I hope that one is acceptable."

"I don't drink with a traitor," she scorned. She looked around then added: "This meeting should have been handled much differently. You realize that the chances of us being watched are high."

"I will remind you," Ryker said, "that you insisted on this location."

"We should not be meeting in Evansville," she pointed out. "We should have met in another city, but since I had no choice, this is better for our purposes than the place you chose. Also, it is the wrong time of the month. There will be a full moon tonight. The moon will be our enemy if we are forced to flee."

Again, Ryker seemed unworried. He was a hellish apparition, a killer made more dangerous because of a total lack of fear, mercy, or regret when he had to fight his way out of trouble. Six feet tall and heavily muscled, he was a brute whose coarse facial features and dark, pitiless eyes gave him a monstrous air. Even tough men gave Axel Ryker a wide berth.

Ryker was Heinrich Himmler's top Gestapo henchman, and Himmler sent him to America to kill Erika Lehmann. Ryker himself was not sure why; it seemed to be some sort of personal vendetta on Himmler's part, but it did not matter—that was his mission. He enjoyed killing, but he was no mindless automaton. Ryker was wily and realized early on that this mission would have consequences. He knew that this woman was a valued spy for German military intelligence and her father was connected at the highest levels of the Third Reich—an old personal friend to Hitler himself. If this mission came to light, all those involved would surely draw the full wrath of the Führer. Himmler would, of course, realize this and he would have to eliminate any connection between the murder of Erika Lehmann and his Gestapo; Ryker knew he would be at the top of Himmler's list of those to be eliminated after the deed was done.

So Ryker decided to make a deal with this female Abwehr spy. He broke in on her at her apartment, and although he amused himself by beating her, he did not kill her. Instead he took the top secret items she had stolen the night before from the Americans; he would return them to her in exchange for enough money to start a comfortable new life in South America. At least that was the stated deal. Erika Lehmann's suspicions were correct; Ryker's plan was to eliminate her as soon as he had the money. Like his boss Himmler, Ryker knew it was prudent to clean up loose ends.

"So, you have my package, yes?" Ryker asked about the money.

"Yes."

"It is in your auto?"

"Yes, and the things of mine you took are in your car I assume?"

"Of course," Ryker said after a drink of his vodka.

"What is your plan for the exchange?" she asked.

"We will drive away in our separate autos. You will follow me. I have found a safe place for the exchange. We will make the exchange and go our separate ways."

"Very well." Erika realized he might be lying about having her items in his car, but it was the only chance she had to regain them, and she believed Ryker's confidence in his killing skills were such that he was not much concerned with her turning the tables. She reasoned that Ryker was vain enough to believe no one could best him, and that was about all she had in her favor. Erika knew she would have to strike first, and that she would have only one thrust with the knife. It would have to be true. If he survived her first strike and got hold of her, she was done.

Ryker finished his drink and stood up. "Shall we go?"

Erika rose without answering. Normally in this type of situation she would take the man's arm as if they were a couple, but she could not bear to even act the part with Axel Ryker, so she followed him through the crowd.

Outside, night was now total with swiftly moving clouds passing now and again in front of Erika's full moon, but the parking lot was well lit by the blinking moon and security spotlights mounted high on the building's corners and aimed toward the cars. Others were walking in and out of the nightclub, and Erika and Ryker were no more than forty feet outside the door when they heard the shout behind them.

"FBI, STOP!"

Erika spun to face the voice. A young man held out his identification in one hand with a gun in the other. She did not recognize him, but only a step behind was another FBI agent she did know. She met Charles Pulaski at the Trocadero three weeks ago—the same night she was later unfortunate enough to meet Axel Ryker. Pulaski happened to be in the bar having a drink. She was at a table with the shipyard scientist who was her mark. Pulaski had interviewed the scientist (as he had many others) the previous month, recognized the scientist at the Trocadero, and stopped by their table to chat. At that time, Pulaski was unaware that the young woman across the table was the spy he was looking for.

The next few seconds seemed to pass in slow motion. Ryker pulled his gun before he turned around then immediately took aim at the young agent. Erika saw Pulaski push the young man out of the way; Ryker fired, and Pulaski slumped to the ground. Two more agents rushed in and Ryker fired at them. The young agent whom Pulaski saved and the two other agents dove behind the nearest parked cars. Using the cars for cover, the FBI agents took aim at Ryker, but Ryker quickly grabbed a young woman cowering nearby and used her as a shield.

The original plan to drive separately was instantly abandoned. Erika knew her only chance of escape was to stay near the hostage. Ryker's car was nearby. He ordered the FBI men to stay where they were or he would kill the hostage, and then he dragged the screaming woman to his car, keeping her between himself and the FBI guns. Ryker opened the driver-side door and roughly pushed the young woman into the front seat. He quickly followed and started the engine. Erika rushed to the other side of the car and jumped in, forcing the hostage between her and Ryker who shifted into first gear and stomped on the accelerator, spraying gravel on the surrounding cars. As they sped from the parking lot, Erika looked behind. The young agent whom Pulaski knocked out of the way tended to the wounded agent, while another agent stood outside a car talking into a radio.

"Please don't hurt me!" screamed the hysterical hostage.

"Shut up!" Erika ordered, then she shouted to Ryker: "Turn right! It's our only chance."

Tires squealed as the car slid out onto the highway. Ryker turned right, which took the car south and toward a bridge that crossed the Ohio River into Kentucky. The bridge was not far and with the gas pedal floored the iron work of the bridge appeared quickly in the moonlight. In an instant, the car was on the long bridge and over the water.

"Please don't hurt me!" the young woman again begged. "I'm getting married next week."

"Kill her," Ryker told Erika.

"No! Please!" the young woman screamed.

"We need her," Erika countered.

"Kill her," Ryker repeated. "The people pursuing us will not know she is dead. Her use to us as a hostage will not change and she will be less trouble."

Their attention was immediately diverted from the hostage when they saw the flashing red lights ahead. Nearly across the bridge, the roadblock ahead ended any hopes of escaping into Kentucky. Ryker slammed on the brakes and the car did a half turn as the tires locked. When the car came to a stop, Erika opened the door, grabbed the hostage and pulled her across her own body and pushed her out of the car. The young woman landed on her side, rolled twice from the momentum, then sprang to her feet and ran for her life.

"You fool!" Ryker shouted. He would have killed Erika Lehmann then and there, but at that moment he had no choice other than to turn the car around and head back toward Indiana.

"Going back will do us no good," Erika said. "The FBI will be coming for us from the nightclub; they probably have the other end of the bridge already blocked. When we get to the middle of the bridge stop the car. We will have to jump. In the dark we might have a chance to swim out of the river and escape. It's our only choice."

"That fall is how many meters, Sonderführer?" Ryker almost laughed. "The fall will kill you, and I cannot swim. I will take my chances on land. And if we are fated to die together, it will be a glorious death for the Fatherland. Would not our Führer be pleased?" said Ryker with heavy sarcasm. He cared nothing for patriotism, and he held no allegiance to anything.

Ryker had made a critical mistake. He told Erika Lehmann he could not swim.

The dagger was taped securely to her lower leg, but she would have to raise her pant leg and pull the tape. Ryker would see and never give her the time, so she flung herself on Ryker and tried to jerk the steering wheel to crash the car into the guard-rail, but Ryker's power was almost superhuman. He held the wheel steady with one hand and easily tossed her off of him with the other. Again she attacked. This time her thought was to block his vision for as long as she could so perhaps he would steer the car into a crash himself. Erika put him in a headlock and held on for as long as possible, using her upper body to block his vision. She looked down and pushed in the cigarette lighter with her foot, but again Ryker violently pushed her off. This time her head hit the metal dash.

She had to stop the car while it was over the water. Ahead on the bridge, two headlights grew brighter as a car raced toward them. Erika pulled the hot cigarette lighter from the dash, and pressed the business end lighter into Ryker's face. He barely reacted to the lighter searing his flesh, and for the third time he tossed her away like a ragdoll. But this time, when Ryker took one hand off the wheel to fend her off, she managed to kick the steering wheel hard with her right foot and the car careened left and smashed into the bridge guard-rail.

With the car stopped, Erika fought to get out. She knew she could not last long in a close quarters fight with Axel Ryker once he was no longer driving and could focus his full attention on her. She kicked away from Ryker and managed to open the passenger door, but she did not escape cleanly. Even though Ryker was in an awkward position to deliver a punch, he managed to deliver a back-handed blow to her side that knocked the air out of her as she fell from the car. Ryker followed her out the same door. Erika saw him reach for the gun in his belt and at the same time try to kick her as she lay on the road.

She rolled hard into his legs causing him to stumble, and then she kicked the heavy car door into him. The blow from the door barely jostled Ryker, but he had not yet gotten a full grip on the gun and fumbled it. The gun dropped to the road. Despite that her breath had not completely returned, Erika turned on her stomach and went for the gun but Ryker was too close and he grabbed her hair and pulled her to her feet. She saw too late his hand coming and the open-handed slap to the face from the brawny Gestapo hit man sent her reeling backward into the guard-rail. Ryker bent over and picked up the gun as a spotlight lit the area around Ryker's car.

"FBI! Stop right there, you're both under arrest!" It was the same voice from the Trocadero parking lot. Erika looked. The car that had approached them on the bridge was now stopped about fifty feet away. Erika made out a silhouette of a man standing behind the open car door with his gun aimed at Ryker. She heard other voices, but could not see the men because the FBI car's bright headlights and the spotlight were trained on her and Ryker.

Ryker ignored the command and raised the gun toward Erika. Two shots rang out from the direction of the FBI car. Both bullets hit Ryker in his side. He staggered and dropped the gun but did not fall; instead, he shrugged off the wounds and came after Erika.

She had to even the odds. Although she was skilled in hand-to-hand combat and in the past had won fights with some men, she had no hope of winning a blow-to-blow fight with Axel Ryker, even a wounded Ryker. Her side was sore from Ryker's swipe in the car, but her lungs had finally filled. She was much quicker than the heavy, muscle-bound Ryker, and she easily avoided his advance. She jumped up onto the ironwork near the edge of the road and began climbing.

Ryker followed.

Ignoring more shouts from the FBI, the two Germans climbed upward in the wind and over the water far below, their climb illuminated by the moon and the spotlight from the FBI car. The odds were now more in Erika's favor; she scaled the ironwork much faster than Ryker, but she did not want him to abandon the chase, so she slowed, adjusting her climb to stay just out of his reach.

Erika neared the top of the ironwork and put some extra distance between herself and Ryker to allow time to draw her dagger. She stopped climbing, pulled up her pant leg, ripped the dagger off her leg, and waited for Ryker. A moment ago, her plan was simply to get him in the water, but Ryker suddenly made another error. He looked down at the FBI agents on the bridge road below. Erika saw her chance. She jumped down onto Ryker's back and buried the dagger in his neck. Blood flew from the wound onto her hand and arm. Even with his jugular vein severed, Ryker still clung to the iron with one hand and attempted to reach back with the other to grab her. Blood continued to rush from the knife wound, soaking them both. Finally, Axel Ryker began to lose consciousness, lost his grip, and the two Germans began the long fall to the Ohio River. Erika held on to Ryker and the decision paid off. During the lengthy fall, gravity rotated Ryker's heavier body, and Erika entered the water on top. Still, the violent entry into the river nearly knocked her unconscious as they went to the bottom and slammed into the soft mud and silt of the riverbed. She released Ryker who was not struggling. Despite the high intensity of the moment, it flashed through her mind that the world no longer had to deal with this plague of a man.

Erika stayed underwater as long as possible. She could feel the direction of the river current and swam with it knowing that would put more distance between her and the FBI on the bridge than if she swam against the flow. When forced to surface, she gasped as quietly as she could, and spun in the water to find the bridge. She had emerged about two hundred feet downriver. High overhead on the bridge, the FBI men had moved their car and were sweeping the river with the spotlight. They chose the correct side of the bridge, thinking bodies, dead or unconscious, would float downriver, but luckily for Erika, the sweeping light was hampered by the bridge's ironwork and brightened the river only here or there. She began a routine of swimming underwater and coming up only briefly to the salvation of the air. One time, the edge of the spotlight caught her for a moment, but she had by then moved farther away and, unknown to her, the gleaming moon was now her ally. The lunar light, instead of aiding the FBI's vision, added a sparkling shimmer to the wind-ruffled waves and prevented her white face from standing out.

At last Erika rounded a bend and left the line of sight from the bridge. Now she had to choose which state to swim toward. She reasoned the FBI might assume that a survivor (if that was possible), would seek Kentucky, away from where they came, but Erika was familiar with the area and knew if she left the river in Kentucky it would be into open farmland with miles to walk under a full moon.

She swam toward Indiana.

A gang of scrub oaks welcomed her as she came out of the Ohio River. The tension of the night left her drained and the fight with Ryker sore. She sat on a log in the moonlight shadows and shivered in wet clothes. *At least the water washed away Ryker's blood.*

Erika thought about what to do next. If things went terribly wrong on her Evansville mission, she had but one hope for getting help in America. Her father had told her about a man she could rely on. This man and her father were old friends and fellow members of a secret brotherhood—and someone Abwehr, and more importantly Himmler, knew nothing about.

Her father had told her the man lived in Cincinnati.

Epilogue

Chili or She-Crab Soup?

Charleston, South Carolina—Saturday, June 28, 1980

The 1980 Lincoln Continental Mark V pulled into the driveway of an ivy-covered bungalow. A tall, dark-haired man in his mid-30s emerged from the Lincoln, walked around the back of the car, and opened the rear passenger-side door. Two children leapt from the car: a six-year-old girl and a four-year-old boy.

An elderly woman watching from a window stepped out onto the porch.

"Grandma!" the girl shouted. Both children ran to the woman who knelt to hug.

"Hi, Mom," said the man. He kissed the old woman's cheek.

"Hello, Erik."

Inside, the boy ran to the sofa, climbed on, and began jumping.

"Frank, quit jumping," said the father. "Sit down and be good." The boy reluctantly obeyed and the girl, Victoria, joined her brother on the sofa. The man turned to his mother. "Are you settled in yet, Mom?"

Elizabeth Ault said, "Pretty much. I have a few more boxes in the garage to unpack, but there's no hurry. I have everything out I need for now."

Dr. Erik Ault accepted a research position at the Medical University of South Carolina three years ago. At the time, he and his wife tried to persuade his mother to move to Charleston with them, but she had resisted until now.

"Do you miss Cincinnati, Mom?"

"I'll be okay as long as I can find a place with good chili."

Erik laughed. "There's a café on Halsey Street that serves pretty good chili. I'll take you there. I don't know if it meets Cincinnati standards; you'll have to be the judge. Down here they eat she-crab soup. I think that's their substitute for chili."

"Sounds interesting." Elizabeth had not lost her willingness to try new things.

Erik put his arm around his mother. "I'm glad you're here, Mom. Everyone in Cincinnati is gone: Grandma and Grandpa . . . and Dad. All your family is here now. Do you need anything?"

Elizabeth smiled and hugged her son. "No, I don't think so." Reporters and policemen do not enter those professions for the salaries—but she and Frank had built a nest egg, and Elizabeth received both her own and Frank's pensions. Now retired, she lived comfortably.

Elizabeth watched her grandchildren and smiled. Both had dark hair like their father and grandfather. Big sister tried to mash down a cowlick on her younger brother's head, but he wanted no part of that and tried to wrestle his sister. Elizabeth turned to her son. "Where's Nancy?" Nancy was her daughter-in-law.

"She's volunteering at the museum today," answered Erik. "I'm picking her up at four."

True, everyone in Cincinnati was gone. Erik never knew Frank's parents: both died before the war. Elizabeth's brother was killed on Iwo Jima in 1945. Her father passed in 1959 and her mother nine years later. Frank died of a heart attack four years ago at age 70.

A day never passed that Elizabeth did not miss her husband. The spark between them never grew weak. Elizabeth always knew her marital indiscretions during the time of her great adventure in 1943 was something Frank never forgot. No one would forget. Yet he never mentioned them again—not once.

Frank never saw his grandson and namesake, born two months after his death, but Elizabeth was thankful her husband had two years to enjoy his granddaughter. Frank fawned over Victoria. Around his granddaughter, the tough-as-nails, no nonsense detective melted and never hesitated to make a fool of himself—anything to make the child laugh.

Elizabeth joined her grandchildren on the sofa, sitting between them. They immediately attacked, fighting each other for position on her lap. The boy, who like his grandfather took great delight in anything rough and tumble, won out. Elizabeth put her arm around her granddaughter who snuggled against her.

"Grandma," the girl said excitedly, "tell us again about Grandpa."

"I've told you the stories about your grandfather many times."

"Tell us again."

Elizabeth laughed.

Victoria became more specific. "Tell us about when the gun shot you and Grandpa saved you."

"Yes, your grandfather saved me. He was very brave. . . ."

Erik Ault sat in a leather chair while his mother told an abbreviated version of the night in Kentucky so long ago. He knew the children would not hear the whole story. Erik was in college before his mother told him any of the details about that long night and about the woman she called Anne. He glanced at his mother's right hand and saw the Ring that was part of the story. His mother called it the Ring of the Slain and told him what it represented. But there the mystery began; a mystery his mother, to this day, refused to reveal. Many years ago, his mother told him, she had given the Ring to Anne's grandfather—Sir Louis—at the restaurant in the Netherlands Hotel. His mother asked Sir Louis to return the Ring to his granddaughter the next time he saw her. Sir Louis agreed. Erik had read the yellowed letter his mother received from England in 1944. Sir Louis wrote that he had visited his granddaughter and given her the Ring. In the letter, he related how his granddaughter, who was not named but referred to only as *granddaughter,* smiled and placed the Ring on her right hand. Sir Louis wrote that when he and his granddaughter parted, the Ring was still on her finger.

And that was the great Ault family mystery.

The Ring, returned to the mysterious woman, Anne, in England during the height of the war, had for years been on his mother's right middle finger.

Afterword

Adalwulf von Krause's wartime activities on behalf of the enemy apparently never came to light during the war, at least there is no record of him being arrested or even questioned by the United States government. After the war, von Krause returned to Germany (the year he left the USA is unclear) where he died in 1968 in his late eighties. I learned nothing of his grandson's fate, but it appears Willy left the United States with his grandfather.

Appendix A

Pursuing Lorelei

Records listing the names of staff who worked at the German embassy in Washington before the war were sealed soon after Pearl Harbor. Those records included names and photographs of family members the Germans brought with them (wives and children were allowed to accompany the German embassy staff members during their time in America). After the war, the embassy records were again made accessible, but certain records from the mid-1930s are missing and officially categorized as "not available."

Over 70,000 workers were employed at the United States Naval Shipyard in Evansville, Indiana, during the Second World War. In October of 1947, what acreage of the shipyard remained (small portions of the land had been sold earlier) was purchased by a private company. After the purchase, thirty boxcars full of shipyard records were transported to an alternative location in Evansville and stored in Quonset huts. Those records included engineering blueprints (top secret during the war), thousands of shipyard photographs, daily logs, payroll receipts, purchase orders, invoices, and the majority of personnel records. The blueprints, photographs, and records remained stored in the Quonset huts until 1953 to satisfy government requirements for archiving wartime records. When the imposed government archiving mandate expired, the property used to house the records became available for other uses and the thirty boxcars of World War II Evansville shipyard records were unceremoniously taken to a local dump and burned. The bonfire drew quite a crowd, and the next day's news reports described a blaze seen for miles.

But not all Evansville shipyard personnel records survived until 1953. In mid-January, 1946, less than five months after the Japanese surrendered on the battleship *Missouri,* a small number of personnel records were removed (there is no record of who removed them) from the mass of records in the shipyard administration building and placed in a locked and guarded storage building in another area of the shipyard compound. Less than two weeks later, on a Saturday night (January 26, 1946), a mysterious fire swept through the Evansville shipyard. The administration building that housed the bulk of the personnel records escaped the fire. The storage building where the small number of select personnel records was taken burned to the ground along with all contents.

Appendix B

About no other event in human history have more books been written than the Second World War. Biographies of Adolf Hitler alone number in the hundreds and grow annually: some well-researched, some not. Many highly regarded World War II historians consider *Adolf Hitler,* by John Toland, the definitive biography of the German leader. Anyone seeking to learn more about Hitler and the Third Reich should begin by reading Toland's work and *Mein Kampf.*

For those who wish to learn more about other historical topics relating to *Blood of the Reich,* their quest need take them no farther than to their local library or bookstore. In addition, vast stores of information are accessible on the Internet. The World Wide Web is a minefield of misinformation—much is poorly researched and a great deal simply invented on the spot—and all wise researchers or seekers of information using the Web will remain wary and keep their guard up. Nevertheless, treasure troves of diligently researched data and reliable records are available on university and government archive websites.

Related History

I.   German agents in America
They were numerous from the years 1938 to 1942. The most widely publicized was the infamous Operation Pastorius: eight German saboteurs were sent to the United States with a cache of explosives to wreak what havoc they could on certain American war industries. One summer night in 1942, U-202 delivered four of the Pastorius saboteurs to an isolated beach on Long Island; a few days later, the other four members of the team came ashore in Florida off U-584. A well-known case later in the war was Abwehr's Operation Magpie: German spies Erich Gimpel and William Colepaugh were delivered by U-boat to a remote shore near Bar Harbor, Maine, in 1944.

And then there's the intriguing Operation Vinland involving a female Abwehr agent, brought to a dark North Carolina shore by U-boat 260 in August of 1942; her mission: to infiltrate a U.S. Navy shipyard in the Midwest. Records concerning her mysteriously disappeared or were suspiciously destroyed at more than one location in the United States soon after the war.

II.   The British SOE during the war

Unlike their shadowy brethren of the British SIS/MI-6 during World War II who sought to work quietly and remain invisible, agents of the Special Operations Executive received a directive from Churchill to "set Europe ablaze" by engaging in *irregular* warfare. SOE agents were schooled in armed and unarmed combat, disguise, sabotage, subversion, terrorism, and assassination. SOE agents conducted numerous search-and-destroy missions behind German lines. Women SOE agents were common. Famed WW II American spy Virginia Hall worked with the SOE behind enemy lines in France—farmed out, so to speak, to the SOE by the OSS. While at Dachau in the summer of 2008, I read the plaque honoring four female SOE agents captured in France who died at Dachau: Madeleine Damerment, Elaine Plewman, Yolanda Beekman, and Noor Inayat Khan.

III.   SOE assassination plots

That the British formed *hit squads* to assassinate various Nazi officials during the war is a matter of historical record. Operation Anthropoid—the 1942 assassination of Reinhard Heydrich (Himmler's right-hand man) in Prague—was sanctioned and bankrolled by the British and carried out by Czech nationals trained for the mission by the SOE at one of its secret compounds in England.

The bomb used in an attempt on Hitler's life during the summer of 1944 by Claus von Stauffenberg in the famous yet unsuccessful Operation Valkyrie of Tom Cruise movie fame contained explosives and other materials manufactured by the SOE.

That same summer, the British considered sending their own agents to assassinate Hitler and gave the SOE the job. The plot the SOE hatched involved parachuting agents into the woods surrounding the Berghof. The SOE knew that when Hitler was at his mountain retreat, a Nazi flag was raised that could be seen from a certain café in Berchtesgaden, the nearby town. And through intelligence, the SOE learned that Hitler took a twenty-minute walk each morning down a hillside path, insisting on solitude to contemplate or on no more than one walking companion if important business needed thrashing out—

easy pickings for a trained sniper hiding in the nearby woods. The SOE had everything in place and awaited the go-ahead, but Operation Foxley was never implemented by the British Chiefs of Staff for several reasons, including the fear of turning Hitler into a martyr to the German people and the apprehension that Heinrich Himmler would be Hitler's likely successor.

IV. Mysterious deaths

Beginning in the late spring of 1944 and continuing through the summer of 1945 (even after the war in Europe ended in May) several prominent and not-so-prominent members of various Himmler-controlled organizations including the SS, Gestapo, and SD (the intelligence branch of the SS) mysteriously disappeared or were found dead. One body was found on a train, two in cars, others at home or other everyday locales. In October 1944, one notorious Gestapo sycophant, Conrad Gerber, who was by all accounts a Himmler favorite, always serving his master faithfully regardless of the gruesomeness of the chore, was found on the floor in the ladies restroom of a Munich beer hall, his jugular severed. The hysterical woman who found Gerber lying in his own blood told Kripo (German criminal police) investigators that on her way into the *Toilette* she passed a Bier Fräulein (waitress) coming out. The witness told the Kripo that the woman smiled at her in passing. All the waitresses were lined up but none was the woman seen leaving the restroom.

V. Nazis working for the CIA and MI-6 after the war

Neither the American nor British intelligence communities displayed any qualms about bringing Nazis into their clandestine societies after World War II.

During the Cold War, both the CIA (the post war OSS) and MI-6 made use of Nazis (some boldly unrepentant). Furthermore, records show both organizations went out of their way to recruit Nazi agents, especially if the Germans could offer experience or expertise in working against the Russians. The CIA not only maintained a close working relationship with Reinhard Gehlen, they helped him set up shop. During the war, Gehlen served as the German Army's intelligence chief for the Eastern Front. With backing from the United States after the war, Gehlen assembled a large intelligence organization staffed with numerous ex-Nazis and known war criminals—at least 100 of Gehlen's operatives were former SD officers or Gestapo agents. Gehlen's organization eventually became the official West German intelligence agency—the BND.

Records (available on-line) from the National Security Archive of The George Washington University show that "at least five associates of the notorious Nazi Adolf Eichmann worked for the CIA, and 23 other Nazis were approached by the CIA for recruitment."

MI-6 was as willing as its American counterpart to sign-up former enemies, and the roll call list of former Nazis who worked for the British Secret Service during the Cold War is long. One name on the British list is Klaus Barbie, the *Butcher of Lyon*. Another name is Horst Kopkow, an SS officer who during the war ordered the executions of approximately 300 spies (many were British and most were tortured before execution). After the war, Kopkow was arrested as a war criminal but ended up being recruited into the British intelligence fold in 1948. The British even faked Kopkow's death to deceive a war crimes tribunal.

VI. The End of the Reich

Adolf Hitler and Eva Braun married on April 29, 1945. The next day, the newlyweds committed suicide in the Führer Bunker below the Reichschancellery in Berlin.

Incredibly, news of their Führer's demise shocked many of Hitler's top paladins.

For months, the fate of the twelve-year Thousand Year Reich had to have been obvious to even the most diehard Nazi fanatics. By the spring of 1945, the once-mighty German Luftwaffe had been reduced to an anemic flock barely capable of flight due to lack of planes, fuel, and pilots. Eighty percent of the U-boats, three years earlier the feared *Wolfpacks*–scourge of the seas, now served as coffins for crews eternally at rest on the bottom of the Atlantic. By that last spring of the Reich, the Kriegsmarine (Navy) was relegated to barely more than a ferryboat service evacuating German civilians and military personnel trapped behind Russian lines along the Baltic Sea.

Nevertheless, many Germans, including some of the most powerful members of Hitler's inner circle, appeared flabbergasted at the news that the Führer was no more and scratched their heads about what would happen next. Even with Germany a wasteland of flattened cities, some of the Nazi high-and-mighty such as Hermann Göring and Karl Dönitz, whom Hitler had named his successor, still clung to the belief that a deal could be struck with the western Allies. Göring and Dönitz stayed put near their respective headquarters while they sought dialogue with the British and Americans.

But not Heinrich Himmler; he was a man fleeing from something—or someone.

VII. A Man from Another Planet

When the war in Europe ended on May 8th, 1945, Heinrich Himmler was on the run. He shaved his moustache, jettisoned his pince-nez eyeglasses in favor of an eye patch, donned a Wehrmacht sergeant's uniform and spent a fortnight driving around Germany looking over his shoulder. For posterity, Himmler's falling into British hands was recorded officially as a *capture*. The truth is that on May 21st, Himmler and his two adjutants (disguised as privates) voluntarily walked into a British checkpoint at a bridge over the Oste River at Bremervörde—a checkpoint they could have easily avoided. The British failed to recognize Himmler and the three men were taken to a camp at Westertimke, near Bremen. Himmler and his adjutants, still thought to be common enlisted men, were again moved, this time to an interrogation center at Second Army headquarters outside Lüneburg.

The official version of Himmler's death is that he committed suicide on May 23, 1945, after biting down on a cyanide capsule hidden in his mouth. Hitler's most notorious henchman, Heinrich Luitpold Himmler, the Grim Reaper's file clerk, architect and champion of the Holocaust, a man German Panzer General Heinz Guderian referred to as *"a man from another planet,"* was dead.

But Himmler's body was not yet dust before eyewitnesses to the events at Lüneburg, including the British sergeant ordered to take Himmler's body into the forest and bury it where it would never be found, began doubting the official version of the Reichsführer's demise. And ambiguities regarding British actions at Lüneburg haunt historians till this day.

A slipshod autopsy was performed and the corpse buried in a hidden location as soon as a shovel could be found. And always looming has been the mystery of the cyanide. Himmler had been strip-searched twice and his clothes taken. A phial of cyanide was recovered from his garments. Moreover, a few hours before his death, wearing clothes given him by the British and wrapped in a blanket, Himmler, while supposedly hiding another cyanide capsule in his mouth, ate a thick bread and cheese sandwich washed down with a large glass of tea while being watched carefully.

◊ ◊ ◊

The testimonies of those at Lüneburg on the day Heinrich Himmler died are a hodgepodge of inconsistencies and conflicting accounts, and myriad questions remain. Not in question is Himmler's odd demeanor after coming into British hands. The British failed to recognize him and witnesses said later that Himmler might have gotten away with his disguise. Other high-profile Nazis such as Adolf Eichmann and the infamous Auschwitz Angel of Death, Dr. Josef Mengele, were captured, but their false identities held up and they were soon released to begin life on the run (Eichmann remained free until 1960; Mengele was never recaptured and died in South America a free man in 1979). But to some of the British witnesses at Lüneburg, it appeared being released was the last thing Heinrich Himmler wanted. On his own accord, Himmler removed his eye patch, donned eye glasses, and identified himself to his British captors, giving some the impression that his disguise was not meant for them. At first, British officers at Bremervörde thought the man claiming to be Heinrich Himmler was joking; this frail-looking, meek and disheveled sergeant could not possibly be the feared lord of the dreaded SS, SD, and Gestapo. But Himmler finally convinced them and seemed relieved to be under guard. One British interrogator, Captain Thomas Selvester, wrote Himmler "appeared almost jovial." It was as if Himmler felt he had finally found safe haven after fleeing from some terrible avenger.

We will not have an opportunity to learn the truth until the year 2045. The British government placed the records concerning Himmler's death under seal for 100 years. Perhaps, when the time comes to open the records we will find blank pages, the truth purged long ago. Then again, perhaps we'll learn if Heinrich Himmler died by his own hand or someone else's.

Valhringr

According to ancient lore, the Valhringr (Old Norse for *Ring of the Slain*) granted certain powers and benefits to any deserving warrior who wore it and believed in the Creed of the Ring. Wearing the Ring ensured that the wearer/believer would win many battles before finally falling. But all great warriors must eventually die, as do we all, and when it came time for death the Ring ensured the wearer he would die gallantly (the ultimate hope of all Viking warriors). We know from Norse mythology that one task Odin gave his warrior daughters, the Valkyries, (the Viking angels, as it were), was to escort all valiant warriors to Valhalla, the Viking Heaven. The Ring lore contends that the Valkyries kept a special eye out for those who wore the mystical Valhringr. Brunhild herself, the most powerful, fearsome, and beautiful Valkyrie personally escorts Valhringr wearers to Valhalla—the Hall of the Slain.

Ring tenets and legends include:

o   The Ring is to be made of silver and have the midnight stone (a black stone, probably onyx or obsidian). Black emits no light, therefore granting its possessor invisibility against negative influences. The Ring is to be worn on the right hand (a certain finger is not specified).

o   On the Ring are the symbols of **Hrungnir's Heart** (the Valknot. i.e. *knot of the slain*), and **Gungnir** i.e., Odin's Spear, or the Spear of Valhalla.

o   Those who hold Hrungnir's Heart swear to honor those slain in battle, including noble enemies.

o   Those who display Gungnir proclaim they are defenders of Heaven, their native land, and family. A Ring wearer swears to defend to the death noble causes.

o   The Ring must never be purchased or sold by the wearer. It must be bestowed upon the wearer by a worthy Ring wearer who feels confident the person granted the Ring is equally worthy to wear the Ring.

o   Both men and women can wear the Ring if worthy. The Ring Brotherhood acknowledged that women were equally entitled to strive for a splendid death (perhaps because the Vikings preferred not to offend the fearsome Valkyries).

o   Those who wear the Ring must be skilled with a weapon (apparently of their choice).

o   Those who wear the Ring are brothers and sisters unto death.

o   Upon death of the Ring wearer, the Ring should be burned or buried with the corpse (Germanic/Nordic peoples practiced both cremation and burial).

o   The Curse: anyone who wears the Ring but does not believe in, or does not honor, the Ring's doctrine is doomed to a dishonorable death and the loss of Valhalla. And the creed stresses that great woe will befall anyone who steals a Ring or acquires one through surreptitious means.

 Hrungnir's Heart

 Gungnir

Author's Note

One of my goals with *Blood of the Reich* was to write a story that stood alone. I did not want readers who have not read *Invitation to Valhalla* (an earlier novel in which Erika Lehmann appears) to be forced to do so or be lost; therefore, I included the flashback chapters for back story. Recent readers of *Invitation to Valhalla* might recognize two of those chapters—Lorelei and The Bridge. In *Invitation to Valhalla*, Erika's battle on the Evansville bridge with Axel Ryker was told from an FBI agent's point of view. In *Blood of the Reich*, the scene is told from Erika's point of view. This last chapter of *Invitation to Valhalla* is where the Cincinnati story in *Blood of the Reich* begins.

However, even though I attempted to relate as much back story as possible for the sake of those who have not read *Invitation to Valhalla*, I had to stop somewhere or risk swamping the reader with two separate stories. For those who have additional questions, such as the grudge between Heinrich Himmler and the Lehmanns, more on that can be found in *Invitation to Valhalla*.

Blood of the Reich is a work of *historical fiction.* That genre term is more than simply ambiguous—it seems on the surface to be an oxymoron, as if it can't make up its mind what it wants to be. I can only define *historical fiction* as it applies to *Blood of the Reich.*

Some of the characters, places, and events in *Blood of the Reich* are real; some are fictional. A few names of actual persons have been changed for an assortment of reasons, including requests from family. Where events are a matter of record no revisions or embellishments for the sake of the story have been made. But unlike *Invitation to Valhalla* where several key witnesses to events in Evansville during the war were still alive and available for interviews when I conducted research in the mid-1990s, none of the key participants in the Cincinnati story were still among us a decade later when I began research for *Blood of the Reich*. Thus, many more holes in the Cincinnati story required my imagination to fill than did the Evansville story in *Invitation to Valhalla*. In the end, *Blood of the Reich* is a novel to be read as a novel, not a history textbook.

— Mike Whicker, 2009

Acknowledgments

Authors of historical fiction, to pass the persnickety tests of verisimilitude, must engage in arduous and many times very challenging research to avoid throwing themselves under the unforgiving wheels of the literary ineptness bus. To avoid this, a wise author will assemble a crack team of experts to check his/her work. I doubt if I am as wise as I am lucky and it makes little difference to me, for watching my back is an impressive platoon of bodyguards, all experts in their fields.

If I thanked them properly here, and listed their individual accomplishments, this would become the longest chapter in the book. None of these remarkable individuals would hanker after that; in fact, just the opposite—they are individuals who frown on flowery accolades. So I will simply list my guardian experts by category and in alphabetical order by last name.

Medical: Dr. H. Dan Adams, Dr. Steven Elliott, Dr. Michael Harrison

Law Enforcement: Frank Gary, Daren Harmon, Zach Whicker

Shortwave transmissions: Darrell Davis, Larry Hahn, Bob Pointer

Great thanks to my copy editor, William Barrow, and my proofreading/review readers: H. Dan Adams, Cookie Barrow, Dr. Sherry Darrell, Darrell Davis, Tom Egan, Gisela Fischer, Janice Harris, Nancy Higgs, Dr. Susanna Hoeness-Krupsaw, David Jones, Lauren Jones, Shelley Kirk, Steve Kweskin, Susan May, John William McMullen, Kathy Pfettscher, Sheila Reid, Joe Rhodes, Eric VonFuhrmann, Erin Whicker, Josh Whicker, and my inspirational and long-suffering bride, Sandy Whicker. And a special thanks to my editor, Jo Ann Learman. All these generous people did their best to keep me on the straight and narrow. Any Homer nods in *Blood of the Reich* are purely the fault of the stubborn author.

Pre-Vatican II Roman Catholic liturgy: John William McMullen and David Nunning

Translators: Rita Crane (Spanish), Dr. Susanna Hoeness-Krupsaw (German), Dr. Oana Popescu-Sandu (Russian)

Evansville during WW II: Harold Morgan

Meteorology: Jeff Lyons   Swing dancing: James Newman

I also must thank Tom Lonnberg, Leann Masterson, and Stanley Rosenblatt.

And the most heartfelt thanks is due Annie (Komis) Rhodes who forced *Invitation to Valhalla* into the hands of Art Buchwald (the iconic author and writer for the *Washington Post*) and Mike Wallace of CBS *60 Minutes* fame and made them promise her to read it. Thank you, Annie.

My deepest gratitude to all.

— Mike Whicker

About the Author

A native of Colorado, Mike Whicker now resides in the Midwest. *Blood of the Reich* is his third novel. Whicker welcomes comments from readers and can be emailed at **mike@mikewhicker.com**.

Novels by Mike Whicker

Invitation to Valhalla
Proper Suda
Blood of the Reich

website: www.mikewhicker.com

CPSIA information can be obtained at www.ICGtesting.com
Printed in the USA
LVOW080801290412

279557LV00002B/1/P

9 780984 416004